Blood-Borne Series

~Book Three~

A Bleeding Ground

C.R. QUINN

D1452397

A Bleeding Ground is a work of fiction. Names, characters, places,
and incidents are products of the author's imagination or are
used fictitiously. Any resemblance to actual events, locals, or
persons, living or dead, is entirely coincidental.

Designed by C.R. Quinn
Cover created by C.R. Quinn
Front cover photo by ExCharmCityCub/Flick   m
Back cover photo by from Lijuan Guo/Stock   .com
     photo by Marie C. Fields/Shutterstock m
www.creativecommons.org\licenses\by-nc\2.0\legalcode

Printed in the United States of America

Library of Congress
ISBN-10: 0692685146
ISBN-13: 978-0692685143

A Bleeding Ground

For Meme, the strongest, funniest,
and brutally honest woman I know

...and yes, I am working on a non-vampire
book for you to read

Prologue

Brianna

Cameron sat in the SUV next to me, his arm securely around my shoulder squeezing me tightly into his side. He had not stopped touching me since we left the hospital, which would usually never be an issue, but now I could feel every fiber of the cotton medical scrubs rubbing and scratching at my skin. When I would try shifting out of Cam's arms he would merely shift with me. I couldn't get away and I was on tactile overload while Alex drove us through the streets of Boston to our home. Every car horn and bang from a pothole sent lightning bolts through my head making me well aware of my current condition. I had been Turned.

So much had happened in the last twenty-four hours that I could hardly get my head around it. I had become a mother and a predator within hours of each other. Dozens of medical professionals were Glamoured to forget that I had died, medical records destroyed, and a lie about destructive vandals in the morgue was created. All actions performed because Cameron couldn't live without me. A notion that most women would fawn over, but I couldn't bear that I had been turned into a monster. I wasn't even allowed to be with my babies. I had been shuffled out of the hospital without even the slightest glance. But I didn't blame my father's and Victor's judgment, how could I be trusted around two precious babies. I had fought with my last breath for my children, and now I was forced to keep my distance because of Cameron. *He* had taken my choice away, *he* had turned me into the one thing I never wanted to be and he was well aware of that fact when he did it.

"Love," he said softly as his fingers moved from my arm to his temples, "you are Pushing me again."

I didn't apologize. I hadn't realized I was using my gift, but I also didn't care. Let him feel a little of what I was at the moment.

Kyla turned and glanced at me over her shoulder with a sympathetic yet hopeful smile. "Almost home, honey."

"It won't be home until my babies are with me," I snapped and suddenly Cameron's body was slammed against the passenger door. I had to have done it, but I barely felt a twinge as the Push left me. I still didn't apologize.

Alex caught my glance in the rearview mirror, his eyes squinting in silent pleading, but I looked away. Cameron rubbed his face as he shifted his body away from me and looked out the window. A minute later Alex pulled up in front of our house and Kyla opened my door.

She wrapped her arms around my neck, burying her face in my hair as she whispered, "You have to forgive him, Bri."

"I can't do this now," I answered, feeling the corners of my eyes begin to burn at the threat of tears. I pulled her arms down from my neck and fled towards my house. There were only two problems – one, I barely blinked before I was standing at my front door; two, I couldn't go inside because I didn't have a key. So now I was standing awkwardly on the front stoop of my house and having to agonizingly wait for Cameron to come and let me inside.

I watched as both Kyla and Alex gave Cameron reassuring hugs before they looked up to me and waved goodbye. It wouldn't be for long, though. The threat of Aidan still loomed around us, and our home would be under constant surveillance with the two of them taking the first shift. The rest of our family was at the hospital providing protection for the babies. Just the thought of them tore away at me. Everyone got to be with them but me, their mother.

Cameron strolled up the front steps of our brownstone, his eyes focused on his hands as he fiddled with the keys between his fingers. I watched as he slid the key in the lock, hearing the pins inside click and release, the smell of wet autumn leaves and burning pine filling my nostrils as he stepped by me and opened the door.

The house looked so different with my new eyes. I could see every paint stroke on the walls, every imperfection in the wood of the stairs in front of me, as well as the obvious fact that we needed to change the garish lighting in the foyer. How did Cameron stand it?

The front door shut behind me, making me flinch from the sound.

"It is jarring at first, I know," he whispered and gently glided his fingers down the sides of my arms. "But you will get used to the sights and sounds."

I shrugged away from him. "I don't want to have to get used to anything, Cam. I want things to be the way they were."

"Brianna, you changed everything the minute you died."

I whipped around to face him. "Don't you dare put this on me!"

My face scrunched up as the sound of my voice bounced loudly off the walls around me. I was so distracted that Cameron took me by surprise and pushed me flat up against the wall. His lips pried my mouth open, forcefully thrusting his tongue inside and pulling at clumps of my hair with his fingers. In some ways it was almost like kissing another man. I had been kissing Cam for almost a year and had memorized the feeling of his cool lips and tongue. But now he was warm and not as smooth. I could feel every slight wrinkle, every taste bud as his tongue searched my mouth.

I pushed him away, shoving him as hard as I would any other day, but today I was a Vampire, and Cameron flew across the foyer and into the living room, leaving a dent in the wall before falling to the floor. After a moment or two he pressed himself up onto his knees, shaking his head and allowing bits of dry wall to fall from his hair.

"Is that going to pass too?" I said condescendingly as his cell phone rang from his pocket.

Cameron stood slowly, smoothing his white t-shirt down his stomach and letting the cell phone continue to ring.

"I do NOT forgive you, Cam."

"I love you, Brianna."

"I still do not forgive you," I shouted again.

"Always, Bri. Remember? Always. How do we keep our promise to one another if you are dead? I know now that I can never live without you. I will *always* love you, and now you will *always* be at my side and with our children."

My eyes began to sting as bloody tears fell down my cheeks. "Will you answer that damn phone?"

Cameron lowered his head as he put his hand in his pocket and eventually placed the cell phone up to his ear. Although Cameron was roughly twenty-five feet away I could hear Victor's distinctive raspy voice coming through the phone. Cameron's head shot up as he looked at me in horror.

"Cam, what does Victor mean my children have fangs?"

Three and a half years later

Chapter One

Jonah

"Jonah," Greg whined through the earbud of my phone, "how much longer do we have to wait?"

Greg was sitting in the car in front of me, and through the windshield of the Facility's SUV I could see him pretending to bang his head against the steering wheel. I never minded the waiting part, being a chauffeur for a while helped with that. But for three years I had been the transportation coordinator for Facility East. I came up with that title myself, head driver just sounded lame. But overall, I loved the job. It paid well, I wasn't stuck behind a desk, and the people I worked for were awesome. They were Vampires, and could snap me like a twig in seconds, but awesome all the same.

I pushed the talk button on my phone, "Greg, their flight only landed ten minutes ago. Maybe they got caught in the baggage claim."

"I think we should declare professor law. You know, like in college. If the professor doesn't show up in ten minutes, you get to leave. At least that's what I heard happens."

"First off, it's usually twenty minutes for a professor. Second, this isn't college."

"Kevin has a crappy car for a Gatherer," Greg said as he began peeking into the various compartments within the car.

"It's more than you have. What did your Gatherer pick you up in?"

"You think I can remember that far back?"

"Greg, you've only been at Facility East for a year."

"Well, I was kind of in shock. I didn't pay attention to her car."

"That's because you were checking her out the whole time, I'm sure."

"Who wouldn't! Leslie was smokin' hot. I wonder why she doesn't come and check on me anymore?"

I shook my head and laughed to myself. "I don't know, Greg, maybe it's because you kept trying to shove your tongue down her throat."

"She almost bit it off the last time."

"And you've made my point."

"Hey, douchebag security guard is walking this way," he said and I looked in my rearview mirror to see that the airport security guard was indeed heading back in our direction and looking at his watch. Thankfully at the same time Kevin, a Gatherer, stepped through the glass double doors pulling a young hybrid girl by the arm. Kevin looked like a typical Vampire, at least in my opinion – tall, muscular, perfect everything, every girl's dream. His hybrid, on the other hand, was the complete opposite. Her long blonde hair was messy and sticking to her face and neck. Her sweatshirt was at least three sizes too big and her jeans hung low on her hips with what looked like days, maybe even weeks, of dirt and grime soaked into the knees and thighs.

"They're here," I said and opened my door. It was odd that Kevin had such a tight grip on his hybrid. She looked miserable, almost on the verge of tears as Kevin steered her toward the SUV. "Hey Kevin, how was the flight?"

"Eventful," he replied impatiently and gave a sideways glance to the hybrid squirming in his grip. "Our hybrid here almost got me detained by a U.S. Marshall because of her antics."

The hybrid didn't react, but merely tightened her ragged hoodie around her waist. Not knowing what else to do in the sudden awkward silence, I opened the passenger door of the SUV and the hybrid wretched her arm out of Kevin's grip and climbed inside.

I looked to Kevin who rolled his eyes, but also seemed relieved. "She's all yours, Jonah."

"Oh thanks. No bags?"

He shook his head. "She has nothing."

"Does she at least have a name?"

"Ashlyn. And I'll give you fifty dollars if you can get anything else out of her. I thought she'd be a little more grateful for getting her off the street."

"So you just came across her on some street in Atlanta?"

He shifted his weight uncomfortably, obviously hiding something. "Yep. Just happened upon her. Never did find the hybrid I was looking for. Can you let Seraphina know? I know she always gets worried when that happens."

"Sure will. Well, your car is all gassed up. You should be good to go for your next assignment," I said as I waved Greg over and began to walk back around to the driver's side of the SUV.

"And Jonah," Kevin shouted after me, "keep your eye on her. She's a runner."

"Ok, thanks for the heads up," I replied and eyed the security guard tapping his watch. A moment later Kevin was speeding away and I put our SUV in gear.

Greg sat in the backseat but was leaning over the center console, not wasting any time hitting on Ashlyn which was an interesting decision on his part considering the pungent smell that was wafting off of her. "So, welcome to the Facility East express. I'm Greg, special guide to all new hybrids, and your new best friend. You need anything, anytime day or night, you come find me. It gets pretty cold up here, so if you ever need anyone to keep you warm…"

"Greg," I warned and elbowed him off the console. "Ashlyn, don't mind him. He's obnoxious to everyone. My name is Jonah…"

"I don't give a shit," Ashlyn snapped as she turned away from us and looked out the window.

Greg patted my shoulder before sinking back into his seat. Through the rearview mirror I could see him giving me a sly smile.

"So Ashlyn, welcome to Connecticut. It'll take us about forty minutes to get to Facility East, do you have any questions before we get there?" Ashlyn didn't answer. "Ok then…uh…well…Facility East was open a little more than three years ago when the original Facility out in San Francisco became overcrowded. It's about half the size of Facility West, but I think it's homier. You'll meet Seraphina and Eris when we get there, they run the place, at least for the next month. Everyone is pretty upset that they're moving away, but at least you'll have some time with them. Eris is a Vampire, but Sera is a hybrid, like you."

Ashlyn whipped around causing her messy blonde hair to fall in her face. "I am not a…a whatever you call it. That other guy tried to feed me that bullshit, too. You've got the wrong girl, let me out of this goddamn car!"

Greg and I exchanged glances through the rearview mirror. When I didn't slow the SUV down, Ashlyn began pulling at the door handle. When the door didn't open she began banging on the window and dashboard.

"Whoa, whoa, whoa," I shouted and grabbed her flailing left hand. "I know you're freaked out, but stop hitting the company car. Just calm down and give this a chance."

Ashlyn brushed her wild hair from her face and wiped a tear from her eye. Nothing melted me like a crying woman. You'd think living with my mother and sister would have made me immune.

"Please don't cry," I begged.

"I'm not, asshole."

"Yeah, and you're not a hybrid," Greg chimed in from the backseat.

"I'm not!" she screamed.

"Ok, ok," I shouted over them. "Greg, shut up. Ashlyn, I know this is a lot to take in all at once, but sorry to tell you, you are a hybrid. Your eyes give you away."

Ashlyn flinched and sank back into her seat. "What's wrong with my eyes?"

I smiled. "There's nothing wrong with them, Ashlyn. It's just that all hybrids have the same dark eyes. They're almost black like Vampires' eyes."

"But your eyes are blue," she replied snidely.

"Thanks for noticing," I replied, trying to ignore her tone. "I'm not a hybrid. I'm just a plain old human. But I've been working at Facility East for over three years, and I promise, you're really going to like it there."

Ashlyn turned back to look out the window. "I don't give a shit about your promises."

I let the statement hang in the air for a few minutes before I finally turned on the radio. I might not be able to ignore a crying woman, but I could tune out an ungrateful, bitchy girl any day of the week.

Chapter Two

Jonah

I looked at the clock on the dash as the guards of Facility East waved me through the gate. It was almost 5:45pm which meant I would be late for my weekly family dinner at Mable's, or as most knew it, The Maple Inn. Six o'clock on Wednesday nights I had a standing table with my mother and my sister, Katie, whenever she was home from college. It was a tradition started shortly after my friend, Brianna Morgan, had stayed there. I had met Brianna while I was working as a chauffeur. The day she got into my car, my life changed. I gained a big sister in Brianna, a second mother in Mable, and eventually a job that provided financial security for my family.

Originally, Wednesday night dinner at Mable's provided the chance to eat out, which until I started at Facility East was a very rare occasion. My father's death had really left us financially strapped, and my mother barely came out of her bedroom. I dropped out of college in order to support my girls and put food on the table. Brianna's recommendation to work at Facility East enabled us to keep up all the household expenses, pay for my mother's therapy, and send Katie to a state university. Not bad for only being twenty-four, even if it meant I sacrificed my college education and most of my social life. But whenever I would get angry or depressed about it I always heard my father's voice in my head telling me, *We have to take care of our girls, Joey, no matter what.*

Sometimes I wondered if that was still the case now that my mom had a boyfriend. I considered myself accepting of most people, but Dr. Paul Redding was a douchebag, and not just because he was dating my mom. I disliked him because of who my mom turned into when she was with him. Thankfully the long hours at the Facility meant I didn't have to watch them together all that often.

But all of that, and the added stress of an angry hybrid, couldn't bring me down today since as soon as I dropped Ashlyn off I was starting my vacation. Five days in Boston with Brianna and Cameron, and their kids – Livy and Jack-Jack. Half the fun of going to Boston was spending time with the kids. Not a situation that most people my age would consider a vacation, but I couldn't be too far from the Facility, and I was poor. Besides I loved them all, and like Eris and Seraphina they were moving back west. After they left I wasn't sure where I'd be able to escape to.

But I couldn't dwell on it a second longer since I was pulling into the large garage where we housed all the company cars – three SUV's, one sedan, and then my baby Camaro. More specifically my silver 1969 Chevy Camaro Z28 with black racing stripes on the hood. It was under a tarp and I never drove it anymore, but it was still mine. Yet another thing given to me by Brianna. I wondered if I would ever be able to pay her back for everything she had done for me. The list was pretty overwhelming.

Once I placed the SUV in park, the child locks disengaged and Ashlyn was quick to step down from inside. Wasn't sure where she thought she was going, you couldn't get inside the building without a keycard, which I had in my pocket.

Throwing the keys to Greg, I made my way toward the security door and pulled the key card out of the back pocket of my jeans. "Greg, take Cole and make sure that all vehicles are topped off for tomorrow morning."

Greg scrunched his face and sighed. "Why do I need to go with Cole?"

"Because he's a Vamp, and you know hybrids can't go out by themselves."

"Nothing ever happens," he complained.

"Take it up with Sera and Eris. It's not my rule." I turned away and scanned my card over the security reader. "Ashlyn, you can follow me."

Although Ashlyn didn't acknowledge me, at least I didn't have to drag her inside kicking and screaming. Quietly she followed me up the flight of stairs and into the lush setting of the Facility's upscale common room. It was full of thick couches and soft chairs where hybrids would congregate to play games, practice their gifts, or just hang out with one another. Everyone at Facility East acted as though they were extended family. They were all in the same boat, so they were the perfect support network for each other.

Eris came toward us with a wide smile as we snaked through the common room, "Joh-nah," he said with his thick Italian accent, "I take it this is our new hybrid?"

"Yes sir. Ashlyn, this is Eris. He runs the place with his wife, Sera. Where is Sera, by the way?"

Eris looked offended as he pulled his long hair back. Eris always looked out of place, especially in New England. He dressed as though he was still out on his island with his white pants and loose fitting button up shirt. Last year he even wore his sandals during a snow storm.

"Mr. Thorne, are you implying I cannot greet our new hybrid and take her through the paces?"

"Er…it's just that you never have before," I teased, and he thankfully smiled.

"My Sera is conferencing with Dian-na about some last minute details. Only a few weeks left until she takes over."

Diana Stewart, or the Ice Lady as I called her, would be taking over for Eris and Seraphina. No one was happy about the change, but there wasn't much we could do about it either.

"Well, Ashlyn, I'll leave you with Eris then," I said and leaned toward her. "Just so you know, Eris is much faster than Kevin and usually not as nice, so be good." I winked at her and she rolled her eyes angrily. Looking at my watch I turned on my heels. "Sorry, Eris, I need to get going."

"Ah yes, it is Wednesday. Go, go, I can take care of Miss Ashlyn. Will we see you tomorrow before you go?"

I nodded. "I'll do the weekly schedules in the morning and submit them before I leave for Bri's. Is it ok if I take the sedan up to Boston?"

"Of course, you know you never have to ask. Buono sera."

Eris gestured for Ashlyn to follow him to the dormitories and as she turned away I could see the absolute fear in her eyes. That was a look I was used to seeing from the newbies.

The usual twenty-five minute drive home took over thirty because I hit every red light possible. My mom wasn't answering her phone, and when I turned onto my street I knew something was up. Only the light from the kitchen was on, making the driveway very dark as I pulled around the back. Thankfully my mother's car was parked in the back part of the driveway, but was she seriously just sitting in the kitchen by herself?

I unlocked the side door to the house and stepped through the mud room which led into the kitchen.

"Mom?" No answer. "Hey Mom, where are you?"

Just as I stepped into the hallway, a blur of light brown hair came at me as arms wrapped around my neck, effectively scaring the shit out of me.

"Jesus, Katie Bell," I shouted as I pulled my sister off of me.

"Ha! I got you," she said happily as she continued to jump up and down.

"You do remember that Dad died of a heart attack."

Katie glared at me. "Not funny, Joey."

"What are you doing here?"

"Why aren't you happy to see me?"

"I'm always happy to see you, but don't you have classes the rest of the week?"

"You're such a killjoy," she whined. "I decided to ditch class for a long weekend at home."

"Well I'm glad I'm working my ass off so that you can ditch class whenever you want to."

"Yeah, yeah, Jonah the martyr works more than anyone else."

"Yes, actually I do," I affirmed. "Where's Mom?"

"*She's* where we're supposed to be. They went on ahead to Mable's so we wouldn't lose our table."

"They?"

"Mom and creepy Dr. Redding."

I could feel my blood pressure rising. "But…but Wednesday is…*family* night! Not dinner with Mom's douchebag boyfriend."

"You call him that a lot, you know."

"That's because I can't think of anything else that would better describe him. I can't believe Mom was too chicken shit to wait for me."

Katie raised an eyebrow. "Because you wouldn't have gone if you had known Paul was coming."

"That goes without saying."

"Come on, big brother, let's get this over with."

Once Katie was securely tucked into the SUV we made our way to

Mable's, and I had to admit I did miss her. Having her in the passenger seat while she flipped through dozens of radio stations looking for the perfect song reminded me of every ride to school, friend's house, and sports event she had to attend. Even when she was home from school during the summer and winter breaks we barely saw each other. Between her social schedule and my job, moments like this were rare.

During the next twenty minutes Katie gabbed about her new classes, and in my opinion spent a little too much time talking about a guy in her Chemistry lab. When we finally arrived at The Maple Inn I pulled around the back to the kitchen's entrance since if I dared to enter through the front door I would have my ass handed to me. Mable insisted that family and guests enter in the back through the kitchen, that way she could greet everyone personally while she was cooking.

My mouth was already watering from the smells that were wafting from inside as we crossed the gravel parking lot. When I opened the door for my sister, I heard Mable's squeal before I stepped inside. She was also a hugger and was very busy suffocating my sister.

"Mable, don't kill her, I already paid for a full semester. She needs to finish it."

Mable let go of Katie and put her hands on her hips. "Don't go gettin' all jealous, I never get to see Miss Katie Bell now that she's in school. Now give me my hug and let me get back to cookin', we're hoppin' tonight."

I did as she asked and squeezed her tightly into my chest. I could easily see over her into the dining room, and she was right, it was packed. But through the crowd I could see my mother leaning in and whispering something into Paul's ear. The intimacy of the gesture made my skin crawl.

"All right, get on in there," Mable said as she let go of me and went back to her stove. "Your mom and her friend have already ordered. Katie, I'm assuming you want your turkey sandwich?"

"Do I ever want anything else? You put crack on your turkey sandwiches, that's why I'm addicted to them."

Mable laughed as she looked at me down the bridge of her nose. "I kept some meatloaf for you from last night."

"Do I get seconds?"

"Have I ever not saved you enough for seconds?"

"What about thirds?"

"Inside," she warned and waved us both away. "Oh, and I made some treats to take to Brianna tomorrow when you go up to Boston. Don't forget to take them when you leave tonight."

"Sure thing," I replied, even though I knew everything would either be eaten by me or the kids. Brianna admitted that since she had been turned into a Vampire she thoroughly missed Mable's famous maple cake.

After giving Mable another hug I led Katie through the dining room. My mother's head popped up from Paul's shoulder as we approached the table. Her eyes were seeking forgiveness, but I just sighed and kissed her cheek. Katie took the seat across from her, meaning that unfortunately I needed to sit in front of Paul. We nodded to each other cordially.

"So, Jonah," Paul began in a smug tone, "from your attire, I take it you didn't have to work today?"

I looked down at my faded blue jeans and maroon shirt. "No…I worked today, it's why I was late. I had a late pickup."

"Really?" he replied, turning his nose up a little as he pulled at the lapel of his brown blazer. "My father always used to tell me to dress for the job I wanted to have. Otherwise, how will your employer know that you want more from your career?"

For my mother's sake I swallowed my true response and instead replied, "Well, Paul, I think my employer wouldn't take me seriously if I came to work in my baseball uniform, since that's the job I always wanted, right Mom?"

She laughed and nodded, but as usual kept any opinion to herself.

Paul cleared his throat. "All I am saying, Jonah, is that you don't want to be a bus driver forever, and that starts with respecting yourself. Take how I dress, I walk into my practice and command respect."

"First of all," I began harshly, but Katie dug her fingernails into my thigh. I licked my lips and tried again in a softer tone. "First of all, Paul, I am not a bus driver, I'm the transportation coordinator for my security firm. Second, if I were a psychologist with my own practice, I still wouldn't dress like you."

"I am a psychiatrist, Jonah."

"Well there you go, neither of us knows what the other one does."

"Jonah, Paul," my mother warned across the table, "let's have a nice dinner. Ok?"

Paul placed his hand over my mother's and squeezed it until she sat back in her chair. "Jenny, I am only concerned about your son's future.

Jonah has established no real career path. He should be worried about that."

"Paul, the reason I don't have a career path is because for four years I've had to support my mother and sister practically on my own. And the only thing I can worry about now is how I'm going to pay the end of year property taxes *and* Katie's tuition in a couple of months. So I'm sorry if my plan isn't acceptable to you, but that's all I'm going to say about it so that I can give my mother the nice dinner she wants." Even though she already ruined it by inviting your sorry ass, I finished in my head.

Thankfully before Paul could insert yet another dig, Mable and her server came over to our table with four large plates. "Turkey sandwich for Katie Bell, meatloaf for Joey, and lamb shanks for the adults."

Paul cleared his throat again. "Excuse me, Mable, is it?"

Mable turned around politely with a fake smile she only gave when she was annoyed. "Yes, I'm Mable. Can I get you anything else?"

"Well yes. Meatloaf wasn't on the menu, and I would prefer that over the lamb."

"Oh, well Wednesday is the lamb shank special, which I know isn't Jonah's favorite. So I always save some meatloaf for him from the night before."

Paul snickered. "The wonderful thing about meatloaf is that it comes in a loaf, not just two slices, so you must have more. I will have what Jonah is having. Thank you."

Paul lifted his plate and held it up to Mable to take away. Just as I flinched, Mable squeezed my shoulder gently with one hand while she took Paul's plate with the other. "I will fix you a new plate right away."

"But…" I began to protest, but Mable shook her head firmly.

"It just means no second helpings tonight," she replied with a reluctant smile before disappearing into her kitchen.

I needed to stuff my mouth with food before nasty things came out. Katie seemed to feel the same way since she shoved half her sandwich in her mouth.

"Kids," my mother begged, "we should wait until Paul gets his dinner. It's only polite."

Katie put her sandwich back down on her plate and I dropped my fork making it clang loudly. Mom flinched and then searched for something to say to break the tension. "You know, Joey, I remember when you used to want my meatloaf like you do Mable's. I just can't seem to compete anymore when it comes to her cooking. I bet you wouldn't even eat it if I made it. Between Brianna and Mable, I feel pretty useless nowadays."

The piece of meatloaf still lodged in my mouth was turning into mush as I was struck dumb by her comments. Unfortunately, the torture didn't stop when Paul took my mother's hand and kissed it.

"Jenny, since we're waiting, do you think we should tell them?"

My mother's eyes grew wide as a fake smile stretched across her lips.

"T-tell us what?" Katie asked, her voice already trembling with worried anticipation.

Mom held up her hand in front of her to display a round solitaire diamond ring on her finger. "We're getting married."

Katie and I were completely silent, both of us looking at the ring on my mother's hand and the cocky expression on Paul's face. Mom looked between her two children, searching for the acceptance she desired, but then her expression changed when she didn't see it.

"I know this is a lot to take in," she began, "but this will be really good for all of us. We'll be able to be a family again."

Another silence fell upon the table just as Mable came back to the table and placed Paul's plate of meatloaf down in front of him. *My* meatloaf. *My* mother. *My* family.

"Is there anything else I can get you all?" Mable asked.

"Are you fucking kidding me?" I said in shock.

"I guess that's a no," Mable said and turned quickly from the table.

"Jonah! Language!" my mother shouted at me.

"Mom, have you completely lost your mind?" Katie shouted across the table.

Mom placed her hand on top of Katie's, but my sister snatched it away. "Katie Bell, please listen…"

"Jenny," Paul began, "you cannot coddle her. Katie, that is no way to talk to your mother. I will not stand for that kind of attitude in my house."

"It's not your house!" I yelled as I stood from my seat, causing the chair to fall over backwards and startle the other patrons. My heart was beating out of my chest. I took a breath before I looked at my mother's mortified expression. "God, you're such a…a…"

"Douchebag," Katie interjected.

"Right, a douchebag. He's a douchebag, Mom. How can you do this to Dad?"

"Jonah, your father has been dead for four years."

"Yes, Mom, I distinctly remember the day I lost my dad, because I also lost my mom. The day after Dad's funeral you went to bed for three months and I had to drop out of school because child services was threatening to take Katie away…"

"Jonah, please not here…" my mother begged.

"I made sure she had clean clothes, I made sure there was food in the house, and that she had lunch money. Me, Mom, not you, not Dr. Dipshit, me. While you sank into your depression, I went out and got a job so they wouldn't take away the house, and four years later I'm still paying for everything and having to watch you turn into a fucking zombie any time you're around Paul. I'm sick of it, Mom, and I'm sick of keeping my mouth shut."

Paul stood from his chair and threw his napkin down onto the table. "Jonah, this is neither the time nor the place, and I will not allow you…"

"Listen asshole, you are not my therapist and you are certainly not my father, so don't even begin to think you can tell me what to do. Screw this!"

I stepped away from the table, ignoring the stares from the other patrons as I passed, but then another thought took over and turned me back around. "Brianna has been good to me and our family. We'd be in a shelter if it weren't for her and you know it. I go to Boston because for a few days someone takes care of me for a change.

"You know what else, Mom, I remember your meatloaf too. And to tell you the truth it's better than Mable's, but you can't lay a guilt trip on me when you haven't made a meal for your kids in four years. If anyone stepped away from our family it was you. Katie and I have been waiting for you to come back to us, and yet you decided to choose Dr. Dipshit."

"Douchebag," Katie corrected.

I looked at my sister and gave her a wink before I turned away again. From the corner of my eye I saw Paul sit back in his chair and point his finger at Katie. Once again I turned around and rounded on him. "One last thing, Paul. If you ever talk to my sister like that again I will break your fucking jaw!"

I could hear gasps around me, and all my anger was suddenly replaced by guilt. This was Mable's restaurant, her business and home. When I entered the kitchen Mable was standing against a counter using her apron to wipe the tears from her eyes.

"I'm sorry, Mable," I said softly and ran outside, unable to address her fully because of my embarrassment.

"Joey, wait!" Katie cried after me, but I ignored her and fished through my pockets to find my keys to the SUV. I could hear my sister crunching through the gravel while I fumbled my way into the driver's seat. Just before I was able to close the door, I felt her hand on my arm. "Joey, you can't leave me alone with them."

I sighed as I turned to look at my sister. "Katie Bell, I'm sorry. I can't stay here."

"Then take me with you."

"I need to go and have a drink or something."

Katie pursed her lips. "I could use a drink."

"You're underage."

"Oh come on, Joey, I've had alcohol before."

"And I don't want to hear about it. Now come on, let me go."

"Can you at least drop me off at home? There's no way I can stay in there with the two of them. Please, Joey."

Like I said before, a teary woman melted me, even more so when it was my baby sister. "Ok, come on. I need to pack anyway."

Quickly she walked around the back of the SUV and then climbed into the passenger seat next to me, placing a shopping bag on the floor between her feet.

"What's with the bag?"

"The stuff for Brianna from Mable, remember? She practically threw it at me as I left."

I put the SUV in reverse and slowly began backing down the driveway. "It's a shame Bri can't eat any of it."

"Why's that?" Katie asked

Shit! My brain was on overload. "Uh...er...diabetes. She's on that special diet."

But honestly I couldn't give my explanation a second thought since Katie exploded into hysterical tears. I leaned her over the center console and hugged her tightly into my side as she sobbed over my mother's engagement to Paul. For four years we had all just trudged along in order to survive. Tonight, Katie and I were hit by a freight train of reality.

"I miss Daddy," she cried and it tore at my heart. My nose and jaw flexed with emotions I didn't want to release.

"Me too, Katie Bell. I don't see how Mom can go from Dad to Dr. Douchebag?"

"Dr. Dipshit was a pretty good one, too," she said with a snotty laugh.

"I think Dad would have liked that one."

"Yeah, then he would have given you the eye for swearing."

"Oh yeah, the eye…" I laughed as the vision of my father giving me his critical but amused squinted eye made me smile and tear up.

"Are you still going to go to Boston?"

"After tonight I definitely need to go."

Katie sniffled and wiped her nose with her sleeve. "Can you drop me back at school?"

"No."

"Please, Joey!" she begged as she rose from my side. "I can't stay in that house all weekend!"

"Hey, you decided to cut class, this is your punishment."

Katie crossed her arms in front of her chest and pushed out her bottom lip. "Don't go out tonight, then."

"Oh hell no. I need a drink. Or twelve."

"Then stay home," she pleaded as she squeezed my arm tightly to her chest. "There's beer in the fridge. Can't you just hang out with me tonight? We can watch movies, *you* can have a few beers, and I don't have to be alone. After what you did tonight, you know Mom will stay at Paul's. Please Joey, stay with me?"

I sighed knowing there was rarely a time I could completely deny Katie of anything. *We have to take care of our girls*, my father's voice rang in my ears.

"Fine. But no chick flick crap."

"Deal. Can we get a pizza? I'm starving."

Chapter Three

Jonah

I never thought I could get so drunk just sitting at home on the couch watching movies with my sister. Katie Bell kept feeding me bottle after bottle of beer, and I drank them gladly, anything to shut out the image of my mother holding her hand up with an engagement ring on her finger. But sadly the morning came and the sun's rays punished me severely from where I had passed out on the couch. My head was pounding, and my stomach couldn't even handle my usual tureen of coffee.

Knowing Katie would try to stop me from going to Boston, I quietly packed a bag and left the house before she woke. After everything that happened last night, Boston was looking better every second. My vacation couldn't have come at a better time. Only a quick stop at the Facility and I'd be on my way.

After I parked the SUV in the Facility's garage I was greeted by an enthusiastic Greg that my hangover was not prepared to deal with.

"Hey man," he said as he stepped in line behind me, "I was wondering when you'd be coming in."

"I'm just here to submit the schedules and then I'm taking off," I replied as we trudged up the single flight of stairs.

"Yeah, that's what I wanted to talk about. But hey, weren't those the clothes you left in last night?"

"Yep."

"So someone got lucky last night," Greg teased. "I hope she was asleep when you left, because you look like shit."

"Didn't get lucky. I'm just hungover. What do you want, Greg?"

Greg stepped in front of me and opened the door to the large common area where smells from the cafeteria were wafting throughout, making me nauseous as hell.

"Well, I was thinking that maybe you could put me as primary driver while you're gone."

I sighed, but continued my way across the common room. "You know I can't."

"Yeah, but I know tomorrow is a supply run and Cole hates doing that stuff."

"That's because Cole doesn't like having to talk to humans."

"Exactly. Let me do it. I know there's a pick up at Bazzuto's, and Mike B. knows me better than Cole. And remember what happened the last time he went to the pharmacy? You had to flirt with the owner for months to get back on good terms."

A shiver went through my body at the memory. I thought I'd never get the smell of mothballs out of my clothes from that dirty old lady. "Fine, fine. But you still have to take a Vamp with you."

"Can I go on pickups, too?"

"You're pushing it, Greg, but uh…if Sera says it's ok, then yeah," I replied as we approached the hallway that led to the dormitories. "Are we all set then? I need to grab a shower before I take off."

Greg nodded and took off in the other direction. I ducked into the stairwell to my left and went down to the basement level where rooms for the staff were located. Even though I lived only twenty minutes away, there were times when my hours were so long and late it was just easier to stay on-site. My room was like a small hotel room with a queen-sized bed, dresser, TV, and a small bathroom. Nothing fancy, but not cheap either. Thankfully I always kept a few changes of clothes and plenty of toiletries.

My head was clearer after the hot shower, but once the steam from the mirror began to dissipate I could see how tired I looked. The dark circles under my eyes seemed to sag near my cheeks which were starting to look gaunt. Even my scraggly hair was evidence that I hadn't been taking care of myself. Brianna had said to me on more than one occasion that I was always too busy taking care of everyone else, and eventually it would catch up to me. The events of last night seemed to have put me over the edge. Besides being angry, I think I was more upset over how easy it was for my mother to throw our family away.

Shaking off the demons that were beginning to soak back into my skin, I squirted a large amount of gel into my palm and combed it through my hair. It was so long on top that instead of the spiked look I was going for, it was beginning to look like a hair helmet. I certainly wouldn't be scoring with the ladies in Boston. Not that I'd been scoring with the ladies in Connecticut either. Working day and night didn't leave time to meet anyone outside of the Facility, and I certainly didn't want to hook up with anyone here. Others didn't have such hang ups, but I felt that you shouldn't screw where you ate. Well, something like that.

With a clean pair of jeans and a polo shirt, I headed out of my room in order to get the schedules submitted for the next week and finally get out of here. When I entered my small office, roughly the size of a walk-in closet, I found Seraphina spinning herself in my desk chair.

"Good morning, Sera," I said unable to stop my lips from stretching into a smile.

"Salute, Jonah," she replied as she stood from the chair.

"Yep, sallwoo to you too."

"Non, non, sa-loo, loo. Say it with me. Salute!"

"Did I forget we had a meeting this morning?"

Seraphina shook her head and fixed the back of my shirt collar. "Non, non. I wanted to drop something off with you, but now I wonder if you are ok."

I sighed knowing nothing got past her. "It's just family crap. Nothing I want to lay on my boss."

"I hope I am more zhan your boss, Jonah."

I smiled and wrapped my arms around her. She was more than my boss, she was family and I needed all the family I could get. "You know you are, but if I don't submit those schedules before I leave for Bri's you'll pull me back to Connecticut by my ear."

"Zhis is true," she winked and pointed to a gift bag sitting on my desk. "I got a little somezhing for you to give to zhe bébés."

I shook my head. "Brianna said you need to stop bringing the kids gifts."

A sly smile stretched across Sera's face. "But I am not giving zhem zhe gifts. You are." Sera kissed my check. "Bon voyage."

The trip itself usually only took two hours, and I was happy to see the sign saying Boston was only another fifteen miles. With only a short time until I reached Brianna's, I rifled through the pockets of my weekend bag for my cell phone and turned it on. I was determined to have a quiet and relaxing ride up to Boston without any distractions from my family or work.

"Call Bri," I said to my phone and a couple of seconds later the cabin of the car was filled with the sound of the other line ringing.

"Hello? Dis is Mama's phone," a young girl's voice answered.

"Wivy, don't answer like that," a young boy's voice said over her, "if it's him, he has to think you're Mama."

"Livy? Jack?" I said as the phone was shuffled between the two of them. "It's me, Jonah."

There was a pause. "Jack-Jack says you can't be Jonah."

"And why is that?"

There was another pause. "Jack-Jack says he doesn't know. But our Jonah is coming to see us today."

"He is, is he?"

"Uh-huh. Uh-oh, gotta go now."

"Livy wait! Don't…" but it was too late, the phone line died. With a sigh I called Brianna's number again, and after the third ring I was ready to leave a voicemail.

"Hel-hello? Hello? I'm here! I'm here, don't hang up!" Brianna said anxiously into the phone.

"Hey! It's Jonah!"

"Hey honey! Sorry about the kids, I heard them talking to someone and then I found them running out of the coat closet."

I laughed. "Is it usual for them to answer your phone while in the coat closet?"

Brianna sighed and laughed. "It is since I told them they couldn't use my phone, and when they asked why, I mistakenly told them it was because that's the number Santa Claus calls me on to check up on them. Since then, they have been hiding my phone and waiting for him to call.

The other day I found the two of them huddled inside one of the kitchen cabinets talking to a telemarketer. So how close are you?"

"About half an hour. Is that ok?"

"Of course! We're waiting for you. Oh, and remember if you don't find any street parking, go into the parking garage down the block. Cam and I will pay for it."

"Bri, I have money."

"I know you do. I'm just saying we'll pay for it. It'll get expensive, and the only reason you'll have to go in there is because there is never any parking in this freakin' city."

"Ok, ok, I'll let you know what happens. See you in a few."

"Great! I can't wait. Really, I mean it. These kids are driving me batty. Oh, I gotta go. Jackson Thomas, don't think I can't see you, you put those fangs back up in your mouth…Olivia stop hissing at your brother…I don't care who started it…"

Unfortunately the line went dead again. I really wish I could have listened to the end of that confrontation. As I cleared the call from my cell phone's screen, four voicemails and seven text messages chimed. I couldn't check them, I couldn't even think of checking them. They would suck me right back to where I had escaped from.

Just as I pressed the power button to turn the phone off again, two cars cut in front of me. I slammed on my breaks and swerved into the emergency lane causing a loud thump to come from the trunk. Wondering if it was just a fluke or if something was wrong with the car, I sped up and slammed the breaks. The noise came again, but this time it was accompanied by a yelp.

Immediately I pulled the car over and put it in park. Just as I stepped out of the car, the trunk unlatched and a flash of blonde hair came out from inside.

"Ashlyn!" I shouted as I wrapped my arm around her waist and pulled her around to the side of the car and away from the traffic whizzing by. "What the hell…" I yelled when she tried running around me, and again I grabbed her around the waist and pressed her up against the car and held her wrists to her chest. "Stop, just stop!"

"Let go of me," Ashlyn growled and jerked her wrists out of my grip.

"Ashlyn, what the hell! Were you seriously hiding in the trunk? You could have suffocated in there!"

Ashlyn rolled her eyes and huffed loudly as she pulled her tattered hoodie around her. "There's a trunk release inside, idiot. As soon as you got to where…"

"You knew I was leaving today. Oh my god, you knew I was taking this car, didn't you! You were standing there when I told Eris."

"Look, just go. I'll find my way."

I dragged my hands down my cheeks. "You're insane."

"I've been called worse."

"Stop with the tough girl act."

"It's not an act," she replied loudly as her eyes flared with anger.

"Bullshit. No wonder my phone was blowing up. Do you have any idea what you've done? You probably have half a dozen Vampires scouring Connecticut looking for you thinking you've been taken or something. You have no idea the dangers…"

"Trust me, I know the monsters that are lurking out there."

"You don't know shit!" I shouted at her as my frustration with her attitude took over. Turning away from her, I walked several paces down the highway and kicked small rocks out of my way. "Half hour away," I yelled to myself then turned back around to see Ashlyn's sullen expression. "Just a half hour away! I haven't had time off in months, let alone four consecutive days away from the Facility. Now I have to drive all the way back. I'm losing a whole day because of you. And that's if they even let me leave again. I cannot believe this shit. Eris and Sera are probably flipping out."

Ashlyn ran to me and placed her hand on my wrist as I scrolled through my missed calls. "If you hadn't slammed on your brakes you wouldn't have known I was in the trunk and I would have snuck out once you finally stopped. All I'm asking is that you look the other way. Once I get into the city I can take care of myself."

Ashlyn shivered in front of me, her hoodie not thick enough for the New England weather.

"Can you get in the car please?" I said flatly as I pulled her hand from my wrist.

"Please, Jonah…"

"Just get in the car," I snapped at her but she didn't move. "Ashlyn, you've never been on the streets in New England. You're standing here shivering and it's only noon. What are you going to do tonight? You have no money, you don't know where you're going, and you are putting yourself at risk when you don't need to."

Ashlyn shook her head and I could see her eyes filling with tears. "I can't...I can't go back there. You don't understand what it's like for me in places like that."

"Ashlyn, please, just get in the car."

We stared at one another for several seconds before two tears streaked down her cheeks and she sighed in defeat. Without saying a word I walked to the passenger side of the car and opened the front door. Slowly Ashlyn walked toward me and eventually sank into the seat before I closed her in. As I walked around the front of the car, my cell phone rang in my hand and Eris's name flashed across the screen.

I waited until I was inside the car before I answered, being sure to turn up the heat in order to warm Ashlyn's still shivering body. "Hello, sir."

"It is about time!" Eris said angrily. "I have been calling you for over an hour."

"Sorry, sir. My phone was off, but I know why..."

"The hybrid you brought in yesterday has gone missing," Eris interrupted.

"I know..."

"Security is looking everywhere for her..."

"Eris, sir, I..."

"Sera thinks she may have run away, but others are afraid..."

"Eris! I have her. Ashlyn is with me."

There was a pause on the other line, but finally he replied, "You could have said that earlier. Jonah, you know you must have permission in order to take a hybrid from the Facility."

I sighed. "I didn't take her with me, sir. She stowed away in the trunk. I just found her."

"Oh, I see. I will call off the search then. How long until we can expect you back?"

Through the side of my eye I could see Ashlyn's pleading eyes staring at me. I shook my head as a hundred conflicting thoughts ran through my head. With a long sigh I replied, "Sir, I'm only a few minutes outside of Boston...I'll...I'm going to see if Brianna minds that I bring Ashlyn with me. I really don't want to have to make this drive three times today."

Eris pondered my suggestion for a few moments before answering, "Very well. But mind you, if that hybrid causes my daughter or her family any trouble, you are to bring her back here straight away. Is that clear?"

"Yes, sir," I replied as I put the car in gear. "Thank you."

"Don't thank me yet. We will have a discussion about not letting something like this happen again."

"Yes, sir," I answered, but was groaning on the inside.

Once I hung up the phone I hit the gas and eventually got back onto the highway. After a few minutes of silent driving, Ashlyn turned and looked in my direction. "Where are you really taking me?"

I gave her a quick glance, and then concentrated on the highway in front of me. "You heard me. I'm taking you with me to Brianna's, and if she freaks out I'll get a hotel or something. I refuse to go back to Connecticut until Monday like I'm supposed to. I will not let you ruin my time off."

"Who…who is she?"

"She's a friend of mine. She also happens to be Eris's daughter, so I'd appreciate it if you would behave yourself."

"You don't have to talk to me like I'm a child."

"Then stop acting like one."

Ashlyn became quiet again, choosing to look out the window as we came upon a toll booth. Once through the gate I could hear her sniffling.

"Why are you crying?" I asked, choosing to keep the window cracked because of the smell that was wafting from her side of the car.

"I'm embarrassed."

"About what?"

"You're forcing me to go to this woman's house, and I'm…this homeless person. Most people don't want girls like me coming to stay in their house. I have a toothbrush and a stick of deodorant," she said as she patted the colorful bag she had strapped across her chest. "That's all I have to my name, and once your friend realizes that, it'll get awkward. It always does."

"Ashlyn," I began in a much softer tone, "first of all, Brianna is really cool. She's been through a lot too, and knows what it's like to be a hybrid. Believe me when I say she'd be the last person to ever judge you. She'll go out of her way to make you feel comfortable. And second, we'll get you some clothes and stuff."

"I don't want your charity," she snapped.

I clamped my jaw in order not to snap back, but I knew now that it was the chip on her shoulder talking. "It's not charity, and it certainly isn't from me. There's a fund that helps hybrids like you get on your feet. You need to start realizing that there are people in this world that want to help you and don't need anything in return for it."

"Everyone wants something."

"Dammit, Ashlyn, can't you just…"

"Shouldn't you call her or something?" Ashlyn shouted as she propped her elbow on the window and rested her head in her hand.

Knowing she was right and I couldn't delay it any further, I called Brianna's number once again.

"You can't be here already," Brianna said cheerily.

"Uh, no. Still about twenty minutes away. So, hey, how much do you love me?"

Chapter Four

Brianna

Lunch in the Burke home was usually the quietest time of the day, mainly because the children were stuffing their faces. Generally it was my favorite time of the day, not just for the silence, but because I loved watching how a peanut butter and jelly sandwich could create absolute joy on the faces of my three little angels as they sat in the tall chairs at my kitchen's island. Olivia, Livy, was my baby girl with a head full of long soft black curls, rosy cherub cheeks and big dark eyes. Jackson, my Jack-Jack, was the spitting image of his father from his curly hair to his formal nature. Then there was William James Ryan, Will, or Wills as most of us called him. He was the son of Renee and John Ryan, my and Cameron's godson, and brother in the eyes of my twins. He was nine months younger than his counterparts, almost to the day. Renee and John didn't waste any time during the honeymoon.

"Mama?" Livy asked as she licked her fingers free of strawberry jelly.

"Yes, baby girl?"

Livy sucked in the corners of her lips in a cute pleading smile and batted her long lashes as she asked, "Can I have more sandwich?"

"No, honey. You've had both halves of your sandwich. You can have more carrots if you want them."

Olivia's bottom lip jutted out immediately and began to tremble. I knew the tantrum would soon begin. "But I'm still hungry."

"And carrots will help with that."

From the twinkle in my son's eye I knew he was about to stir the pot. His mission in life was to torture his twin sister. "Mama, can *I* have more sandwich?"

Little shit. Unfortunately I had to say, "Yes, honey."

I took the other half of Jack-Jack's sandwich and placed it on his plate and waited for my daughter's head to explode.

"Why does he get more!"

"Olivia," I said calmly, "you finished your sandwich, Jack-Jack didn't. Now you can have more..." but that was all I could say before the meltdown began. No amount of carrots would console my baby girl now.

"Awbie?" Wills called to me. It was how he had said Aunt Bri when he was younger and the name stuck.

"Yes, Wills," I answered over Livy's wails. "Do you want the rest of your sandwich?"

He nodded his head and held out his little hand. Once he had taken his sandwich he leaned over Jackson and stretched his arm out in Livy's direction. "Here, Wivy, you can have mine."

Wills was always the peacemaker between the twins, though his gift was generally used on Olivia. Not to say that he didn't often participate in the twin's antics. Just a little while ago he was the lookout while the twins confiscated my phone and hid in the coat closet. My little darlings were smart, above and beyond others their age, but there were certain things they thankfully hadn't figured out yet. Such as, if Wills was left by himself, that meant the twins were up to no good. Wills would never voluntarily be without them unless he had been given a mission, which he always took very seriously. Also, the twins didn't count on the fact that Will's eyes gave everything away. Somehow between Renee's emerald green and John's stunning blue, Will was blessed with the biggest, almost turquoise eyes that showed even the most minuscule amount of deception.

Olivia's tears finally stopped and she happily took the rest of Will's sandwich. "Fank you, Wills," she said and quickly began to eat with a smile from ear to ear.

"Awbie, can I have more carrots?"

I placed a handful of carrots on his small plate and he eagerly began to devour them. "One day, Wills, I think you're going to turn into a carrot."

He smiled at me for only a second before his carrot became an airplane.

With the three of them happy and quietly eating again I could begin to clean up before Jonah came bursting through the door, with an added guest mind you. I certainly couldn't wait to hear that story. I really wanted to know what could have happened in the ten minutes between phone calls.

Placing the jelly and bag of carrots in my arms, I stepped over to the refrigerator and opened the double doors to find two bottles of blood staring back at me. Fabi had dropped them by yesterday after I let the last two bottles go to waste. Cameron would not be happy when he found out that I hadn't fed like I promised. It wasn't like we hadn't had the argument before, it was a regular occurrence whenever he would return from San Francisco. The sum of it all, I didn't like being a Vampire. Plain and simple. Even though it had been three and a half years since I had been Turned, it had happened against my wishes. I didn't like having to drink blood, I felt it was wrong. I didn't know who the blood belonged to. What if it too had been taken against their will? What if they died giving it? I had a lot of time on my hands to dream up all kinds of anxiety.

Actually, I had yet to drink directly from a live person, much to everyone's dismay. Most times I fed from Cameron, which in the beginning was easy enough because we were always together. Unfortunately Victor had laid on significant pressure for Cameron to be in the manor more and represent the Warriors in various matters across the country. Honestly I felt like Victor was reneging on his deal of allowing us to stay in Boston in order to raise the kids, and Cameron didn't push back as much as I wanted him to. Personally I felt that even though Cam didn't like being away from his family, he liked the work he was doing for our coven.

Usually he wasn't away for more than a week or so, but this time he had been gone for three weeks and we all missed him terribly. This trip was longer because he was preparing the manor for the twins. He was also purchasing Daddy O and Maddy's new home, and even scoping out a few properties for Renee and John. In a few weeks' time there would be a mass exodus of the Burke, Morgan, and Ryan clans from the East Coast. We were obviously moving so that Victor could have Cameron readily available to him, and allow the kids to be with their father. Maddy, having left Facility West to be with Daddy O, moved to the North Carolina house shortly after the twins were born. Now that we were moving across the country, we had convinced them to come with us so they would be closer. Eris and Sera were moving back to their island, mainly because Sera refused to be further than two hours from her grandchildren. And lastly, John (with the recommendation of Cameron and Maddy), had been offered the chief physician position at Facility West. With a huge raise in pay, opportunities to do research, and a regular schedule that would allow him to spend more quality time with his family, the decision for him was simple. Plus Renee wasn't too keen on us moving to California without her. But I had to admit that the feeling was mutual.

"Mama?"

"Yes, Jack-Jack," I answered, blinking back from my thoughts and closing the refrigerator door.

"Are you going to have some of your special wine?" he asked, meaning blood.

"No, baby, it's too early for wine."

Although my babies knew what I was, and consequently what they were, there were some terms we used code for. My children had fangs, although we couldn't explain why, therefore it was pointless to hide our lifestyle from them altogether. They were smart enough to know their family wasn't like those they went to school with, and they also knew to keep it to themselves. Wills was also very smart for his age, not like the twins, but brighter than many other three year olds. But his two best friends made sure he didn't slip up around others. Thankfully all three of them had been accepted to the same preschool, and even assigned to the same class. On the first day of school Renee took a tranquilizer and went home while Cameron and I stayed perched around the corner waiting for a phone call from the school or the sudden evacuation of the building. But neither came. Days came and went, and we realized our children didn't need us, much to our chagrin.

School was only two days a week, and the other three days the Burke home was daycare for Wills and the twins. Yes, sometimes it was overwhelming, but it was also absolutely fulfilling. However, today instead of providing daycare for Wills because Re was working, she was taking the day to begin packing up the house. Begging the question, why could I hear her singing on my doorstep?

The front door unlatched, and suddenly the voice of my dearest friend rang through the house. "He-llo?"

"Mommy!" Will squealed as he lowered himself to the floor.

A moment later Renee was stepping up to the landing and Wills dove into her arms. "Oh, little man, you're getting too big for that. How did you get heavier since I dropped you off this morning?"

Will simply shrugged and curled himself under Renee's chin as she stepped into the kitchen.

"It must be all the carrots he ate at lunch," I said as I wiped away the peanut butter and jelly from the faces of my children with a wet cloth.

"Will Ryan, one of these days you're going to turn into a carrot."

Will poked his head up. "That's what Awbie said too!"

"Of course she did, we almost share a brain." Will's eyes widened as he looked between his mother and me. "Just kidding, little man, go play."

Wills jumped out of Renee's arms and followed the twins to the dining room we had converted into a playroom. While the kids played, Renee helped me clear the lunch dishes.

"Not that I'm judging," I began.

"But you're going to anyway," she interrupted as she took the bread from the counter and placed it in the pantry.

"How exactly can you pack up your house while you're standing in mine?"

She shrugged and rolled her eyes. "I checked things out at the storage unit and then went and got boxes. After that I just wasn't feeling it."

"Ah, well, if you weren't feeling it," I laughed.

"Speaking of not judging, have you…uh…fed lately?"

"Why?"

"Frankly, you look like p-o-o-p," she said softly.

"Re, my children can spell."

"Oh please, they can't hear me."

"Mama, Aunt Re said poop," Jackson shouted from the playroom.

"Yes, Jack-Jack," I moaned and eyed Renee, "Aunt Re said poop."

All three kids broke out into hysterical laughter and sang the praises of poop.

"I hate that your kids are smarter than mine."

"Re, my kids have fangs and can control Vamps and hybrids with their minds. Trust me when I say I'd rather they be like Will."

"Well, my kid is pretty awesome," she said proudly. "But hey, back to you. Seriously, you're paler than usual and the circles under your eyes keep getting darker. Are you not eating again?"

I sighed and turned away from her, padding down the hallway to the linen closet to get fresh sheets for Jonah's friend. "I just can't find the time."

Renee stepped into the hallway and followed me into the guest room. "Bri, you can't bullshit your twin. Why aren't you eating?"

"Mama, Aunt Re said bull…"

"Yes, Livy, I know what your aunt said." I looked over the bed and glared at Renee.

"And after knowing me for almost fifteen years, you should know it's almost impossible for me not to swear. I'm surprised Wills doesn't talk like he's from the docks."

We laughed as I pulled the bedspread down to the floor and fluffed out the clean fitted sheet. Renee grabbed the opposite end and the two of us began tucking the corners of the sheet over the mattress.

"Come on, Bri, you still haven't answered my question. Why aren't you eating?"

"To quote you, 'I'm just not feeling it.'"

Renee rolled her eyes. "Don't use my air quotes against me. You have to be the first Vamp with an eating disorder."

"Once Cam gets home…"

"That's not the answer. Plus, he's going out with John and Jonah tonight, there won't be much time."

"It doesn't take long," I replied, urging her to let the topic drop.

"Er…why are we making this bed, anyway? Jonah usually stays upstairs."

"He's bringing some girl with him."

"A girl?! Oh thank god, for a while there I thought he was gay. And dammit, he's just too cute to be gay. I need to be able to fantasize about someone."

"Renee!"

"What?"

A silence fell upon us, and then we burst out laughing.

"Ok, Re, help me finish making the bed," I said when our laughter finally died down.

"Fine," she replied as she grabbed the pillows from the floor while I stretched the comforter across the bed, "but you could make this bed ten times over in the same time it takes for me to help you."

I shrugged. "I know, but I still like doing things the way I used to, especially when you're here. It makes it feel like old times, like things never changed."

"Buuut, they did," she said as she threw the pillows messily up against the headboard. "It could be worse, you could be six feet under." I glared at her. "What? You're the one who's all 'I'm so sad I get to spend the rest of my life with the man of my dreams.'"

"And watch everyone else around me grow old and die," I replied.

Renee chewed on the inside of her cheek. We'd had the conversation so many times, and neither of us ever won. Just then, "Oh good, the doorbell," she said and ran from the room.

The front door unlatched and Jonah's voice echoed up the stairs. "Hello? I know you're home, so stop hiding."

The kids ran out from the dining room and squealed with joy at the sight of Jonah. While the boys took the stairs, Olivia leapt into the air, landed with her stomach on the banister and slid down the railing. When she had reached the end, she launched herself in the air completing a full layout twist and landed in Jonah's arms. All the bags he had in his arms thumped loudly on the floor in order to catch her. Unfortunately this wasn't something she only did with Jonah. This was how my baby girl greeted almost everyone.

Jonah gave my daughter a big hug and kissed her several times on the cheek before putting her down on the floor. He moved the bags from where they had dropped on the floor and stepped aside to allow his friend with extremely dirty blonde hair to come inside.

Renee nudged me with her elbow and said through the side of her mouth, "What's with the homeless girl?"

"Re!"

"Oh come on, we're both thinking it."

I wanted to tell Renee she was wrong, but the smell that was wafting up the stairs since the girl entered the house made me think that perhaps Jonah had picked her up off the street. I know it was rude to ask someone to leave because of the way they smelled, but my Vamp sense of smell was making her presence difficult to deal with.

With a sigh, both Renee and I came down the stairs to greet Jonah and his friend who was now almost cowering in the corner. While Jonah hugged and tussled with the boys, Olivia climbed up my leg and waist until her arms curled securely around my neck.

"Mama, she's a hybie," she said loudly as she pointed to Jonah's friend.

"Livy, it's hybrid, not hybie, and we don't point. I'm so sorry...er..."

"Oh!" Jonah said and stepped to attention. "Ashlyn meet Brianna, her kids Olivia and Jackson, and that's Renee and her son Will."

I extended my hand and Ashlyn tentatively took it, but after only two seconds she ripped her hand from mine and backed herself further into the corner.

"You brought me to a house of Vampires!"

Jonah's eyes grew in confusion. "Uh...I didn't think it mattered. They're not all Vamps."

Olivia climbed down my body and stepped in front of Ashlyn and took her hand without asking. "It's ok, Ashwyn, we're nice. I promise." Suddenly Ashlyn's demeanor changed and she became almost as giggly as the children. "Come on! I wanna show you my princess castle."

Olivia pulled on Ashlyn's arm and the two of them ran up the stairs with the boys following after. Once they were all out of sight, Renee and I glared at Jonah.

"I know, I know," he pleaded, "she might be a little crazy."

"Oh that's comforting," Renee replied sarcastically.

I gestured to the living room behind us. "Let's go in here where they can't hear us. I need to know what you just got me into. Re, can you go and watch the kids?"

"What! Uh-huh, I wanna hear about the crazy chick."

I raised an eyebrow at her and reluctantly she trudged up the stairs while Jonah and I stepped into the living room.

"Jonah, be honest, are my kids in danger?"

"I don't think so, Bri. She's been a little, shall we say, resistant to admit she needs help. She's terrified of staying at the Facility, but won't say why. She hid in the trunk of the car..."

"She was in the trunk?"

He nodded. "The only reason I found her was because two cars cut me off and I had to slam on the breaks. She must have been in there for hours, maybe even overnight."

"Well that would account for the smell."

"Yeah no, she smelled like that yesterday. Bri, she has nothing, and I mean nothing but those clothes she has on and her purse. I was hoping that..." Jonah widened his eyes and he gave me a big cheesy pleading smile, "...maybe...you could give her a change of clothes until I can take her shopping tomorrow."

"You're going to take her shopping?" I replied doubtfully causing Jonah to look offended.

"I spent many a Saturday in the mall shopping with Katie. Please, Bri?"

I sighed, my heart now pouring out for Ashlyn. "Come on, we'll go find something." Gesturing for him to follow me, we traveled back through the foyer and into the master bedroom down the hall. "What's with all the bags?"

"One is from Sera…"

"I knew she'd find a way to get around the no more presents sanction I put on her."

"The other is from Mable, treats for you, which means treats for the kids."

I opened the door to the walk-in closet and began searching through the stacks of sweatpants and workout clothes. "I'm surprised you didn't eat it all on the way up here."

He laughed. "Well, I can't lie, I did eat half of it. So hey, is Cameron back yet?"

"Technically he got back this morning, but he's been in a meeting with the Negotiators all day," I replied just as I found the black pair of newer workout pants I was looking for and pulled out the matching hoodie.

"The Negotiators are still around? I thought they disbanded after Dante's death."

"Er, yes and no," I replied as I stepped out of the closet and placed the clean clothes on the bed next to Jonah. "They've gone through multiple leaders and they're still a mess. Victor sent Cameron to tell them to get their act together, last straw kind of thing. The other covens are pretty fed up with them."

"He's still going to come out tonight, right?"

"Hell ya," I affirmed as I stepped over to my lingerie chest and pulled out a pair of socks and underwear that I had only just bought and not worn. You couldn't put clean clothes on and still wear dirty underwear, and goodness knows how long Ashlyn had been wearing hers. "The last place he wants to be is at this meeting. He said he wouldn't stay past five and he'll fake a sick child if he has to. Only Fabi knows our children don't get sick."

"Speaking of the kids, Livy's gift seems to be working well," he laughed.

"I'm so sorry about that. She doesn't see hybrids very often, unlike Jack-Jack who sees Vamps all the time. The only hybrids she sees are Sera, Jared's skanky girlfriend Nikki, and Nikki's sweet sister Natasha."

"Nikki's still skanky?"

"Nikki will always be skanky. She's the only hybrid I wouldn't mind letting Livy use her gift on. If my daughter only knew what she was capable of."

"She doesn't know?"

I shook my head as I placed the socks and underwear in between the sweatpants and hoodie. "Neither of them do."

"Why not?"

"It's more of a protection from Jack-Jack. I mean if you had a way to control your parents, wouldn't you use it?" Jonah smiled and understood. "Speaking of, want to tell me what happened with your mom?"

"Who told you?"

I laughed. "Mable sent a message, Sera called, even Katie sent me a text."

"Ah crap, I'm sorry. The last thing you need is to be brought into my family crap."

Taking the clean clothes in my arms, I waved him to follow me out of the room. "This is the last time you'll be able to crash at my house and complain about your family. I have cold beer in the fridge, your favorite chips and salsa, and you're officially on vacation. Perfect time to get things off your chest."

Jonah stood, but paused and stared at me for a moment. "Is it weird I'm missing you already?"

I smiled and sank into my hip. "Well, I am pretty wonderful. Now come on, let's find a polite way to tell your girlfriend she needs to take a shower."

"She's not my girlfriend," Jonah said firmly as we exited the bedroom.

"Uh-huh. Any other guy would have turned that car right around and taken her back. You, on the other hand, did not. Now why is that?"

"Er…because I knew you'd have cold beer and my favorite chips and salsa."

"I think it's because you wanted me to meet your girlfriend before I moved away."

Jonah growled. "She's not my girlfriend."

Chapter Five

Cameron

Ormond, the seventh leader of the Negotiator coven since Dante's death, stood at the front of the long table in the Victorian-styled conference room. He was smug, pompous, and nothing like Dante which is probably why I did not care for him. For hours they had been droning on about minute issues rather than discuss any of their real problems. At this point I was ready to find anything silver and jam it into my eye.

"So, in regards to the decision to change the coven's name from the Negotiators," Ormond began, "we have seven for, seven against, and three abstentions."

All seventeen Vampires sitting around the conference table groaned. From what Fabiani had told me, this was a topic that had been voted upon at almost every meeting since Dante's death, and every vote ended in a draw. So it begged the question, why were they still voting on it?

Ormond cleared his throat and shook the tension from his face. "My pupils, you have elected me as your leader. So I beg you to let me guide you. You must see that our coven needs a facelift. We need to move forward and not be blinded by our need to keep things the same. Now, my pupils…"

"We are not your pupils," Fabiani grumbled. All heads turned in his direction. "What? Most of us are thinking it."

Ormond scowled across the table. "And what hypocrisy would that be?"

Fabiani rose from the table with a seriousness I rarely saw, and with all the confidence in the world. "Ormond, you sit at the head of our table preaching how we need to change. Yet you try to copy Dante in almost every way, and may I say you do it badly. We are not your pupils, and you are not our master. Our master is dead, and we have done nothing but embarrass ourselves since his death. The other covens are laughing at us. We've become a joke among our race. We need to get ourselves together, and that doesn't start with changing our name."

"Is that why there is a Warrior among us? To force us get ourselves together?" a light-haired Negotiator I did not know the name of said nastily while he eyed me up and down.

Another Negotiator sitting at the opposite end looked to the fair-haired Negotiator as he said, "He's here because Fabi's in the Warriors' pocket."

To which the fair-haired Vamp replied, "He's in something of a Warrior, but I don't think it's called a pocket."

"Well considering Victor wants to dictate everything, you never know what he makes his assassin call his…"

"That is enough," I said firmly as I slowly stood from my chair, effectively silencing the room. "Ormond, although you have neglected to tell your coven members, you know I was asked by not only Victor but by all the coven leaders to come here today and deliver a message."

Ormond folded his hands together and leaned forward on the table. "And what would that be?"

"To continue on Fabi's sentiment, you need to get your act together. This coven needs to shape up or disband, it is that simple. Your lack of leadership is evident and has caused you to slack on your duties as an established coven."

"All covens have growing pains when a new leader takes over," Ormond replied snidely.

"No coven has gone through seven leaders in their existence let alone three years. I have sat here respectfully all day and listened while you all squabble over pointless issues. Your coven has real problems, both in business and in morale, neither of which will be solved by a change of name. The other coven leaders need to see a successful turnaround within the next six months…"

"And what constitutes successful?" Ormond interrupted.

I could feel the muscles in my face fall in disgust. "If you need to ask, then there are bigger problems here. Ormond, the coven leaders are now your peers and it is your job as head of the Negotiators to convince them that this coven is worthwhile. And yes, I do know the pressure can be daunting. But at the end of the day, you have six months to make a full turnaround."

Ormond's bottom lip disappeared into his mouth, and at the silence Fabiani asked, "And if we don't prove successful, what will happen?"

Slowly I looked around the room and for the first time saw worried and nervous faces around the table. "After six months if you do not voluntarily disband, you will no longer be recognized as an established coven and you will lose all the benefits and protections that it provides you."

The light-haired Negotiator gave a soft harrumph before saying, "And if the leaders no longer recognize us then they lose our annual sponsorships."

"Perhaps the money would be missed if your coven was not default on your obligations for the past two years," I rebutted.

Ormond suddenly looked uncomfortable, as did the other six former leaders that sat in the room. I knew first hand from Fabiani that few of the coven members knew how deep their coven's debt had gotten.

Taking my suit jacket from the back of the chair, I draped it over my arm before saying, "Gentleman, your coven has a great history among our race. Our covens were the first two formally established and I am not here to condemn you. But considering your performance the last few years, six months is a gift. Do not waste it. Good day, gentleman." I stepped away from my chair and turned toward the closed double doors, but then I could not help but turn back around. "One last thing. I may simply object when you make derogatory remarks regarding my brother, but regardless of his sexual orientation he is still the Warrior Assassin. If he ever hears of your comments he will find you, and kill you, and continue on with his day."

With a dramatic turn, I shrugged into my suit jacket and opened the double doors to the foyer just as the room behind me exploded in angry voices.

"I'll walk with you," Fabiani said behind me as I approached the door.

"You do not wish to stay for the fireworks I just started?"

Fabiani snaked his arm around mine and lead me out of the Negotiator's headquarters. "Oh that's nothing. I take it you haven't been home yet?"

I shook my head. "It made sitting in there even worse."

"I tried to warn you."

"Yes you did, but your description was still inadequate. Why have you not raised your hand to lead the coven?"

Fabiani's gate slowed as we traveled along the sidewalk toward a busier street. "I did raise my hand, twice actually."

"And you did not get enough votes?" I asked, very surprised when he shook his head.

"After the second time it was actually Ormond who took me aside and said that as long as I was sleeping with a Warrior I would never be elected coven leader. Apparently everyone sees it as a conflict of interest."

I pulled Fabiani to a stop as we reached the corner. "You were Dante's premier pupil, you of all people should be leading that coven. No one in there is doing his memory justice."

Fabiani shrugged. "Most days I don't mind. It means I get to spend a little more time with Devy, even if it is still behind Victor's back. But having been so close to Dante and learned so much from him, I find comfort knowing that when the coven finally goes to shit I'll still be way better off than my colleagues." Once again snaked his arm through mine. "Now speaking of my honey, how is he really? He can be so manly and unemotional on the phone."

"That could be since every time you call him he is with Father."

"It's not my fault he has daddy issues and is always with Victor." I gave him a skeptical look through the sides of my eyes. "Ok, ok. Maybe sometimes I try and push the issue with him coming out to Victor."

"And how is that working for you?"

"Not well. But I don't want to talk about that. What I want to know is, is he hopelessly lost without me?"

"You have been dating my brother for four years now, you know he never wears his emotions on his sleeve. I am sure he misses you in his own special way."

"Well, I will just have to make him feel better in my own special way when I see him tomorrow," he teased as he squeezed my arm closer into his chest.

"I did not know you were going out to San Francisco."

"Last minute client meeting. It's not until Monday, but I figured I'd get some Devy time beforehand."

"Since we have talked about your love, may I ask about mine?"

"Bri's fine. I made sure her sexual needs were met while you were gone."

I sighed in embarrassment at Fabiani's comment which even made a passerby gawk at us. "Fabi, perhaps we could speak a little softer?"

"Sure," he said even louder than before, "your wife is very aggressive in bed. Thank goodness you have those chains and stabilizing bars hanging from the ceiling, otherwise I would have…"

"Enough," I laughed as I wrapped my arm around Fabiani's head and held my hand up against his mouth. A second later he pushed me away laughing as well.

"But am I wrong?"

"Yes. Brianna is not my wife," I replied in a teasing tone, though begrudgingly on the inside.

Fabiani elbowed me in the ribs. "I knew she was a little sex pistol. The stay-at-home moms always are. Proper lady during the day, porn star at night."

"Fabi, please be serious with me, how has she been? Is she drinking?"

A strained smile came across his face. "I delivered two new bottles of, *you know*, yesterday. But she had the old bottles still there. Honestly, she doesn't look very healthy. I'm sorry, I did try."

I sighed deeply and with disappointment. Feeding on blood was still an ongoing battle with Brianna. "Do not be sorry, thank you for looking after her while I was away."

"Pshaw, we're family. One big f'd up family."

I laughed. "Speaking of, you are still meeting us down at Oliver's, right?"

"Of course. Devy and I will be there Thanksgiving morning. I have a big client meeting in D.C. the day before, so Devy's going to fly to meet me so we can be tourists for a couple of days. But of course he's telling Victor that he's with you and Bri at Oliver's already. Not sure if you're aware of that." I shook my head. "Yes, my life has become very cloak and dagger lately. Anyway, this is where I leave you."

We arrived where Fabiani had to turn to get to his apartment two streets over. He wrapped his arms around my neck, having to stand on his tip toes to do so. I patted him lightly on the back.

"I will see you in a few weeks then." I patted him on the back once again. "You can let go of me now."

Fabiani pushed me lightly away, though he was very dramatic about it.

"I told you not to fall in love with me. I am with your brother now, Cameron. You have to forget about me. Please, for both our sakes."

With a huff and a dismissive hand, he walked away from me and I was allowed to finish my trek home in peace, enjoying the sights, sounds, and even the smells of the city. It would be hard to leave the life that Brianna and I had created, but over the last year I had rarely spent two consecutive weeks here. The traveling and time away from my family was brutal, but most of the time I was enjoying the work. Today was an exception. Though Devin had volunteered, Father was smart enough to know that sending him would have been a disaster. Obviously Devin had ulterior motives for coming out here, but even with all his preventative measures, I had a feeling Victor somehow knew about Devin's relationship with Fabiani. He often reminded me that he knew everything about his children.

I, on the other hand, did not have so much luck with my own children. My twins were made up of constant surprises. I never knew what they would do next, or what would come out of their mouths. Brianna was a much better parent than I was, though she was forced to be since I was away so much. But things would be different now that we were moving back to the manor. At least that was what I had promised and I would work endlessly to make it a reality.

Brianna's transition to being a Vampire had been challenging to put it mildly. She barely spoke to me for weeks after the children were born. Finally one night after the twins had been up most of the night crying, she came out of their room, her fangs extended and dark purple circles under her eyes from lack of blood. I can still hear her tortured voice as she tried to tell me how horribly her throat burned, and how badly her body ached. I brought her mouth to my neck and instructed her how to draw my blood. It was not the perfect solution, and Vampire blood did not provide all the benefits human blood did, but at least it was something.

Since then getting Brianna to drink anything but my blood was difficult. I hated being forceful with her, it was my fault she was a Vampire and I still had some guilt about it. Although it was not even close to the amount of guilt I was stricken with in regards to my children. They were born pure, perfect hybrids. In a moment of weakness and grief I had fed them my blood and created a new breed of hybrids. They ate, breathed, and had heartbeats like their human counterparts, but they also possessed superior strength, speed, intelligence, and fangs.

Though many among our race knew that our children were human-like

Vampires, no one knew how they got that way, not even Brianna. It was my guilty secret, and I had still been too cowardly to tell her. She had been so angry with me over Turning her, I could not imagine her reaction if she knew what I had done to our children.

The twenty minute walk to our side of town went by mercifully quickly. The anticipation of seeing my family was almost overwhelming. As I approached our home, Jackson's voice rang in my head. Not only could my son see Vampires like his mother, he could also distinguish between them. A talent his mother was just learning to do.

As I stepped up to my front door I could hear the excitement bustling on the other side. The sounds made me smile as I opened the door and thrust my arms out just as my daughter's smiling face was coming at me from her graceful dismount from the banister. I caught her in the air and her thin arms wrapped around my neck while she pecked feverishly at my cheek.

"Ada! Ada! I missed you so much!" she squealed and squeezed me even tighter against her warm face.

I petted her soft black curly hair and kissed her forehead. "I missed you too, monkey." Olivia's eyes sparkled as she climbed up on my right shoulder and around to my left where she perched herself, hence my nickname for her. Once Olivia was settled, I was free to see my son and my nephew, William, make their way down the stairs and stand on the final step.

"Atten-tion!" I said firmly causing the two boys to push their shoulders back, holding their chests out and thrusting their arms down at their sides. I folded my hands behind my back and began to pace in front of the boys. "I trust the two of you have protected the homestead."

"Yes sir!" they shouted in reply.

Olivia's tiny index finger poked me in the middle of my cheek. "I helped too, Ada."

I turned my head and winked at her. "I am sure you did, monkey." Sharply I turned back to the boys, causing them to snap back to attention. "In my absence did you watch over your mother? Protect her from harm?"

"Yes sir," Jackson responded.

William raised his hand as he replied, "I watched Awbie, too!"

"Master William, I have no doubt. My boys, I am very pleased with your performance. Now can I get some hugs?"

Jackson and William giggled as they bent their knees in unison and launched themselves into my outstretched arms – Jackson in my right arm, immediately nuzzling his head under my chin, while William sat in the crook of my left. I walked up the stairs with the three children a very happy man.

"Cam, guess what," William began, only one of three people I tolerated hearing my nickname from.

"I simply cannot guess, William, you must tell me," I replied.

"I can wead a new book now," he said proudly.

"Then you will have to read it to me," I replied just as excited for him. It had to be difficult for him to see Olivia and Jackson reading short novels while he was graduating from picture books.

Olivia pulled on my ear. "Guess what, Ada?"

"What, monkey?"

"Jonah brought a friend with him," she said happily as we reached the top of the stairs where I could see Renee sitting at the kitchen island, and my angel putting dishes away in the cabinets.

"He did?"

"Yes I did, and trust me it was a surprise to me too," Jonah said as he came out from the door to the staircase that lead to the third floor.

I laughed lightly, not quite sure of his meaning, but assumed I would be informed tonight during our night out. Placing the children down on the floor, I took Jonah's extended hand, pulled him to my chest, and patted his back as he did mine.

"Good to see you, man," he said as we released each other.

"And you as well," I replied and then looked around the room. "Where is your guest?"

He pointed down the hall. "Taking a shower."

"Thank god," Renee moaned.

Once again I was in the dark and looked to Jonah.

"So, this friend you brought, is she your girlfriend?"

"She is NOT my girlfriend."

"So you say," Renee teased.

Brianna shushed everyone. "I'm sure she can hear us."

As if on cue, the bathroom door clicked open and a young woman with long wet blonde hair came out from within, oddly wearing one of Brianna's outfits. Jonah turned quickly and shuffled down the hallway, gesturing for her to come into the kitchen.

"Ashlyn, come and meet Cameron first. He's Brianna's…er…" he looked up at me as he pulled the girl down the hall behind him, "fiancé still?"

I nodded and ignored Brianna's glaring eyes from the across the kitchen.

"Cameron, meet Ashlyn, she's a hybrid from Facility East."

Ashlyn's long blonde hair covered her entire face as she looked at the floor. She was unbelievably shy and even fearful, you could smell it in the air. Gently I extended my hand to her, causing her to lift her head and her thick hair fall from around her face. Her dark hybrid eyes were in drastic contrast to her light skin and yellowy hair, and yet her face was weathered and tired for a person so young.

Ashlyn's gaze finally reached mine, and just as our fingertips touched she let out a blood curdling scream. Everyone froze as we watched Ashlyn fall backwards and pull herself back across the hardwood floors.

"Ashlyn, what the hell is the m…" Jonah tried shouting over Ashlyn's screams as he followed after her. However, she kicked his front leg out from under him causing him to lose his balance and fall to the floor.

Her screams intensified when I stepped toward her, making her bolt from the floor. "Get away from me, don't touch me!" she screamed as she came to stand near the kitchen island.

"Ok, ok," I said calmly as I held my hands up in front of her. "No one will hurt you here."

"Stay away from me!"

"Ashlyn stop!" Jonah shouted from the floor. "What's the matter with you!"

"Him!" she screamed and pointed at me. "He attacked me and my mom!"

"Ashlyn, stop it. Cameron never attacked…

"Yes he did," she screamed, "when I was eight years old. He threw my mom against the wall and then he bit me! He bit me and drank my blood. I was only a little girl but I remember. I saw you, I remember you! You said you'd kill my mom, and you bit me, I remember."

In the blink of an eye, Ashlyn grabbed a large carving knife from the island's surface and swung it around just as the twins ran around me. I circled my arm around just in time to sweep Olivia out of harm's way, but Jackson was just out of reach.

"Ashwyn, pwease," Jackson pleaded.

"I said stay away!" Ashlyn screamed and swung her knife around again. Just as my arm came around Jackson's waist, Ashlyn was flung backwards down the length of the hallway by an invisible force. Her body flailed like a ragdoll as it came in contact with the doorframe of the twin's room at the end of the hallway.

I looked down at Olivia in my arms and saw that both her hands were extended tensely in front of her. Brianna ran to Jackson as I placed Olivia down on the floor and turned her to face me.

"Olivia," I said sternly, "did you do that? Did you Push Ashlyn?"

Olivia's entire face trembled as big tears dripped from her eyes. "I got scared."

"I know, monkey," I said softly as I wiped her cheeks, "but you cannot do that to anyone." Though I did not know how she knew how to Push Ashlyn at all.

"But…but she was gonna hurt Jack-Jack," she cried.

Unable to take her tears, I lifted her into my arms and held her tightly against my chest while I soothed her and cooed to her that everything would be fine. I looked to Brianna who seemed more upset about the ordeal than my son who was wriggling free from her tight grip. Renee at some point had moved from her seat at the island to the couch, where William sat perched on her lap. Jonah helped Ashlyn slowly stand from the floor, it seemed that my daughter's gift had only stunned her and there was no permanent damage. Once Jonah had secured Ashlyn in the guest room he closed the door behind him and leaned up against it to steady himself.

Olivia's cries finally stopped and she pressed herself up from my chest, her bottom lip still in a pout.

"Are you ok, monkey?"

She nodded and rubbed the back of her wrist into her eye. "Uh-hmm, but I think I need a cookie."

"You need a cookie?"

She nodded. "It will make me feel better."

I looked to Bri who rolled her eyes and headed to the cabinet where the cookies and other treats were kept. She pulled out three cookies and gave one to each child. "Now go play," she said as she pushed all of them into the playroom.

Once the children were safe and playing as though the knife wielding scene had not just occurred, the adults breathed a big sigh of relief. Brianna came to stand next to me and instantly I wrapped my arm around her waist and pulled her into my side. I kissed the top of her head as the sound of Jonah's sneakers squeaked along the hardwood floors back into the kitchen. No one quite knew where to begin causing an awkward silence to fall between us.

Finally Jonah spoke up. "I thought you said the kids didn't know how to…you know," he said pointing to his head and then shooting his fingers away similar to the way that Ashlyn had flown down the hall.

"We've never shown them or talked about it," Bri replied as she unraveled herself from my side. "I guess we need to now."

Renee stood from the couch and walked back to her seat at the island. "Personally, I want to talk about the big elephant in the room."

"Where's an elephant!" the children shouted at the same time.

Renee looked around me and without a second thought she replied, "It's in your room, go find it and keep it in there so it doesn't escape." The playroom emptied quickly as all three children ran down the hall and into the twin's bedroom. "Ok, now we can talk. Cameron, spill."

Before I could open my mouth, the front door opened and John Ryan was bursting into the house. I was happy for the distraction, but Renee did not let it last long.

"John, hurry and get up here. You'll never believe what just happened," she shouted in the direction of the stairs causing John to run up them.

"What! What did I miss?" he said once he reached the landing and was huffing from his lack of breath.

Renee's heartbeat quickened as she began to relay the events with the dramatic flair of her famous air quotes. "Then she grabbed a knife and started swinging it around and almost hit Jack, then Livy used her 'hybrid mind trick' that she didn't know she had and tossed 'crazy pants' down the hall. Oh, and I forgot, before she picked up the knife she starts spouting all this nonsense about how Cameron 'attacked her mom' and how 'he' bit her. Sorry to say, Jonah, but your girlfriend is crazy."

Jonah pulled at the ends of his hair as he sighed. "She's not my girlfriend."

Reluctantly I added, "And she is not crazy."

Everyone's head whipped around to look at me.

"Wait, wait, wait," Renee said as she began opening the cabinets. "I want to make some popcorn. I have a feeling this is going to be good."

Chapter Six

Cameron

Renee had to settle for eating a bag of tortilla chips, which she did with an expression of great anticipation and excitement as I relayed a moment from my past that I had all but forgotten. It certainly was not one of my proudest moments.

"I was under orders," I began but was quickly interrupted by Renee with bits of chips shooting from her mouth.

"Victor told you to attack some woman and bite a kid?"

"Let me go further back. As you know, Victor employs humans to live in the manor as blood donors."

"Blood sluts," Renee interjected.

I shook my head. "Not all of them."

"But most of them, come on be honest," she pressed.

"*Anyway,*" I replied annoyed, "in order to be one of Victor's blood donors you must abstain from drugs and alcohol since they have negative effects on Vampires when in the blood. They are also not allowed to seek out Vampires outside of the manor. Although the rules are simple enough, there are those humans that try and circumvent Victor's authority. There was a woman named Charlotte, Charlotte Shaw I believe, who had been in Father's employ for many years. One day it was discovered that she had made the transition from blood donor to blood whore."

John raised his hand, "Er…can I ask what the difference is?"

Renee rolled her eyes and replied, "Just like it is with humans. Sluts give it away for free, whores get paid."

Smiling sympathetically at him I continued, "Essentially she is correct, John. Apparently Charlotte had a rather large list of clients. Victor kicked her out of the manor and then nine years later Father received a message from her saying that when she left the manor she had been pregnant with his child, a daughter. Afraid for her life and the life of her child, Charlotte kept this secret from him. But hard times had fallen on her and she was willing to fight for financial support that his daughter deserved. If he did not comply, she would expose the coven, the race, everything."

Brianna's eyes widened. "I'm sure Victor took being blackmailed well."

"Although Victor was relatively certain he had not fathered a child, he sent me to verify Charlotte's claims. But regardless of the child's paternity, he wanted Charlotte to understand that blackmailing him, or any other Vampire, was unacceptable.

"I found Charlotte living in a rundown apartment on the outskirts of Atlanta, and though I am not proud of it, I did expose my fangs to her and threaten her. I asked her where the child was, and she refused to tell me therefore I became aggressive with her. When that happened I heard a child scream. I found Charlotte's daughter hiding in a closet, and I…" I sighed knowing how shameful it was, "I bit the girl's wrist and tasted her blood."

I paused, seeing the shock on Brianna's face. Even Renee had stopped crunching her chips.

John cleared his throat. "Why bite her, Cameron?"

"You can taste the Vampire's…how do I explain it…flavor, in the blood. When the familiarity of Father's blood was missing from the young girl's, I knew she was not his daughter. Shortly after the incident we discovered that Charlotte had done this scam on dozens of other Vampires, but had finally become desperate enough to go to the top."

Jonah sighed. "Considering Ashlyn's reaction to seeing you I think we can assume that she is this Charlotte Shaw's daughter. So you're right, Cameron, she's not completely crazy. Unbalanced, maybe bi-polar, but not crazy. Well I know I feel better," he said sarcastically as he fell into the couch. "Can we go and drink now?"

I shook my head and looked to Brianna. "You and John will need to go without me. I should stay here with Brianna and the children."

Renee jumped off her chair, throwing the empty bag of chips onto the island. "No way. You guys were going out, and Bri and I were having a girl's night. We can handle Ashlyn if she gets out of control, or more so Livy can handle her."

"No, it is not right."

"Cam, go. We'll be fine," Brianna said as she squeezed my arm. "It'll probably be easier for Ashlyn if you're not here. Re and I can explain the whole story to her whenever she decides to come out."

I took her hand from my arm and kissed it. "Are you sure?"

She nodded, and then pulled me toward the stairs. "I'll help you find something to wear."

"Which really means she wants to take your clothes off and do nasty things to you while we wait," Renee laughed as the two of us ran quickly down the stairs and into our bedroom. Just as the bedroom door closed, Brianna pushed me up against the wall and her lips were instantly attacking mine. My hands went underneath her shirt and kneaded up her back. Her skin was so soft and even more tantalizing now that it was not blazingly hot like when she was human. Her tongue was slipping in and out of my mouth and with a moan her fangs extended.

Reluctantly I pulled her face away, seeing close up just how deep and dark the circles were under her eyes. Gently I kissed each eye, and I watched as guilt etched into her face. I bent down and pulled her legs around my waist before walking over to the bed. Once I sat down, I brought her mouth to my throat and a second later I felt the prick of her fangs.

Only a few minutes passed before I petted her head and tilted my throat away from her. She licked away the residual blood from her bottom lip and looked at me questioningly as I shifted her legs off of me before rising from the bed.

"Love, you know I have trouble not giving in to your every whim, but that is the last time you can feed from me."

Brianna's face flexed. "But...why?"

Turning away from her in order not to be melted by her hurt look, I stepped into the walk-in closet and began looking for options to change into. "Angel, it has been over three years now, you need to feed like every other Vampire. Father is worried and wants to see you reach your full potential. That will certainly not be achieved by drinking my blood."

"Were those Victor's exact words?" she asked in a mocking tone.

"No," I answered with a laugh as I hung my suit jacket on an empty hanger and began to unbutton my white dress shirt. "His exact words were, 'Child, your coddling of Brianna needs to stop now. Get it in her head that she needs to start living like the rest of us.' Is that what you wanted to hear?"

From her silence, I gathered it was not. I removed my shirt and let it fall to the floor as I peered out into the bedroom. It broke my heart to see my angel wiping a tear from her eye.

"Bri, I did not mean to sound so harsh."

Her head popped up, causing another red tear to streak down her face. "Did you miss me at least?"

In a second's time I ran from the closet, laid Brianna flat on the bed, ripped her shirt open, and smiled at the sight of my favorite lacey white bra. I stretched myself on top of her as she wrapped her legs around me. Her moan was satisfying as I sucked at her neck and squeezed her bra-covered breast tightly. Bri began grinding her pelvis against me as she scratched her nails up my back. Just then I felt her fangs lightly nip at the side of my throat. I whipped my head up and gave her a scolding look.

"What?" she said angelically, though there was a tiny bit of my blood on her lip.

I pushed myself off of her and stood at the edge of the bed while she remained splayed in front of me. "I am guessing there are two full bottles of blood in the refrigerator. So not only can you no longer have my blood, but until one of those bottles is empty, you cannot have me."

Brianna propped herself up on her elbows, her dark straight hair flying in front of her face. "What do you mean I can't have you?"

"Until you drink one bottle of blood I will not make love to you." I stepped back from the bed and went back into the closet knowing if I stood in front of her for another second I would lose my resolve. "This hurts me too, love."

"You're being a jerk."

"You can call me what you want, but it will not change the fact that you need to drink the blood that is in the refrigerator."

"Blechk," she retched, "you taste better."

I smiled to myself as I shrugged into a blue button down shirt and changed the subject. "I inspected Oliver's new house yesterday, all the repairs should be finished by next week. Kyla said she would go over and check on things. Needless to say she is counting down the days until you are back in the manor."

"Aren't you going to miss this place, though?"

"Of course I am," I replied as I pulled a navy sweater over my head and pulled out my collar and cuffs. "But it is not as though we are selling it."

"I know. It just won't be the same knowing other people will be staying here from time to time. It won't be our home anymore. I'm going to miss having a place we can escape to."

"We will have Oliver's new house just a few minutes away, and there is always your father's home on the island," I said as I stepped out of the closet to see her skeptical look. "There will be places for us to escape to, my love. Our lives will not revolve around the Warriors and the manor."

"Did you forget the last time we lived there?"

"This time will be different."

She sighed and from her look I knew she did not believe me. Then she furrowed her brow and shook her head. "Jeans, babe. You need to wear to jeans to the bar, not your suit pants."

Looking down at my pants and high shined shoes, I turned and walked back into the closet. As my suit pants dropped to the floor, Brianna brushed past me and dropped her ripped blouse at my feet. "Don't wear your skinny jeans either. I don't want anyone else checking out your ass. And by the way, you owe me a new shirt."

"Anything else?" I asked as I pulled a looser fitting pair of jeans from within the dresser. Just as I went to put them on, I lifted my head in time to see Brianna unfasten her bra and search her lingerie chest for another one. Feeling my eyes on her she turned straight on with her bare breasts hooking me like I was a helpless fish. "Why…are you…changing?"

Knowing she had me, and wanting to continue her torture, she slid her jeans down her slender thighs and stood in front of me in only a sheer pair of white panties. "Well, since you don't want to have sex with me, I might as well wear something comfortable.

"Angel, it is not that…"

"I hate that bra because it's itchy, but you really like it so that's why I wore it. But since I don't have to worry about that now, I can look like a hobo. That is unless…" she began as she seductively traced her fingers down the center of her chest, grazing the inside of her right breast, "…you want to change your mind."

I had to bite the inside of my cheek and use almost every ounce of energy to keep my feet planted where they were versus leaping over to her and pulling her silky soft legs around my waist. "No…I have…*not* changed my mind," I struggled to say.

"Fine," she snapped and in a blur pulled on a new bra, a pair of pajama shorts, and a zippered sweatshirt.

The sensual moment was over, and I reluctantly pulled on my jeans and slipped on a pair of casual shoes as Brianna ran past me. Following after her, I wrapped my hand around her arm and pulled her to a stop. "Bri," I said as I turned her around to face me, "you know I want to make love to you right now, but for your own health I need you to…"

"Ok, ok, I get it!" she shouted and I could feel a slight Push at the edges of my head. "I don't want to talk about it anymore! Let's just leave it alone. I'll do what you want, ok?"

I tried wrapping my arms around her, but she pushed them away.

"I do not want you to drink the blood simply because I am telling you to do it. I want you to care about yourself as much as I do."

"I do care," she grumbled but avoided my gaze. "I take care of myself and the kids and the house pretty much by myself."

"Brianna, a few minutes ago you were not even fast enough to get Jackson out of Ashlyn's way. If Olivia had not Pushed her, he might have gotten hurt."

Brianna's head jerked up. "We both know he's fast enough that if the knife had gotten close he would have moved."

"This time it was just Ashlyn. What if it were Aidan or some other Vampire standing between you and the twins."

"I'm trying," she cried. "I don't need you throwing Aidan in my face."

Walking over to my nightstand, I pulled a soft white handkerchief from within the top drawer and then returned to my angel and wiped her tears away. "Love, I am going to stay home with you and the children tonight."

She shook her head and took the handkerchief from my hand. "No, you need to go. Jonah's been talking about it all day. Besides I need to work on Livy's Halloween costume, so you can't be here."

"Ah, so our bet is still on?"

"Uh, duh," she said in a very Renee-like way. "Jonah's judging which kid has the best costume, remember? Plus, I'm a little upset with you right now, so you need to go out."

"Yes, love, if you insist." I wrapped my arms around her and this time she allowed them to stay. Before letting go I kissed her hair, and she tilted her head up and kissed me softly on the lips. "Just to quell any doubts you may have, I missed you terribly."

She kissed me one more time and then gave me a devilish smile as she said, "Good."

I laughed as she pulled me out of our bedroom to the foyer where Jonah and John were already waiting. John had changed from his standard medical scrubs and into a pair of jeans and a gray sweater that was stretching over his growing stomach. Jonah shoved his arms into his coat, and the three of us were ready for our guy's night out.

We waved goodbye to the children and ladies, urged them to call if Ashlyn got out of hand again, and then ducked out the door.

"I'm telling you both now, I'm getting hammered tonight," Jonah said as we stepped down onto the sidewalk.

"I hear ya, man," John laughed as he patted Jonah's shoulder. "I'm glad I'm off tomorrow. I need a few drinks in me after today."

"Does this mean I'll be carrying both of you home tonight?" I teased.

"Yes," they replied at the same time.

Jonah nudged me in the ribs. "Personally, it's why I keep you around."

"And all this time I thought it was because I gave you a free place to stay and Bri spoils you."

Jonah laughed and looked sheepishly at the ground as we continued toward the busier street. "Is it my fault that Brianna cannot resist my boyish charms?"

"Jonah," John began as he shook his head, "enjoy it while you can. Your looks will fade."

"Nah, I can't really see that happening."

John looked over at me for support, but then realized he was looking at a Vampire whose looks had been frozen for almost three hundred years. "Ok, fine. Let's talk about Jonah's new girlfriend," he teased and Jonah groaned.

It was the beginning of a fun night.

Chapter Seven

Jonah

The entire bar was buzzing with the Thursday night football crowd. Thankfully our team was winning. Surprisingly enough, of all the times the three of us had gone out together, a football game had never been on. If it had, I would have discovered that Cameron had never actually seen a game, which boggled my mind. It's an American pastime, and he'd been around when America was established. I just couldn't get the thought out of my head.

While Cameron stared curiously at the game, John and I shouted along with the other bar goers at the referee's bogus call.

"Why did he throw that yellow flag?" Cameron asked once the yelling died down.

It was John's turn to explain. "Pass interference. The defender can't put his arms around the receiver like that."

"Then why did he?"

John and I looked at each other and simply blinked. There wasn't really an answer, so both of us shrugged and took chugs from our beers.

When the next set of downs began, Cameron asked, "So each team has four chances to go ten yards?"

"Yes," I replied.

"And if they get ten yards, they get to do it again."

"Yes," John replied.

Cameron scrunched his brow, another dozen curious questions going through his head. "Why not just run it down the field each time and score? It seems easy enough."

"Cameron," John laughed, "maybe you and your brothers could. But the rest of us need four chances to move ten yards, actually sometimes we'd like more... like right now. Shit, come on!" John yelled, as did many around us. "Sorry. So Jonah, you were in the middle of telling us what happened at Mable's."

I nodded and finished what was left of my beer. "Yeah, so basically Mom tells us that she's engaged, and Dr. Douchebag gets all righteous and tries to act like he's my father. I completely lost my temper and started screaming at them. It was just a mess."

"Have you talked to your mother since last night?" Cameron asked as he rose from his stool and gathered several empty bottles into his arms.

"No," I replied. "I can't bring myself to call her yet."

"Not that I have too much experience with this kind of situation, however, I have a feeling that the more you fight and argue with your mother, the more she will run to this other man's arms."

"Funny, that is exactly what Bri said," I laughed.

Cameron smiled sympathetically as he turned to the bar and began chatting up the female bartender while handing her the empty bottles.

John cleared his throat and then gave me a similar sympathetic smile. "Jonah, you do need to talk to your mom, otherwise this whole situation is going to fester and get even more uncomfortable. And I do understand your feelings about Dr. Redding, I never liked the man."

"You had to work with him when you worked in Connecticut?"

He nodded. "Only a couple of times. I always hated when his name would come up on a patient's chart. He was always such an ass. Plus, I never thought he was a very good psychiatrist."

"Obviously he's not since my mom is still a nutcase. You have to wonder about a therapist who starts dating a former patient."

John shook his head in disgust. "That's certainly not...ethical."

Cameron returned to our table with beers and several shot glasses.

"What kind of shots are these?" I asked.

He shrugged as he placed everything on the table. "I do not know, she simply gave them to me."

"Of course she did," John moaned teasingly. "If I'd gone up there she probably would have charged me double. To Cameron's good looks," John toasted and raised his shot glass.

Cameron laughed. "Now John, be serious. She would not have waited on you at all."

We all wailed and laughed over Cameron's burn and clinked the shot glasses before drinking them down. Well, only John and I drank them. Cameron lifted his shot and then slid it over to me. The alcohol was so strong I could feel it burning down my throat.

"So seriously guys, what do I do? I can't let my mom marry this guy."

John exchanged a look with Cameron before taking a beer from the center of the table. "When it comes to how to deal with family, I'm not the one to ask. My parents and I don't dislike each other, but we've just always gone our separate ways."

"How's that?" I asked and swigged my beer.

"I've just always done my thing, they've done theirs – a result of having two extremely academic parents, and a son who didn't want to spend his life in the classroom lecturing. Once I left for college they packed up and moved to London to be guest professors. I got a phone call the day before they left saying if I needed money, email them. That's what my relationship with them is, and yes there have been dozens of times when I could have said something, but I just chose not to because it was too uncomfortable.

"I didn't really care until Wills came along. I could take them ignoring me, but my kid? They've seen him three times since he was born, and yet I can't bring myself to make them feel guilty about it. I wish I could, but this has gone on for so long that really what's the point now? Maybe if I had stood up and screamed at them in the middle of a restaurant when I was in my twenties I wouldn't be looking for a house in San Francisco that has an in-law apartment where I hope I can finagle an excuse for them to stay with us and get to know their grandchild since Wills thinks his grandparents are Renee's mom, and Eris and Sera."

"So what are you saying?" I asked, half teasing, as he drank a long swig of his beer.

"Call your mother, that is what he is saying," Cameron answered for him. "From personal experience in dealing with Victor, there have been times when I will not apologize for my opinion or actions, but regret how they came out. Do you regret the things you said to her?"

"No. I just shouldn't have said them to her in a public place like that."

66 ~ C.R. QUINN

"Then that's what you tell her," John said patting my back. "Now let's talk about the girl in the trunk."

Cameron and I laughed, and my chest lightened as the mood changed. "Haven't we beaten that horse to death?"

John shook his head and laughed. "No, I want to hear about when she jumped out of the trunk on the Mass Pike again."

Our table burst out into more laughter and again it felt good. This was exactly what I needed. Not just drinks with friends, but with older brother type friends with life experience who could really help me through a tough situation. But just then the night got even better when our team scored a touchdown and the entire bar exploded in cheers.

When the noise died down and I knocked back the last of my beer, Cameron slid over the last bottle that stood in the center of the table.

"Cameron, if you can't drink, why do you buy three of everything?" I asked as I gladly took the beer.

"It feels good to buy a drink and be able to toast with you. Plus, I know one of you drunks will drink it."

I laughed at knowing he was absolutely right. "So John, are you excited about the new job?"

John's smile stretched widely across his face. "I really can't wait to get there. I'll still be able to be a doctor and help people, but I'm also really excited about the research aspect. I can't wait to really look under the microscope at what makes hybrids so different, or how we can use V-blood on a grander medical scale."

Cameron laughed. "I am fully expecting to walk into the medical wing at Facility West and find limbs and other body parts strewn about while John cackles like a mad scientist."

"It's your fault," John said accusingly. "If Jared hadn't broken your leg that time..."

"Wait," I interrupted and looked at Cameron. "Jared broke your leg?"

Cameron nodded, though he seemed slightly embarrassed. "Right in two."

"But why?"

"Because I made him," he laughed, as did John. There was obviously an inside joke, and when he changed the subject I knew he didn't want to share. "How is Facility East?"

I shrugged. "It's all right, I guess. The job's fine, I'm just dreading Sera and Eris leaving." Cameron gave me a peculiar expression. "What?"

"I just find it humorous that Eris is preferred over Diana."

"We already call her the Ice Lady and she hasn't even started yet. I can tell I'll be looking for a new job soon. Eris and Sera make that place feel like home. Diana just doesn't have the heart like they have."

"So Cameron," John said before taking a drink, "how's the transition going?"

"To quote Jonah, 'It's all right, I guess.'"

John looked skeptical. "That's it? It's all right? You and Devin are going to lead one of the most powerful...er...companies..." he caught himself carefully, "and you can't be more excited?"

"So far it has meant time away from my family, endless weeks of proving myself to my siblings and almost everyone I come in contact with. Frankly, I am a little tired. The final transition is decades away, and yet Father is pushing me and Devin as if we are taking over tomorrow. Honestly, I am just happy to have these few weeks away from it all."

"How's Bri handling the move?" I asked.

Cameron spun an empty beer bottle between his fingers. "I keep promising Brianna that we can still have a normal life there, but really who am I kidding? Even three thousand miles away from the manor our lives are far from it. Every day brings something...not normal."

John rose from his seat and patted Cameron's shoulder as he said, "Re told me that the kids are having dreams like Bri used to."

Cameron nodded as John went up to the bar. I raised my eyebrows and gulped down my beer before asking, "What's wrong with their dreams?"

"They are having prophetic dreams," he replied as he put his hand through his hair and scratched the back of his neck. "Nothing life-changing like Brianna would have, but they dreamt of their first day of preschool a week before it happened. Scary enough, both of them were having the same dream at the same time."

"Are you sure there's no way you can get drunk?"

"I wish," he laughed just as John came back to the table with two beers in his hands. "They are able to talk to one another using their minds, now they are sharing dreams. What could possibly be next? They are not even four years old."

John handed me one of the beers as he said, "Well, you know I love those kids. I'd do anything for those kids. I'd die for those kids. I'd *kill* for those kids." John paused. "Too much?"

"A little," I laughed as I eyed the female bartender coming around from behind the bar with another round of shots on a tray. "Incoming," I warned and jutted my eyes behind Cameron's shoulder.

John looked behind him and stepped to the side to allow her to place a napkin in front of each of us and then a shot glass.

"You boys enjoy," she said seductively while looking only at Cameron, her fingers lingering on his shoulder as she walked away. I thought John might actually fall over while gaping at the exchange.

"That was awkward," Cameron sighed and slid the napkin and shot in front of me.

I smiled as I looked down at the napkin and then held it up in front of him. "Well it's about to get worse. She gave you her phone number."

Cameron's face fell. "It is times like these I really need a wedding ring on my finger."

"Only you would say something like that," John said with a groan. "Every other man in this bar would kill for that girl's number."

Cameron shook his head. "No woman can compare to my Bri. I just wish she would finally give in and marry me. I want that ring on my finger. It will certainly stop unwanted advances from other women."

"Oh to have such problems," I teased and then took a long drink. "You know Bri loves you. When do you think either of you could stop long enough to plan a wedding?"

Cameron threw his arms up in frustration. "I will make the time. I just need her to say yes. She was all ready to do it before the twins were born."

"A lot has changed since then, man," John slurred slightly. "She's a…you know…and she's raising two kids with super powers and you've been gone a lot."

"Thank you, John, for not making me feel guilty."

"That's what I'm here for," John replied and smiled proudly.

The conversation paused for a few moments, the sounds of the bar and the forgotten football game surrounding us. John and I were already well on our way to being intoxicated, but it didn't stop Cameron from leaving the table and buying another round of drinks. While John and I started downing our fresh cold beers, Cameron once again twirled an empty bottle between his fingers while he got lost in his own thoughts.

Finally he poked his head up and said, "What if I were to plan the whole wedding myself? Get Kyla and Sera to help me? We could do it all ourselves and then the day of the wedding I could just tell her we are getting married."

John's beer was frozen at his lips, disbelief showing in his widened eyes. "You're not serious…are you?"

"She wears my engagement ring so I know she believes in the commitment. She could not say no to just getting married right then and there. Right?"

I placed my hand on Cameron's shoulder, bringing his attention to me. His face was looking for my acceptance, but all I could say was, "If you decide to do that, you have to promise me that I'm in the room when you tell her. I have to see her reaction, because I'm thinking it will be better than anything on reality TV."

"Really?" Cameron answered in a defeated tone and then looked at John. "You think that too?"

John nodded. "Chernobyl will pale in comparison. But hey, I'll support you with whatever you want to do, man. But like Jonah, I want to be there when you tell her."

Cameron shook his head and smiled as he let go of his idea. "Oh look, one of the other players is running clear across the field, I think he might score."

"They should recruit Jonah's girlfriend. She has a talent for running," John teased as the rest of the bar groaned at our team's failure.

"She. Is not. My girlfriend," I said as I banged my head on the table. "Seriously, how many times do I have to say this?"

John laughed loudly as he sat back in his chair next to me. "I don't know, Jonah, I mean she is the first girl I've ever seen you with and now you keep saying she's not your girlfriend. I'm beginning to think…"

"Fine, fine," I interrupted as I lifted my head from the table, "she's my girlfriend. Will that get you off my back?"

John shook his head in judgement. "You locked your girlfriend in the trunk of your car? What kind of boyfriend are you?"

I sighed. "There's no way I can win on this, is there?"

"Nope, not really," John replied.

Chapter Eight

Brianna

It was a good thing my skin could no longer burn from the heat of a glue gun because at this point I would have little skin left on my fingers. I never thought wagering a harmless bet over who could make the better Halloween costume would turn so competitive. Well, really I was the one making it competitive as a defense mechanism. Fashion and sewing were skills Cameron had mastered before he had even been Turned. God only knew what he had made for Jack-Jack. I couldn't sew to save my life which unfortunately meant my poor little girl had to suffer through my sad gluing skills. But as I glued the final sequins onto the fluffy pink tulle of her skirt, her smile made me think she wasn't too disappointed.

"There you go, baby girl. You are now officially a butterfly princess," I said having to duck away as Livy twirled around and almost hit me with her pink glittery wings that hung crookedly no matter what I did, something Renee commented on several times.

Livy took the edges of the tulle in her hands and held her skirt out wide as she posed proudly. "Oh Mama, I do look like a butterfly princess!"

Her thin arms wrapped around my neck as she jumped up and down. "I'm so glad you like it, sweet pea," I replied as I kissed her cheek.

Olivia stepped away and twirled until she stood in front of Renee. "Aunt Re, what do you think?"

"Livybean, if there is such a thing as a butterfly princess, then you're it," she answered as she rose from the couch with her empty wine glass and kissed her goddaughter on the top of her head.

"Mama, are you going to have more special wine, too?" Livy asked as she pointed to my empty glass with a red film.

"Yes she is," Renee answered for me. "I'll bring the bottle over for you, twin."

"*Thanks,* twin." I didn't mean it, and she knew it. But that didn't stop her from bringing the bottle over and pouring the remaining blood into my glass. As she walked back into the kitchen I took a sip and shivered. "Blechk."

"Well if you didn't take so d-a-m-n long to drink it, it probably wouldn't taste so bad," she scolded.

"Mama, Aunt Re spelled damn. That's a bad word."

I narrowed my eyes at Renee and then turned to my daughter. "Yes it is, baby girl, and that's why we don't say it."

"Can I spell it like Aunt Re?"

"No," I replied firmly. "Now let's get you out of this and into your jammies."

I slipped the elastic bands of Olivia's wings off her shoulders as she said, "Mama, I think I need a crown for my costume."

"A crown?"

"Uh-huh. I sparkly princess crown."

"Kyla would be so proud," Renee laughed as she padded back into the sitting area with a full glass of wine.

Olivia's eyes grew wide at the sound of her other godmother's name. The only person she loved more than her Aunt Re was her Auntie Ky. "Mama! Can Auntie Ky come and see my Halloween costume? She could give me princess hair!"

I narrowed my eyes at Renee again. "You had to say the K word, didn't you?" She didn't answer, but merely gave me a smug smile. "Livy, baby, Auntie Ky can't fly out here just to do your hair."

"Why not?"

"Er…because she'll be busy doing her own hair. Arms up, please."

Olivia obliged and I lifted her pretty pink costume over her head. A few minutes later I was zipping her up into her favorite pink footy pajamas. Though my babies were twins, they were so different from each other. Jack-Jack was my little snuggler, always had been. At bedtime he needed his favorite bear, a blanket, and a story while being cuddled. Olivia, on the other hand, had to put herself to bed, and only wanted her hair brushed and then a kiss.

Just as I was about to grab her hairbrush from the coffee table next to me, I heard a door open at the end of the hallway. Livy took off around the corner and a moment later she was pulling a timid Ashlyn into the kitchen, who was surprisingly wearing the clothes she'd arrived in.

"Mama, Ashwyn's awake."

"I see that, sweet pea, but I don't think she wants to be dragged like that."

Livy let go of Ashlyn's hand but waved for her to come into the sitting area. Ashlyn reluctantly followed, looking extremely uncomfortable in her surroundings. I did feel for her. She'd been brought here pretty much against her will, came face to face with a Vampire who bit her when she was young, and then was thrown into a wall by the little girl who was now dancing in front of her.

"Baby girl," I began, "isn't there something you need to say to Ashlyn?"

Olivia stopped her dancing and looked up to Ashlyn with very apologetic eyes. "I'm sorry, Ashwyn. I didn't mean to hurt you."

Ashlyn looked down at Olivia with confusion creased in her face. "You...did that?"

Livy threw her arms around Ashlyn and climbed up the front of her before feverishly kissing Ashlyn's cheek. "Ooo! Do you want to see my butterfly princess dress?"

Ashlyn's previous timid demeanor suddenly changed as she placed Olivia down on the floor and the two of them bounced over in my direction. I gave a side glance over to Renee whose mouth was gaping open.

"Er...baby girl, it's way past your bedtime. You can show off your costume another time." Both girls' bouncing stop, yet only Livy pouted in front of me. When I didn't budge, she stamped her foot and turned her back to me, flipping her black hair out from inside the back of her pajamas. I took the brush from the coffee table and began brushing through Livy's long soft curls.

"Ashwyn," Livy began sweetly, "do you need your hair brushed, too?"

Ashlyn shook her head and took several steps backwards, her solemn mood sinking back into her body.

"Ashlyn, you must be starving. There is some leftover pizza from dinner if you'd like some."

"No…thank you…I left your clothes on the bed. I just came out to say how sorry I am for what happened before. I'm just going to take off before Jonah gets back."

"But you can't!" Livy said in a panic. "I have so much for us to play with tomorrow."

Ashlyn's breath began to quicken, fear visible on her face. "No I really should go before…"

"Cameron's not here, Ashlyn," I said and saw some relief in her. "Look, why don't you sit and eat, and we can talk. Afterwards if you still want to leave, I'll hold the door open for you."

Ashlyn looked nervously around the room before finally nodding and sitting in the armchair at the corner of the room. Renee rose from the couch and headed into the kitchen to fix Ashlyn a plate while I finished brushing Livy's hair.

"Kisses, baby girl," I said and turned her around. Her warm pink lips kissed my cheek before squeezing me around the neck tightly.

"I wuv you, Mama."

I kissed her soft hair and rubbed her back as I said, "I love you too, sweet pea. Now don't wake the boys when you get into bed. All right?"

Livy's floppy curls fell into her face as she nodded energetically. "Night-night, Aunt Re," she said as she danced away on her tiptoes.

"Good night, Livybean," Renee said as she placed a plate of pizza into the microwave.

Livy paused at Ashlyn and gave her a hug before flitting down the hall into the bedroom she shared with her brother, and for tonight, Wills. Listening for Livy to shut the door, I watched as Ashlyn's body slumped and the lines of her face sank deeper into despair. You could tell she was still visibly shaken from the entire day. If her stomach wasn't growling so loud I think she would have already bolted.

I rose from the floor, drank what blood was left in my glass, and shuffled into the kitchen. "Ashlyn, can I get you something to drink? Wine? A beer maybe?"

She shook her head, keeping her eyes focused on the floor. "I don't drink."

"Why the hell not?" Renee asked in an almost disgusted tone.

"My mother was a bad alcoholic. I'd just rather not tempt fate."

Renee's mouth opened and I interrupted before god only knows came out of her mouth. "Soda, then? Water?"

"Soda please," Ashlyn answered.

As I reached into the fridge for the soda, the microwave chimed and Renee removed the two pieces of sizzling pizza. I missed pizza. I missed pizza and a beer. No amount of blood could be as satisfying as a good piece of pizza and a nice cold beer. I hated being a Vampire.

Renee set Ashlyn's plate in front of a chair at the island and I gestured for her to come and sit.

"Wow," she said between bites, "this is amazing." She took several more bites, barely chewing between them. "I've never had pizza taste like this."

I smiled. "That's because you've had pizza in the South. It's just not the same as it is up here. When I was young I thought I hated pizza because it always tasted like cardboard. Then I moved to New England and realized I had never had real Italian pizza before. There's just no comparison."

Ashlyn took a big gulp of her soda and then started on her second piece of pizza. "You're not from here?"

"Nope. North Carolina, actually. But I've lived up here for quite some time. You're from Atlanta, right?"

"Kind of. My mom moved us all over when I was little, but then we finally settled in Atlanta when I was…" Ashlyn froze and eventually dropped what remained of her pizza back down on her plate. "I really should go."

"Wait, Ashlyn," I called to her as she stepped away from the island. "We need to talk about what happened today."

"I'm sorry, ok! I'm so sorry! But I know it's him, I just know it," she cried as she whipped herself back around to face us.

Renee and I walked around the island in opposite directions and came to stand on either side of her. Gently I placed my hand on her shoulder and steered her toward the couch. "You're right, Ashlyn. Cameron is the man you saw when you were young."

Her bottom lip began to tremble. "I knew it was him. I've never forgotten his face."

"And we're all sorry that happened to you," I said softly as I petted her long blonde hair. "But there is more to the story I think you should hear."

Ashlyn sat calmly while I relayed what Cameron had told us about the circumstances of his visit so many years ago. Eventually Ashlyn's fear of

Cameron turned into numb indifference in regards to her mother. That feeling, I knew all too well.

"Blackmail," Ashlyn said with a sigh, "well that's my mom for you."

"Where's your mom now?" Renee asked as she took a sip of her wine.

"Dead, I assume," Ashlyn answered flatly, causing Renee and I to exchange looks. "She left one day to go see a client, and never came home. After a week I figured some Vamp drained her."

Renee angled her head in closer. "So she really was a...a blood whore."

"Re!" I shouted.

"No, it's fine," Ashlyn said as her stomach growled loudly again.

"Would you like some more pizza?" I asked although I was already up and halfway into the kitchen.

"No, no, Brianna. I should really go. I can't be any more of a burden than I've already been."

Renee laughed and tugged at Ashlyn's arm, bringing her to sit back down on the couch. "Ashlyn, you've got a lot to learn about my friend there. She's not about to let you go out there by yourself. Bri's the biggest bleeding heart I know."

"Well my heart's not doing much else now is it?" I teased, making Renee roll her eyes. I turned and warmed up the remaining pizza in the microwave. "Ashlyn, I'll hold my end of the bargain. You can leave if you want, but you're not going without eating and if you don't want to stay here I'm sending you to a hotel until we can figure something else out. You can't stay on the street, it's just not safe."

"I've been on the street this long, I can take care of myself," Ashlyn grumbled as she sank further into the couch's cushions.

Renee shifted sideways to face Ashlyn with a signature impatient dead-eye look. "Ok, we get it, you're the tough girl on the street. Blah, blah, blah. Now if this was a movie, this would be the part where you see that although everyone you've ever known has sucked, other people are generally good and kind, so you take down your defenses and let us help you. Some cheesy ballad starts to play while a montage of your past flashes across the screen. So let's just cut to the point where we help you and I can get back to my wine buzz."

I laughed to myself as I took the pizza out of the microwave and walked back to the couch. "Ashlyn, don't worry. Renee talks to everyone like that. Now, like I said, you can either stay here, which I know I'd prefer, or we can start calling around for a hotel room. But if you do go to a hotel, I'm sending Re with you, and she'll stay with you the whole time you're there."

Ashlyn glanced at Renee out of the side of her eyes and then replied, "Ok, maybe I'll stay here…at least…until Jonah gets back."

Both Renee and I laughed as Ashlyn finally took the plate out of my hand.

"Well, you have to wait until after Jonah takes you shopping tomorrow," I said as I sat down on the coffee table in front of her. "I actually think he's a little excited about it."

Renee coughed her wine back into her glass. "Sorry," she choked. "Jonah's taking her shopping?"

"Yyyeesss," I growled at her. "There's nothing wrong with that. He's going to help her get the basics."

"I feel kind of weird about that," Ashlyn said after swallowing a large bite.

Renee raised an eyebrow in her direction. "How can you feel weird about getting free shit? Hey, if you don't want it, Jonah can take me shopping instead."

"I'm sorry, just because some Vampire knocked up my mom I'm entitled to free clothes?"

"Yes!" Renee replied loudly.

I glared at Renee before saying, "Ashlyn, think of it this way, your biological father skipped out on you and the Facility is basically helping you with back child support."

"It's guilt money."

"Absolutely," I replied. "So take advantage. I remember how scared I was when I went to the Facility, but once you settle in it's really not that bad."

"Yeah, but doesn't your dad work there or something?" she asked with a tone similar to a snotty teenager.

"Actually, I went to Facility West out in California. The one in Connecticut is only a few years old, as is my relationship with my father. Come to think of it, when I left for the Facility I had nothing but a pair of sweats that Renee gave me. Cameron was the one who actually went out and bought me clothes to take with me. So you see, we have more in common than you think."

Ashlyn became quiet, choosing to finish her last slice of pizza before she said, "But you're a Vampire now."

"Well she's observant, I'll give her that," Renee said snidely as she rose from the couch with her empty wine glass.

"Ignore her," I said softly and patted Ashlyn's knee. "Yes, I have been a Vampire for almost four years."

"What made you want to be…"

"I had complications during childbirth so Cameron Turned me."

"Oh yes," Renee slurred from the kitchen, "her Cam couldn't bear to live without her so he did the only thing he knew and turned her into a Vampire. Oh woe is her, woe is her."

"You've definitely had enough," I said over my shoulder.

"Maybe you have," she replied under her breath. "So Ashlyn, if your mother left you high and dry, whadja do for money?"

Ashlyn's upper body retreated into couch as she crossed her arms and pulled in her hoodie. "Whatever I had to," she answered as she looked at the floor.

There was certainly more to that story, but before we could push for more information the front door opened and the house was suddenly filled with the sound of three men laughing. The boys were home, and earlier than expected. As I stood from the coffee table I could see why.

"Angel, I am home," Cameron said as he crested the top of the stairs with both Jonah and John folded over both shoulders.

"Wonderful, babe, you've brought drunks home. But we already have one," I said, pointing into the kitchen where Renee was finding it hard to breathe because she was laughing so hard. "Shhh! You guys are going to wake the kids and then I'm gonna be pissed."

"Uh-oh," Jonah slurred, although I was still looking at his behind. "The southern accent is coming out. That means she's wicked mad."

"Get him upstairs, please," I groaned to Cameron. Carefully he lowered John's feet to the ground, and although John stood solid for a second, he stumbled backwards and fell down on the floor. Cameron simply shrugged and stepped over him, leaving Jonah hunched over his shoulder as he opened the door to the third floor and disappeared. I looked over at Renee and gestured to the laughing and intoxicated John on the floor. "What do you want to do with him?"

"Eh, just leave him there."

"I'll call you guys a cab. Neither of you need to be walking home," I said grabbing my cell phone from the kitchen island.

"A cab…is a great idea," John slurred. "I need to give sex to my wife."

"Yeah, that's not happening," Renee replied snidely.

John rolled over on his stomach and tried to pull himself across the floor. "Oh come on, baby. Bri's keeping the little man, so we can really go at it."

Renee glared at him as he continued to crawl in her direction. "Um, I'm thinking the only thing you'll really be going at is the toilet. It looks like you drank the whole bar."

John stopped at Renee's feet and looked up at her. "It wasn't my fault. Cameron made me drink the whole bar. He forced it down my throat. I tried to stop him, but he's so strong."

"Yes, John, I am very strong," Cam said from the doorway. "I am strong enough to toss you down the stairs after an accusation like that."

John's eyes widened before he turned his head back to Renee and said, "Cameron only made me drink half the bar, I totally chose to drink the other half on my own. Now, will you please have sex with me?"

Renee crossed her arms and rolled her eyes. "Ok fine, but I'm not doing anything kinky. Now come on, I'm sure Bri wants you off her floor."

"Oh crap, I didn't call for a cab yet," I said with a gasp as I began scrolling through the screens on my phone to find the number for a cab company. But a moment later, Cameron wrapped his arms around my chest and nuzzled his lips to my ear.

"Do not bother, love. I will take them up to the corner and get them a taxi."

I patted his forearm that was stretched across my chest, loving the whiff of autumn leaves coming from his skin. "Are you sure?"

"Of course," he replied with one last quick kiss to my temple and then unraveled his arms from around me.

John turned onto his back as Cameron came to stand over him. "Do I get to ride on your shoulder again?"

Cameron simply smiled before easily folding John over his shoulder. Renee scurried around the island and hugged me as she said, "Thanks for taking the kid tonight. "

"No problem, you're taking the twins overnight on Halloween. Wills is a heck of a lot easier to handle than my kids."

"Ain't that the truth," she responded before giving me a quick kiss on the cheek. "Love ya. Now, if anything else happens with…" she gestured with her eyes over to where Ashlyn was sitting on the couch, "…call me. Or better yet, take a video and send it to me."

"Goodnight, twin."

"'Night, twin," Renee replied before taking Cameron's arm and allowing him to lead her down the stairs.

Once the three of them disappeared out the front door I turned to see Ashlyn rising from the couch. "Sorry about that, Ashlyn, things aren't usually like this. Can I get you anything else to eat? Or drink maybe?"

"No," she replied and stepped by me, but then stopped herself and turned back around. "I'm sorry. Thank you for everything, really. I'm just not used to...help."

"Ashlyn, I've been where you are. My circumstances were different, but before I met Cameron I always believed I wasn't worth saving. The Facility and the Warriors gave me confidence and showed me what I was truly capable of. All I'm saying is give it a chance. Give us all a chance for that matter."

Ashlyn nervously began pulling at her long blonde hair and looked at the floor. "I don't do well in crowded places. I get so overwhelmed and anxious, and I end up freaking out and then people think I'm crazy. I just don't want to be locked up in that place with so many people."

I took a step toward Ashlyn, my bleeding heart, as Renee would call it, going out to her, but when she took a reciprocating step back I stopped. "The Facility is a very different place now than when I was there. There are still threats out there, but hybrids aren't being hunted down and found dead like they used to be. Once you're able to defend yourself, or master your gift, the Facility lets you go. They really are there to help you."

Ashlyn crossed her arms in front of her chest. "Look, you seem nice, and Jonah says you're a good friend. But forgive me if I don't trust Vampires very much. They've done nothing but hurt me my entire life." She turned around and began walking to the end of the hallway. Just before she reached her guest room's door she whispered, "They'd never let me go, anyway. You can't master a gift you don't have."

I just wanted to give her a hug. She was so resistant and damaged, unknowing of what real love and caring was. All of which were common traits among so many hybrids. The Facility's purpose was to help, but there was only so much they could do.

Not wanting to spend another listless moment getting myself depressed, I walked to the end of the hallway and popped my head into the children's bedroom. Olivia was laying underneath her perfectly straight princess bedspread, and it would be just as perfect in the morning because she slept so still. Jackson, on the other hand, was surrounded by his favorite stuffed animals, his soft blue comfort blanket wrapped around his arm and tucked underneath his chin while his bedspread was tangled around his splayed little body. Wills was in the trundle bed from underneath Jack's bedframe, as always in the middle of the twins' extremes. My three little angels were deep in sleep, hopefully dreaming of anything but today's events. I could check if I wanted to, but I had to touch them in order to look into their dreams, something my father said would pass as I got older. Not wanting to wake them, I decided to refrain from intruding and closed the door.

The house was very quiet as I padded back down the hallway and turned off all the lights on the second floor causing the tiny nightlights to shine brightly against the hardwood floors. Once I reached the top of the stairs, my Cam was stepping through the front door, looking as stunningly handsome as ever even though he was only wearing a pair of jeans and a sweater. Damn I was lucky, I thought to myself as I slowly stepped down the stairs toward him. With all my hang ups and anger at what he had turned me into, looking at him now I could only feel love for him. He was my Gatherer, my savior, my lover, my everything. And although I stepped down to him in my sweatshirt and pajama shorts, he looked at me with the same incredible desire I felt for him at that moment. Being barefoot in front of him I only came up to his chest, causing him to have to bend down in order to rest his lips on mine. When he lifted his head he cupped my face with his right hand as his thumb brushed down my cheek.

"My angel," he cooed softly.

I rested my hand on top of his as I said, "I'm so glad you're home."

"Not as much as I, love." I smiled as I took his hand away from my face and tried to lead him toward our bedroom when he pulled back on my hand. "Bri, I need to apologize."

I turned around to face him, noticing that his previous look of desire had been replaced by worried eyes. "Apologize for what?"

"For earlier. I did not mean to be so harsh with you. I simply wanted…"

I placed my index finger up to his lips to quiet him. "Cam, I've been a pain, I know I have. But I drank a whole bottle, just like you asked me to even though I should have had the mind to do it myself. You shouldn't have had to treat me like a spoiled child. I'm sorry too. I'll do better."

Cameron took my hand and kissed each finger before flattening my palm over his silent heart. "It is only because I love you so much that I worry about you when you do not take care of yourself. You look so much healthier now that you have fed."

I narrowed my eyes at him before turning around and walking toward our bedroom. "Healthier, huh? You chose that word carefully didn't you, Mr. Burke?" He chuckled to himself as he followed me down the hall. "Did you have a good time tonight?"

"Yes," he replied simply as we stepped into our bedroom.

"Did Jonah tell you the whole fiasco with his mom at Mable's?"

"Mmm-hmm," he replied before the bedroom door clicked closed. Just as I went to turn around, his arm snaked around me from behind while his other hand brushed my hair away from my neck to allow his lips to knead deeply into my skin.

My eyes closed in response and I grazed his arm, surprised at feeling his bare skin under my fingertips. Curious, I let my fingers travel up the length of his arm to his shoulder and then down the length of his waist to his hips that were pressed against me.

"My god, Cam, when did you get naked!"

He laughed in my ear as he slid his hands down the front of my shorts, pressing me back into him where I could feel his growing excitement pushing into my backside. "You said you fed. After that, my clothes could not come off fast enough."

"I knew you missed me," I teased as I reached up behind me and combed my fingers through his thick hair. Cameron's sweet breath wafted across my face as he moaned in pleasure. His hands moved up to the middle of my hoodie and pulled the zipper down until it unlatched itself at the bottom. Gently he pulled the jacket off my shoulders, letting it fall softly to the ground while his fingers unhooked my bra and slid the straps down the front of my arms.

It always amazed me how excited Cameron made me. Until I met him I always thought sex was either disappointing or terrifying, nothing like what you saw in movies. However, the passion Cameron and I generated together challenged anything you saw on the big screen. Proof of which when it felt as though a bomb went off in my body as he clenched my breasts in his hands at the same time his fangs sank into the base of my neck. The act alone made my own fangs extend.

Cameron pulled his fangs from within me and turned me around, his eyes burning with lust while a low growl sounded deep in his throat. My open mouth found his while our tongues fought against each other. His taste, his smell and his touch were fueling my insatiable need to have every inch of him. Not needing any help, I wrapped my legs tightly around his waist while crushing my breasts against his chest. Cameron's left arm wrapped around me while his right hand slid up my thigh and underneath my shorts, pulling at the thin elastic of my underwear. It did make me wish I hadn't thrown a fit and put on a sad pair of white cotton panties. Though Cam didn't seem to mind as he knelt down and lowered me to the floor, not even bothering to try and make it to the bed. My legs released their hold on his waist, allowing him to stretch out on top of me and grip the band of my pajama shorts firmly in his hand.

"Don't rip these," I begged. He opened his eyes quickly and then sighed as the left side of his mouth curled up in a smile. "They're my favorite."

"Yes, love," he answered as he shifted his weight to the side and pulled what clothing remained between us down my legs. When my shorts reached my ankles, I flicked them off and rolled up from the floor causing Cameron to sit up curiously. As I kissed him, I rose up on my knees, causing him to do the same, and walked him backwards until his back was pressed up against the foot of the bed.

His fingers entwined themselves in my hair as I finally lowered myself down onto him. Cameron kissed and sucked at my neck as I reveled in the feeling of him deep inside of me. Our pelvises grinded into one another as we found our rhythm and another fire started to stir within me. My fangs hadn't retracted, and what can only be understood by another Vampire as a tingling and uncontrollable need to sink them into flesh.

I wrapped my hand around the back of Cameron's head and pulled at his hair, causing him once again to moan in pleasure but also tilt his head back to expose his neck. From the look in his eyes he knew what was coming and wasn't about to stop me. With his fingers still tangled in my hair, he pulled my head down to the side of his neck and flinched only slightly as my fangs sank into his neck. His blood was thick and tepid but incredibly sweet as it entered my mouth and ran down my throat. Cameron unfurled his fingers from my hair, letting it fall loosely down my back while he cradled his arm around me. His moans and sighs were so enticing that it was difficult to pull myself away from my him, but with a gentle caress of my cheek, he was silently telling me that I had had enough.

Reluctantly I pulled my fangs from within his neck and licked the wounds clean. Cameron removed his arm from around me, barely allowing me enough time to lift my head before his lips were crushing mine. His fingers tickled my abdomen as he grazed them down my stomach and around to the small of my back where he flattened his palm and kept my pelvis pressed firmly against his. When his fangs bit into the top of my breast I completely lost myself in him. Pressing my cheek into his hair, I cradled his head and allowed him to take total control of me. All nagging resentment I continued to hold onto was forgotten. In moments like these there was only love between us, a deep, though fragile, love that belonged to only Bri and Cam.

Cameron laid with his back pressed up against the headboard of our enormous bed, though I couldn't tell you when exactly we made it up here. At some point the comforter had been tossed into a heap on the floor, so only the silky flat sheet covered me as I curled into Cameron's side, my index finger making lazy circles on his chest while we talked the night away. It had been weeks since we had been in bed together, and the absence wasn't just felt by me. Our love making aside, he could not help but caress me or kiss me or hold my hand against his heart. All gestures of his longing to be home. Even our conversation went from important topics to random tidbits about the goings on at the manor.

Cameron's fingers brushed up my arm as he began telling me about his hellacious meeting with the Negotiators. "I believe Fabiani may leave the coven if Ormond does not pull things together."

"Poor Fabi. Nothing's been the same for him since Dante was killed."

"That is true, but he did tell me today that businesswise he is doing very well."

"I guess that's a consolation. Has he convinced Devin to tell Victor that they are together?"

Cameron shook his head. "I am afraid Fabiani has more faith in Devin than I do in regards to that. And by the way, if Father asks, Devin is with us at Oliver's the week prior to Thanksgiving."

"He is?" I asked as I propped myself up on my elbow.

"No. He will be with Fabiani in Washington, D.C. But if Father asks, we are to tell him he is with us."

"I feel like I'm in high school again."

Cameron's head thumped against the headboard. "I hate lying to Father about someone that is actually making Devin a better person. Father sees it, everyone sees it, and yet Devin simply denies that anything has changed. Then Father comes to me searching for answers and I lie to his face. What if when he finds out that Devin and I hid this from him for years and he decides not to relinquish the coven to us after all? Then all the sacrifices we have made the last two years will be in vain."

"Been holding that one in long?" I said giving him a quirked eyebrow.

"Do not tease me."

I sighed as I lowered my cheek back down on his chest. "I think you need to give Victor a little more credit. He approved your Warrior training program and no one thought that would happen." Cameron shrugged. "Oh come on, it's a big deal. Hybrids really have a chance of becoming Warriors now."

"Well, you were the inspiration, my love."

"Did Natasha Cushlin apply? She told Jared she was going to."

"Yes, she was the first to apply. She really does have potential."

"Unlike her skanky sister."

"Nikki and Jared have been together for almost four years. Are you ever going to accept her?"

I paused, tossed the thought around in my head and then answered, "No."

"Bri, you have to eventually…" Cameron began, but I shot up and put my hand over his mouth.

"There's a child out of bed," I said, hearing the kids' bedroom door creak open. "Well don't just lie there, put some clothes on. Move! Move!"

The sheet flew off of me as I leapt into the closet. Cameron was only a second or two behind me, though he was obviously less stressed about a child coming into our room while we were both naked. I, on the other hand, couldn't get my underwear on fast enough.

Just as I pulled on a clean pair of pajama pants, I could hear a pair of little feet stepping slowly down the stairs. "We have an extra minute or two, it's Wills."

Cameron cocked his head as he stepped into one of his many pairs of silk pants. "How do you know that?"

"He's taking one step at a time, can't you hear it? With Livy you would have heard a swooping noise because she would have slid down the banister. And you would barely hear Jackson at all because he would have run down the stairs so fast."

"You are such a wonderful mother."

"Aah, thank you. Now put a shirt on and pick up all the other clothes out there. I'll take care of the bed."

Cameron did as I asked, pulling on one of his softer grey t–shirts. While he gathered up our clothes that had been discarded all over the floor, I tossed the thick comforter back onto the bed and spread it out smooth.

"Ok, now what?" Cam asked as he threw our dirty clothes into the closet. I grabbed the tattered paperback book that was lying on my nightstand and threw it over him.

"Get in bed," I said as I pulled back the comforter and climbed in.

"I would never read this."

"It doesn't matter! Just get in the bed! He's coming down the hall."

Cameron sighed and got under the blankets while I grabbed my latest trash magazine from inside my nightstand drawer.

"I do not understand why I have to read this sad example of a Vampire novel."

"Would you rather read my magazine?"

"I would rather wear polyester."

"We have to look like we're doing anything else but what we were doing. Parents don't have sex, don't you know that?"

"Parents obviously have intercourse, or else they would not be parents."

"Ew…you had to say intercourse. It just sounds disgusting. Oh, oh, here he comes."

Instantly my magazine went up in front of my face, though Cameron purposely began reading the paperback upside down. Just then little Will Ryan, dressed in superhero pajamas, opened the door having to stand on his tiptoes in order to reach the door handle. "Wills? What a surprise."

"Awbie," he began as he scuttled into the room. "Wivy and Jack-Jack are havin' bad dweams."

Cameron took my magazine from my hand as I pulled the comforter away. "How do you know they're having bad dreams, sweetie?"

"Der cwying and der doin' this…" Will stretched his hand out, his palm tense and splayed, similar to what the twins did whenever they would have a dream between them.

Cameron hit the floor first, sweeping Wills up into his arms before we fled upstairs. Quietly I stepped inside the twins bedroom while Cameron held Will in the hall. The twins were still in their beds, though their inside arms were stretched out towards each other. A cloudy mist traveled between their hands and their whimpers broke my heart. I knelt to the ground and gently held my palms up against theirs. As I closed my eyes I stepped into my children's minds…

With a gasp I was brought into a wooded area where the night was black with only shafts of white moonlight showering down from above. I looked to my left and saw Cameron crouched in a fighting stance with Devin and Alex in similar positions. When I finally looked ahead I saw a dark-clad woman standing at the top of a ridge with one arm stretched out tensely in front of her and the other stretched out behind.

It was me.

Jackson was clinging to my left leg while Olivia was draped over my shoulder with her arms around my neck. Both of them were shaking and whimpering in fear. As I stepped closer to the ridge I could see the clearing below. It looked like a sea of people, but right in the middle, clear as day, was Aidan Pierce. His eyes were focused on me, not the woman in the dream that the children were clinging to, but me. And he winked.

In a panic I blew the dream away and the only piece that remained were the twins floating in solid white clouds. Slowly the two of them turned around, their frightened little faces changing quickly as they saw me.

"Mama!" they said in unison as they ran to me.

Jack-Jack crossed his arms in front of him as said, "Mama, I did not like that dream."

"It was scary," Livy pouted.

"I didn't like it either, babies. I thought you might want to see Eri."

"Oh yes, yes!" Olivia squealed, though Jackson seemed to echo her feelings in his expression.

In a flash I imagined my father's house on the ocean cliff, the turquoise water expanding in front of us beyond the wide balcony. The twins began to run around me, peeking their heads into the open balcony doors shouting for their grandfather. A moment later a hand wrapped around my arm and when I turned, my father's smiling face was there to greet me, though his smile fell when he saw that I did not return it.

"Daughter, was it?"

"I need you to watch them for a little while," I said quietly in his ear.

"What is the..."

"I'll explain later, just please don't let go of them."

He nodded just as the twins finally saw him.

"Eri!" they shouted as they ran to him and jumped into his arms.

Slowly I stepped away, feeling the shift in control as my father took over the children's dream.

With another gasp I was brought back into the twin's bedroom, their arms still outstretched towards each other. Cameron was hovering close behind me with Will now asleep in his arms, a small drool mark forming on Cameron's gray shirt.

"Well?" he said anxiously.

"We've got a problem."

Chapter Nine

Jonah

The toilet was cool against my cheek. The acidy smell of vomit was in the air since I couldn't keep myself upright long enough to flush it down. The floor wasn't that cold so I wondered if I could handle sleeping here. What possessed me to keep drinking? Seriously, what didn't I drink? My head was pounding as the room began to spin. Just as my stomach started to churn again I heard the shuffle of feet come into the bathroom.

"Bri...sorry...here...stay...toilet...cool," I said incoherently.

Brianna didn't answer, but instead stepped over me to get to the sink and turn on the water. I rolled onto my back and had to put my hand over my eyes to hide them from the blaringly bright bathroom lights. Brianna grabbed me underneath my shoulders and slowly pulled me upright against the toilet. I flinched at the feeling of the cold washcloth being wiped down my chin and neck.

"Bri...don't," I whined sloppily, resting my hand on her wrist but then pushed my eyes open at the feeling of her warm skin. Where I expected to see Brianna, I found Ashlyn giving me a sympathetic smile. "Wh-what?"

Ashlyn pulled my weak hand from her wrist and continued to wipe down my mouth and neck. Did I have vomit all over my face? Great.

"Ashlyn...you don't..."

"Stop," she said quietly. "Just let me finish, ok?"

"But…this is gross."

She snorted. "Hardly. When you're *lying* in your own puke, now that's gross, and unfortunately how I usually found my mom. So you're lucky you made it to the bathroom." She took the cool washcloth and wiped my forehead before throwing it back in the sink. "Come on, big guy," she grunted as she crooked her arms underneath my armpits and hoisted me up to a standing position.

Unfortunately I didn't help her much as she wrapped my left arm over her shoulder and walked me back into the bedroom. I could barely see the bed in front of me as she lowered me down onto the corner of the mattress. "Do you have another shirt?"

"Why?"

I heard her sigh as she took the edges of my polo shirt and pulled it up to my chest. "Ok, arms up. You've got to help me a little."

I did as she asked, though both of my arms felt floppy. "You just want to see me without my shirt."

"Oh yeah, that's it," she replied snidely and pulled my shirt over my head. "Seeing you in your boxers just isn't enough."

"Wh-hat!" I slurred, finally looking down and seeing my navy boxers with white moose scattered around. "Don't judge. These aren't…my best pair."

"I'm just glad you don't go commando." Ashlyn stepped around the bed and pulled the blankets out from under the pillows. A moment later Ashlyn was back at my side and pulling me up to the head of the bed. "Mooses?"

"Moose."

"Really?"

"Yep. Moose. English major. Me."

"Yep, you sound it," she said as she pulled the comforter over me and fluffed a pillow under my head.

"Well, I didn't finish." The city lights lit the room enough that I could see Ashlyn walk around to the other side of the bed. "Why're you here?"

"Uh, you brought me here, remember?"

"No, up here. Right now."

The mattress sank as she sat down and swung her legs up onto the bed and stretched out next to me on top of the comforter. "Something's going on downstairs."

"Is everything…" I started to say as I bolted up from my pillow but then had to fall back down in hopes that I wouldn't throw up again. "Wh-what's going on?"

"I don't know. I keep hearing Cameron on the phone, and he and Brianna keep going in and out of the kid's room."

"I should go down there."

"I think you should stay right here," she replied, pulling down the thick comforter and lifting my arm out from underneath.

"What are you doing?"

"Just trust me," she replied and began squeezing her thumbs into my palm. "This was how I always helped my mother."

"I-I don't understand," I sighed just before I felt the blood rush out of my face. "I'm...oh no...I'm going to..."

Ashlyn squeezed my arm tightly and held it so that I couldn't move. "No, you're not going to be sick. It just feels funny for a second and then it'll pass."

"What?" I sighed before the pounding in my head and uneasy feeling in my stomach started to drain away in waves. When she finally released my palm I was shocked at how good I felt. Then it hit me. "Is this your gift?"

Ashlyn crinkled her brows together. "It's just pressure points, Jonah. I told you, I don't have a gift."

Suddenly I was flooded with feelings of anger and annoyance, at her, her tone, this blanket, my stupid moose boxers. "Everyone has a gift, Ashlyn!"

"Well I don't! My mother was more than clear that I was less than nothing," she said in a raised tone as she sat up from her pillow.

"Why are you so angry?!"

"Why are you?!"

Our noses almost touched as we yelled at each other for absolutely no reason. Suddenly my stomach started to churn again and the bile started to rise in my throat. Ashlyn jerked back and took my hand again, pressing into my palm uncomfortably. As my sickness began to wane, so did the anger I had felt only a minute ago. How did things get heated so quickly and then just stop? And how did she know I was about to be sick again? I glanced over at Ashlyn and could see that she had calmed down as well, looking peaceful as she continued to squeeze my palm. The initial thought was of course that she was crazy, but then another thought hit me.

Slowly I removed my hand from hers and watching Ashlyn closely, I quickly thought about the time Katie Bell and I were fighting over the

Mexican dip and she grabbed the bowl and accidently poured all the dip down her shirt. Or the time she thought the yellow down marker she saw watching a football game on TV was real, and couldn't believe that the football players didn't trip over it. Or the time she wanted to dye her hair red and I forgot to set a timer and her hair turned neon orange. In my head I was laughing hysterically, but right in front of me Ashlyn was holding her sides she was laughing so hard.

Testing further, I quickly switched my thoughts to the sight of my father lying motionless in his casket. Finding Katie Bell's soccer video where Mom had dropped the video camera and inadvertently taped my father having his heart attack. Coming home for the first time in my life and not hearing my father's voice calling to me, or no longer finding the pile on the kitchen counter where he emptied his pockets from the day. My eyes started to burn from the tears I wouldn't let come out, but Ashlyn's cheeks were glistening with them.

With a deep exhale I shot away all memories, good and bad, clearing my head, and effectively bringing Ashlyn out of her sadness. Frantically she began wiping the tears from her cheeks.

"What is wrong with me? I'm not crazy! I'm not! But...oh my god, what's wrong with me!"

Carefully I wrapped my hands around Ashlyn's wrists and brought her hands away from her face. "I know you said you don't have one, but I think this is your gift, Ashlyn."

"*What*," she said snidely, "my gift is that I'm a freak?"

Feeling the anger begin to seep back into my body, I took a deep breath and said, "Just hear me out. Right now you're upset, but I am going to think about something that makes me really happy, ok?"

Ashlyn crinkled her brows again. "Oh good for you...I'm glad you can..." but she didn't finish and a huge smile started to form across her face as I thought about my car and driving through the Connecticut countryside during the fall.

"Ok, do you feel happy?" She nodded, though I could tell she didn't know why. "Good. Now I'm going to think of something that makes me really angry."

Through Ashlyn's smile I could see her confusion and reluctance, but her face fell and turned into a snarl as I began thinking about Paul, Dr. Douchebag, and how much I hated him. How I despised him when he held my mother's hand that now had a ring on her finger.

"Stop, stop!" Ashlyn begged as she pulled her wrists out of my grip. "I don't understand, what's going on!"

Taking another deep breath and exhaling all my bad feelings about Paul, I gently nudged Ashlyn to lie back down.

"I'm not crazy," she whimpered.

"No. You're not crazy. I think you're an Empath."

"I don't know what that means."

"An Empath can feel what others are feeling. Like what just happened. When I was feeling happy, you felt happy. Then I thought of things that made me angry, and you felt those things too."

"Maybe that's why I hate crowded places. An...Empath?"

I nodded. "Yeah, like Sera. Oh wait, you didn't meet her. But she can always tell how I'm feeling, even if I'm trying to hide it, and she can also take your feelings away by touching you. But unlike Sera, you seem to also be able to reflect your feelings onto others."

"What do you mean?" she sniffled and wiped her nose with the sleeve of her sweatshirt.

"Earlier when we were yelling, I was feeling anger that wasn't mine. I think you were projecting your feelings onto me."

Ashlyn sighed and rubbed her face. "So now I make everyone around me just as crazy as I am. That's great."

"At least you won't be alone," I kidded and thankfully she smiled.

"Well I guess my mother was wrong. At least I'm not *less* than nothing, just your average nothing."

"You're not nothing, Ashlyn. If anyone is, it's your mother." She wasn't convinced and buried her head into her pillow. "So, speaking of your mom, did uh...Bri talk to you...about..."

"Yes...she did."

"So Charlotte Shaw is your mother?"

She nodded. "Was. She *was* my mother. She *was* a blackmailer, *was* an alcoholic, *was* a blood whore."

"Did you know about the blood...thing? Sorry, I can't call your mom a whore."

"Why not, that's what she was. I didn't know that's what people like her were called, I just knew what she did. She was never shy about it, even told me where not to let Vamps bite, and how to count through it so you don't get drained."

I blinked with surprise. "Why would she do that?"

Ashlyn paused for a moment, swallowing hard and avoiding looking at me as she said, "My mother taught me those things so that I wouldn't die while a Vampire drank from me."

"Your mother let you..."

"There wasn't much of a choice, Jonah. It's not like I volunteered for it. But when your mother says, 'Ashlyn, if you don't do it, we'll have no money for food,' or 'Ashlyn, you have to do this or they'll turn off our electricity again.' She was such a bad alcoholic toward the end that no one wanted to drink from her so we did what we had to in order to survive."

"But you were just a donor, right?" I asked, but suddenly being flooded with an overwhelming feeling of shame I had a sense I was wrong.

"At first," she finally replied. "I was only seventeen when my mom disappeared. Her clients kept coming and I needed the money. For a while I only let them feed, but eventually I couldn't make ends meet so...if they wanted more...I'd let them. I'm not proud of it but I just didn't have a choice."

"But how did you end up on the street?"

"The hole I lived in got condemned. Clients couldn't find me, or didn't want me anymore, so I started living on the street and made connections where I could."

"It's a good thing Kevin found you."

Ashlyn's face fell. "Jonah...Kevin didn't just happen to find me. He was a client...well he was supposed to be, but when he saw me he freaked out and forced me onto that plane."

Ashlyn's eyes were becoming droopy as she nuzzled her cheek deeper into the pillow. I could feel the veil of exhaustion hitting me as well, but I couldn't stop with my questions. "But Kevin was helping you. He was getting you off the street. Why did you keep fighting him? Why did you keep telling me we had the wrong girl?"

"If all you know of Vampires is sucking and screwing, and one of them forces you to come with him onto a plane, you think sex trade. Ok? What would make me think any different?"

"Ok, so you freaked out on Kevin because you thought he was kidnapping you. You hated being at Facility East because there were so many people around. So why did you freak out when you met Brianna?"

"My guard was down," she said as she yawned widely. "You said you were taking me to a friend's, I wasn't prepared for a Vamp so I panicked. I was afraid that I'd be trapped here and fed on. You hear stories about that.

Then I saw the kids and all that fear went away."

"Well I think we know why that is, now. But why the freak out on Cameron?"

"You make it sound like I do nothing but freak out."

"So far you've done nothing but."

She punched me weakly in the shoulder, her hand limply gliding down my bare bicep and resting in the crook of my elbow. "I've had nightmares about him since I was eight years old and then he was standing in front of me. I think you would have freaked out too."

"Well at least one good thing came out of today," I said yawning.

Ashlyn didn't open her eyes as she answered, "What's that?"

"I know your last name now."

"Yeah, yeah," she yawned.

"Ashlyn, you can't sleep here."

"I won't," she replied but didn't move from her position.

"Ashlyn," I said nudging her, "come on."

"I'm going," she muttered, but still didn't move.

"Five minutes. That's it."

"Mmm-hmm. Five minutes."

Chapter Ten

Jonah

Even through my closed eyes I could see the sun shining through the windows. It was morning and I suddenly hated the fact that I'd promised to take Ashlyn shopping. I probably could have slept all day if I had the chance. As my brain started to wake up I was suddenly aware of two things – one, my right arm was asleep and pins were tingling in my fingers, and two, there was a weight pressing against my bare chest. I lifted my head and stretched my heavy eyelids open to see Ashlyn tucked into me, tangles of her thick wavy blonde hair splayed around her and on both our pillows.

Ah, fuck.

"Ashlyn," I whispered, nudging her shoulder gently. "Ashlyn, wake up."

She moaned and brushed her hair away from her face, but instead of waking up she nuzzled her face deeper into my chest. Surprisingly I didn't mind that she was curled into me. It had been a really long time since I woke up next to someone, but it wasn't right. I somehow needed to get her back into her guest room without Bri or Cameron knowing.

"Ashlyn, wake up," I tried again, carefully rolling her away from me.

The movement made her whine and jut out her bottom lip in a cute pout as she rubbed her eyes with the heels of her hands. "What happened?"

"We both fell asleep. We need to get you downstairs before Bri catches us."

Ashlyn rose up onto her elbows, looking around the room anxiously as she got her bearings. "I'm sorry. I've never slept like that before."

"Nothing to worry about, we just can't get caught sneaking you back downstairs."

Ashlyn slid from the bed while I bent down to the floor for my jeans. I ruffled through my duffle bag and pulled out a clean t-shirt and stretched it over my head. As I opened the door, Ashlyn was at my side though she avoided my gaze and looked to the floor.

"I'm glad you slept," I said softly.

Ashlyn looked up at me, a hint of a smile forming at the corners of her lips. "I'm sorry if I get you in trouble."

I waved her down the stairs with me, being careful to walk as quietly as possible down each carpeted step. When we approached the door at the bottom of the staircase I turned the door handle slowly and peered out down the hallway. Coast clear.

But just as I opened the door and waved Ashlyn to follow, from behind me I heard, "Jonah!"

It was Olivia, her cute little voice echoing through the kitchen causing me to freeze and Ashlyn to slam into my back. When I opened the door fully and turned around I could see Cameron sitting on the couch with Will sitting on his lap reading a children's book while Olivia was stretched across the back of his shoulders against the cushions and Jack-Jack curled into his side. Both Burke children, mind you, from the recognizable illustrations on the covers were reading novels I didn't read until I was in middle school.

Olivia was still waving at me when she said, "Good morning, Jonah. Good morning, Ashwyn. Did you have a sleepover? Ada, can I have a sleepover like Jonah and Ashwyn?"

Cameron's raised eyebrow and judgmental expression made me feel worse than anytime I was ever scolded by my own parents.

"You already had a sleepover last night with William, monkey." She pouted and brushed her hair out of her face. "All right now, lovie, read your book. William, where did we leave off?"

Will turned the page of his children's book and slowly began reading the page to Cameron. "T-the c-cat…sat on…the mat."

While Will continued to read I waved Ashlyn toward her bedroom, but after a few steps she turned back and squeezed my arm while she whispered in my ear, "Please don't tell anyone what I told you last night. You know, about what I did…"

I took her hand from my arm and squeezed it reassuringly. "I won't. Go get ready and we'll go shopping like I promised."

"We don't…"

"We're going," I replied firmly and gently pushed her down the hall.

When I turned back toward the kitchen, Cameron's eyebrow was still raised in my direction while he listened to Will stutter through his book. "Well done, William. I am very impressed."

"Weally?" he replied hopefully.

Cameron nodded. "You'll be reading with the twins in no time. All right children, how about you finish your reading time downstairs in the living room."

"Can we watch a movie?" Olivia asked as she jumped down from the back of the couch.

"No, monkey," Cameron said firmly as he placed Will down on the floor. "It is reading time, not movie time."

Olivia pouted as she crossed her arms, and followed her brother and Will toward the stairs. "Can we have a snack?"

"No, monkey. You just had breakfast."

"But I'm a growing girl!" she whined.

Jack-Jack rolled his eyes and started down the stairs while Will took Olivia's hand and whispered something in her ear that I couldn't hear, but it apparently made her happy enough to run with him down the stairs to the living room. A moment later Cameron was in the kitchen opening cabinets and pulling out bowls and boxes of cereal.

"What did he say to her?" I asked as I opened the silverware drawer and pulled out two spoons.

Cameron laughed as he pulled the milk out from the fridge. "He told her he had some peanut butter crackers in his bag downstairs. I swear he would give her the shirt off his back if she asked for it. He will also probably starve to death since he is always giving her his food. Speaking of food, I will have to apologize because I know Brianna usually goes out of her way to make you breakfast, but unfortunately you are stuck with me and I only know how to make cereal."

"Is everything ok?" I asked as I tore open one of the boxes of cereal and poured it into my bowl. "Ashlyn said you guys were up pretty late."

Cameron's face was strained even though he was trying to hide it. "Brianna is fine, however, she was concerned with a dream the twins were having and stayed with them until they woke this morning. She is resting in order to regain her strength."

"But everything's ok, right?"

Cameron paused a second before he answered. "We shall see, I suppose. I am sure it is nothing. Will Ashlyn be joining you for breakfast?" I nodded as I swallowed down the fruity ringed cereal. "Oh, good. Since she joined you in bed the least she can do is join you for breakfast."

My throat didn't know whether to choke on my cereal or spit it out across the room, unfortunately it kept going back and forth. When I was finally able to swallow I said, "I'm sorry, man. Nothing happened I swear. We just fell asleep talking."

"And yet she is not your girlfriend," he laughed. "Can I request, for the sake of the children, that the two of you refrain from anymore sleepovers?"

"Yep, yep, no problem. Won't happen again, I promise."

"So what is your plan for today?"

"Not really a solid plan. I just need to take Ashlyn to get some clothes and stuff. Any suggestions on where I can go that won't cost a fortune around here?"

"I'll write down some areas where you can get all the things she may need in one or two places. You know what else might be...uh hold on..." Cameron stepped around the island and stood near the top of the stairs as he said, "Olivia?"

There was a brief silence before she yelled from the living room, "No, Ada, we're not watching a movie."

"Olivia Sera," Cameron warned in a very stern voice.

"Ada, how do you always know?!"

"Because I am your father," he replied. "It is still reading time."

I thoroughly enjoyed the sly smile on Cameron's face as he pulled out the stool next to me and sat.

"With your hearing they can't get away with anything."

Cameron's smile fell quickly. "Do you think I am being too hard on them?"

I shook my head as I shoved a mound of cereal into my mouth. "Not...yet. They'll be miserable as teenagers, though."

"Yes, but that is when they can get into real trouble. I think I can live with that. So as I was saying," he began as he reached into his back pocket, pulled out his wallet, and then handed me a wad of cash, "I think Ashlyn would benefit from a day of beauty."

I blinked. "A day of what?"

"A day of…well that is what women call it when they get a haircut, get their makeup done, facials, things like that. At least the women in my life do."

"So that's what this is for?" I asked as I held up the cash and he nodded. "And there isn't the slightest bit of guilt connected to this?"

"She does not need to know who the money came from."

"You could just apologize to her."

"Of course I will, but she still seems a little skittish."

"Well there's a little more than just being skittish. Can you do me a big favor?"

"Of course."

"I think Ashlyn is an Empath." Cameron looked skeptical. "I'm serious, but she's even more than that. She can make you feel what she's feeling. It's pretty freaky and cool at the same time. Anyway, that's why she's so against going to the Facility, there are too many emotions flying around. If I mention the Facility again, she'll take off, I just know it. So I'm hoping that maybe…you could…call Sera?"

Cameron twisted his lips back and forth as he crossed his arms in front of his chest. "So you need me to convince Seraphina to leave Facility East two weeks before it changes hands to give personal attention to a hybrid who has escaped from her care once already?"

"Y-y-yes?"

He sighed, but then cracked a smile. "Actually both Seraphina and Eris will be here late this afternoon. Having Eris closer to the children will ease Brianna's fears over the dreams the twins are having, and heaven knows Seraphina cannot pass up an opportunity to see her grandchildren. I will be sure to prepare her to work with Ashlyn."

"That worked out nicely," I laughed. "So since I didn't have to cash in my chits for that, can I ask for a new favor?"

"I suppose."

"Explain a day of beauty to me again?"

In this moment I was thankful for several things. One, I was thankful for Renee coming over to Bri's to pick up Will and then calling her hairdresser for, in her words, an emergency haircut. Two, I was equally thankful that one of the other hairdressers had enough time to squeeze me in. Now my hair was efficiently light and spikey. Lastly, I was thankful for a hangover-free morning, because if I had one I wouldn't have been able to enjoy the bright rays of sun shining on my face through the salon's display windows while I waited for Ashlyn's hair appointment to finish.

Unfortunately the downtime gave my mind the opportunity to rehash all of last night's revelations. Yesterday afternoon Ashlyn was a pain in my ass, an unstable homeless girl who was going to ruin my vacation. Now she was a girl who'd been forced into horrible circumstances by her alcoholic mother and fought tooth and nail to survive. Did it bother me she had been a blood donor? No. Did it bother me she had developed into a blood whore? Yes. Was it her fault she had to resort to such means? No, although I wasn't all that confident in my answer. Why did it bother me so much? Why did I keep thinking about her with so many other men…or women I guess. We never did get into details. Honestly I didn't want to know. But why was that? I'd heard dozens of sob stories from the other hybrids I'd taken to the Facility, and I knew intimate details. But why was I putting up such a wall when it came to Ashlyn?

The shopping bags that were gathered around my feet crinkled, making me slowly lift my head and stretch my eyes open to see a smiling young woman standing in front of me. I shook my head and blinked my eyes in a double-take when I realized it was Ashlyn. Her previously waist-length wavy blonde hair was now straight and resting at her shoulders. Between the haircut, Brianna's borrowed clothes, and her new makeup, she looked like a completely different person.

"So, whadaya think?" she said sweetly as she twirled around. "I never thought my hair could be this straight."

"You look a lot lighter," I replied and then wanted to hit myself in the face. Lighter? What an asshole. "Er…uh…what I meant was…they took off a lot…meaning it must feel lighter…oh god…"

"Honey," the female hairdresser said over Ashlyn's shoulder, "when a man stutters and makes an ass of himself, it means he really likes it."

Ashlyn smiled sweetly at me before looking at the floor. It made me wonder if she could feel my embarrassment, or that now I was worried she knew I was embarrassed or right now when…oh dear god make it stop.

"How much?" I asked the hairdresser and got up from the leather couch. The hairdresser waved me over to the front counter, and I almost lost my shit over how much Ashlyn's haircut cost. But I didn't argue and took the wad of cash out of my back pocket that Cameron had insisted on giving me. Just as I stretched my hand over the counter and was about to give the hairdresser her money, Ashlyn rested her hand on top of mine with a questioning look on her face.

"What?"

"Are you…" she began, her face suddenly flooded with worry.

"Cameron," I corrected.

Ashlyn turned away and began gathering the shopping bags. "I'll pay him back."

"It's not to be paid back."

"Then why?"

"Guilt. What else."

Ashlyn became very quiet as we left the salon and made our way through the bustling city sidewalks. I found it sad that all the life she had in the salon seemed to have been blown out of her with the cool fall breeze that was causing her to shiver.

"Our next stop should be to get you a coat," I said trying to keep up with her pace.

"I don't want anything else. Can we go back now?"

Gently I took her arm and pulled her to a stop. "First, you're not going to last up here without a coat. Second…"

"I said no," she shouted and then crossed the street without me. Passersby looked at me as though I was a predator.

With the shopping bags banging into my legs, I ran across the street to catch up with her, narrowly missing being hit by a taxicab.

"Ashlyn, wait," I yelled in her direction, and thankfully she stopped once she got on the other side of the street. Her arms were crossed in front of her chest and she couldn't stop pacing. "What's wrong?"

"I don't want anything from him!"

"Ok, ok, just calm down. He's trying to make up for what he did. It's not for forgiveness, it's just to help you."

Ashlyn's pacing stopped as the number of people around us started to grow with the lunchtime crowd coming from the buildings around us, and it seemed as though the walls were closing in on her.

"Are there too many people around?" She nodded nervously. "Are you hungry?" She nodded again. "Ok. There's a great little place just up ahead. We'll duck inside, have a bite to eat, and you can clear your head."

"Sorry," she said almost breathlessly.

"Don't be sorry. We'll get you feeling better in no time."

A few minutes later I wish I could have taken those words back. When I opened the door to the small bistro there was wall to wall people. I felt Ashlyn tense under my arm, and without a word I closed the door and steered us back down the sidewalk. Thankfully only a few doors down was a small diner that had only two other patrons inside.

"Well, we either go to a crowded place with good food, or a place that's empty because the food's terrible. Your choice."

"I don't remember the last time I went to a restaurant."

"Don't base your opinion on this experience. I don't have high hopes."

I laughed hoping she would laugh too, but she merely sank deeper inside of herself as we stepped inside. The place itself was dark, very little natural light coming through the windows even though it was a sunny day. Everything in the restaurant had a sheen of grease and grim on their surfaces while a haze hung in the air. There was no hostess, only a sign telling us to seat ourselves and two waitresses with scowls on their faces. But even with their attitudes, the lack of people caused Ashlyn to relax enough to come out from underneath my arm. Taking her hand, I led her to the back section of the restaurant.

The younger of the two waitresses pushed off the back wall and headed in our direction with two menus in her hand. As we sat down she threw the menus down on the table and pulled out her pad of paper. "Drinks?"

Ashlyn's eyes were wide as she looked up to the waitress, suddenly dumbfounded.

"Two cokes," I answered and Ashlyn sighed with relief when the miserable waitress left. "You ok?"

Ashlyn shook her head as she replied, "Wow. She *really* hates her life."

"Do you blame her? Look at this place?" I laughed as I held the menu up in front of me causing Ashlyn to do the same. "So do you want to talk about why you got so upset?"

She looked up from behind her menu and answered, "No one gives something for nothing."

"Uh…well that's not true. Cameron does. Brianna does. Pretty much their whole damn family does. You just need to…" but I didn't get to finish since the rude waitress slammed the two sodas down on the table. If the food wasn't keeping people away, it could definitely be the people.

"Do you want anything else?" the waitress snipped.

Ashlyn's menu started to shake so I had a feeling that she wouldn't be the first to answer. I hadn't even had the time to look at the menu, but I wasn't about to have to deal with this waitress any longer than I had to.

"Turkey club," I answered, seeing it listed at the top of the sandwich list and handed her the menu.

"And you?" the waitress said impatiently to Ashlyn.

"The same," Ashlyn responded. As soon as the waitress disappeared into the kitchen, Ashlyn leaned over the table and asked, "What did I just order?"

"You don't know what a turkey club is?" She shook her head. "Then why did you order it?"

"There were so many things on that menu, and I really just wanted her to leave."

I couldn't help but smile. "All right. Do you like turkey?"

"I think so."

"Bacon?" She nodded. "Tomato and lettuce?" She nodded again. "Then you'll love a turkey club. Now whether you'll like a turkey club from this place, that I can't promise. So, is this place helping you clear your head?"

"Yeah, a little. I'm sorry about before, it was just so…so…"

"I know," I interrupted, seeing the strain begin to seep back into her face. "Actually, I wanted to talk to you about that."

Ashlyn straightened up from the table, but then slumped against the bulkhead. "I have a feeling I'm going to hate this."

"Ok look, based on what happened last night, let's face it, you need some help."

"I'm not sure how to take that," she said and crossed her arms.

I sighed. "You know what I mean. You need help with your…your gift…your Empath thing. Cameron called Sera and she's agreed to work with you one on one to get you comfortable enough to go to the Facility."

"Why would she do that?"

"Er…uh, because Cameron asked her to."

"And why would he do that?"

"Because I asked him to, because he wants to help, Sera wants to help. Are you seeing a pattern here? We all want to help you, Ashlyn. What I can't understand is why you're so against it!"

"Because nothing comes for free, Jonah. If I've learned anything in my life, it's that. Everybody wants something from you and if you don't give it to them they just take it."

"Why can't you just believe that there are good people in this world who only want to help you."

"I don't trust anyone because no one has ever given me a reason. Unlike you, Jonah, I haven't lived a fairytale my whole life!"

Just as I was about to open my mouth and lose my temper, the rude waitress stepped up to our table and placed our turkey club sandwiches in front of us. "Could the two of you keep it down?"

Having no patience, I replied, "When you start being nice, we'll keep it down. Got it?"

The waitress rolled her eyes before turning away. Even though my stomach was growling at the sight of the double decker turkey club sandwich, I knew this conversation needed to finish.

"Frankly, Ashlyn, you don't know me well enough to say that to me. I know about fear and loss..."

"Oh really?" Ashlyn interrupted snidely. "What, you didn't make the football team? Daddy didn't buy you a car on your birthday?"

"My dad died," I replied angrily causing the skeptical look to be wiped from her face. "Four years ago. He had a heart attack during my sister's soccer game. I was twenty years old and suddenly a parent of a teenage girl because my mom couldn't cope. I dropped out of college and at one point I was working almost a hundred hours a week in order to keep a roof over our heads. I know the overwhelming fear of losing everything. I've had to ward off debt collectors and decide whether to pay the electric bill or buy groceries. And I did it because I loved my mom and sister, I sacrificed everything for them and now..."

I stopped myself, swallowing down the lump forming in my throat and taking a well needed breath. "But then I met Brianna Morgan, and my life changed. She didn't know me from Adam, but when she found out I was having a hard time she helped me and my family. And a few months after that she helped me get a job at Facility East that could really allow me to support my girls. But even after all of that, she keeps welcoming me into her family and shows me this world I never knew existed, a world that you are a part of, a world that is waiting to help you."

"But…" Ashlyn began but then sighed in frustration. "But why would she do all that?"

"Because she's a good person. Everyone just wants to help you, Ashlyn, and they want to help you because they're good people. Cameron, Bri, Sera, Eris, all of them."

"So what is it you want me to do?"

"I want you to trust me, Ashlyn, and take the help," I answered and picked up my sandwich.

"Is this Sera person nice?"

"Nicest woman I know," I answered before finally taking a big bite of my turkey club. But as I chewed, I knew there was something wrong with the taste. When I looked up, Ashlyn was about to take a bite of her sandwich and I waved my hand in front of her to stop. I took a napkin from the holder and spit the sandwich out into it.

"Don't eat that," I warned and she dropped her sandwich back down onto her plate. "Sorry, I don't know if Mable's spoiled me with her cooking, or if this place is really trying to kill people."

"Those people are eating their food," Ashlyn said, pointing to the only other couple in the restaurant.

"Then they don't have taste buds. Look, if we're working on getting you to trust me, then I cannot let you eat that."

Chapter Eleven

Cameron

"Ada?" Jackson asked as he stood on a stool while I knelt in front of him pinning the hem of the dress pants for his Halloween costume.

"Yes, son?" I replied through the straight pins between my lips.

"Do you think my costume will be better than Wivy's?"

The left side of my mouth lifted in a smile as I pulled one of the pins free and threaded it into the fabric. Guessing that this was the start of my son's many topics of conversation (since he always had so many), I took the remaining pins from my mouth and stuck them into the cuff of my sweater. "Have you seen your sister's costume?"

"No," he sighed.

"Then how can I possibly answer your question?"

"Because you're Ada. You know everything."

I smiled and looked up to see his precious face smiling down at me. Sometimes it was hard to believe my life without seeing that cherub face with his black unruly curls similar to my own. "When you become older you might feel differently."

"Never, Ada. You are the smartest person in the world," he said proudly but then added, "besides Mama."

I laughed quietly and began to pin the hem of the other pant leg.

"Ada?"

"Yes, son?"

"I'm sorry I grew again."

"There is no need to apologize, my boy. If you do not grow, how are you going to fit into your father's and uncles' shoes?"

"I have to wear your shoes?"

"No, son, it is just a saying. It means that someday you will grow up to be like me and your uncles."

"Whew! I don't think I'll ever be big enough to wear Uncle Alex's shoes. They're huge!"

"Yes they are," I laughed as I rose from the floor and stepped over to the guest bed to get Jackson's cape.

"Ada?"

"Yes, son," I replied and tied the cape around his neck.

"Do I have to be a Warrior like you and Mama? And Devy? And Uncle Alex and Uncle Jer? And Grandfather?"

I paused for a moment waiting to see if he was going to list the remaining Warriors, he certainly knew all their names. "If you do not want to be a Warrior, you certainly do not have to be."

A tiny smile formed across his face along with a sigh of relief. "Oh, good. Because I know what I want to be when I grow up."

"You do?"

"Uh-huh. I want to be a hybrid helper."

"A hybrid...helper? Do you mean like a Gatherer?"

"Nuh-uh. A hybrid helper. I would help hybrids that need help."

Slowly I nodded my head, not fully understanding the career he had created for himself. From the dresser behind me I took the Edwardian collar that I had constructed and placed it around Jackson's neck to begin pinning it to the cape. "Jackson, if you want to help hybrids, I believe you have chosen to do something very noble. You and Olivia are technically Warriors by birth, but that does not mean you have to do what we do. It merely means that you will always have people to help you and protect you if you need it. Understand?"

He nodded vehemently. "Yes, Ada. Ada?"

"Yes, son?"

"Does Mama know I'm showing my fangs tomorrow?"

I licked my lips as I pushed one of the straight pins into the collar. As part of Jackson's costume I had agreed to allow him to keep his fangs extended. I did not, however, tell Brianna about it. "Since your fangs are part of your costume I felt it should be part of your unveiling. But, what did we talk about?"

"I can't chase Wivy with my fangs out."

"You give me your word?"

"I promise, Ada."

I cupped Jackson's cheek and kissed his temple. "You are my dearest boy." Jackson's chest swelled as he straightened his posture and allowed me to get back to work on the collar of his cape. "Son?"

"Yes, Ada?"

"Do you remember the dreams you had last night?"

"Mm-hmm. Eri took us swimming in the ocean with the dolphins. My dolphin was named Daisy."

I smiled as I took a step back to check the alignment of the collar. "Do you remember your dream before you swam with Daisy?"

Jackson nodded reluctantly. "Kinda. I didn't like it, Ada. Everyone was so angry, and Mama was yelling. It was...am I allowed to be scared?"

"Of course you can be scared, Jacky."

"But you don't get scared. My uncles don't get scared. Grandfather and Eri don't get scared."

"Well that is simply untrue," I said as I placed the final pin into the stiff collar then untied the cape from his neck altogether. "I have been scared many times in my life, as have your uncles and grandfathers."

"Really?" Jackson replied with tremendous surprise.

"Absolutely. Everyone gets scared from time to time, it is how we handle our fear that defines us."

Jackson looked to the floor as I began to unbutton his white dress shirt. "I might have cried a little."

"You are only three years old."

"Three and a half!"

I laughed. "Yes, Jacky, three and a half, and you are allowed to cry if you are scared."

Carefully I removed Jackson's dress shirt and then the dress pants in order to finish the alterations later. He was more than happy to be able to get changed back into his play clothes. While I helped him tug on his small rugby shirt, I asked, "Now son, in this scary dream, did you recognize anyone?"

He nodded as his head popped through the shirt's collar. "Wivy, and Mama, and you, and Devy..."

"Anyone not part of our family?"

"Oh yeah, lotsa people."

"Did you know anyone? Did any of them speak to you?"

"No, Ada," he answered and jumped down off the stool. At a non-human speed Jackson quickly scooped up his sneakers and headed toward the door.

"Jackson Thomas, I will require you to wear pants." Jackson stopped abruptly. Slowly he turned around, his shoulders now slumped as he walked begrudgingly back to me. He took the small pair of jeans out of my hands. "Now son, you do remember what your mother and I have taught you about talking to strangers, correct?"

"Yes, Ada. I *don't* talk to strangers. I don't go anywhere with strangers. And if someone I don't know tells me you sent them, I ask for the password."

"Which is?" I groaned.

"Pickles!" he replied happily before bolting from the room.

"Ah yes, pickles, a legacy password from your mother," I said to no one as I placed the pieces of Jackson's costume into the closet until I found the time to finish. Eris and Seraphina would be here within the next hour and they would be occupying this bedroom, subsequently the only remaining guest room unless you counted Jared's windowless room down in the basement. We had a full house, and knowing Brianna the way I did, I knew she was itching to get in here and freshen up the room before her parents arrived.

Once Jackson's costume was hidden in the closet, I stepped from the room into the hallway just as Jonah and Ashlyn were coming up the main stairway. Jonah's hands and arms were heavy with different sized shopping bags, while Ashlyn was free of bags as well as almost twelve inches of her hair.

"The shopping day seems to have been successful," I said as I met them in the kitchen.

Ashlyn nodded shyly while Jonah placed the bags on the couch as he said, "It was like pulling teeth, but I think she got what she needed."

"Jo-nah," Ashlyn groaned in a soft, embarrassed tone.

"What? I've never met a girl who hated shopping as much as you do," he teased and stepped over to the kitchen island. "Did you hear from Eris?"

"Yes," I nodded. "He and Seraphina should be here within the hour." I looked over to Ashlyn who was still keeping an obvious distance. "Seraphina is looking forward to working with you, Ashlyn. Having been isolated for so many years, she is very excited to meet someone with a similar gift to her own."

Ashlyn nodded nervously and retreated down the hallway toward her guest room.

"Well hopefully she'll open up a little with Sera," Jonah sighed.

"Has she been like that all day?"

Jonah shook his head. "No. She had a little meltdown earlier, but overall she was good. Frankly, it's you, man. She's still really nervous around you."

"I know I need to speak with her," I replied. "But it is difficult to find the words, and even more so when…"

"Jackson Thomas, you get back here right now!" Brianna yelled from downstairs.

At the same time my son came running up the stairs in a blur. I pushed myself from the kitchen island and caught him as he sped toward the hallway. He wriggled in my arms until he realized he had been caught, and suddenly I noticed that his fangs were prominently displayed.

"Retract those fangs this instant," I growled.

From downstairs I could hear Olivia crying while Bri shouted up the stairs, "Cameron, can you…"

"I have him, love," I interrupted as I placed Jackson down on the floor. His fangs had disappeared although tears began to stream down his cheeks. "To the timeout step, son."

Sniffling and wiping his face with his sleeve, Jackson walked over to the staircase and sat down on the first step, his little curly head bent down into his chest. As I stepped over to my son, Jonah took Ashlyn's shopping bags from the couch and left down the hall toward her room. When I sat down on the step next to Jackson he immediately draped himself over my leg and out of habit I began rubbing his back. Since they were tiny babies, Jackson had always been the more sensitive of the two.

"Jacky, why were your fangs out?"

"I…was…chasing…Wivy," he cried into my leg.

"And why were you chasing your sister?"

"We were…just playing."

"But we just spoke about not chasing your sister with your fangs."

Jackson lifted his head, leaving behind a wet spot on my pants from his tears. "But they just came out, Ada. I didn't mean to. I just got…my heart was just beating too fast, I couldn't help it! Doesn't your heart beat too fast sometimes?"

My heart did not beat at all, although it was breaking at the moment. My son was being punished for something he could not control, and it was my fault. I had done this to him, and to Olivia. My little boy was crying over something no other child in the world had to contend with, and all because I had a moment of weakness and fear.

Jackson was still looking up at me with his flushed cherub cheeks and teary eyes. "I'm sorry, Ada."

"I am not the person you need to apologize to."

"I'm sorry, Wivy," he said loudly down the stairs.

There was no answer from the living room, even though I could hear Brianna urging Olivia to accept her brother's apology.

With a sigh I stood from the stairs. "You will need to stay there until your mother says you can come down."

"Ada?"

"Yes, son?"

Jackson closed his eyes and his voice was suddenly echoing in my head, *Ada, can I still use my fangs for my costume?*

"We shall see," I replied and I continued down the stairs while a tremendous amount of guilt began to weigh heavily on my chest.

"Cam?" Brianna called after me once I turned toward the back door.

"Jackson is on his step," I replied and continued down the hallway.

"Where are you…"

"I just need some air."

"You don't breathe, babe."

I sighed as my hand wrapped around the doorknob. "In your words, I need to be moody-broody and I would rather do it outside."

"I love you."

"Always, love," I replied and shut the door behind me.

Chapter Twelve

Brianna

Moody-broody my ass, Cameron was being downright depressive. I knew when he needed to be alone, but usually it was fifteen or twenty minutes. He'd been out on the patio for almost an hour – pacing, sitting, talking on the phone, and then pacing some more. With the kids upstairs with Jonah, and my parents only minutes away, Mr. Burke's moody-broody time was over. Looking through the backdoor's lattice window I could see that he had returned to pacing, but he abruptly stopped when I opened the door.

"You're gonna wear away our paving stones, babe," I said as I crossed over to him.

"Sorry, love. I just have a lot on my mind."

"Anything you want to tell me?" He shook his head. Jerk. "Did you hear anything from Alex?"

"No. They are coming up as empty as they have the last three and a half years."

"That's really not what I wanted to hear."

Cameron stretched his arms open and I immediately melted into his chest. "And I certainly did not want to have to tell you. We just have nothing to go on."

"A random forest big enough to hold an army of enemy Vamps isn't enough to go on?" His laugh rumbled in his chest beneath my ear. "Our babies could be in danger, Cam."

"I know, love."

"Is this when it starts? They're only three, Cam. How can the future of Vampires be placed upon their shoulders?"

"I do not know, love."

"Why does it have to be them?"

"I do not know, love."

"Why hasn't Sera said anything? She's had to have seen something, right?"

"I do…"

"Oh don't tell me you don't know," I said impatiently, though half kidding as I pushed away from his chest. "Tell me something you do know."

The left side of his mouth lifted into my favorite smile. "I know I love you."

"Well someone has to," I laughed. "My parents should be here any second, so prepare yourself."

"There is never enough time to prepare for your father."

"And don't I know it," I replied and walked back toward the house.

"You know he likes to torture me by asking if we have set a date for our wedding." I stopped just in front of the backdoor, able to see Cameron's pleading reflection in the window pane. "It would be nice if we could say…something."

"Soon, Cam. I promise. Things just need to settle down."

Cameron didn't respond before I stepped back into the house. When I was halfway down the hall, a car horn echoed from outside. I didn't need to look out a window to know it was my father. Through the walls of the house I could sense his radiant Vampire essence, as well as that of his driver, Vlad.

When I opened the front door a white SUV was parked outside, effectively blocking the one-way street. My father exited the SUV and extended his hand to Sera. Her blonde hair was perfectly quaffed as always, however, deeper age lines decorated her face. I actually didn't notice Vlad until he appeared at the back of the truck and lifted the tailgate.

"Vlad, I didn't know you were staying with us too."

"I'm not," he replied firmly as he removed several pieces of luggage from the back. "I am supposed to be on vacation."

Eris rolled his eyes in my direction before turning and taking the bags out of Vlad's hands. "I have only delayed your vacation by several hours. That is what makes having a private jet so convenient, you can leave whenever you want. Besides, most people would not complain to the owner of the jet they are getting to use for two weeks."

There was an awkward silence as they stared each other down in the middle of the street but Sera didn't seem fazed as she stepped away from the SUV with two gift bags banging against her knees.

"Those better not be for the kids," I warned as she wrapped her arms around me and kissed me several times on the cheek.

"Zhey are from Vlad, not me," she replied with a sweet smile.

I looked past her shoulder to see Vlad finally break face and smile as he shook his head. "Sera, do not bring me into this. Take care, Eris," he said as he patted my father's back.

"We will see you in a couple of weeks, old friend," Eris replied before stepping toward the house as I stepped off the curb to say goodbye to Vlad.

"Honestly, I take the same two weeks off every year and he makes me delay my plans," he said kiddingly as I hugged him tightly.

"I'm sorry, Vlad. This is my fault."

"Which is the only reason I'm doing it," he replied before turning back to the SUV and pulling out several large plastic bags from a major toy store chain.

"There's more?! I'm gonna kill her. How did she shop so fast?"

A sheepish grin stretched across Vlad's face as he held the bags out to me. "Actually...these are from me. Tell the kids Uncle Vlad says hello."

"Are you sure you don't want to come in?"

He shook his head vigorously. "The quicker I get out of the country the better," he replied giving me a quick kiss on the cheek. "I'll see you in North Carolina before you know it."

Vlad gave me another quick kiss on the cheek and then closed the tailgate before running around to the driver's side door. When I turned back toward the house, Eris had disappeared inside but Sera was still standing on the front steps, smiling like the Cheshire Cat as she eyed the hulking plastic bags hanging from my arms.

"Petite chute, do not be angry," she said sweetly in her thick French accent. "We all just love zhe petites bébés so much."

"Words are better than toys."

"But I am zheir Mémé, it is my right to spoil zhem," she laughed as we walked through the front door, but suddenly Sera tensed and gasped.

"Mom?"

"I am fine," she said as she stepped into the foyer and rested her hand against the wall.

Dropping the bags to the floor I quickly stepped over to her, gently petting her arm and noticing her face losing its color. "You don't look fine."

I watched her take in a deep breath and transfer her weight from the wall to my supportive arm. "I can feel your Empath."

"Ashlyn? She's upstairs, you can…feel…her?"

She nodded. "She is very strong, and…" she took another deep breath as I led her over to the staircase, "…and extremely nervous."

A shiver went up Sera's spine as we continued up the stairs and I noticed that her hand was clenching the handrail tightly. As the second landing expanded before us, Ashlyn stood front and center wringing her hands nervously in front of her waist.

"Ashlyn, this is my mom, Seraphina, but we all call her Sera."

Sera smiled weakly and extended her hand toward Ashlyn whose hand was shaking as it rose in the air. Just as their fingertips touched, Sera gasped loudly and took a large step backwards, forgetting that the stairs were right behind her. At the same time my father and I flew to Sera just in time to catch her in our arms before her back hit the stairs.

"Protections," she said through labored breath while squeezing my hand tightly and pointing at Ashlyn.

"What? Protections from what? From Ash…"

I looked in Ashlyn's direction who was now sobbing on the floor with a very confused Jonah trying to console her.

"Non, non," Sera replied impatiently as she ripped her hand out of mine and squeezed her head. "La montrer comment protéger. Protéger, protéger!" she continued to shout as she hit the heal of her hand against her forehead.

"Shields, Brianna!" Cameron shouted over Sera's screams and Ashlyn's sobs. "Show Ashlyn how to use a mind shield, like you use."

I looked down at Sera who nodded as she shook in my father's chest.

"Shields? Ok, shields…" fucking shields, I thought to myself as I slid across the floor to sit in front of Ashlyn who was a shivering mess. Shields were so natural now that I couldn't think of how to explain them to Ashlyn, or how to create a shield insider her mind. "Ok Ashlyn, first you need to calm down."

"I'm killing her, oh my god I'm killing her!" Ashlyn sobbed and in return caused Sera to make similar moans behind me.

Gently I began stroking Ashlyn's arm and hand, looking up at Jonah for any suggestions on how to calm her down, but he looked just as dumbfounded as I felt.

"You're not killing her, sweetie, you're just…your emotions are…

"Killing her!" Eris shouted behind me.

"You're not helping, Dad!" I yelled over my shoulder, but then brought my voice back down when I said, "Ashlyn, I need you to close your eyes and breathe, sweetie. Just breathe." She did as I asked, but she was almost hyperventilating while tears continued to leak from her eyes. "Ok, now…think of…of a steel door…think of it like a garage door closing…"

"Daughter, tell her how to do a shield this instant!"

I whipped my head around and growled at my father. "It took me two days to learn how to do a shield and you want me to do it in two minutes!? Now shut up and…" Cameron cleared his throat in the kitchen where his arms were protectively draped across the twins' shoulders. Then an idea hit me.

"Livy, come here, baby girl."

Cameron gave me a cautious look as Olivia freed herself from her father's arm and flitted across the floor to my side. "Yes, Mama?"

I pulled her down onto my lap and held her tiny hands in mine. "Ok, sweet pea, can you see Ashlyn's light?"

"Yes, Mama, it's really red."

"Good girl," I said relieved as I took my own shield down and felt an energy connecting me to my daughter. I could easily see Ashlyn's hybrid essence hovering in front of me and using my daughter as a conduit I forced a shield to develop inside Ashlyn's mind. After only a few seconds the room felt lighter, and it was certainly quieter now that Ashlyn had stopped crying and Sera's moans had also ceased. Afraid to let go of my hold on Ashlyn, I stayed on the floor with Olivia in my lap while I slowly turned my head to see Eris helping Sera to her feet. Eris supported her limp body as she slowly shuffled into the sitting area.

"Mom?"

"I will be fine, petite," she replied weakly while Eris lowered her onto the couch. "Cameron, some wine, s'il vous plait."

Cameron affirmed something in French and quickly pulled a bottle of Sera's favorite white wine from the fridge. Olivia began wriggling in my lap which meant her attention span was waning. When I turned back to Ashlyn her face and body were relaxed with relief, but I wondered how long it would last. Jonah could see my hesitation and placed his hands on her shoulders.

"Ok, Ashlyn," I said calmly, "do you feel the shield?" She nodded tentatively. "Now, Livy and I are going to let go, but I need you to remember that feeling. Just concentrate...and we'll slowly...let...go."

Once I removed my hand from Olivia's, she immediately jumped up from my lap. Thankfully Ashlyn remained calm and there were no screams coming from Sera so apparently the shield was working.

"I'm sorry," Ashlyn said softly and then looked over my shoulder. "I'm sorry, Sera."

I looked over to where Sera sat on the couch and watched as she drank an entire glass of wine without taking a breath. When she was done she shook her head at Ashlyn's apology and tapped the lip of her glass for Cameron to pour her another. "Do not apologize, young one. I was simply not prepared for you. Zhe alcohol will help."

"The wine will dull her sensitivity," Eris added.

"Well if I knew that, I would have gotten Ashlyn drunk before you guys got here," Jonah joked and helped Ashlyn to her feet. Thankfully even Ashlyn laughed and yet another layer of the thick atmosphere was shed.

I had to laugh to myself as my stepmother downed her second glass of wine. I wondered if she would be plastered during her entire visit. As I rose from the floor, Jack-Jack was suddenly at my side and pulling on my shirt sleeve.

"Mama, when's it my turn?"

"Your turn for what, baby?"

"To help Ashwyn."

I blinked. "Uh...help Ashlyn with what?"

Jack-Jack's bottom lip jutted out in a pout. "Wivy got to help Ashwyn, now I want a turn."

"I think she's ok now, Jack-Jack. But you can't help hybrids like Livy..."

Well that did it, not that I knew what the heck I'd done, but Jack-Jack let out a painful high-pitched wail.

"BUT I WANT TO HELP!" he screamed and stamped his feet loudly on the hardwood floor before he fled down the hall toward his bedroom. "I CAN HELP TOO!"

"Ok. What just happened?"

"You might have just crushed our son's dreams," Cameron replied.

"Oh good. I thought it was something small."

The children had been asleep for almost two hours and had been dreaming for almost the same amount of time. To avoid exhaustion, my father and I had spilt the dream watching, each taking a twin. After Jackson's complete meltdown he had been in constant need of attention and reassurance and snuggling. Who knew a three-year-old would be so settled in his future career. Most little boys his age would say they wanted to be a fireman or a policeman, but not my Jack-Jack. Oh no, he wanted to be a "hybrid helper". His overt caring and love for others could even be seen in his dreams tonight as I watched him help people cross the street, carry their groceries, even save a young woman from an oncoming car. Although I couldn't say with complete certainty, I assumed to him they were all hybrids in need.

At the present, Jack-Jack was walking alone down a brightly lit city neighborhood, similar to one you would see here in Boston. The streets were shiny with a previous rain causing the moonlight to shimmer along the asphalt. But beyond that, nothing was happening. It seemed as though he was waiting for something, or possibly someone, which of course made the hairs on my arm stand on end. I was taking in every detail of the street, the houses, even the trees that lined the sidewalks. But besides Jackson kicking rocks in front of him, his dream was actually a little boring.

I sat on a bench and observe my son unobtrusively. He knew I was there, but kept on as though I wasn't. Just then someone's fingers brushed my forearm causing me to jump and look defensively to my right. My guard instantly relaxed when I saw Cameron sitting next to me.

"You know you're going to zap my energy," I said taking his hand and pulling his arm around me.

One night Cameron stumbled upon the fact that by touching me while I was Dreamwalking my body acted as a conduit for him to come into the dream as well. My body was very conduit-ty? By touching Olivia I could see hybrids as she did, and in Jackson's case his gift only strengthened my own. The only problem with being used as a conduit was the amount of energy it drained out of me.

"I apologize, angel. I am merely checking in. Anything substantial?"

I shook my head. "Nothing so far, but the night is young."

"You cannot monitor the twins' dreams all night every night, love. Your strength will simply not hold out."

"Dad can."

"Your father is over three thousand years old. You are…" I gave him a deadly squint which made him clear his throat, "…not."

"But what if the one time I'm not watching, something happens, or Gorgin…Godan…whatever his name is…what if he takes control over the twins? He was able to find me, what's to say he couldn't find our babies? Dad couldn't break through his hold on me…"

"Yes, but you did, remember?" Cameron interrupted, taking my left hand and kissing its back before placing it over his heart. "You broke through once, I am sure you could do it again if the situation presented itself, especially if it involved our children."

"But how do we…" I began but stopped at the sound of Olivia shouting her brother's name. I looked past Cameron and saw our daughter running down the empty street toward her brother. She was wearing her butterfly princess Halloween costume, although the pink ballet flats I had purchased for the outfit had been replaced by her favorite red rain boots.

"What in the world is our daughter wearing?" Cameron said as his eyes followed Olivia down the street.

"You know Livy, so…creative." Cameron accepted my explanation although he would definitely be quirking his eyebrow at me tomorrow when the twins showed off their Halloween costumes. Just then another figure shimmered in the distance. "Dad?"

"Daughter, did you bring their dreams together for a reason?"

My face fell. "I assumed it was you."

He shook his head. "One minute Olivia is giving a recital to a large group of butterflies then she simply skipped off and I followed her here."

"They must be doing it," I said as I bolted up from the bench. "That could mean that…"

"Aidan!" Jackson cheered, causing all three of us to whip around.

And there he was, the one man who almost destroyed our family, and our children were running to him. I lurched forward in response only to have my father clasp my arm and pull me back next to him.

"Figlia, we watch. That is all," he said firmly.

"I will not just stand here while…"

"Bri, your father is right…"

"What!?" I yelled in total shock as I ripped my arm from my father's grasp. "You of all people know…"

"Yes, love, I know," he interrupted in a soft tone and placed gentle hands on my shoulders. "But I watched your dreams and they helped us learn and prepare for what was to come. We must watch and not interfere."

I looked between the two of them, their eyes full of sympathy and wisdom, and yet I just couldn't accept it.

"I'm sorry," I said before running to where Aidan was standing with my children in his arms, one on each hip while he spun them playfully around. "Put. Them. Down."

Aidan's cocky smile spread across his face as he slowly put the twins down onto the ground. "Hey kids, let's play a game."

"Babies, come to Mama," I ordered but they stayed next to Aidan, mesmerized by his charm and his prospect of a game. "Please babies, just come to Mama."

Aidan knelt down between the twins and pointed at me. "Now let's see who can make your mommy fly."

My eyes grew wide as Livy and Jack joined their inside hands together and thrust their arms out in front of them causing me to fly backwards roughly fifty feet and slam into Cameron and Eris, knocking them down like bowling pins. Immediately I stood from the ground only to be lifted off my feet and held in midair while Cameron shouted at the twins to stop whatever it was they were doing.

Suddenly the entire scene froze – the twins still as statues with their arms held out in front of them, Cameron reaching for me above his head, and my father simply watching the chaos. The only movement came from Aidan who was gliding towards me, his devilish smile still plastered across his face as he looked up at me. I was frozen in the air, unable to move or talk, almost as though I was paralyzed but fully aware of everything happening around me.

"Looking good, Morgan," Aidan said as he reached up and grazed my cheek with his fingertips. "And all this time I thought I'd lost you. It's not too late you know, all of this can stop. Isn't that what you want?"

"Go...to...hell," I managed to say through my clenched teeth.

Aidan's smile fell from his face and the evil that was within him took over. "The twins are mine. It's only a matter of time. How does Olivia Pierce sound to you? Jackson Pierce? Oh, you prefer calling him Jack-Jack, don't you? I think I will prefer to just call him...son."

"NO!" I screamed and feeling not only my throat burn but my head exploding.

My back slammed into Cameron as the two of us went flying into the front wall of the twins' bedroom. Both Livy and Jack sat up in bed screaming and crying at the same time Eris and Sera came running through the door.

"Figlia!" my father shouted as he rounded on me while Sera quickly began comforting my crying children. "You know you cannot disengage from a dream like that, you could have hurt the children."

Cameron stood from the floor and firmly grasped my father's arm and pulled him out of the room. I couldn't look at Sera or listen to the sounds of my sobbing children. I pushed myself up from the floor which caught the attention of the twins.

"Mama?" the two of them said at the same time.

I stepped over to where both of them were clinging to their grandmother and kissed each of them tenderly on the tops of their soft curly heads. "Stay with Mémé. I need to talk to Ada and Eri."

When I stepped out of the room my father and Cameron were having very tense words, although they were half whispered.

"Daughter, we need to..." Eris said angrily as I passed by.

"I need a minute," I interrupted and opened one of the French doors that led to the balcony.

"No, no minutes. We are talking about this now."

"No, we're not!" I shouted back. "I know what I did, Dad. I know I could have hurt the babies. Don't you think I feel awful right now? All I am asking is for a few minutes and then you can scold me and tell me what a horrible Dreamwalker and mother I am. Ok?"

I didn't give him a chance to answer before I stepped outside onto the balcony and slammed the door behind me. I stood at the edge of the balcony, grasping the handrail firmly while I closed my eyes and tried to calm all the sights and sounds that were running through my head. Roughly five minutes passed before one of the French doors behind me opened and Cameron's arms wrapped around me and pulled my back into his chest.

"Your father *will* apologize to you once you come back inside."

"Why should he? I know better. But hey, Brianna Morgan loses her cool again and screws everything up! What else is new?"

Cameron pulled my hands from the handrail and hugged them into my chest. "Bri, this would be difficult for any parent to handle. Your father is definitely an exception."

"Did you hear what Aidan said?"

"Yes," he growled.

"I think we should call off trick or treating tomorrow night." Cameron lowered his arms and turned me around. "You disagree?"

"I believe you might be overreacting a little."

"But what if…"

"We will protect our children from whatever Aidan puts in their path."

"And what good is our protection if our children simply run to him?"

"We will talk with them again."

I melted into his chest, tucking my head in my usual spot underneath his chin. "Nothing can happen to them, Cam."

"Nothing will as long as we look for the signs, just like we used to do with you." Cameron kissed the top of my head and then began petting my hair. "There is something else we should talk about."

"Besides figuring out how we're going to protect our children from a psychopath?"

He tilted my chin up with his index finger. "You are a wonderful mother, Brianna. If you ever say otherwise again, we will have words."

"We will, huh?"

"Try me."

Chapter Thirteen

Brianna

Olivia stood beaming in front of my full-length mirror while I put the final bobby pins in her hair. Kyla had given me step by step instructions over a video chat on how to give Livy "princess hair", and with only a little criticism from my daughter I was able to recreate it rather successfully. Her crooked wings flapped against my legs as she twisted left and right admiring her sparkly pink Halloween costume, her vision of what a butterfly princess should be minus one item.

"See, Mama, with my princess hair I *need* to have a crown," she begged as she hugged my right leg.

"Baby girl, if I had a crown I'd give it to you. I just ran out of time."

She looked up at me with a pout and squinted her left eye. "Is that because you keep resting? Why do you keep resting, Mama? Are you sick?"

"No, sweet pea, I'm not sick," I replied as I removed her hands from around my leg and knelt down in front of her. "I've been watching your dreams the last few nights and that makes me very sleepy so I need to rest."

"Eri doesn't need to rest when he does it."

"That's because I'm not old like Eri."

"But Mama," she began and gently patted my hand, "you are old."

I pressed my lips together before straightening her crooked wings. "Now what did Ada and I talk to you about today?"

"Don't talk to strangers," she said loudly and proudly.

"That's right, don't talk to strangers. Never, ever, ever talk to strangers."

"Mama, I never talk to strangers. Never, ever, ever. Just like you and Ada always say," she said dismissively as she rose on one foot and began pirouetting.

"So last night in your dream why did you talk to that man?"

Olivia stopped her twirling and looked at me curiously. "You mean Aidan?" The sound of his name coming from my daughter's lips made my fangs tingle inside my gums, but I bit down to prevent them from extending and nodded. "Oh Mama, Aidan's not a stranger."

"Wh-what do you mean, baby?"

"Aidan is Jack-Jack's friend," she replied nonchalantly and resumed her twirling.

"How long has Aidan been Jack-Jack's friend? When did he start seeing him?"

"Silly Mama, Jack-Jack doesn't see him for real."

"Livy, honey, please stop twirling and tell me why your brother doesn't see him."

Livy froze in mid-twirl, her arms stretched high above her head. "Because Aidan isn't real. He's Jack-Jack's imaginary friend. Can I twirl now?"

I was about to say no and press her a little harder when the door to my bedroom opened and Sera poked her head inside. "Petites? Can I come in?"

"Mémé!" Livy squealed. "Do you like my costume?"

"Ah oui, petite singe," she replied as she stepped inside the bedroom carrying a small white box.

"Didn't you buy the kids enough stuff already?" I whined as Olivia took the box from her grandmother's outstretched hand.

Sera cupped my cheek and replied, "Petite chute, just one more zhing, I promiss."

Olivia giggled as she began to open her gift.

"What's so funny, baby girl?"

"Mémé calls me little monkey, but she calls you a little cabbage. You're a cabbage, Mama," she laughed to herself.

"Oh yes, I'm well aware that Mémé calls me a cabbage," I replied, raising an annoyed eyebrow in Sera's direction.

In the next second my bedroom was flooded with the sound of my daughter squealing so loudly I thought my ears would bleed. From within the small white box she removed a tiny crown with rhinestones that rose in a small point in the center.

"Mémé, how did you know!"

Sera leaned down to be eye to eye with Livy and said slowly, "Parce que Mémé sait toujours."

Livy licked her lips as she translated the statement in her head. Finally, and with a twinge of uncertainty she said, "Because Mémé knows…always…oh, always knows! Right, Mama?"

I laughed. "I wouldn't know, baby girl. I can't speak French like you do."

"Why not? It's easy!" she replied as she handed me her little crown and then turned to face the mirror so that I could place it on her head. Once the combs were secured tightly in her princess hairdo, Livy jerked away and began twirling a new happy little dance.

While she was distracted I turned to face Sera who smiled at the sight of the joy she had given her granddaughter. When she finally noticed that I was looking at her she covered her reddened cheeks. "It is worth zhe grief you give me to see zhem so happy."

"Mom, at this rate even the manor isn't big enough to hold all the gifts you buy them."

She laughed and slipped her arm around my shoulders. "But zhat is not what you are so worried about. What is it, petite?"

Knowing I couldn't hide anything from her, I turned my back on Livy and lowered my voice as I said, "Is this a good idea? Letting the twins go out tonight? You would tell me if you saw something, wouldn't you?"

"Of course, but…" she began, but a sudden sadness sank into the wrinkles on her face, "…I have not seen anyzhing."

"Nothing?" She shook her head and my patience became thin. "Mom, I love you so much, but why is it you know when Livy needs a crown for her costume but you don't see if her life is in danger?" Sera's eyes became glassy with tears. "I'm sorry, I didn't mean…"

"My visions have become so scarce since zhe bébés were born. I haven't seen anyzhing, petite, I promiss."

"I believe you, Mom, I do. I'm just…"

"Worried, I know. Your guard should be up, zhat I know."

But before I could press any further, my attention was brought to the far side of the bedroom where Olivia's dancing had abruptly stopped. I watched as she tilted her head slightly to the left as though she was listening to someone, and in her case she most likely was listening to Jackson speaking inside her head.

Livy straightened her head and looked over to me as she said, "Mama, Jack-Jack's ready. Can I show my costume now?"

"Yes, Livybean, you can show your costume now," I replied and pulled Sera from the bedroom to follow my very excited butterfly princess into the hallway. "Mom, you look tired."

Sera sighed as she crooked my arm around hers. "I zhink my age is catching up with me."

"It's not your age," I scolded as we stepped into the hallway. "Working with Ashlyn is draining you."

"To say zhe least," she replied as we came to the foyer where Olivia was twirling around in front of Jonah and Eris explaining every detail of her sparkly costume.

As we came further into the foyer I noticed that Ashlyn was purposely keeping a safe distance by standing in the corner of the living room while watching from afar. I didn't need to be an Empath to know she wanted to be with everyone, and it did make me sad to see her self-induced exile. However, I was happy to see that the defiant-tough-girl attitude she had when she first got here had pretty much disappeared. And although she was still refusing to go to the Facility, she had been very accepting of Sera's training.

"Mama!" Livy squealed. "Jonah loves my costume!"

"Good, baby."

"I think we might win!"

"Well, we'll have to wait and see. Your brother isn't here yet…"

"Here I come," Jackson announced from the second floor.

The stiff black collar of his costume was visible first, but when he finally came to stand at the top of the stairs my jaw dropped and everyone in the foyer became silent. Even Ashlyn came in closer to see what everyone was gawking at. Cameron came to stand just behind Jackson's right shoulder and he was already giving me a pleading look of forgiveness.

"Mama, I'm Dracula!" Jackson said proudly as he took the edges of his cape and held his arms up high. Underneath his cape was a perfectly tailored pair of black pants, white satin vest and pristine tux shirt. The gold medallion that hung from a red ribbon glistened and bounced off his chest as he skipped down the stairs. "And look, Mama, I'll be better than any other Dracula because I have real fangs!"

Jackson opened his mouth wide and snapped out his fangs to my horror and to everyone else's amusement as they snickered around me. "Jack-Jack, what have I told you about..."

"But Ada said I could," he interrupted while pointing up to Cameron who was slowly coming down the stairs.

"Cameron!"

"Angel, listen," he replied, holding his hands up in front of him. "He knows there are rules."

He doesn't follow the rules when he's in the house, you expect him to follow them when we're out in public, I forced into Cameron's head making his eyes wince.

Jackson pulled on the cuff of my shirt. "Mama, I won't chase Wivy. I won't chase anyone, I promise."

I looked down at him with pursed lips and a very skeptical look. "If you want to show off your fangs they're going to have to stay out the entire time. We can't have them coming in and out, we'll never be able to explain it. Cameron, I can't believe..."

"Brianna," Cameron began, pumping his palms out in front of him again, "this was a very creative choice on our son's part. It is very tongue and cheek."

"It's hysterical!" Jonah said loudly through his continued laughter. "Ok, I'm ready to rule." Jonah pushed himself off the foyer wall, while Livy and Jack-Jack stood very straight and proud on the last step of the staircase. "Ok, I have to say that the prettiest and pinkest costume winner goes to...Livy Burke!"

Olivia squealed as she jumped off the step and twirled wildly around. However, Jackson's face fell in utter disappointment causing his fangs to retract slowly.

"Oh, but I'm not done," Jonah announced, causing Jack-Jack to cautiously lift his eyes up. "But this year's best costume award goes to...Jack-Jack Burke for his very creative and I'm sorry, f'ing hysterical costume."

"Yeah!" Jackson shouted as he stuck his tongue out at his sister.

"Poop!" Livy cried in response.

"Olivia Sera," Cameron said sternly, "what have we said about that word?"

Olivia pushed her bottom lip out into a pout. "You don't like it."

"You should remember that next time, monkey."

"Sorry, Ada. Mama, can Ada make my costume next year?"

I laughed. "Ada can make both your costumes for the rest of your lives!"

But the laughter from my comment was drowned out by the sound of another wailing child coming up my front stairs. Quickly I turned around and opened the front door to see Dr. John with his fist up about to knock while Renee was struggling with a puffy-eyed Wills in her arms. Instantly I waved them in, and even though Dr. John looked exhausted and weary from his son's crying, it didn't stop him from bursting out into laughter as soon as he saw Jackson standing in the foyer.

Renee rolled her eyes and grimaced as she stepped through the doorway while Wills, dressed in what looked like black pajamas, continued to sob. "He's laughing while Wills' is having a full on meltdown."

"Oh Wills, tell Awbie what's the matter," I cooed as I rubbed his back.

With a loud wail he leapt out of his mother's arms and into mine as he cried, "I wanned…to be…a…Warrior!"

Wills buried his face into my shoulder and I looked to Renee for an explanation. Dramatically she threw her arms up in the air. "Ok, ok, I completely screwed up. He's been obsessed with those karate lessons that Devin got him into and he said he wanted to be a ninja. Then last week he said he wanted to be a warrior, I thought he meant a 'ninja warrior', not a 'Warrior'… like you kind of 'Warrior'," she said, air quoting like a crazy woman. "So now he looks like a…a…"

"A kid in black pj's?"

Renee glared at me while John sneakered behind me. "Ok, 'Miss Glue Gun', what do you suggest?"

"Cam?" I asked, looking at him pleadingly. If anyone could make something out of nothing in minutes, it was him.

With a crooked smile he stepped down from the stairs. "Come, William, let us see what we can do."

Cam quickly took Wills from my arms and raced up the stairs, causing Wills to instantly squeal with glee.

"Well let's hope he can do something," Renee sighed and then finally noticed Jackson's costume. "Ok, so someone needs to explain this."

"Aunt Re," Jack-Jack groaned in frustration, "I'm Dracula, can't you tell?"

Everyone broke out in another fit of laughter, but then I noticed that Eris was the only one not joining in.

"Dad, did you know about this?" I asked quietly as I pointed to Jackson who was now growling at his Uncle John and showing off his fangs.

Eris scoffed loudly, causing the others' laughter to die down. "If I had, my grandson certainly would not be dressed like that. I find it preposterous. Never in his life did Vlad dress like that. And a cape! Please."

"Ok wait," Jonah said in about as much shock as I was in. "Did you just say…"

"Is Vlad, *the* Vlad," I interrupted.

"Oh my god," Jonah began with excitement. "As in Vlad the Impaler, the man they've always said was the inspiration for Dracula."

When Eris didn't answer, I looked over at Jonah and then back to my father. "Dad, you can't be serious. Vlad can't be…he…just can't."

My father dismissed me as he replied, "If that makes you feel better then so be it. But costumes like that are why Vlad takes the same two weeks off every year."

"Oh my god, I know Dracula," Jonah muttered to himself. "So f'ing cool!"

"Attention all," Cameron announced from the top of the stairs. "We have a new Warrior with us."

Everyone turned to look at Wills who was now smiling from ear to ear. His black sweatpants were now tucked into a pair of black boots that I knew were Jack's, as was the black winter vest that was similar to the Warrior's combat vests. The final touch was the communication unit that was strapped around Wills' neck and the earbud tucked inside his ear. I think Will would have been happy to run around in his underwear as long as he got to wear Uncle Cam's comm unit.

"William, ask you aunt for the finishing touch," Cameron said as he placed Wills' down on the ground.

Will looked up at me with his stunning blue-green eyes and asked, "Awbie, can I wear your pin?"

"My pin?" I looked up at Cameron and he gestured to the collar of my shirt. "Oh! My Warrior pin?"

Wills nodded hopefully. "Pwease?"

I reached underneath my collar and undid the backing of my gold Warrior pin. Will's smile couldn't have been any bigger as I clasped the pin to his vest. After me three little angels posed for pictures we were finally ready to head out – one butterfly princess, a wannabe Warrior, one fake Vampire, three real Vampires, and two humans. Typical family outing.

"Jack-Jack, can I have your red licorice?" Livy asked as our group slowly crossed over to the next neighborhood street where many of the children's classmates were gathering.

"Nope," Jackson replied as he peeked into his candy bag.

"But you don't like red licorice," Livy whined.

"Yes I do."

"No you don't! Ada, can I have Jack-Jack's red licorice?"

"No, monkey. That is Jackson's, and if he does not want to give..."

Livy stopped firmly in her tracks and began wailing at the top of her lungs. Unfortunately we were all used to it, and everyone had their own reaction. Renee rolled her eyes, John ignored her, Cameron and I sighed, and my father laughed. With a gentle hand Cameron pushed her forward, only to have her stop a few steps later, causing Cameron to push her forward once again. This happened several times before she finally stepped back in line with her brother and Wills, though her crying did not cease. This was hysterical to my father, even causing other parents to turn and look at him curiously. But no amount of soothing or negotiating would stop her crying, this much we had learned over the years. Either she had to calm herself down, or...

"Wivy, you can have my wed wicowish," Wills said sweetly as he held out a piece of wrapped red licorice. Olivia's sobbing stopped instantly.

"William," Cameron began, "you do not need to give away your licorice."

"It's ok, Cam," Wills replied as he turned to look up at his uncle, "I want to."

Cameron shook his head as Wills handed his licorice to Olivia and then ran to the next set of endless brownstones. "Renee, I will see that William's supply of licorice is restored."

"Oh Cameron, stop your nonsense," Renee replied.

"But I know it is his favorite. He should not give away his things just because my daughter is throwing a fit."

"He's been doing it since they were babies, so I don't think there's a way to stop him now. Besides, he has plenty of candy."

Cameron sighed again. "Today it is just candy, what will it be in the future?"

"He'll grow out of it," John replied. "In a few years he'll realize girls have cooties and he'll ignore her just like other boys his age."

I laughed. "I doubt Olivia will ever let him get away with that."

"And she speaks!" Renee said dramatically.

"What are you talking about?"

Renee pulled on my arm and pursed her lips tightly with her famous are-you-freaking-kidding-me-right-now look. "Ever since we left your house you've been on edge. Seriously, what's up your butt?"

Without taking my eyes off the children while they rang the doorbell I replied, "The twins are having dreams."

"Yeah, so? They've always had dreams."

"But these have Aidan in them."

"Since when?"

"The last couple of nights. But last night…"

"Mama!" Olivia squealed as she jumped down from the stairs, "that lady said she loved my crown!"

"Oh good, baby girl."

"And Mama," Jack-Jack shouted as he ran to me, "she thought my fangs looked real!"

John laughed. "Well howdaya like that! Hey, little man, why the frown?" John said and extended his arms down to his son who eagerly climbed onto his father's hip.

"Daddy, what's swat?"

"Huh?" John replied as we all began to inch back down the sidewalk.

"Dat lady said I looked like I was in swat. What's dat?"

"Oh, you mean S.W.A.T., they're like really special cops."

"But I not a cop, I a Warrior. Like Cam."

"Yep," John sighed, "just like Cam."

Eris patted John on the shoulder and gave him a sympathetic smile. "I feel your pain, John. There aren't too many things worse than being a Warrior."

"Dad!" I growled, but Cameron wasn't insulted. He was pretty used to my father's abuse and even gave a crooked smile.

"Come on, Wills!" Jack-Jack shouted. "I'll race ya to the next house!"

Wills squirmed out of Dr. John's arms and ran after the giggling twins.

"Ok, ok," Renee interrupted as soon as the children were away. "Twins, dreams, Aidan, go!"

I rolled my eyes slightly. "He was playing with the kids, telling them to use their gifts against me. Cam and I have been telling them not to talk to strangers and then Livy tells me tonight that Aidan isn't a stranger. He's Jack-Jack's imaginary friend."

"What!" Cameron shouted as he stopped and turned around.

"Er…guess I forgot to tell you that. Great, right? Aidan somehow got his hooks into our son without us even knowing."

"Well, you guys'll just have to use your magic powers to get those hooks out. Just do what you always do," Renee said firmly.

"And what's that?"

"Fucking kick some ass!"

"Re!" John scolded. "There are kids around."

"Yeah, but not mine. God that felt good. Fucking fuck fuck. Fucking shitty ass bitch bastard. Whew, that's been festering inside."

"Wait, where are the kids?" I said in a panic and pushed myself between Renee and Cameron. I looked up at the brownstone where they were supposed to be and they were nowhere in sight. "Jack? Livy!"

Cameron brushed past me as I spun wildly around looking for a glimpse of a pink wing or shiny black cape. Parents everywhere froze, some holding their own children to their sides while others looked around in a panic. Suddenly I noticed a small wooden bench to my right, similar to the one I had sat on in the twin's dream last night. When I looked down the street my jaw dropped at the recognition. I could have slapped myself for not seeing it before. I had been so wrapped up in watching the kids that I hadn't looked at my surroundings as a whole.

"Cameron! This is it," I shouted, causing both him and Eris to sink into their offensive modes.

"Aidan!" Jackson shouted in the distance.

Cameron's ears perked up and his head turned to the right. I didn't wait for anyone and ran down the sidewalk faster than I should have in public. Cameron and Eris were right on my heels as we ducked and pushed people out of our way. Finally, I caught a glimpse of a pink wing peeking out from the side of a man's leg. Abruptly I took the man by his shoulder and pulled him back to reveal Olivia, Jackson, and Wills talking to a young boy about their age.

Jackson turned around with a fang-filled smile as he said, "Look, Mama, it's Aidan from school. He's dressed like Dracula too!"

Slowly I stood from the ground looking at Aidan's parents who had terrified expressions on their faces, the father rubbing his left shoulder where I had grabbed him. I was such a moron. Moron!

"I'm so sorry. I'm the twin's mother, Brianna Moron...ah...Morgan. Brianna Morgan."

"And she's back," Renee laughed behind me.

Chapter Fourteen

Jonah

"Sera, are you sure you don't want to watch the movie with us?"

Sera eyed me and shook her head. "The two of you have spent enough time with an old woman like me for one evening. Enjoy zhe movie by yourselves like you should."

"Sera, it's not like that…"

"Besides, I have a lovely book waiting for me until Eri comes home, which shouldn't be too long. Enjoy your movie."

Sera waved goodnight and I headed back down to the living room with a fresh bowl of popcorn. I could hear Ashlyn laughing at whatever program she had switched to while I made us more popcorn for our Halloween movie marathon. It shouldn't have surprised me that she had little exposure to…well…everything, including classic scary movies.

"Ok, hopefully this bowl will last longer than the first," I laughed and slid down onto the couch. "Maybe I can actually eat some this time."

Ashlyn smiled slyly but immediately buried her hand into the hot popcorn. "I can't help it," she said and then shoveled the whole handful into her mouth. "Wi ro ruw."

"Try again?"

She took a second to swallow and laughed again. "Sorry…it's so good."

I went to put my hand into the bowl but was cut off by Ashlyn's hand. "Slow down, tiger. You'll make yourself sick."

"Can't help it. I've never had popcorn this good."

"Some people think it's the butter that makes it, but it's really all about the salt. Shake it up a little, more salt, shake a little more, more salt. It'll kill ya faster, but it's a good way to go."

"Did Sera go to bed?"

I nodded as I shoved a handful of popcorn into my mouth. "Mmm-hmm."

"I feel so bad," she said, taking the whole bowl of popcorn from me and placing it on her lap. "I'm killing her, just like Eris said."

"You are not," I replied. "It just takes a lot out of her. She knows what she's doing."

"So..." she began before swallowing another handful of popcorn. "...Sera isn't really Brianna's mother, right?"

"Stepmother, but no one really looks at it that way."

"Is her real mother not around or something?"

"Eh...the easy answer is no."

Ashlyn narrowed her eyes at me. "What's the hard answer?"

I scratched the back of my neck at the uncomfortable question. "Well, when I first met Bri we talked a lot about our families and we had a whole conversation about her mother and how rotten she was. Then I didn't see her for months, I got the job at Facility East, and shortly after that she had the twins. A few weeks later I came up for a visit to see her and meet the twins, and of course the first thing I notice is that she's...well...not human anymore. So we're hanging out here at the house and talking back and forth, I'm just about to ask her if things were better with her mom when Cameron's sister-in-law Kyla grabs my arm, pulls me into another room, and tells me not to mention anything about Bri's mom...ever. It's the same with bringing up that she's a Vampire, you don't."

"She mentioned something about that my first night here, something about complications during childbirth?"

I nodded and took a handful of popcorn before it was gone. "She bled out or something, no one is really keen on giving the details, but Cameron Turned her in time."

"She doesn't seem very happy about it."

"Nope," I replied and then shoved the popcorn into my mouth. "Dat's why...we don...talk...abou it."

"I've heard it's rude to talk with your mouth full," she laughed.

"You started it," I replied after forcefully swallowing the popcorn down. "Ok, no more talking. The ultimate scary movie is about to begin."

Ashlyn bit down on her bottom lip and sighed nervously. I pushed myself up from the couch and stepped over to the entryway to turn the lights off when the front door opened and Eris quietly came inside.

"Sir? Is everyth..." I began but Eris put his finger up to his lips. A moment later Cameron came through the door with Olivia asleep and draped over his shoulder while Brianna carried Jackson diagonally across her chest. Both of them went immediately up to the second floor without even the slightest acknowledgment. Eris closed the door quietly behind them, and once Cameron and Bri were out of sight I asked, "Is everything ok? I thought the kids were staying at Renee's."

For the first time in my memory Eris actually looked weary. "There was an...incident."

"What happened? Are the kids..."

Eris put his hand up in front of him to stop me. "Everyone is fine, just shaken. Mia figlia could not bear to be separated from the children. Did Sera retire?"

"Yes sir, just a few minutes ago."

"Thank you for keeping her company this evening."

"The pleasure was mine. I...uh...let me know if there's anything I can help with...with the twins I mean."

Eris nodded as he ran up the stairs in a blur. I flipped the living room lights off and made my way back over to the couch where Ashlyn was already giving me a questioning look.

"Everything ok?"

I shrugged. "Not really sure. Something happened tonight, but no one's talking."

"That seems to be a theme of theirs."

I laughed. "You got that right. Ooo, ooo! The movie started already, crap. Shh! Shh! You have to pay attention right from the beginning."

Ashlyn sank deeper into the cushions and was only quiet for a few seconds before she asked, "Do the lights really have to be off?"

"Mmm-hmm, it makes it scarier."

"We don't need to give it any help," she muttered to herself before she started eating her popcorn one piece at a time.

I had watched this movie every Halloween religiously, and knew that in just a few seconds the killer's enormous knife would be plunged into the unsuspecting teenaged babysitter. The underscore music became tense and through the side of my eye I watched as Ashlyn's popcorn eating became slower and slower. Now in three, two, one...

Ashlyn let out a blood curdling scream echoing that of the babysitter in the movie. Her arms flew up to cover her face causing the bowl in her lap to go flying into the air, covering us and the room in popcorn. My uncontrollable laughter was louder than her scream and I didn't even mind that she started hitting me in the arm. Suddenly the lights were turned on and both Eris and Cameron were standing angrily in the entryway.

Quickly I stood from the couch, now realizing my mistake. "I'm so sorry, Cameron. I didn't even think..."

"Both of you are all right?" Cameron interrupted impatiently.

"Yes," Ashlyn and I answered at the same time.

Eris grumbled as he left the room while Cameron shook his head and said, "For the remainder of the evening we would all appreciate it if you could reserve all screams for real emergencies?"

Both Ashlyn and I nodded vigorously.

"I'm sorry, man, really."

"Just bad timing on your part, Jonah. Well then, I shall bid you both goodnight," he said as he turned on his heels and disappeared up the stairs.

Ashlyn and I just stared at each for a couple of seconds before bursting out into laughter.

"We should clean up this mess," she was finally able to say after taking several needed breaths. Once she placed the empty bowl onto the coffee table we got on our hands and knees and began scooping up popcorn by the handful.

When the bowl was half full of dirty popcorn, carpet lint, and a candy wrapper, I looked up to see Ashlyn only an inch away, a piece of popcorn caught in her wavy blonde hair. Her pin straight hairstyle from the salon only lasted the day, but the natural wave to her hair made it shorter and even more youthful. In just a couple of days she had turned into a pretty girl, a pretty girl whose eerily dark eyes were boring into mine. If this had been our own movie, the romantic music would be swelling and I would reach for her cheek and pull her lips to mine.

My head flinched as I shook the sudden feelings out. I barely knew her, what the hell was I thinking? But as I looked into her eyes again, my desire to kiss her returned. Slowly I reached my hand out, wanting to feel her soft cheek and perhaps even more. Just as my fingertips grazed her skin, she closed her eyes and tilted her chin up, positioning herself perfectly to be kissed. But just as the feelings had come over me, they disappeared and suddenly I was frozen with my hand inches from her face. Not wanting to be too awkward, I moved my hand to her hair and pulled out the piece of popcorn that had embedded itself. As soon as Ashlyn realized what was really happening, her eyes shot open and she placed her hands up to her red cheeks to hide her embarrassment.

I tossed the piece of popcorn into the bowl and sat down on the floor with my back against the couch. "Maybe we should leave the lights on for the rest of the movie."

Ashlyn nodded as she shifted to sit down on the floor as well, still trying to hide her reddened face from me. "Or maybe not watch a scary movie at all?"

"No way, this is a classic."

"Jonah, I can't guarantee that I won't accidently scream again. And then Cameron will get upset and..."

"Ashlyn," I interrupted, "you have to see this movie at least once. I promise it doesn't get any...worse...than that. Come on, Ash, you'll be fine."

She pursed her lips in a skeptical pout, although as she turned to face the screen I could see a tiny smile develop at the corner of her lips. It was the nickname, gets the ladies every time.

As promised I left the lights on, although only after another few minutes both of us decided that sitting on the floor was uncomfortable. I had to admit that Bri's couch was amazingly cushy, and from experience was an excellent place to nap. What I had yet to experience was how conducive it was to cuddling, not that I had much choice in the matter since Ashlyn curled right up into the left side of my body.

Silently we watched as the movie's main character was oblivious to the fact that she was being followed by the crazed mental hospital escapee, narrowly missing opportunities where she could have been harmed. All of which made Ashlyn flinch as it was supposed to, but also caused her to creep closer into me, not that there was much room left. Oddly I didn't mind it, the opposite actually. I liked the feeling of her pressed into my side, the smell of her shampoo wafting around me when she finally rested her head on my shoulder. Butterflies were churning in my stomach while a tiny voice inside me was telling me all of this was wrong. She was so vulnerable and damaged that nothing good would come of this.

Of this? For fuck sake she's just resting her head on my shoulder.

Unfortunately, the time of mere anticipatory scares was over and the next round of murders in the movie was about to begin. I also had a pretty good idea that Ashlyn would be unable to keep her scream to herself. As to not give it away, I lowered my arm from the back of the couch and let it rest gently around Ashlyn's shoulder, which gave an unexpected result of her turning into my chest and draping her arm across my stomach. Her movement made me relax, so much so that I forgot why I had moved my arm in the first place.

My eyes shot open at the sight of the killer suddenly appearing behind his victim causing my entire body to tense and react to keep Ashlyn from screaming. Funny enough it wasn't the movie that made her scream, but the fact that I had scared the shit out of her when I slapped my hand across her mouth causing her hands and arms to flail about.

"Shhh! Shhh!" I whispered and laughed in her ear while pulling her tightly into my chest to muffle the sounds of her screaming that eventually turned into soft laughter.

She reached up for my hand and pulled it away from her mouth so she could breathe and laugh, but another moment later the laughter dwindled and an awkward silence fell upon us. Ashlyn was looking into my eyes like no one had ever looked into them before. Just then an uncontrollable feeling came over me and before I knew it I was kissing her. My hand went from holding her cheek to tangling my fingers in her thick hair, pulling at it and kneading the base of her neck. The sound of her moan, the feeling of her hot breath on my face, the feeling of her hands on my chest, everything about her was intoxicating in a way that surprised me and I just couldn't get enough.

I didn't stop her when she stretched her leg across my waist, straddling me and pulling me up to her. Suddenly her hands ducked underneath my shirt and a rush of desire flooded over me. My hands traveled up her thighs around to her back and brought her up against me. I could feel the heat coming from between her legs and I wanted to be inside, I needed to be inside her, it was the only thing that would extinguish this insatiable fire that was burning inside of me. My fingers fumbled with the zipper of her yellow hoodie while she tried pulling my shirt up my chest. Finally her zipper released and I pulled the jacket down around her shoulders, exposing a white tank top so thin that her small breasts shown through. I slid my hand underneath her shirt and squeezed her breast tightly causing a delicious moan to escape from her mouth and into mine. I wanted more of her, all of her, right now or…or…I would stop breathing.

When Ashlyn began grinding her pelvis into mine all foreplay was over. I was going to take her. I didn't care that I had just met her. I didn't care that she was slightly neurotic. And I certainly didn't care that Cameron or Brianna could come down at any minute. I had to do this, I had to be inside her, I had push and grind into her, feel her hot skin engulf me from all sides.

Reluctantly I released her breast and tried pulling her hoodie down her arms, but with her hands still up my shirt it was impossible. I didn't want her to stop rubbing my chest and pressing her nails into my skin, but I needed her sweatshirt off. I wanted to feel her breasts pressed up against me more than I wanted anything in my life. Noticing my struggle with her jacket, Ashlyn slipped her hands out from underneath my shirt and allowed me to pull her hoodie down her arms. But just as I thought I was home free, somehow her sleeves got tangled at her hands and no amount of pulling could get them free.

Ashlyn's giggle tickled my lips as she shifted her weight back onto the couch. Quickly I took the opportunity to pull my shirt over my head and smiled as Ashlyn continued her struggle with her hoodie. Just as my hands went to unbutton my jeans I suddenly realized I didn't have any idea what the hell I was doing. The desire, that unbelievable yearning to take Ashlyn right here on the couch had completely disappeared. Even when Ashlyn finally freed herself from her jacket and pulled her tank top off, fully exposing her breasts to me, I simply froze and stared at her unable to move.

I didn't understand what was happening. Two seconds ago I was getting ready to lie on top of her, but now I couldn't figure out how we'd gotten here. I pushed Ashlyn off of me and rose from the couch, insensitive of the hurt and confusion in her eyes.

With my back to her I said, "Do you have your shield up?"

"Wha-at?" she replied.

I turned around to see her awkwardly pulling her tank top back over her head. "Did you…did you do that to me?"

"Jonah…I don't…"

"DID YOU PUT THOSE FEELINGS INTO ME," I shouted, causing Ashlyn to flinch and tears instantly fill her eyes.

"I didn't mean...I...I thought you wanted..." she stuttered as she shoved her arms back into her hoodie and pulled the sides around her chest.

"What, you thought I wanted you to take advantage of me? Manipulate me into having sex with you?"

"No! Jonah, I'm sorry it just got away from me."

"Oh, I'll say," I said as I yanked my shirt from between the couch cushions and pulled it over my head.

"Jonah, please, I didn't realize what I was doing it's still..."

"Ashlyn just save it," I interrupted as I stepped toward the entryway. "I have enough women in my life who manipulate me into doing what they want. I don't need another."

I opened the front door to the house and stepped outside without glancing back at Ashlyn as I shut the door behind me. I was fuming. My entire body was shaking so badly I had to sit down on the front steps. I kept raking my hands through my hair trying to wrap my brain around what had just happened, and even more so what could have happened if she hadn't been distracted for that brief moment. Dozens of horrible scenarios were racing through my head when the front door behind me opened.

"Jesus, Ashlyn, leave me alone for one goddamn minute."

"What if I am not Ashlyn?" Sera's distinctive French accented voice said behind me.

Instantly I stood from the steps and turned around, mortified that I had yelled at her. "Oh my god, Sera, I thought..."

"I gazher you and Ashlyn had a tiff?"

"Yes, ma'am. Did we wake you?" She shook her head and directed me to sit back down. "Then why are you out here?"

She sighed. "I detest menopause. Only a cold night like zhis can cool me down."

"I'm...uh...sorry. My mom went through that, she said it was awful."

"Oui, oui," she replied as she sat down next to me. "You know being an Empath can be very difficult."

I smiled slyly to myself wondering how much of the argument she overheard. "Really? How so?"

"Even with zhe strongest of shields, you have greater instincts zhan most. Even if your lover says he is not mad, you know he is. You can feel when someone is lying to you about zhe most hurtful zhings. Ashlyn has it even harder since she cannot only feel ozhers, but can push her feelings onto ozhers without knowing."

"Exactly," I replied flustered. "You'd never know if your feelings were real or what she put into your head. You could never trust her. You'd spend all your time second guessing yourself."

"Ah, oui. Just zhink of zhe zhings she could make you do."

"I know, right!" I stood from the step and turned to look at her. "I was out of control in there, Sera. If she hadn't gotten distracted I could have..." hurt her, gotten her pregnant, gotten an STD from her, the list was endless and I couldn't bring myself to verbalize it. "It just...I'm just so..."

"Angry?"

"Yes! Yes, I'm angry, I'm furious! It's just wrong to force your will on someone like she did."

Sera nodded her head slowly. "Oui, very wrong. Who knows how long she has been doing zhis, she probably forced you to bring her here."

"Er...no. That was my idea. She wanted me to just leave her on the street."

"Ah, I see. Well zhen, she must have forced you to take her shopping for her clothes and such."

I sighed. "Nope, that was me too. She didn't want any of it, she was pretty guilty about it."

"Oh. Hmm, zhen it must have been her idea to bring me here to help her."

I shook my head. "Me again."

"Hmm," Sera huffed as she stood from the step. "It seems you are forcing your will on her versus zhe ozher way around. It seems as zhough she hasn't had much choice zhe last few days. I find zhat interesting, don't you?"

I had no answer for her, not that she waited for me to give it since she turned and went back inside. She made me sound like a douchebag. But I was helping Ashlyn, wasn't I? What she did to me was violating, nothing like what I did. Right? Right?

Best vacation ever.

Chapter Fifteen

Brianna

"Again, figlia, again," my father shouted.

My small courtyard had been turned into a makeshift training ground where Eris was trying to remind me of the skills he and Devin had taught me several years ago. Sadly my refresher course was going as poorly as my initial sessions with my dad which was causing him to lose his patience with me. Sera was having much better success with Ashlyn, although the young hybrid was certainly less chipper compared to yesterday. And then at the edge of the courtyard the twins were playing and coloring the brick walkway with bright colored chalk, although more of it seemed to be getting on their hands and eventually on Cameron's pants and black sweater.

"Figlia!"

I shook to attention. "Yeah, yeah. I'm ready," I lied.

The daggers in my hands still felt foreign after a solid hour of working with them. The main reason? They weren't mine. *My* daggers were in their velvet lined box tucked away in my closet. Why? Because *my* daggers were now poison to me. Their silver handles gave them an added defense when I was a hybrid, but now I couldn't even touch them without burning my skin away. And trust me, I had tried holding them many times. The daggers I had now had leather-wrapped handles that didn't mold or curve with my palm like my silver daggers did. These stand-ins were stiff and felt like toys.

Suddenly I jumped back just as my father's sword grazed the tip of my nose and continued its trajectory downward. I shuffled backwards with my daggers drawn as Eris's sword began traveling back up. I blocked the long blade with my right dagger and then tried hitting it away with my left, however, it only resulted in both of the daggers being hit out of my hands. Not wanting to hurt my dad (or my wooden fence) I only Pushed him hard enough to take him off his feet and give me enough time to grab my daggers from the ground.

I barely had enough time to put my daggers up in front of me when my father's sword was once again coming down upon me. I crossed my daggers above my head and struggled to hold the sword away from my face.

Stand up, Mama, stand up! Jackson's little voice rang in my head.

I looked to my left through the corner of my eye and saw both my babies cheering for me. The pride in their faces forced me to push my sneakers into the ground and lifted my father's sword away from me. It took less than two seconds for him to rear it around again, however, I met each of his strokes with my own, feeling a bit of my old rhythm coming back to me. Right, left, right, up. Left, right, left, down. Over and over again, finding new speed I had never used before.

My strokes pushed my father back a few paces only to have him spin around and begin to push me back until we reached the end of the narrow courtyard where the wooden fence was now only inches from my back. Eris froze with his sword held between my crossed daggers in front of my chest and held my gaze with his fiery eyes. Silently they were telling me to fight and bring out the fire my father was used to seeing, but it wasn't there and he knew it. With a frustrated grunt, Eris took a step back and threw his sword on the ground. The twins, thinking that he had surrendered, jumped up and down and cheered for me.

"Mama you won!" Olivia squealed

"She did not!" Eris snapped, causing both of my children to immediately stop their bouncing. "I withdrew for lack of…everything!"

"Eris," Cameron said in a warning tone, "there is no need to be so harsh with her."

"There certainly is! Her footwork is a mess, her technique has disappeared, and she has no confidence in what she's doing."

"Of course I don't!" I shouted. "Everything is new, Dad, nothing feels the same. I thrust forward like I used to and I overshoot because I'm stronger. I take a step forward and I pass you because I'm faster. I can't…I can't do what I used to do, and I certainly can't do it with these," I said and threw the daggers to the ground.

"Daughter, it shouldn't matter what you have in your hands! With your skills you should be able to take a blade of grass and turn it into a deadly weapon. Excuses are no longer an option. Now pick up those daggers and show me that the old Bri-an-na is still in there."

My father's eyes blazed with anger at the same time Sera placed a hand around my father's arm. She might have been able to take my father's anger away, but not mine. I was fuming and I could see Ashlyn growing uncomfortable in her chair.

"Sorry, Dad," I replied. "The old Brianna is gone just like my fighting skills. Let's just add that to the list of how I'm failing as a…" Cameron's eyes grew large, I'm assuming because he was afraid I would say Vampire loud enough for all our neighbors to hear. But he didn't have to fear, I didn't want to say what I was. I also didn't want to cry bloody tears in front of everyone.

"Figlia!" my father shouted as I ran past him. "We are not finished."

"Yes we are."

"Figlia, this is not the time to give up, you've seen…"

"I know what I've seen, Dad. I can't do it anymore!"

"That's preposterous! Warrior, take my side on this one."

Cameron sighed as he looked between me and my father. "Eris, perhaps that is enough for today."

Eris snarled. "When it comes to my grandchildren there is never enough we can do in one day. If I have to defend them twenty-four hours a day I will…"

"Because you think I can't?!" I shouted.

"Not in this state!"

Anger was radiating from my father as Sera tightened her grip around his arm. "Eri, give the petite some time."

"We all know…there isn't…time," he replied through strained lips as Sera took the intense emotions from him.

"You know what," I yelled as I threw my arms up, "we don't *all* know that. And why? Because you two won't tell us anything. So how much time do we have, Dad? Mom? What are we talking, months? Weeks?

What!" My parents merely stared at me with worried faces as I threw a tantrum similar to my children who were quietly hiding behind their father's legs. "Great, just great."

I turned away so I could disappear into the house when I almost ran into Jonah's chest. I looked to the ground in embarrassment wondering how long he had been standing there.

"Er, sorry, Jonah," I said and stepped around him to get to the door before I completely broke down in front of everyone. "I'll...uh...make you breakfast. Just give me a few minutes, ok?"

Jonah shook his head nervously as he said, "Bri, you don't have to..."

"Yes I do!" I yelled before ducking through the door and hurriedly walked to my bedroom.

What was wrong with me? Why couldn't I get my feet under me? Why wasn't I better at sword fighting now? What would happen if Aidan came through my door this instant, could I save my children? Could I live with myself if I let something happen to my babies?

No. The answer was no. I wouldn't be able to forgive myself, and neither could Cameron, especially knowing that I was better than this. Frustrated, I ran into my closet and frantically started pulling down box after box from the top shelves causing them to burst open and their contents to spill on the floor at my feet. Finally I saw exactly what I was looking for – a thin rectangular wooden box. Carefully I slid the box from its hiding place at the very back of the shelf and melted into the debris on the floor.

Red tears dropped on the box's silky wood finish. My right hand was shaking as I flipped the small metal latch and lifted the lid to reveal my beautiful silver daggers. I couldn't help but trace my index finger along the swirling pearl and silver pattern on the face of one of the handles. I didn't care that the skin of my finger was burning, but I needed more pain. I pulled the dagger from its green velvet inlay and wrapped my hand around it. My palm sizzled as the silver handle seared my skin. The pain was excruciating but it didn't stop me from taking the other dagger into my left hand and allowing the silver to burn through multiple layers of my skin.

I had been Turned when everyone thought I was dead. I had no sun sensitivity. Why couldn't I be insensitive to silver as well? That was what I really needed. I needed to be able to use the daggers, they gave me my strength and power. Without them I couldn't defend myself or my children. I could make myself suffer through the pain, I could learn to handle it. I *would* learn to handle it, I had to, for the sake of my children.

"Brianna!" Cameron shouted in a panic as he knelt down in front of me. "What are you doing!"

"I can do it, Cam," I cried both in desperation and pain. "I can suffer through it."

Cameron grabbed my wrists firmly. "Brianna, stop this! Let go of them!"

"No!"

"You are torturing yourself, Bri."

"I know," I screamed nastily in his face.

In a flash he disappeared from the closet and returned a second later with a towel in his hand. Without a word he knelt back down to the floor and placed the towel over my right hand. I screamed as he ripped the dagger from my hand bringing with it a thick layer of my skin. But my scream didn't have time to fully leave my throat when he ripped the second dagger from my left hand leaving behind a bloody swirling brand on my palm.

"Why, love?" he asked as he gently took my wrists and held my hands up in front of me.

My bottom lip quivered as I looked into his sad and worried eyes. "I need them...Cam. I...can't do it without..."

"Yes, Brianna, you can," he pleaded. "I know you, I have seen you do extraordinary things when you were only..."

"*Human*, Cam. When I was human," I replied as an uncontrollable wave of emotion came over me. "He's gonna take them, Cam. Aidan's gonna take our babies and I won't be able to stop him, and if I can't stop him I won't be able to live with myself, but I will! I will have to live forever and be reminded every day of what I let happen, what I couldn't stop, every day, Cam."

Cameron released my wrists and cupped my cheeks. "Aidan Pierce will NOT get to our children."

"He already has."

"Brianna, stop this madness! You are stronger than this, I know you are, my love. Find that strength again, Bri, find that confidence you had when you battled your father, or saved Jared and the coven at the manor, or used yourself as bait to capture Elaina while you were eight months pregnant."

"Why didn't you just let me die?"

Cameron's head jerked back as though I had slapped him in the face. "What? H-how can you say that…"

"It was my fate, Cam. I'm not supposed to be like…this," I yelled and knocked his hands away from my face. "Look at me, I'm a…a failure at everything. How could you do this to me?"

I folded myself over, my head quickly finding my hands. The debris shifted as Cameron stood in front of me though I couldn't look at him.

"Our children have had their mother at their first three birthdays. You have seen their smiling faces as they opened their Christmas presents, rocked them back to sleep when they woke in the night, watched them take their first steps, heared them say their first words. That is why I did it."

Finally I lifted my head to see Cameron towering over me. I was still such a mess that I couldn't find the words I wanted to say. Gently he wiped my wet face, staining the towel red. When he was done he wrapped his hand around the back of my neck and pulled my forehead to his lips.

"I love you, angel," he said after he finished his kiss and stood from the floor. "As I have said many times before, I am sorry that what I did upsets you so. But I do not regret having you with me or that my children have their mother versus having our family relay stories about the kind of person you were. So please, accept my apology this one last time, for I will not be doing it again."

When I didn't respond, Cameron took a step out of the closet just as Sera came to stand in the doorway.

"Oh, ma petite chute," she cooed.

"Perhaps you can help her," Cameron said softly as he lowered his head and left the room.

Sera stepped further into the closet and held out her hand with a loving smile. I took her hand and pulled myself up before she tucked me under her arm and walked me out of the closet.

"Mom?"

"Oui?"

"I'm so messed up."

"Aren't we all?"

I shook my head as she sat me down on the bed. "Not like me. I'm really, really messed up."

"I believe you get zhat from your fazer."

"I think you're right about that," I laughed and then it melted back into a cry.

"Oh, petite chute," she said as she pulled me into her chest. "I miss being able to make you food to comfort you."

I gave a snotty laugh. "Yes, I'd like to go back to the days when food would cure all things."

"Oui, oui, I find food and sex get us through most things."

"Mom!" I said and rose from her shoulder.

She gave me a smile and I couldn't help but laugh.

"Now zhere is my petite chute," she said and cupped my cheek.

"How do I get back to who I was before? I don't want to be this crazy person anymore."

"Petite, you need to find what is keeping you back. What is fueling you to stay on zhis path?"

I shrugged and shook my head. "I don't know."

She raised an eyebrow and I leaned back in surprise since she had never challenged me before.

"How about your anger towards Cameron?"

"I don't…"

"Petite, do not lie to yourself."

"Going right for the jugular, aren't you, Mom."

"Zhat is my job, petite."

I sighed and put my cheek back on her shoulder. "So how do I get around the anger thing with Cam?"

"Oh, zhat I do not know. You must figure that out yourself."

"Your guacamole would have had the answer."

"Oui, oui, it cures all."

Chapter Sixteen

Cameron

Thank goodness Seraphina came in when she did. There was no telling where the argument with Brianna could have gone. My lover was hurting, but it angered me when she said she would have rather been dead than be with me and her children as a Vampire. It was not only infuriating, it was hurtful. Extremely hurtful.

Leaving Seraphina to do what she did best, I quietly stepped into the hallway and shut the bedroom door behind me.

"Hey," Jonah said as he came through the backdoor. "Is uh...Bri, ok?"

"Honestly, Jonah, she is not, but I have faith in Seraphina. Are you hungry?"

"Don't worry about it, please. I can fend for myself."

"Absolutely not. Brianna made pancakes this morning and I believe there is batter leftover just for you. Perhaps you can show me how to make them?"

Jonah laughed. "There's a reason I eat at the Facility or at Mable's, but I'm sure we can figure it out."

With a fake smile I gestured toward the stairs and followed Jonah up to the second floor.

"Before I forget, I believe this is yours," I said as I pulled a cell phone from my back pocket. "Jackson found it between the cushions in the couch. It has been ringing all morning." Jonah's cheeks became flush as he slowly took the cell phone from my hand. "I take it you had a good night."

"No...er...not exactly," he sighed as he took one of the stools out from underneath the kitchen island while I stepped over to the refrigerator for the bowl of leftover pancake batter. "Can I...can I vent for a sec?"

"Consider me your Brianna stand in."

"Oh come on, I vent to you."

I raised an eyebrow. "Not like you do to Brianna."

He laughed, but then his face fell. "Something happened last night with Ashlyn."

While Jonah paused in thought I took the opportunity to turn on the electric griddle that Brianna had left out. Of course I was only doing what I had seen her do. I truly had no idea what to do next and was hoping Jonah would help me, although he remained sullen on his stool.

"When I saw the two of you last night you looked pretty close."

"Yeah, until she forced me to make out with her," he snapped.

"How is that?"

Jonah's hands brushed through his unruly dirty hair that had a severe cowlick on one side. "She made me feel...I don't know where I stopped and she began, seriously I almost had sex on your couch."

I blinked. "I could have done without that knowledge."

"When I finally came to my senses I was so angry at her, and then Sera started saying all these things to me..."

"Seraphina was there?"

"No...uh, I went outside to get some air and then she came out and made me second guess everything that I have done for Ashlyn and really made me feel like a piece of shit."

"Seraphina is very good at that," I replied with confidence from personal experience. "Did Ashlyn do this on purpose? Or was it an accident?"

Jonah shrugged. "She said it was an accident, but I don't know..."

"Jonah, you have to remember this is very new to her."

"I know, but..." Jonah's hands raked through his hair again, "I'm just so...mad and confused, then I think about what Sera said then I get angry at myself. I just can't get over..."

"How hungry are you?" I interrupted as I heard the sound of sneakers squeaking up the stairs. Jonah furrowed his brow in confusion before I gestured toward the stairs and said, "Ashlyn, just in time. Jonah and I have discovered neither of us knows how to make pancakes, yet here we are."

"I'd probably burn them," she replied as she came to stand next Jonah, noticeably uncomfortable with Jonah's cold shoulder.

"Not any worse than I will," I joked but no one laughed.

The tension was thick and growing, and the only thing to cut it was the sound of Jonah's cell phone ringing.

"It's my mom, I'd better take this since she's called a million times already," Jonah said as he jumped off the stool and walked out the French doors that led to the balcony.

Ashlyn watched as he answered his phone and closed the door behind him, but then quickly looked at the floor when she noticed me watching her. "I think your griddle is overheating."

I looked over at the griddle which now had thin wisps of smoke rising from its surface and quickly turned down the temperature. When Ashlyn turned on her heels and began to walk away I cleared my throat and said, "Ashlyn, wait. I have been meaning to find a moment to speak with you."

Slowly Ashlyn turned back around, her eyes darting uncomfortably in order to avoid looking at me. "Ok."

"I wanted to apologize to you."

"For what?"

"For what I did to you, biting you when you were so young. I was a very different person back then, never questioning anything Victor told me to do. I just want you to know that I am sorry for scaring you like that. I truly feel terrible about it and hope that somehow we can put it behind us."

A small smile began to form at the corner of her mouth. "Uh, yeah. We can do that."

"Are you sure? You seem a little...hesitant."

She shook her head. "No, it's just...I wasn't prepared for that. Brianna told me what my mom did, and you didn't have a choice really, I guess."

"Yes I did and I chose badly. You did not deserve what I did to you. So please accept my apology."

"Yes, apology accepted, all in the past."

The two of us smiled awkwardly at each other for a moment. "Would you mind helping me with this? Brianna is definitely the cook in the family but she is...indisposed at the moment."

"She was so upset, is she going to be ok?"

"She will be," I responded trying to keep the doubt in my voice to myself. "So where do I start?"

"Do you have butter?"

I nodded and removed the butter from the refrigerator. "Ok, now what?"

"Just spread some of the butter on the griddle, and we'll need a scoop or something for the batter."

I did as Ashlyn instructed, allowing the butter to melt while I looked in the various drawers around me for a large spoon. Finally seeing a metal ladle, I pulled it out and held it up. "Like this?"

"Yep. Now just scoop and pour it out."

Just as I placed a heaping scoop of batter onto the hot griddle, Jonah could be heard shouting from outside. I looked sideways at Ashlyn to see if she heard him as well, and by her widened eyes I suspected she had. When I had created my second pancake, Jonah's shouts were so loud that I was sure my neighbors could hear him.

"He said he was talking to his mother?" Ashlyn asked as she pulled a long plastic spatula from the utensil holder.

"That is what he said," I replied and took the spatula from her extended hand. "They have been having some communication problems lately."

"I'll say. At least I'm not the only one he's mad at," she said sadly. "I'm sure he told you what happened last night."

"Not as much as you think," I answered, trying to ease the worry that was settling into the fine lines around her eyes. "Things happen, Ashlyn, especially for a hybrid just learning about her powers. Brianna experienced the same thing when I first met her."

"And the Facility helped her?"

"Yes," I replied with a slight hesitation. "The Facility will help you attain the resources you may need, but you are lucky to have someone like Seraphina who can assist you firsthand."

She nodded as she chewed the corner of her lip. "Sera's a really nice lady. She doesn't need to be doing all of this for me."

"But she wants to. That is what makes her such a wonderful person."

Ashlyn cleared her throat and nudged me slightly in the side, then pointed to the pancakes that were both bubbling on the griddle. "You need to flip them now."

"Yes. Now this I have seen Brianna do."

Carefully I slid the spatula underneath the first pancake, lifted it and flipped the spatula sideways just when the batter began to seep off the sides. However, instead of flipping the pancake over, the half-cooked-half-batter circle flew across the room and hit the wall, sticking for a moment before sliding down slowly and finally landing on the floor. Ashlyn exploded into laughter and I was thankful that she was the only one to witness my lack of flipping skills.

"Ok," she began through her labored breath, "maybe try flipping up and over instead of sideways."

Wanting to prove to her that I could do this simple task, I slid the spatula under the last pancake and took her advice of flipping up and over. I was definitely successful at the up portion since the pancake went flying upwards and stuck to the ceiling. Ashlyn barreled over with laughter, cushioning her head with one arm on top of the island. I stood staring at the pancake for several seconds when Jonah came back inside from the balcony. His cheeks were pink, though I was unsure if it was from the cool weather or the anger that he was trying to suppress.

"What's going on?" he said impatiently.

Ashlyn stood up straight at the sound of his voice and I pointed up to the ceiling where the pancake still clung, but he had no reaction.

"Come on, Jonah, it's funny," Ashlyn said brightly.

"Yeah, real funny."

"Things didn't go so hot with your mom?" she asked as she tentatively placed her hand on Jonah's shoulder.

In an unkind way, Jonah rolled his eyes before roughly rubbing his face with his hands. "You are perceptive, Ashlyn, I'll give ya that."

"Do you want to tell me about it?"

Jonah yanked his hands from her grip. "And how could a prostitute help me with my problems?"

If it were not for the sounds of the twins coming up the stairs, you could have heard a pin drop across town after what Jonah had said. Tears instantly filled Ashlyn's eyes before she turned and ran from the kitchen.

Jonah stood from his stool, realization suddenly hitting him. "Ashlyn, wait, I didn't mean..." But Jonah could not finish his sentence as the sound of Ashlyn slamming her bedroom door echoed down the hall. "Shit."

"Ada, Jonah said a bad word," Jackson announced as he and Olivia crested the top of the stairs with Eris who stood between them.

"Yes, son, and you know not to repeat it."

"Ada, what's a prostitute?" Olivia asked sweetly.

Jonah whipped around and looked me apologetically.

"Oh yes, Warrior," Eris began with a wicked smile, "I cannot wait to hear your response to this."

My children's dark angelic eyes stared at me with curiosity while I tried to figure out how I would phrase my answer. "A prostitute…is someone who is paid to…" I paused trying to find the right word, "…love…someone else."

"Ooo! I want to be a prostitute," Olivia squealed.

"Oh dear god," Jonah moaned behind me, definitely echoing my own feelings, and causing Eris to place a hand up in front of his mouth to contain his laughter.

"No, monkey," I said as I knelt down in front of her, "you cannot be a prostitute."

"Why?"

"Because it is not considered an honorable profession."

"Why?"

"Well…because you should love people for free."

"But Ada, I could be a prostitute for free."

"Me too, Ada!" my son replied and the two of them joined hands and began bouncing around in a circle.

I stood from the floor and felt Jonah pat me on the back. "Cameron, I'm really sorry."

I sighed. "Eris, can you watch the children for a little while?"

Eris nodded. "Of course. Where are you going?"

"Jonah needs breakfast and I am sure some coffee." Jonah stepped toward me shaking his head, but I put my hands up before he could speak. "And I need some air."

In a matter of minutes Jonah was donning a baseball cap, choosing to stay in his sweatpants and t-shirt even though it was a cool November morning. The sky was gray, yet smooth like a fine silk, and as was usual in New England at this time of year always keeping you guessing as to whether it would rain or snow. As I closed the front door behind me, trying to ignore the sounds of my children begging their grandfather for sugary treats which he would absolutely give in to, I noticed Jonah pacing on the sidewalk.

When I stepped down onto the sidewalk he immediately popped his head up and started walking. "All right, go ahead, lay it on me. Tell me what a horrible example I am."

"Jonah, I am not your fa…" I stopped myself, but it was too late.

Thankfully Jonah gave a forgiving smirk. "Yeah, Cameron, I know you're not my father but…but after what I just did…if my dad were alive he would have ripped me a new one. Maybe that's what I need to kick me back into place. Maybe you could pretend to be my dad for the next hour and yell at me like he would have for saying that to Ashlyn."

"I was not aware that Ashlyn had followed in her mother's footsteps."

Jonah nodded shamefully as we rounded the corner to one of the busier areas of our neighborhood. "Only after her mother didn't come back. Christ, she was only seventeen and she did it to survive. Of course she told me in confidence and I promised her, *promised her*, that I would keep it between us. Damn it, I am such an asshole."

Squeezing Jonah's shoulder I pulled him into the first deli we came across. "My question, Jonah, is why? It is not like you to say such a thing."

"I know," he groaned as we stepped up to the counter and ordered the largest and most meat-filled breakfast sandwich they made along with the tallest coffee they offered. The coffee arrived first, and Jonah did not continue with his explanation until he had taken a large gulp. "Do you ever feel like your life is spinning out of control?"

I gave a terse laugh. "Yes, it has happened often in my life."

"You see, I was still mad at Ashlyn for last night, and then my mom was really laying into me."

"About?"

"About what happened at Mable's, and being up here with you guys."

"Us?"

He nodded as I took the hot breakfast sandwich from the woman behind the counter, and then directed Jonah back towards the exit.

"She was so…jealous? She's never been like that before, but today she was yelling at me to come home and that we needed to talk, which I agreed but that we could talk at Mable's on Wednesday as long as Paul didn't come. Well, that just sent her into a rage and she started saying these awful things like 'why don't you just stay up there then', and then I got mad and said I'd like to but that you guys were moving to San Francisco, to which she said 'I'm sure you'll want to move out there with them then' and then it just got nasty. I don't remember what I said to her after that and then she hung up on me.

"Then I come inside and out comes the worst thing I could have ever said to Ashlyn. Did you see her face? What do I do?"

"Apologize."

"Then what?"

I smirked. "Apologize again."

"But what if she won't talk to me?"

"Then you keep apologizing until she does." Or unlike me, wait until she is in hysterics with silver daggers burning into her hands and tell her you are done apologizing. I felt like such a hypocrite.

"I didn't mean it," Jonah sighed as he tucked his coffee into his arm in order to tear open the paper around his sandwich.

"Of course not."

"I'm such a douche."

"In this scenario, yes you are. But in general, you are a gentleman, something that is rare in your generation. Be honest with Ashlyn and accept her reaction. There is not much else you can do."

Jonah groaned and took a bite out of his sandwich. After swallowing and wiping the egg yolk that had dripped down his chin he asked, "Why did you tell the kids what a prostitute really was? My parents would never have told me in a million years."

"Yes, but if I had tried to hide it, they would have gone onto the internet and found out the truth in seconds. But as you saw, it still did not go well. I cannot imagine what Brianna will say if she finds out."

"Well send her to me," Jonah replied guiltily. "It was my fault. I said it in front of them."

We walked silently for a minute, purposely passing our street since I did not want to go back to the chaos just yet. I was telling Eris the truth when I said I needed some air. I did not need to breathe it in of course, but more so to clear my head.

"So what's really going on with Bri?" Jonah asked before taking another bite of his sandwich.

I sighed. "Brianna is struggling with many things right now."

"Does this have anything to do with last night? Not that I even know what happened, but everyone's still on edge about it."

"Some of it is about last night, but there is a lot more going on."

"Like?" When I did not answer he pushed again. "Look man, you needed to get out of that house too, so you might as well get it out."

"And get off the subject of Ashlyn?"

"Mmm-hmm," he replied as he drank his coffee.

"Where to start," I sighed and then gestured down a quieter street. "All right, do you know why we built Facility West?"

"To protect the hybrids?"

"Correct, but do you know what from?"

"Wasn't there a gang or something?"

"Sort of. There was an unrecognized coven headed by a woman named Elaina."

"Oh yeah, I remember that name. She was hunting hybrids or something, right?"

"At first. Then she zeroed in on her real target, a certain daughter of Eris."

Jonah stopped in his tracks. "Bri? Your Brianna?"

"Yes. My Bri." My scared, stubborn, little hybrid. "At first we thought Elaina was only after Brianna, but later we came to find out that it was really the twins she wanted."

"Dude, why have I never heard about any of this?" he asked as I put my hand on his back and prodded him down the sidewalk.

"Honestly, we were all hoping it was over."

"It isn't? I thought Elaina was dead."

"She is dead, but while Brianna was pregnant we discovered that Elaina had a partner, a man by the name of Aidan Pierce, a man who had been a good friend of mine for many, many years."

"Are you serious?" he asked as he crumpled up the wrapper of his sandwich and plunged it into the pocket of his sweatpants.

"Unfortunately, yes. I am not sure when exactly he changed sides, but he betrayed us and was successful in kidnapping Brianna."

Jonah stopped again. "When did this happen!?"

I turned and looked at him. "Shortly after you met her."

"For how long?"

"Almost two months." Six weeks, six days, twenty hours to give a closer estimate. "For three and a half years we have had people looking for him without even the slightest sign, and then like a bolt of lightning our walls begin to crash in on us."

"So he's back?"

"Unfortunately. He has somehow found a way to make a connection with the twins through their dreams and we cannot seem to convince them he is not a friend."

"So why the twins?"

I took a deep breath before answering, "Because my two darling children are somehow the key to my race's future."

"How do you know that?"

"Because it has been prophesized."

"By whom?"

I smiled. "By a great prophetess named Seraphina Dubois."

"You're shitting me."

I could not help but laugh. "No, I am quite serious."

"Is that why Eris was trying to teach Bri how to fight? What's with the swords and stuff? That seems so unlike her. What? Why are you laughing?"

"Sometimes I forget you did not know her before she was pregnant. You see, Jonah, Brianna is actually quite talented with her daggers. It is in her blood."

"From Eris?" he asked and I nodded. "So why was she freaking out this morning when I came out?"

My hand went mindlessly through my hair and pulled at its ends. "There are a lot of underlying reasons, one of which is that she has lost the confidence she once had in herself." I pulled Jonah to a stop, feeling my frustration and temper stirring. "Brianna could beat any one of us any day of the week when she was human. She won against Eris – Eris! – in a dual. But she has it in her head that because she has been Turned she cannot do the things she used to."

"Can she though?"

"Of course she can! The only limitation she has is herself. Brianna has convinced herself she no longer has the skills that are truly engrained in her. Add to that the stress of Aidan coming back into our lives, and possibly the children being harmed, she is beside herself. I need her to be the Warrior I know she is, but...my Bri does not cope well with change."

"And there's been A LOT of change in the last few years."

"To say the least," I smirked as I released his arm and we began our walk again. "She believes she can only fight with her old daggers, as if they hold the power of her sword fighting skills."

"Why can't she use her daggers?"

"Because the handles are made of silver."

"Ah," he responded and then took a long sip of his coffee. "Why can't she wear gloves?"

I froze. "What?"

Jonah stopped and looked nervously back at me. "I just asked why she couldn't wear gloves. I don't mean winter gloves, you know something with grip. Could she use the daggers then?"

I was stunned. "Jonah, you are a genius. I cannot believe none of us thought of that."

Jonah smiled, but with some humility. "Eh…sometimes it just takes someone on the outside to take a look in. We could probably find something at a sporting goods store."

"There is actually one just a few blocks over," I said as I started walking without him. I only took a few steps before my cell phone began to ring from my back pocket. When I looked at the screen, Brianna's picture was smiling back at me. "Hello, angel."

"Where are you?" she answered with an urgency in her voice that made my muscles tense.

"Are you all right? The children?"

"We're fine, but why are the kids talking about being prostitutes?"

"Oh yes, please hold," I replied and handed the cell phone to Jonah. "It's for you."

Chapter Seventeen

Jonah

My bag was half packed when Bri knocked on the bedroom door and stepped inside. "You're packing already?"

"Yeah," I sighed sadly. "Eris wants to get an early start tomorrow. Figured I pack now and sleep in a little longer. Whatcha got there," I asked as I pointed to her arm that was hiding something behind her back.

"Beer," she replied simply as she pulled a six pack holder with only three beers left. "None of us are going to drink it so you might as well finish it. Pouring it down the drain seems like alcohol abuse."

"Well since you put it that way," I laughed, taking the beer from her hand and twisting open one of the bottles. "I take it the kids are asleep?"

"Thank you for that," she said as she picked up a dirty t-shirt from the floor. "You thoroughly wore them out."

I laughed. "Well they wore me out too. It's not even nine o'clock and I'm barely able to keep my eyes open."

"Are you sure you don't want me to wash your clothes? It's a small load, it won't take long."

I took the dirty shirt from her hand and placed it in the pile on the bed. "I think this is the third time I'm telling you no, but thank you," I replied as I sat on the edge of the bed and took a long drink. Brianna sat next to me and placed her cheek on my shoulder.

"I'm sorry this visit has been so crappy."

"It hasn't been crappy."

"It hasn't been good," she groaned and straightened up. "We haven't had any time to hang out and talk. There's so much on your shoulders, I can see it."

I took another drink and stared at the wall instead of her. "It's not your job to listen to all my problems."

"It's not? Hmm, and all this time I've been listening to you drone on about all your crap and I didn't have to?"

"Some scam, right?" I laughed.

"Seriously, though, are you ok?"

"Nope," I answered and took a drink. "My dad would have beaten the crap out of me for how I talked to my mom today and for what I said to Ashlyn."

She squeezed my hand. "Did you *really* call her a prostitute?"

"Yep." I took a final drink and placed the empty bottle back into the cardboard holder and took another bottle.

"But why, Jonah? Even if she was one, what you did was shitty."

"I know, I know!" I said flustered. "I've been apologizing all day to her, begging like an idiot at her door. She won't let me in, she won't talk to me…"

"Do you blame her?"

"No, but…"

"But what?" she asked with a very motherly raised eyebrow.

"She…hurt me…first," I sighed as I opened the cold beer that was sweating in my palm. "It's a sad excuse, I know. She won't even come out to eat."

"Eh…well not exactly. She came out when she heard you playing with the kids downstairs."

"How did she look?"

Brianna smirked. "About as good as you do. It's sad that we tend to hurt the ones we love the most."

"But I don't…" I shouted and placed my beer on the nightstand, but I stopped what I was going to say because I was sick of denying it, especially to myself. "I don't…*love* her."

"But you don't dislike her either," Bri retorted with one raised eyebrow.

"There are many levels in between dislike and love, Bri…but it doesn't matter, the timing's terrible."

"Love always finds you at the worst times."

"I work all the time."

"Good thing she lives where you work."

"But she pushed her feelings on me."

"Only once, and she'll get better at her shields." I opened my mouth but nothing came out. Instead Bri snapped her fingers and said, "I can do this all day. Jonah, face it, you like her. And it's been awhile, hasn't it?"

I nodded. "Nothing serious since Dad died."

She smiled kindly. "So don't you think it's about time to let yourself go and let this happen?"

I didn't answer right away as I paced in front of her. Back and forth. Back and forth, with no real rebuttal except, "But she *hates* me."

"Hate is a strong word, honey. All of us have seen that there is something brewing between you two. Maybe she just needs some time. She's been bombarded with so much the last few days."

"Yeah, I know," I sighed and then came to sit down on the bed next to her. "I hear you've been bombarded these last few days too."

Bri's eyes widened and she blinked slowly several times before she could speak. "Cam told you?"

I nodded eagerly. "Cam told me A LOT."

When she asked what I knew I told her absolutely everything that Cameron had divulged to me during our walk this morning, and I certainly wasn't shy about criticizing her for never telling me. "For almost four years I've bitched to you about everything, I feel like such an asshole now that I know how much you and Cameron have had to deal with. Maybe that's what I really am, I'm really just an asshole."

Bri squinted her left eye and pursed her lips. "That's not true, and you know it."

"Then why? Why have you never mentioned anything?"

She shrugged. "Jonah, you deal with so much, the last thing you need is for me to unload on you. And honestly, hearing about all your problems gives me a chance to forget about my own."

"Well I'm glad I could help," I laughed along with her.

"By the way," she said once our laughter died down, "I want to thank you for the gloves. You deserve the…the…I don't know, Nobel Prize?"

"Oh come on, they're just gloves."

"But now I can defend my babies like I need to, Jonah. You don't know how much relief I feel right now because of those gloves. Thank you." Her voice cracked as she wrapped her arms around my neck and hugged me.

When she released me she immediately stood and turned her head away, her hand going up to her face to wipe away a tear she didn't want me to see.

"Hey, Bri," I said as I stood from the bed, causing Brianna to stop her advance toward the bedroom door. "I don't know what it's like being a parent...I mean a real parent, like you, but I know that if anyone tried to hurt Katie I'd fight to the death to save her and I can't wield around a sword like you can." Slowly Brianna turned around, her arms crossed tightly in front of her as she reluctantly looked up at me. "I have no doubt that if this Aidan creep even comes close to those kids your instincts will kick in and you'll kill the bastard. Just stop letting your brain get in the way."

She gave a tight smile. "When did you get so smart?"

"I met a really smart lady four years ago who told me to take care of myself otherwise I wouldn't be able to take care of those that I love."

Brianna walked over to me with her arms stretched and I leaned down in order for her to wrap them around my neck. "I really am going to miss you, Jonah," she said through her sniffling.

"Me too," I replied feeling my nose tingle with similar emotions.

"I already told Cameron we have to fly you out to San Francisco."

I laughed. "And what did he say to that?"

"Anytime," she answered as she released me. "Sorry, Jonah, you've become a part of the family whether you like it or not."

"Trust me, Bri, I don't know what I would do without you guys."

She nodded as she pressed her lips together and began to back up toward the door. "Well...I'll let you get back to packing. I'm not saying goodbye..."

"Because you'll cry?" I said snidely to which she gave me the stink eye.

"Because we'll see you in a couple of weeks when we come down to pick up Dad and Mom from the Facility."

"Wow, it's here already. You're all really leaving."

Brianna sighed as she pulled the bedroom door closed. "Yes it is. Unfortunately."

After Brianna left I didn't bother packing the rest of my things neatly and just threw my dirty clothes in the bag. I was exhausted and didn't care that I was going to bed at nine o'clock. Problem was after an hour I woke right up. I couldn't keep my eyes open an hour ago and now it seemed as though they'd never close. I tossed, turned, put a pillow over my head, nothing worked. Then to make matters worse, my brain was going a million miles a minute, all mind you, about Ashlyn.

It was now after eleven and no hope in sight of getting back to sleep without resolving what was keeping me up – I liked Ashlyn more than I wanted to admit, and I'd hurt her. With a growl I flipped the blankets off of me and headed down the stairs to the second level. All day I had begged Ashlyn to let me into her room with no luck, but maybe now she'd be a little more forgiving. Even better, maybe she would be asleep.

Once I reached the bottom of the stairs I opened the door slowly, poking my head out to see if anyone was in the area but the kitchen was dark. As I stepped down the hall towards Ashlyn's room I noticed a light coming from underneath her door. Crap. She was awake.

Lightly I tapped on the door, but she didn't respond. I knocked again. Nothing. After a third knock I gave up and turned the doorknob. I had tried it during the day as well and every time it had been locked. This time, however, it turned easily in my hand and my stomach flipped over as I inched the door open.

"Ashlyn?" I whispered as I slowly stepped inside the room seeing the blankets bunched up on her bed, but she wasn't underneath them. "Ash?"

"What are…"

"HOLY SHIT!" I yelled and jumped almost three feet forward. When I turned around, Ashlyn was standing just inside the doorway with her arms full of shampoo and other toiletries. "Sorry, Ashlyn, you scared the shit out of me. Where did you come from?" I asked still catching my breath and now noticing the scowl on her face.

"I was in the bathroom getting my things. Now get out."

"Ashlyn, wait," I begged as she blew past me and threw her things on the bed. "We need to talk."

"I said get out."

"Not happening."

"Excuse me?" she growled as she whipped around to face me.

"Ashlyn, come on," I whined and took a step toward her. "I'm tired of apologizing to the fucking door. We leave tomorrow and I don't want to have to sit in a car for two hours with this...this...shit between us."

"Oh yes it would be terrible if YOU had to be uncomfortable."

"Ashlyn, I'm sorry!" I said loudly and then realized the door to her bedroom was still open. Breaking the eye contact I had with her, I turned and stepped over to the door and shut it quietly. "I am sorry, Ashlyn. I really am sorry for what I said to you. I was mad at you..." I began but stopped at her loud huff, "...which I believe I was allowed to be. But then my mom got me so angry that I...took it out on you. I'm sorry for exposing you like that. I said it in anger and it was wrong."

"I find that people tend to say what they really think when they're angry."

"I didn't mean it, Ashlyn, I swear."

"You're sorry, fine. Now leave."

"No."

Ashlyn grinded her teeth as she threw her arms up in the air. "Why are you doing this?!"

"Because...I...I...*like* you. Ashlyn. I like you. A lot."

Ashlyn froze for a second and then a look of disgust came across her face as she walked over to the only window in the room. "You have got to be kidding."

"Ashlyn, I know today was a mess and I can't take back what I said. But I am sorry, and I'm telling you the truth when I say I...want to...to be with you."

"Oh, and the next time you get mad you'll call me a whore again only it'll be at the Facility in front of hundreds of people."

"Ashlyn, I would never..."

"You did! You did already. You said you would never tell anyone my secret, but look at what you did," she shouted before turning her back on me, her shoulders shaking from her sobs. "You have no idea what happens when people know you're a whore."

"You are not a whore," I said firmly.

"Well, I was and once people know, they think they can do whatever they want to you. You did it once, why would you care if you had to do it again. It's not like I woke up one day and decided I wanted to whore myself out. I didn't want to! Christ, I lost my virginity to a fucking stranger who nearly drained me dry and then just left me on the floor."

Ashlyn completely broke down, resting her head against the windowpane. Quietly I stepped up behind her, carefully placing my hands on her shoulders. Immediately she flinched and pushed me away from her.

"Don't touch me," she cried and then took a deep breath as she wiped her wet cheeks. "I trusted you, Jonah."

"I know."

"No you don't," she growled. "The hardest thing I've ever done was trust you and come here. And STAY here! You have no idea how many times I've looked out this window and wondered if I could climb out and hit the ground without breaking my ankle. Or how many times I've gotten as far as the front door and stopped myself from leaving. Every time I stayed was because of you. I kept telling myself to trust in you, and look where it got me."

"Ashlyn," I begged, "it was an accident. I made a mistake."

"So did I," she replied. "When we were on the couch, I made a mistake and you wouldn't even hear me out. I didn't know I was doing it. You called me a prostitute on purpose because you wanted to hurt me, that's the difference here. So don't expect me to stand here and take your apology seriously."

"Is your shield down?" I asked and took a step up behind her.

"What?" she replied weakly. "No."

"Take it down for a minute," I said as I wrapped my arms around her and pulled her back into my chest.

"Jonah, let go of me," Ashlyn grunted as she squirmed in my arms which made me tighten them around her.

Without arguing with her I closed my eyes and concentrated on thinking about every ounce of guilt, regret, shame, and remorse I felt for hurting her. I'm sorry, sorry, sorry, I kept thinking. Forgive me, please forgive me.

"Ok, ok," Ashlyn cried and broke from my arms. "I get it, just stop."

I must have underestimated how intense my emotions were since now Ashlyn was panting and shaking her head.

"Sorry. I'm sorry. About that...and...before, of course."

Ashlyn finally caught her breath and fought hard not to look at me. "Fine, I believe you. Does that make you feel better?"

"Yes, but let me show you how I feel..."

"Please, don't. I'll be sick if I take any more."

"Fine then," I said nervously before placing her face between my hands and resting my lips gently on hers. Her lips were tight as she held her breath, but finally I felt her body relax, and as it did I pressed harder into her mouth. I could feel her pulse racing underneath my fingertips.

Not wanting a recreation of last night, I reluctantly pulled away from her lips, but continued to hold her face in my hands and reveled in the sight of her struggling to stretch her eyes open. But only a moment later her lazy expression faded as her eyes became watery, and my stomach flipped over.

Slowly I pulled my hands from her face and turned away. "I'm...sorry. I'll leave you alone."

"Jonah, you don't want to be with me."

"I don't?"

Ashlyn's hand came over the top of my shoulder causing me to stop and turn into her arm. Tears were once again trickling down her cheeks. "You deserve someone...not...like me."

"Ashlyn, I..."

"Do you know how many people I've been with?" she cried as she wrapped her arms tightly around her chest. "You should be with someone...cleaner."

"I know your past..."

"You think you know my past. You'll make yourself crazy thinking about it."

"That's not true."

"You're doing it now," she said softly as she sank down onto the edge of the bed.

"Don't read me, Ashlyn."

"Be honest with yourself, Jonah!" she snapped back.

Unfortunately she was right. It was one of the issues that kept circling in my head all day. How many men had she been with? How were they? How would I compare? Could I compare? I was only human and she'd been with Vampires, ultra-males, better in every way.

Except...a little voice in the back of my head whispered...I cared for her. Even better, I believed she had feelings for me too, and I didn't have to pay her for them.

Ashlyn looked at me wearily as I came to stand in front of her. "Ok, I'll be honest. Your...experience...we'll work through it. You think you're the only one with baggage here? Crap, some days I need a bellhop to help me carry my shit around."

Ashlyn laughed with a mixture of humor and tears. "I don't know how to do this."

"There are no real rules, Ash," I said and knelt down in front of her. "We decide what feels right. I mean, most guys don't tell a girl he likes her while standing in his boxers, but here we are."

Ashlyn smiled. "It seems to be normal for us since this is the second time I've seen you in your boxers."

"See! We're already making our own rules."

"But can you trust me?" she asked seriously. "I heard you, last night with Sera. How do you know I'm not making you feel this way? Or that I didn't make you kiss me just then?"

I rose from the floor, holding myself up by my fingertips on the edge of the bed while I leaned down and kissed her gently, then again, and again. Short, soft kisses that made Ashlyn melt before my eyes. "This is me, I know it is because it feels different from last night. I'm in control of myself and I know why I'm doing everything I'm doing right now."

Gently I put my hands underneath her arms and pulled her into my chest.

"What if it happens again? I can't promise…"

"We'll just take things slow, ok? Give you some time to work on your shields. And just be honest with me if you think you can't control it. Ok?" She nodded against my chest. "But can I ask one thing?"

"Mmm-hmmm," she replied nervously.

"I know you won't always be able to help it, at least that's what Sera says, but I would appreciate it if you wouldn't read me. We all need privacy, but with someone who has gifts like you that can be hard."

"Sera's been helping me with that too," she replied and then looked up at me, biting her bottom lip. "Are you sure you want to do this?"

"I am very sure," I smiled. "What about you? You hated me a little while ago."

"I didn't hate you." I raised a skeptical eyebrow. "I was trying to, but I couldn't. I think that made me the angriest."

"So you do like me."

"I would have left days ago if I didn't," she answered seriously. "So what happens now?"

I shifted Ashlyn out of my arms and let her stand on her own. "Well,

I'll kiss you goodnight, let you get a few hours of sleep, and then drive you to Connecticut insanely early tomorrow."

Ashlyn smiled as she tucked a section of her thick curly hair behind her ear. "I like the kissing part."

"Me too," I said and kissed her forehead and then one last time on her lips. "Goodnight, Ashlyn."

Ashlyn leaned into me, this time putting her hands on either side of my face, pulling me down to her and letting her lips linger on mine. It was my turn to lose myself in her and be disappointed when she pulled away. "You won't change your mind tomorrow, will you?"

"No way," I replied. "Especially not after that kiss."

Ashlyn blushed as she pushed me away gently. "Goodnight, Jonah."

Reluctantly my feet retreated and brought me over to her bedroom door. I glanced back one last time before closing the door behind me, thinking how Ashlyn and I had crossed the gambit of emotions in a matter of minutes. But it was done, everything was out in the open and we could start fresh.

I sighed with relief as my body fell back against the door, my heart still racing with excitement over kissing Ashlyn. It wasn't until I heard a noise coming from down the hall did I realize that the kitchen light was on. When I looked down the hall I saw Sera's smiling face duck back around the corner. Shit. And from the sounds in the kitchen she wasn't alone. With another sigh I pushed myself from Ashlyn's door and quietly walked down the hall, purposely not making eye contact with anyone as I came to the door that led to the third floor, although from the corner of my eye I could see everyone was there – Bri, Cameron, Eris and Sera.

Just as I stepped up on the first step Cameron cleared his throat and said, "So does this mean we can call Ashlyn your girlfriend and not have you jump down our throats?"

I paused on the step and turned slowly. "Yeah, I guess it does."

Chapter Eighteen

Brianna

"Daughter, you must practice every day, no excuses," my father scolded. "I will monitor the twin's dreams every other night beginning tomorrow. If anything interesting shows up I will let you know."

"Thanks, Dad," I smiled and gave him one last hug. "We'll see you in a couple of weeks."

"And?"

I rolled my eyes like a teenager, and considering he missed those years of my life I figured he could use some catching up. "*And...*I'll practice every day. Happy?"

"Mia figlia, I am always happy," he said brightly as he pulled his shoulder length brown hair back into a hair tie.

"That's a lie if I've ever heard one."

"It is not a lie," he replied, his brows scrunched tightly together. "I have a wife I adore, a daughter who loves me, and grandchildren that are the definition of joy. Of course I am always happy."

"Except when you lose your temper at the daughter that loves you."

He sighed. "Perhaps you could stop doing things that make me lose my temper."

"And maybe I could shoot rainbows out of my ass."

He laughed and kissed my cheek. "Daughter, I know the great things you are capable of. It makes me angry when you don't think the same."

Just then the front door of my home opened and a head of bright red hair came through. "We're here! We're here! Please tell me we didn't miss them."

Eris smiled as we watched Renee carry a sleepy Wills up the stairs. "Figlia surrogata, you have just made it. And William, my boy…"

"Bye E-we," Wills said as he rubbed his eyes and then easily transitioned into Eris's outstretched arms. It looked as though Wills would fall right back asleep on my father's shoulder until he noticed Olivia running down the hall towards us. "Wivy!"

"Come on, Wills! We're playing a new game," Livy said as she waved Wills down to the floor.

Wills, now wide awake, looked over to me and asked, "Awbie, can I go play?"

"Of course, but…" I began but didn't finish before he squirmed out of Eris's arms. "Olivia, did you say goodbye to everyone?"

"Bye Eri!" she squealed before racing down the hall with Wills in tow.

"Livy, what game?" I called after her.

"Sorry, Mama, secret game," she replied right before she closed the bedroom door behind her. I looked over at Renee. "We're in so much trouble when the three of them are teenagers."

She cocked an eyebrow. "I intend to be sedated during that time. Anyway, gotta get to work. Bye, Sorta-Dad," she said kissing Eris on the cheek and giving him a quick hug.

"And to you, figlia surrogata."

"You two are so weird," I said looking between them.

"Hey Renee!" Jonah said cheerily behind me. "I thought I heard your voice."

"Yeah, yeah, wanted to come say goodbye," Renee began as she stepped past me and Eris, and threw her arms around Jonah's neck. "Besides, I needed to check out your ass one last time before I moved across the country."

"Re-ne!" I yelled.

Thankfully Jonah laughed. "It's ok, Bri. I'll miss being checked out by an older woman."

Renee hit him in the chest and then noticed that Ashlyn was standing behind him. "Hey crazy girl!"

"Renee!"

Renee ignored me as she continued, "Heard you were going to the Facility, good for you. Maybe you're not as crazy as you seem."

"Renee Alexandra…" Sera scolded as she came down the hall with her bag over her shoulder.

Renee looked like a dog in trouble. "Sorry, Sera."

"How come you apologize to her and not me?" I asked.

Renee shrugged. "Because you're my twin, everything is always forgiven. It's an unwritten law. Anywho, gotta go!"

Renee gave Sera a quick hug before racing down the stairs as fast as she could in her four-inch heels. When I peeked over the top of the second floor landing I noticed Cameron opening and closing the door behind her, and then buffing the scuff marks left behind on the hardwood stairs.

"Where did you go?" I asked him when he finally came up the stairs.

Cameron gave a sheepish grin. "One last game of find your car. Jonah, the car is now in front of the house."

"I never get to see the people when they have to actually find their car," Jonah said with a slight frown.

"Well," Cameron began, "if you go out now the gentleman from two doors down is roaming aimlessly along the sidewalk."

Jonah didn't wait a beat before he was running down the stairs.

"Hey!" I called after him causing him to stop halfway down and turn to look at me.

"What?! You said we weren't saying goodbye today, remember?"

Jonah gave me a boyish grin before he ran down the rest of the stairs and through the door. Eris was quick to follow, proving that no matter how old he was, he could still be a boy at heart.

When I turned back around I was happy to see Ashlyn hugging Cameron goodbye, and my feelings seemed to be echoed by Sera's warm expression. When Ashlyn stepped away from Cameron she came to me, and looking at her now she was a completely different young woman than the mess that had walked through my door a few days ago. It wasn't just her haircut, clean clothes, and absence of body odor; the enormous chip on her shoulder was gone. Her need to be tougher than anyone else in the room was replaced by a smile and a sense of gratitude.

"Brianna…" Ashlyn started to say, but the rest was choked up in her throat as her eyes became watery. Knowing the signs well, I pulled her into my arms and rubbed her back like I always needed at times like these.

"Are you scared?" I whispered in her ear and she nodded. "You're doing the right thing, and it's really a great place. There's nothing to be scared about, they'll take great care of you."

Ashlyn lifted her head and wiped her cheeks with the cuff of her sweater. "I know they will. I'm just glad that Jonah will be there."

I smiled. "I'm very happy for you. I just love that kid. Now you call if you need anything, even if it's just to talk. Ok? Jonah knows how to get ahold of me."

"Thank you," she said through her tears. "Seriously, for...everything. I've never known this...any of this. Thank you."

I put my arm around her and turned her toward the stairs. "You are so welcome, sweetie. But you have to promise me you'll take care of my boy. I can't tell you how much I'm going to miss him."

"I will," she smiled and blushed. She gave me one last hug before retreating down the stairs, leaving only one person left to say goodbye to.

"Je t'amie, petite chute," Sera said as she hugged me tightly.

"I love you too, Mom. Be safe going back."

"Oui, oui. Jonah is always a safe driver. I am more worried about you."

"I'm fine," I replied with little confidence.

"Petite, petite, you really do need to start believing zhat."

Well nothing gets by her. Damn Empath.

"I'm trying, Mom. Just...if..."

"What is it, petite?"

I looked guiltily into my stepmother's eyes as I replied, "I know you feel that sometimes you have to let things play out, but if you see anything, good or bad, if you see anything will you please tell me?"

Sera squeezed my hand. "I want nozhing but you and my petite bébés to be safe. Je t'amie, ma petite chute."

I had hurt her feelings, but it had to be said. She patted me on the cheek and then made her way down the stairs. Moments later Cameron and I were standing on the front stoop waving goodbye as the black sedan from the Facility pulled down our street. Cam wrapped his arm around my shoulder and squeezed it when their car finally disappeared around the corner. When I sniffled he kissed my temple and pulled me back inside the house.

"You will see Jonah in a couple of weeks, love."

"I know," I answered as I closed the front door.

"What a wonderful feeling," Cameron said with a sigh, gazing up the stairs to the second floor.

"What's that, babe?"

Cameron turned with a devilish crooked smile. "We finally have the house to ourselves."

In a flash Cameron was pressing me up against the front door, his lips kneading my mouth open while his tongue declared war on my own. I put my hand through his hair and pulled at his thick curls since it would be the only way I could lift his lips from mine. "The kids are upstairs."

Cameron's eyebrows knitted together pleadingly. "That means there is an entire floor between us. Besides they are playing diligently in their room."

"But we need to leave to take them to school in half an hour."

"We can be quick," he replied as he kissed down the side of my neck.

"Just what a girl wants to hear."

Cameron lifted his head, my message ringing loud and clear. "It is not my fault you are so irresistible."

"Mmm-hmm," I replied skeptically. "I think I was pretty resistible yesterday."

"A blip in your history."

"Ha! Lately I've been a freakin' radar." Cameron smiled, however, he did not find my comment as funny as I did. In response I snaked my arms around his neck and pulled his head down until his forehead rested on mine. "Did I thank you for the gloves?"

"Only four times so far. Did you use them yet?"

I nodded as our tones became even softer and more intimate. "I think they'll really help me, Cam."

"Then that is all I need to hear, my love."

"I'll be the old Brianna again, I promise."

Cameron lifted his forehead from mine and looked intensely into my eyes. "Gloves or not, you are still my Bri, *the* Brianna Morgan."

"*The* Brianna Morgan, huh?"

"Well, I do wish it was Brianna Burke."

I groaned. "Cam, not this again. I told you, once things calm down we'll take the plunge. But seriously, don't you know me well enough to know that if you keep pushing I'm just gonna keep taking steps back?"

"Unfortunately I know it all too well."

"You weren't supposed to completely agree with me."

Cameron took my hand and kissed the tops of my fingers, a gesture even after all these years still made me swoon.

"Angel, I only ever want to make you happy."

I cupped his cheek with my hand. "Cam, you do make me happy."

"Lately it does not seem that way."

Quickly I pushed myself off of the door, grabbed Cameron's hand and pulled him down the hallway toward our bedroom. "Come on, I'll show you how happy you make me."

"But we have to take the children to school."

I turned to face him. "You said we'd be quick."

With a feral growl Cameron picked me up and wrapped my legs around his waist as he carried me into our bedroom. Just as my hand reached under the edge of Cameron's shirt, a high-pitched wail echoed from the second floor. We both froze, knowing what was inevitable. Without saying a word, Cameron put me down on the floor and the two of us begrudgingly made our way back to the foyer.

Olivia stood at the top of the stairs, her cries bouncing off the walls on either side of her. As soon as she saw the two of us she swung her leg over the banister and slid down, turning before she hit the bottom and flying into her father's waiting arms.

"Whatever is the matter, monkey?"

Livy lifted her head from Cam's shoulder, her wails choked out intermittently by her heaving breaths. "Ada, the boys...won't let me...play...with them."

"Why not?"

Olivia's precious cherub cheeks pulled her entire face down into a pout. "They said boys only. That I couldn't play with Aidan 'cuz I'm a girl."

The sights around me blurred as I reached the top of the stairs before Cameron. The doorknob to the twins' bedroom crumbled in my hand causing me to thrust my shoulder into the door. Jack and Will were jumping in midair when the door burst open and splinters of wood flew across the room.

"Where is he!" I yelled in Jack's direction. "Where's Aidan?!"

Cameron stood in the doorway, Olivia still clinging to his chest. "Jackson, answer your mother!"

Jack stood from the floor, his face confused and petrified as he pointed to the corner of his bed. "He's right there, Mama."

"What?"

"Aidan is on the bed," Jack replied and then pointed to the corner. "Now there, and there, and there."

Jack kept pointing around the room at nothing. Finally I looked to the one person who would tell me the truth. "Wills, do you see Aidan?" He looked at Jack and then nodded. "Do you really see him?"

Wills looked back at me and shook his head slowly. "No, Awbie."

"Jack? Tell me the truth, is Aidan a real person in this room with you?"

Jack pouted. "No, Mama. He's not here, we were just playing."

My chest was heaving, I probably looked like Devin did before he exploded. But these were my babies, and I needed to leave the room before that happened. "Let your sister play in here, no more closed doors," I said quickly as I ran out of the room.

I couldn't get out onto the second floor balcony fast enough. I took in gulps of cold air, making my throat and lungs burn. In less than two minutes I had lost my mind. Aidan was in my house, and then he wasn't. My children were in danger, and then they weren't. Aidan was making me go insane and he wasn't even here.

The doors behind me opened, and a waft of rustic autumn leaves swirled around me seconds before Cameron's arms came around my chest. "No one is going to school today, or for the remaining two weeks we are here."

"Does that make us horrible parents?"

"Other parents do not face the troubles we do. Besides, our twins are smarter than any of the other children at that school. We only enrolled them for the socialization. I will call Renee, if she has a problem with keeping William here, I will take him over myself."

I patted Cameron's arm. "Our son couldn't have picked another name for his imaginary friend?"

"I think we would be foolish to think that our son's name choice was chosen at random."

"That's comforting."

A quiet laugh rumbled in Cameron's chest. "Shall we go back inside? For the scare we inflicted I am sure that the children deserve some pancakes."

"Are you offering to make them?" I said as I turned in his arms, seeing the loving eyes and crooked smile that I needed.

"Do you want more pancakes on the ceiling?"

"Ah, good point."

Chapter Nineteen

Jonah

Before I knew it I was pulling our black sedan into the Facility's parking garage, and moments later I was leading Ashlyn up the back stairs and into the main lobby. As usual, hybrids were sitting in big cushy chairs drinking coffee, eating breakfast, and gossiping about whatever had happened the night before. However, as Ashlyn and I walked through the crowd, much of their conversation ended while they gaped at the two of us, hand in hand and walking toward the dormitories. From the death grip Ashlyn had on my hand, I didn't dare say a word. She was either terrified or concentrating on keeping her shield up; though it was probably a little bit of both. When the doors to the elevator finally closed, Ashlyn let out the huge breath she must have been holding in while we were walking through the lobby. Her entire body collapsed into my side and I easily held her there until the elevator doors reopened minutes later.

Thankfully her room was only the fourth one down on the left. After pulling her down the hall, I punched in the code on her room's keypad and quickly got her inside. Before I had barely opened the door, Ashlyn ran inside the room and into the bathroom, slamming the door behind her.

"Ash?" I said quietly as I put my ear to the door, but I could hear her retching inside. Suddenly I had a sinking feeling that bringing her here may not have been a good idea after all.

Not knowing what else to do, I put her bags on the bed and unzipped the bigger one to begin unpacking. I was surprised to find that Ashlyn was an immaculate packer, every item pristinely folded and categorized, completely the opposite of my bag. I opened the drawers of the small dresser and began placing her clothes where I normally would. Shirts, second drawer. Pants, bottom drawer. Underwear, top drawer. Ha! How many guys got to touch his girlfriend's underwear after dating for less than twenty-four hours? Then again I was the one who bought it for her too, so double points.

Just then the bathroom door opened and Ashlyn was standing in its doorway, her expression changing suddenly as she noticed that I was holding her neatly stacked bras in my hand.

"I...uh...was just..." but I didn't bother trying to explain myself and simply sighed and put the bras in the drawer. "Feel better?"

She nodded tentatively. "Sorry."

"Nerves or people?"

"Nerves...I think."

"Nerves, you think?" I said, allowing her to rest her forehead on my chest.

"Why was everyone staring at us when we walked in?"

I snickered. "Because you're the girl who escaped. Of course people are going to stare."

Ashlyn tilted her head up and for the first time I realized just how short she was. She didn't even reach my shoulders.

"You didn't have to hold my hand."

I paused as my face fell with disappointment. "If you didn't want people to know about us you should have told me. I just thought..."

"No, no! I meant you didn't have to hold my hand if you didn't want to. You work here, and people know you, and if you..."

"Ash," I interrupted and put my finger on her quivering bottom lip, "I want everyone to know about us. I'm going to hold your hand and do whatever else you're comfortable with doing in front of other people. I'm not ashamed of you, Ashlyn."

"But..."

"But what?"

Ashlyn's forehead fell back onto my chest. "What if I do something stupid or humiliating? I don't want to embarrass you or cause you to lose your job."

Placing my finger under her chin, I tilted Ashlyn's head back so that I could look her in the eye. "Trust me, I embarrass myself all the time. Stop worrying, you're going to do fine. Trust me, trust me, trust me. Are you seeing a theme here?"

Ashlyn forced a tight smile as she fought back the tears that were forming in the corners of her eyes. Just then a knock came at the door and Ashlyn flinched violently in my arms.

"It's just Rebecca, she's your guide today. Remember?" She shook her head and I started to feel her panic radiate into me. "Ash, before you step out there I need you to take a moment to get calm, ok?" Ashlyn released her pent up breath, and then closed her eyes as I continued to speak to her in a low, soft tone. "Rebecca is going to take you to the clinic so the doctor can give you a checkup." Ashlyn's shoulders tensed underneath my hands. "Nothing invasive, Ash. Normal stuff, maybe some blood work, that's all. Then you'll go to a welcome-to-being-a-hybrid class, and if I can work it I'll meet you for lunch in the cafeteria, ok?"

Ashlyn nodded and opened her eyes, worry still lying deep within them. "What happens after lunch?"

"Er...not really sure, but Rebecca will get you acquainted with everything. Then once I'm done working I'll come get you and we'll do dinner, and then just hang out."

"Just you and me?" she asked hopefully and I had to smile.

"Yes, just you and me."

"No scary movies this time."

"I'll see if I can dredge up some popcorn," I laughed and suddenly Ashlyn rose on her toes and pressed her lips against mine. She wrapped her hand around the back of my neck, her nails tickling me gently at my hairline. I couldn't wait for tonight.

Another knock came from the door which seemed to pressure Ashlyn to lower herself back down to the floor. "Ok, let's get this over with."

"You'll be fine. And if something goes wrong, have someone find me, or Sera, or even Eris. We're all here for you."

Ashlyn smiled as she stepped past me and slung her patchwork messenger bag across her chest. "I don't think you'll need your purse."

Ashlyn's eyes darted quickly to the floor, a look of embarrassment creeping into her face. "I...It's one of those things, I never go anywhere without it. It's kind of my life."

"What is it with girls cramming their lives in their purses?"

Ashlyn shook her head and held the bag up in front of her chest. "No, I mean...I made this, Jonah. Every piece of fabric and charm is from something in my life, things to remind me of good times. It's like a security blanket, I don't go anywhere without it."

Of all the times I had seen this bag of Ashlyn's, I never bothered to look at the detail. Everything from the pouch to the strap had a special meaning, and whereas before it looked like a mishmash of fabric, now I could see distinct patterns in the swatches and even tiny messages she had written to herself. Charms and key chains dangled from the zipper, each tarnished and chipped, but obviously significant to her.

I lowered Ashlyn's arm, allowing the patchwork bag to stretch once again across her chest. "Someday, when you're comfortable, I would love to know the story behind every patch."

"That could take a while," she replied.

"Good thing we have time."

When I opened Ashlyn's door I found Rebecca propped up against the opposite wall with her arms crossed in front of her. I assumed that the annoyed expression on her face came from the fact that Greg, owner of the worst pickup lines I had ever heard, was standing next to her talking about something she wasn't remotely listening to. When Rebecca noticed the door open, she promptly pushed herself off the wall.

"Hey, Rebecca, sorry to keep you waiting."

"It's alright, I could hear you talking so that's why I waited," she said as she stepped up to me and then lowered her voice. "I just didn't count on the company."

I snickered and brought Ashlyn around to my side. "Sorry about that, too. Ok, so Ashlyn, this is Rebecca. Rebecca, this is Ashlyn Shaw."

Rebecca extended her hand which only caused Ashlyn to sink back into me. Thankfully Rebecca didn't seem offended. "I get it, you're nervous. The first day is always the hardest. But I promise I'll take good care of you today."

Ashlyn shook her head. "I'm sorry, I just have trouble around people, especially when I'm nervous. I-I'm an Empath."

Rebecca's eyes flashed. "An Empath? That's awesome," she said and I could feel Ashlyn relax as Rebecca waved for her to come out into the hall. "So there's this guy that I'm totally crushing on, and I can't tell if he's into me or not. Girl, you could totally save me some time."

The girls' conversation continued down the hallway and Ashlyn only gave me one look back, but she was smiling. When Greg took a step to follow them I placed my hand on his shoulder and turned him the opposite way so we could take the stairs. Really it was to save him from the embarrassment I knew would be coming his way from Rebecca. Greg was a good kid, but calling him socially awkward when it came to girls was an understatement.

"Dude, you're totally cock blocking me," Greg whined as I pushed him slightly down the hall.

"Greg, you and Rebecca will never happen."

"How do you know? You don't even know her."

"I know enough. Now come on, I've gotta get to work," I said as I opened the door to the stairs and waited for Greg to step ahead of me.

"Yeah, by the way, you have the boringest job ever."

"Thanks?" I replied as the two of us began our descent down the first flight. "Slow weekend?"

"Not one pick-up. Cole let me come with him on the supply run, but that was it. Oh, and don't worry, I did all the talking with the lady at the drugstore, you won't be having to do any...a...favors," he said in a slimy tone while he waggled his eyebrows.

"Really? Not one pick up?"

"Nope. There were supposed to be two, but I guess one guy got cold feet, and the Gatherer canceled the other one."

"Canceled? Canceled why?"

"I don't know, ask Cole." Greg waited until we began to walk down the third and final set of stairs to ask what must have been his most burning question. "So I have to know, the Ashlyn chick, did you really sneak her into the trunk of your car so you two could have a wild kinky weekend?"

"What!" I yelled and pulled him to a stop. "Is that what people are saying?"

"Uh...er...some people. Some say she ran away, others think you snuck her out. And since the two of you came walking in holding hands, it's kind of swaying people that way."

"She ran away, Greg. I didn't know it until I was almost in Boston, and then we just...connected. You believe me, don't you?"

"Sure, man. Sure."

I rounded on him again, making him flatten himself up against the wall. "It's the truth, and you're going to spread that around, understand me?"

Greg nodded his head nervously as I stepped back from him and began pacing in a circle. Damn I hated rumors and gossip. Ashlyn hadn't been in the building more than twenty minutes and people already thought bad things about her. Hopefully people would only talk behind her back and quietly enough where she couldn't hear it. More importantly I hoped that people would actually listen to Greg for once.

"So," Greg said with his voice slinking back into slimeyville, "did you get any? I mean, she's pretty hot now…"

"Go," I replied angrily and pointed toward the stairwell door. "Go before I kick your ass."

Greg flinched and ran into the main lobby with me only a few steps behind him before I turned toward the offices. I longed for a little peace and quiet to get caught up. Greg was right, when pick-ups were slow, my job could be boring. But downtime allowed for car maintenance and detailing, all things I liked, and catching up on paperwork, which I could do without.

Just as I rounded the corner, someone called my name behind me. When I turned around I saw Warren, the Facility's Head of Security, waving me over to him.

"I've found him," Warren said into one of our walkie-talkies. "Where have you been? We've been calling you on the walkies for the last five minutes."

"I just got here. I don't even have a walkie on me. What's going on?"

"Come with me," Warren growled and escorted me back through to the main lobby. "By the way, thanks for showing my security team up with your little prank. Did Eris put you up to that?"

"Prank? What pran…oh, you mean, the hybrid in the trunk thing. That wasn't me, your beef is with Ashlyn."

Warren released a huff through his nose. "Either way it is being addressed. But for now you have an irate guest at my front gate," he replied flatly. When we stepped out the front doors three of Warren's human security guards fell in line with us across the front turnaround of the main driveway.

"Are you going to tell me who's at the gate?" I asked finding it hard to keep up with his pace.

"His ID says his name is Dr. Paul Redding…" I stopped in my tracks at the sound of Paul's name causing Warren to turn back. "So you know him. Good, then we can put this to rest quickly."

"Why didn't you just tell him to leave?"

Warren lifted his brow and I flinched back a little. "We did, but he is putting up a bit of a fight."

"If he's putting up a fight, can't you shoot him or something?"

"Jonah, he's human, you know we can't touch him. Is he a threat?"

"Just to my mother," I replied to blank stares. "He's my mother's boyfriend. I don't know why he's here and frankly I don't want to speak with him."

"Jonah, I do not pretend to understand what's going on here, but he is refusing to leave until you speak with him. Because he's local, I don't want him creating any trouble for us in the community. So nut up and find out what he wants."

I grinded my teeth as all four security members stood and waited impatiently for me to do or say something.

"Here's the thing, Warren, I hate this guy. I mean HATE this guy. I called him Dr. Douchebag to his face last week." The human security guards laughed under their breaths. "He's turned my mother into a zombie, he thinks what I do here is a joke, and he's tearing my family apart. Can't we go down there like…like total bad asses and scare the shit out of him or something?"

"Jonah, we are not in the business of meddling in family relations…"

"Please!" I begged. "Just this one time. I'll…I'll…I'll even get Ashlyn to tell you how she was able to sneak into the trunk of the car unnoticed."

Warren's eyes were fixed on me, the debate in his head effectively showing on his face. Finally, "Well if we're going to do this, we're going to do it right."

With a circle of his index finger in the air he signaled all of us to follow him to the security team's armory and outfitting area. Ten minutes later Warren had eight security guards, both human and Vampire, dressed in light combat gear. Even I was given a black t-shirt and combat vest, though only the security members strapped on their machine guns. We piled into one of the SUVs, Warren at the wheel with me in the passenger seat, the human security guards in the backseat, while the Vampire security members stood on the running boards and held onto the roof rack of the truck.

Warren sped down the long winding driveway bordered by the young trees that were relocated there. At the speed Warren was driving the front gate came up quickly. Paul was leaning against his late model silver Audi on the other side of the tall metal security gate. As our SUV approached, the two guards who were standing in front of it kept their positions, not even flinching when Warren slammed on the breaks and the truck stopped only inches from the back of their legs. I guess it paid to have Vampire eyesight.

After the Vampire guards jumped off the running boards, the rest of us filed out of the SUV and I reveled in the fact that Paul's pompous grin fell. As I walked toward him the security guards fell into a V-formation behind me, making Paul look like he might piss himself.

"You better have a damn good reason for being here, Paul," I said as I came to stand at the nose of his Audi.

Paul adjusted his coat's collar as he eyed the security team behind me. "I think this is something better discussed inside. Perhaps…"

"You're not stepping an inch past that gate. You have five minutes before these gentleman force you off this property, so tell me what is so damn important that you make a scene at my workplace."

"Fine, we can do it in front of your friends if you so insist," Paul replied, puffing his chest out slightly. "Your mother is quite distraught. Your behavior at Mable's last week was atrocious, and I will not stand for it. Your father would be ashamed."

"Don't you dare talk about my father," I shouted as multiple hands squeezed my shoulders and held me in place. "Everything I do is for my family! You know it, and my mother knows it. Besides raising my voice to my mother, I've done nothing wrong."

"Jonah, all I am here to do is bring peace to the family."

"Bullshit! You're the one destroying my family."

"No, Jonah," Paul replied in a condescending tone, "you are. Your mother and I are getting married, we are creating a new family, one that can include you or not. Katie follows your lead, and by behaving as you did the other night, you are driving a wedge through this family. In essence, you are taking your mother's children away from her. You, Jonah, not me."

My cheeks were flush with anger while my nose and throat burned from the cold air I was heaving in and out. "If my mother…" I began slowly and then paused to keep my tone in check, "…Katie doesn't follow my lead or anyone else's, and from day one she saw you as the snake that you are. Deep down inside my mother sees it too, I know she does, but she's too scared to be alone so she stays with you.

"Mom knows what she needs to do if she wants to talk with me about what happened last week, so frankly your help is not needed or wanted." I took two slow steps towards Paul, the security team moving with me like a shadow as I stood nose to nose with him. "Now get back in your car and get out of here before these gentlemen show you what they're trained for."

As I turned away, I felt Paul's hand on my shoulder as he said, "We're not finished…"

Before I could turn around two of the guards flung Paul back against his car and held him there.

"This is my house, Paul, my rules," I shouted. "Now get into your fucking car and don't even think of coming back." I turned and waved the security team forward. As a group the team surrounded Paul's car while Warren came to stand next to me.

"What now, sir?" Warren asked seriously, and I was happy with the power he'd given me, even if it was for just a moment.

"He has one minute to leave the property. If he doesn't, do to him what we do to everyone else."

"So we have your permission to shoot him?" Warren asked as he quirked a curious eyebrow.

Paul's terrorized expression was priceless as I replied with a devious smile, "Permission granted."

Chapter Twenty

Jonah

"Katie Bell, just remember this food is for you to get through exams, not to feed your whole dorm," I said as I dropped the four grocery bags onto her twin sized bed. When I turned around she was sticking her tongue out at me.

"Yes, Joey, for the ten millionth time, I know," she replied.

"That also means no sharing with Chemistry boy."

"Who? Oh him. Goodness, Joey, that's so two weeks ago. Now I'm seeing this guy from my history class. His name is…"

But I stopped listening. Since our dad died she had never had a boyfriend for more than a few weeks, two months tops, and when one relationship ended another began soon after. She and I were drastically different in this department, but it was different for girls when their dad died. It seemed like Katie was always searching and never happy with who she found. No one was able to measure up to her expectations, nor did she want to give them a real piece of her heart. It made me worry about her, more than a brother should about his younger sister, but that was my role now whether I liked it or not. That also meant that I needed to ensure she was protecting herself.

While she continued her babbling and began unpacking the junk food she claimed was needed for exams, I peeked inside the top drawer of her nightstand, the jewelry case next to her lamp, the basket filled with junk next to the jewelry case next to the lamp.

"Joey!"

"Wh-what?!" I said, frozen like a child caught with his hand in the cookie jar.

"What are you looking for?"

"Um...things?"

She rolled her eyes. "If you want to know if I'm using protection..."

"I'd rather not have to verbalize it."

Katie huffed and stepped over to the nightstand, opened the bottom drawer, and then slid a magazine to the side to uncover her stash. "See, condoms and my birth control. Happy?"

"Are you using them?" I said as I picked up her birth control.

"Yes. Can we put it away now," she answered, yanking the pills out of my hand and throwing them back in the drawer. "This is not quite the thing I want to talk about with my brother."

"Trust me, your brother didn't want to catch you having sex in the house and have to take you to get this stuff in the first place."

"A day I'd rather forget, Joey. More like a whole week I'd like to forget."

"Just remember, Katie Bell," I said and squeezed her hand, "there's nothing wrong with saying no to a guy. If he really loves you, he'll wait until you're ready. Don't be one of those girls who believes she has to give it away in order for a guy to like her."

Katie slid her hand out of mine, shaking her head as she turned to finish unpacking the rest of her groceries. "Don't worry, Joey. Mom gives me the same speech all the time. That and the, please don't come home pregnant. At least that's something you'll never have to worry about."

"Why's that?"

Katie gave me an annoyed look. "Besides the obvious fact that you, Jonah, my brother who I assume was born with male parts, cannot get pregnant. You also never have girlfriends with which to have children with."

"Well..." I replied as I shoved my hands into the pockets of my jeans. "...that's not exactly true."

Katie's head flinched. "Which part? That you don't have a girlfriend? Or that you don't have male parts? Or...oh my god, have you gotten a girl pregnant and not told Mom? Holy shit, Joey..."

"Katie! I have a girlfriend, I just have a girlfriend."

Katie's worked up expression softened and she flung her arms around my neck. "Joey! Oh I'm so happy for you! How long? What's her name? Has Mom met her? When do I get to meet her?"

By the time her questions were over she was jumping up and down so I pulled her arms from my neck. "Calm down, Katie Bell."

"Calm down? How can you tell me to calm down! Joey, this is huge for you. Tell me about her, tell me everything," she said excitedly as she pulled me down onto her bed.

"Uh...well...her name is Ashlyn."

"Cool name, like her already. What else?"

I smiled and wondered what else I could possibly tell her since there was so much I had to keep secret. "She's uh, short. Blonde. Shy."

"You're horrible at this," Katie said with disgust. "How long have you been together?"

"Almost three weeks now."

"Ah, so right after the whole flip out at Mable's."

Being Wednesday, it had been exactly three weeks since the "flip out" at Mable's, and I had yet to go back. "Yes, just a few days after that. She...a...works...where I do."

"Oh. Really? She's in private security?"

"Yes, girls work there too."

"But are they real women? Is she...manish?"

"No! Jeez, Katie. She's..." I paused feeling shy, "...beautiful. I've never met anyone like her."

"Ooo!" Katie squealed as she kicked her legs and clapped to herself. "You really have it bad, Joey, I can tell. Do you love her? Did you tell her you love her?"

"No," I laughed shyly. "Not yet. We're taking it slow."

"Does Mom know?"

"How would she? I haven't talked to her in weeks."

"You've stood her up at Mable's the last two Wednesdays too."

"I did not..." I said frustrated as I stood from her bed, "...I told her I would speak to her without Paul, and she just won't do it."

"I know, but if she knew about Ashlyn you know she would...oh! Bring Ashlyn to dinner tonight at Mable's."

"No way," I replied firmly and then bent down to kiss her forehead. "Love you, Katie Bell. Good luck on your exams. If you need anything..."

"I know, Joey," she said as she stood from her bed and hugged me. "I always call you when I need you. You're the best brother I have."

"Only brother you have," I replied as I hugged her tightly.

"Only one I need," she sniffled. "Talk to Mom. Please."

I didn't reply and instead gave her one last kiss on her cheek before I ducked out of her embrace. If I didn't leave now, I never would. When it came down to it, I always missed my baby sister.

An hour later I had made my way back to my niche in the northwest corner of Connecticut, even completed the usual supply run from the various stores around town. The SUV was full and I had nowhere else to go but back to the Facility for a nice evening with my girl. Ha! My girl. It still made me smile.

Although the last three weeks had been upsetting familywise, my time with Ashlyn had been amazing. Most days we met for lunch, and almost all of our evenings were spent together unless Ashlyn's newfound friends were declaring a girls' night, which I was happy for. Not only had Ashlyn adjusted to the Facility, she was thriving. She had made friends and had become very close to them in fact, which was something she had never had before.

The evenings we were together were spent mostly watching TV in either her room or mine, and yes, exploring our boundaries. Every night we got a little bit further. She was fighting to keep her shield up, and I was fighting to keep her past out of my head. But Katie had been right, I was falling in love with Ashlyn. At least I assumed I was. I had never been *in love* so to speak. I had had girlfriends, but I never felt the way I did when Ashlyn was in my arms, or even worse the loss I felt when she wasn't. That was how I knew this was different. With others I could have cared less what they were doing when we weren't together, but on the days Ashlyn would stay with her friends I found myself disappointed only because I wouldn't hear about her day until I showed up at her door to escort her to breakfast the next morning like a pitiful puppy.

Was this love? That was what I needed help with. Honestly it's what I needed my dad for. He would have been the one to talk about this with. Even after four years my nose still tingled at the thought of him.

Just then the radio stopped playing my favorite station and displayed that a call was coming through. The number was familiar and unexpected, causing me to clear my throat and shake away all thoughts of my father.

I pressed the button to accept the call. "Mom?"

There was a soft gasp on the other end of the phone before my mother spoke. "Joey? I...I didn't think you would answer. I was preparing to leave a voicemail."

"You can if you want."

"No, no! That's not...I was just surprised that's all."

"Ok, well your sister just called me. She says you're dating someone?"

I could kill my sister. I loved her, but I could kill her. "Uh...yep, I am. Is that why you called?"

She sighed through the phone. "No, I...I was calling to see if you were going to come to Mable's for family dinner tonight."

I slammed on the breaks as I came to a red light that I wasn't paying attention to, gripping the steering wheel tightly and looking in the rearview mirror hoping the dark blue car behind me wouldn't hit my rear bumper.

"Joey? Did you hear me?"

I waited for my adrenaline to wear off before I answered. "Yes."

"You're coming!"

"No, I heard you."

"Oh...so are you coming?"

"Will Paul be there?"

"Yes, he will be there."

I stepped on the accelerator, lurching the SUV forward and causing the back of my head to hit the headrest. "Then no."

"Joey, please," my mother whined.

"Mom, you and I need to talk..."

"I know, honey, I know we do but..."

"*Without* Paul," I interrupted as I continued through town, trying to concentrate on the road while I turned off Main Street and headed into the hills.

"Honey, I miss you. Can't we do dinner tonight, and then we'll talk tomorrow. Just you and me, I promise."

I was growling under my breath as I approached a stop sign. "Fine, Mom. I'll come to dinner," I said at the same time a nagging feeling urged me to look in my rearview mirror and notice the same dark blue car from earlier still behind me.

"Oh Joey, thank you. I can't wait to see you."

"Uh-huh," I answered as I pulled away from the stop sign, the dark blue car following several seconds later. "Tell Mable to give us a table for four."

"Four? Are you going to get Katie Bell?"

"No. I'm bringing Ashlyn," I replied as my eyes darted back and forth between the road ahead of me and the rearview mirror where the dark blue car was still following several feet behind.

"Ashlyn? Is…is that your new girlfriend?"

"Yep."

"It's not that I don't want to meet her, Joey, I do. But it's family dinner night."

"Exactly my point, Mom. Paul is not a part of our family."

"Honey, he will be soon. I need you two…"

"Mom, I'm not going to dinner with just you and Paul. Either I bring Ashlyn, or I don't come at all. I'm sorry but it has to be that way."

The line went silent for only a few seconds, although it felt like much longer. Finally, "Fine. I'll tell Mable 6:30?"

"Sounds good."

"Now if you could just promise that tonight you'll try and get along…"

"I really have to go, Mom. I'm on the road."

"Oh, ok. Well I love you, honey."

"Love you too, Mom."

I pressed the button to end the call so quickly I'm not even sure if my salutation came through. I did love her, I didn't want to hurt her feelings, but for some reason I had a bad feeling about this dark blue car that was still following me.

When I got this job I made it a point to know every turn and back road within a ten mile radius of the Facility. I had yet to use them, except for when the monotony of driving the same route became unbearable, but today it seemed as though it would pay off. As I headed deeper into the suburbs tucked deep within the hills, the dark blue car followed me at every turn. My fingers hovered over the button that would call the Facility directly, but I was hesitant to push it. What if this person just happened to live up here? If I called the Facility now, a security team would be on us so fast that this potentially poor bastard wouldn't know what hit him.

I stopped at the next stop sign where turning right would take me to the Facility, a left would go into a housing development. I didn't bother turning my blinker on and made the right turn, ready to press the call button when the dark blue car turned the opposite direction. Once the car disappeared from my sight I stopped my SUV, putting it fully in park and taking the time to catch my breath and allow my heart to stop beating out of my chest. In the three years that I had driven hybrids to and from the Facility, never had I ever felt that someone was following me. Warren's security team trained me and all my other drivers on what to look for, and how to lose a tail, but I had never had to use it.

What was it about that stupid car that had the hairs on my arm standing on end? Why was I so paranoid? Sadly just sitting here on the side of the road wouldn't give me any answers, so I put the SUV back into drive and continued the three miles to Facility East.

When I pulled up to the tall metal gate a few minutes later I had never been so relieved. The driveway stretched out before me and by the time I reached the massive garage my breath and heart rate were normal. I felt a little stupid for the reaction that I had about that car. When Cole and several other members of my staff came down to unload the SUV I didn't bother getting in their way. Being Vamps they could unload the truck and get it to where it belonged faster than I could, and honestly I needed to talk to my girl.

The lobby was buzzing as I walked through, several hybrids choosing to conduct an impromptu yoga routine while others merely watched them and ate snacks. A few of Ashlyn's friends had pushed some of the cushy chairs together in order to play a game of cards. When I stepped over to their group, Rebecca's head popped up.

"Hey Rebecca, have you seen Ashlyn?"

She nodded. "She's practicing with Eris. Training room B, I think. Oh, there's Sera, she'd probably know," she said pointing behind me.

I turned my head and caught a glimpse of Sera's blonde hair flowing behind her, similar to the flowing pink blouse she was wearing. I thanked Rebecca, ignoring the girlish giggling as I left their group, and called to Sera.

"Ah, Jonah, I take it zhat we have our supplies?" she asked.

"Yes ma'am. Is Ashlyn training with Eris again?"

"Oui, all afternoon. I am sure she wants you to rescue her from his torture. Follow me, I know where zhey are," she said as she crooked her arm around my elbow and led me down the hallway toward the training rooms. "I hope your sister is doing well?"

"Yes ma'am. She has a sufficient amount of junk food to get her through exams. I hope you don't mind me driving down there, it's been so slow here lately."

"Of course not, Jonah, you work so much longer than you are required.

I feel guilty when you do not take more time to see your family."

"Speaking of," I said with a sigh, "may I ask a favor?"

"Absolument," she replied.

"Huh?"

She smiled and patted my hand. "It means absolutely. Absolutely you can ask me a favor."

"Well, I was hoping I could take Ashlyn to Mable's tonight to meet my mother. I know you don't typically let new hybrids leave the premises..."

"Oui, oui, oui, you can take her. Jonah, zhat is wonderful. I zhink she will need it after her session with Eri today," she said, pulling me to a stop in front of training room B. Through the window I could see Eris standing at the far end of the room facing Ashlyn who had her back turned. "She seems to be having some difficulty today, poor dear. Perhaps you can help her."

"Me? What can I do?"

She smiled before turning away and continuing down the hallway. "I zhink you would be surprised, Jonah. Have fun tonight."

I loved Sera, she really was great to work for, but sometimes she was so mysterious it was eerie. When I looked through the slim training room window again, I saw Eris crouching to the ground, his teeth and fangs exposed, and I could hear the growls through the door. Immediately I opened the door and ran in.

"Wrong! Wrong, Ashlyn," Eris shouted. "Shield...up..."

"Eris what is..." but I didn't finish my thought as he fell over at his waist, resting his head on the thick blue canvas mat. The air in the room was thick and uncomfortable, and I realized it was probably from whatever Ashlyn was emitting. As soon as she heard my voice she turned in my direction and I could see the tears welling up in her eyes. While Eris remained crouched on the ground regaining control of himself, I walked slowly to Ashlyn and held my arms out in front of me. Her forehead easily fell onto my chest as I wrapped my arms around her.

"I can't do it, Jonah. I just can't do it."

"What is it you're trying to do?"

"Defense training," Eris answered instead as he stood from the mat and adjusted his shirt. "The thought is, if she can make people feel what she is, perhaps she could use it as a weapon."

"Since I can't use any other weapon they've given me," Ashlyn said begrudgingly from my chest, and thankfully she couldn't see Eris nodding his head in agreement. "Problem is, I can't do this either."

"That is not the problem, Ashlyn," Eris corrected. "You can do this, but you are emitting the wrong kind of emotions. I am the last person you want to make feel angry."

Ashlyn's head popped up from my chest, her eyes still a little teary. "I try feeling sad or scared, but then when nothing happens I get so mad at myself and then Eris has to hold himself to the ground he's so angry. I just can't think of the right things at the right time."

"*You* can't feel sad?" I asked shocked.

Eris took a step forward. "The feelings need to be debilitating to her opponent, Jonah."

"Oh, yeah, she can do that," I said positively and turned her around to face Eris.

Ashlyn squeezed my hand that rested on her shoulder. "Jonah, wait…"

"Ash, just trust me," I interrupted. "You do trust me, don't you?"

"Mmm-hmm," she replied tentatively.

I bent my head down to nestle into her ear. "Concentrate on where Eris is, then close your eyes." Ashlyn sighed but closed her eyes like I asked. "Can you picture where he is?" She nodded. "Ok, now think way back when you were little. Picture that rundown, moldy apartment you lived in with your mother, can you see it?" She nodded again.

"Now think about what it was like living there – hot in the summer, cold in the winter, empty cabinets, no food in the fridge. Think about going to school with dirty, ragged clothes that don't fit, the kids picking on you about the way you looked, the way you smelled. Coming home from school and finding your mother either passed out or with a client. Remember how you felt when you saw her being fed from, time and time again, watching her deteriorate right before your eyes."

Her breath became staggered and I squeezed her shoulder. "Remember that moment when she let a Vampire drink from you, sat and watched him sink his teeth into your neck. Made you feel guilty if you didn't do it, blamed you for not having food to eat because you wouldn't do it."

I looked forward and saw Eris sink down on one knee, his face contorting uncomfortably. It was working, but there needed to be more.

"Now think of that day you came home and your mother was gone. Waking up the next day and the next alone and with no money. You were scared and hungry, landlord screaming for rent, Vampires knocking at your door looking for a blood donor, and then those looking for more."

196 ~ C.R. QUINN

I took a deep breath and lowered my voice even further as I said, "And the time you gave in, letting that Vamp take the innocence from you and then leave you on the floor bleeding and sore. Desperate for money taking Vamp after Vamp, but then having your apartment condemned, having to live on the street, alone, scared, stripped of everything…"

"Stop…please," Eris begged from across the room. "For the love of all that is holy, please stop."

When I looked up again Eris was curled in a ball on the mat, red tears streaking his face and neck. From several feet away I could see that he was visibly shaken, literally shivering in front of us. I looked back down at Ashlyn and noticed that she had finally opened her eyes, her cheeks and neck just as wet as Eris's but with clear tears.

I kissed the side of her face and wrapped my arms tightly around her chest as I rocked her gently from side to side. "Now, think about how you'll never have to deal with any of that again. Now you have a roof over your head, three meals a day, new friends…"

"And you," she interjected as she twisted her head up and stole a kiss.

"Yeah, and me," I replied. "I told you that you could do it."

She gave a skeptical laugh. "When I have you in my ear I can."

"Those are your memories, Ash. You just have to tap into them at the right time. Just think, you are now the second woman to take Eris down, you should be proud."

Eris laughed from across the room. "And discrete, I hope. Ashlyn, I believe we are onto something. We shall practice more tomorrow."

Once Eris moved to gather his things, I took the opportunity to turn Ashlyn fully around in front of me.

"How do you feel?" I asked as I wiped her cheeks with my fingers.

"Ok. A little tired."

"Too tired to come out with me tonight?"

Ashlyn's eyes sparkled. "Come out where?"

"Now just breathe," I began, which only prompted her to hold her breath. "I need you to come with me to Mable's tonight and have dinner with my mother and her douchebag fiancé."

Ashlyn froze except for her eyelids that blinked slowly. "You want me…to meet…your mother?"

"Yes, and…well frankly be a buffer."

"When?"

"In about an hour."

"What!" she yelled. "You want me to…in an hour? An hour! What am I…I don't have anything to wear. Look at my hair, I'm a mess. Jeez, Jonah, give me a little more notice than an hour, it's your mother! I need a shower, and an outfit, I don't even have makeup…" Ashlyn continued to yell as she stepped around me, grabbed her bag from the floor, and walked toward the door.

"Ash? Come down to my room when you're ready?"

"Yeah, yeah. Your room, got it," she mumbled as the training room door slammed behind her.

"Damn I'm glad I'm a boy. I couldn't deal with everything she just threw at me. Did you feel that?"

Eris shook his head. "Thankfully, no. I believe I have had my fill of Miss Shaw's emotions today. Now you do know that you need to ask permission to take a hybrid from the premises," he asked lightly as he held the door open for me.

"Yes sir, I do. That's why I asked the boss."

Eris smiled and nodded. "Ah, good. My Sera-phin-a is definitely the boss, in every way. That is how we have stayed married so long."

"That's funny, I would think that you being, you know, *the* Eris, would make you the boss."

Eris patted me on the back as we began down the hall. "My young Jonah, you have so much to learn. Did your supply run go smoothly?"

I licked my lips, debating on what to say. But in the end, "Yes, everything went fine."

Chapter Twenty-one

Jonah

Once I was in my room it only took me twenty minutes to shower, shave, re-spike my hair, and put on a clean set of clothes. What I wasn't quite ready for was waiting around for another forty minutes. The TV was on in the background while I splayed out on my bed, staring up at the ceiling and thinking about all the ways this evening could go terribly wrong. Many scenarios ended with me punching Paul in the face. I liked those, except for the fact that Ashlyn would see me do it.

At the forty-four minute mark I could hear the tones of my room's code being entered on the keypad on the other side of the door.

"Finally," I muttered under my breath as I sat up from the bed and found my very flustered, although beautiful, girlfriend stepping through the door. Her hair was straightened and she looked incredibly sexy in a skirt, something she had yet to wear since we met.

"Boy you've got nice legs," I accidently said out loud, but it made Ashlyn drop her shoulders and laugh. "I'd apologize, but I wouldn't mean it. You look beautiful."

Ashlyn blushed as she stepped over to my bed. "The skirt is Emma's, the shirt is Lindsay's," she said as she pulled at each piece of her outfit. "The scarf and cardigan are Rebecca's. The only thing I'm wearing that is actually mine is my underwear."

"Thank goodness for that," I joked as I placed my hand on her hip and pulled her in front of me. "You really do look nice, too nice really. This isn't a fancy place or anything."

"But I'm meeting your mother, this is a big deal. I need to look...no, be perfect for you."

Ashlyn's hands were shaking at her sides, as was her bottom lip. I cupped her cheeks with my hands and pulled her face down to mine. "You are perfect. And there's nothing that my mother or anyone else could say that would ever change that in my mind. Ok?"

She nodded, though less than confidently. "I wore that perfume you like."

"You did, huh?" I replied, although I could smell it on her the minute she came through the door. I slid my hands from her face and pulled down on the center of the bright pink and blue scarf, freeing it completely from her neck. I tucked my head into the crook of her neck as I kissed her soft, fragrant skin. "Here?"

"Mmm-hmm," she moaned softly as I grazed my lips down the side of her neck and kissed lightly across her chest.

"And here?"

"Jonah, we don't..." she began but stopped her protests when my dissent down her chest reached the collar of her low cut shirt.

My fingers glided up the outsides of her thighs, not daring to go too far under her skirt, although I surely wanted to. Her fingernails were combing through my hair and scratching at the back of my neck, and in that moment I completely forgot about everything ahead. I loved her, and my heart was racing at the thought of saying it out loud.

Just as I lifted my head from her chest, thinking I could tell her at that moment, Ashlyn stepped away from me. "We're going to be late."

"I'll cancel. Let's stay here and see where this goes," I said with a devilish smile which unfortunately did not work.

Without another word Ashlyn picked her scarf up from the floor and tied it back around her neck. Next she pulled out the collar of my shirt which I hadn't noticed was flipped under and kissed me on the cheek. "Thank you for wearing my favorite shirt."

"Yeah, well...uh...I missed you today."

Ashlyn leaned down, brushing her nose against my cheek. "Maybe I could...a...stay in here tonight?"

I pulled my head back slightly to look her in the eye. Had we finally made it to that step? We'd been floating around it, especially the last few days, but was she hinting at it now?

"Jonah?"

"Yeah! Uh…yes…sorry," I replied and then kissed her nose. "I'd really like that."

Ashlyn smiled and pulled me up from the bed, as usual only coming up to my chest when she wore her flat shoes. I bent down to pick up her colorful patchwork bag from the floor and handed it to her before guiding her to the door.

"Wait," she said and pulled away from me, "I need to freshen up."

I looked at my watch and worried about the time. "Your makeup is fine, Ash."

Ashlyn stepped into the bathroom but turned around and looked at me from the doorway. "No…uh, much lower than my face."

Oh. Awesome.

"Sorry," I said, feeling the blood rush into my lower body.

"No you're not," she replied with devilish smile and disappeared into the bathroom.

And she was right, I wasn't sorry that I'd made her wet. Just the thought of it coming from between her legs made me bulge and have to adjust myself. Damn it. I started thinking about work, rotting meat, maggots coming out of the rotting meat, anything to get this damn erection to go away. Boy I wanted Ashlyn bad. This was just the thing I needed before going to see my mom. My mom! Ah, that did it. Problem solved. Now I just needed to do the hip shake for the final adjustment.

"What are you doing?" Ashlyn asked behind me.

I fixed my shirt and turned around to see her giving me a coy smile. "Just tucking in my shirt. Ready?"

She nodded and hung her bag across her body, giving me a look that said she didn't believe my explanation. I took her hand and pulled her from my room, suddenly a little nervous myself. I hoped that Ashlyn had her shield up and she wasn't reading me.

A few minutes later I was securing her into my Camaro, choosing to take her for a ride in my real car making tonight feel more like a date, sadly something we hadn't had. Of course she had seen my car, sat in it and admired my pristine interior. But tonight I would be driving my girl in my silver baby, I couldn't be more excited.

Ashlyn laughed at my goofy smile as I revved the engine and tore down the long tree-lined driveway.

"I can't believe Brianna just gave you this car."

"Hey now," I corrected, "I paid a dollar for this baby."

"You were pretty lucky to meet Brianna."

"You don't have to tell me," I sighed. "I'm not sure where I am going to escape to when I need a break from my family."

"Speaking of," Ashlyn began as she placed her hand on top of mine on the gearshift, "are you sure you want me to come with you tonight?"

"Of course I do," I replied.

"But it's the first time you're seeing your mom since…"

"My flip out?"

"That's not what I was going to say."

"That's what Katie called it," I laughed and downshifted to make the right turn onto the main road that would bring us into town. "I need you there tonight, Ash. I just need you there to help me…not…blow up again."

Ashlyn looked out the passenger side window as she squeezed my hand and placed it on her bare knee. Although I loved the feeling of her leg, I hated feeling it shake with nerves underneath my hand.

"Ash, the last thing I want to do is make you feel this way. I'll turn around right now if you want me to."

Through the corner of my eye I could see her shaking her head. "No, I need to do this. It's just…"

I squeezed her knee when she didn't finish her thought. "Talk to me, Ash."

"Can you turn on the heat? My legs are freezing."

I did as she asked, and while we waited for the heater to warm up I hoped that she would open up. Just as we entered the more incorporated part of town, she finally said, "It's just something that Emma said while she was doing my hair."

"And that was?"

She hesitated again. "Just that…she said that when it comes to sons, mothers can see into the soul of his girlfriend and see all her sins."

Thank goodness we had come to a red light, otherwise I would have slammed on the breaks. "First of all, that was a shitty thing for Emma to say. Second, my mother doesn't have any kind of psychic or x-ray vision. The only sins she'll know about are the ones you tell her."

"Mothers always know. They can tell when their son is dating…"

"A blonde? A Pisces? A short person?"

"I am not short."

"Ash, some children are taller than you."

"Not true," she said and hit me in the arm.

"Hey! Face it, you're tiny. And my mom is going to love you. Now Paul, he may like you but you cannot like him in any way. I mean that."

"How was Katie?" she replied, obviously changing the subject when the light turned green and I had to start shifting again.

"She's good. She can't wait to meet you."

"Oh god," she groaned. "I have to get through your mother *and* your sister."

"And Mable," I corrected as the driveway of The Maple Inn came up on our right.

Ashlyn leaned forward toward the dashboard, her eyes wide and mouth gapping open as she gazed upon the large Victorian home with its intricate and colorful detailing. It was the most beautiful place I had ever seen, inside and out, and from the look on Ashlyn's face I think she agreed with me.

"I thought we were going to a restaurant."

I shook my head as I pulled into the driveway. "It's an inn and restaurant. Breakfast is for the guests, but teatime and dinner is open to the public. Unless you're me, I get to eat anytime I want."

Ashlyn pointed behind her as I drove around to the back of the house. "Don't you need to park in front?"

I laughed loudly as I pulled into a parking spot nestled in the corner. "Mable would tear my hide, her words not mine, if I dared to park in front. Family and guests are asked to park here and come in through the backdoor." After putting the car in park and turning it off, I watched the color drain from Ashlyn's face. "Ok, last chance. I can still take you back to the Facility since you look like you're going to throw up."

"No, I'm ready," she replied and went to open her door.

"No, no, wait, wait, wait," I said, quickly unbuckling my seatbelt and opening my door. Through the windows I could see Ashlyn watching me as I ran around the car, finally coming to her door and opening it. I extended my hand and she looked at it and then up to me. "You're supposed to take my hand, Ash."

Slowly she placed her hand in mine and I helped her out of the car, once again enjoying the sight of her beautiful legs. She stood next to the car while I closed her door, and every part of her body was shaking with nerves. Ashlyn crossed her arms tightly in front of her chest while she chewed on her bottom lip.

I wrapped my left arm around her and tilted her chin up with my right. "Don't be nervous. You look beautiful and you have nothing to worry about. You're not prone to fighting in this place like I am."

When she smiled, her shoulders relaxed and she uncrossed her arms. I took her hand and pulled it through the crook of my arm before escorting her across the gravel parking lot to the backdoor that led right into Mable's kitchen. Ashlyn was squeezing the crap out of my hand, and I don't think she was breathing. I looked down at her, seeing that she was chewing on her bottom lip again.

I took one of the many charms that hung from the zipper of her bag and shook it. "What's this one from?"

"Hmm?" she replied looking up me, and then at the red, white, and blue ribbon that held a gold medal at its end. "Uh…that one? Um…middle school spelling bee."

"And what's that from?" I asked and pointed to a fuzzy pink patch of fabric.

"My baby blanket," she replied and rubbed it in such a way that it seemed to comfort her. "I wasn't joking when I said it was my life."

"That's why I like it." I kissed her temple. "Ready?"

"Not in the slightest."

I laughed as I opened the door and pulled Ashlyn into Mable's small, but well-oiled machine of a kitchen. Mable was at her large stove wiping her hands on her apron when her face lit up at the sight of me and Ashlyn. I held my arms out wide as I said, "Please tell me there's a piece of meatloaf for me in the fridge."

Mable raise one eyebrow and pursed her lips in disapproval. "Don't you even think about asking for meatloaf tonight. If you want meatloaf you need to come on Tuesday nights from now on, you hear me?"

"Yes ma'am," I nodded.

"Missed you, honey," she said and patted my back.

"Sorry I haven't been around, but there's someone I want you to meet." I opened up to face Ashlyn, and I was happy to see that the fear had finally left her eyes. "Mable, this is Ashlyn Shaw, Ashlyn this is…"

But I couldn't finish since Mable pushed me behind her and immediately hugged Ashlyn. "I'm sorry, Ashlyn, I'm a hugger. Welcome, welcome, welcome," she said as she patted her back. When she released her, Mable was bubbly with laughter as she checked out Ashlyn from head to toe and then finally patted her cheeks. "Jonah, she is just the cutest little thing I've ever seen. When yur mama told me you were bringin' a girl, I just about lost my drawers."

While Mable continued to gush and giggle over my girlfriend, Ashlyn began to scarily mimic her. Was her shield down already? Afraid that I needed to quickly take over the situation, I put my arm around Ashlyn and said to Mable, "Are they here yet?"

Mable's mood instantly changed. "Yes they are. Can you promise me everyone'll be on their best behavior? I don't want people thinkin' this is one a them reality TV shows."

"Yes ma'am," I replied before giving her a kiss on the cheek. Quickly I pulled a still giggling Ashlyn into my side and pulled her into the dining room. I looked down at her and whispered in her ear, "Is your shield down?"

Ashlyn put her hand up to her mouth to hide her laughter. "Sorry, I just couldn't help it. She is very…spirited? She poked right through my shield and I just had to feel it. I'll put it back up now."

"Yeah, I would since there's my mother…standing and waving like a crazy woman."

My mother was waving at us from across the room like we couldn't see her from thirty feet away. Ashlyn's bubbly mood quickly turned back to a nervous ball of energy. My mother stepped around to the front of her table while Paul remained in his chair up against the wall. Tentatively my mother's arms stretched out in front of her, and for a moment I could see she was worried I wouldn't reciprocate. But she was my mom, I couldn't help but want her affection.

"Hi, Mom," I said as I hugged her and she gave me her signature two kisses on my cheeks and a rub up my back.

"I'm glad you came," she said as she stepped back and looked over my shoulder. "And this is?"

I opened up and pulled Ashlyn forward. "Ashlyn, this is my mother Jennifer Thorne. Mom, this is Ashlyn Shaw."

"Nice to meet you, Ashlyn," my mother said as she extended her hand and Ashlyn shook it nervously. "But please call me Jenny. I'm so happy you're here. I can't remember the last time Joey brought a girl home to meet me."

"Joey?" Ashlyn replied confused.

"Oh, that's what we've called Jonah since he was a baby. He's our little Joey, aren't you, honey?"

"Mom," I whined and looked away, causing both my mother and Ashlyn to laugh.

My mother put her arm around Ashlyn and pulled her over to the table where Paul finally stood from his chair. "Ashlyn, this is my fiancé Paul Redding."

My jaw clamped down as douchebag Paul extended his douchebag arm and shook my girlfriend's hand.

"*Doctor* Paul Redding," he corrected.

Doctor Douchebag was more like it.

Ashlyn forced a smile as she shook Paul's hand, and a moment later sat down in the chair I held out for her across from my mother.

"So Ashlyn, are you from around here?" my mother asked.

"Um, Atlanta actually," Ashlyn answered in a timid voice.

"Really?" Paul responded skeptically. "You don't have an accent."

I wanted to punch him in the face, but Ashlyn took it in stride. "I moved around a lot."

"What brings you up here?" my mother asked as she looked at her menu, which prompted me to do the same since Mable hadn't saved me any meatloaf from the night before. But when I noticed that Ashlyn was giving her menu the death grip I answered for her. "She works at the Facility, Mom."

My mother raised her eyebrows in surprise. "Really? You do private security? You look so harmless."

"Mom," I whined again and eyed my mother.

"What?" she replied defensively. "I was just saying that…"

"Interrogations," Ashlyn interrupted. "I'm training in interrogations."

It was Paul's turn to raise his eyebrows in surprise. "Interesting. What drove you toward that career choice?"

Ashlyn swallowed before saying, "I can…read people."

"Well, at least you have a plan, Ashlyn," Paul said but looked at me.

I felt Ashlyn's hand on my thigh, and I instantly felt a wave of relaxation and warmth helping me to keep my mouth shut. Thankfully the waitress came to our table at that exact moment.

"Good evening, my name's Kim and I'll be taking care of you," she said as she flipped open her small writing pad. She had to be new because I'd never seen her before, and must still be in high school since she didn't look more than seventeen. "Also, Mable told me to tell you all that there is no meatloaf tonight…no, that there is no meatloaf in the entire place so, and these are her words, 'don't go askin.' I hope you know what that all means." Everyone at the table gave a quiet laugh and nodded. "Ok good. So what can I get everyone?"

Paul handed his menu to Kim. "The lady and I will both have the shepherd's pie."

I looked over the top of my menu and watched my mother's face fall before surrendering her menu, but she instantly put on a fake smile when she caught me looking at her.

"I'll have the burger," I said, keeping my eyes on my mother for another few seconds until I realized Ashlyn wasn't giving her order. I looked down to my left and noticed that Ashlyn's bottom lip had disappeared into her mouth while her eyes darted up and down the one page menu. "Ash?"

"Uh…um…." she stuttered, "uh…the…turkey club?"

Kim happily took Ashlyn's menu and stepped away from the table.

"That's so funny, Ashlyn," my mother began, "Mable's turkey club is my daughter's favorite too."

"Jonah's been trying to get me to try a turkey club since we were in Boston, but we ate at this terrible place," Ashlyn said with a laugh, but a second later her face fell and she quickly looked back at my mother.

"Oh, Jonah took you to Boston? So Brianna meets your girlfriend before I do," my mother said snidely.

Ashlyn looked worriedly at me. "Was I not supposed…"

"Mom, not that it matters, but Ashlyn and I didn't start dating until after we got back from Boston. Ashlyn was in Boston for training, it was just a coincidence that we were both staying with Brianna. What's your beef with her lately? Brianna has been very good to our family. If it weren't for her and Cameron we wouldn't have a roof over our head, and Katie wouldn't be in college."

"Joey," my mother responded in a flustered tone, "you make it sound like we owe everything we have to her."

"Because we do! If Bri and Cameron hadn't helped me get the job at the Facility, who knows where we would be."

"Oh that place," my mother huffed loudly.

"Now you have a problem with where I work?"

"Paul told me about the guns, Joey."

"It's private security, Mom. Of course there are going to be guns."

"But to draw them on innocent people? Paul was only there to see you and he was nearly killed."

"Innocent?" I replied, almost laughing. "Is that what he told you? He..."

"So Paul, what are you a doctor of?" Ashlyn interrupted, causing me and my mother to go back to our corners so to speak.

Paul adjusted the collar of his shirt as he proudly answered, "I am a doctor of psychology. I have a practice in town. Now how long have you been working as an interrogator?"

Ashlyn licked her lips nervously before she answered, "Not working yet, just training. But I've been at the Facility for a few weeks now."

"And you live there as well?"

"Yes, but everyone does."

Paul crossed his arms in front of him, and had that cocky smirk on his face that I hated. "It isn't against the rules for staff and students to be dating each other? It seems to me that..."

"Ashlyn isn't a student, Paul, and I am not a teacher," I interrupted. "I do think, however, there are rules about patient doctor relations, but you didn't seem to really care about that now, did you?"

"Jonah!" my mother hissed and looked around to see if anyone had heard my statement. "You promised..."

"Did you make *him* promise?" I fired back.

Ashlyn squeezed my hand as she said, "How was your visit with Katie today?"

I sighed and let my temper die down. "It was good," I replied and then looked at my mother. "She looks good."

"I always worry about my Katie Bell near exams," she said to Ashlyn. "Last year she barely ate during her finals and came home just skin and bones."

"Which is why I made sure she had groceries today, Mom."

"But if she needed groceries, why didn't she call me? I would have gone down."

Because I am the one who always takes care of her. I am the one she can count on if she needs something. She didn't need to call me, I knew she'd be getting low on her groceries and that her exams were coming up. And she didn't eat last spring because you had told her that you were dating your therapist and in her eyes you were replacing her father with a tool bag named Paul, oh sorry, *doctor* Paul.

Ashlyn's hand was squeezing mine so hard I couldn't feel my fingers. I must have been putting out some angry vibes. Although I had wanted to tell my mom all those things I only responded, "I don't know, Mom. She probably thought you were working."

Thankfully at that moment Kim and Mable came alongside our table with plates in their hands. Mable put my plate down in front of me first, and immediately I knew something was up. I had ordered her classic burger, but what was sitting in between the bun on my plate was not a burger. Actually, it looked like meatloaf. When I looked up, Mable gave me a wink.

"Pardon me, Mable," Paul began and pointed to me as I took a bite of my meatloaf sandwich, "that looks awfully like a piece of meatloaf."

Mable smacked Paul in the shoulder. "Now Paul, don't go callin' me a liar. I told you all I didn't have any meatloaf tonight. Now that there is my signature burger."

"Tomato sauce is leaking out of it."

"It's ketchup," Mable said giving Paul a stink eye. "Now, Miss Ashlyn, Katie usually finishes that whole sandwich, so you got some competition."

Ashlyn couldn't answer because her mouth was already stuffed.

"Trust me, Mable, Ashlyn has a big appetite. I bet she'll beat Katie's record by five minutes."

Ashlyn nudged me in the side with her elbow, her sandwich never leaving her hand.

"So, Ashlyn, will you be joining us here for Thanksgiving? Or spending it with your family?"

Ashlyn cleared her throat and reluctantly put her sandwich down. "I…uh…don't have any family."

"Oh dear," Mable moaned as she placed her hand on her heart. "I didn't…I hope I didn't upset you."

"Not at all. My mom's been gone for a while now."

"Then that just means you'll be with us," Mable said cheerily. "And I make the best pies in a twenty mile radius. I'll go ahead and put down a reservation."

"Actually, Mable, I think we'll be staying home this year," my mother chimed in and I almost snapped my neck turning to look at her.

"Why? Why would we be staying home?"

My mother looked at me as if I had asked an absurd question. "I thought I would cook this year. I used to do it every year, remember?"

"But it's been our tradition the last few years to come here."

"And before that, our tradition was to say home," my mother replied sternly. "We can talk about this later, Joey, we're keeping Mable."

"You're right, Mom. Mable put in a reservation for me and Ashlyn. We'll be here on Thanksgiving."

Mable wrung her hands in her apron as she excused herself from our table. For the first time in years my mother's face was contorted into the expression she usually gave me when she was about to lay out my punishment.

"Joey, what has gotten into you?"

"Me? Why are you suddenly trying to make us out to be the family we're not? Is it because Ashlyn's here? Because we don't need to pretend in front of her, she knows what our life has been like since Dad died."

"Jonah," Ashlyn warned softly at the same time my mother went to defend herself, only Paul put his hand up in front of her.

"Jenny, let me handle this," Paul said in a cocky tone. "Jonah, your mother is tired. These last few years have been extremely difficult for her, and your constant need to push her aside and fill her role with other women has been detrimental to this family. Putting this family back together begins with you choosing your mother over this Brianna woman and even Mable."

My cheeks were on fire while Paul spoke down to me like a child. My mother was looking down at her napkin, the floor next to her, her plate, everything else but me. My heart was beating out of my chest, and I could feel Ashlyn's pleading stare burning a hole into the side of my face. With a slow breath I stood from my chair and gestured for Ashlyn to follow me. Although my breath was slow, every nerve in my body was on fire. It took every ounce of control I had to turn and step away from the table with Ashlyn clinging to my arm.

My back was barely turned when Paul had to finish with, "Your attitude is killing this family, and we're tired of it, Jonah."

I slipped my arm out of Ashlyn's grip and turned quickly back to the table, instantly pointing my index finger inches from Paul's face.

"You know what I'm tired of?" I growled. "I'm tired of you." Then I looked to my mother. "I'm also tired of being made to feel guilty for taking time for myself. I go to see Brianna because she takes care of me for once since every other goddamn day I have been taking care of you and

Katie. I come here to see Mable because she makes me happy, she makes me feel like I matter to her."

"You matter to me, Joey," my mother whined. "If you were so unhappy why did you…"

"Because I had to, Mom! I kept up the house because you looked to me to do it. I took care of Katie because you left me to do it. I sent Katie to college because you expected me to do it. I gave up everything for you – my education, my friends, everything! And you don't even seem to care. You spit on those few people I have in my life and what they do for me, and us. The only thing worse was letting this snake into…our lives…" I stuttered as an uncontrollable laugh came over me. "He's…why Katie…doesn't come home."

Suddenly the entire dining room burst into boisterous laughter, including my mother although it didn't stop her from talking. "You…could have…said something," she said through her laughs.

"To whom?" I replied, holding my sides since it sounded like the funniest thing in the world. "You weren't around."

"My husband died!"

"I know…but Katie and I lived."

"But I…wanted him."

I couldn't understand why I was laughing so hard, or why everyone was joining in like we were all inhaling laughing gas. I also didn't care that Ashlyn jerked me away from the table, pulling me through the dining room and into the kitchen where Mable and her staff were holding themselves up against the walls while they laughed uncontrollably.

When we finally got outside, the cold air seemed to clear my head a little as we made our way to my car. Ashlyn took my keys from my pocket since I was still laughing too hard to find them. Eventually she opened the driver's side door and lowered me into the seat. When she finally closed the door and began to walk around the car all my laughter stopped.

By the time Ashlyn got in the car and handed me my keys I almost felt like myself again. Silently I started the car and once I pulled out of the driveway of The Maple Inn all my anger from earlier had settled back into my bones. I peered over at Ashlyn who was looking out her window and wiping her eyes.

"Did you do that in there? Make everyone laugh?"

From the corner of my eye I could see her nodding. "Y-yes."

I clamped my jaw and swallowed as I shifted gears. "Why?"

"I couldn't let you do it. I couldn't stand and watch you all destroy each other like that. I just couldn't, Jonah."

She continued to cry and I gripped the steering wheel so hard I thought it might bend in my hands. When I hit the second red light in a row, I turned off the main road and headed down a back road that would add a few minutes to our trip, but frankly I didn't care just as long as I could keep driving. Tonight was such a bad idea. I knew I should have waited to talk to Mom one on one. But no, I had to give in and bring my girlfriend into my warped family dynamic, and then she went and made the entire dining room sound like we were in a comedy club. How in the world would I explain what happened? How would my mother and I recover from this?

She thinks I replaced her with Brianna?! And Mable? We stayed afloat because of Brianna. We started family dinner night at Mable's and it helped us reconnect. I've given up four years of my life for her, doing things she should have been doing and she says I'm the reason for our troubles? Me? Me!

"Are you fucking kidding!" I yelled and hit the steering wheel. The right hand shoulder widened into a dirt pull-off and that's exactly what I did. As soon as the car was in park I turned the engine off, unbuckled my seatbelt, and stepped out of the car, unfortunately slamming the car door behind me. I stepped around to the back of car, kicking the first rock I saw into the adjacent woods.

"FFFUUUUCK!" I screamed as loud as I could up to the sky. My chest began to burn as I heaved the cold autumn air in and out of my lungs. Years of pent up anger and resentment and sadness were finally coming out of me. I let my love for my mother and sister, and my devotion to my father, determine my life for the last four years never once taking a step out to look in and see how messed up things had gotten.

A shiver went up my spine as a cold breeze went through my shirt. After taking a few deep breaths I slowly made my way back into the car. When I closed the door and reached to start the car again I realized that Ashlyn was still sniffling at the passenger side window.

"Ash…"

"Jonah, I'm sorry," she whimpered. "I know you said never to do that to you, but I couldn't help it. I couldn't let you and your mother say those things to each other in front of all those people. Please, please, just forgive me, I won't do it again. I promise."

Ashlyn's body was shaking as she huddled into the passenger side door, propping her head in her hand as she cried into it.

"Ash, do you think I'm mad at you?" Slowly she turned her head and nodded with tears streaking down her cheeks. I unbuckled her seatbelt and pulled her into my chest, putting my hands into her hair and kissing the top of her head. "Ashlyn, I'm so sorry. I'm not mad at you, not in the slightest. If you hadn't done that who knows what would have happened."

Ashlyn tilted her head up to look at me. "You're not mad?"

"I am mad, but not at you." I wiped the tears away from her cheeks with my thumbs, cursing the center console for not allowing her to get closer. "I'm sorry I ruined everything tonight."

"She doesn't love him, you know," she said sadly.

"Who? My mother?"

She nodded. "She doesn't love Paul."

I blinked. "How…how do you know that?"

"Her body language for one," Ashlyn replied. "Didn't you see how far away she sat from him? Every time Paul started to talk she would look away, and most of the time she felt embarrassed or angry at what he said but there was this…this…" She took a breath as she tried finding her words. "I don't know, a block of some kind. She's…I don't know, resolved? She doesn't want to be with him, but she accepts it."

"Then why is she marrying him," I growled. "She loved my father so much, she knew what a real marriage was about. Why in the world would she go to the complete opposite?"

Ashlyn grazed my forearm with her fingertips, causing another wave of warmth and relaxation to rush through me. "I don't know. I just know she doesn't love him because…she doesn't feel the way I feel when I'm with you."

The car became quiet and serious as we stared intensely into each other's eyes. My heart was racing, once again struggling to verbalize my feelings for her.

"Do you know how beautiful you are?" I said as I moved my hand deep into her thick blonde hair.

"I know how beautiful you make me feel," she replied as she slowly pulled her scarf from around her neck and tossed it in the floor.

It was difficult to swallow the lump in my throat as I watched her take off her cardigan, showing the simple black camisole and her slim, pale shoulders. I grazed my fingers down the length of her arm, excited by the goosebumps that formed. Slowly she leaned across me, her lips sucking at my neck and climbing up to the edge of my jaw. My breath quickened as Ashlyn's fingers combed through my hair causing a fury within me to kiss her.

In mere seconds the passion between us exploded as our mouths, lips, and tongues collided and fought for more of each other. I wrapped my arm around Ashlyn's waist and pulled her clumsily across the center console. Her bare legs straddled me on either side creating such heat between them it made things stir underneath my pants. Both of my hands immediately went to her legs, rubbing up the outside of her thighs and following where they bent into the dimples of her hips.

Ashlyn's kisses softened as she sighed pleasurably on the tops of my lips while her fingers fumbled to unbutton my shirt. I kneaded my fingers deeper into her hips, slipping my thumbs under the lace edge of her underwear, the action of which was causing her inner thighs to tremble. I wanted her so bad, and from the force at which she pulled my shirt open and slid her hands underneath my T-shirt I had a feeling she wanted me as well.

When my fingers slid underneath the straps of her camisole she rose up in front of me, her eyes blazing seductively into mine. I pulled the straps off her shoulders bringing the top of the camisole to rest at the base of her stomach. She hadn't worn a bra and her small, perfect breasts were shining right at me. Up until now I had only snuck my hand into the cup of her bra, but now the most perfect breasts I had ever seen were inches away from me. Ashlyn looked at me expectantly, seemingly wondering if I was going to do anything or not.

Not wanting to keep her waiting a second longer, I wrapped my right arm around her waist, bringing her closer to me as I sucked her right breast into my mouth. My tongue played and flicked around her nipple until it constricted and rose into a firm point. A loud moan came out of Ashlyn, the timbre which I had yet to hear in any of our make out sessions, and also one that made me fully aroused. My free hand went up the backside of her thigh, once again going underneath her skirt around to her backside.

Ashlyn pulled me away from her breast, bringing my lips back to hers as she began rolling her pelvis into mine. Although her movements were incredibly arousing, they were also grinding my zipper into my hard penis which was already being mushed in the wrong direction.

"What's wrong?" Ashlyn asked breathlessly as I winced in pain.

"Yeah," I replied with another wince as she shifted her weight in the wrong place. "I just need...to adjust."

With a seductive smile, Ashlyn took my hands away from the button of my jeans and replaced them with her own. "Let me."

Gently she rested her lips on mine, being sure to keep her eyes open to watch my reaction as she unzipped my jeans and slid her hand down into my boxers. Firmly she took my penis into her hand and pulled it upright. Gingerly she began to stroke me up and down with her fingers, her breasts grazing my chest as she did so. This was going to happen. All the foreplay from the last few weeks led naturally to this, and yet it was exciting to finally be in this moment. With my left hand I pulled one side of her underwear down her leg as far as it would go, causing Ashlyn to have to adjust slightly to bring her leg up far enough to be able to slip them down and off her ankle. The front of my boxers quickly became wet and sticky, and the heat coming from between her legs as she rested herself on top of me made it difficult to wait another second to be inside of her.

I pulled my boxers and jeans down from my hips while Ashlyn leaned across to the passenger seat where her hand disappeared deep inside her patchwork bag. A few seconds later she came out with a condom between her fingers. I cannot describe what came over me at the moment, but it certainly wasn't what I assume most guys' reaction would have been. Instead of thinking, oh good I'm glad you have protection, all I wondered was where she had gotten the condom from. Did she always carry them with her? To which another thought came along that of course she had to always carry them in her former line of work. These thoughts of course we're helped by the sight of Ashlyn tearing the condom wrapper with her teeth, pulling the condom free from the package, and then unrolling it down the length of my penis in seconds. To say the least, she was a pro.

I looked up at Ashlyn as she rose up on her knees, effectively preparing herself to slide down onto me. All the excitement and nervousness I felt before had left me, and in its place were horrible thoughts and comparisons to what her experience really was. The worries I had had for weeks were making my stomach turn. Suddenly I felt horribly inadequate, and the fact that our first time together was inside my car on the side of the road disgusted me.

"Jonah?" Ashlyn asked softly as she hovered near my lips, her eyes full of worry as she slowly lowered herself back down onto my lap. "What's wrong? What did I do wrong?"

"Nothing," I replied immediately as I cupped her cheeks with my hands. "Absolutely nothing, it's…it's me, Ashlyn. It's totally me."

Tears quickly filled her eyes, cresting her bottom lids and dripping down on my hands. "I knew it. I knew my past would get in the way."

"Just let me…"

"That's it, isn't it?" she said angrily as she pushed my hands off her face.

"Yes…" I began, causing her to sob into her own hands. "And no. Just let me explain." I exhaled slowly and hit the back of my head into the headrest while Ashlyn's cries grew louder. "I'm sorry, Ashlyn, I am. I feel like such an asshole."

Ashlyn shook her head and wiped her tears away with her fingers. "No you're not. You deserve better."

"No, Ashlyn, you deserve better," I replied firmly as she leaned down into my chest. "That's what I'm trying to say. I want our first time…no, I need our first time to be special. I need it to be memorable for you. You deserve candles, and rose petals, not a gear shift digging into your leg. This just isn't right, it needs to be special."

"Our first time will be special no matter what, don't you see?" she said as she rose back up in front of me. "It'll be the first time I do this because I want to. I can't think of anything more special than that, but…"

"There are no buts," I said as I cupped her face firmly once again between my hands. "We are going to do this, Ashlyn. You are the sexiest thing I have ever seen, and saying no to you right now goes against every urge I have. But…I need to stop because you shouldn't be treated like some piece of tail, you are a lady."

Ashlyn's breath caught in her throat as her bottom lip trembled uncontrollably. "A…a lady?"

"Well…a really hot lady," I replied with a laugh and got her to laugh with me. "I need to do for you what no one else has, and that is respect you for the woman you are. Can you let me do that?" Ashlyn nodded as her stomach growled loudly, causing us both to laugh again. "I need to get you back and get something to eat. It won't be a match for Mable's turkey club, though."

Ashlyn laughed again, and at the same time her face was illuminated by a pair of bright white lights. Immediately she covered her chest with her arms and ducked down into my chest. "Someone's coming," she said as she peered through the back window over my shoulder.

I ducked down as well, looking into the side mirror and watching the headlights cut off and the car pull in roughly fifty feet behind us. "I think it might be a cop. We should get dressed, and quick."

Ashlyn pulled her camisole back up over her chest, and struggled to get over the center console to her seat. While we finished dressing ourselves I kept an eye on the car through the rearview mirror, but no one got out of the car. Was this really a cop, or a voyeur who just happened to be passing by? I put my car in gear and waited for lights and sirens to blare, but nothing. Not knowing what else to do, I slowly pulled back onto the road.

"Everything ok?" Ashlyn asked nervously.

"Yeah, I think we're good. He's not coming after us. Probably just wanted to scare us into moving on."

Ashlyn curled her body around my arm, nuzzling her head into the crook of my shoulder. "So…can I still stay with you tonight?"

"Hell, yeah!" I replied excitedly. "But I have an early morning. Diana's coming tomorrow. The ice queen cometh!"

Ashlyn laughed but at the same time my stomach dropped slightly when the mystery car pulled a U-turn. Not only did he not turn his headlights on as he drove in the opposite direction, but the moonlight caught his path and it was now easy to see that it was not a cop car, but a dark colored sedan.

"Jonah? Are you sure everything's ok?"

"Yeah. That car just seemed familiar, but it's nothing to worry about."

It was the first time I had flat out lied to my girlfriend.

Chapter Twenty-two

Cameron

Moving day had finally arrived. With it came tears, irritability, and arguments, which I had prepared myself for and my Bri more than delivered. Could we have moved ourselves? Certainly. Did I hope that hiring professional movers would ease Brianna's stress level? Absolutely. Was I correct? No. Having strangers in the house only made Brianna more paranoid about being exposed for what we were. However, having been a Vampire for several centuries I knew very well how to keep our secret. Rule one was to stay calm and not draw attention to the fact that you were trying to hide something. Now I loved Brianna very much, but frankly she was horrible at this. She was so overbearing about everything the movers did that I chose to stay out of her way and read the newspaper as slow as I possibly could at the kitchen island.

Because we were reducing from a four bedroom house to merely three rooms at the manor, only personal items, a few of our favorite furniture pieces, and the children's bedroom sets were going to California. Everything else would be kept here to maintain a fully furnished residence for whenever a Warrior or family member needed a place to stay. In a way I think it was even more difficult for Brianna to handle that strangers would be in the place she had made our home while she was across the country sharing a mansion with sixty other people. Anyone could understand her sadness and anxiety, but it did not change what we needed to do.

While the movers kept busy downstairs in the living room, Brianna came up to the second floor with several flattened boxes underneath her arm. When I gave her a questioning look over the top edge of my newspaper she said, "I know they're professionals, but I just don't trust them with the crystal."

"We have crystal?"

Apparently that was not an appropriate question since she glared at me in response. "Yes we have crystal. What do you think all those glasses in the china cabinet are?"

"I thought you and Renee found those at a flea market," I responded and slowly folded down my newspaper.

"That doesn't mean it's not crystal."

"Love, each glass cost a dollar. I think that the movers…"

"I'm going to pack it, ok!" she shouted just as the twins ran from their bedroom squealing at the top of their lungs. Having incredible hearing of their own, it always surprised me how our twins did not understand how painfully loud they could be. Their volume and running down the hall when they should not have been was not lost on their mother and she simply snapped. "What did I say about today!"

The twin's joyful sprints stopped abruptly, their eyes large and fearful as they looked up at their mother and replied in unison, "No running."

"And?" Brianna said sternly.

"No screaming."

"Mama and Ada need you to stay out of the way of the movers," Brianna said in a more guarded tone. "Now back to your room, please."

Without another word the twins turned around and took several slow steps down the hall before looking devilishly at one another and running back into their bedroom. Brianna paused for a moment before she threw the flattened boxes down on the floor and pushed her hands up her face and through her long straight hair. "I didn't mean to yell at them."

"Of course not, angel," I said as I pushed myself up from the kitchen island and stepped over to the dining room. When I came to stand directly in front of her she rested her forehead on my chest and I instinctively wrapped my arms around her. "I know this is hard."

"Very hard," she replied sadly. "And I have to do it again when we get to Daddy O's. I don't…" she paused as she lifted her head, quickly wiping a reddish tear from her eye before it could drip down and stain her cheek, "…I'm not sure how I'm going to make it through."

I brushed away her bangs that always seem to fall into her eyes and tucked them behind her ear. "Everyone knows how difficult this is for you. You just need to trust that we are all here to help."

"Are you ready to kick me to the curb yet?" she laughed.

"Maybe just to the front porch."

Brianna laughed again as she bent down to pick up the flattened boxes from the floor. "The movers are almost done downstairs. The only thing left is the kids' room."

"And the crystal," I corrected and got smacked in the chest.

"Smartass. I told Renee we'd be over as soon as we finish up here, so probably around dinnertime? It's only three o'clock now."

"So we will definitely feed the twins beforehand so they do not have to eat Renee's cooking."

"You are so smart," she said with a smile and began to pack up the so-called crystal.

Just when I thought that Brianna had finally calmed, I heard the children begin their squealing from down the hall. Within seconds they were once again running down the hallway, this time Jackson chasing after his sister while he yelled, "Aidan is coming! Aidan's going to get you!"

The glass Brianna was holding in her hand shattered on the floor as the children approached the stairs.

"No, no, no!" she screamed as she ran in front of the children. "What did we say…"

Suddenly Jackson flung his arms out in front of him and at the same time an invisible wave pushed Brianna back to the edge of the stairs. Her face contorted in pain as she was lifted almost four feet off the ground.

"Jackson, put her down!"

"Wow, Ada," Olivia said in awe as she watched her mother float above her, not quite understanding the amount of pain Brianna was suffering. "Mama's flying! Jack-Jack, you're making Mama fly."

"PUT HER DOWN NOW!" I shouted causing Jackson to flinch and his concentration to be broken.

Brianna fell to the floor in a heap as though the invisible strings holding her up had been cut. It was only then did I see one of the movers standing on the stairs. His eyes were wide, his jaw slack from the scene he had just witnessed. Slowly he began to retreat down the stairs backwards.

"Jackson, to your room."

"But Ada..."

"This instant!" I shouted, giving him a look that scared him more than I had intended. Quickly Jackson ran down the hall while I stepped over to Brianna and knelt in front of her. "Love? Are you all right?"

She shook her head that was cradled in her right hand. "I'm sorry for every time I've ever done that to you or anyone in our family, that freakin' hurts."

I tried to smile as I helped her slowly to her feet. "Yes, angel, I know too well how much it hurts." Brianna opened her mouth to apologize, but I held my finger up to her. "There was a witness," I said as I pointed downstairs where I could hear the gentleman relaying what he saw to his coworkers. "Can you Glamour them while I take care of our son?"

"Don't be too hard on him," Bri replied before lifting Olivia into her arms. "Come on, Livybean, let's go see how Mama's Glamour skills are."

Once Brianna disappeared down the stairs I turned and headed down the hallway to the children's bedroom. When I pushed opened the bedroom door Jackson was sitting on his stripped bed, his body turned into the corner of the wall with his head hung low. His sniffles and jagged breath pulled at my heart but at the same time I was still very angry with him. I stepped over to his bed and sat down on the edge of the mattress.

"Jackson," I began, causing him to quickly turn around and crawl across the bed. He draped his legs across my lap and nuzzled his left cheek into my chest. "Not this time, Jacky. You need to stand like a little man now," I said as I placed my hands underneath his arms and placed him on the floor. As he wiped his eyes with the back of his hand, I pulled down his shirt over his exposed round stomach and in that moment I remembered he was still my baby boy. His powers and intelligence often made him seem older, but in reality he was not even four years old, barely standing past my knee.

"I'm...sorry...Ada."

"I am not the one you need to apologize to."

"I'm sorry, Mama," he sobbed loudly toward the open door but then looked at me. "Are you going to give me away?"

It was difficult not to crack a smile since he was absolutely serious. "Son, of course we are not going to give you away. But why you would do such a thing to your mother?"

"Well...Wivy did it to Ashwyn..."

"Just because your sister did it, you feel that gives you permission?"

"I…I didn't…didn't know if…I could," he stuttered as he wiped his runny nose with the cuff of his shirt, effectively making me cringe.

"Jacky, do you know how much pain you caused your mother?"

Jackson's breath caught in his throat. "It hurt? I hurt Mama?"

"Yes you did," I replied firmly. "In the same way that Olivia caused Ashlyn pain."

This brought on a whole new wave of cries. "I didn't mean to! Mama, I didn't mean to."

"Then why, Jacky?" I pleaded as I knelt down in front of him. "Please tell me, son, I cannot believe you would do something like that just because your sister did."

"He told me to practice," he cried and then flinched when he caught himself.

"Who?" I growled.

Jackson lowered his eyes to the floor while his hands picked nervously at the edge of his shirt. "A-aidan."

My hand reflexively began rubbing my chin and bottom lip. "How did he tell you?" Jackson looked down at the floor. "Jackson Thomas Burke, do not keep this from me. How is Aidan speaking to you? I know it is not through your dreams, you must tell me this minute!"

"In my head," he replied softly.

"W-what?"

"In my head," he repeated, finally looking up at me. "Like how I can hear Wivy."

"What did he just say?" Brianna said from the doorway with Olivia on her hip. I had been so focused on Jackson I had not heard her come down the hall.

Jackson's eyes widened, his expression suddenly very fearful. "He talks to Wivy too!" he said pointing accusingly at his sister.

Brianna's head whipped around to look at Olivia. "Olivia? Is that true?"

Olivia furrowed her brow tightly and gave her brother a nasty look. "Yes. But I stopped listening to him because Mama and Ada don't like him."

"Jackson," I said softly, placing my index finger under his chin and turning his head back to face me, "why did Aidan tell you to practice?"

"To help the hybrids," he replied very matter-of-factly. "Aidan says to be a hybrid helper I need to learn how to use my powers."

From the corner of my eye I could see Brianna place Olivia down on the ground and walk down the hallway.

"Did Aidan say he has hybrids?" Jackson scrunched his brow in confusion. "To help, Jacky, to help. Does Aidan already have hybrids that need your help?"

He shrugged. "I don't know. He just said I had to practice."

"Ada, I didn't listen to Aidan like Jack-Jack did," Olivia said proudly.

"Thank you, monkey," I replied, giving her a slight nod but then turned back to Jackson. "Jackson, you need to listen to me, Aidan is not your friend."

"Yes he..."

"No he is not," I snapped, causing him to flinch. Taking a breath and placing both my hands on his arms, I leaned in close and looked into my son's dark eyes. "Jacky, I know you want to believe Aidan is your friend, but he is not. Would a friend tell you to do that to your mother? Would a friend purposely get you in trouble? He is a bad man, son, a very bad man, and I do not know how he is able to talk to you, but you must stop listening. Tell him to leave you alone. Tell him if he does not stop, your father will k..." kill him, that is what I wanted to say, "...or your father will stop him. Do you understand me, Jacky? Do you understand that I am ordering you not to listen to Aidan or talk back to him? Are we clear?"

Jackson nodded his head out of fear, his entire bottom lip sucked into his mouth. "Yes, Ada."

"Very well. Now, I need your book, Jacky."

"Why?" Jackson replied as his head shot up.

"Because you are being punished. All of your toys are packed, so that leaves your book," I said holding out my hand.

Dragging his feet, Jackson walked over to the nightstand, picked up his copy of *Treasure Island,* and reluctantly placed it in my hand. "When do I get it back?"

"You may have your book back at my leisure," I replied as I stood and walked out of the bedroom. Even from the far end of the hallway I could smell and feel the cold outside air coming in from the terrace doors that Brianna most likely left open in her frustration.

As I neared the kitchen I concentrated on the sounds coming from downstairs, and the movers seemed to be working with easy conversation. As I had thought, when I turned into the kitchen both terrace doors were wide open with Brianna standing between them. Her back was to me, her body rigid and still while her brown hair blew around her.

"Bri…"

"By the way, we're professional illusionists," she said without looking at me as I came to stand next to her.

"Pardon?"

"The mover saw me floating in the air. The only thing I could think of was to tell him we were professional illusionists working on a new act."

"Why not simply remove the memory?"

Bri paused for a moment before looking at me. "I can do that?" I gave a nod. "Did you show me how to do that?" I nodded again. "Well, just put that on the ever-growing list of Vamp things I'm bad at."

"Come on, love," I groaned and wrapped my left arm around her shoulders, but she pushed it away and stepped onto the terrace.

"He's hearing Aidan in his head? Aidan is speaking to our son, and there's nothing we can do about it. Aidan doesn't have those kind of powers, how the hell is he doing it?!" she shouted.

"I do not know, love, but…"

"What are we going to do?!"

"Why do you think I have the answer!" I shouted back, causing her to whip around.

"Because you always have an answer."

I sighed as I opened my arms and she instantly tucked herself into my chest. "I am all out on this one, love. We just need to be diligent."

"And make Livy rat out her brother."

"Absolutely," I laughed lightly. "I believe Olivia will be a useful asset."

But my laughter turned quickly into a groan when my cell phone rang with Victor's ringtone. Brianna did not waste a moment before she stepped out of my arms and went back inside. She knew I had to take the call, whether I wanted to or not. "Yes, Father?"

"Child, I need you at Facility East," Victor said urgently.

"Today is our moving day, Father."

"How long will it take you to get there?"

I sighed. "We are two hours away, but at least three hours from being able to leave the house. Why?"

"Make it less, and get there as soon as possible. You and Brianna are the closest Warriors we have."

"Father, we were already planning on being there tomorrow…"

"There has been an attack."

Chapter Twenty-three

Jonah

Today I honestly became concerned that there wouldn't be enough tissues in Connecticut let alone inside the Facility with the amount of tears being shed over Sera's last day. Not all the tears were clear, either. Many of the Vampires were having difficulties with the Facility's transfer of power to Diana Stewart.

I had called her the ice queen, but even that couldn't describe her distant and uncaring nature. Her speech to the hybrids basically told them that change was here and to get over it, whereas her speech to the staff informed us to accept the changes coming or get out. For the first time in years I thought about whether I should look for another job. Not only was Diana different than Sera, she wasn't even on the same planet and I don't mean just in personality. Sera always had an easy look to her, soft and sweet like a grandmother should be. Diana's jet black hair was pulled back in a bun so tight it gave her a facelift, and her tight gray suit was as sharp and cold as her demeanor.

After giving a greeting we all could have lived without, Diana announced she would be meeting with each member of the Facility East staff beginning with the managers, and unfortunately my time had come. I'd been waiting outside Sera's office for almost fourteen minutes and I knew it was fourteen minutes because I kept looking at my watch afraid I would be late for the pick-up I needed to make. It was the first pick-up in almost a week and I was itching to get out of here for more than one reason.

Just as I was about to give up and leave, the door to the office swung open and Warren stepped out with a flustered look on his face. Facility East's Head of Security was always in control, so this was a sight to see.

"Hey, Warren, everything ok?" I asked as he stepped past me.

"Wait there, Jonah, I'll go and get you one of our bullet proof vests," he replied with his back to me.

"What for?"

"Trust me, kid, you'll need it."

"Mr. Thorne?" Diana's voice called from inside the office just as Warren disappeared around the corner. If Diana Stewart could chew and spit out a man like Warren, what the hell was she going to do to me? "Mr. Thorne!"

I jumped to attention and adjusted my uncomfortable dress shirt underneath my even more uncomfortable suit jacket. When I stepped inside I instantly noticed that Diana had removed the soft lamps Sera had placed around the room and chose to use the harsh overhead florescent lighting which didn't soften her appearance in the slightest. As I took another step inside, Diana rose from her chair behind the desk and extended her hand.

"Welcome, Diana, I'm Jonah Thorne," I said as I shook her cold bony hand.

"You're human," she replied wide-eyed and slowing our handshake.

"Uh...yes?"

"I didn't see that in your file."

"I also love asparagus and long walks on the beach, but I doubt that's in the file either," I replied with an awkward laugh which did not go over well.

"Shall we begin, then?" she asked flatly, gesturing for me to sit in one of the chairs behind me.

I looked at my watch as I sat down in the chair closest to me. "Not to be rude, but I need to leave for a pick-up in about ten minutes."

Diana looked down her nose at me as she replied, "There is no one else on your team who can take it?"

"Um...well, it's my turn in the rotation...and...I...I like to be fair."

Diana tightened the corners of her lips and exhaled slowly. "Very well then, let me be frank. Now seeing that you are human, I am more than convinced that your continued connection to Brianna Morgan and her family is the reason you have the position you do. Looking at your previous experience you never should have been hired, so why do you believe you should stay in your current position? Because I am telling you now, your relationship with Brianna Morgan only hinders you in my eyes."

Where was Warren with the bulletproof vest? He wasn't kidding. Screw the vest, I needed an athletic cup. Diana's stern black eyes were staring me down for an answer. I swallowed the lump that had formed in my throat and said, "Diana, I'm not going to lie, Brianna and I have become close friends over the years. But we were just acquaintances when I interviewed with Dante. I don't think Dante would have given me this job if I had come to him under false pretenses. From what I was told, Dante could size up a man without him saying a word. Did you know him?"

"I knew of him. However, you're..."

"I am good at my job, Diana," I interrupted while trying to keep my voice sounding calm. "I brought structure to my department which had no definition whatsoever. I'm a good driver, I care about every hybrid I pick up, I have a good rapport with the Gatherers, I pull more shifts a week than anyone else because I'm always covering for one member of my team or another, and some of those shifts are overnights and I'm the human. So you ask why I should stay in my position, I am the position. There isn't anyone who steps up to the plate like I do, and I'm not being a pompous jerk, that's just fact. I do what needs to be done, whether it's part of my job description or not because I love this place, this job, and everyone I work for."

My brain finally caught up with my mouth and slammed my jaw shut. Looking at the expression on Diana's face I had never been so afraid of being fired in my life.

Diana released a slow sigh as she closed what I assumed was my file in front of her. "Is it true you drive Facility vehicles for personal use?"

"Yes," I replied. "As do other members of the staff, with permission of Seraphina of course."

"Do you also take hybrids off campus?"

It was obvious this woman was out to get me, and someone was providing her with plenty of ammo out of context. "Sera and Eris have allowed certain hybrids to accompany drivers on occasion to help with vehicle swaps and pick up supplies from the local stores."

"And your girlfriend? Is she one of these select hybrids?" Diana said with a cocked eyebrow and condescending smile.

"Diana, you have an excellent source giving you the dirt on all of us. So yes, last night I took my girlfriend out to dinner on my time, in my own car, and with Sera's permission. We've released dozens of hybrids this year, as has Facility West. If we're releasing them back out into the world, what's the issue with me taking my girlfriend around the corner for dinner?"

"I think the bigger issue is that you're dating a hybrid in the first place."

I looked down at my watch and noticed that I had officially run out of time, so I stood from my chair. "Well, I certainly hope you pry into everyone else's love life during your interviews with them because compared to some people I'm practically a monk. Unfortunately, I need to leave for my pick-up. If there are any further questions you know where to find me."

Diana picked up the file in front of her and threw it onto a pile at the far end of the desk. "I don't think that will be necessary. I'm sure someone from your staff can fill in any holes. Would you say that Cole would be a good resource?"

My jaw tensed as my fingers fumbled to unbutton my suit jacket. "I'm sure he can help you," I replied. But I'm sure you've already been talking to him, I thought.

Before anything inappropriate jumped out of my mouth, I turned on my heel and left Diana's...no...no...*Sera's* office, it was still technically Sera's office until tomorrow. After that meeting I may not see it become Diana's office. What did she have against humans? Humans who knew Brianna Morgan, that was. Diana hated me before I even walked through the door.

"Son of a bitch!" I yelled as I threw my jacket into my office as I passed.

"Hey!"

I jumped and quickly took a step backwards to see my girlfriend pulling my suit jacket off her face. "Ash!" I said as I ran inside. "I'm so sorry, I didn't know you were..."

"I know," she laughed as she placed my jacket on the desk in front of her. "You're a pretty good shot."

"Damn, this day just keeps getting worse."

Ashlyn took my hand and squeezed it tightly as she said in a tentative voice, "I came to see how your meeting went, but I'm afraid to ask."

"I can't even talk about it right now...I..." I looked down at my watch again and shook my head in frustration. "Shit, I'm so late. I really do have to go, baby, I'm sorry," I said as I cupped her cheek and gave her a quick kiss on the lips. "I'll be back in a couple of hours, did you want to grab some dinner?"

"I promised Emma and Rebecca I'd eat with them tonight."

"Ah, I see how it is. You get a jacket in the face, and I get stood up for dinner."

Ashlyn wrapped her arms around my neck and pressed her body up against me, causing me to naturally rest my hands on her hips. "I'll come to your room after dinner, and you can tell me everything about your horrible meeting. Ok?"

"Sounds perfect," I replied and leaned down to kiss her softly. "Ashlyn, I..." Love you. Three little words, Jonah. I love you. "I...I'll see you in my room later then. Don't be too late. I mean, have fun with the girls, but I..."

"Jonah, I want to be with you too. Now go! Get out of here," Ashlyn said as she turned me around and pushed me out the door.

By the time I left the Facility I had twenty-seven minutes to make a forty-five minute drive to the airport. In this part of the state there was no highway to make up time on. It was all backroads, beautiful mountains and lakes all around, but backroads all the same. When I finally pulled into the airport's arrival terminal I could already see one of my favorite Gatherers, Leslie. She was funny and down to earth, not like many of them who thought they were above all others. Leslie had also been Greg's Gatherer, and he still had a hopeless obsession with her. But I couldn't really blame him, she was hot, especially in the tight black short-shorts she was wearing. She looked completely out of place in Connecticut in the middle of November, but she didn't seem to care that people were gawking at her. The only person Leslie was paying attention to was the young brunette she had her arm around who looked like she couldn't be more than seventeen. A pang of guilt hit my stomach seeing that the young hybrid was wearing only a light sweater with her hands tucked up under her arms.

As I pulled up in line to the curb Leslie gave me a happy wave and whispered something into the hybrid's ear. Quickly I put the SUV in park, bolted out of the driver's seat, and ran around the front of the truck. "Leslie, I'm sorry I'm late."

"Look at you all dressed up," Leslie said with a mischievous smile. "Was it because you knew I was coming?"

"I wish that was why," I laughed as she gave me a quick hug, making me the envy of the other business men standing around.

"When I saw it was you, I told Lyla here that she was lucky because Jonah is the best driver Facility East has. And you're pretty cute, too."

My cheeks instantly became flushed. "Leslie, what am I going to tell Greg?"

Leslie immediately looked over my shoulder to the SUV. "He isn't with you, is he?"

"No," I laughed and saw the relief on her face.

"He's a good kid, but last time I almost broke his fingers off. *Anyway*, I'm not here to gab about my old charges, Jonah *this* is Lyla Jane. Lyla is her given name, Jane being the name I've given her since I like the sound of Lyla Jane," Leslie said as she handed me Lyla's large red suitcase and matching duffle bag.

After slinging the duffle bag over my shoulder I extended my hand to Lyla and I was shocked at how warm her hand was. "Lyla Jane, or just Lyla, I'm Jonah. Let's get you in the truck where it's nice and warm."

Lyla smiled shyly and tucked a large section of her hair behind her ear. "Don't worry. I never have issues with the cold. Leslie, I guess this is goodbye," she said sadly as she hugged her Gatherer.

"Take care, kiddo, it's been a fun trip. If you need anything, you just find Jonah, he'll take good care of you, but I know you're going to be just fine," she said tenderly as she released Lyla and petted her hair.

I turned and opened the front passenger door, and once Lyla was securely inside I gave a quick goodbye hug to Leslie. "It was good to see you, Leslie. I'll tell Greg you said hello."

She laughed. "You know I'd do anything for that kid. He just needs to find a girlfriend. Speaking of which," she said with a coy look. "I know she's young, but a...Lyla really is a pretty cool kid, and trust me she's not like any hybrid you've ever met before. Besides, she's beautiful."

"Er…I appreciate the thought, but I have a girlfriend."

"Since when!" she said, hitting me too hard in the arm.

"Almost a month," I said proudly.

"Is she a hybrid?"

I nodded. "Ashlyn Shaw."

"Ashlyn Shaw, Ashlyn Shaw," she muttered under her breath while her eyes searched her memory. "Oh…wait, that was Kevin's case, wasn't it? Crazy girl, almost got him arrested."

"Yeah, that's probably her," I admitted reluctantly. "The Facility has really helped her."

Leslie smiled sweetly. "Good for you, I really mean that. I think you'll need the distraction now that Diana's taken over."

"Tell me about it," I moaned.

"Believe me, Facility West had a party the day that woman left. I'm sorry you have to deal with her now."

I shrugged. "Considering how my meeting with her went today I may not have to deal with her for very long."

"Not that I'd want to lose you," Leslie pouted, "but I wouldn't want to work for that snatch."

"Ok, that's my cue," I said uncomfortably and stepped off the curb. "Now don't look at my ass, I have a girlfriend."

"Oh now you're just guaranteeing that I'm going to look at that behind of yours, crazy girlfriend or not."

After I placed Lyla's bags in the backseat, I closed the door and looked across to Leslie. "She's not crazy, Leslie, maybe you could spread that around."

Leslie blew me a kiss as I stepped up into the driver's seat and closed the door. "Do you need me to turn up the heat, Lyla? I really am sorry you had to wait outside so long. No one has ever had to wait for me, it's usually the other way around."

"Jo…Jonah, right?"

I nodded as I pulled away from the curb.

"Seriously, don't worry about me in the cold. I'm used to it, and…my gift…keeps me plenty warm."

"Are you a portable heater or something?" I laughed lightly and she did the same.

"Well…sort of. I'm…a…Firestarter."

"A what?" I asked looking at her through the side of my eyes.

"A Firestarter. You know, one who starts fires."

"I thought those were pyromaniacs."

Lyla laughed. "Well, most pyros don't have their own flame," she said at the same time she snapped her fingers and a small orange flame rose from the center of her palm.

"Holy shit!" I yelled, and then swerved back onto the road. "Leslie was right, you really aren't like any other hybrid I've seen."

"Thanks," she replied proudly and closed her palm to extinguish the flame.

"I've never met a Firestarter."

"Sadly enough, most hybrid Firestarters don't live very long."

"Why's that?"

"Uh…well…most tend to blow themselves up. Ever heard about spontaneous combustion?"

"I thought that was a myth."

"Isn't everything that Vampires and Werewolves and other mythical creatures don't want you to know about?"

"Wait…Werewolves are real?" I said with a slight hitch in my throat.

"Uh…duh. How long have you been working for the Vamps?" Lyla said in a snide, adolescent way.

"They don't tell me much," I retorted. "So it'll take us about forty minutes to get to the Facility and usually what I like to do is get to know you and answer any questions you may have. So what do you know about the Facility?"

"Everything!" Lyla replied enthusiastically. "Its predecessor, Facility West, was getting crowded and everyone was having to be schlepped to the West Coast, so they built Facility East to give hybrids a choice of where they'd like to go. However, Facility East tends to be where most of the less powerful hybrids go which is why there's less intense security. But the best thing is that Facility East is run by Seraphina Dubois, which is cool, but that means that her husband, Eris, is also there. Like seriously, it can't get better than that. It's not every day you meet an Ancient."

"You know about Eris?"

"Of course I do, it's one of the reasons I decided to come to F.E."

"F.E.?"

"F.E., Facility East. Isn't that what you guys call it?"

"Er…no. How old are you?"

"Eighteen," she replied dismissively. "My dad is flipping out that I'll get to meet and do stuff with Eris. I mean, it's a really great privilege to even be in his presence. My dad said he'd been in hiding for like forever, but came out to help his daughter, Bria…"

"Brianna Morgan!" I interrupted, wanting to get one up on her, but then realized how stupid I was.

"And I thought they didn't tell you much."

"Eh, well there's a lot I still don't know. But I'm actually good friends with Brianna, which is how I got mixed up in this crazy Vamp world." The SUV suddenly became very quiet. So much so that as we approached an oncoming red light I slowly looked over at Lyla who was staring at me wide-eyed and with her jaw dramatically held open. "Lyla?"

"Oh. My. God. Are you telling me that you know Brianna Morgan personally? *The* Brianna Morgan?"

I smiled as the light turned green. "Yes I do, but I know she wouldn't consider herself *the* anything. She's just Bri."

"OH! MY! GOD!" Lyla suddenly shouted at the top of her lungs causing me to jerk the wheel and making the SUV swerve. "That means you know Cameron. Please tell me you know Cameron Burke!"

"Yeah, of course I do, and their kids too in case you want to scream again."

Lyla fell dramatically back into her seat. "Is Cameron as hot as people say he is?"

"I'm not going to answer that," I replied as I turned onto the rural highway.

"Oh, but their story is so romantic. Cameron, the handsome Gatherer, takes Brianna from her boring suburban housewife life to the Facility where she'll be safe from the Vamps that are hunting her down. As they journey across America, they fall madly in love despite threats of death from the Warriors. But Cameron defies the Warriors and chooses Brianna over his coven. So in the end love reigns, and Brianna gives birth to twins and Cameron Turns her so they can live happily ever after for all eternity." She swooned. "Isn't that just the most romantic story you've ever heard?"

"I guess so," I replied, although I didn't have the heart to correct her on a few points. "How do you know all of this? You make it sound like there's some Brianna Morgan comic book or something."

"When you live in the middle of nowhere, and the only visitors you have are other Vamps, you take all the gossip you can get."

Just then my cell phone rang, the LCD screen displaying Katie Bell as the caller. Not wanting to take the call with a hybrid next to me, I sent the call to voicemail and felt extremely guilty about it.

"Your girlfriend?" Lyla asked sweetly.

"Nope. My sister."

"Take the call, I don't mind. Really I don't."

"Nah. I'm sure she's just calling to yell at me about something."

"Oh that's so cute," Lyla whined. "I wish I had a brother or sister. It certainly would have been less lonely on our farm. I mean, I told all my problems to my horse and my potbelly pig, but they never answered back."

Just as I about to look in Lyla's direction over the potbelly pig comment, my eyes caught a glimpse of a dark blue sedan in the rearview mirror. With a second and longer look I swore it was the same dark blue sedan that I had seen yesterday. It didn't seem like a coincidence, but I had to make sure while trying not to alarm the teenager sitting next to me.

"So where are you from?" I asked, trying to keep my tone level and calm.

"Montana," she replied shyly. "My dad promised that if I was able to control my fire that I could leave home and go to a Facility once I turned eighteen, and well, here I am."

"Why did you come all the way out here? Facility West was much closer."

She paused a moment before she answered, "Well...Firestarters aren't very welcome at Facility West. A girl almost got killed there a few years ago because a Firestarter couldn't control himself during...ah...well..."

"Sex?" I answered for her. "Yeah, I know the girl who survived."

"Really?" she answered extremely interested.

"Met her a few times, actually. Natasha Cushlin, though you have to call her Tosh or else she'll punch you in the arm."

"So she's...ok?"

"It's not something she talks about, and if you ask her about it she changes the subject. To look at Tosh you'd think she was completely healed which makes sense since she's a Healer, but Brianna told me there's a section of her torso that's badly scarred. Kind of like an Achilles heel, but ah...her stomach. Did you know the Firestarter?"

"I knew of him. I guess he was like a cousin?" she shrugged. "His dad and my dad had the same maker. Obviously his dad didn't train him like mine did, though Dad did say it's harder for guys because of the...a...big moment, which is another reason Dad was so happy I was a girl."

"Sounds like you're close to your dad," I said, continuing the idle conversation as I turned left and watched the dark blue sedan follow.

"I'm close with both my parents, they're actually pretty cool. There aren't a lot of teenagers who have parents who can wield fire."

"Both parents?"

"Mm-hmm. My dad Turned my mom last year. Her first week she almost burned down the barn, but now she's a stronger Firestarter than I am. But that's another reason why I left."

"You were jealous of your mom?"

"Oh heck no," Lyla laughed. "It's just that when my mom was finally a Vamp, it was like my parents were falling in love for the first time. I almost felt like I was intruding. So, last week on my birthday I told them I was ready to go. I would have been here last week if Dad hadn't thrown a fit and tested my control for almost three days."

"How did you do it? Control yourself, that is," I said as I took another left and the sedan followed.

"It's so lame," she whined. "But my fire started when I was really young, so my dad used to sing me this song to calm me down, and well it just turned into this thing."

"Can you sing the song for me?"

"No!" she laughed. "It's way too embarrassing."

"Oh come on," I begged since I needed her as calm as possible.

"Ugh, all right," she sighed and then began to sing in a soft voice, "Ly-la, oh Ly-la, my diamond in the sky-la," Lyla stopped and began to laugh. "My dad is an awful poet."

"No it's fine," I replied as my opportunity to determine whether the blue sedan was truly following me neared. "Are you buckled up?"

"Yeah, why?"

I looked in the rearview mirror as I pressed the accelerator down and unfortunately watched as the sedan kept up with me. "Just hang on," I said as the fork in the road came into view less than a mile ahead.

From the side of my eye I could see Lyla grip either side of her seat tightly. "Jo-onah, what's going on?"

"Could be nothing, just don't look back. Hey!" I yelled as Lyla flinched her head around to the back window. "I said DON'T look back."

"But…"

"Lyla, I need you to do as I say, ok? This is just a precaution, so I need you to relax back in your seat because I'm going to be swerving."

"When!"

I pushed the accelerator down again, noticing that the blue sedan was not only keeping pace but I couldn't even see its front bumper he was so far up my ass. Although my heart was racing, I took a deep breath as the fork came closer. "Now!"

I tightened my grip on the steering wheel and pulled it quickly to the left. The SUV's tires squealed as it crossed the divide, dove down the sloped grassy embankment, and swerved onto the asphalt of the lesser traveled road that I knew all too well. The blue sedan sped past the fork in the road, but I could see his brake lights illuminate for a second before speeding away again. Having traveled this road before, I knew that it connected back up again a couple of miles ahead, so now it was either come out ahead of him or behind, and I was hoping for the latter.

I reached for my cell phone that was sitting in the cup holder and pressed the speed dial which I had never had to do in all my time at the Facility.

"This is Warren," the Head of Security's voice rang through the SUV.

"It's Jonah, I'm being followed."

"Are you sure," he replied in a firm voice.

"Yes. I've lost him for a few minutes but he's bound to catch up. We're about a half hour out."

Warren said something to someone else in the room then brought the phone back to his mouth. "We're pulling your GPS up now. Just stay your course, I'm going to call you right back. I need to gather a team, ok? Two minutes."

I nodded to myself as I heard Warren's line disconnect and suddenly the smell of burnt leather filled the cabin of the truck. Not wanting to take my eyes off the road at this speed, I gave a quick glance in Lyla's direction and saw smoke coming from her hands which were holding her seat tightly.

"Lyla!" I said urgently. "Lyla, your hands!"

Without a word she balled her hands up in her lap as she began muttering something to herself. Perfect. If the car chase didn't kill us, Lyla might prove the theory of spontaneous combustion next to me.

"Lyla, we're going to be fine," I said quickly. "I just need you to calm down."

Lyla's breathing became fast and loud. "Does this happen all the time?"

"No," I replied and looked to see that her hands were almost glowing red. "Trust me, this never happens. We'll get through this as long as you can calm down."

"I'm trying!" she shouted.

"Why don't we sing your song?"

"What?!"

"Your song, Lyla, your song! The one your father made up to keep you calm. I think this is the perfect time to try it out."

"Uh...um...Ly-la...Ly-la," she stuttered as she opened up her palms and small orange flames grew from inside them.

"Ly-la, oh Ly-la," I began to sing as we careened down the road. "Come on, Lyla, sing with me. Ly-la, oh Ly-la, my...diamond in the sky-la..."

"Diamond in the sky-la," she sang softly. "With her hair so brown, going all over town, my little, little, Lyla."

Lyla was right, her father was a horrible poet, but the song seemed to be working since the orange glow from her hands was beginning to disappear. "Good Lyla, just keep singing. Ly-la, oh Ly-la," I sang as my cell phone started ringing again and I quickly accepted the call.

"Jonah, are you singing?!" Warren said from the other side of the phone.

"Long story. Lyla keep going," I said to her as the intersection I was dreading was now visible up ahead.

"The team is assembling, Jonah. We're tracking your location, just keep driving and we'll get to you as soon as we can. I'm staying on the line until..."

"Ah shit!" I interrupted just as the blue sedan turned onto our road and was coming right at us. "Lyla, hold on!"

I slammed on the brakes and turned left onto a residential street, the force of which slammed Lyla up against the passenger side window. I think the only thing lacking in my defensive driving course was having a screaming woman next to you. The noise made it almost impossible to concentrate.

As I straightened out the SUV, I could see that the blue sedan was still right behind me. The residential street was like an obstacle course with garbage cans littering both sides and cars parked sporadically throughout. But neither the trashcans nor the cars were a hindrance to the blue sedan as he slammed into the back of our SUV. Lyla screamed and grabbed the dashboard with glowing red hands.

"Jonah!" Warren screamed into the phone. "Jonah!"

"Busy! Busy!" I yelled in reply. Between him and Lyla, I couldn't hear myself think. I swerved around a parked car and saw another street coming up on my right and got an idea. "Breathe, Lyla! Breathe!"

"I'm…trying," she cried as she began to sing her song again.

"Sit back in your seat, I need you to prepare yourself."

"For what!"

"Just do it!" I yelled as the upcoming street drew closer. Lyla sat back in her seat just as the blue sedan sped up again to ram us, however, I turned the wheel to the right just as his bumper hit ours and launched us down the side street. Lyla's screams were almost as high-pitched as our squealing tires.

"Jonah, report!" Warren yelled through the phone.

"We're here, Warren. I'm trying to lose him. Shit!" I growled as I turned down another street and saw the blue sedan coming at us from a perpendicular street on my left. I put the pedal to the floor but we were sent spinning when the blue sedan crashed into the back side panel of the SUV. My body rocked from side to side once the SUV finally stopped after its second rotation. We were facing the blue sedan head on. Warren was screaming through the phone, but I didn't have time to respond as the other driver got out of his car and began walking toward us.

Slowly my hand went up to the gearshift and put the car in reverse as I said, "Lyla, open the glovebox, you should see a can in there. Take it out."

She did as I asked and as soon as she sat back in her seat I put the accelerator to the floor causing the tires to spin until they caught traction and pulled us backwards down the street.

"What is this!" Lyla screamed as the man began to run at us. When he started to gain on us Lyla pointed and screamed, "He's a Vamp!"

"I know!" I yelled and looked through the back windshield to steer us around the residential street hazards. "You're holding aerosol silver, now roll down your window."

"Why?!"

"Just trust me, will you!"

Once again Lyla did as I asked and rolled down her window completely. "Now what?"

"Use your fire," I told her as the Vampire was almost in line with the front corner of the SUV.

"How!"

"Like a fucking blow torch!"

"With this?" she asked as she held up the aerosol can. "I've never…"

"Lyla please! I need enough time to turn around!"

Nervously Lyla undid her seatbelt and with a shaking hand she held the can of aerosol silver out the window. With a deep breath she released a shot of flame from her hand, but it was so small that it didn't reach the Vampire and she didn't press down on the can.

"Again, Lyla! You can do it!"

With another deep breath, Lyla pressed down on the nozzle of the can and suddenly a long stream of sparkling silver and orange flame flew from her hand and hit the Vampire square in the chest.

"I got him!" she cheered as the Vampire stopped, dropped, and rolled.

But the Vamp was only on the ground for a moment or two before he shook his head and came running after us again. Those few seconds, however, were enough for me to slow down, put the SUV in drive, and turn it around to face forward. As I pressed the pedal down, I looked in the rearview mirror and saw that once again the Vamp had caught up to us.

Just as I was about to swerve, the Vamp punched his hand through the back passenger door. Lyla screamed, of course, but I picked up our speed causing his feet to fall underneath him and allow us to drag him down the road.

"Lyla!" I yelled to get her to stop screaming. "Do you have more in you?"

She nodded nervously. "Yeah. Yeah, I do."

"Good girl, now melt his ass!"

Lyla gripped the can in her right hand as she leaned out the opened window. Suddenly a burst of flame came shooting out of her left hand, hitting the Vampire right in the face and neck. I could hear him screaming in agony as the silver mixed with fire melted his body layer by layer. The Vamp pulled his arm from inside the SUV, releasing his anchor to the truck but not before Lyla gave him one last blast. Finally the Vamp was set free from the SUV, his body flipping and rolling down the street like a ragdoll.

I slammed on the brakes, unfortunately causing Lyla to go flying and hit her head on the dash. I stared at the Vampire in the road waiting to see if he would get up. When he didn't I said, "Warren?"

"Jonah," he said with a sigh of relief. "Are you two ok?"

I looked over at Lyla who was shaking uncontrollably. "We're alive, but not ok. Do you have my coordinates?"

"Yes, we see you."

"There's a dead Vamp in the road."

"Don't wait there, come home. My guys will handle it. "

Carefully I helped Lyla back into her seat, my hands shaking as much as she was from the adrenaline. Once she was buckled in I put the truck back into gear.

"You did good, Lyla."

"My dad never trained me for that. He always taught me to control myself, not actually use...I...I killed that Vamp. A Vamp like my mom and dad. What am I..."

"Lyla," I interrupted, "that Vampire was going to kill us, or take you, or who knows what. I think your mom and dad will understand."

We were roughly twenty minutes away from the Facility when three black SUVs came speeding down the opposite side of the highway. The lead SUV passed us while the other two screeched through a U-turn and sped up behind us.

"Oh my god, not again!" Lyla cried.

"They're with us, Lyla. We're safe from here on out, I promise."

Just then the backseat filled with thick black smoke, and a few seconds later Eris was sitting behind me. "Jonah, you gave us quite a scare."

Lyla gasped as she turned in her seat and gaped at our new passenger. "You're...you're..."

"Eris, young one. My name is Eris. And you are?" Instead of answering, Lyla fainted. "I can't say that is the first time that has ever happened."

"Lucky you," I replied in a short tone.

"You did well, Jonah," Eris said as his hands rested on my shoulders.

"We could have died, sir. There were a couple of times I thought..."

"Do you need me to drive?"

"No sir."

"Good," Eris replied cheerily. "Because I actually do not know how to. That is why I have Vladimir. Good man that Vladimir."

I looked in the rearview mirror to see Eris smiling at me. "Is this the part where you try and distract me from all the shit I just went through?"

"Yes. Is it working?"

"No."

Chapter Twenty-four

Jonah

Facility East looked like Fort Knox with armed security stretched across the front gate and spaced sporadically along the driveway to the building. Lyla still lay unconscious in the passenger seat while Eris continued spouting nonsense to keep me distracted, but I wasn't listening. There was only one thing on my mind and getting to her was my only goal at this moment.

I was relieved when the driveway curved around to the tall front doors. The tires of the SUV skidded to a stop as I hit the brakes and pulled the steering wheel sharply to the left. The SUV was still settling back and forth when I jumped from inside and ran up the front steps where I was met by Diana and another set of guards. I could hear Diana calling after me as I blew by her and ran inside the large lounge where many hybrids were gathered, several of them holding and comforting one another. Frantically I looked around the room searching my girl, and after several seconds of panic I finally found her crying in Sera's arms.

"Ashlyn!" I shouted across the room over the noise of the crowd. Her head popped up from Sera's shoulder looking for me as I pushed through the crowd. When I finally reached her, I grabbed her hand and pulled her into the adjacent stairwell. As soon as the thick metal door shut behind us I turned Ashlyn to face me and pressed her up against the wall. My lips slammed on top of hers so hard my bottom teeth hurt, but that didn't stop me from kissing her as if I would never get the chance again.

When I finally needed air I pulled away from her, placing my hands on either side of her face tightly as I looked into her eyes and said, "I love you, Ashlyn. I've been trying to tell you for the last few days and I was just too chicken shit to say it. But as I was driving back here all I could think about was that I could have died and you would never have known how I truly felt about you and…" I had to take a breath and rest my forehead on Ashlyn's when flashes of my brush with death replayed in my head. "…I couldn't get to you fast enough, Ash. I'm sorry I didn't tell you sooner, you don't deserve being told like this."

Ashlyn placed her hands over mine. "You love me?" she sniffled as I lifted my head to see her eyes begin to water.

"I do," I replied, feeling a lump begin to form in my throat. "I love you, Ashlyn, and I don't expect you to say it back if…"

"Oh no…no, I…love you too," she said with half a cry and half a laugh. "I was waiting for you to say it. But then today…" Ashlyn couldn't finish her statement as she broke down in a full hysterical crying fit. Her arms wrapped around my waist as I tucked her head into my chest and allowed her to soak my shirt with her tears.

"Ahem," I heard next to me making me lift my head to see Diana standing in the doorway. "Mr. Thorne, we need you."

"I just need a couple of minutes," I replied.

"Now, Mr. Thorne."

"I barely escaped death a half hour ago I think I've earned another goddamn minute!"

Diana huffed loudly as the door slammed behind her. Ashlyn's whimpering lessened as she looked up at me. She swallowed and pursed her wet lips before saying, "You need to go."

I shook my head and kissed her, her mouth opening easily and letting my tongue slip deeply inside. My hand caught the wall as I pressed her up against it. I had no idea how long we stood there kissing when I heard the stairwell's door open again. Reluctantly I pulled away from Ashlyn's lips, but did not take my eyes off of her.

"Jonah," Warren said softly from the doorway. "I'm sorry, but we need you."

I squeezed Ashlyn's hand tightly. "I won't be long. Wait in my room?"

Ashlyn nodded before stealing another quick kiss. "I'll bring some things with me. I don't want to be away from you tonight."

I gave her a gentle kiss on her lips before saying proudly, "Love you."

"Love you too," she whispered with a smile before ducking under my arm and leaving the stairwell.

I stared at the wall for another few seconds, taking several deep breaths before finally turning to Warren who was giving me a sympathetic look.

"Jonah, I am sorry…"

"No, I understand," I interrupted as I followed him back out into the hallway. "Where are we going?"

"We need to debrief you while the details are fresh in your mind. Do you need medical attention first?"

I shook my head as my cell phone began to ring from my pocket. When I pulled it out I noticed it was Katie again and for the second time today I ignored the call. I felt like a horrible brother, but under the circumstances there was no way I could talk to her right now.

"Jonah, I'd turn the ringer off of that thing if I were you. Diana is showing her true colors and they aren't pretty." Just as we approached Sera's office Warren grabbed my shoulder and pulled me to a stop. "Now listen up kid, I'm warning you that Diana is not on your side for whatever reason. What you did today was nothing short of phenomenal performance and you brought a young girl here unharmed. Just stick to that, got it? You did your job and the hybrid is here safe. There's nothing else you could have done. It's not like you had any warnings."

My eyes grew wide as my brain began to catch up and process Warren's statement. "Well…at the time…they didn't look like signs."

Warren was silent for a moment as he squeezed my shoulder again. "Ok, we'll handle it. I'll defend you as much as I can, as will Sera and Eris."

"Whoa, wait a minute, is my job on the line here?"

"I don't know, kid. All I know is that she's looking for a reason to get rid of a bunch of us and you might have just given her one. Come on," he said as he opened the door to Sera's office.

Eris and Sera were already seated in chairs in front of the desk while Diana stood behind it.

"Mr. Thorne, have a seat," Diana said, gesturing for me to come inside. "We have lots to discuss."

Although I would never admit it out loud, after an hour and a half of Diana's grueling questions I wished I had been injured in the attack today. Warren had tried to warn me but I felt so beaten down I thought I'd break through the chair. The only thing adding to the ordeal was my phone constantly vibrating from Katie's texts after I continued to ignore her calls.

"Mr. Thorne, you didn't think it was appropriate to report that you were being followed?"

I sighed. "At the time…"

"What about now? Do you think you should have reported it now?"

Warren put his hand up covertly signaling for me to calm down while Sera gave me a look conveying something similar. "Hindsight is 20/20, Diana. The first time I saw the car I did take actions to see if it was following me and it turned into a sub-division. The second time I saw it, I didn't know for sure it was the same car because it was pitch black outside."

Diana folded her hands on top of the desk as she leaned over and said condescendingly, "Again, after being suspicious twice in one day you didn't see fit to report what you had seen?"

"Like I said before, I didn't put it together. In each case I was in a different car, he didn't give chase, and yes now I wish I had said something but I didn't want to start something over nothing. This guy could have been following the other four drivers…"

"Yes, but they weren't being followed," she answered snidely.

"Or they just didn't notice," I snapped back.

And as if on cue, my phone vibrated on my lap. When I gave a quick glance I saw it was one line from Katie: I need you!

It wasn't often that Katie Bell *needed* me, and put it in the pile of missed calls and other texts begging me to call her made me worry.

"Mr. Thorne," Diana said in a raised voice, "will you please put that thing away! Just because it is on vibrate does not mean I can't hear it."

"I'm sorry, ma'am, but may I make a quick call? I think there might be something…"

"Certainly not," she snapped and Sera let out a frustrated sigh. "Now let's talk about why you involved the hybrid…ah…um…"

"Lyla," I answered for her. I could see that Sera shared my level of disgust at the fact that Diana didn't even know the name of the girl who almost died today. "Her name is Lyla."

Diana looked down her nose at me. "And what possessed you to instruct a young hybrid to put herself in danger. You could have gotten her killed."

I could feel my nostrils flaring as my cheeks started to burn. "When a Vampire is chasing after you and punches through the door of your SUV you do whatever comes to mind to defend yourself. I couldn't drive and spray him with silver on the other side of the vehicle. I had a hybrid who was a Firestarter, the Vamp was on her side of the SUV, I made a call. One, by the way, that worked. Warren's guys confirmed the Vampire is toast and Lyla survived unharmed."

"You brought her here unconscious!" Diana yelled.

"She fainted at seeing Eris," I corrected. "Lyla was fine until she saw him."

All eyes went to Eris who merely shrugged.

My phone vibrated and once again it was from Katie: Come home! 911.

I immediately rose from my chair. "I'm sorry, I have to go."

"Sit down, Mr. Thorne," Diana yelled as she slammed her hand down on the desk. "We are not done here."

"There is a family emergency, I need to get home."

"We are on lockdown. No Facility vehicles are leaving the premises."

"I have my own car. You can't stop me."

"But Warren's men will!"

"No zhey won't," Sera said angrily as she rose from her chair. "Jonah, go. Go to your family."

Diana rose from behind the desk and leaned on the tips of her fingers. "Seraphina, you do not have the right…"

"Do not tell me what my rights are," Sera said firmly. "Until midnight tonight I am still in charge, and you, *madam,* can sit back down in zhat chair." Diana slowly sat back down, her lips clenched shut. "Warren, be sure Jonah gets through zhe gate. Eri, put away your fangs." Eris gave her a very challenging look as his fangs hung over his bottom lip. "S'il vous plait, mon amour."

Sera kept her eyes on her husband as she waved me away and I didn't look back. The hallway to the garage was a blur as I ran to my car and dialed Katie's number which went right to voicemail.

"Hey, hey, it's Ka-tay, leave a message, eh."

"Katie, what the hell? I'm coming home. Call me."

By the time I hung up the phone I was roaring my silver Camaro to life and the tires were squealing out of the garage. The large front gate nearly clipped my side mirror as I drove through because I was driving faster than it could open. Even my back end fishtailed as I turned out of the driveway. I kept calling Katie's number, and when I heard her message for the third time I banged on the steering wheel.

"Katherine Elizabeth Thorne, don't you ever text me a 9-1-1 message and then NOT ANSWER YOUR PHONE!"

I waited to curse at her until after I had hung up the phone. It was at that point I called the house and my stomach sank when the answering machine didn't pick up. Did I call the police now? What if the Vampire who was following me had associates? What if they knew where I lived? Could Vampires be attacking my family right now? Was that the emergency that I'd been so casually ignoring for the last couple of hours?

I went through red light after red light continually pressing redial and still no answer from either my sister or my mother. When I finally turned onto my street I could see our house and the lights were on. There were no emergency vehicles in front of the house, and everything looked surprisingly innocent as I pulled into the driveway. I didn't waste a moment getting out of the car and bolted into the side door of the house.

"Katie?!" I shouted as I ran into the kitchen only to find Paul standing up against the counter eating a sandwich. "Where's Katie? Katie!"

Paul didn't answer, but my mother's voice came from the hallway. "Joey?"

"Mom, where's Katie?"

"What are you doing here?" she asked as she finally stepped into the kitchen, her cheeks red and splotchy while her eyes were puffy from crying. "I thought you had to work…"

"Mom, what is going on? Katie's been calling me all afternoon and then she sends me this 9-1-1 text telling me to come home…"

"I told her not to bother you. I knew I should have taken her phone."

"Where is she," I said as I tried to step past my mother, but she took a step in front of me. "Mom, what is going on? Why is Katie home?"

"Joey, listen," my mother began just as Katie's bedroom door opened and my sister's head poked out.

"Jonah!" she sobbed as she came running down the hall. I stepped around my mother and held Katie at arm's length to see that she too had been crying. "Joey, please don't let her do it. Don't let her make me come home."

"What?" I replied as I looked at her confused. "Katie, you said this was an emergency. What the hell is going on?"

"SHE," Katie growled as she pointed to our mother, "comes and picks me up from school today with this 'hey let's go shopping and have dinner' line, and then turns around and says that I have to move home next semester because you're not paying for my school anymore."

"Since when!"

I turned to my mother who responded, "Since now."

"But why? I…"

My mother put her hand up to my face. "You made it perfectly clear you resent having to drop out of college and now pay for your sister's education."

"I didn't mean…"

"Joey, is that true?" Katie whimpered. "You resent it?"

"Wha…a…no," I stuttered in reply. "Mom, that's not what I said."

"Actually, honey, it is. I got the message loud and clear. You're tired of paying for everything so I'm taking it off your plate. Only I can't afford the full tuition, so letting go of the room and board brings the cost down to where I can. I'm sorry, Katie Bell, that's just the way it has to be."

"But I have friends," Katie cried. "I won't ever see them. I'll miss out on everything! Joey, please! I'll do whatever you want me to do, just please help me stay on campus, please!"

I looked between my sister and my mother completely dumbfounded. I didn't want to pay Katie's tuition, but I also didn't want her to miss out on all the things I did.

"Mom, I'll still help with Katie Bell's school. Let me pay for the boarding, that way she can…"

"No, I've made up my mind," my mother replied although she was looking at Paul for validation.

"Fine then," Katie said angrily. "Joey, Mom's selling the house."

"Katie!" my mother yelled back. "I told you I wanted to wait to tell your brother."

"Hold it, just hold it," I interrupted as I stepped between the two of them. "What do you mean you're selling the house? This house? The house *I'm* paying for?" My mother swallowed as she looked over to Paul. "No, no, don't look at him, look at me. Look me in the eye and tell me that you were seriously going to try and sell this house out from under me."

"Joey, it wasn't like that, I was going to tell you," she pleaded.

"When? The day I drove up and saw the for sale sign in the front yard? How could you do this? How could you even think of selling this place?"

"Joey, please listen…"

"No! No! You're not selling the house. I pay the mortgage, and the taxes, and almost all the utilities. If you want to leave, just sign everything over to me."

"I can't do that," she said softly.

"Why not?!"

"Because I need the money," my mother snapped as tears ran down her cheeks.

I blinked. "Money? For Katie's school? I already said…"

"No, Joey, I need the money from the sale to…" my mother paused as she took a staggered breath "…for a new house with Paul."

I put my hands on my hips and looked up at the ceiling trying to keep my anger inside. Katie slipped her arm around my elbow and cried onto my arm.

"That's why I kept calling you," Katie whimpered. "You weren't picking up and then my phone died."

I opened my mouth, but my mother spoke first. "Look kids, I know this is hard. I know these last few years have been so hard, but I need to do this, *we* need to do this."

"We do?" I countered as I pulled away from Katie. "*We*, Katie and I, do not need to do this. You're forcing this on us so you can go play house with Dr. Douchebag."

"Jonah!" my mother shouted. "I'm tired of you calling your soon-to-be stepfather that name!"

"He will never be anything to me," I yelled as I pointed and looked directly at him. "Father, stepfather, doctor, nothing!"

"Then get a place of your own," my mother shouted.

"Ah," I said with a non-humorous laugh. "So, you're making Katie come home, selling the house we have memories of Dad in, and then kicking me out. Wow, Paul, you've had quite a productive day."

"Joey, this wasn't all Paul," my mother said in his defense.

Katie was sobbing next to me as I began turning in my own little circle of disbelief. When I came to face the dining room I noticed two stacks of boxes sitting on the floor. "Have you packed my things too?"

My mother didn't answer, but her bottom lip began to tremble.

"Mom," I said through my teeth, "whose stuff is in the boxes?"

"Joey," she replied, unable to look at me, "we need to move on. It's been four years..."

I didn't bother to listen to anything else she said and ran to the boxes. Behind me I could hear my mother and sister arguing as I tore open the box on top of the pile. A whiff of my father's smell hit me in the face as I looked into the box filled with his old shirts and suits. I rummaged through to the bottom not finding what I was looking for and threw the box to the ground. When I started in on the second box my mother began pulling on my arm.

"Where is it, Mom!" I shouted at her.

"Joey, let's not do this now," she begged.

"Where is it!"

"Where is what, honey?" she cried.

"Where is Dad's watch? Did you just throw it away like you did everything else of his?"

"Honey, I need to move on. I kept all of this for four years, it's time."

"Then why pack it up and throw it away?"

Gently my mother wrapped her hand around mine. "It's best this way."

"Screw you!" I shouted as I wretched my hand from hers. "This stuff is mine and Katie's to go through. You have no right deciding what to do with Dad's things, he's our father."

"He was my husband," she snipped.

"That's right, Mom. And you're throwing him in the garbage for Dr. Douchebag."

"Jonah, I told you..."

"I know what you told me. I have heard everything you've told me tonight. One, I don't have to pay for Katie's school anymore. Ok, great. Second semester bill is due at the end of the month, have fun getting that together. Two, you're giving Dad's things away. Sorry, not happening, I'm taking it all, and Katie and I will go through it and determine what we want since it's our birthright. Three, you're selling the house out from under me. Again, great. Until it's sold, the mortgage is due at the first of each month, taxes are due at the end of the year. Boy, don't I have a lot of money to spend now that I don't have to deal with all of that crap. Four, I need to move out. Fine. No time like the present."

I held onto the box of my father's things and walked quickly to my bedroom at the end of the long hallway. I turned the harsh overhead light on as I entered the room and immediately dug through my closet until I found the large duffle bag I used to use for hockey and placed it on the bed.

"What are you doing?" Katie cried.

"Leaving," I replied as I emptied my underwear and sock drawer into the bag.

"Joey, don't do this. You can't…"

"I'm sorry, Katie. I can't live like this, and Mom doesn't want me here."

"That's not true." But it wasn't Katie who answered, my mother had stepped into the room quietly.

"Dad's watch?" I asked firmly without looking at her.

"I…I'm not sure."

"Bullshit," I replied as I walked aggressively to stand in front of my mother. "Dad left me that watch. It was Granddad's, and then it was Dad's, and now it's mine. Since Dad died you've kept it in your nightstand so you can look at it every night before you go to bed, and don't deny it. I've never asked for it for that very reason, but now I'm too afraid you'll throw it in the garbage if you haven't already. Now, either you give me that watch or I go and pull it out of your nightstand, and then you'll have to explain to Paul why it's still there and not in one of those goddamn boxes out there."

Anger was pulsing through my veins as I turned back around and began filling the large duffle bag with shirts and pants. I was like a machine. Not even the sound of Katie's whimpering stopped me.

"Take me with you," she begged.

"I can't," I answered truthfully. "I'll have to live at the Facility for a while and you can't stay there."

"I'll stay at school. I'll live in the dorms, even do intersession classes so I don't have to leave campus. Just please don't leave me with the two of them. You know Paul creeps me out, I can't live with him. Please, Joey, I'm begging you, I'll do anything."

At that point the duffle bag was full so I zipped it up, threw it over my shoulder, and stepped over to my baby sister who was tearing my heart out with her tears. I had to swallow the large lump in my throat before I said, "Katie Bell, I'm sorry. I can't watch and see what Paul turns Mom into, and she won't listen to either of us. She's letting him call all the shots, and pushing me away is one of them."

Just then my mother came through the door, my father's wide-faced stainless steel watch in her hand that shook as she extended it to me. Even looking at it made my heart beat faster and my chest swell with emotion. I had seen that watch on my father's wrist growing up and I never had the heart to take it from my mother's drawer once he died. Taking it now seemed so…final?

My mother's lip trembled as I debated whether I could take the watch from her hand. Instead, I wrapped both my hands around hers and looked her directly in the eye. "Mom, you don't have to do all of this."

She shook her head. "The watch really is yours. I should have given it to you years ago."

"No, that's not what I mean," I replied as I lowered my voice. "Mom, I know you don't love Paul."

My mother's breath caught in her throat as her eyes flinched. "That's not…why would you say that?"

"Because it's true! You don't love him, and you're doing all of this because you think you have to. I know the things I said last night hurt you, and I'm sorry, they just came out wrong. Maybe I am a little more resentful about having to support us than I thought, but really all I've ever wanted from you was some appreciation for what I've done for our family. Some kind of acknowledgment or understanding from you that maybe it would difficult for me to see Katie getting to do all the things I had to give up."

"Joey, don't you see? I am trying to make things right…"

"And you're doing it the wrong way. You're making it worse by forcing Paul on us. He's tearing us apart, Mom, don't you see that? Look at what he's made you do? In less than twenty-four hours you're selling the house you've lived in for over twenty years, throwing Dad's things in the garbage without telling us, and…"

"Stop it, just stop it," my mother shouted and ripped her hands from my grip. "Joey, when you finally love someone you'll realize that sometimes you have to make concessions."

"I am in love, Mom. I love Ashlyn, and not only would I never make the concessions that you are, she would never ask me to."

My mother's eyes filled with tears once again as she cupped my cheek. "You deserve to be happy. If you love Ashlyn as much as I loved your father, then you need to cherish that every day because it can be taken away so quickly."

"Mom, you can find that kind of love again. You don't have to settle for Paul."

She removed her hand from my cheek and wiped her face. "I found my true love when I was seventeen years old and he was taken from me too soon. I've accepted that I will never find that again."

"Then why marry Paul!"

"Joey, I am a middle-aged woman. There aren't men lined up and down the street waiting to sweep me off my feet. I'm a depressed widow with two grown kids, it's not particularly a dating calling card. And Paul is...willing."

"But Mom," Katie Bell chimed in, "you deserve better than that."

Mom smiled as she placed her arm around Katie's shoulders. "Thank you, Katie Bell, but I've accepted this and I'm sorry it means things will change, but I think it'll be best for all of us."

"You've accepted to marry a man you don't really love," I snapped as the anger began to rise in my chest.

"If it means my son can finally be free of the burden he's had to endure for four years, then yes, I will marry Paul. I can't move on without him, and that means neither can you."

I could see in my mother's eyes that she had made her choice and there was no going back. She was marrying Paul and saying goodbye to her previous life with all its strings.

"I will never accept Paul, and I refuse to watch you willingly do this to our family." Reluctantly I held out my hand and with tears still in her eyes my mother placed my dad's watch in my palm. "I'll get by with what I have in my bag, just put everything else in storage and I'll pay for it until I get a place of my own."

"Joey..."

"Goodbye, Mom," I said as I gave her a kiss on her cheek.

When I finally took a step into the hallway I could almost hear my heart ripping apart. As I stepped into the kitchen, Paul was still against the counter finishing his sandwich without a care in the world.

When he noticed my presence he gave me a cocky smile as he wiped his mouth with a napkin. "This really is for your own good, Jonah."

"Fuck you," I growled as I took a step forward, but then stopped and looked at him one last time. "If you even look at my sister sideways I will have you killed and make sure no one ever finds your body."

"JONAH, WAIT," Katie Bell screamed from the opposite end of the hallway.

I adjusted my heavy bag's strap on my shoulder and trudged out of the house. Katie's cries continued as I walked to my car. I wanted to get out of here before she caught up to me, but of course I couldn't be that lucky. As soon as I opened the door of my car Katie was grabbing my arm.

"Joey, please," she cried as she pushed me away from the car and hugged me tightly around the waist. "I don't have to go to school, I'll…I'll take a break and get a job. Just please! Please take me with you!"

Between her grip and her sobbing, I found it hard to talk. I had never said no to my baby sister, but now it was for her own good. My arms found their way around her as my chin rested on top of her head. "Katie Bell, you need to stay in school. We don't need two Thorne children dropping out of college."

"I'll go back, I will."

"From experience, that's easier said than done. You need to go back inside, Katie Bell."

"No," she cried. "I don't want to live with Mom, I want to live with you."

"Katie, I have no place to live."

She pushed me hard in the chest. "Then where are you going?!"

"I told you. I'm going to crash at the Facility until I can find a place."

"Then take me there!"

"I can't take you anywhere, Katie."

"Why not!" she screamed in my face.

"Because I don't want to!" Katie's crying suddenly stopped as she stared at me in stunned silence. "I'm your brother, not your parent and…now I can…I can finally have a life. I don't want the responsibility of you anymore, I want to have my own life and do things a guy my age is supposed to."

"You don't mean that."

"Yes I do," I lied as I threw my bag into the car. I had to get out of here before I completely broke down and begged her forgiveness for saying the most heinous lies to her. "Now go inside, Katie."

"Don't leave me, Joey," she whimpered.

"Take care of Mom," I responded, unable to look at her as I sank into the car.

I started the engine as soon as I shut the door and just as I put the car in reverse Katie kicked the front left fender. "I hate you!" she screamed and kicked the same spot again. "And your stupid car!"

I didn't wait for Katie to come around again. I pressed the accelerator to the floor and screamed down the driveway. When I finally pulled out onto the street I could still hear Katie screaming profanities at me. What she didn't know was that she couldn't hate me as much as I hated myself.

Chapter Twenty-five

Jonah

The ride back to the Facility was a complete blur. I didn't even remember turning onto the Facility's street let alone the twenty minute drive. This entire day was the worst of my life and that included the day my father died. I couldn't take anymore, I was done. My body was aching from the attack, and my heart was heavy from everything that happened with my family. I knew that if I let out even the slightest bit of emotion I would find myself in the fetal position in a corner somewhere.

The car behind me flashed its lights causing me to look in the rearview mirror and then at the speedometer. I flinched when I saw that I was barely driving twenty-five miles an hour. Immediately I pressed down the accelerator because I wanted to be in the safety of the Facility and I just didn't have time for the asshole behind me.

When I pulled into the Facility's driveway I was quickly greeted by several armed guards, one of which instructed me to roll down my window.

"Identification," the guard whose name I couldn't remember instructed while the others looked underneath my car and through the windows. I handed the guard my Facility ID just as another vehicle pulled in behind me. The guard gave my ID a quick glance before handing it back to me and giving the signal for the gate to open. "Sorry, Jonah, we have to check everyone. You're all clear, go on up."

Without another word I drove up the long driveway for the second time today. When I finally pulled in front of the garage I released a sigh of relief. Not only did I feel safer, but I knew I was only moments away from being able to lock myself up in my room and release everything that I was keeping inside. I stepped out of the car and just as I pulled the large hockey bag onto my shoulder someone called my name. My stomach dropped when I saw Brianna coming around the front of a large SUV that had just pulled in behind my car.

"Jonah, wait!" she called before she was a blur and suddenly throwing her arms around my neck. "When Victor said it was you...I...I was afraid..."

"I'm fine," I replied softly as I patted her back. When I looked over her shoulder I saw Cameron open the back door of the SUV allowing the twins to climb out from inside. "Do the kids know what happened?"

She shook her head as she untangled her arms and took a step back. "No. We just told them that the hybrids needed our help so at least Jack-Jack wasn't too upset about missing a sleepover with Wills. Livy on the other hand cried for the first forty-five minutes. Are you sure you're ok?" she asked with a quizzical eye.

"Yeah," I lied as I looked down at my shoes and wondered how much longer I could keep my cool. "Just a little shaken up."

"What's with the bag?"

My nose and eyes began to burn as I watched Brianna's face change from curiosity to concern, but it became almost impossible to keep my emotions inside when she cupped my cheek.

"Jonah, what happened?"

"I..." I tried to say but my voice cracked causing me to clear my throat.

"Another fight with Mom?"

I nodded my head while keeping my eyes back on my shoes. "She's choosing Paul and selling the house, so I just left. I can't watch her destroy our family anymore."

"What about Katie?" Bri asked softly, but the sound of my sister's name suddenly became too much to handle.

"You know...I...ah...gotta go," I replied, backing away from her and adjusting the bag on my shoulder. I threw a quick wave to Cameron and the kids while Brianna pleaded for me to stay, but I didn't want to be a blubbering mass on the floor of the garage. I needed to get to my room and fast, and thankfully there was no one around when I ran across the lobby. Before I knew it I was opening the door to the basement floor and my room, my new home actually, was only a few doors down.

Quickly I punched in the code on the keypad, pushed my way in, and then slid down until I hit the floor. Finally I was where I could let it all go in private and my eyes didn't wait to start burning as they became blurry with rare tears. Just as my head bent down into my hands I heard a squeak from my bed that was tucked around the corner. Looking through my fingers I saw Ashlyn come around the other side of the wall and freeze when she saw me.

"Jonah?" she asked tentatively. When I finally lifted my head to look at her she flinched as if something hit her in the face. "Oh…my god, what happened? Jonah!" she cried as she ran to me and kneeled down in front of me. "Please tell me."

Slowly I pushed myself up to a standing position with Ashlyn following with wide teary eyes.

"Mom chose Paul," I said flatly. "And you were right."

"About what?"

My jaw flinched several times before I was finally able to say, "She doesn't love Paul. She admitted it and she is still choosing to stay with him. Actually choosing to sell *my* house so she can use the money to buy a house with him and make Katie live with them which is the last thing she wants to do, and Mom couldn't give a shit because she has some asinine thought in her head that she's doing this all for me but then she's looking at Paul to answer everything for her and she's standing there trying to lie about putting all my Dad's…"

I stopped abruptly at the thought of my father, and suddenly I felt ill.

"Jonah?"

When I didn't answer her, she took a step toward me and I matched her with a step away. "I just need…I need…"

"Tell me, baby, what do you need? I can feel how much you're hurting…"

"I just need to take a shower," I said and held my hands up in front of me as I took the few steps into the bathroom. I shut the door behind me and didn't give Ashlyn the slightest glance. Immediately I turned on the shower and then fumbled with unbuttoning my shirt. When I got down to the last two buttons I just ripped my shirt off causing the buttons to bounce off the walls around me. When I went to take off my watch I froze. I was looking down at my father's watch and had no idea when I had put it on. It looked so foreign on my wrist since I had only seen it on my father and his father before that. I had demanded it from my mother and now I felt unworthy.

"Always take care of your girls, Joey", he would say to me all the time. *"You can tell a good man by the way he treats others, especially his wife and kids." "Being a big brother will always carry the burden of protecting your sister."*

I couldn't keep his voice from ringing in my head; it was as though he was standing right next to me. I could even imagine the disappointed look stretched across his face for everything I had said to my family. My fingers fumbled at the watch's worn clasp trying to get it off my wrist. After wanting to wear it for as long as I could remember, now looking at myself in the mirror I didn't deserve it and couldn't get it off fast enough.

In one evening I had thrown my family away and suddenly I couldn't breathe. I flung the shower curtain open and stepped into the scalding hot water. My stomach was churning while my father's voice continued to shout every promise I had broken and every way I had disappointed him. His statements kept repeating and repeating until the frustration became overwhelming causing me to slam my fists into the wall and growl like an animal.

I was finally ready to let go of everything inside me when the bathroom door clicked open. I froze and held my breath, waiting for some kind of noise, but none came.

"Ash?"

"Yeah," she replied simply, but said nothing else.

When the awkward silence lasted another few seconds I finally said, "Everything ok?"

"Yeah," she replied in the same tone, but honestly it was pissing me off.

"I'll be out in a few minutes."

"Take your time," she said as the sound of her voice moved toward the back of the shower.

It was at that point I felt a sudden cool breeze behind me and the shower curtain opened. I turned to look over my shoulder just as Ashlyn stepped into the shower, the sight of her bare breasts catching my eye first. Instantly I stood up straight and whipped my head forward. She wrapped her arms around my chest and pressed her amazing breasts into my back.

"Ash, I…"

"Just let it out, baby," she interrupted as she rested her cheek on my back.

"I've asked you not to read me," I replied, having to put both my hands back up against the shower wall.

"When your emotions practically slap me in the face I don't need to read you. If you don't let it out I'm afraid you'll explode."

"I can't."

"Why not?"

"I've never…I can't lose it in front of you."

"Good thing I'm behind you then," she replied and squeezed me back into her chest.

"I'm just upset about the house."

"That's not it, Jonah. You have nothing to be afraid of."

"Nothing to be afraid of?" I laughed sarcastically. "I walked out on my family and who knows when I'll see them again. I…I've left my sister to live with…with that *snake* and nothing I said to my mother changed her mind in the slightest, not even when she admitted she didn't really love him. What kind of mother…" I stopped as my voice cracked and the inside of my nose burned. "She…I wasn't her son anymore…and then I…" The tears I had been dreading finally came as my head rested against the shower wall. "Oh my god I abandoned…Katie Bell."

"No you didn't, Jonah."

"Yes I did!" I yelled as I beat my fists against the wall. "She begged to come with me and I…I yelled at her, I lied to her…I said…I told her I didn't…she hates…*hates me*…then the watch…goddamn boxes…" I cried unable to form complete sentences.

"Your boxes?"

"No," I sighed, trying to control my breathing, but just thinking about those fucking boxes stacked up on each other brought on another whole wave of emotion that I had been keeping inside for four years. I didn't cry for my father when he died. My sister was hysterical, my mother catatonic, which meant I didn't have the luxury of grieving. There were arrangements and bills, school for Katie and therapy for Mom, they needed me to be strong for them and I did that. But between almost being killed and seeing my mother throwing away my father's things cut a gash into my heart that was finally releasing everything I had never allowed myself to release. "She was going to throw him away, Ash, like garbage! He was my dad…my…my hero…he loved her…he loved all of us, he doesn't deserve to be…to be…"

"You're there, baby, you can say it," Ashlyn prodded as I struggled to find the words I needed to say.

"Seeing those boxes," I began as I finally lifted my head from the shower's wall and covered my eyes with my right hand, "…it was like…I was…like I was burying him all over again…putting him in another goddamn box."

My chest began heaving as emotions drained from every cell of my body. I was making an absolute ass of myself, but I couldn't stop it even if I wanted to. I had lost control, something I had always prided myself on being able to maintain. My hysterics lasted another five or six minutes before my breathing finally began to settle down. It was at that point that I remembered whose arms were around me. Slowly I rose to be fully upright when my body was suddenly flooded with a feeling of warmth and comfort.

I placed my hands on top of Ashlyn's. "I love you too."

As soon as the words were out of my mouth Ashlyn choked on her own tears. Everything I was feeling was seeping into her, more so I'm sure because so much of our bodies were touching. This was not how I ever pictured being naked in a shower with my girlfriend, and I felt even guiltier at the fact that she was enduring my emotional turmoil physically. Gently I unfolded her hands from around my waist and turned around to face her. Her eyes were red and sad as she tried to force a smile with a trembling bottom lip.

My fingers grazed down the side of her face, tangling themselves into her wet hair and around her neck. "I'm sorry you had to see…*feel* all of that."

Ashlyn wrapped her arms around me, once again pressing her warm wet body up against me. "I couldn't let you shut me out."

"I wasn't trying to. I've just never let any of that out."

"I could tell," she said with a slight smile.

"You need to put your shield up."

"I'm trying to," she laughed, "there's just so much…"

"I need you to try harder, Ash," I interrupted impatiently as my forehead rested on hers. "I need…you. That's all, I…I really need you."

She took my face into her hands and tilted my head up slightly. "You have me, all of me."

My lips rested gently on top of hers for only a moment when all the anguish that had been stirring within me turned into an unbelievable passion. Ashlyn's mouth opened freely to allow my tongue inside, even releasing a soft moan as I pushed her up against the opposite wall of the shower. My left hand immediately began massaging her right breast while my right hand pulled her leg around my waist. My hips curled under with a slow elongated pulse, grinding myself into her and feeling the hot wetness between her legs.

Reluctantly I released her lips causing her eyes to open in surprise. "Jonah? Do you not want…"

"No, I do," I interrupted immediately. "I just…uh…Ash, I want you so bad…and I don't think I'll be able to control myself."

"I don't want you to," she replied so intensely that I quickly turned around and shut off the water, opened the curtain, and stepped out of the shower.

"Come 'ere, baby," I said as I bent down, allowing her to wrap her arms around my neck and then lifted both of her legs around me. She was so tiny that I could have wrapped my arms around her twice, but despite her size she had amazing inner thigh strength and tightened her legs around my waist as I walked us out of the bathroom and into the bedroom. It looked so easy in the movies, but in our reality I stumbled into the wall twice before finally making it to the bed and laying Ashlyn down upon it. Sensually she stretched herself out, showing me just how beautiful she was.

"Condoms?"

"My bag," she replied and pointed to her colorful patchwork bag sitting on the dresser behind me. Quickly I grabbed the bag and handed it to her knowing I would never find them. By the time I laid down beside her she had an unwrapped condom in her hand and was unrolling it down my hard shaft. I wrapped her soft leg around my hips and slid my hand between her legs, slipping a finger inside of her. Ashlyn gasped, her eyes a mixture of surprise and desire for more.

Nothing was said as I rolled her on her back and took position between her legs, only a loving and wanting gaze between us. Ashlyn placed her hands on my ass as she spread her legs further and pulled me inside of her, both of us releasing a moan of relief. Through her touch I could feel a pulsing heat vibrating through my body causing me to push into her harder and faster. Her breathless high-pitched sighs intensified when I took her breast into my mouth, sucking and flicking her hard nipple with my tongue. I don't think I had ever enjoyed a pair of breasts so much in my life.

At that moment Ashlyn's hips began tilting and curling in a whole new gear, her warm insides coming at me from amazing and new angles, making it almost impossible not to echo her rhythm. Problem was, we were going too fast, I could feel it in my pelvic muscles as they tightened and stiffened, but I couldn't find the strength to stop. Ashlyn crooked her arms under my shoulders as she bent her legs up and wrapped them around my back. It was at that point I knew it was over.

Her breath quickened as I pounded myself into her. I tried thinking of baseball, football, anything to slow down the progression of the oncoming climax, but of course when you have a beautiful blonde sighing your name in pleasure there's nothing you can do when you feel every muscle in your body contract and explode.

Ashlyn's body froze underneath me as I released an awkward grunt. Several silent seconds passed before she unfurled herself from around me and said, "Did…you…"

I opened my eyes and saw her questioning eyes looking back at me. "I'm sorry," I sighed as I pulled out from within her and rolled over to the edge of the bed. "This was not…goddamn it. Can anything go right today?"

"Baby, it's ok," she said comfortingly. "It happens. It's nothing…"

"No, this needed to be perfect," I snapped as my head fell into my hands. "Christ, it needed to be better than that."

"Who says?"

"I do!" I snapped again as my head shot up. "I'm competing with Vamps, Ashlyn, you have no idea what kind of pressure that is."

Fuck.

She pulled away from me abruptly. "This is what you were feeling yesterday, isn't it?"

"Stop reading me!"

"I'm not!" she shouted back. "I don't have to read you when you're like this. I'm not an idiot."

The tension hung in the air as the two of us sat on opposite ends of the bed with our backs turned to one another. She didn't understand the pressures of competition that all men faced when sleeping with someone new. It was bred into us and not something that could be relieved by saying 'this time would be different', it just didn't work that way.

"I can't help what I am," Ashlyn cried softly behind me.

Her statement and her cries made me stand and walk around to her side of the bed, kneeling in front of her. "*Were*, Ashlyn."

"It doesn't seem to matter when we get to this."

I sighed in frustration at letting my pride and insecurities ruin our first time together. "I can do better."

"I don't need you to do better."

"But Ashlyn, *I* need to do better. Honestly, I am much better at this than…that…was. It's just with everything today…and there was a lot of nakedness in the shower and…I," I sighed in embarrassment, "…it's been longer than I hate to admit since I've done this, especially with someone that I care about, and you are just so damn sexy and gorgeous that I couldn't slow myself down…"

Ashlyn placed her hand over my mouth, her eyes still glassy with tears. "Don't you see? All I've ever had are men who don't care. The minute you turned around in the shower you had me, I didn't care what we did or for how long, no one has ever looked at me the way you did. I've never seen that kind of fire in anyone's eyes, and the way you touched me…"

Ashlyn shook with a sudden shiver as goose bumps rose up on her skin. Gently I brushed my fingers down the outline of her collarbone, continuing down the front of her chest, and then grazing the inside of her left breast causing her to completely collapse into herself. "That tickles."

I returned her smile and gently pulled her face down to mine. "I just need a little more time."

She nodded and then rested her forehead on mine. "We can slow down. I completely understand."

"No," I laughed. "That's not what I meant. What I mean is, I need a few more minutes before we can do this again."

"Oh," Ashlyn replied in a surprised tone. "Again, huh? We're going to…" she giggled a little to herself, "…make…love?"

I nodded. "Again, and again, and again," I replied sensually and then joined in her coy laughter. "As long as that's ok, of course."

She nodded vigorously. "Mmm-hmm, very ok."

"So in the meantime," I began as I pulled her hands away from me. "Lay back."

Ashlyn's face fell into a terrified look. "Why?"

With a comforting smile I leaned into her and kissed her deeply, pressing up slightly as I laid her down on the bed. Before she could tangle me in her arms I kissed down the center of her chest, resting in between her breasts and even squeezing them into my face causing Ashlyn to release a loud breathy sigh. Her arms once again tried to wrap around me, so I continued my dissent down her chest and to the edge of her stomach. Slowly I rose up, gently placing my hands between her inner thighs and spreading her legs open to me. She truly looked like a piece of art.

I bent down and gently began flicking my tongue up her inner thigh to where it met her pelvis. I expected a moan or a sigh, but instead Ashlyn popped up on her elbows causing her hair to fly messily in front of her face. "Jonah! What...what are you...doing?"

With a mischievous smile I replied, "Do you trust me?" She nodded nervously. "Just lie back and let me take care of you."

"Wh-wha...how?"

Gently I brushed the back of my fingers between her legs and watched as her eyes closed and her body shivered. "Just relax."

Ashlyn laid back tentatively, her thighs shivering with nerves as I lowered myself back onto my knees and pressed my lips against her.

Once again Ashlyn shot up on her elbows. "You're going to...do...that?!"

"Yes!" I laughed. "I'm going to...do...this."

"But...people do that?"

My smile felt as though it was touching both ears. "Yes, Ashlyn, people do this. Probably not as much as most women want."

"But...it's...down there."

"Yeah, baby, that's why I really want to."

"Why?"

I paused with a proud smile. "Because it's obvious I'll be the first. Now lay back so I can make you feel something you've never felt before."

Ashlyn smiled nervously as she laid back down, her moans starting instantly as I explored her inside and out. From this point on all the men she'd had, all the Vamps with their superior stamina and physique, didn't matter because I'd won. I'd done what no one else had ever done to her- loved her.

Chapter Twenty-six

Cameron

"Diana, what is it exactly you want?" I asked, tired of her wretched whining.

"What do I want!?" she replied, slamming her fist down on the desk. "I want real security. This place should be crawling with Warriors after what happened today, and yet, I'm only given one."

"Two," I corrected. "Brianna, as you know, is a Warrior. She scanned the perimeter and there are no Vampires within ten miles, and you have a tremendous security team that has been on their guard since the incident. Perhaps they were only after this particular hybrid..." I gestured to Diana to fill in the name of the hybrid that was currently escaping me, but surprisingly she shook her head with uncertainty.

"Her name is Lyla Firino," Seraphina answered with a loud frustrated sigh.

"The Warrior is right," Eris said as he placed his hand gently on his wife's arm. Usually the gesture was the other way around, but I could see the upset in Seraphina's face over Diana's lack of knowledge. "Perhaps they wanted her because she is a Firestarter."

"Yes, but how did they know she would be coming in today?" Diana rebutted.

"Diana, you said yourself that Jonah reported being followed yesterday.

Maybe they had an idea of when she was coming and merely waited until they saw her," I said trying to calm the room.

"But why wait until now? Why not just go and grab her from home? Why did they need to come here and jeopardize *my* Facility."

I saw Eris's hand squeeze Seraphina's arm again.

"Ma'am, if I may," Warren, the Head of Security, began from the far corner of the office, "the Firino's are known to be powerful Firestarters. No one in their right mind would go there willingly. It would be less dangerous to take her when she's away from her parents' protection. But Diana, as I have been assuring you, we are very well protected. My team…"

"This is just ridiculous!" Diana interrupted. "Lanashell never had these kind of troubles at Facility West. She would snap her fingers or merely say the words Brianna Morgan and the place would be surrounded by Warriors. But no, when I have a real crisis I'm left with a mishmash human/Vampire security team, two Warriors, and two creepy little Vampire kids."

I felt my fangs itching the insides of my gums, desperately wanting to come out at the mention of my children, but instead my cooler head prevailed. "Diana, Lanashell has settled several crises without the help of the Warriors, but when she has needed us, the proximity of Facility West to our headquarters has made it easier. This could very well be an isolated incident, but if not, four Warriors are coming to take our place tomorrow morning. You will be well protected."

"You're leaving?!" Diana said in a panic as she rose from her chair and then looked to Eris. "Are you leaving as well?"

"I no longer have ties to Facility East, Diana," Eris replied with a slight smile. "I go where mia familia goes."

"I will not allow it!" Diana slammed her fist down on the desk again causing Eris to stand and expose his fangs to her.

"Do not begin to think you can give ME orders, madam," Eris growled as both Warren and I put a gentle hand on his shoulders. After two percussive breaths Eris's temper seemed to lessen. "Trust in your security team."

"But there are humans on the team!"

Warren held his hand out defensively in front of him. "The humans on my team have strength and talent, and would very well give their lives defending each and every hybrid here."

"That is precisely the issue," Diana snapped back as she sat down in her chair. "If we were to be attacked, the humans would be killed instantly, providing no line of protection, causing the Vampire members of your team to have to work doubly hard."

"But…that is…simply not the case," Warren stuttered. "My humans…"

"Are now fired," Diana interrupted without the slightest bit of emotion. "As are all humans currently employed at Facility East."

"Pardon?"

"You heard me, Warren," Diana answered in a snotty tone. "Effective immediately, all human personnel are henceforth terminated and will be asked to leave the premises. And in case you need me to be specific, Mr. Burke, that does include your friend Jonah. I think we all know he should never have been allowed to be in the position he has, especially after today's events."

"But you cannot," Seraphina shouted as she came to stand next to Eris. "We need zhe humans as much…you simply cannot…"

"Well pardon me, but I can," Diana interrupted as she looked at her watch. "It is now a quarter after midnight, meaning this is now my Facility and I have the right to do whatever I see fit. The humans go. Perhaps you can lead the charge tomorrow when you leave, preferably with your freaky little grandkids in tow."

The lovely French lady, whose manners and poise were engrained deeply into her DNA, lost all her control and lunged across the desk with her hands stretching out towards Diana. Eris wrapped his arms around her waist and pulled her from the desk and then from the room altogether as French expletives spewed from her lips.

"What did she say?" Diana yelled as she patted her hair down and pulled her chair back to its original position. "What did she call me! One of you tell me what she said!"

"I do not speak French," I lied, trying not to smirk at Seraphina's comment.

"Well good riddance," Diana huffed as she pulled her poorly cut blazer back down to its proper place. "Now, Warren, I believe you have some layoffs to do."

"Diana, please," Warren begged. "The humans make up almost half of my team. I cannot protect the entire Facility with so few."

"Then you should have thought about that before you hired so many humans."

"But many of them are also blood donors."

"Then they can visit when we need blood, otherwise their services are no longer needed. You have until noon tomorrow to replenish your team. Hopefully the other Warriors will be here by then. You are dismissed."

Warren's lips disappeared into his mouth while he and Diana stared each other down. After several seconds Warren finally turned on his heel and slammed the door behind him.

"Diana, this truly is madness."

"Madness, Mr. Burke?! There isn't one human security member at Facility West. What is madness is how many there are here! Lana would never have allowed…"

"Facility East does not house hybrids as dangerous or unstable as Facility West. Diana, I understand you are trying to make your mark as a leader, but I am telling you for your own good that terminating all humans from Facility East is a disastrous move."

Diana dug her knuckles firmly into the wooden desk as she slowly rose from her chair. "Don't think for a moment that I don't know who you are really trying to protect here. You could give a flying flip about the other humans, all you really care about is the fact that your little Jonah is now out of a job."

"What do you have against…"

"Never in a million years would Lana have hired him in his position. Dante was a fool."

"Diana, you must understand that Jonah was well vetted by Dante and has exceeding all expectations, even surpassing his Vampire co-workers whom you see as so superior. Jonah has sacrificed both life and family for this Facility. He is a supervisor, unlike the other humans, and deserves more consideration especially because of his actions today."

"You have got to be kidding!" Diana replied. "He put that hybrid's life in danger simply by being in the car. If one of our Vampires had been in that SUV they would have fought instead…"

"Fought and perhaps lost," I interrupted. "Jonah staying in the car most likely saved Lyla Firino's life, and I am sure that is the only thing that both she and her parents care about at this moment. Jonah is a hero and should be recognized for his actions, not…"

"What do you want then?"

"Jonah's continued employment."

"Absolutely not."

I sighed. "Then a severance."

Diana's eyes narrowed as she considered it. "How long?"

"One year."

She laughed. "One month."

"Six months."

"Three months is more than generous."

"Five months, and I convince Victor to give you one additional Warrior."

"Four months, one additional Warrior, but *you* have to tell him."

I truly hated this woman and her cheap suit, but it was for Jonah and I would rather tell him the bad news than for him to hear it from her rancid lips. "Four months, one Warrior, and he retains free room and board during that time."

"And you will tell him?"

"Yes," I growled.

Diana's lips twisted over her teeth as she considered the offer. "Fine. You can tell him in the morning, but none of the other humans can get wind of his severance."

"Very well," I replied and then turned to leave.

"I will hold you to your word, Mr. Burke."

When I turned back around she was displaying a sly, but victorious smile, as though she truly thought she had me by the balls.

"Diana, I will hold up my end of the bargain as long as you do. But if you try to shirk Jonah's severance in any way, you will quickly see the Warriors' support taken from you. However, even at this rate I cannot see you sitting behind that desk for too long."

"How dare you…"

"You sit there thinking you are running things as Lanashell does, as if you are her equal. But having worked with Lanashell over the years I can tell you that you do not have even one-tenth of her leadership skills. It is true that Lanashell manages her Facility with a firm grip and that it runs like a well-oiled machine, but she has something you obviously do not possess – compassion. You watched Lanashell while you worked with her, but you certainly did not pay attention and learn from her. Knowing her as I do, she would be appalled at your actions today.

"Once Jonah has everything he needs out of you, I will see to it that your future here is limited, although I have a pretty good idea that you will do enough damage all by yourself."

I opened the office door, but stopped just before stepping out. "One last thing. If you dare to insult my children or their mother again, you will truly see how closely related I am to the Warrior Assassin. Do we understand each other?"

Diana nodded nervously before I stepped into the hallway and slammed the door just as Warren had. And speaking of, he was standing just to the left of the door, holding his mouth to restrain his laughter. When he saw me, he straightened up quickly like a soldier in front of his commanding officer, but when I smiled he relaxed his shoulders. "Could you do that again so I can record it?"

I gave a short laugh as I began to walk down the hall with Warren following in line behind me. "Would you like to do another pass around the perimeter?"

Warren nodded. "Please. It'll postpone having to fire half my staff. And thank you, by the way," Warren said as he pulled back on my shoulder. "Most Warriors I feel would look down on my team, human and Vampire. I appreciate you trying to defend us."

"Little good it did. Your team respects you, they are talented, and they would sacrifice themselves to protect these hybrids. Any Warrior would respect that and despise the bureaucracy that decides to break that bond. Understand, Warren, the Warriors coming tomorrow are only here to help. They will not be looking to take over, only to give counsel and a fighting arm when needed."

"Tell that to Diana," he growled. "I believe she's gunning to have them replace me altogether."

"I will be sure to debrief them, but they know the boundaries. These particular three Warriors are not looking to have the responsibilities you do."

"I believe you mean four," Warren corrected with a raised brow.

"What I do for that kid," I sighed as my hand raked through my hair.

"Jonah's a good kid. He's lucky to have you in his corner."

"I merely worry about what will happen to him when we leave."

"I will look after him as much as I can," Warren replied, extending his hand and I shook it. "Ready for that pass?"

"Give me ten minutes. I would like to check in on Brianna and the children first."

"Meet you at the gate in ten," Warren nodded and we both disappeared in clouds of black mist.

A second later the darkened inside of the small hotel-like guestroom developed around me. When I turned to face the bed I smiled at the sight of my little ones curled up on either side of their mother's chest. I wish their sleep was always this peaceful.

"That took a while," Brianna said softly as I sat on the edge of the bed.

"Diana Stewart will run this place into the ground in a matter of months."

"That bad?"

I released a cynical laugh. "Your father had his fangs extended most of the time, I threatened to kill her, and your stepmother leapt onto the desk trying to attack her."

"Please tell me you recorded that."

"You are not the only one who has asked."

"What got Mom so upset?"

"Diana was being very free with her insults, and…" I paused again as I turned and folded my leg up on the bed. "Bri angel, Diana is terminating all the human staff."

"What? Wait…all…humans?"

"Yes, love, unfortunately including Jonah."

"Did the bitch give a reason?" she asked as she covered the children's ears.

"She feels that humans have no business working here."

"How much more is he going to have to take?" she said, wiping away a red tear escaping from her right eye. "Does he know?"

"Not yet," I replied. "He deserves a good night's sleep."

"Cam, this could break him. He just left his family, he doesn't have anywhere to go. What is he going to do now? We can't just leave him here, we need to help…"

"Shh, angel," I interrupted and placed my hand on her leg. "I made a deal with Diana. He will be able to live here with full pay for the next few months. Hopefully that will be enough time for him to either get on his feet or make up with his family."

"You did that for him?"

"For you, too. I knew you would worry."

"Like I don't have enough to worry about," she replied, petting the heads of the twins sleeping on her chest. "We haven't had a second to talk about what happened today with Jack."

"I know," I sighed and rose from the bed when Bri grabbed my arm.

"Cam, we need to talk about…"

"Not…" I snapped in a whispered growl but then caught myself as I watched Bri narrow her eyes, "…now. I need to meet Warren for another security run."

"This is our son, Cameron," she whispered. "And if Aidan is behind today's attack that could mean he's been building a whole new coven just like we saw in the twins' dream. This whole thing could have been a trap to get us here so he could get to the kids."

"That is why I need to be with Warren," I replied and successfully stood from the bed this time.

"You *need* to be with your children right now. *We* need to figure out what we're going to do with Jack-Jack. Warren has had you all night, we…I get to have you for a couple of hours to figure out how we're going to protect our children from Aidan."

"Brianna, I am well aware of everything I need to do and I am doing my best to give everyone the attention they need. Today has been…" I paused and exhaled in order to bring both my tension and my volume down. "Today has been overwhelming."

"Try going through it alone," she mumbled under her breath.

"You are NOT going through this alone," I snapped.

"Really," she challenged, but then our argument stopped abruptly as the twins joined their hands across Brianna's chest. Suddenly everything we were arguing about was moot.

"I should take a look."

"Are you strong enough to let me watch with you?"

Bri nodded and I climbed up next to her on the bed. The twins' faces twitched as they released soft whimpers. I wrapped my hand around the back of her neck causing her to tilt her head up to me.

"I'm sorry," she said.

"I am as well," I replied, pulling her closer to me and kissing her forehead. "Whatever we see, we will handle together."

She nodded nervously before placing a hand on each child's cheek. After taking a deep breath, Brianna closed her eyes and a few seconds later her body was rigid and stoic meaning she was fully inside our children's dream. I brought her head to rest against my cheek and flattened my palm against her chest. A moment later I was enveloped in a cloud of darkness as my consciousness was sucked into my children's minds.

The darkness that had initially surrounded me began to fade, but the scene around me was almost as dark. The only source of light came from the full moon shining down on the trees that surrounded us.

"Cam," Brianna called as she stepped over to me, taking my hand and pulling me further into the scene around us.

As we had seen before, another Brianna stood at the edge of a small ridge with one arm stretched out tensely in front of her while the other was similarly behind her. Jackson was wrapped around Brianna's left leg while Olivia stretched herself across her mother's shoulders, both of them holding on for dear life. But what were they doing? What was Brianna doing? And now that my attention was on them, why were the Warriors scattered around, including myself, gripping and tearing through the ground as if we were being blown back by an invisible wind.

"What do you think is happening? What am I doing up there?" Brianna whispered beside me.

I squeezed her hand. "I was thinking the same thing," I replied and then pointed into the distance where Aidan stood with his followers. "Does it appear that Aidan's group has gotten larger?"

Brianna scanned the scene in front of us and nodded slowly. "A lot bigger. How come there are so few of us?"

Just then, the other Brianna fell to the ground and instinctively I leapt forward to go to her, but my Brianna, my true Brianna, pushed her hand into my chest.

"It's not me, remember?"

Together we watched as the other Cameron went to the other Brianna's side, took Jackson into his arms, and pulled Brianna up into a standing position with Olivia on her hip. Together they ran away from the chaos of fighting that ensued around them, running in our direction as they each clutched a child to their chest. Brianna and I fell in line behind, dodging the flying bodies and branches and earth being kicked up by the battle.

As we ran I tried taking in as many details as possible, but truly there was little unique about the wooded area. It could be one of a thousand places in the United States, let alone the world.

The other Brianna and Cameron began to slow, so we did the same, staying behind them but close enough to hear the conversation.

"Baby girl, you have to go with them," the other Brianna said as she finally came to a stop.

"No, Mama, no way, no way," Olivia cried as she snaked her arms tightly around her mother's neck.

"Livy, please!" the other Brianna begged. "You have to go."

The Brianna next to me gasped and lunged forward when Aidan appeared before us and began pulling Olivia from her mother's arms. Reluctantly I clamped my arms across my Brianna's chest, whispering to her that what we were seeing was not real, that we needed to watch and learn. But no amount of comfort could be given while Olivia screamed and flailed at Aidan trying to tear her away from her mother. Jackson, however, climbed down from my counterpart and merely stepped alongside Aidan.

"No!" the true Brianna screamed and broke free of my hold. Running to Jackson, she pulled him away from Aidan who was still struggling with a screaming Olivia.

"Mama no! I need to go! I need to help!" he yelled and ripped his hand away. Brianna swept her arms out in front of her...

With a snap, the dark hotel-like room was surrounding us once more but with the sounds of our children's cries. Brianna unhinged herself from my side, checking each child and wiping tears from their cheeks.

"Mama, I don't like that dream," Olivia cried.

"Neither do I, baby girl," Brianna replied.

"Then why do we keep havin' it?"

"I don't know," Brianna lied as she gave me a fearful look.

"Ada, do I have to go in time out again?" Jackson said guiltily. "You were making Wivy go with Aidan, so I thought I had to."

Brianna gasped loudly. "We did not..."

I held my hand up to stop her seeing how emotional she was. "Son, we were not making Olivia go with Aidan."

"Yes you were," Olivia whined.

"Monkey, we would never do that. It was just a dream. We never want you to go with Aidan, remember?" Olivia nodded pitifully against Brianna's chest. "Right, Jackson?"

Slowly Jackson nodded his head, although I was not overly confident in his response. With a frustrated sigh I climbed off the bed and held out my arms to him which he quickly jumped into.

"Where are you going?" Brianna asked worried.

"I still need to help Warren with a security sweep. It will give Jackson a chance to practice his skills, and give us a chance to have another conversation about not trusting Aidan."

"Cam, I don't think…"

"We could make it a family affair," I urged as I held my hand out.

However, it was Olivia who took my hand and climbed up my arm to rest atop my shoulder. "Come on, Mama! I don't wanna sleep anymore."

Brianna sat reluctantly on the bed so I extended my hand to her again. "Together, love. I cannot do it alone."

"I hate when you use my words against me," she said, taking my hand and rising from the bed.

"I hate when we argue and I act like a jerk."

"Me too," she winked and transferred Olivia from my shoulders to her hip. "Midnight family outing it is."

Chapter Twenty-seven

Jonah

I practically needed a crowbar to tear me from Ashlyn this morning. I had admitted to her that it had been a while since I'd had sex, but it had been even longer since it had been meaningful. We might have gotten off to a rough start, but once my dick and my brain began working together, if Ashlyn or I even flinched in our sleep we were attacking each other. Every condom she had in her purse now littered the floor around the bed. I guess I was hoping the condom fairy would come in and clean before I got up, but nonetheless I had the dirty job. I did catch myself smiling a little at the number I had to pick up, we were maniacs last night.

Awesome.

My shower was quick, my hair left wet and flat as I threw on a pair of jeans and an old t-shirt I found in my bag of clothes from home. Even with all the euphoria from hours of making love to Ashlyn, deep in the pit of my stomach was still the ache and burn from everything that had happened with my mother. But every time a thought or image came into my head I shook it away. There wasn't time to wallow like I had started to last night. There were bigger things happening today, or at least I thought there would be.

After grabbing a hoodie from the closet, I went back over to the bed where Ashlyn laid completely unconscious in a fetal position. Leaning down, I gently kissed her bare shoulder that stuck out over the comforter.

"I'll be back soon," I whispered in her ear and then kissed her cheek.

"Mmmm," she moaned.

I kissed her once more on her temple. "I love you, Ash."

"Mmmm," she moaned again, but this time with a warm smile. The smile only lasted a second before she was asleep again. Goodness knows she needed it. I couldn't imagine how sore she was going to be when she woke.

Awesome. I did that.

With a sigh, and half a woody, I adjusted myself and walked out the door.

The hallway was quiet, oddly quiet. But perhaps everything was under control? I shrugged to myself and continued up the stairs to the main floor where again the halls and the gathering areas were completely empty. It wasn't that early. Again I shrugged. I could use a quiet day after the hell of yesterday.

Turning down the corridor for the offices I noticed Warren walking in my direction with his head down and muttering to himself. He was so deep in his own world that he didn't even acknowledge me when I said good morning. Well I supposed that the Head of Security would have a lot on his mind so I brushed it off and walked towards my office. Not that I knew what I was going to have to do when I got there. It wasn't like we were going to be doing any pickups for the time being.

When I turned into my office I jumped backed, startled by a figure sitting in my chair, but then relaxed when Cameron lifted his head.

"Hey man, you scared me," I said, catching my breath and stepping inside.

"Good morning, Jonah. Did you sleep?"

"Yeah, a little," I smiled. "How was your night? Looks like you're wearing the same thing you were in when I saw you last night."

Cameron adjusted his shirt's collar that lay underneath his dark sweater, and oddly he looked nervous as he stood and gestured to the chair. "Yes well, it has been a long night. Have a seat, Jonah, there are some things we need to discuss."

I did as he asked and sat in my chair. "It's so quiet, is everyone still on lockdown?"

"Yes, it is easier to account for everyone that way."

When Cameron didn't say anything else after a few seconds I clapped my hands together and said, "So what did you need to talk to me about? I already know we're shutdown for pickups so…"

"Yes, all new hybrids have been diverted to Facility West," he interrupted as he stood abruptly from his chair. "But that is not what I need to…" Cameron paused again, turning his back on me.

"Listen man, whatever it is…you're kinda freaking me out."

Cameron turned around, his hands firmly on his hips while his face settled into a conflicted expression. "I apologize, Jonah. I did not think it would be this difficult." He licked his lips and resigned to sitting back down in the chair next to me. "Jonah, last night Diana made a decision to let go of all human staff."

I blinked slowly, my heart suddenly beating through my ribs. "Let…go?"

Cameron sighed and glanced at the floor. "We fought for you, Jonah, you must believe me. Eris, Seraphina, Warren, we all fought for everyone but especially you."

My cheeks and ears started to burn as Cameron went on, but I wasn't listening. How dare Diana fire me after everything I have done for this place. After all the hours I spent away from my family, giving up any kind of social life for the past four years, and then almost losing my life protecting Lyla.

"I brought that girl back here alive," I interrupted angrily as I stood from my chair so fast that it hit the desk behind me.

Cameron remained seated as he calmly replied, "Yes you did, and you are to be commended."

"Yeah, and I'm being fired instead," I snapped as I turned my back on him, facing my desk and seeing the picture of my mom and sister on its surface. Then everything hit me. "Oh my god…I…left my house. I'm…homeless. Where…where am I going to go? How am I going to get another job! I can't list this place. Who's going to hire me? I can't do anything…and Ashlyn…what am I…"

Suddenly I couldn't breathe and my hands hit the desk as I keeled over.

"Jonah, listen to me," Cameron began with a hand on my back, "I negotiated a severance for you. Four months, full pay and benefits, and you can stay here during that time. Bri and I will help you, Jonah, whatever it is you need we are here for you."

Slowly I rose from the desk and turned to Cameron. "You did that for me?"

"Of course I did."

"How long do I have again?"

"Four months," he replied. "I fought for longer but…"

"No, no, thank you. Really, thank you, man. I didn't mean to get so…"

Cameron squeezed my shoulder. "You have every right to be upset, Jonah, everyone is."

"I'm guessing that's why Warren ignored me."

"Probably. I know he has been speaking with his staff all morning. He is now very short-handed."

"Wait a minute," I said shaking my head, "did Diana…make you…tell me?"

"I thought it best to hear it from a friend."

"So that's a yes," I responded. "I really hate that bitch. Maybe it's a good thing I'm not working for her anymore." My stomach flipped and the blood suddenly drained from my head. "Holy shit, I'm not working for anyone."

"But you will," Cameron replied, squeezing my shoulder again. "And remember you are not alone. Brianna and I…"

"Have done enough for me," I interrupted. "Well I guess I can go back to bed then. Make sure Bri finds me before you guys leave."

Cameron smiled and nodded. "I do not think you have much choice in the matter."

With a sigh and one last glance at my office, I stepped out into the quiet hallway and headed back to my room. My mind was racing and my stomach was still doing flips as I thought about all that I had lost since yesterday. What the hell was I going to say to Ashlyn? We finally took that big step in our relationship, but we were still new. Would she still want to be with a guy who didn't have a job or a place to live, limited opportunities and prospects, basically an all-around loser?

While the endless worries swirled in my head, I was on autopilot as I crossed the lobby and didn't even see Brianna until her arms were around my neck.

"Ohmygod, Jonah, are you ok?" she said very quickly as she stood on her toes and hugged me tightly.

"Not really."

"I'm so sorry, honey. Cameron fought…"

"I know he did."

"Sera and Eris would never…"

"I know they wouldn't."

"Diana's a bitch."

"You got that right."

Brianna released my neck and lowered herself to the ground as she cupped my face between her hands. "Don't be too proud to ask for help. If you need anything, Cam and I are here."

I pulled her hands away. "Like I told Cameron, you guys have done enough. I'll…figure something out. Besides you're leaving today. You have enough to deal with right now."

"Then come with us," she said.

"Bri…"

"Seriously, Jonah, come with us down to Daddy O's. It'll be crowded as all get out, but we're having a big Thanksgiving dinner. You'll be surrounded by friends and you'll be away from this place."

"I can't leave Ashlyn here all alone."

"Of course I meant Ashlyn should come too, silly. Diana can't say she won't be protected, there'll be more Warriors down there than there will be here. Just…just promise you'll think about it, ok? I'm not saying I don't want you to mend things with your mom, because I do. I think it's really important that you do. But putting some time and distance between you might help calm things down a little."

Honestly I just wanted to go back to bed. It was warm. Ashlyn was there. Naked. That alone would help take my mind off this really shitty morning. But Brianna wouldn't let me go without some kind of answer.

"I'll think about it."

"Really think about it," she said and hugged me tightly. "We're not leaving until the other Warriors get here later this afternoon. If you decide to stay, at least come and say goodbye. The kids definitely want to see you."

"I wouldn't dream of disappointing them," I replied before turning away and ducking down the side stairs to the basement.

I couldn't get to my room fast enough. Fucking Diana. Fuck her that fucking sour-faced fucking fuck. When I finally stepped inside my room the curtains were still drawn, but I could still find my way to the bed. I immediately stripped down and climbed underneath the comforter where I followed the warmth radiating from my girl. Sliding up behind her, I wrapped my arm over the curve of her waist and pulled her back into my chest.

"Back already?" she yawned as she tried to turn around, but I clamped my arm down to keep her where she was so that I could say what I needed to.

"Ashlyn, I...do you think you can be with a guy who has no family, no place to live...and no job?"

Ashlyn's body flinched. Quickly she pulled my arm away from her waist and turned around to face me. "My god, Jonah, what happened?"

"Diana fired all the humans."

"Oh my god, are you serious?"

"Ash, I know we haven't been together that long so I wouldn't blame you for not wanting to stay with someone who has nothing."

With a flustered grunt Ashlyn rolled me onto my back, climbed over me, and turned on the light from the nightstand. "Ok, so last night you tell me you love me, but today you're telling me to get out?"

"Wh...uh...no! That's not..."

"Then why would you say that," she said angrily as she unfortunately pulled the comforter around her bare chest. "I can't believe you would say that to me after last night."

"I have nothing!" I replied loudly as my hands covered my face in frustration. "No family, no job, no place to live, nothing! You deserve better..."

"Oh stop with that shit, Jonah!" she yelled. "Will you at least look at me?" Reluctantly I pulled my hands away from my face and saw her beautiful dark eyes staring back at me. "I don't deserve anything, Jonah. I've never done anything in my life to deserve a guy like you."

"Don't say..." I began but she put her finger up to my lips.

"Baby, you are so much more than I deserve. Every day we're together is...it's like I'm stealing you away from the good girls you should really be with. If you're saying I shouldn't be with you because you don't have a job or a family or a place to live, then why the hell are you with me? It's not because I have a family, because big surprise I don't. I really don't, I am completely alone unlike you. Jonah, you have a family. Your mother and sister are still here, and yes, you're fighting, but if something were to happen to any one of you, you would be at each other's side."

"But..."

"So you lost your job. You'll find another one. At least you have a chance out there. I should be telling you it's ok for you to leave me, not the other way around."

I shook my head. "I could never do that."

"Then don't say that shit to me," she replied resting her cheek on my chest and hugging me with her draped arm. "We'll figure it out. If there's something I know how to do, it's how to survive on nothing."

I wrapped my arms around her tiny body, rubbing her soft bare back up and down. I didn't want her to have to go back into survival mode. I promised her she'd never have to live like that again, and now…

"Jonah, stop worrying."

"Ashlyn, stop reading me," I replied in a snarky tone and then felt guilty. "Sorry."

"Don't be. I promised not to, and I'm…just trying to help."

"I know you are. I just feel like I've been stripped of everything. I…I just feel so alone."

"But you're not," she said kindly. "You have me, and Brianna and Cameron, and Eris and Sera, even Mable. You just have to tell us what we can do for you."

I wrapped my hand around the back of her neck and pulled her up to my lips. Her breasts grazed my chest as she draped herself on top of me while my free hand traveled down to her thigh. Holding her tightly I rolled her onto her back and instantly began sucking her neck while I massaged her small right breast. Her moans became louder as my pelvis began grinding against her.

I released the skin of her neck and crushed my lips against her again, plunging my tongue deep inside her mouth. When I finally did come up for air I lifted myself up onto my forearms as I said softly, "Please let me inside you."

Fear suddenly crossed over Ashlyn's face. "But we used everything I had."

Fuck.

"I'm sorry, baby, but…

"No, you're right," I replied, angry at myself once again for not being prepared. Pressing myself up, I started to roll off of Ashlyn when she suddenly grabbed my hips and held me in place.

"Just…this once," she said nervously.

"Ash, it's ok…"

"No, I want you too just…we just need to be careful."

I nodded nervously. Slowly I lowered myself back onto my forearms as Ashlyn widened her legs and guided me inside of her. She was warm and wet and surprisingly I could feel that she was swollen. In fact, I could feel absolutely everything and it scared me at how difficult it would be to control myself. As I moved in and out of her, Ashlyn's moans were driving me crazy as were her lips that were kissing and sucking my neck and earlobe.

"Do you want to go away with me?" I asked trying to distract myself.

Ashlyn pulled away in order to look at me. "You really want to talk about that now?"

"If you want this to last, then yeah, we should talk about it now."

Chapter Twenty-eight

Brianna

Thanksgiving was finally here. We left Facility East over two weeks ago, and with each passing day came new guests. At this point there were six Vampires, five humans, four hybrids, three kids, and a partridge in a pear tree. Wait, that's Christmas. The biggest hurdle was finding room for people to sleep in Daddy O's small one level ranch in the North Carolina mountains, and of course there was always drama in the morning over the bathroom. I guess there were some advantages to being a Vampire now.

"Uh…Bri, that looks an awful like stirring," Kyla said with a challenging tone. "Renee's in charge of chopping, and I am in charge of stirring. You are stirring those potatoes so that is infringing on my job. So stop."

Kyla desperately wanted to help cook the Thanksgiving meal. Knowing she didn't know how to cook, I gave her the fake important job of stirring. Then of course because Kyla had a job, Renee insisted on having a job. They were my second set of twins, and acting just as old as my children sometimes.

I gave another dash of salt to the big bowl of mashed potatoes and handed it across the center island to Kyla. "Maddy's been chopping off and on for the last hour and you don't hear Renee complaining."

"That's because I'm on wine number two," Renee replied.

"Number three, actually," I corrected.

"Three? What happened to number two?"

"Er…you drank it while I made sweet potatoes," I laughed as did Sera and Maddy. It was definitely a women-only kitchen, and they were certainly four of my favorite. A few times I even caught myself thinking Mama Jo's spirit was with us too. Hell, I was using her cookbook, she was probably looking over my shoulder making sure I was preparing everything correctly, and then probably checking out Maddy. Even though Maddy and Daddy O had been together for four years now, there were times it was hard to see her in the house. Daddy O had been alone for so long and Mama Jo's imprint was so strong that I had to keep reminding myself how wonderful Maddy was. Madeline Forebush was a saint, and even though saying goodbye to the only real home I ever knew, she and Daddy O deserved a new home of their own that was absent of old ghosts.

"So Maddy," Renee semi-slurred, "still enjoying retirement?"

"Oh yes," Maddy replied as she poured her homemade cranberry sauce into a serving bowl. "I've enjoyed it down here, but I'll be happy to be back in San Francisco."

"You'll be happy to be closer to Jared," I joked and she gave me a sly wink.

"I hear ya, Maddy," Renee said. "Though I've always been partial to Jonah."

I raised my eyebrow at her. "You've been partial to his backside."

"Do you blame me?" she replied before drinking back the last of the wine in her glass.

"Well, it's not yours to look at anymore," I chided. "It belongs to Ashlyn now."

"Oh yes, crazy girl has stolen his heart away from me," Renee sang dramatically, almost hitting Kyla in the face with her unruly arms.

"Shhh, she's not crazy," I nagged as the timer for the turkey went off.

"Well she used to be."

"I zhink she has come very far," Sera replied defensively and handed me the thermometer for the turkey. "Ashlyn and Jonah make a very good match, don't you zhink?"

"Sickly-sweet-perfect," Maddy replied. "Especially compared to Jared and that girl."

All the women around the island groaned in agreement with Maddy. Nikki was here because of Jared and we had no way around it.

Just as I pulled the turkey out of the oven, Daddy O's recliner creaked from the living room.

"Is that the turkey I smell?" he asked as his head popped around the corner.

He was old, but his sense of smell was always dead on. "Daddy O, in all your years, have you ever gotten to eat the turkey right out of the oven?"

"Only when Jo wasn't lookin'," he smiled.

"Go sit down, Ollie, it has to sit for a half hour," Maddy scolded. "You may have gotten around Jo, but your granddaughter is much faster."

Daddy O shifted his pleading eyes to me. "Lil' Bri, I'm an old man…"

"Go sit down, you old coot," I interrupted as I stretched two large pieces of foil over the turkey, and with a loud harrumph my grandfather shuffled back into the living room.

"Ok, so now that Ollie is gone," Kyla began in a devious tone, "we were going to start complaining about Nikki."

"Don't we complain enough about her?" I groaned as I began filling the oven with all the side dishes that needed to bake.

Kyla laughed. "You got to be in Boston for four years while I had to live with the girl."

"Why can't she be more like her sister? Natasha is a wonderful young woman."

"You mean Tosh," Renee corrected snidely, only because Natasha had corrected her about a dozen times. "She's a bit tomboyish, but I do like her more than her trickster sister. Why can't Jer date her instead?"

Maddy gave a little sigh. "She's convinced herself that no man will ever want her because of those scars she has."

"I don't get that," Renee said shaking her head. "She's a Healer. How does a Healer not heal?"

"Everyone has their limitation," Maddy replied. "I guess a Healer's is having a Firestarter burst into flames on top of you. But that is what your husband will be looking into, isn't that right?"

Renee shrugged. "Yes? I have no idea what my mad scientist husband is planning on doing."

"Shh," Kyla interjected, "someone's coming up the front steps."

I peered through the kitchen archway in time to see Jonah approaching the front door. "Oh no, Jonah has his cell phone again."

"Oh I hope it is his mozer," Sera said softly.

But we all shook our heads once Jonah stepped through the door and said, "What do you mean Cole didn't pick up the turkeys? They've been ordered for months, all he had to do was pick them up from Bazzuto's yesterday."

"How many times has Diana called now," Renee asked softly.

"Nine," I replied while Sera and Maddy grimaced. "Yesterday she called three times because she couldn't figure out how to turn on the heat."

"That woman has always been useless," Maddy whispered. "Jonah needs to stop taking her calls."

"He would if he didn't care about the hybrids so much," I replied while Jonah paced angrily into the dining room.

"Well, what food *do* you have?" he paused. "I don't think you can feed two hundred hybrids potato chips and cheese slices for dinner." Every woman around the kitchen island squeezed her hand over her mouth to keep the laughter from exploding. "Then go to the gas station for all I care and get some lunchmeat. I'm sorry, Diana, I wish I could help, but you fired me. So…" and he hung up the phone and threw it on the dining room table. When he finally found his composure he turned around slowly with a flabbergasted look on his face. "Potato chips, cheese, and some olives. Now that's a Thanksgiving meal to remember."

"And it is not your responsibility, Jonah," I said firmly.

"I know, I know. I seriously need to stop answering the phone but…." he sighed, shaking away the feelings. "I'm going back out to play some football."

"Wait, where's your coat?" I nagged as he turned to go back outside. "There is four inches of snow on the ground."

"Not when you have a team of Vampires to plow the side yard to make a small football field."

"Who's winning?" Kyla asked, finally finishing whipping the potatoes.

"Our team," he replied happily. "Tosh and Ashlyn have no idea what they're doing, but it doesn't matter because whoever has the ball Alex just picks them up and runs them into the end zone."

"Well, tell him he can run into my end zone anytime he wants," Kyla said causing everyone to laugh but Jonah.

"And that's my cue to leave."

"Tell everyone we'll be eating in twenty minutes," I said before he walked back out the front door.

"For goodness sake, Kyla, do you ever not think about sex," I said as I measured out the sugar for the pumpkin pie and poured it into the mixing bowl.

Kyla pondered for a moment. "No. I pretty much think about sex with Alex all the time. We'll see if you're that lucky after eighty years of marriage."

Renee snorted. "Sera, Maddy, and I will be dead, and Bri would actually have to get married."

"Re!" Kyla whispered harshly between her teeth.

"What?" she replied defensively. "It's true."

"Maybe you should cool it on the wine," Kyla scolded as I tried concentrating on measuring the pumpkin filling.

"Oh come on," Renee scoffed. "If I can tie the knot then anyone can. Sorry to be the only one willing to say something about it."

Kyla opened her mouth, but I put my hand up. "Ky, it's fine. It's just the wine talking."

"That's right, twin, just deflect it," Renee said rolling her eyes and making me throw the wooden mixing spoon into the bowl.

"I am sick and tired of you bringing this up! You know why I'm not married? Because for three and a half years I've been raising two babies with superpowers and fangs and trying to figure out just how one even raises two babies with superpowers and fangs! And all the time worrying if today is the day that Aidan comes and steals them away from us, and doing everything I can to protect them without smothering them so they can have some semblance of a childhood.

"And mind you, because Victor just can't seem to be able to live without Cam, I'm doing most of this alone while trying to figure out how to live as this creature that I didn't want to be in the first place! So Re, for today of all days, I'm asking you to back off. Ok? It shouldn't matter to you whether I'm married to Cam or not."

"But it does matter to him," Cameron's voice rang from behind me. With an embarrassed sigh I turned to my left to see Cameron standing inside the foyer with melting snow dripping from his hair. I opened my mouth to say something, but Cameron interrupted me as if the previous moment hadn't just happened. "Devin and Fabiani have arrived."

Without another word, Cam turned and stepped back out on the front porch to greet his brother and Fabi. After I untied my dirty apron from around my waist, I made my way out of the kitchen, but not before pausing next to Kyla and whispering, "Thanks for the warning."

Kyla looked away guiltily, and I knew full well she could have warned me that Cameron would be coming in if she wanted to. Was everyone against me?

A moment later Devin stepped through the front door looking surprisingly casual in an olive colored t-shirt and black blazer, meaning Fabi most likely dressed him since Fabi Fabulous himself was wearing something similar, although Fabi's jeans were twice as tight and he was sporting his signature scarf. Just the sight of Fabi caused a flurry of activity as Renee, Kyla, and I fled from the kitchen and draped our arms around our friend.

"The four twins are back together at last," Fabi announced happily as the four of us laughed and hugged. "We've been more like a tripod without you, Ky. Now let me look at you."

As we released each other, Kyla took a step back and showed off her latest ensemble while she spewed designers' names I had never heard of. Renee rolled her eyes at me over the two of them, and then placed her cheek on my shoulder. She was silently asking for forgiveness, if not for her words at least for her timing, and like the chump that I was I patted her other cheek with acceptance.

"I suppose I could have just sent Fabi by himself with all the greeting I'm getting," Devin grumbled.

Renee laughed as she lifted her head from my shoulder. "So even the mighty Warrior Assassin gets jealous."

"I do not," Devin replied, narrowing his eyes at Renee as she gave him a rare kiss on the cheek.

Once Renee stepped away it was my turn to hug Devin.

"How was D.C.?" I asked as I removed my arms from around his neck.

"It was very interesting," he replied, but then looked over at Cameron. "Did Father call?"

Cameron shook his head. "Your secret is safe, Brother."

Devin's shoulders and chest lowered with relief, although Fabi gave a perturbed side glance. Just then the hallway behind us echoed with the sounds of the children squealing as they ran through the living room and into the foyer.

"Devy!" the three of them cried as they prepared to jump into their uncle's arms, but Devin held out his hand firmly and his expression became extremely stern.

"What is the meaning of this?"

Olivia stuck her bottom lip out as she said, "Didn't you miss us, Devy?"

"Of course I did, monkey, but you know the rules." Devin gave a firm nod as he flattened his palm and held it out in front of him at hip level. "Let us see how your technique has held up since my last visit."

All three children smiled excitedly as they each took their stance. Jackson was the first to go, looking adorable as he took a deep breath and concentrated on the height of Devin's hand. A second later he jumped in the air, spun 180 degrees, and kicked out his right leg hitting Devin's palm. When my son landed on both feet, his smile was as big as his father's. Next was Livy, and as usual she shared her brother's skill although she made it look like she was floating in mid-air she was so graceful. William, my precious baby Wills, tried desperately hard, but he was nine months younger and human. However, I was always amazed at how Devin was with him. Wills took a step forward, jumped around in a circle, and flung his little leg out as Devin lowered his palm to meet it. And as was also usual, we all cheered louder for Will's effort.

"Well done, children!" Devin cheered as he scooped all of them up into his arms. The Warrior Assassin was a ball of mush when it came to his niece and nephews, and yes, Wills was just as much of a nephew as Jackson. "So what is all this activity I saw outside?"

Cameron patted Devin on the shoulder as he said, "Jonah has taught us the game of football. We could certainly use you on our team. Alex is killing us."

"Ooo! Who's shirts and who's skins?" Fabi said as he finally pulled himself away from Kyla. "Because Devy'll play for the skins and I'll watch."

Devin gave Fabi a killer look as Olivia scrunched her face and said, "Devy, what is skins?"

"It's a...uh...Uncle Fabi's favorite team," Devin grumbled.

"Oh honey, you got that right," Fabi laughed loudly. "So seriously, there is a skin's team, isn't there?"

Once everyone came in from the wintery football game outside there were twenty of us seated around multiple tables pushed together with anything that could be used as a chair. Food was spread from one end of the table to the other, although many glasses were already filled with warmed blood. Daddy O stood at the head of the table, the carving knife and fork at the ready. However, just before plunging the fork inside the turkey breast, Daddy O stopped and held the utensils out to Cameron.

"Son, I think it's time you did the honors."

Cameron froze, shaking his head slightly as he said, "Da, you are the patriarch of the family, you always carve the turkey."

"I know, but you're really the head of the family now and the head of the family carves the turkey. Now come on, son" Daddy O said shaking the carving utensils at Cameron once again.

"Babe, don't put too much thought into it," I began, seeing Cam's reluctance. "Daddy O really just wants the first piece of turkey instead of having to wait until he's done carving it for everyone else."

Daddy O narrowed his eyes at me. "No one is talking to you, little girl."

"If the Warrior is shy about it, I can certainly carve the turkey," Eris said lightly.

"Ain't no one talkin' to you either," Daddy O warned. Needless to say Daddy O had only warmed up slightly to my father over the years.

Thankfully Cameron took the carving set from Daddy O's hands and stood nervously at the head of the table while my grandfather showed him where to cut the first piece.

"That's right, son, just put that piece right here," Daddy O said as he eagerly held up his plate and the flurry of dishes began to make their way around the table. "Now even though I ain't carvin' the turkey, we're all gonna say what we're thankful for."

"Why don't you start, Daddy O. What are you thankful for?" I asked as I dished out carrots onto Livy's and Wills' plate.

"Well," he smiled, "I'm thankful that after eighty-three years, I finally get a piece of hot turkey before anyone else."

"I told you," I said to Cam who laughed while he struggled to cut the turkey breast away from the bone.

"All right, 'Lil Bri, you know I'm thankful for all this new family ya done brought me. Not to mention my Maddy here."

"Oh, Ollie," Maddy blushed as she scooped a heaping serving of mashed potatoes onto Daddy O's plate.

"What are you thankful for, Maddy?" Jack-Jack asked next to her.

"Oh I'm thankful for being a part of this family," Maddy replied as she held out the bowl of mashed potatoes and Jackson nodded.

"I'm thankful for mashed potatoes," my son replied as his eyes grew wide at the mound Maddy put on his plate.

"Jackson, I believe you can be a little more creative than that," Cameron said as he threw down the carving knife and pulled out the turkey legs by hand.

Jackson sighed as he quirked the corners of his mouth in thought. "I guess I'm thankful that Ada says I can be a hybrid helper when I grow up."

"A hybrid helper," Eris said sounding impressed. "It sounds like a very honorable profession."

"I know," Jack-Jack replied nonchalantly and then plunged his fork into his mashed potatoes.

"Sera-phin-na, we are up to you," Eris said before taking a long drink from his glass. "What are you thankful for, my dear?"

Sera placed her fork down on her plate and wiped the corner of her mouth with her napkin. Finally with a sigh she replied, "My island. I cannot wait to get back to my island."

"Ah, my dear," Eris cooed as he kissed my stepmother's temple. "I too am happy to go home again, and to not be bogged down by so many hybrids and their problems."

"Oh thanks," Ashlyn scoffed, but with a smile while others around the table laughed under their breath.

"Miss Shaw, you were a pleasure more often than not, but there were many others I could have done without. Now what about you, Kyla? What are you thankful for this year?"

Kyla smiled happily as she flipped her long wavy orange hair over her shoulder. "Well, I have to say I'm thankful that Bri and Cameron are moving home where they belong since living in Boston all these years has just been silly. Now we can all be a family again. Alex, don't you agree?"

"Uh...yes?" he replied looking awkwardly to me and then to Cameron.

"Shall we move on to Jared," Cameron interceded as he awkwardly broke off one of the turkey wings and placed it on the platter with the other jaggedly cut meat.

"Thanks, bro," Jared responded before swigging back what blood was left in his glass. Slowly he rose from his chair, smoothing his classic concert t-shirt down his abdomen before saying in a very serious tone, "It can be very hard being the baby of the family, and I know that I don't always make it easy to take me seriously. But I'd like to thank Cameron and Devin, my dear older brothers, future leaders of the Warriors, for listening to me and agreeing to create the technological command center that we so desperately need and that I deserve."

While others oohed and awed, I noticed Devin look down the table at Cameron who had stopped cutting the turkey. "Brother? Did you..."

Cameron shook his head. "Little brother, you know very well we did not agree to build your command center."

"We said we would discuss it with Father," Devin continued sternly. "Were you hoping that if you said something in front of everyone we would feel pressured to give in?"

Jared shrugged. "Yeah pretty much. So?"

"No!" Devin and Cameron replied in unison.

With a loud huff, the strawberry-blonde Warrior sat back down in his chair dramatically. "Fine. Your turn, Nik," he said putting his arm around her.

Nikki swallowed nervously. "I am thankful for...I'm thankful for finally being accepted into the family."

Renee choked on the sip of wine she had just taken in, causing her to cough it back into the glass. "Sor...ry..." she said as Dr. John wiped away a dribble of red wine from her chin, "...big ass tannin."

Nikki pursed her lips, giving Renee a look I'm sure she thought could cut glass. Problem was she was going up against a pro who hated her. Poor Tricky Nikki, still stupid.

"Anyway, I'm also thankful for my sister, Nat, for giving me a second chance to be her big sister."

Natasha scrunched her eyebrows together as Nikki took her hand and squeezed it. Once again Nikki underestimated her prey since Natasha twisted her hand out of her sister's grip.

"Well, I'm just thankful to be alive," she said not acknowledging her sister whatsoever. "And I have Maddy to thank for a lot of that."

From the other end of the table Maddy gave Natasha a loving smile. "It was mostly you, Miss Tosh, you're the Healer after all."

Natasha narrowed her eyes. "You know what I mean. You wouldn't let me give up, and because of that..." she said with a questioning tone and then looked to Devin, "Can I tell them?"

Devin smiled and nodded his head. "Yes I suppose so."

Natasha's smile stretched from ear to ear as she sat up proudly in her seat and announced, "I was just told that I have been accepted into the Warrior Training Program!"

Applause and cheers erupted from everyone around the table with the exception of Nikki whose expression was a mixture of fear and sadness. Jared gave his girlfriend one look, rolled his eyes, and stretched across her to give Natasha a congratulatory hug.

When the congratulations towards Natasha finally tapered, Jonah took a swig of his beer and cleared his throat. "I'm so glad I have to follow that," he laughed. "Um...well...I'm...uh..."

"You're really starting off well," Renee said snidely.

"Thanks, Renee, as always you give me the shot of confidence I need."

"Anytime, kid," Renee toasted.

Jonah smiled as he sighed and tried again. "Not to sound too hokey..."

"Too late."

"Re! Let the kid speak," Dr. John chided and then gestured for Jonah to continue.

"Ok, so not to sound too hokey," he paused and looked at Renee, but when she didn't say anything he continued, "but I'm always thankful for Brianna and Cameron. You both have helped me so much I don't think I'll live long enough to ever repay you. Without you, I would have never gotten the job at the Facility, and yes Renee I know I got laid off."

"Damn it!" Re replied, causing another round of laughter. "I couldn't say it fast enough."

"Well, I thought I'd get it out there before you could," Jonah joked. "But really, it was a great adventure, and it's where I met Ashlyn. So whatever happens from here on end, I'll always be thankful for the day Bri got into my car. So cheers." Jonah held up his bottle of beer and then gave Ashlyn a quick kiss on her cheek. "Your turn, baby."

"Well thank god," Renee replied instead. "I just lost three years of my life. Come on, Ashlyn, show your man how it's done, ten words tops."

Ashlyn swallowed nervously as she thought for a moment. "I'm thankful for being shown what I am. How'd I do, Renee? I did it in eight."

Renee smiled at getting caught. "That a girl. You can have a few more words I guess."

"Oh good," Ashlyn replied happily. "Because I'm really thankful for Jonah showing me that there are good people in this world, and I'm so happy to be celebrating my first thanksgiving with all of you."

"Does that mean we get a patch on the purse?" I asked much to Ashlyn's surprise. "Jonah has a big mouth. So seriously, do we get a patch?"

Ashlyn laughed and nodded. "Yes, I think this definitely constitutes a patch, but it means you'll be missing a napkin or a piece of your tablecloth."

"Oh how lovely," Fabiani replied next to her and patted her hand gently. "Now who are you?"

"Fabi!" I yelled.

"What? I've been traveling, I don't know who she is." Fabi turned to Ashlyn as he stood from his chair. "Don't worry, honey, we'll catch up later I'm sure. So now back to me. Today, my Devy has made this the happiest day of my life."

Devin froze for a second in confusion and then looked sideways at Fabi. "I have?"

"Oh Devy, don't be so modest," Fabi cooed as he rubbed the back of Devin's neck. "Devin has made me the happiest man alive because he has decided to come out to Victor."

"I decided no such thing!" Devin announced angrily.

"Come out of where?" Jackson asked innocently.

"The closet," Fabi replied, causing both Devin and Cameron to stand from the table.

"Fabiani, this is not an appropriate conversation around the children," Cameron warned.

"Why do you like the closet so much, Devy?" Olivia asked with curious eyes.

"Because he likes the coats," I replied quickly and then gave Fabi a dirty look. Thankfully Livy was more interested in her turkey than pushing the subject further. "So what are you thankful for, Devin?"

Everyone could see Devin's chest heaving up and down. "I will be thankful if I get through the day without killing a Negotiator."

"Oh please," Fabi huffed as he sat back down in his seat, "you'd be lost without me. I mean seriously, you can barely dress yourself."

"I dressed myself just fine for five hundred years before meeting you."

"Yes, I'm sorry, you are very capable of looking like you are going to a funeral. So really, tell everyone how thankful you are for me."

Devin gritted his teeth, and flexed his jaw before speaking again. "Yes, Fabi, I am very thankful for how much you test my patience."

"Ah, honey, any time."

Devin gave Fabi one last sideways glance before continuing, "But I am most thankful for my brother and Bri coming home to the manor. Now Cameron and I can really start establishing ourselves as leaders in the coven."

"And build my command center!" Jared cheered. "Ok, doc, your turn."

Dr. John placed his fork down on his almost empty plate. "Ok, well of course I'm thankful for Re and our little man."

"I'm fankful for you too, Daddy," Wills said proudly.

"Thanks, champ," Dr. John replied and winked at his son. "But I'm also really excited about this new opportunity at Facility West. It should be quite an adventure."

"What are you fankful for, Mommy?" Wills asked next to her.

"You of course, little man, and your father. But I'm also thankful for not having to live in a cramped apartment anymore, and being thousands of miles away from my mother. Yee-ha!" Renee cheered before drinking down the rest of her red wine, hopefully her last for the evening.

"Mommy, is it my turn?" Wills asked hopefully and Renee nodded. "I'm fankful for Mommy, and Daddy, and Awbie, and Cam, and Wivy, and Jack-Jack, and Devy..."

"Wills, baby," Renee interrupted, "are you thankful for everyone at this table?"

"Mmm-hmm," he nodded enthusiastically.

"Well good, little man, let's move on to Livybean."

Olivia didn't sway her concentration from the food on her plate as she said, "I'm fankful for butterflies and pink," she said before putting a forkful of green beans into her mouth.

"Pink what, baby girl?" I asked pulling her fluffy black curls away from her face.

"Just pink, I love pink."

"Wivy," Jack-Jack said from across the table, "aren't you thankful for tatoes?"

Livy looked up from her plate just as Jack-Jack scooped up his mashed potatoes in his hand and threw them across the table. My hand instantly shot out and stopped the majority of the potatoes before they hit Olivia in the face.

"Jackson Thomas Burke!" I shouted as I flicked the potatoes onto Olivia's plate. "What are you doing?"

"I was helping, Mama," Jack-Jack squealed with laughter.

"That is enough of that, Jackson," Cameron scolded.

"Jack-Jack should get a time out, Ada! And I should get more tatoes!"

"Here, Wivy," Wills said sweetly, "you can have mine."

William had spoken those exact words probably as much as he had said mommy and daddy. What was completely shocking was when William James Ryan, my little angel, slapped Olivia in the face with a handful of mashed potatoes. Livy froze for a moment in shock and then had a complete meltdown causing both Jack and Will to laugh hysterically.

"That's enough!" I shouted as I stood from my chair. "Both you boys, go wash your hands and then go sit in…"

Now…I saw the mashed potatoes coming at me, but my brain apparently stopped working and I didn't duck out of the way before the potatoes splattered against my chest and into my hair. When the shock faded I looked to the far end of the table and saw creamy mashed potatoes dripping slowly from Jared's hand.

"You little sh…"

"Come on, Beebs, lighten up."

I looked down to see the bowl of green beans just to the side of me. Slowly I reached down and pulled the bowl into the crook of my arm. Suddenly everyone was on guard, grabbing for any food items they could.

"Wait, wait!" Daddy O shouted as he slid his chair away from the table. "For the love of all that's holy, just let me save the turkey before ya'll start actin' like heathens."

Carefully Cameron removed the platter of turkey from the center of the table and gave it to Daddy O who ran as best he could to the far side of the kitchen with Maddy just behind him.

Scooping a big handful of green beans I yelled, "Oh it's on, ya'll!"

Chapter Twenty-nine

Brianna

It would definitely be a Thanksgiving for the history books. Daddy O was disgusted over the waste of a great meal, but he kept his turkey safe and the pies were unharmed. Afterwards another storm front came over the mountains bringing a fresh inch of fluffy white snow. The top step of the front porch made for the perfect perch to watch the flakes float down to the ground in a haunting silence. The only noise came from behind me in the living room where I could hear Jonah, Ashlyn, Nikki, Tosh, and Jared, or as Daddy O called them "the youngins", creating a ruckus as they continued to bond with each other. It warmed my heart to see the new developing friendships, even if they wouldn't be together for very much longer. Beginning tomorrow, our full house would be leaving in groups over the next week. To me, it was the beginning of the end.

The front door opened behind me, and from the whiff of autumn leaves I knew it was Cameron. He had volunteered to hose down the children to allow me the quiet time I needed. The days to enjoy my childhood home were dwindling, and he knew I wasn't doing well with it. I hated change more than anyone, and right now my life was fraught with it.

"The children are clean and tucked in between Oliver and Madelyn," he said as he sat behind me and nestled his head on my shoulder.

"So Daddy O and Maddy won't get a lick of sleep tonight."

"Not a bit," he laughed.

"I finally got the potato smell out of my hair."

Cameron sniffed my hair. "Well, almost." I nudged him in the ribs with my elbow, and he laughed again. "Did you have a nice Thanksgiving?"

"It was nice having everyone together."

"That is it?"

"Yes, *that is it*," I said as I rudely imitated him. "What do you expect me to say? That my Thanksgiving was great except that I keep thinking that I need to soak up every memory possible because I won't ever have another Thanksgiving here ever again?"

"Yes, love, you should say that if it is how you feel."

"Of course that's how I feel!" I replied angrily and stepped off the front porch into the falling snow. "Everyone knows I feel like that and they're tired of hearing it. I know you have to be."

"Bri, you know…"

"This house has been the only constant in my life, Cam. No matter where I was with Shelby or Sam, I could always come back here. Everything good in my life happened here – Daddy O, Mama Jo…you. This is where we fell in love, Cam, aren't you going to miss it?"

Cameron stood slowly from the front porch and glided down the stairs to where I stood. The white snow was in drastic contrast to his dark clothes and black hair as it collected on him. Even though I was being a brat, his eyes were still loving as he kissed the back of my hand and placed it over his heart. "Brianna, I thank God every day for making you as stubborn as you are and demanding that I bring you to your grandfather's home. If that had not happened…"

Just then Cameron swept me off my feet and ran us to the street. When we reached the bottom of the hill he put me down on the ground and came to stand behind me as he whispered, "…then we would never have taken a walk, and you would not have held my hand for the first time." Tenderly, Cameron touched my fingers, much like he had that very night and somehow still caused butterflies to flutter in my stomach.

Then a moment later he scooped me into his arms and ran us back to the front of the house and placed me down on the bottom step of the porch. "And then, we would never have had our first kiss."

Cameron's left hand caressed my cheek as he drew his face closer and his lips finally rested on mine. He pulled away slightly and took my face with both hands and kissed me again with more intensity, making my stomach flip just as much as it did the night he had first given me those kisses.

When he pulled away again, he revealed his signature crooked smile which never failed at melting my heart. "Then of course, there was the time you were standing in your bedroom with nothing on but my shirt."

"I was wearing underwear."

He smiled again as the fingers of his right hand traveled down the length of my neck and chest. "Fine, but your breasts were bare and the shirt was not buttoned. That I remember very well."

"And all this time I thought you were being a gentleman and not looking."

Cameron shrugged with a forgiveness-seeking look. "What man would not take a little peek, especially at your perfect breasts?" I smiled with slight embarrassment and looked at the ground. "Now we have one last stop."

"We do?"

In the blink of an eye Cameron lifted me into his arms and ran into the woods that surrounded my grandfather's house. Less than fifty feet in was a warm glow of candles peeking through the trees. As we drew closer I could see a large blanket stretched out on the ground with several lanterns weighing it down at each corner. I looked up at Cameron who was already giving me a hopeful smile.

"It's lovely," I said as he lowered me to the ground.

"We have barely had a minute alone since we arrived so I wanted to do...something." Cameron shrugged as his confidence waivered. "I know it is not much..."

"Babe, it's perfect. I'm sorry I was such a bitch before."

He kindly ignored my statement and bowed deeply. "M'lady," he said, gesturing to the blanket and extending his hand.

Taking his hand, I allowed him to lower me down onto the blanket. I stretched myself alongside him, wrapping my left leg around his hips and nuzzling into the nook of his chest. It was our usual position, two puzzle pieces finally connecting like they were supposed to.

"Angel, are you ready for the best part?"

I lifted my head up from Cam's chest and looked him in the eye. "I'm looking at the best part."

"Thank you, angel, but look up," he said and pointed upwards.

I turned my gaze toward the sky and saw exactly what Cameron wanted me to see. The dense tree canopy above us provided such cover that the majority of the snow never reached the ground. Instead, the small flakes fell lightly but dissolved before reaching us. It was as if we were in our own snow globe.

"Ok, you're right. That is the best part," I conceded and rested my head on his shoulder so that I could continue to watch the snow.

We laid in silence for several minutes, Cam's fingers gliding through my hair. "Bri?"

"Hmmm?"

"Can we talk about the things you said in the kitchen today?"

"What all did you hear?"

Cameron's fingers stopped petting my hair which wasn't a good sign. "Do you really feel as though you have raised our children alone?"

"Cam," I whined trying to backpedal, "Renee was really going overboard and I lost my temper..."

"Brianna, you are avoiding the question."

"Because I don't want to talk about it!"

Cameron sighed as he slid me off his chest and hovered over me, his dark wet curls falling in front of his face. "Angel, I know you are hurting. I know leaving all of this behind is very difficult for you, but you are not alone. You have never been alone. Our whole family has been there to help you..."

"To nag me is more like it," I snapped. "Why can't you fight like you used to, Brianna? Why aren't you married yet, Brianna? Have you fed today, Brianna?"

"Have you fed today?"

"Jesus, Cam!" I shouted as I pushed him out of the way and folded myself over the top of my knees. "I would have if Jared hadn't thrown potatoes at me."

"Then let me get you some blood now."

"No!" I shouted again and grabbed his arm just before he took off. "I will eat when I want to. I need you to trust me to take care of myself, Cam."

"I do trust you."

"Then why doesn't it feel like that?"

Cameron bit his bottom lip as he released my hand and cupped my cheek. "Because I am horribly overprotective and a failure at expressing my fears and worries in a better way. Bri, I cannot lose you or our babies, especially not to Aidan. I need you to be at your full strength at all times so that you can handle anything that comes your way, especially when I am not with you."

"Then stay," I pleaded and Cameron instantly replied with a sigh. Not letting him answer, since I knew he'd give me some excuse as to why Victor needed him, I sighed myself and like a spoiled child I flopped back down onto the blanket. A moment of silence fell between us, although I could hear odd sounds in the distance. "What is that noise?"

"I believe it is Kyla and Alexander."

"Are they seriously up in a tree somewhere?"

Cameron quirked his eyebrow. "Are you that surprised?"

"I guess not," I laughed. "I did scrub the ceilings after they visited."

"Well," Cameron began as he grazed his fingers across my forehead and down my cheek, "we could give them a run for their money."

"Um...I don't think I've ever made *those* kinds of sounds," I replied as it started to sound like there were monkeys having sex in the distance.

"Oh yes you have," Cameron laughed.

"When!"

With a sheepish grin Cameron replied, "When we made love while you were pregnant."

If I could have blushed I would have, but instead I leaned back against Cameron's chest and looked back up at the snow. "I couldn't help it."

"I was not complaining, love."

"Do you ever wish we could have another baby?"

"The two we have do not keep you busy enough?"

"Lord knows they do, but...wouldn't you want to try again? Maybe I could do it right this time."

"What is that supposed to mean?"

"Cam, come on," I sighed as I sat upright, "you can't say our children are normal."

Cameron sat up and tilted my chin up with his fingers. "Our babies are precious...and...perfect."

"Our babies have fangs."

"Olivia and Jackson are smarter, stronger, more talented than any child on Earth, and are already more powerful than most hybrid adults."

"And they are being hunted because of those powers. The powers that I gave them. I made Vampire children just like Elaina said I would, and now Aidan is coming after them because of something I did."

Cameron raked his hand through his hair, looking as defeated as I felt. We sat in another uncomfortable silence for several minutes, and with each passing second my guilt grew. After everything he had done to create a romantic night together I had to shit on it like I always did.

Just as I began to curse myself, the snow that had previously been dissipating above us was now coming down in a light blanket of sparkling white. Mad at myself and tired of the constant grunting still echoing in the distance, I stood from the blanket but Cameron grabbed my ankle.

"Angel, I need to say something."

"No, you don't..."

"Our children are not the way they are because of something you did," Cameron said as he stood and looked down at me with sad eyes.

"Cam, forget what I said. I'm just in one of those moods, and as usual I've ruined our time together."

"Please let me say this..."

"There's nothing to say, Cam," I interrupted once again, but this time brushing off the snow that was collecting on his shoulders. "You know how I get. When's there too much going on I just...shut down." Cameron didn't reply, but I could see in his eyes that he painfully agreed. "You know you could help distract me."

"Anything, my love."

Slowly I crossed my arms in front of my waist, grabbed the ends of my sweater, and pulled it over my head. "Well, I've never made love in the snow," I said, thinking that of course I hadn't since I would have died of hypothermia or something.

"Neither have I," Cameron said licking his lips as he fumbled with his belt buckle while he watched me unhook the front clasp of my bra and peel it away from my breasts. In a blur, Cameron scooped me up into his arms and laid me gently down upon the blanket as the snow began to create a white sheet around us.

"You do know there's a lot of pressure for you to perform here."

"How so?" he replied as he removed his shirt.

"Cam!" I replied flustered as I unbuttoned my jeans and pulled them down to my ankles. "We have to beat Ky and Alex! We have to show them we can have sex like animals too."

"If you say so," he said before removing my jeans completely, wrapping his arm around my hips, and flipping me on my stomach.

"Cam, what in the world are you doing," I gasped, looking back at him over my shoulder as he slid up behind me, wrapping his arm around my waist, and pulling me back against him.

"I am doing what you asked, love," he said in a low, husky voice as his hand began pulling down the waistband of my underwear. "Like animals, you said. Well…"

My lady parts began to tingle even before he reached around me and plunged his fingers inside of me.

"Holy shit I'm glad you listen to me."

Chapter Thirty

Jonah

Whatever possessed us to go shopping on Black Friday I'll never know; maybe because it was an opportunity to get out of Oliver's house. Don't get me wrong, I was happy to be down here but there were times I felt trapped in a package of sardines. The crisp cold air of the outdoor outlet mall was refreshing, and even the snow from the day before couldn't keep the crowds away on this infamous shopping day. Ashlyn was snuggled firmly into my side while we all waited for Nikki to emerge from the store she had ducked into almost twenty minutes ago. I wouldn't have minded waiting if it weren't for the fact that Jared was wearing a thick jacket over a hooded sweatshirt with the hood up, a baseball cap, sunglasses, and thick leather gloves. Frankly he looked like a terrorist and other shoppers kept glancing at him as they passed.

"Is it the gloves?" Jared asked when a woman stared at him intently and tried to hide the fact that she was taking a picture of him with her phone.

"Yeah, that's it, the gloves are causing people to turn you in to Homeland Security," Tosh laughed.

"It's not like I can help it," Jared replied, tightening his hood to cover his face. "I'd rather not burn my precious baby-soft skin. Why can't people look at me like I'm a celebrity?"

"Sorry, Jer," I said. "You're just not that pretty."

"I take offense to that," he said seriously and then couldn't keep a straight face.

"So Tosh, when exactly do you start your training with the Warriors?" Ashlyn asked, peeking out from my side.

Tosh's eyes lit up at the topic. "First thing Wednesday morning. I seriously can't believe it's real. I'm so excited even though I know it's going to be hell at first."

"Nah, it won't be that bad," Jared replied. "As long as you last the first year or so I'm sure they'll Turn you."

My head flinched with the sudden realization. "Wait, what? You'll be Turned?"

"Duh, Jonah. It's not like they have hybrid Warriors."

"Brianna was," I answered plainly.

Tosh shook her head and rolled her eyes. "Brianna was special. Victor won't do that again, especially for someone like me. But it's what I want anyway, so…"

"You *want* to be a…that?"

"Why do you think Nikki's freaking out? She totally laid on the 'we're finally reconnecting and now you want to go and kill yourself' blah blah bullshit."

"Nikki really does care about you, Tosh," Ashlyn corrected softly as she sat up completely. "You may not believe it sometimes, but she can't hide her feelings from me."

"Fine, she cares. But she has no right to judge me on my life decisions. That's all I'm saying. I mean come on, I don't judge her over being with this dirt bag for four years."

"Hey!" Jared shouted defensively as he stood. "The two of you wouldn't even be talking if it weren't for me, Na-tash-a."

Tosh smiled mischievously, and we all knew how much she hated being called her full name. The banter between Jared and Tosh reminded me of how it could be with Katie Bell, and immediately a wave of sadness washed over me. She still wasn't talking to me, and yesterday was the first time we hadn't been together for Thanksgiving. Just then my body was flooded with a warm feeling and I could feel Ash's concerned eyes boring holes into the side of my face. Not wanting to give it another second's thought, I quickly changed the subject.

"Did you guys hear those animals out in the woods last night? Was it a full moon or something?"

Jared burst out laughing, even causing a few shoppers to look over. "What?"

"I just...just...I just," Jared tried to say through his laughter. "I think it's hysterical you think...those...were animals."

"But if they weren't animals..." I began but Tosh shook her head warningly. "I don't want to know?"

"Not unless you want to be sick," Jared laughed again, but his mood quickly changed when he noticed Nikki struggling to come out of the store in front us due to the number of bags hanging from her arms. "Damn woman, I am not made of money."

Nikki rolled her eyes and loaded Jared's arms with the bags. "It's not my fault you have such a big family."

"I certainly don't like them this much."

"And that's only Alex, Kyla, and Devin. You still have Cameron, Brianna, the kids, and then you said you wanted to get something for Renee and her family, then there's Maddy, and Victor..."

"Jeez, Nik, I hate when you get all crazed like this. It's a month until Christmas, we don't have to get everything today, for crying out loud. Honestly you look a little crazy right now."

"And you look like the Unabomber," Nikki replied as she crossed her arms. "You don't see me complaining, do you?"

"Actually you were complaining on the car ride over," Tosh said with pride.

"Now that's what I'm talkin' about, Tosh," he said, giving her a fist bump. "Bros before ho...er...your sister." Nikki raised one eyebrow at her boyfriend and bore through him with one look. "I'm gonna run this shit to the truck. Maybe I can actually get a signal out there and see how things are goin' up at the house."

"Good idea," Nikki replied curtly and then pulled Tosh up from the bench. "Come on, we have a lot more shopping to do."

Tosh groaned as she stepped alongside her sister, but she wasn't the only one groaning. Ashlyn sounded twice as bad when we stood from the bench and followed the two Cushlin sisters.

"Are you feeling all right?" I asked, looking down at her as she pulled her patchwork bag across her chest.

"It's just my stomach," she shrugged and curled back into my side as we made our way through the crowds.

Nikki looked over her shoulder as she said, "No offense, but you did have two full plates of Thanksgiving yesterday. That's like eight thousand calories, so…"

My mouth opened to say something, but Ashlyn was quicker. "Well considering there were days in my past where I didn't get to eat at all, I like to think I was making up for lost time."

I bit my bottom lip and squeezed Ash's hand. There were times I forgot about the spunky homeless girl I first met.

"I just meant that maybe it was too much," Nikki replied in a snarky tone. "Nat, let's go in here."

"In there?!" Tosh replied pointing to a store whose window display was sparkling with crystal. "You can't afford anything in there…no sorry, Jared can't afford anything in there."

"Could you please not argue with me for one minute? I just want to go in and look. Is that so terrible?"

Tosh rolled her eyes and allowed Nikki to pull her into the store. I glanced down at Ashlyn who suddenly looked tired and pale. "Do you want to go in?"

She shook her head. "It's hard enough being around the two of them out in the open. I don't think we want to test my control with breakable things all around."

I laughed and kissed the top of her head. "You're stronger than you think, Ash."

She smiled as she looked up at me and then pursed her lips which I instantly rested mine upon. When I stood back up she was still smiling and searching my face. "Are you as excited as I am about going back tomorrow and finally having a room to ourselves?"

I rested my forehead against hers, and thought about everything I wanted to do with her, trying to push to her all the excitement, love, and desire to make love to her again. I heard her giggle underneath me and when I lifted my head I could see the blush in her cheeks, but then a second later her expression changed as she placed her hand over her stomach. "Maybe Nikki was right, maybe I did eat too much."

"Do you want to sit down?"

"No, I'll be fine," she replied with a slight groan as she pulled me toward a vendor's kiosk. "So what time are we leaving tomorrow?"

I shrugged as I watched her look through the various trinkets dangling from the racks. "Whenever we want really, it's not like I need to get back for anything." Ashlyn gave me a warning look. I'd been laying on the woe-is-me act pretty thick, and she'd all but told me to shut up about it. Like I said, the spunky homeless girl was still kicking around. "Are you going to be able to handle a twelve hour ride?"

"Trust me, baby, I can handle it. It's having to spend twelve hours alone with you that's got me worried."

"Wow," I replied insulted. "I take back all those feelings I just sent you." Ashlyn's eyes grew wide and gave a quick look over to the vendor sitting in a chair across from us who was giving me a peculiar look. Not knowing what else to do, I took one of the shiny charms shaped like a snowflake and handed it to him. "We'll take this one."

"Jonah, I was just looking. I don't need..."

I squeezed her panicked hand that was gripping my arm. "Do you like it?"

"Yes," she replied meekly.

"Good. It'll remind you of our time here, and I think I should have something on your bag."

She smiled and removed her hand, allowing me to take out my wallet and pay for the charm. Within two minutes there was snowflake charm hanging from my girl's patchwork bag. I was officially a part of her life.

I put my arm around Ashlyn's slender shoulders and steered us away from the kiosk in order to keep track of the Cushlin sisters. "Now, you were just kidding, right?"

"Of course I was, silly," she teased. "I can't wait to have you to myself."

"Good, because uh...I want to talk to you about something," I began nervously as I pulled her to a stop. "So as soon as we get back it's nose to the ground looking for a job, and everything I'm getting from my severance is going into savings. I've got a pretty big nut already saved since I don't have to pay Katie's tuition or the taxes..."

"Jonah," Ashlyn said putting her gloved hand on my chest, "you don't need to tell me about your finances, that's your business."

I took her hand from my chest and squeezed it tightly between both of mine. "I just want you to know that I have a plan. I want to get out of the Facility as soon as possible, and I want you to come with me."

Ashlyn froze. "With you? Like live together?"

"It won't be anything grand, probably a shitty apartment, but at least we'd be together. I get nauseous when I think I won't be with you when my severance is over. If this is too much or too soon, I understand. I just want you to know that I'm serious about us. I really do love you, Ash."

"Yes!" Ashlyn shouted and then realized everyone was looking at us. Quickly she hid her face in her hands until I cradled her into my chest.

"So what are you trying to say?" I laughed.

"I'm thinking you're nuts, but…" she paused and gave me a quick kiss with her cold lips. "…I go where you go, baby."

I went to kiss her again but our little love fest was rudely interrupted by the screaming Cushlins exiting the crystal store behind us.

"Why must you always create a scene," Nikki yelled at Tosh as they walked toward us.

"Because you're being absolutely ridiculous," Tosh retorted. "Jared cannot afford that stupid crystal bowl in there."

"Cameron and Brianna love that stuff. Jared wouldn't mind."

"Buying them an expensive bowl will not make them like you, Nik," Tosh snapped, causing Nikki to freeze and glare at her sister.

"Tosh," I warned quietly, "that's enough. Maybe we should go find Jared."

"And you've found him," Jared said as he approached from behind. "Couldn't get a signal in the parking lot either, so…er…Nik, you ok?"

Nikki nodded with a forced smile and turned away from the group.

Jared just shrugged and continued, "Well, like I said, I couldn't get a signal in the parking lot so I haven't checked in with Alex in a while. So…"

Suddenly Nikki gasped loudly and turned back around to face us. "We gotta go," she whispered as she pushed through the middle of us and continued on without a glance back.

"Uh…that's just what I was gonna say," Jared said rolling his eyes, but frankly none of us understood what was going and merely followed after Nikki who had quickened her pace drastically.

Ashlyn grabbed my hand and whispered, "Something's really wrong, Jonah. She's…she's terrified."

Squeezing Ash's hand, I pulled her along to catch up to Jared who was actively pulling on Nikki's elbow to slow her down. We sped up when the two of them ducked around a corner of shops, but in the few seconds that passed Nikki must have doubled-back since the five of us collided in a moment that should have been put up on the internet.

"Nikki, what the hell," Jared said loudly.

"Shh!" she hissed and ducked into the middle of our group in a panic.

Jared was frustrated, Tosh was annoyed, I was confused, only Ashlyn seemed to have any sense and actually tried to talk to the terrified girl in the middle of us. "Tell us what's happening, Nik."

Frantically Nikki looked around, peering and ducking through the small spaces between us. "I saw...they're here."

"Who's here," Jared said with sudden concern.

"Two Vamps," she whispered. "I know them, well...I think."

"Know them how," Tosh pressed and Nikki looked at her with tears in her eyes and unable to answer. "Are they E's?"

Nikki nodded as she sucked her lips into her mouth. Jared immediately went on the defensive, looking around us while stuffing one hand into his jacket. In a flash he pulled out a concealed handgun, drew the slide back to chamber a round, and then secured it in his jacket pocket. Tosh pulled down one of the straps of her backpack, unzipped the front pocket, and began stacking wide silver rings on each of her fingers. When her hands were covered in silver she reached inside the main compartment and wound a length of half-inch wide silver chain around her wrist. Ashlyn stood next to Nikki trying to comfort her and keep her calm, while I stood there with my thumb up my ass.

Ok, not literally, but I certainly felt completely useless.

With Nikki in the middle, Jared directed us forward while Tosh took position behind. I had never seen this side of Jared, or Tosh for that matter, and they seemed to flip on the Warrior with a switch. Ashlyn kept giving me worried looks back as we made our way across the large courtyard in the middle. Finally finding the courage, I looked over my shoulder at Tosh and whispered, "Where are we going?"

"I'm guessing the car," she whispered back and I could hear the nerves in her voice as she continued to survey our surroundings.

"Who's E?"

Tosh shook her head as she placed her hand on my back and urged me forward. "Later."

"Stay close," Jared whispered behind him, "we're goin' into the crowd."

We did as he instructed, and like salmon fought through the waves of people coming at us from all sides as we approached a major intersection of shops. We pushed through the crowd trying not to draw attention to ourselves, though it was hard with the Unabomber look-a-like leading the charge. As the parking lot neared, and the crowd thinned, Jared took an abrupt turn to the right and ducked down a small alley with several Dumpsters lined up against one of the brick walls. Hurriedly we ran to the back of the alley and hid behind the furthest one.

Jared pulled Nikki to him, placing his hands on either side of her face to keep her focused on him. "Nik! Nik, listen to me. I'm going to Project..."

"NO!" she yelled in a panic and grabbed at his hands. "Don't leave me, don't..."

"I have to Project to the truck," Jared interrupted, trying to keep his voice low but firm. "Otherwise we're sitting ducks out in that open parking lot. I'll Project to the truck and bring it around. There's a loading dock on the other side of this alley, that's where we'll meet. Just stay with Nat."

"Tosh," Tosh corrected.

"Are you fucking kidding!" Jared snapped back, causing Tosh to look at the ground, but he quickly took her chin between his fingers and lifted her head to his eye level. "Do not be brave, do not be stupid. Stay here, I'll honk the horn and you guys come running."

Tosh nodded nervously as she placed her arm around Nikki's shoulders and pulled her away from Jared. A second later the area in front of us was filled with black smoke as Jared disappeared like a character in a comic book. The four of us squatted down next to the Dumpster, Tosh keeping Nikki tucked close into her chest to keep her choking sobs muffled. Ashlyn was shaking underneath my arm as I pressed my cheek into the top of her head.

"We're gonna be ok," I whispered into her hair and she squeezed my hand tightly in reply. At the same time Tosh looked our way with a nervous expression and I extended her my free hand which she quickly wrapped her silver-clad fingers around.

"Where'd she go?" a man shouted in the distance, causing Nikki to flinch in her sister's arms.

The curious voice in the back of my head gnawed at me to take a look. Slowly I peeked around the edge of the Dumpster, Tosh's hand squeezing mine tightly with a warning. Standing just at the edge of the alley were two everyday looking men. None of the other shoppers that were walking by showed any concern with them even though they were shouting at one another. Little did they know that both of them were extremely lethal.

"How could you lose her," the same man shouted again as he thrust his hands into the other man's shoulders sending him backwards and out of my view. "I am not losing this bounty because of you."

"Me!" the other guy shouted. "You wouldn't have found Nikki here if it weren't for me."

"And you wouldn't have found out about the hundred-grand if it weren't for me. Now let's find the bitch, turn her over to Aidan, and get our money before someone else does. Ok? She can't have gone too far."

The two men turned, looking around them for any sign of Nikki which caused me to jut my head back behind the Dumpster again. We huddled silently together for another few seconds before Tosh peeked around to see if the coast was clear and by her sigh of relief I assumed it was.

Nikki rose from her sister's chest, tears still coming down her cheeks as she looked between the three of us. "Did he say bounty? A one-hundred-thousand dollar bounty...on...me?"

"Shh," Tosh warned, "they might still be around."

"No! No!" Nikki replied in a panic as she shot up out of Tosh's grip. At the same time the sound of three loud honks came in the distance. In a flash Nikki was tripping over her sister and darting down the alley. I pulled Ashlyn up off the ground and the three of us chased after her Nikki. Just as she reached the end of the alley an arm came out of nowhere and clotheslined her. Nikki's legs swung over her head as her back and head hit the concrete with a loud thug. In the next second one of the men I'd seen was hovering over Nikki, wrapping his arm around her neck and pulling her up from the ground while she kicked and screamed.

Tosh kicked into a higher gear, taking three long strides before leaping into the air and landing on the man's back. Quickly she wrapped her legs around his waist and pressed her silver-clad fingers into the man's face causing his skin to hiss and burn.

"Run Nikki!" Tosh yelled and Nikki obeyed by digging her heels into the ground and backing out of the alley. Unfortunately Tosh and the Vampire's tussle was blocking any way for me and Ashlyn to get out.

Tosh released the Vampire's face for a brief second before unwinding the silver chain from around her wrist and tightening it around his throat. The Vampire howled as he pulled at the chain around his neck, burning his fingers in the process. Tosh growled in pain as she tightened the chain once again, effectively burning a deeper slice into the Vampire's throat, but in the next second the Vampire thrust his back into the brick wall behind him. Ashlyn screamed as we watched Tosh's head bounce off the wall, leaving her disoriented and bleeding. The Vampire reached behind him and swung her up and over his head to the ground like a ragdoll.

At the same time shots rang out in the distance and suddenly dozens of people were screaming and running. The Vamp stood up quickly and ran to the edge of the alley to check out what was happening so I took the opportunity to run to Tosh's aid. The puddle of blood underneath her head was growing although she was looking up at me and blinking in confusion.

"Jonah!" Ashlyn screamed behind me and I looked up just as the Vampire reached down and then lifted me off the ground by my throat.

"I'm not here for you, human," he growled as my head pounded from the lack of oxygen. As I scratched frantically at the Vampire's hand I watched as red tears began to flow from his eyes. His face contorted with emotions he didn't understand, but my eyes darted to my right and saw Ashlyn standing with her hands outstretched, her eyes tightly closed. I suddenly realized my girl must be trying to help.

"What the hell is happening to me," the Vamp cried out as he dropped me to the ground.

While I coughed and gasped for air, the Vampire was slumped on the ground wailing next to me, his face streaked with bloody tears. Ashlyn eyes were tightly closed as she desperately concentrated on inflicting as much sorrow and pain as she could onto the Vampire, but he was like the monster that just wouldn't die.

"If I...can't have Nikki...I'll just take her sister," he said as he painfully began to drag himself along the ground towards Tosh.

"No!" Ashlyn screamed as her eyes shot open and ran to Tosh's side, falling down and draping herself across Tosh's limp body.

"Ashlyn, no!" I yelled just as the Vampire's hand came down on Ashlyn's chest and suddenly the two of them disappeared in a cloud of black smoke. I shook my head and squeezed my eyes shut for a moment expecting to see Ashlyn lying across Tosh when I opened them. But only Tosh was in front of me moaning.

"Ash?" I called out quietly into the empty space and when she didn't answer I yelled to the back of the alley. "Ashlyn!"

"Jonah!" a voice called behind me and when I turned I saw Jared coming down the alley with this handgun drawn. "You ok? We gotta go...shit, Tosh!"

"I'm fine," she groaned as she rolled over onto her side, her hair still wet with blood though her injury had completely healed. Jared rushed over to her, lifting her up to a standing position. "What happened to Ashlyn?"

"She…she threw herself on Tosh and then…then…he touched her and they…they vanished. He Projected…but…with her."

"That's impossible," Jared replied shaking his head.

"Do you fucking see her here?" I shouted. "I know what I saw, Jer. She went up in smoke just like you guys do."

"He's right, Jer," Tosh interjected as she unwrapped herself from his side. "I felt her on top of me and then she was gone."

"Come on, we've got to find her."

"How?" Jared replied in an agitated tone. "If you're saying she Projected, she could be anywhere."

"We can't leave without her, we can't just leave! We have to look for her," I yelled again, but this time placing my hand against Jared's chest to stop his progression down the alley.

"Jonah, I just shot a Vampire in broad daylight and stuffed him into the back of the truck. We have to get out of here now!"

"No," I growled, shaking my head nervously.

Jared crushed my hand. "Jonah, I don't want to hurt you."

"I'm not leaving without her."

"Don't say I didn't warn you," he replied a split second before his fist came in contact with my face.

Chapter Thirty-one

Brianna

At last the house was no longer bursting at the seams. Cameron and Devin left at the butt crack of dawn with Fabi, Renee, John and a sleeping Wills. Jonah and Ashlyn were shopping with Jared, Nikki, and Tosh. Alex and Kyla were hunting in the woods nearby. Sera and Maddy were taking naps in their respective bedrooms while Eris was driving Daddy O nuts with conversation in the living room. Olivia was jumping into slushy puddles in her favorite red rain boots with Jack-Jack only a few feet away diving head first into the big mounds of snow his uncles had created the day before. It was a wonderfully peaceful day, perfect in its simplicity as well as productivity. It was amazing what you could get accomplished when there weren't a million people around to get you off track.

"Daddy O, can I make you a sandwich?" I asked.

Daddy O winked at me over the top of his newspaper which, by the way, was not a deterrent to my father's incessant talking. "And that's why yur my favorite granddaughter, sugar."

"Thanks, Daddy O, but there's not much competition," I replied before opening the front door and taking a step out. "Livy, Jack-Jack, it's lunchtime. Time to come in."

I stepped back inside, only slightly affected by the whines of my children. They had been prisoners in the house since we got here, and never out of anyone's sight, especially mine. Even today's play outside was short and really only at the behest of Sera. Who cares that they were having frightening dreams as recent as last night. The romp in the snow with Cam didn't last past round one since Eris began shouting into the woods for me to come inside. Poor Maddy and Daddy O had to be woken up in the middle of the night so I could get to the children who were sleeping between them. All the stress that had been released with Cameron came right back at seeing Aidan pulling Olivia out of my arms in the children's dream, but even worse having to see Jack-Jack go with him willingly.

"'Lil Bri, make sure you give me a good mix a white an' dark meat," Daddy O called from his recliner.

"Ok," I replied as I pulled out the large container of leftover turkey.

"And a scoop of stuffing."

"I know," I answered, and then said under my breath, "And just a touch of cranberry sauce."

"Oh, and maybe just a touch of cranberry sauce."

I smiled and laughed to myself since he was giving me instructions as if he hadn't made his customary day after Thanksgiving sandwich the same way for over fifty years. I removed the bowls of stuffing and cranberry sauce from the fridge and began preparing lunch when Daddy O's landline rang. Based on the caller ID I figured it was for me.

"Home already?" I answered.

"Pulling up to the manor now, love," Cameron replied. "And even though I know Devin will tease me, I am not embarrassed to say that I miss you already."

"Only a couple more days and then you'll be sick of the sight of me."

"Impossible. How are the children?"

"Happy to be playing outside."

"Did they mention anything about their dream last night?"

"Nope, nothing. When I tried to talk to them about it they claimed they didn't remember and changed the subject."

"There is no question they are your children," he laughed lightly as the sound of car doors opening and closing echoed through the phone.

"Yes, well, even though they are my children they're still not listening to me, as usual," I replied and held the phone away from me before yelling back outside, "Kids! Lunch! Now!" When I put the phone back to my ear I could hear Cam chuckling. "Sorry."

"Speaking of lunch," he began but then lowered his voice, "did you feed?"

I sighed dramatically as I looked at the empty bottle of blood sitting next to the sink. "So far today I have dressed and fed your children, made breakfast for the seven remaining humans, packed eleven boxes, thrown away fifty pounds of junk, coordinated with the donation center for a pickup, finished three loads of laundry, cleaned the bathrooms, changed all the sheets on the beds, and now I'm making lunch for everyone. Now after having done all of that..."

"Mama," Livy interrupted as she came through the front door and began stomping her red rain boots on the entryway's carpet, "can I have carrots and turkey for lunch?"

"Yes, baby girl. Tell your brother to come in," I responded and placed the receiver back up to my mouth. "Now like I said, after doing all of that..."

"I tried, Mama," Livy said, her wet boots squeaking loudly on the hardwood floor as she entered the kitchen. "I told him he'd get in trouble, but he wants to play with Aidan."

With the phone still pressed to my ear I ran past Olivia and through the opened front door. By the time I stepped onto the porch, Eris was standing just behind me and looking directly at our sworn enemy standing in the front yard. It wasn't a dream, it wasn't a vision, Aidan Pierce was holding my son's hand and had no white light glowing from his head for me to grab hold of.

The phone fell to the ground, and I could hear Cameron screaming through it as I slowly stepped down the porch steps. "Jack...baby, c-come to Mama."

"But Mama, Aidan came! He came like he said he would," Jack-Jack said excitedly causing a devious smile to stretch across Aidan's face.

Eris kept flinching behind me, having difficulty keeping control but worrying as I was that Aidan would hurt my baby boy if either of us jumped. Slowly I took another step down, extending my hand and trying to keep it from shaking. "Jack-Jack, please...remember what Ada said. Just come to Mama, please baby."

Jackson's lips twisted from side to side as he looked up at Aidan curiously. "Ada said you're a bad man."

"Me? Come on, Jacky boy, I have all these hybrids that need your help."

"Jackson, don't listen to him!" I shouted as I rushed down the remaining steps.

"Are you ready to play our game, Jacky boy?" Aidan said as he lifted my son into his arms. "Remember what you have to do?"

"Don't you touch him," I screamed as I struggled to get traction on the slippery wet snow. Eris grabbed my arm and pulled me forward as Aidan clutched Jackson to his chest and ran across the driveway.

"Now, Jacky!" Aidan shouted as he crossed the street and headed up the steep side of the mountain. Jackson looked over Aidan's shoulder and I could see the wave of white light coming from Jack-Jack's hands before it hit us, thrusting Eris and I backwards into the steps of the front porch. I dug my fingers into the ground and launched myself forward across the driveway, not even bothering to wait for my father. From the corner of my eye I could see Alex and Kyla emerging from the woods on the side of the house and quickly changing their direction to follow me.

"Stay with Olivia!" I shouted as I crossed the street and began climbing up the mountain, following the scent of my son that hung in the air. By the time I had crested the hill Eris was next to me and the two of us were flying down the slope of the mountain. Roughly fifty feet ahead of us I could see Aidan winding through the woods while Jackson's giggles bounced off the trees around him. In tandem, Eris and I leapt over a large fallen tree, flying through the air to gain lost ground. Unfortunately our landing caught Aidan's attention and suddenly another wave of white energy sent Eris and I through the middle of the dead tree.

Only a second later Eris was rising from the ground and pulling me up to a standing position. My head felt as though I'd been hit by a sledgehammer. Eris had to pull me along for a few steps before I caught up with his stride, running down to where a stream cut into the base of mountain. Frantically I looked both ways, sniffing the air and unable to find Jackson's scent.

"Figlia, this way," Eris shouted as he grabbed my elbow and pulled me to the left. Snow flew up from our footsteps as we followed the stream around a sharp bend, but our progression was quickly stopped as another wave of pain threw us back into the craggy rocks.

When the stars cleared from my eyes I looked up to see Jackson with his hand still outstretched in front of him.

"Nicely done, Jacky boy," Aidan said, resting his hands proudly on my son's shoulders.

I flinched forward, but Eris grabbed my arm and brought me back down to him. Initially I glared at him, but then quickly followed his gaze behind where Aidan was standing and saw another ten or so men coming toward us, one of which was smaller and hunched over moving more like an animal than a man. I lowered my mind shield and none of them were displaying a white light, but from the fangs that were hanging from their mouths I knew they were Vampires.

"Oh don't worry, Morgan," Aidan began, "we've had enough hybrid blood to protect ourselves against you."

Slowly I pushed myself up from the ground, my father matching my movements. "Aidan...please. I'll give you whatever you want..."

"Oh but I think this is more about what Jackson wants," Aidan interrupted and knelt down next to my son.

"N..." was all I got out before being hit by another wave of pain, however, this time the stream of white mist wasn't coming from Jackson, but from the creepy, thin, hunched Vampire. Looking at him now I realized I was being tortured by my Vampire great-grandfather. Goram? No, Gorum. Right? It's generally better to know the name of the Vamp that's torturing you.

Fighting against the hold Gorum had on me, I struggled to look to my left to see that Eris was trembling with the same pain I was. With a force that was not our own, both Eris and I were brought to our knees, our torsos held upright and rigid, and our mouths forced firmly closed.

"Now, Morgan," Aidan began coolly, "you wouldn't want Jacky here to give up his dream of helping hybrids, now would you?"

"Mama?" Jack-Jack said looking at me with conflicted eyes. I tried opening my mouth to scream at my son, but every movement brought new levels of burning pain. When Jackson didn't see any opposition from me he responded, "I'm just gonna go help the hybrids, and...then I'll come right back, I promise, Mama. Tell Ada I'll be good, I'll make him really proud."

"Oh I'm sure you'll make everyone proud, Jacky," Aidan replied smugly as he extended his hand and my son took it happily. "Now hold on tight."

My body was racked with pain as I tried resisting with everything muscle, every fiber within me. Eris was also fighting and groaning next to me, and I could see Gorum's hand shaking slightly to keep us under control. But in a flash our struggles were made useless as I watched

Jackson and Aidan disappear into a cloud of black smoke. My body froze as I stared stunned and mystified at what I had just seen. It was impossible, absolutely impossible. Jackson couldn't Project, he was a hybrid, a little more Vamp than human, but still he couldn't so…what…how…where the hell was my son!

Gorum stood over me, the other remaining Vampires standing a few feet behind him, all with wicked smiles. Gorum put his long, thin fingers through the stream of white mist connecting the three of us together.

"Beautiful, isn't it?" he said in a sickly, raspy voice. "So pure, yet so painful. I wonder, did you think you and your children were the only ones with this ability?" he continued as his fingers brushed down my cheek with a burning chill before shifting his attention to Eris. "Though my gift seems to have skipped a couple of generations. Poor Eris, such a disappointment, but so was your sister's blood."

My father's fangs extended with great effort, his body shaking with pain as a feral growl came from deep within him. Gorum smirked as he thrust his palm against my father's cheek causing him to scream in agony.

"For thousands of years your father's debt has been outstanding," Gorum yelled over my father's screams. "Perhaps your grandson can pay it on your behalf."

"NO!" I screamed, fighting through the excruciating pain and using all my power to cut the connection Gorum had on me, and by some miracle it worked. It shouldn't have because of the hybrid blood he had ingested, and Gorum was just as shocked as I was when the white mist snapped back like a whip, knocking him down to the ground.

The other Vampires took a fearful step back as Gorum stood quickly and uttered one word, "Leave!"

My sneakers slipped in the snow as I leapt forward, my fingers grasping at the black smoke of Gorum's Projection. I screamed as I pounded my fist into the ground. Suddenly a hand grabbed my arm and I instantly jerked my elbow back, making contact with the person's face. Unfortunately that person was my father, but there wasn't time to apologize.

"Olivia!" I screamed as I pushed up from the ground and tried to gain my footing in the slippery mess I had created.

In an instant I closed my eyes and pictured the front porch of Daddy O's house. With a deep breath, and as Cameron always instructed me, I pushed my spirit toward the image in my mind. My body stretched and floated freely until the sight of the small ranch-style mountain house was focusing in front of me. Alex was standing on the top step of the porch, Olivia peeking from around his right leg.

"What's the matter with you?! Why isn't she inside!" I screamed at him as I swept my daughter up into my arms and ran inside the house where Daddy O and Maddy were clinging to each other on the couch. Olivia squirmed out of my arms and ran to them as Alex turned me around to face him.

"Brianna, where's Jackson!" Alex's deep, booming voice reverberated in my chest. "Brianna!" Alex yelled again, but this time grabbed my shoulders firmly and shook me to attention at the same time Kyla walked into the house with the phone I had dropped to the ground pressed firmly to her ear. When my eyes focused on Alex he continued softly, "Where is Jack-Jack?"

"A-aidan," I heard my voice say, and then it hit me – my son was gone, vanished in a most unexplainable way. I could feel my chest heaving with panic. What was I supposed to do now? My son was with Aidan. I couldn't track either of them. What was I...How would I...

"Aidan?! Here!" Alex continued.

I nodded vacantly. "He...took...him. He took Jack-Jack," I cried as my knees gave out from under me. Alex quickly took my weight and lowered me to the floor as he continued to ask questions I couldn't process.

Kyla knelt beside me and handed me the house phone. "It's Cameron, honey."

With a shaking hand I took the phone from Kyla and as I brought the phone up to my ear I could hear Cameron's raised voice coming through the receiver. "...the alarm and get Father. I knew it, I knew this would happen, Brother. She never feeds, and now look what has happened, the very thing we have been...h-hello? Ky...Bri?"

Shocked and angered, I allowed the phone to slip out of my fingers and crash loudly on the floor, plastic pieces scattering in all directions. Quickly I rose from the floor, tripping over my own feet trying to get around the couch to where Olivia was snuggled into Daddy O's chest. With more force than I care to admit, I pulled Olivia off my grandfather's lap, holding her arms firmly at her side. "Where did they take your brother?"

"Jack-Jack's ok, Mama."

"Where did they take him!" I shouted at her and suddenly Daddy O's hand was squeezing my forearm.

"Now, 'Lil Bri..." he began but I shook my arm free of his grip.

"She is the only one that can talk to him," I growled and then turned my attention back to my daughter. "Olivia, tell your brother to tell us where he is."

"But Mama…"

"NOW! Or…or…you will be punished."

"No, no, petite," Sera said with a quiver in her voice from across the room with my father standing next to her. "Do not yell at her."

"And you!" I said angrily as I released Olivia and flew over to my stepmother only to be caught mid-stride by Kyla clamping her arms around my chest. "Did you see it?" I shouted at Sera as I flailed in Kyla's arms. "How could you let them take my son!"

Tears instantly began to fall down Sera's cheeks while my father took a protective stance in front of her. "Figlia, how dare you throw out accusations…"

"She always sees things! She always knows when there's trouble, especially when it…"

"I did not see anyzhing, I swear, petite," Sera interrupted.

"Bullshit! Total bullshit," I screamed as I pulled at Kyla's arms, causing Alex to cover me as well. "You kept danger away from me long enough for me to have the babies, and then what? Hand them over to Elaina? Was that the plan all along! You just didn't plan on Elaina getting killed, so are you working for Aidan now?"

"Brianna!" Kyla shouted.

"Why else would she allow Aidan to take Jack without the slightest bit of warning? She could have done something if she wanted to, but instead…she told me to let them play outside. You're a part of it, aren't you?!"

"Daughter!" Eris growled through his extended fangs. "Do not test me…"

"Now that's enough!" Daddy O shouted from behind me. "Brianna Marie…Marilena Morgan, you stop actin' like a heathen this instant. Eris, you put them fangs away right now. I'll not tolerate any a this in my house, especially with my great-grandbaby standin' right here."

I stopped my struggles, but Kyla and Alex tightened their grips when I tried to move toward Olivia. "I swear if you don't let go of me I will Push both of you through the back wall of the house."

Slowly and cautiously they loosened their hold enough for me to run to Olivia and lift her into my arms much to her dismay, causing Daddy O to take a step forward. "Sugar, maybe you should leave Livy with us."

"She is *my* daughter, and the only connection to Jack-Jack," I snapped as Livy squirmed in my arms. "Now leave me alone, all of you!"

"Bri, please," Kyla pleaded.

"Stay away from me!" I yelled and backed down the hallway. "And if anyone comes through that door so help me I don't care who you are I will not control myself."

Before another word could be said I quickly ducked into my childhood bedroom and closed the door behind me. The living room erupted in shouts and cries as I slid to the floor.

"Baby girl, you have to tell me where your brother is."

"I don't want to, Mama."

I jerked her up from my chest and held her at my eye level. "This is not a game, Olivia! You talk to your brother this instant!"

My ears rang painfully as Olivia wailed in front of me. I was a horrible mother. One child kidnapped, the other terrified by my hysterics. I didn't deserve to be their mother, I didn't deserve anything. I had failed in every way and this was my punishment.

Gently I cradled Olivia back into my chest, wiping her tears and cupping her cheek with my hand. "Sleep, baby girl, sleep," I cooed as I fought against my daughter's will and induced her sleep. Absentmindedly I was rocking back and forth, petting her hair and stepping into her mind.

Jack-Jack? Baby, please answer me.

Chapter Thirty-two

Jonah

I wasn't sure what hurt worse – my heart, or my face. Ashlyn was gone, literally disappeared into thin air. I don't think the word "impossible" had ever been used so often. No one, not even Eris who was an Ancient, had ever seen a dual Projection, and even that term had just been made up. Even witchcraft had been debated, but honestly I didn't care to argue about it. My girl and Jack were gone, who gave a shit about how it happened, let's just get them back.

With Warriors in the living room, and the other bedrooms occupied, I was left to take solace in the only place remaining in the house – the bathtub. The icepack Kyla had made me was now just a bag of water but my cheek was still throbbing and swollen. Even with the lights off and a towel underneath my head I couldn't relax enough to sleep. Every time I closed my eyes all I saw was Ashlyn's terrified face looking back at me.

Just then someone burst into the bathroom and shut the door. Suddenly I could see the issues with my choice of hiding place. Now I could tell it was a woman, and to make things more uncomfortable she was crying. But really, what woman wasn't crying in this household. Before another awkward moment passed I cleared my throat, making the woman gasp and flip the lights on.

"Jonah?" Tosh said as my eyes squinted to adjust, causing my cheek to twinge with pain. "What are you doing in here?"

"Only place left," I replied and then gasped at the pain.

Tosh wiped her eyes as she pushed herself off the bathroom door. "Let me take a look at your cheek, it looks like it's getting worse." I didn't object as she knelt in front of the bathtub, took my face in her hands, and gently turned my left cheek toward her. When she whistled I knew it looked as bad as it felt. "I think Jared might have broken something."

"Great," I groaned, trying to move as few muscles as possible.

"I should have fixed this earlier, I'm sorry."

"Huh?"

"Just remember this is just as awkward for me as it will be for you."

Before I could ask what she meant, Tosh leaned over the edge of the tub and ran her tongue up the length of my cheekbone, and then did it a second time. Yep, actually licked my face. I was still in shock by what just happened when the throbbing started to subside. Carefully I put my hand up to my cheek and could feel that the swelling was going down.

"How did you do that?"

"I'm a Healer," she replied like I was an idiot.

"I know, but I thought..." I said pointing awkwardly to her torso causing her to roll her eyes.

"I'm not defective, Jonah. My body has limitations," she replied as she self-consciously pulled her shirt down even though it hadn't ridden up. "How are you holding up?"

I shrugged and shook my head. "I can't even..." I began but couldn't find the words and let the back of my head fall up against the tub's wall. Tosh sighed and rested her forehead on my arm as a sad silence fell between us. "Why were you crying?"

"Because I hate my sister."

"Most people do, I hear," I said, causing her to laugh lightly, lift her head, and wipe a tear from her eye. "What did she do?"

"She wants us to promise not to say anything about the bounty."

"Why not?"

Tosh sighed again and lowered her voice. "Because she's afraid one of the Warriors will cash it in. She doesn't even trust Jared enough to pass it up. And so she's asking me to flat out lie to the people who just inducted me into their training program and if I don't, she's going to tell them that it's my fault Ashlyn was taken."

"Whoa, wait a minute, it isn't your fault."

"Isn't it?! If I hadn't engaged that Vamp we could have stayed hidden and waited for Jared to come find us."

"Maybe you should remind her that she decided to make a run for it which is why you had to engage that Vamp."

"Nikki is really good at spinning things to where you don't know what's true anymore. She'll probably get me…kicked out of…the program and then what will I do?"

I let Tosh collapse into my chest, although the edge of the tub was cutting into both of us. "They won't kick you out, Tosh. I'll defend you, I saw what you did, and I promise they'll believe me more than her."

Tosh lifted her head and wiped her eyes again. "But if I tell the Warriors about the bounty, and someone cashes it in, it'll be my fault. She already blames me for everything that happened with our dad that…" Tosh stopped abruptly, tears still caught in her eyes as her expression changed to an apologetic one. "I'm sorry."

I shook my head and gave her the hug that she needed. "Your sister is such a bitch."

Tosh flinched beneath my arms with a laugh and stayed in my hug for another minute before sniffling and pulling away. "Don't say anything about the bounty for now, ok? I know it doesn't make any sense, but let me try and talk to her."

I nodded reluctantly. "Sure."

"Now, I feel bad, but I really do have to go to the bathroom."

I smiled and pushed up painfully from the hard tub and walked out of the bathroom. Just as I shut the door and stepped into the hallway, Kyla came running out of Brianna's bedroom with her hands squeezing her head tightly.

"Ok! Ok! I'll stay out," she cried as the door swung closed and she slid down to the floor. "Bri…stop."

As I went to go to her, Alex's big frame flashed by me and pushed me face first into the wall. "Ky, what happened?"

"She attacked me, Alex. Bri actually Pushed me. Me!"

Alex tucked his wife into his side. "Ky, you know she's not her in right mind. She won't even talk to Cam."

"Has she said why," I asked, knowing I was butting in on their conversation.

Kyla shook her head. "She attacks anyone who tries to go in, even Sera. With Bri's powers, and being able to use Livy's, no one is safe to go in there, but we need to talk to her. We need to check on Livy, she's been held hostage in there since this afternoon. I know I don't understand what she's going through, but I'm still her friend and..." Kyla paused as an obvious idea cut into her speech. "Jonah...you could talk to her."

"But you said..."

"She can't attack you, you're human," she replied as she unraveled herself from her husband's side. "Plus she might talk to you because you lost someone today too."

My nose started to tingle, making me rub my face roughly in order to keep my emotions inside.

"I'll try."

Kyla sighed with relief. "Wonderful. Oh, wait you'll need something before you go in there."

Kyla quickly disappeared around into the kitchen as Alex squeezed my shoulder and said, "It might be a touchy subject, but you need to let her know that we'll be leaving for California before sunrise."

I blinked, stunned. "But shouldn't we stay here and look for..."

"Wherever Aidan has taken Jackson and Ashlyn, it is not around here. It is dangerous for us to be so exposed and unprotected. We need more resources than what we can get here. Understood?"

I nodded nervously, suddenly realizing I had no idea where I fit in anymore. "Yeah, understood."

Just then Kyla came from around the corner, a bowl of water in one hand and a dish rag in the other. "Here, you're going to need this."

"Why?" I asked, taking the bowl and rag from her.

"Oh you'll see," she replied in an unsettling tone.

Slowly I turned in the direction of Brianna's room and walked to her door with all eyes watching to see if I'd be kicked out like everyone else. With a deep exhale, I turned the doorknob and cautiously entered. The light from the hallway cast a beam of light that illuminated the edge of the bed just enough for me to see Brianna lying with Livy unconscious on her chest.

"What don't you people understand," Brianna said in a flat, low voice.

"I just do what I'm told," I replied.

"So they sent you in because I can't attack you."

"Pretty much."

"I just want to be left alone."

"I can understand that," I replied and closed the door behind me before stepping around to the far side of the bed. "They just want to see how you are and check on Livy. Let me do that and I'll be out of here, and everyone will leave you alone for the rest of the night. I will make sure of that."

"I don't have much of a choice, do I?"

"No, not really," I replied as I sat down on the edge of the bed next to Bri and leaned over to turn on the lamp that sat on the nightstand. When the light came on I nearly choked on my own spit when I gasped at the sight of my friend. Vampires cried red tears, diluted bloody tears, and Brianna had been crying so hard and for so long that her face and chest looked as though a maniac with a knife had gone to town on her. I could see where newer tracks of tears had cut into older ones that had dried and crusted over. She looked like I felt. "I guess that's what the water is for."

"I'd say leave it if I didn't think it would scare Livy so much," she said as she caressed her daughter's hair.

"Is she…"

"She's sleeping."

"Will this wake her up," I said as I placed the bowl on the nightstand and dipped the rag into the water.

"Not as long as I'm touching her," Brianna answered as I wiped her cheek. "I've never forcibly used my power on my children, but I need to hear from Jack…"

More red tears stained Brianna's cheek that I had just wiped and I realized I might need another bowl of water at this rate. "Does it hurt her?"

"I don't think so," she replied with uncertainty.

"Then keep her asleep for the time being. She really shouldn't hear everything going on out there or frankly see you like this."

"That bad?"

I huffed as I wrung out the rag and started cleaning her other cheek. "If my brain could work at all right now I'd come up with some funny comparison, but yeah, you look bad."

Bri pursed her lips as she tilted her chin up so that I could wipe underneath.

"They blame me, you know."

"Who does?" I replied as I soaked the rag again into the darkening water.

"Everyone. My dad, Alex, especially Cameron."

I paused with the rag on her collarbone. "No one blames you, Bri, *especially not* Cameron."

"You didn't hear him on the phone, Jonah. I heard him, I heard him say it was my fault...that...that he *knew* this would happen."

"Maybe you heard him out of context..."

"I know what I heard, Jonah," she snapped and I quickly jerked my hand away from her. "How do I forgive him for that? I realized today that everyone who supposedly loved me really thought I was just weak and crazy this whole time. If Eris hadn't seen Jackson disappear no one would have believed me. How do you think that makes me feel?"

"It feels like a punch in the face," I said as I wrung out the rag, thinking it might be safe to proceed again. "Oh wait, that's just when Jared actually punches you in the face."

Bri gave me a sympathetic smile as I resumed wiping away the red tears from her chest. "I'm sorry, here I am going off and I didn't even ask you how you were doing."

I shrugged as I cleared the threatening emotions from my throat. "I keep thinking I'm gonna wake up, or she'll come around the corner like it was all some stunt and then...well, she doesn't. And now thanks to Tosh, my broken cheekbone is healed but I no longer have the distraction of the pain so it's all just there in front of me, ya know? I was a stupid, weak human going up against a Vampire. Of course I was going to lose, and now she's gone."

Knowing I couldn't hold in my emotions any longer, I tossed the bloody rag into the bowl of water and turned away. Brianna squeezed my elbow gently, which didn't help me with the tears I was trying to keep from escaping.

"Sorry," I said, wiping my eyes with the back of my hand.

"We both had someone taken away today," she sniffled as she tangled her fingers around mine. "Most of the people around us can't seem to sympathize with that. They just do what they're told – pack up and leave, by force if you have to."

"Oh yeah," I said with a sarcastic laugh, "I'm supposed to tell you that you're expected to leave tomorrow, but I'm guessing you know that already."

"I heard Alex tell you in the hallway. I'm a freakin' Vampire, for cryin' out loud, I can *hear* everything. Of course, maybe since I'm 'not in my right mind' they think I'm..."

I turned my head when Brianna stopped speaking and noticed the new tears staining her face. Quickly I began wiping her face again.

"You have to trust that they know what they're doing, Bri," I said in everyone's defense. "Alex is right, wherever they took Ash and Jack, it's probably not around here. At least tomorrow you and Livy will be safe and surrounded by Warriors. I'll be...hell I don't even know. Do I honestly drive back to Facility East alone? What do I do when I get there? How will I know when you guys get Ashlyn back, do I get a phone call or something? What the hell happens now!" I paused, knowing I had raised my voice. "Sorry. I didn't mean..."

"You have nothing to be sorry about," she interrupted. "I'm surprised you haven't spoken up."

"Technically I couldn't because Jared broke my face, so..."

Bri squeezed my hand tightly. "There's no question where you should be, Jonah. You're coming with us."

"To San Francisco?"

Bri lifted an eyebrow. "To paraphrase you, if my brain was working I'd come up with something funny to say. Yes, to San Francisco, to the manor. I..." she paused as red tears lined her eyelids, "...I need you there. You're the only one who believes me, and I...just need you there. Besides you're all that Ashlyn has, so you have every right to be there.

"Oh, Jonah, I'm so sorry," Brianna suddenly began sobbing. "I'm sorry I ever introduced you to all of this. I thought...I just wanted to...help...you and your family, and now look."

"Bri, no..."

"None of this would ever had happened if I hadn't..."

"And I never would have been able to really provide for my family, and I never would have eaten all of Mable's good food, or been able to send Katie Bell to college. Most importantly I never would have met Ashlyn, and...despite...what's happened...I...wouldn't take that back for anything." I cleared my throat again and finished wiping Brianna's face. After putting the rag back into the bowl I leaned over and kissed Livy on the head before saying, "I'll tell everyone Livy's ok and that you know about tomorrow. Hopefully Tosh is out of the bathroom and I can try getting some sleep."

"Don't tell me you're sleeping in the tub."

I shrugged. "Only place left."

"Just stay here," she replied and jutted her chin to the other side of the bed.

"I think Cameron might object to that."

Bri gave a nasty look. "I don't give a shit. You need a place to sleep, I have a place for you to sleep."

If I wasn't so tired and didn't want to sleep in the bathtub I would have said no flat out, but the bed looked too inviting. I walked over to the bedroom door and when I opened it Alex was waiting.

"Livy's fine. Bri knows about tomorrow, I'll make sure she's ready," I said and went to shut the door.

"Wait, you're staying in there?"

"Goodnight, Alex," I replied and shut the door.

Chapter Thirty-three

Cameron

Even with the kidnapping of my son, Victor required some routines to stand. Therefore, Devin and I were being forced to attend Julian's daily morning meeting, though it was more like a daily flogging. Victor had already eyed me several times to stop my fidgeting, but could I help it? No. The answer was plain and simple. It was torture having to sit and listen to my least favorite sibling drone on about irrelevant things that only he cared about. Victor had always entertained him and expected Devin and I to do so as well when the time came, though that was the last thing on my mind.

"So Father, with that said," Julian continued, "we will release Anasio and Dobbs this afternoon, and then move up the fang extraction on Walters to today so we can free up a few cells."

"Very good, child," Victor replied. "Be sure that the prisoners are all released through the back tunnel entrance. I do not want any accidental interactions with William or Olivia."

"Of course, Father. Now I'd like to discuss getting new surveillance equipment. We are working with very old cameras and monitors…"

Victor held up his first two fingers. "Child, as I said last week, we have just contracted to update all the external surveillance equipment for the manor. I am afraid the funds are simply not there."

"Then what about my request for new bed linens?"

"Are we seriously discussing bed sheets for prisoners?!" I said loudly in a voice I could not contain and received a critical eye from Victor. "There are more important things happening to this coven at the moment."

"You mean more important things happening to you," Julian chided. "There are others in this coven besides you and your family, Cameron. I am requesting the bed linens for the lesser violators, those who do not need to experience as much indignity as others."

I groaned and stood from my chair. "They are criminals. If they did not want to face indignities, they should not have broken our laws."

Just then, Connor burst through the door. "Father, I apologize for the intrusion. Cameron, the convoy is pulling up."

Without a second's hesitation I ran from Victor's suite with Devin and Connor close on my heels. "Connor, any updates?"

He nodded and quickened his step to keep up with me. "All the Trackers have been deployed. Several of them have underground contacts, so they are hoping there are some grumblings to go off on since we have no starting point. Cameron, you do realize since we basically have the entire country to scour this is going to cost a fortune."

"Money is no option, I told you that," I snapped as we turned onto the main corridor. "Total team members?"

"Twenty-five for now, but that's mainly for operations. You know Father will deploy everyone once we have something."

"Twenty-five is fine. Tell everyone to gather in the library in twenty minutes. I want everyone coming from North Carolina debriefed within the hour so that we have all the facts. Do we have rooms ready for Jonah and Natasha?"

"Yes sir. Fabiani volunteered to bring Tosh's things from the Facility since he was already staying there. I meant to ask earlier, should I have someone prepare a room for him here? It seems odd for him to stay…"

"He's fine at the Facility," Devin said abruptly causing Connor to look confused, but I pressed on to take the heat off of my brother.

"Connor, can you have someone wake the Ryan's? I promised Renee I would notify her as soon as Brianna arrived."

"Yes sir, and I will begin notifying the team about the meeting," he said quickly as he turned and ran up the stairs to the living quarters.

"Brother," Devin said in a warning tone as we approached the front door, "you do not need to take care of every little detail. Let me…"

"Please, Brother, no lectures. Not now," I said as we stepped out onto the front landing just as Brianna's convoy pulled down the long driveway.

"I have said it to you before, Brother, sometimes you need to bend a little so that you don't break."

"I really hate it when you say that to me."

"Perhaps if you listened, I wouldn't have to keep saying it. I hate to point it out, but there are some glaring similarities to a few years ago..."

"Say nothing of the kind," I shouted as I gave Devin a warning look. But when the three black SUVs stopped in front of the manor what passed between us did not matter anymore. Alexander stepped down quickly from the passenger side of the middle SUV and opened the rear door to reveal Brianna sitting with Olivia wriggling in her lap.

"Ada!" she squealed as she slipped out of Brianna's grip and ran up the few stone steps into my arms.

I hugged her tightly to my chest and took in every bit of her – her warm baby soft skin, the fruity smell of her long bouncy curls, the sound of her bubbly laughter in my ear. After kissing her several times on her cheek, I caught myself looking for her bookend. Where there was one, there was always the other, but now there was the heartbreaking absence. "Monkey, have you heard from your brother?"

"No-wah," she whined with a dramatic sigh. Before I could press her further she pushed down on my shoulder and launched herself behind me to Devin who of course caught her. "Devy, do I have to do kicks today for a hug?"

Devin gave her a loving smile as he petted her soft hair, and from the tone of his voice I could see that he too was having difficulty seeing one twin without the other. "No...monkey, not today."

When I turned back to the SUVs I was struck by the sudden absence of Brianna. I looked around in every direction in a panic until I came back around to Olivia. "Where did your mother go?"

She shrugged. "I dunno know. Mama's really, really sad, Ada. She wouldn't let go of me the whole time. I wanted to sit wif Auntie Ky on the plane, but Mama wouldn't let me."

"Your mother misses your brother very much, monkey, that is why it is important for us to know if Jackson has said anything about where he is."

Olivia crossed her arms and pouted. "How come everyone wants to talk to Jack-Jack? I didn't break the rules, how come you don't wanna talk to me?"

"Olivia, of course I do..." I began but I was quickly forgotten at the sight of Connor stepping outside. My daughter wriggled out of Devin's arms and ran to Connor because she knew that in his breast pocket were sticks of chewing gum specifically for her. While Olivia jumped into his arms I turned back around to see Kyla walking up to me. "Where did Brianna go?"

"Like she would tell me," Kyla snapped. "Bri has completely lost her mind. Where's Renee? We need all the help we can get to snap Brianna out of this. Seems like the only person she's talking to is Jonah. He even came out of her room this morning."

"He spent the night in her room?" I asked and she nodded. My fangs prickled inside my gums and over Kyla's shoulder I could see Jonah approaching. I had to remember that Jonah was my friend. We had known him for years and he would never betray my trust. As Jonah came up the stone steps he extended his hand to me with sympathetic eyes. Unable to control myself, I took his hand forcefully and jerked him forward. "You slept with my Brianna?"

"Uh...w-what?" he stuttered. "No! Of course not!"

"Why were you coming out of her room this morning?"

Jonah's jaw trembled as I squeezed his hand tighter. "Er...uh...because...I slept...no, not like that...I mean...I was sleeping in the tub, and then Tosh had to go to the bathroom, then I...no, uh Kyla, yes Kyla asked me to go and talk to Bri, so I did and then instead of having me sleep in the tub again Bri told me I could...stay...*stay*...in her room. That's all that happened, Cameron, I swear. I would never...NEVER, do that to you or...or to Ashlyn."

Quickly I let go of his hand, realizing what an ass I was being. "Jonah, I am so sorry..."

"Don't be," he replied as he shook his hand out. "We're all going through a tough time right now."

"I am sorry about Ashlyn." Jonah nodded uncomfortably and shifted his bag back up on his shoulder. "Welcome to the manor, then. I wish it could be for better reasons. Kyla, could you show Jonah and Natasha to the human wing? We have rooms prepared for them."

Kyla extended her arm and Jonah took her direction with Natasha following close behind, though oddly she kept her eyes focused on the ground.

I turned back toward the front door just in time to see Olivia pulling several sticks of gum from Connor's pocket. "Look, Ada!" she said cheerfully, waving the silver wrapped gum in front of her. "Can I have them now?"

"Later, monkey. We need to..."

"I want to see Grandfather," she interrupted as she jumped out of Connor's arms.

Quickly I lunged and grabbed her hand to hold her in place. "Olivia, Grandfather is very busy, he may not..."

"Pwease?" she begged, blinking her big black eyes at me. "I know he will want to see me."

I was putty in her hands. I stiffened my arm and allowed her to climb up and drape herself over my shoulder. "I am sure he will be delighted to see you. Brother, would you care to join us?" Devin nodded. "Connor, we shall meet you in the library shortly."

Connor parted ways from us as we passed through the front door of the manor and walked down the main corridor. The manor was a flurry of activity, and more people than usual were clogging the corridor, although many of them slowed and took notice of Olivia on my shoulder, and even she noticed after a while.

"Ada," she whispered in my ear, "why is everyone looking at me?"

"Possibly because they are not used to seeing you without your brother," I replied sadly, feeling his loss with every step.

"No, I don't think that's it," she said with absolution.

"Well, then perhaps it is because you are so beautiful."

My daughter's eyes brightened as she smiled and brought her cherry cheeks to life. "Yes, that must be it."

As the hallway to Victor's quarters approached, Julian came walking around the corner with a severe scowl which deepened when he saw me. "I suppose that we are all to bow down to you and anyone associated with your so-called family?" he growled.

I counted to three before responding since I could not say what I wanted with Olivia on my shoulder. "Julian, you remember my daughter Olivia." Julian pursed his lips and gave her a curt bow to which Olivia waved in return. "I do apologize about leaving earlier..."

"My time is valuable, Cameron, and I do not appreciate being treated as though what I do is not important. You and Devin leave before we are adjourned, and then your wife...or whatever she is, comes barging in on my time with Father. That is my designated time..."

"Brianna is with Father?" I asked, but did not wait for a reply as I ran to Victor's quarters while Olivia giggled with glee at the speed.

Without knocking I opened the door and saw Brianna sitting in one of the antique upholstered chairs with her head in her hands. Victor was kneeling down in front of her, his hand on her back trying to comfort her while her body flinched with violent sobs.

"Ada, there's Mama," Olivia announced.

Brianna's head flinched up to look at me and through her blood-soaked eyes I could see my presence was not wanted. Quickly I pulled Olivia down from my shoulder just as Brianna fled to the opened terrace doors at the far end of Victor's room. In four steps I intercepted her, my fingers just grasping hers before she stepped out onto the terrace. "Bri, please...what is..."

"Let go of me," she growled softly without turning to face me.

Tentatively I wrapped my other hand around her arm and slowly tried to pull her toward me. "Love, please come back inside," I pleaded, keeping my voice low and soft, my movements slow and steady. "I need you, Bri. We need each other right now."

Suddenly Brianna wrenched her arm from my grip and slapped me across the face almost knocking me to the ground. When I straightened up, all that was left of my fiancée was a cloud of black smoke.

No. No! This was not happening...again. Not only had my son, MY SON, been kidnapped, but Devin was right, this was just like four years ago. Her unexplained and sudden hatred for me was exactly as it was when we rescued her from Aidan.

That man. That god-forsaken man has messed with my life for the last time. He needed to die, and I needed to kill him. There could be no more mistakes, no more missteps, either he died or I died trying and I was not ready to leave my children fatherless. So that meant Aidan would need to be found and killed, slowly, painfully slow, begging for mercy slow. Perhaps a live skinning, or...

"Brother?"

I flinched back to reality as I felt a hand on my shoulder and heard Devin's voice behind me. When he stepped around to face me I realized I was panting like he often did before he exploded into a vicious rage, and from his expression he recognized it all too well. Painfully he squeezed my shoulder and held me firmly inches from his face.

"Your daughter is ten feet away, you need to calm yourself down," he whispered forcefully. "Do you hear me, Brother?"

"You are going to preach to me," I growled causing him to squeeze my shoulder to an uncomfortable level.

"Olivia has already seen her mother hit her father. Do you want her to see more?" I shook my head stiffly. "Then get ahold of yourself."

My teeth were grinding together when Olivia called to me. "Ada? Are you all right?"

I took in a long, deep breath and put on the best smile I could before turning around to face my daughter. "Yes, monkey, everything is fine."

From her pout and furrowed little brows I could see she was not convinced. "Why did Mama…"

"She was testing me," I interrupted. "Your mother was testing me like Devy does to you. I…unfortunately…failed."

The words rang true in more ways than one, though I had no inkling as to why I deserved such a blow from Bri. But apparently my answer to Olivia was sufficient since her expression changed to a happier one as she turned to Victor.

"Grandfather," she began as she stood proudly and looked up at him, "when are we having our special breakfast?"

Victor sighed playfully as he rested his hands on his hips and placated his granddaughter. "Well, little one, you arrived a few days earlier than expected, but I will see what I can do."

"I want waffles, lotsa waffles."

"Is that all?" Victor said as he lifted Olivia into his arms.

"Oh no, Grandfather, I want fruit, and syrup, and juice, and milk…"

"Olivia," I interrupted, "I am sure your grandfather will provide quite a spread. But I know he has more pressing matters to attend to."

"Grandfather, is that true?" Olivia said with a pout which obviously tore at the great Roman general's heart.

"Unfortunately it is."

"What matters do you have to press?"

Victor had to bite his bottom lip to keep from laughing. "Nothing you need to worry your pretty little head about. But I promise that I will have everything your heart desires at our special breakfast. Now you be a good girl and go with your uncle for a moment while I speak to your father." Olivia gave Victor a kiss on the cheek before launching herself in the air and leaping from his shoulder to Devin's arms like a wild cat. Once the two of them were out of the room, Victor closed the short distance between us and kept his voice low as he said, "Child, I am afraid things with Brianna may be more worse than any of us ever thought."

"Based on her actions a moment ago, I would certainly agree," I said as my hand touched my jaw that still ached from her hand.

"But I fear it is deeper than Jackson being taken, or even her resentments at being Turned. She gave me this," he said as he opened his hand to reveal a gold Warrior's pin.

"It is hers?" I asked as I took the pin from his palm and held it up to my eye. One of the rarest sights to ever behold was to see Brianna without her Warrior pin.

"I am sorry, child," he replied gravely. "I know it is her grief talking, but she was adamant that she be released from the coven."

"What?!"

"Yes, child, I was just as shocked. She was telling me how unworthy she was when you stormed in. I have never had a Warrior in such a state."

"You have never had a Warrior lose a child, Father," I replied and handed the pin back. "Only you can bestow this, besides I do not think she would want it from me anyway. I must go now, Father, we are convening the team shortly."

"Child, we will get through this."

"Not soon enough," I replied as I exited the room and found Olivia sparring with Devin in the hallway.

At my presence, Devin lowered his hands and stood straight. "Where to, Brother?"

"The library. We should prepare for our meeting."

"Oh, I love the library," Olivia squealed as she ran several steps ahead before I leapt forward and grabbed her hand.

"Olivia, you cannot run off," I said firmly. "You must stay with me or one of your uncles at all times. Do you understand me?"

"But Ada…"

"No, Olivia, do you…"

"Ok, ok," she whined as she tugged me forward.

Together the three of us walked back through the corridors toward the library, however, as we approached I knew something was awry when I saw Connor and Alexander standing awkwardly in front of the library door.

Alexander went into immediate action once he noticed us coming down the corridor, his hands up defensively and speaking in a calming voice.

"Cam, we should find another place to meet."

"Is she in there?"

He nodded. "Ky is trying to talk to her, but…"

"Then we should not disturb them," I replied just as a flash of red hair came around the corner.

"Jesus, this place is too effing big," Renee shouted from the other end of the corridor with John just behind her and William pulling on her arm to get to Olivia who was doing the same to me. Eventually we both gave way and the two children met each other with squeals and a hug. "We've been wandering the halls trying to find everyone. Where…where is she?" she asked half out of breath.

But before I could answer, the remaining member of the twin gang also came running around the corner. Fabiani, dressed as a muted version of himself, slowed and stiffened his posture at the sight of us. It saddened me to see how much he felt, or perhaps was asked by Devin, to change when in the presence of those not in our immediate family.

Once Fabiani came to Renee's side I addressed both of them. "Bri is in the library with Kyla. To say she is distraught is…" I had to pause as the vision of her slapping me in the face flashed in my head. "Please…please help her, she will not speak to me."

After giving each other a concerned look, Renee and Fabiani stepped past me toward the library while everyone else looked at me for what to do, and sadly I had no answer. All I could do was watch Olivia smiling and laughing with William. The sight was so wrong without my little boy skipping along with them. How could they be so happy at a time like this? How could they laugh and sing in the corridor as if nothing happened - as if my son was merely down the hall instead of with a madman.

"Olivia, enough!" I shouted, causing both children to freeze abruptly in place. I knelt down in front of her and tried to ignore her scared eyes as I wrapped my hands around her thin arms and concentrated on calming my voice. "Olivia, it is really important that we hear from your brother. Could you try and talk to him again?"

"Why?" she pouted which caused me to exhale a slow sigh to keep my calm.

"Olivia, your brother could be hurt, scared…"

"But he's not, Ada," she interrupted plainly.

"But we do not know that."

"I do," she replied. "Ada, I always know when Jack-Jack is scared."

"How?"

She shrugged. "I dunno. I just do. I'm hungry, can we have lunch now?"

"Olivia, it is still morning," I said as my hand raked through my hair in frustration.

"Can I have more breakfast, then?"

This child would be the death of me.

"John, could you take the children down to the kitchen for some breakfast?" He nodded as he lifted William into his arms and held out his free hand to Olivia.

"Brother, perhaps we could use your meeting room for the debrief?" Devin asked next to me.

"Oh...yes, of course. I will need to move a few things around..." I began, but he stepped in front of me and placed his hand on my shoulder.

"Go with John and the children..."

"But..."

"*Brother,*" he interrupted and lowered his voice, "take your daughter to the kitchen. We can handle the rest. Bend, Brother, I am begging you."

I could see in my eldest brother's eyes that he was truly begging me, and it was out of love.

"Fine. I bend."

Chapter Thirty-four

Cameron

"We were hiding behind a Dumpster when the two Vamps came down the alley," Nikki relayed in front of the team members crammed into my small meeting room. It was a tight squeeze to say the least, but Olivia and William still found room to play quietly in the corner, and I could not help but watch them.

"And they were the same Vampires you recognized from Elaina's coven?" Alexander prodded her from the front of the room.

"Yes," Nikki replied softly. "But like I keep saying, I don't know their names. I just...saw them around."

"All right, then what happened."

"I heard Jared blow his horn so I ran out of the alley and one of the Vamps followed me. Jared shot him just as I got to the truck and he put the body in the trunk. Then he went to get Jonah and them."

After several moments of silence, it was obvious Nikki was not going to divulge any more information. Alexander realized the same and looked to Jonah. "Jonah, after Nikki fled what happened?"

Jonah looked down at Natasha and exchanged a nervous glance before he said, "The...uh...other Vamp came down the...uh...alley. We tried to run, but...um...he...uh...pushed Tosh down on the ground and she hit her head. I tried to rush him and he started choking me. Then um...Ashlyn used her Emo gift to affect him enough to let me go, and when he did he went after Tosh again. Next thing I knew Ashlyn was running to protect Tosh, but the Vamp grabbed Ashlyn instead and they disappeared."

"For now, we are calling it dual Projection," Alexander informed the room. "Somehow they were able to Project not only themselves, but whoever they were touching. I've done some outreach and no one has ever heard or seen anything like this."

"And we are sure the witnessed accounts are accurate?" one of the team members asked, although I did not look away from Olivia soon enough to see who.

Alexander nodded. "Yes we are. The one witnessed by Jonah was almost verbatim to what was witnessed by Eris and Brianna. Our assumption is that this is a gift that is being shared through blood since Aidan Pierce has not shown this ability in the past. Jonah, are you sure there isn't anything else you can share with us about what happened? Something they said maybe?"

I looked over just in time to see Jonah's pupils dilate. He was hiding something, but it was also very obvious that Nikki and Natasha were also involved by the nervous expressions on their faces while they waited for Jonah to respond.

"Uh…no," he said unconvincingly.

"Tosh?" Alexander asked and she shook her head guiltily. Alexander gestured for them to sit as he gave Devin and I a skeptical glance before saying, "I'd like a couple of volunteers to help me research further."

"Nikki will help you," Devin announced, much to her surprise of course, although Alexander did not seem too thrilled about it either. Knowing Devin as I did, I could see two reasons for his action – one, it was a way for Nikki to earn her keep, and two, a slight punishment to Alexander for allowing Aidan to get to my son. I was not overly opposed to either.

Alexander nodded to Devin and then continued with, "The remaining team members will report to Connor since he will be coordinating the operations. Similar to our Trackers, we know several of you have assets underground. Contact them immediately to see if they are hearing any grumblings about yesterday's attacks, or even better, anything about Aidan Pierce's new coven, but be discreet. We want accurate information, not paid-for nonsense. Brothers, anything else?" Alexander said as he gestured in our direction.

Devin took the invitation and stood with a very stoic expression as he said, "Everyone in this room is on-call at all times. This is not only an attack on hybrids, it is a direct attack on our entire family. Jackson is the first grandson of our dear father, and none of us should feel whole until he is with us again. Rarely in our history as a coven have we had a priority such as this, so there is no room for error. You are dismissed, except Jonah, Tosh, and Nikki, the three of you stay."

While everyone else muttered curiously and filtered out of the room, I watched as the three young adults' eyes grew large with fear. Thankfully my brother waited until the only people that remained were Alexander, Connor, and Jared before laying into them.

"Now that we're alone, how about the three of you start telling us the truth about what happened yesterday."

Natasha looked at the floor, Nikki looked at Natasha, and Jonah's eyes wandered around the room.

"Everyone in this room could see through that bullshit you tried to feed us. Now someone needs to start talking and I mean immediately. None of you have seen me truly lose my temper and I don't care…"

"Brother," I interrupted as I stood from my chair. "There is no need for you to lose your temper. Hopefully now that it is just us in the room they will tell us the truth, and perhaps why they felt they needed to keep things from us." Jonah's eyes fell to the floor, but Natasha's slowly came up to mine. "Natasha, part of being a Warrior is being able to trust one another. And I assure you, Devin and I were not the only ones who could tell you were hiding something."

Natasha swallowed hard as her jaw clinched and her eyes began to water. With a sudden burst of energy she shouted, "There's a bounty on Nikki!"

"Nat!" Nikki screamed as she turned to her sister.

"She didn't want us to tell you," Natasha continued to sputter, but Nikki quickly retaliated.

"It was Nat's fault Ashlyn was taken!"

Then all hell broke loose as all three of them began to squabble with one another, the sound of which grated on my raw nerves.

"Enough!" I shouted, and they immediately silenced themselves. "How do you know there is a bounty on Nikki?"

Jonah sighed while the two Cushlin girls glared at each other. "While we were hiding we heard the two Vamps talking about the bounty."

"And when the hell were you going to tell me this," Jared said angrily as he tried to get Nikki to look at him, but she merely began to cry into her hand.

I looked back to Jonah. "Did they mention how high the bounty was?"

He nodded. "A hundred grand."

"Damn," Devin said appalled. "I don't even get that for a hit."

"Brother," I whispered warningly as I shook my head tersely. "Nikki, why would you keep something like that from us?"

"Yeah, Nik," Jared began, "I'd really like to know that too."

With tears streaming down her cheeks she looked at Jared and then turned her eyes to me. "Because I didn't think any of you would pass up the chance to turn me over."

I sighed knowing that the amount would be tempting to some. "Nikki, it is evident that your life is in danger and the safest place you could be is here at the manor. I know that we have all moved on from your past indiscretions, as we have said many times."

"Saying it and meaning it are two very different things," Nikki replied snidely, causing Jared to pull on her arm.

Connor, who stood at the edge of the room, cleared his throat to bring our attention to him. "Not to sound glib, but in some ways this is good news." Jared jerked his head in Connor's direction with a venomous expression. "Jer, all I'm saying is that with a bounty that high, there are certain to be grumblings about it. It's something we can have our underground contacts keep an ear out for. If someone is capturing Nikki, they'd have to deliver her somewhere. And considering the past, I'm sure Aidan would want Nikki brought right to him." This time Nikki jerked her head around and glared at Connor. "I'm...a...just saying."

"Thank you, Connor," I responded calmly. "Please update everyone, but make sure they are aware of Devin's wrath...threat of death...fire and brimstone...that sort of thing."

Devin turned his head slowly toward me, and from the side of my eye I could see his raised brow. Connor nodded and left the room which prompted me to move on to the next issue that was presented. "So pray tell, how is Ashlyn's disappearance Natasha's fault?"

"It isn't!" Jonah shouted in Natasha's defense.

"Jared told her not to do anything stupid, but she attacked that Vamp which is why Ashlyn was taken," Nikki shouted.

"She attacked him because *you* freaked out and got clotheslined by that

Vamp," Jonah yelled, his face blood red with anger. "Tosh saved your life!"

"Well she sure didn't save your girlfriend's, Jonah. I'd think you'd be a little more upset about that," Nikki replied nastily.

Jonah was growing angrier by the second, and Natasha was gasping for air trying to keep her emotions under control. Slowly I stepped in front of her, putting my index finger under her chin and tilting her head up. "Natasha, did you attack the Vampire in order to help your sister?"

"Yes sir," Natasha answered in a weepy voice. "Nikki ran, and he came out of nowhere and he up ended her. I jumped on him so she could get away."

"Yeah, and then the bastard smashed her into a brick wall," Jonah said. "Her head was cracked open and he slammed her into the ground. Like an idiot I tried to help, and that just ended up with him straggling me. Everything that happened after that was exactly as I told you."

I looked to Devin who was giving me a similar curious look back. "What part of that story was necessary to keep from us?"

Natasha's eyes grew wide. "Be...because I disobeyed an order, I wasn't strong enough, and...and Ashlyn's gone because I wasn't good enough."

Devin crossed his arms but had a surprising caring look on his face as he said, "Tosh, you are human. You are a hybrid, but you're still a human. If you weren't a Healer you'd be dead."

"I know, but..."

"Regardless," Devin interrupted as he held his hand up in front of her, "you jumped into action, forsaking your life in order to protect others. There aren't a dozen hybrids who would have done that, and that's why we only have ten in the Warrior training program. And of those ten, I would guess only you would have been brave enough to do what you did."

"Natasha, you did well," I said, causing her to smile and wipe her cheeks dry of her tears. "Need a hug?" She nodded and I obliged, thinking I needed it as much as she did. "But please do not keep things from us again, understood?"

She nodded, and Nikki took the opportunity to flail her arms in exasperation and flee the room with Jared following after her.

"Uh, Cameron?" Jonah said softly, causing me to glance over at him. "I'd really like to help. My girlfriend's out there, I can't just sit here like an asshole waiting for her to come back. Please just let me do something."

Being able to personally relate to what Jonah was feeling, I looked over to Alexander. "Alex, I am sure you could use more hands."

"Of course. I've been thinking about what Jackson said to Eris and Bri." Alex paused when I flinched at the sound of my son's name, but then continued, "Eris said Jack kept saying he wanted to go and help the hybrids. What if Aidan has been acquiring hybrids right under our nose?"

"I have been suspecting that myself," I replied.

"Both Facilities have been releasing hybrids for over two years now," Jonah said. "Once they've left, we're not tracking them anymore. This Aidan guy could have picked them up on the street and we wouldn't have known."

"Jonah, I believe you have found yourself a job," I replied. "We should see if we can get our hands around how many hybrids they may already have."

Just then Renee and Kyla came bursting into the room, both Brianna and Fabiani noticeably absent. The sudden commotion also caused Olivia to jump up from the floor and grab William by the hand.

"Come on, Wills!" she squealed as she pulled William up from the floor and ran for the door.

"Olivia Sera Burke!" I shouted as I flew past Kyla and Renee, and stopped my daughter just as she was about to step out into the hallway. "What did I tell you?!"

Olivia flinched from the volume of my voice and then froze in place. "Not to run off."

"Twice I told you, Olivia, twice!"

"But I'm bored, Ada," she whined. "I wanna go play wif Wills."

"You cannot right now, we are…"

"BUT…I…WANNA…PLAY," she wailed at the top of her lungs causing a shiver to run through my body. This was when her mother would step in and calm her down in seconds. Bri was a miracle worker when it came to Olivia's tantrums. My daughter stood in front of me crying as if the world was over and I did not know what to do in the slightest. Finally, a hand tapped me on the shoulder.

"I can watch her," Natasha said, causing Olivia's cries to soften.

"Thank you, Natasha, but I cannot ask you to do that. You have your training…"

"But it doesn't start for a few more days. I don't mind, Cameron, really I don't," she said as she stretched her hand out to my daughter.

"Thank you," I replied. "Just bring her to my bedroom for now."

Olivia pulled on Natasha's arm. "Can Wills come too?"

"Of course," Natasha replied, but then looked behind her to Renee and John. "As long as that's ok?"

Renee nodded. "Yeah, take him. We need to talk to Cameron anyway."

Her tone was anything but pleasant or reassuring. Natasha took both kids by the hands and lead them through the room to the inside door which opened directly into my bedroom.

As soon as the door closed, I turned to Renee. "Where is she?"

"She's with Fabi and Victor. Things are bad, Cameron. She's a..." she began but struggled to find the word she was looking for, "...I don't know, sicker? She's more than depressed. I mean, it's no surprise to any of us that she's been resentful about being Turned, but it's just exploded into this all-encompassing anger about everything. And obviously at the heart of it all is Jack-Jack being kidnapped, and..." Renee gave a cautious look to Kyla before continuing with her hands ready in the air for her air quotes, "...and that you 'blame her' for it."

"She said...that I blame her?" Renee and Kyla nodded, but when Jonah joined in, I said, "Did she say that to you last night as well?" He nodded again. "How could I blame her? Why would she say something like that?"

Renee sighed. "Something about how you 'accused' her of not feeding..."

"She said she did not have time," I interrupted.

"Well apparently she did."

"No...no! She told me...I asked her if she fed and she began telling me all the things that she had to do which prevented her from feeding."

Kyla took a cautious step forward with sympathetic eyes. "I saw her myself, Cameron. She fed right after you all left. She made a point of showing us so that no one would pick on her."

"Then why would she go on like that..."

"Cameron, you know how Bri is," Renee said. "She was being dramatic and was telling you everything that she'd done, and then in spite of all of that, dot dot dot, yada yada yada, 'I still fed, Cameron, pooh pooh on you.' But before she could finish, Livybean interrupted her and then the shit hit the fan."

"But..." I began, but Kyla continued over me.

"When she came back with Eris, she picked up the phone and heard you say you knew something like this would happen because she wouldn't feed."

I reached back into my foggy memory of yesterday. "I...I do not remember that."

"I'm sorry, Brother," Devin interjected, "but you said precisely that. I was standing right next to you."

"I was in shock!" I shouted.

"I know, Brother..."

"No you DON'T! None of you do," I growled so harshly my fangs extended. "My child, *my son,* was ripped away from me and who knows what is being done to him. The only person who knows what I am going through right now refuses to speak to me. I need *her.*"

I turned my back on my family and Devin suggested that everyone clear the room. The only person not to comply was Renee. I scratched my scalp roughly before turning around and seeing Renee standing in front of Devin with her arms crossed and her hip popped while giving him a challenging look. She knew so little about how lethal he was.

"Renee," I said weakly, "what do I do? You know her better than anyone."

Renee looked away from Devin and relaxed her stance. "Honestly, Cameron, I don't really know how to handle *this* Bri. She's given up on everything. And..." she paused and furrowed her brow, "...I didn't want to say anything in front of everyone, but...the coven isn't the only thing she's talking about leaving."

I froze. The only sound in the room was Renee's heartbeat which quickened as more time passed until I finally said, "She wants to...leave me. Leave me?"

"Brother, I'm sure she didn't mean it. She's in a delicate state," Devin said as an odd sensation came over me and I started to laugh nervously.

"So she is going to leave me," I said with still a hint of awkward laughter. "For almost four years I have endured her hateful comments and angry fits over being Turned, and I have taken them as my punishment. And before that I suffered through her hatred of me for things I had not even done after we rescued her from Aidan. Yet, she is going to leave me for something I said in the heat of the moment? The fact that she *had* fed is a shock."

I turned away from them, placing my hand up against the wall and having to control the urge to bang my head up against it. "I do not have the strength to do this anymore," I said honestly, which burned me to the core.

"Cameron, don't you give up too," Renee said behind me. "Just give her some time. You know she always calms down after a couple of days."

"Renee's right, Brother. Let Father and Fabi counsel her, I'm sure they'll help her through this."

"I need to be with my daughter," I sighed, not wanting to talk about anything anymore. I walked toward the inside door that led to my quarters where I could hear Olivia's joyous laughter echoing from the other side. When I finally opened the door I smiled at the sight of my daughter twirling around in front of Natasha and William, but the instant she saw me she stopped her lovely little dance. Her frightened expression was yet another reason to bang my head up against the walls.

Slowly I knelt down to the floor, waving my finger at her to come to me. With a scared pout, Olivia dragged her feet across the stone floor toward me.

"Lovey, I am sorry I raised my voice."

Olivia looked behind her where Natasha was urging her on. When she turned back around she said, "I'm sorry I didn't listen, Ada. I won't run off again, I promise."

Placing my hands under her arms, I pulled her up onto my lap, and held her to my chest. "I know this is all difficult for you to understand, but I need to know you are safe. That is why you need to be with one of us at all times. Comprends, petite singe?"

 She giggled, as she always did when I spoke French to her, though I never understood why. "Oui, Ada, je comprends," she replied as she gave me a quick peck on my cheek. "Ou est Mama?"

Where is Mama, she asked. Where indeed.

"Your mother is with Grandfather. I am sure she will be up here soon enough," I said hopefully. "Have you heard anything from your brother?"

She shook her head. "Nope."

"Have you told him it is very important that he talk to us?"

Olivia sighed dramatically, very much like her Aunt Renee. "I *did*, Ada," she said as she slid down from my lap. "Can I have lunch now?"

Chapter Thirty-five

Jonah

"Jonah, wake up," a voice whispered in my ear causing my eyes to flutter open. Tosh was standing over me, her hand on my arm nudging me to wake.

I lifted my head from the desk in the library I had fallen asleep on and rubbed my eyes. "Sorry, just resting my eyes."

Tosh gave me a challenging look. "You were snoring."

"I don't snore."

"Uh, yeah ya do," Jared replied where he stood with Connor in front of an enormous monitor that displayed a map of the United States. It must be around 7:30am the way the two of them were making marks on the map and fielding messages from the dispatched Trackers combing the country.

I rubbed my eyes again and looked back at Tosh as I said quietly, "Have they heard anything?"

"Not yet," she replied, shaking her head just as Connor touched the monitor and turned a portion of South Carolina red. Red meaning the Trackers had found nothing in the area, yellow showing where they were going, and green meaning a solid lead. Sadly there was no green showing on the map at all, only growing splotches of red and yellow. "Wait…wha…what day is it?"

Tosh scrunched her face. "Wednesday. You should go and get some sleep. Nikki will be here soon." She looked over Alex's barrowed laptop to a pad of paper I had shoved underneath it. "How much luck have *you* had?"

I looked down at the paper where there were a handful of names in my cramped handwriting. "I've only found five hybrids so far that were released from one Facility or the other that haven't been seen or heard from in a while. Not sure what I was thinking when I said I would…wait a minute, today's Wednesday?" Tosh's eyes were wide as she nodded. "Today's your first day, isn't it?"

She nodded again, this time with a nervous smile. "Yep. In twenty minutes I'll be making a complete fool of myself."

"Natasha," Cameron said, though I couldn't see him from behind the wings of the tall chair he was sitting in, "you will do very well. Am I right, Connor?"

"She'll be great, and we all know it. She knows it, too," Connor said as he turned away from the monitor and gave Tosh a quick wink.

What the fuck? When did that start? But any further questions I had about Tosh and Connor were quickly diverted by Devin and Kyla coming into the library. Both of them went immediately to Cameron's side, although Devin gave the monitor a cursory glance before saying, "Brother, you are missing Julian's debrief with Father."

"As are you, Brother," Cameron muttered from his chair.

"Actually, Father allowed me to duck out to remind you about his breakfast with Olivia."

"Damn!" Cameron exclaimed as he stood from the chair. The front half of his button-up was hanging out over his pants, his hair sticking up on one side from resting his head up against the chair. As if he could feel our critical eyes on him, he ran up to one of the decorative mirrors and began combing his hair down with his fingers.

"Cameron," Kyla said, "I can get Livy ready for you."

"I know I am a failure at many things, but one thing I can do is dress my daughter."

"Cameron, I didn't mean…" Kyla began but stopped when Cameron held up his hand.

"Sister, I merely meant that I can get Olivia out of bed."

Kyla flipped her hair over her shoulders as she turned toward the door. "The movers came yesterday and I put as much as I could in your rooms, but there are a ton of boxes in the hallway. I'm sure you can take care of

THAT as well," she said just before slamming the door.

Cameron sighed as he gave up on his shirt, and pulled it out all the way around. He gave one last look at the map, shook his head, and left the library as well.

Tosh quickly turned to me and said quietly, "Cameron looks awful."

"Is there anyone that looks good?" I replied as I closed the laptop.

"Have you seen Brianna?"

I shook my head. "Not since we got here. You?"

"She's peeked in on Livy and Will a couple of times when I've been with them, but I only saw her for a second. But what I saw…"

"Tosh, don't you have somewhere to be?" Devin warned from across the room.

"Yes sir."

"Good," Devin continued, "perhaps you can see that Jonah finds his room since it looks like he hasn't slept in a bed in days."

Well that was certainly the truth. Tosh eagerly pulled me up out of my chair and lead me out of the library. Only halfway down the corridor Tosh pulled me to a stop. "Do you seriously not hear your cell phone ringing?"

I patted down my front pockets and then my back ones, pulling out my ringing cell phone and noticing my mother's name flashing on the screen. I stared at the screen for another second before I looked up at Tosh and said, "I should really take this."

Tosh looked down at her watch and bit her bottom lip. "I have to get to the training room then. I wanted to be a few minutes early."

"Sure, sure," I nodded. My mother's call went to voicemail as Tosh turned to walk down an adjacent hallway. "Hey, come find me afterwards and tell me how it went."

Tosh turned back around, a surprised smile on her face. She took the two steps between us, rose up onto her toes, and kissed my cheek. "Thank you."

"For what?"

"For caring," she said and turned away again. "My sister told me to fuck off."

I laughed to myself, although it was only at Tosh's reaction, not what Nikki had actually said to her. God that girl was a bitch. With a reluctant sigh I pressed redial and put the phone up to my ear. My stomach was growling and shaking with nerves as I pushed my feet back down the corridor in the direction I was pretty sure my room was. I hadn't actually found it successfully on my own yet, I'm sure today wouldn't be any different.

"J-Joey? Joey?"

"Hey, Mom," I replied as I came into the foyer.

"I was just leaving you another message. Honey, where have you been? I've been calling you for weeks, you had me so worried."

"Mom, you made your choice very clear, and I thought I was just as clear that I wouldn't be around anymore."

"But Mable said you didn't even come in at Thanksgiving."

"I couldn't I'm..."

"Joey, I'm sorry, you can't just go on ignoring me like this, I'm your mother. And what about your sister? She's been an absolute terror since you left..."

I took the phone down from my ear as I turned up the large staircase that wound widely up through the floors of rooms. At the mention of my sister my feet became very heavy. What my mother probably didn't know was that I had tried calling Katie Bell endless times and she was ignoring me as much as I was avoiding our mother. When I put the phone back up to my ear my mother was still ranting away.

"Joey, that night at the house was...was really bad for all of us. I just think if we all sat down together and talked..."

"Mom, I can't..."

"We could meet at Mable's if it's more comfortable. Please, honey, just give this a chance."

"Mom, I can't..."

"Why not!"

"Because I'm in San Francisco!" I yelled, causing a Warrior coming down the stairs in the opposite direction to look at me strangely.

"You're...you're where?"

"I'm with Brianna's family in San Francisco."

"But why? Why in the world would you go all the way out to California? What about work?"

"I was laid off."

"What!?" she yelled into the phone. "You get laid off and don't tell me!"

"We're not speaking!"

"Joey, you don't lose your job and go on vacation to California with your friends."

"I am n..." I stopped as I hit my forehead with my cell phone several times before bringing it back to my mouth. "I am not on vacation. Ash is..." I cleared my throat, "...she's...uh...Ash is in trouble."

My mother's tone changed very quickly. "What kind of trouble?"

A crazy Vampire kidnapped her along with my friend's son, they disappeared into thin air and could be anywhere, I thought to myself, unable to think of a plausible cover story.

"Was she working?" my mother said, unknowingly coming to my rescue.

"Uh...yeah, she was on a job...and it went bad. Now they're keeping her and some others hostage."

"Oh my god, Joey. Is she all right?"

"We don't know. That's why we came out here. Cameron's family is working on getting her back."

"When did all this happen?"

"Does it really matter, Mom? She could be hurt, they could be torturing her for all we know."

"Then why are you there? Joey, this isn't safe."

"Where else would I be? She's my girlfriend, Mom."

"But you've only known her for a few months."

"What the hell is that supposed to mean?"

"Joey, I'm just saying that you've only been together a short time, is it worth all this?"

I was stunned into silence. Was she worth it? Was Ashlyn worth it, asks the woman marrying a man she didn't love. It didn't matter that we'd only been together for a short time, I loved her. No, I didn't just love her, I needed her, every day, with every breath in my body. "Abso-fucking-lutely."

"But Joey..."

"Goodbye, Mom," I said as I hung up the phone, and if I could afford another one I would have thrown it at the wall. It was at that point I looked at my surroundings. "Where the fuck am I?"

Chapter Thirty-six

Brianna

Livy danced around the meadow in front of dozens of colorful butterflies, a princess performing for her subjects. Rarely was my daughter happier than when she was her vision of a butterfly princess. Watching her dance around brought tears to my eyes, but honestly what didn't.

From across the meadow I could see my father gliding through the velvety grass. As he came in line with Olivia and her butterflies, he bowed deeply with respect before continuing on to stand in front of me, blocking my view of Olivia. I took a step to the left so that I could see her again, and he matched me. When I tried again the other way, he squeezed my arm tightly to keep me in place.

"Let go of me," I growled softly so that Olivia could not hear. "Or I will…"

"What will you do, Bri-an-na? And with what power?" he challenged as he forcefully turned me around to see the faded and jagged edges of the meadow, as if someone had torn a picture in half. Eris pointed ahead of him to the vacant area. "That is your Dreamwalking, figlia, hardly visible. If it were not for me you would be ripping a hole in your daughter's mind."

"Let go," I said as I pried my father's hand from my arm. "I have enough people telling me how rotten I am, I don't need you to…"

"Figlia..."

"Stop talking to me like that! After everything that's happened to me in the last few days the least you could do is be your pompous, condescending self in your real voice."

While my father sighed through tight lips I stepped around him to get my view of Livy back. After a few seconds of silence, Eris returned to my side, his fake Italian accent stripped from his voice. *"Daughter, you have gone through something very traumatic and I am trying to understand your behavior, but I cannot. You are neglecting yourself, your Warrior, and you have injured Seraphina in ways I never thought possible."*

"But she..."

"It is unacceptable! The fact that those accusations came across your lips disgusts me."

"That's right," I said snidely, *"just keep laying it on."*

"And I will as long as it takes to get through to you."

"Get through to me!"

"This depression you are in is a detriment to Jackson's recovery. So tell me what needs to happen to get through that stubborn head of yours! Warrior, help me here," he said gesturing behind me.

I jerked around to see Cameron walking up behind me through the faded scene of what was my weak half of Olivia's dream. If Cameron was here, that meant he was with me in Livy's room, next to me, touching me. His gate quickened as I took several steps back, eventually closing my eyes and breaking the connection I had with Livy.

My eyes snapped opened and I could feel the weight of Cameron's hand resting on the nape of my neck. I knew I didn't have enough strength to Push him, so instead I gave him an elbow to the gut which flung him backwards. Immediately I bolted from the floor and had my hand on the doorknob when I felt Cameron grab my wrist, although his grip wasn't firm.

"Please, angel, talk to me," he pleaded softly as he brushed the fingers of his other hand down my forearm. "Please come back to me, I need you…"

"And I needed you," I replied as I ripped my arm out of his grip and flung the door open. His fingers fumbled after me as I stepped out into the hallway among the stacked up moving boxes that I recognized from our home.

"Awbie!"

I looked to my left to find Wills running toward me, Renee and John a few steps behind. Cameron stayed frozen in the doorway in order not to make a scene in front of our nephew. I knelt down on the ground as Wills ran into my arms and allowed me to scruff up his soft brown hair, filling my nose with the scent of baby shampoo. When he straightened up, his bottom lip was pushed out into a pout.

"What is it, Wills?"

"You wook sick, Awbie. Are you sick?"

My face fell, realizing that my appearance must be atrocious. I petted his soft hair again, my silent heart melting at his big blue eyes. "You are so dressed up, honey, where are you off to?"

"I goin' to school, Awbie!" Wills shouted proudly. I froze in place, realizing that today was one of several school interviews we'd scheduled for all the children. Wills didn't notice my change in mood so he continued, "I wish Wivy could come wif me, but Mommy says she and Jack-Jack have to go together cuz der twins. Is that twue, Awbie?"

Just then, from inside the twins' bedroom Olivia cooed, "Ada? Where's Mama?"

Cameron took a quick glance behind him and then back to me with another pleading expression. Feeling all eyes on me, I gave Wills a quick kiss on the forehead and ran across the hall into my room. After I slammed the door behind me I almost ran into the boxes that filled the room. I hadn't stepped foot in our bedroom since I had arrived at the manor, and I was instantly flooded with memories. Nothing had changed, not even the comforter or the drapes. My fingers grazed over the raised embroidery of the fabric of the comforter as I sat down on the bed.

My throat was on fire, my limbs heavy with fatigue, and I felt as though there was a gaping hole in my chest. To a mother, losing her child was more than cutting out her heart, it was having it cut out and then realizing you weren't going to die.

"Ok, that's it!" Renee shouted as she burst into the room and then plowed into the stack of boxes I had only narrowly missed myself. If I had any energy or feeling I would have fallen on the floor laughing, especially as her legs dangled in the air. After pushing away two of the boxes in front of her, Renee regained her footing, straightened her skirt and blouse, and then popped her hip as she crossed her arms. "Ok, that's it!"

"You said that already," I snipped at her in a flat tone.

"That's because I really mean it, Bri," she began as she walked toward me. "I'm done with the crying, and the hiding, and avoiding Cameron, and the general 'crazy woman' you're being right now. The pity party's done, as of today, done. Jack-Jack was taken, I know it's hard, I know it is, but it doesn't mean you just lay down and die."

"I am not…"

"Have you looked at yourself? Your eyes are all sunken in and purple, you're paler than pale, wearing the same clothes you came here in, and now you've got freakin' stigmata coming down your face."

Self-consciously I wiped my face, the blood merely transferring from my face to my hands. "I look how I feel, Re. And not you, or Kyla, or anyone else in this friggin' place knows what I'm going through. So if I want to cry and make a spectacle of myself, I will!"

"Oh trust me, Bri, you are doing a 'spectacular' job," she said with a slight smile at her own pun, but then changed her expression as she began to lay into me again. "You know very well that Cameron is feeling every bit of pain that you are."

"Don't even sa…"

"What, say his name? Are you fucking kidding me?" she shouted and then took in a deep breath of satisfaction. "Fuck it feels good to curse."

"I'm so glad you can make jokes right now."

"Fuck you, you fucking drama queen."

"How dar…"

"Dare I?"

"Stop finishing my sentences!"

"Fine, how about, 'get off the cross, Bri, we need the wood,'" she said flinching her fingers at each word. "Is it the pity you need? Do you always need everyone to feel sorry for you?"

"I can't believe you would say something like that to me."

"Why wouldn't I?" she said shrugging freely. "First it was years of abuse from Sam, then the whole leaving Cameron when you were pregnant, then giving yourself up to Aidan and Elaina which in turn got you killed, and now it's wah, wah, wah, oh he Turned me, woe is me. 'I'm Bri, and I can't be happy unless I'm miserable.'"

I flew from the bed. "You bitch…"

"You're gonna come at ME with fangs!" she shouted.

Instantly I took a step back, putting my hand up to my mouth. "You need to back off, Re."

"Bri, that is the last thing I need to do," she interrupted, her eyes filling with tears as her voice became shaky. "You know that I love Jack-Jack...as if he were...my own son. And God forbid if Wills was ever..." she cleared her throat and wiped the corner of her right eye, "...if he were ever...missing...I would want you to be yelling at me if I didn't have my head on straight.

"I meant what I said before, and frankly I am sick and tired of seeing you feel sorry for yourself and punishing Cameron. If I were Cameron, I would have left you years ago rather than have to suffer through the shit you keep slinging at him."

"And all this time I thought you were on my side."

"There are no 'sides' here, Bri!"

"If you support what he did to me, then you're on HIS side."

"Fine!" she yelled as she thrust her arms out in front of her dramatically. "Then I'm on Cameron's side! Thank you, Cameron! Thank you for Turning Brianna. Thank you for having miracle blood that brought her back to life so that she could be in her children's lives. Thank you, Cameron Burke, for loving my best friend so much that you couldn't live without her, and because of that my godchildren get to have a great mother in their lives."

"But I'm not a great mother," I whimpered as my head fell into my hands. "I'm not, Re, I'm not."

"What are you talking about?" she said and knelt down in front of me. "You're a great mom, those kids love you so much."

My face scrunched up as my bottom lip trembled. "I watched him, Re. Aidan gave him a choice, and my son chose him over me. Jackson looked me right in the eye and said he'd rather be with that psychopath than his own mother. Now what does that tell you?"

Renee reached over to the nightstand next to her and pulled a tissue out of the box that rested on top. She blotted my cheeks as she said, "Sweetie, he's three-years-old. Aidan knew Jack-Jack's weakness for hybrids and he preyed on that. It had nothing to do with you."

"It has everything to do with me!" I shouted as I stood from the bed. "I gave birth to true Vampire hybrids and Aidan took Jack because of it. And because Cameron fucking Turned me, I had to watch it happen."

Renee wrapped her hands around my arms and gently lowered me back down on the bed. "Sit down, I'm going to tell you something I've never told anyone." I looked at her with a worried expression. "It's about the night you...you died."

"Re, I don't want..."

"You are going to sit there and hear what I have to say," she snapped, pointing her index finger at me. "Lord knows I've listened to you enough the last few days," she said rolling her eyes, but then a solemnness came over her as she sat next to me. "That night when John came out of the operating room, I instantly knew...I knew...something had gone wrong. He couldn't even look at me while he told everyone that you were gone, and I remember hating him in that moment. We'd only been married for a few hours and I couldn't imagine how I was going to be able to stay with the man that let my 'twin' die."

"Re, I'm..."

She put her hand up to me as she continued, "John and Dr. Taylor pulled all sorts of strings and got the babies put into a room immediately so that we could be alone with them. I...I don't even remember how long Daddy O and I were in there before Cameron came in, but I do remember how he looked. I was holding Olivia and I could see his reflection in the glass of the window, and he...he was...walking death. He had no emotion, he looked...hollow.

"At one point it was just me and him, and he told me that even though John and I were godparents along with Kyla and Alex, that if anything ever happened to both of you that you wanted the babies to be with us." I nodded slowly, remembering the very conversation with Cameron. "Of course I said yes, and then I went to leave, but something stopped me. I remember turning around and suddenly having this nervous ache in my stomach. I looked him right in the eye and told him that nothing could happen to him because he's all the twins had left. Just the way he looked and was talking, I was scared that he was going to go and do *something*."

"Do something?" I said skeptically. "He's a Vampire, Re, there's no *something* he can do."

"Oh yeah?" she replied defensively as she stood from the bed. "So a little time after that, Cameron comes running out of the room and the boys had to pull him outside because he was freaking out so bad. John told me that he was trying to avenge your death or some romantic shit like that, and that when Devin was holding onto him he was literally 'disintegrating' because he'd given all his blood to you."

"Re, I still don't see what this has to do with anything."

"He was the only one who heard you!"

I shook my head in confusion. "Heard me when?"

"Ok, felt you, I don't know…when you were…were…coming back to life," she replied. "Since that day I've been convinced that everything happened for a reason."

"Really, Re?"

"Don't look at me like that, I know it's cliché, but I mean it. Now shut up and pay attention because I'm gonna get really deep. So let's say he didn't give you all his blood, only gave you a little, he never would have been able to feel you because he wouldn't have been weak enough. You could have woken up in the morgue and someone else could have found you, and goodness knows what would have happened.

"Now, if Cameron had listened to you and my husband, you wouldn't be here. You would have missed every birthday, every Christmas with the twins, and you would have never met Wills. Or hell, Wills may have never been made. Would you be willing to give up all of that? Or even worse, Cameron goes out and ends up getting himself killed, the twins come to live with me, and Aidan gets both kids because John and I couldn't protect them. So what's worse, you rotting away in the ground not being able to do anything for your son, or being a Vampire who can kick Aidan's ass?"

I couldn't answer, so she continued, "Jackson needs you, Bri. Your daughter needs you, Cameron needs you, we all *need* you to get your shit together. And frankly you just scared the shit out of my son, so do whatever it is you need to do to 'look' better. Please…twin."

I nodded as my head fell into my hand, my hair falling down like a curtain on either side of my face. A moment later I felt the weight of Renee's body resting on top of me, her arms rubbing down the length of my back as she nuzzled her forehead on my shoulder.

"You know I'm only doing this because I love you, right?"

"Mm-hmm," I responded weakly as I lifted my head.

"So don't hate me that I have to leave to take Wills to his school interview."

I shook my head. "I don't, it's just hard because we were supposed to go together."

"Frankly, I'm glad you're not. I don't need your kids showing up mine like they do every other time," she said in her I'm-half-joking-and-half-serious tone. With one last kiss on the cheek, Renee clonked her way out of the room but not before saying, "Talk to Cam. It's the least you can do."

The brat closed the door before I could say anything. She was right, but it didn't make me feel any better. Everything had fallen in on me and now there was no other option than to do all the things I didn't want to. I didn't want to feed, I didn't want to talk to Cameron, and I didn't want to face the reality of my actions.

Feeling the anxiety building in my stomach, I flopped backwards down on the bed. Something brushed up against my arm and I looked over to see that Cameron's overnight bag had rolled over. Never had I hated a bag so much as I hated this one. For years this dark brown leather bag had been a symbol of him leaving us for bigger priorities, leaving me to trudge through my new life as a Vampire alone. Shitty, shitty, goddamn shitty bag.

My anger towards the innocent bag was released when I grabbed it and threw it against the wall opposite me, causing several items to fall out of the main compartment including a book I had never seen before. Curious, I walked over to where the book was splayed opened and was taken aback at the sight of a picture of me with the twins when they were only a couple months old. I picked the book up from the floor and flipped the plastic covered pages to the beginning where there was a matted picture of me and Cameron with the babies both covered in cake from their first birthday. Below it read "The Burke Family" in Cameron's scrolling cursive.

Slowly I began to turn the pages as I made my way back to the bed, all the while wondering why I had never seen this. It started with my favorite picture from my Claiming ceremony where Cameron is dancing with me in my beautiful white dress, and underneath it the caption read, "My Angel". The next two pages were the ultrasounds of the twins followed by the pictures he had taken at their birth. I was horrified by how I looked, my face swollen from pregnancy and pale from blood loss, my eyes wet with tears as I held my babies for the first time.

I flipped through the next few pages, seeing more pictures I had never seen before – me sleeping in the nursery with both swaddled babies on my chest, Jackson pulling at and trying to eat Cameron's black curls, Olivia laying on her back smiling and reaching for her father who was above her taking the picture. Shot after shot of the twins growing from infants to toddlers to preschoolers. Then there were the family gatherings, birthday parties, Christmases, and even cuter candid shots. This was our life in pictures. Was this his reminder of what he'd left at home?

As I continued to flip through I could see light brownish stains on certain pictures. Had he cried? Had he truly missed us so much that these images would bring him to tears? Was I truly as big of a bitch as Renee made me out to be? Carefully I placed the book back in his bag and placed it on the bed. My sulking time was over. I had to do the one thing I hated more than anything else in the world - confront my problems.

Though dragging my feet, I left our room and stepped into the hallway with every intention of finding Cameron. I peeked into the twin's room across the hall, but there was no sign of Cameron or Olivia. When I turned back into the hallway, Jonah was roaming aimlessly a few feet ahead looking dead on his feet.

"Jonah?"

His head instantly whipped around and a look of relief came over him. "Bri, thank god, I'm so lost."

"Where are you trying to get to?"

"My room," he replied. "I'm so tired I was about to just curl up on the floor somewhere and hope someone found me."

"You do look tired," I said as I took him by the arm and slowly turned him back around toward the wide spiraling stairs.

"You don't look so good either."

My hand self-consciously went through my hair as I led him down one flight of stairs. "Trust me, Renee more than described how shitty I look."

"Have you..."

I pulled him to a stop. "If you are about to ask me if I've fed, I'm going to leave you here to rot."

Jonah immediately closed his mouth tightly and gestured for me to lead the way.

"Wait a minute, why are you going to bed now?"

"I can't sleep," he replied sadly. "Every time I close my eyes I still see Ashlyn, and then I can't get back to sleep. So I go down to the library to do some more searches and end up passing out and then apparently bothering everyone with my snoring, which I think is a lie."

"Nope, you do snore," I replied, having heard it firsthand. "You can't do that to yourself, Jonah. You need to keep your strength up."

"That's a little hypocritical, isn't it?" he said, gesturing to me from head to toe. When I didn't come back at him he allowed me to take him the rest of the way in silence.

When we reached his room he opened the door slowly and peeked in to verify that it was indeed his room. When he recognized his things, he held the door open for me to come in behind him.

"I know you hadn't intended on coming out here with us, and we left Daddy O's in such a hurry," I began and closed the door, "do you have everything you need?"

He nodded. "Yeah, I think so. For now, that is."

"Well, if you need anything, anything at all, you just let me know. I'll make sure you get it."

"Honestly what I really need is sleep," he said rubbing his face with his hands before yawning widely.

"I'm sorry I can't help you with that. I'm so weak I don't think I could put an ant to sleep right now."

Jonah snickered as I went to leave, stretching his arms out and I welcomed the comforting hug. I basked in the warmth of his arms around me, the heat coming from his neck as my cheek pressed against it, the sound of his blood pumping and pulsing against my skin. The pain in my throat suddenly turned from a nagging burning to an insatiable thirst. I felt my fangs prick through my gums first, and I was able to push away from him by the time they were fully extended.

"I'm sorry, I'm so sorry," I said in a panic as I cupped my mouth with both hands. "I should go."

"Bri, wait," he said as I went for the door. "Bite me."

"Excuse me!"

"No, no, not like that...I mean...doesn't a Vampire's bite make you sleep?"

"Well...yeah. It can relax you enough to..." I stopped as I saw the question being asked in Jonah's eyes. "No. No! Absolutely not!"

"Why not?" he whined. "You need the blood, I need to sleep. It's a win, win."

"No, it's a lose, lose. I drain you or prick your artery, you die, and I have to face your mother and sister. No, not happening."

"Come on, Bri, please."

I shook my head nervously. "Jonah, I've only fed from Cameron or from a bottle, never from anyone who was alive."

Jonah sank down onto the corner of the bed. "Bri, I'm begging you. I'm useless right now. Please, Bri, I know you can do this. I trust you more than anyone else in the world. Please? Please do this for me...and you.

You need this just as much as I do."

My brain was screaming at me to leave the room, but my body glided over to him. Jonah sighed in relief and adjusted nervously on the bed as I side-stepped and front-stepped and tripped over my feet. We were like two pre-teens trying to coordinate our first dance. Finally I sat down, the awkwardness building uncomfortably between us.

Jonah turned to face me, pulling at the collar of his t-shirt. "How...do you...want to..."

"Maybe from behind," I blurted out and then flinched. "I mean I'll get behind you. That way we don't need to look at each other."

Jonah nodded as he turned his back to me, keeping one foot on the floor and the other leg bent across the bed to steady himself. I crawled up behind him, sitting back on both knees and pulling him into my chest. "You're a Vampire, you can do this. You know how to do this, just drink his blood."

"Bri, maybe cut the commentary."

"Sorry."

You're a Vampire, you can do this. You're a Vampire, you can do this. Carefully I cradled his head into the crook of my left shoulder and I could already see his jugular vein shining blue underneath his skin. I had to remember this was Jonah, I couldn't hurt him. Don't kill him, don't kill him. Prick the vein, wait for the pop, let it flow, count to ten, retract, lick it closed. Quick and simple.

"Bri," Jonah said softly, reaching up behind him and touching my arm, "I trust you."

I exhaled and repeated what Cameron had said to me the first time, "Just stay still, so you don't tear."

Before Jonah responded I sunk my fangs into his vein, felt the pop, and let his blood flow into my mouth. As soon as the hot blood hit my throat it soothed the burning, but also created an unbelievable need to drink more.

Count to ten, count to ten, I quickly reminded myself. One, two, three, four. Jonah's blood was fresh and flowing with life. Five, six, seven. It wasn't thick or lukewarm like Cameron's, or starting to coagulate like bottled blood. Eight. Retract Brianna, the voice in my head shouted, but my body was starting to hum with power. Nine. I could feel my hardened blood vessels soften and come to life with each swallow. I was passing up on this? The huntress and predator inside of me was suddenly coming to life, and I wanted more. One human now, then another, and...shit, ten!

Quickly I retracted my fangs and licked the two circular wounds closed, catching the dribble of blood that leaked down Jonah's neck. I watched his chest continue to move up and down, the sound of his heartbeat steady and strong. I wrapped my arms around him, thanking him softly for giving me his blood and receiving an unintelligible moan in response.

I reached behind me and pulled down the comforter and sheet, and then tucked his legs underneath. Jonah was completely asleep by the time I pulled the blankets up to his chin. In seconds everything had changed. My head was clearer, as was my sight and other senses. I had fought feeding from a human for almost four years, and now I would have to admit that it was probably my first step, in Renee's words, to 'getting my shit together.'

Quietly I backed away from the bed and silently slipped out into the hallway.

"Bri?"

I flinched to attention as Devin came up behind me. "Devin, w-what are you…uh…doing here?"

"A couple of the new trainees didn't show for their first day. I was coming to find them," he answered as he looked past my shoulder and into Jonah's room. "You?"

I stepped into the hallway and closed the door. "Jonah was lost, so…"

I couldn't think of anything else to say, and Devin could tell I was holding back. With a curt nod he stepped away as he said, "I'm glad to see you're looking better."

"Dev," I said and he turned only his head in my direction. "If you see Cam…tell him I need to talk to him. I'll be in our room."

Devin gave another curt nod and continued down the hallway without another word. As he disappeared into the stairwell I realized I should have added one more thing and that was not to mention where he found me. Not so much for my sake, but for the life of the young man who was sleeping on the other side of this door.

Chapter Thirty-seven

Cameron

"Now, monkey, I understand that you wish to look unique for your grandfather," I began as my precious daughter skipped down the stone hallway in her favorite red rain boots, a very full purple petticoat, white sweater, pink boa, and her tiara from Halloween, "but perhaps this is a little much."

Olivia held my hand as she began jumping between the large stone slabs in order to avoid the cracks. "Ada, I told you, it's special breakfast. If I don't look special, how will Grandfather know?"

"Yes, but..."

"Mama lets me dress up," she interrupted matter-of-factly. "Mama also lets me wear lip gloss."

"You do not *need* lip gloss, lovey. Your lips are already perfect."

"But it tastes good," she smiled, melting my heart as she always did and making me miss her brother in the same moment.

As we approached Victor's wing, Julian was walking towards us, his face frozen with his usual disdain. He averted his gaze a second after our eyes made contact.

"Good morning, Juwian," Olivia said happily.

Julian's head shot up, but his face relaxed once he saw Olivia. Not knowing exactly what to do, he gave a curt bow in Olivia's direction.

"Olivia, what have I taught you about when a gentleman bows to you," I said and then watched as she tucked her left foot behind her and curtsied. Julian's face melted, and I found myself having a moment of weakness. "Julian, I have been thinking about your requests to Father."

"Father has made his feelings very clear, as have you."

I paused a moment to let the tension die down before saying, "Julian, Father will never agree to spend that kind of money for our prisoners."

"Cameron, you more than…"

"Let me speak," I interrupted. "Father will never approve new linens, but what about torn or damaged ones? Instead of discarding them, you could ask the housekeeping staff to give those items to you."

Julian shifted his weight uncomfortably as he thought about my proposal. "You don't think Father would object?"

"Why would Father have to know?"

Julian shifted his weight again. "But what about the cameras? We practically have antiques."

"The new surveillance equipment among other things has stretched our coffers. But…" I said, trying to urge him on.

Suddenly Julian's eyes flashed with an idea. "What about the old equipment? What are they doing with the old cameras?"

"Knowing Jared, they will probably be stored somewhere in his room. He can be quite a hoarder with electronics. Perhaps I could connect with him on your behalf. The old cameras would certainly be better than what you have."

"And you would…do that? For me?"

I sighed quietly to myself, knowing I was responsible for his doubt. "Certainly. I will make sure I find some time to do it today."

Julian took a step back, uncertainty and doubt still hanging over him. Finally, "Thank you…brother," he said giving me a nod and then nodding down to Olivia. "Miss Olivia."

"Bye, Juwien," Olivia said happily as he began to walk past us. "But you can call me Wivy, like my friends do."

Julian stopped and turned around, a curious look on his face. "And we are friends?"

Olivia giggled. "Of course we are."

Then the most miraculous event happened – Julian smiled. It was thin and small, but it was definitely a smile. My daughter could melt anyone. Julian clicked his heels and bowed deeply while he brought his right fist to his heart, the Warrior salute. "Good day, Miss Livy."

Once again Olivia tucked her left foot behind her and curtsied. A second later she wrapped her fingers around my thumb and pulled me back down the hall.

"Come on, Ada, Grandfather's waiting," she whined. When we were only a few feet away I allowed her to break from my side and run to into Victor's suite. "Wow!"

There in the center of the room was my maker standing in full Roman General regalia. From his draped gold-embroidered red cape, detailed cuirass covering his chest and torso, and red plumed helmet that was tucked under his arm, he was every ounce the intimidating Roman leader of our coven. His prideful smile over Olivia's reaction was the only thing that made him appear even remotely mortal.

Olivia pulled on my sleeve and looked at me with challenging eyes. "See, Ada, I told you we dressed up," she said with a smart smile. She bounded into the room and jumped into Victor's waiting arms, unable to stop from petting the red plume of his helmet.

"Come, come, little one," Victor said as he brought Olivia over to the elaborately decorated table that had been brought in especially for this event. "Everything you asked for is here as promised. There is fruit and yogurt and dreadfully smelly eggs…"

"And waffles?!" she cried.

Victor freed his right hand from underneath Olivia's legs and lifted the dome lid of a large platter which displayed a mound of waffles. My daughter's eyes sparkled as she wiggled her way out of Victor's hold and down into the chair closest to her.

"Child, please join us," Victor said gesturing to a chair opposite him.

"Ada didn't dress up, Grandfather," Olivia said as Victor placed a thick Belgian waffle onto her plate.

"Yes, little one, your father is a tad underdressed for our breakfast."

Olivia nodded as she stabbed her fork into the center of the waffle and brought it to her mouth where she began biting the edges. "I tried to tell him," she said between chews. "Grandfather, may I have some eggs, pwease?"

I took the fork from Olivia and placed the waffle back down on her plate to cut it into pieces while Victor gave her a large serving of scrambled eggs. "Monkey, please eat like the lady you are."

Olivia twisted her lips back and forth as she propped herself up on her knees in order to reach the table. While Olivia stuffed her cheeks with waffles and eggs, Victor poured a glass of blood for both of us.

"Dare I ask the team's progress?"

"Still nothing to report," I grumbled.

"And how is my newest Warrior today?" he asked, purposely refraining from saying Brianna's name in front of Olivia.

"The same."

Victor sighed. "I saw a lot of Dante in Fabiani, I was hoping he would have better luck."

"Fabiani is very talented, but I doubt even Dante could help her this time."

"She'll come around, child, she always does in her own time," he said, taking the last sip of blood from his glass and then pouring another. "Now in general, Fabiani seems like a good man. What are your feelings about him?"

I tried to remain steady, consciously trying to keep my eyes from widening in fear as to why Victor was asking about my brother's partner. "I think Fabiani is a very good man, Father. He is very successful in his business, one of the few that are keeping the coven going. He has fought very hard to keep Dante's legacy alive, unfortunately he is often met with resistance."

"Without Dante I'm afraid the Negotiators will simply implode. They may be excellent mediators, but I have a feeling no amount of work on Fabiani's part will save them."

"I wuv Uncle Fabi," Olivia said happily, making me jerk slightly in my chair at what else she might say.

Victor narrowed his eyes. "Uncle?"

"Grandfather!" Olivia shouted as something else suddenly caught her attention and she pointed to Victor's desk in the far corner of the room. "Are those new crayons?"

Victor smiled as did I over Olivia's keen sense of sight, especially for things that might be for her. "Perhaps. There might also be a new coloring book and drawing paper if you eat all of your breakfast."

Olivia's eyes sparkled as she shoved a very large helping of scrambled eggs into her mouth. A second later Devin came into the room causing Olivia to leap from her chair and run to him. Just as she was about to jump into her uncle's arms, Devin crossed them in front of his chest.

"Monkey, you know what you have to do," Devin said in a warning tone and then held his hand out in front of him at shoulder height.

"That high!" Olivia cried. "But I have my boots on!"

Devin gave her a challenging look. "Monkey, what if you were being attacked in real life and you had your rain boots on? Do you think your attacker would wait for you to take them off?"

"No," Olivia whined with a pout.

"Then come on now."

Devin put his hand back out in front of him and Olivia took her preparatory stance. After exhaling a deep breath, she jumped up and spun into the air, kicking her right leg out and hitting Devin's hand, and then continued her rotation down to the floor. As a father, I could not be happier that my brother had taught his niece how to do a roundhouse kick, and even more so that she had perfected it.

Devin stood proud and waved her toward him. Olivia quickly jumped into his arms and kissed him on the cheek as he carried her back to the table and placed her down in her chair.

"Father, I'm happy to announce our first group of Warrior Trainees have been inducted into the program," Devin said, giving me a side glance since we were supposed to induct them together. "All have been accounted for, although two need to invest in better alarm clocks, and another needs to cleanup his vomit from the corridor outside of the training room."

"Eeew," Olivia whined as she scrunched up her face, but then dug into the mound of fruit Victor had put on her plate.

"Well then, child, congratulations are in order," Victor said toasting his glass of blood to Devin and then to me. "Since your brother has been detained, I assume you gave our trainees some inspirational words?"

"Yes, Father," Devin nodded as he stepped around to the far end of the table and sat down in the last vacant chair. "I told them not to die or cry while in training. I do not have patience for either." Victor smirked as he brought his glass back up to his lips and drank. As Devin poured himself a glass of blood a thought suddenly came to him. "Brother, I almost forgot, Brianna is looking for you."

I was out of my chair before he finished his sentence. "She is…whe…when did you see her?"

"About fifteen minutes ago while I was searching for the missing trainees. She said she would be in your quarters."

"And you are just telling me this now!" I shouted as I turned away from the table and ran toward the door.

"At least we can say she's fed now."

I froze and slowly stepped back to the table. "Say that again, Brother."

Devin straightened up awkwardly in his chair. "Just that it...appeared she had fed."

My fingernails dug into the palms of my hands. "And you saw her in the human wing?"

"Yes," he replied tentatively, "she was coming out of Jonah's room. Brother, wait..."

But it was too late. Victor's suite faded away as I Projected directly into our bedroom. As the black mist dissipated around me, Brianna came into view. She was in the middle of changing her clothes at the side of our bed in only a pair of dark grey panties and an oversized yellow hoodie. Even from twenty feet away I could see the rosiness in her cheeks and the disappearance of the dark purple circles under her eyes. Devin was right, she had fed and for the first time I was furious about it.

"Bri?"

"Jesus!" she shouted as a ripple ran through her body. When she caught her breath, so to speak, she looked at me with a very perturbed expression. "Christ, Cam, you scared the..."

"Is this what you want?" I interrupted.

"Wh-what?"

"Him!" I shouted. "Jonah! I know you fed from him." Brianna grimaced and looked at the floor. "You feed from him, talk only to him. If he is who you want then just tell me. There is no need for you to lead me on like this any further, and the two of you can get on with it."

Brianna looked up at me slowly, one eyebrow cocked and her opposite eye squinted in a vicious look. "Are you accusing me of something?"

"You let him sleep in your bed," I shouted as I flew to her side. "No, our bed! We laid in that bed together, it was the beginning of everything for us, and you go and let him take my place. If I am accusing you of anything, it is throwing away everything we have together."

Brianna's Push came quick and threw me face down into the floor.

"First of all, *Mr. Burke*, I let Jonah sleep next to me because all the other beds were taken and he desperately needed to sleep. Did I think that perhaps it would hurt you just a little bit? Yes. I was hoping it would make you feel even a sliver of the hurt you caused me."

"Brianna, I have tried to apologize about the phone call but you will not give me the chance. I was upset..."

"It wasn't just the phone call, Cam!" she shouted as another Push hit me like a punch in the chest and flipped me on my back. "You doubted me, you blamed me for losing my child!"

"Our child!" I shouted back as my anger pulled me up to a standing position. "I am suffering as well, Brianna. The loss of Jackson is killing me, too. I had to stand with a phone in my hand and listen helplessly as disaster struck our family. The last thing I heard from you was how busy you were that morning. How was I supposed to know you had fed? For almost four years you have fought me about feeding, what was I supposed to think? You could have easily told me you fed that morning rather than be dramatic and try to play on my guilt."

Brianna paused again and I braced myself for the Push, but surprisingly it did not come. When the silence lasted for nearly thirty seconds I realized it was worse than a Push. I preferred the pain over the anger that was festering inside of her.

Finally, in a very curt tone, she said, "Well, Cameron, I fed that day. I fed today, and still you're not happy."

"No, Bri, I am not happy," I replied in an exhausted tone. "And obviously neither are you. I do not know what else to do. I have given you everything you have ever asked for. Endured your hatred over Turning you. And now this? I no longer wish to live this way, I simply cannot. I love you and I thought it was enough, but it is obvious to me now that I was wrong. Once we retrieve Jackson we will go our separate ways. You will always have the protection of the Warriors but you can live wherever you choose. I will certainly more than provide for the children."

"That's your solution?" she said angrily. "After four years just send me and the kids on our way and throw some money at us? You think your money is going to make me forget all you've done?"

"Why not? It made you forget about what Sam was doing to you."

Brianna rushed at me and slapped me so hard across the face I fell down onto one knee. "You son of a bitch!"

"Not compared to him, and yet you stayed," I growled and received another hit causing my hands to hit the ground. My fingers dug into the fibers of the rug while my cheek burned and healed, but still I went on as I looked up into her black and very angry eyes. "For fourteen years you stayed with that monster while he beat you, destroyed every piece of you. How many times did he actually rape you, Brianna? Over that many years, how many? A dozen times a year? Maybe more than that? How many times did he hold you down and make you take all of him? I have felt the scars inside you, Bri, and there are times I wonder how you survived. And yet here I am, guilty of being unable to live without you that I had a moment of weakness. I have always confessed that in that hour I was a weak man and did what I knew was against your wishes. Had I demeaned you, or kept you like a caged animal, maybe I would have gotten many more years with you."

I will admit that after all the words escaped my lips I could not believe what I had said. Years of frustration and nagging feelings rotting inside of me came out in three breaths. Brianna stood frozen in silence. No longer could I use the sound of her heartbeat as a gage for her feelings. Her face was like stone, smooth and cold and unmoving. After what seemed like an eternity, a small red tear leaked from her left eye. Her mouth twitched as she tried to speak, but another tear bled from her right eye. Her shoulders slumped and she sank down into the floor in front of me.

"That's the second time today I've had Sam thrown in my face," Brianna said and wiped her bloody tears away with the cuff of her hoodie. "Despite what you and Renee think, I stayed because I had no other choice. I was weak…and stupid and…scared. Everything changed when you took me away. I found I had a voice, I could stand up for myself. I didn't have to accept what I didn't like. I'm not just mad that you Turned me, Cam, it's that you did and then left me alone."

"I did not leave…"

"You kept running off to the manor to play Warrior and left me home to raise two babies while trying to come to terms with being…this!" she cried as she gestured to herself. "I didn't want to be this, I wasn't prepared to be this with two babies who were spouting fangs of their own. You were hardly home and then a lot of times when you were, you weren't really there, and I just lashed out because I could! Because I knew you…wouldn't…hurt me."

I let Brianna cry for a few moments before my hand finally rested on her bare calf, but even then she flinched and turned away.

"Victor promised three years," she said. "That's the only reason I agreed to you taking his place. I was given an exclusive three years with you, and that lasted, what? Six months? Then you were at his beck and call for weeks at a time. Why didn't you fight it? Why didn't you fight for us? For me? For our children?"

"I have been fighting for us. Since we met that is all I have ever done.

Do you think that Aidan is the only threat to you and our children?"

Slowly she looked over her shoulder. "Other threats? Since when?"

"Since about six months after the twins were born," I replied and she shook her head in disbelief. "Angel, you are the first Vampire ever to be sun resistant as a newborn. At one point or another every coven leader has come to Victor demanding the release of how it was done. Warriors have been attacked for this information. Two years ago several covens formed an alliance to convince the others that our coven should be forcibly disbanded unless we reveal how you were made."

"Why didn't you tell me?"

"And add to the stress you were already under? Shortly after we calmed the coven leaders it started getting out about the twins' Vampire traits and it started all over again. Devin has killed and injured more Vampires in the last three years than he has in the last three decades in the name of protecting you and our children."

Brianna pushed herself up from the floor and walked toward the bed. "And that's why you've been pushing the move to the manor."

"Yes."

"And all the family visits while you were away."

"Yes," I sighed as I pulled my knees up in front of me and stretched my arms across the tops, my head falling weakly into my chest.

"You could have just told me."

"And it would have sent you over the edge."

Brianna turned around as she laughed. "Cam, I've already fallen off the cliff and drowned in the ravine."

"That is not true, love," I replied firmly.

"I think everyone else in the manor would disagree with you." She wiped her eyes again and rested her hands on her hips. "I'm tired of being unable to do anything right."

"What do you mean?"

Brianna's arms flew out in frustration. "I can't fight the way I'm supposed to, I'm a rotten Vampire, hell I can't even make normal babies."

I paused as a twinge of guilt pulled at my heart. "Bri, it is not your fault..."

"I keep replaying that night in the limo with Elaina. She told me I would give birth to Vampires and I didn't believe her. I kept telling her she was wrong because I had looked at the ultrasounds. If there were fangs I would have seen them, but then here we are. If it weren't for me, our children wouldn't have the special powers they're being hunted for and our son would be with us right now. Our kids were damned the second I became their mother."

Brianna collapsed onto the bed, her hands catching her head as she wept. No longer could I let her suffer from my cowardice. I had no reservations about her leaving me after this, she already had one foot out the door. My stomach filled with dread as I stood from the floor and stepped over to the bed. I was surprised when her hand searched the air in my direction and I immediately took it and kissed the tops of her fingers.

As I knelt to the floor I placed her hand over my heart and held it there for a moment before I said, "Love, the children are not true hybrids because of you."

Brianna scoffed as she wiped her eyes with her free hand, although it only succeeded in smearing the tears across her cheeks and staining them red. "Cam, they were in me, connected to me for eight months. It's my blood that made them that way."

I sighed as I licked my lips and prepared for the worst. "Brianna...I...it is not your blood that made the twins the way they are. Jackson and Olivia came out of you perfectly normal hybrids." When I finally looked up, Brianna's eyebrows were knitted together. "It was me, Bri, not you."

Brianna blinked several times and pulled her hand out of mine. "I don't understand...what do you..."

"Brianna, I activated them," I said quickly.

"Act-activated...no...activated? No...how's that poss...when!?"

"After you passed. I was with them and..."

Brianna thrust both her hands into my chest sending me flying into the wall across the room. Crumbling bits of stone fell down on my neck and shoulders as Brianna came toward me.

"You activated our babies!" she screamed. "You gave our newborns Vampire blood! What were you thinking?"

"I had not planned on doing it."

"That's your defense! You didn't *plan* on opening a vein and making them drink your blood," she shouted and turned me onto my back. "You-son-of-a-fucking-bitch-whore," she yelled as she pummeled my chest and abdomen with her fists. "You-turned-them-and-made-me-think-I-did-this-you-bastard-fucking-bitch! Why didn't you tell me!"

"I tried," I yelled and caught her wrists. "I tried so many times."

Brianna leaned her weight into her arms as I held them a few inches above my chest. "Bullshit. You've had almost four years to say something. You're a coward, Cameron, a fucking coward!"

"I know," I growled as I began pressing her arms away from me. "Is that what you want to hear?"

Quickly I let her go and my hands flew up in front of my face and chest trying to protect myself as she hit and pounded me with every ounce of anger she possessed.

"How-could-you," she shouted and cried. "They-were-just-babies-we're-supposed-to-protect-them-not-turn-them-into-monsters-like-us-how-could-you-how-could-you-do-that-to-them-you-son of a bitch, why!"

Finally I caught both of Brianna's wrists in mid-air and pushed her down to the floor with me sitting on top of her. She resisted as I held her wrists forcible over her head, dividing my weight between her arms and her pelvis in order to secure her down on the floor.

"Because you died, Brianna!" I shouted at her, causing her body to stiffen. "You died! Sam had you for fourteen years and I barely get you for one. WE were supposed to raise our children together. WE were supposed to cherish the day that they were born. But no, you decided to fight Aidan and Elaina on your own and it contributed to your death. For three-and-a-half years you have spit your venom at me when it is I who should be angry at you!"

Brianna pushed her pelvis up from the floor causing me to lurch forward and lose my grip on her wrists. Quickly she rolled to her side and started to crawl away from me. I grabbed her ankle and pulled her back toward me, but she kicked me in the face causing me to fall back. Brianna took the opportunity to push up to a standing position and run toward the bathroom. I did the same, and just as she ran inside I wrapped my arm around her waist and pulled her back into the bedroom. She kicked and screamed and clawed at my arms as I dragged her to the bed and threw her down upon it. She looked up at me with wild eyes as I stepped toward her, her zippered hoodie now half open and hanging off her shoulders displaying even more of her body only covered by a thin bra that matched her dark grey panties. A sudden animalistic urge surged through my body and my chest noticeably began to heave.

Brianna climbed further up the bed as my hand went for my belt.

"You wouldn't dare," she challenged, and it was definitely a challenge. There was no fear in her voice, only anger and provocation.

"You put the lives of our children in danger," I began as I popped the button of my pants. "You persuaded my father and brothers to betray me," I continued as I pulled my zipper down and grabbed Brianna's ankle when she tried pushing away again. Her yellow hoodie rode up above her head as I dragged her down to the edge of the bed. She fought and kicked me as I pulled her legs around my hips.

"I did what I had to do," she yelled as I dodged her jabs to my chest.

I pressed my weight into her pelvis as I laid on top her, holding and catching her flailing arms as I could. "You fight for everyone else but us!"

"You Turned me!"

"You died on me! You fought for the babies and then gave up."

"I was supposed to die! Sera never saw me in her visions with the children."

"As a human!" I replied as I held her face firmly between my hands and pulled it up to mine. "She did not see you because you were meant to be a Vampire, Brianna, with me and our children."

"Not like this!" she screamed and clawed at my hands. "I can't be what you want me to be."

"You are everything I want, Bri," I responded before pressing my lips firmly down on hers. She opened her mouth for a split second before becoming angry again and shaking her head violently. Suddenly she swung her left elbow and broke my cheekbone.

I howled like a true wild animal before returning to Brianna, whose eyes burned with rage and desire. I plunged my hand down between her legs and ripped her underwear from her body. Brianna snarled as she took my cashmere sweater in her hands, ripped it down the middle, and pulled the sides down past my shoulders. I nipped at the base of her neck and pulled her bra down, exposing one of her breasts and squeezing it firmly.

When I tried moving down to her chest, Brianna locked her grip around my neck. Before I could react she plunged her fangs into the side of my throat and began sucking veraciously. I tried pulling away, but Brianna tightened her grip and chewed deeper into my neck. Knowing she could drain me dry in a matter of seconds, I combed my hand through to the back of her head and wrapped my fingers around a large section of her hair. As I pulled her forcefully away from me her fangs tore a hole in my neck spilling my thick Vampire blood down both our chests.

"There," she growled. "I've fed. Happy now?"

I tightened my fingers around her hair and held her there securely as I pulled down the waistband of my pants.

"Is this how a coward feels like a man?" she said snidely. "Just like Sam, forcing your wife to have sex."

"You are not my wife," I replied angrily as I entered her, thrusting myself inside her rougher than I ever had in our history together.

Brianna moaned and grimaced as I continued to pound against her. I could feel the muscles deep inside her begin to twitch as she tilted her pelvis up and down at the same rhythm. She ripped her bra in two and I immediately took her left breast into my mouth and squeezed her right very tightly. Brianna let out a feral wail and dug her nails into my shoulders. From the way her insides were contracting I knew I was getting her close to climaxing. I released her breast and licked a clean trail through my blood that had smeared down the length of her neck and chest. I could feel the pressure building within me, finding it difficult to control myself any longer. I sank my fangs into the skin of her neck and Brianna released a high-pitched moan causing me to explode within her as her blood filled my mouth.

When our bodies finally stopped convulsing I licked the wounds on her neck closed. Brianna went limp underneath me, prompting me to slide off of her. She curled up into a ball as I crumbled into the floor. Nothing was said between us for nearly five minutes. The only noise in the room was the sound of Brianna's quiet whimpers. I felt absent of every feeling except guilt for what I had done to my children, and shame for what I had just done to the woman that I truly loved with all of my heart.

Brianna stirred on the bed behind me, the springs in the mattress creaking as she melted over the edge and into the floor next to me. I took one look at her red-streaked face and had to turn my head the other way. She waited a moment before nuzzling into my side and pulling my arm across her.

"You took their choice away, Cam," she said softly.

"I know," I replied as my own red tears welled up in my eyes. "I did not know it would transform the children."

"All this time I thought it was me. All this time, Cam. But..." she began, but then paused as she turned my head to face her. "What made you do it?"

I sighed. "I was...lost. One minute you were holding Olivia and in the next you were fading away. Hearing them call your time of death I...I was furious. Angry at John for letting you die, angry at you for not fighting. I was a madman. I made everyone leave the operating room, even threatened John. I cursed you for leaving me and our newborns. Deep down the only reason I gave you my blood was because I did not think it would work. You were dead, they called it. There were no signs of life on the monitors. When Eris and Victor came in I begged them to give you their blood as well. Father fought me at first, but I believe he only gave in because he too thought it was a lost cause.

"When I finally left the operating room they took me to a room where they had taken the twins. Madelyn practically had to push me inside I was so resistant. I kept thinking we were supposed to see the children together, you and I as their mother and father. Everything felt wrong when I went inside that room."

"Renee said you looked like walking death."

"That sounds like an accurate depiction," I replied as I thought back to that awful day. "I could only hold Olivia for a few minutes. I could already see so much of you in her and it killed me. Renee placed Jackson in my arms before she left the room and I had never felt so alone. I kept thinking about how useless I was to them.

"At some point Jackson started to cry and that caused Olivia to start crying, and I gave up on everything. There was no way I could be their father, I knew Renee and John would take them in, and Kyla and Alexander would protect them."

Brianna clasped her hands around her mouth, more red tears trickling from the corners of her eyes.

"The children were screaming at an ungodly volume, no one would help me, and so many horrible thoughts were going through my head that I bit my fist to keep from screaming along with them. I drew a little blood and suddenly both children stopped crying." Brianna gasped and her eyes widened. I pointed at her face as I said, "That was my reaction as well. It was so instantaneous I knew that it could not be a coincidence. I looked down and Jackson was even sucking his lips, like he was ready to feed. I was already convinced I would not be around long enough to activate them as adults, so I told myself that I was simply activating them early."

"And they drank it?"

I nodded. "Very easily. I practically had to rip my finger from Olivia's mouth," I said with a one-sided smile. "But they were fine when I left them."

"What made you leave? Renee said you bolted out of the room."

"Aidan called," I growled. "Somehow he found out that you had died and gave me a one-time opportunity to kill or be killed and I took it."

"You had no blood in you, you would have been killed."

I paused. "Most likely."

"Why would you leave them?"

"I would not live without you."

Brianna pulled away and wiped her red-stained face. "But Cam, as a human I wouldn't have lived…"

"I was prepared to have at least forty years with you, not just one. With you gone…"

"But our babies!"

"Bri, in that moment they would have been better off with Renee and John."

Brianna chewed on her bottom lip as her eyes darted back and forth, goodness knows how many thoughts were spinning away in her head. Finally, "But you didn't go."

"Devin stopped me," I replied, shaking my head. "He kept shouting that you were alive, that with his gift he would have felt your looming death, and he did not. And that, my love, was when I heard you," I said as I caressed her forehead with the tips of my fingers, brushing the stray hairs out of her eyes. In that moment I saw in those dark eyes the spark that had been missing ever since I Turned her.

"If you hadn't given the children your blood, you never would have heard me," she said, and her words surprised me.

"Yes…I…suppose so."

"If Devin hadn't stopped you, you would have gotten killed and I would have woken up without you."

"Well, I definitely had not thought about that."

"So earlier after Renee handed me my ass, she started telling me about that night at the hospital. She said that after things settled down, she thought about how everything happened for a reason. And I think she was right."

My eyes fluttered with surprise. "How did that taste coming out of your mouth?"

She narrowed her eyes. "Awful. And I'll deny it if you ever tell her I said so," she replied with a smile, but then brought a seriousness to her voice. "But she was right. Even if the slightest thing was off by a second it would have been a Vampire-style Romeo and Juliet and our children would have been down a parent, if not…" she had to pause for a moment to collect herself before she could finally say, "I can't even think about our children being orphans. But...why have you never told me any of this?"

"I knew you would leave me."

Brianna shifted uncomfortably. My statement was harsh but true and altogether sad for both of us to admit.

"Can we start over?" she asked timidly.

I shook my head as I squeezed her hand tightly in mine. "No, I would rather come out of this stronger than we were before. That is, of course, if you can forgive me for all that I have done."

Brianna looked down as she chewed on her bottom lip, and my stomach sank. What was probably only a few seconds seemed like hours before she finally responded, "I can...accept...what you did." She looked back up at me, conflict still etched in her face. "I hate that you considered...well more like decided to leave the children. But..." she began, but looked down in the floor again, "...but having felt that low myself, I understand."

I placed my finger underneath her chin and tilted her face up to me. "That is at least a beginning."

"Does anyone else know what you did?"

"No," I replied, shaking my head. "Though I believe Father and your parents might suspect something."

"Why do you say that?"

I shrugged. "Sometimes I feel there are double meanings in things Seraphina has said to me over the years."

Brianna laughed. "Doesn't she always?"

"Also, it is the lack of inquiry on Father's part. Even with the backlash we received, never once did he question me about it. I believe he did not want to know the answer."

"Well, I think that might be best," she said with a sigh. "I don't think we should tell anyone, at least for now. If it were ever to get out that anyone could make true hybrids this easily...my god, if Aidan only knew."

"Thankfully he does not, and neither does Jackson."

At the sound of our son's name Brianna became teary again, and for the first time since his kidnapping I let my guard down. In the safety of my Bri's arms I finally let the tears and feelings of loss flow out of me. Brianna held me tightly, her cries echoing mine as I buried my head into her shoulder.

When our sorrow finally calmed, I lifted my head and looked into Brianna's black eyes and no longer saw hatred in them. I combed my fingers through her hair and felt her body relax.

"Bri, I just need to know if you…"

"I didn't sleep with Jonah," she interrupted and I had to close my gapping mouth. "That is what you were going to ask, wasn't it?"

I nodded shamefully. "Can you promise me one thing?"

"Sure," she replied timidly.

"Feed from anyone else you want, just not Jonah." Brianna gave me a smirk. "Do not make me go on about this," I begged, hating to admit that I was a bit jealous.

Brianna leaned in slowly and placed a gentle kiss on my lips. I kissed her back and slid my hand inside her hoodie, pulling it down off her shoulder. Her mouth opened to mine, her fingers tentatively grazing down my chest. Just as I wrapped my arm around her waist, about to pull her onto my lap, I heard the voice of the one person with the worst timing.

"Brother!" Devin shouted from the hallway.

Brianna groaned. "I swear he has freakin' radar."

"Devin, do not…" I shouted, but Devin burst into the room. "…come…in."

"Goddamn it, Dev!" Brianna yelped as she tried hiding behind me.

I did not bother moving or even covering myself. "Brother, you cannot keep…"

"Livy's talking to Jack," he interrupted causing Bri and I to go silent. "I thought I could break the rule just this once."

Brianna shot up from the floor. Thankfully Devin dove in front of her and shut the door before she could run out.

Brianna slid to a stop and screamed, "What are you doing?! I have to get to Livy!"

Devin looked up at the ceiling as he held his hand out in front of him. "I know, Bri. But not until you put something on."

Brianna looked down at herself and suddenly realized that she was naked except for her yellow hoodie. Mortified, she clinched her hoodie shut and ran to the bathroom, slamming the door behind her.

Devin was still looking up at the ceiling as he said, "Brother, I'm sorry but I thought this was important enough…"

"Yes, Brother," I laughed lightly as I pushed up from the floor and pulled my pants back up to my waist, "this is very important. We will meet you in Father's quarters in a minute, we need to freshen up."

Devin nodded and slipped back out. When I opened the door to the bathroom Brianna had shed the hoodie and was standing in front of the sink vigorously scrubbing away the dried blood on her neck with a washcloth. Since I needed to do the same, I stepped up next to her and began splashing water up on my chest.

"You could have stopped me before I ran up to your brother half-naked," she said angrily as she rinsed the washcloth and then began washing her face.

"You were more than half-naked, love. It is a good thing my brother is gay," I teased as I dried my chest with a hand towel and began to examine the healing hole in my neck. "You really did a number on me."

Bri narrowed her eyes as she looked at me in the mirror. "Then we're even."

Chapter Thirty-eight

Brianna

I have to say I am a master at embarrassing myself, although standing naked in front of Devin was pretty high on the list of all occasions. Thank goodness Dev was gay, and also that he loved me enough to stop me from running out the door. Jonah's blood had cleared my head so effectively that I thought I could handle anything. Had I known that "anything" would entail all of Cameron's confessions I might have opted out, at least for a day. Although opting out all the time is partially what got us in this mess.

It scared me to think where Cam and I would be if Jackson hadn't been taken and forced us to confront the nastiness that had been growing between us. So many times we fought with no resolution, only nicking the surface until there was just a layer of scar tissue. But now, we'd cut the tumor out at its core. No more lies stood between us, but forgiveness hadn't come yet. I could accept what Cam did, but that didn't mean he should have done it. Who knows what I would have done if our roles were reversed. But as Renee said, everything happens for a reason, and right now because of Cameron's actions we could at least talk to our son through Olivia.

Cameron and I dressed quickly, choosing to rinse off the red stains on our bodies from dried blood and tears. As we went to leave the room, I took Cameron's hand and pulled him to a stop.

"I'm nervous," I said.

He squeezed my hand reassuringly and kissed my forehead gently. "There is nothing to be nervous about. We are merely talking to our son."

I quirked my eyebrow. "You say that, but I know your insides are doing backflips right now."

"But if I admit that, then who will keep you calm?"

I smiled at him as I rose up on my toes and kissed him. "Still love me?"

Cam gave me his crooked smile. "Always. You?"

"I'll never let you doubt it again."

"And I won't let you feel that alone again, I promise."

Cameron squeezed my hand and we ran together to Victor's suite. As soon as we burst through the door, Victor was there with his hands up cuing us silently to be calm.

"We are merely drawing some pictures with our new crayons," he said slowly and deliberately. Olivia was sitting at her grandfather's antique desk on the upper level of the suite, eagerly coloring on a large piece of art paper. There was a long table in the middle of the room, and by the amount of food and Victor's odd choice of clothes it must have been a special breakfast date. By the irritated pout on Livy's face she wasn't too happy about it being interrupted.

Victor lowered his head and gestured for us to come closer as he spoke in a whisper. "Apparently Jackson has been talking to Olivia pretty regularly since he was taken."

Cameron squeezed my hand tightly. "I feared as much. I believe she is enjoying being an only child."

I tightened my lips and took an angry step forward, but Victor put his hand to my chest. "Brianna, child, we are standing on a very delicate thread and she can snap it at any time. Now, I know you want to talk to Jackson, but tread carefully. That is my only warning."

I nodded and slowly walked over to Olivia, Cameron's hand still firmly clasped in mine. Devin was standing over Olivia's shoulder, his arms crossed in front of his chest, although the fingers of his left hand were worrying a patch on his chin. I knelt to the floor next to Olivia's chair, her little left leg hanging over the edge and kicking the air while she colored.

"Hi, Mama," she said with a hint of dread.

I combed my fingers through her soft, black curls and kissed her temple. "Hi, baby girl," I said as I glanced down at her drawing. "What are you drawing?"

"Grandfather asked me to draw where Jack-Jack was," Olivia said, dropping her brown crayon and picking up a green one. "So I'm drawing trees, lotsa trees."

"Do you mean woods?" Cameron asked. "Like a forest?"

"Mm-hmm," she replied as she began to draw lollipop trees across the majority of the page.

"So Jackson is staying in a wooded area," he pressed again.

She nodded and pointed to four figures standing next to each other in the middle of the page. "That's Jack-Jack, that's Aidan and Gorum, and that's Ashwyn. I don't like Gorum, he's cweepy."

"Yes, baby girl, he is very creepy," I replied as steadily as I could. "Is Jack-Jack talking to you now?"

She pushed out her lip in a dramatic pout. "Yes."

My hands were almost shaking as I slowly reached for my daughter. "May I talk with him?"

Livy sighed. "I already told him he was in trouble."

"Jackson is not in trouble, monkey," Cameron corrected as he knelt down behind me. "We just want to make sure he is all right."

"Fine," she sighed again as her attention went back to coloring in the trees she had outlined.

Cameron squeezed my shoulder as I placed my hand on Olivia's back. I closed my eyes and lowered my shield in order to let my daughter's consciousness flow into me. With a deep breath, I was sucked into the unknown where my twins communicated.

"Jack-Jack, Mama's here," Olivia said into the dark emptiness.

A few seconds of silence passed before I finally heard, "Hi, Mama."

"Hi, baby," I replied, trying not to breakdown at the sound of my son's voice. "Are you ok?"

"Yes, Mama, I'm fine," he answered in a soft and unsure voice. "Wivy says I'm in trouble, am I in trouble?"

"No, baby, we just want you home. Can you tell us where you are?"

"I dunno, Mama. Aidan says it's like camp. I have my own cabin."

"Mama," Olivia interrupted, "can I go to camp?"

"Not today," I replied in a short tone. "Jackson, please tell Mama and Ada where you are."

"Ada's there?"

"Yes, baby, he can hear you."

"Is he mad? I know I broke my promise."

"Jack-Jack, no one is mad. We just miss you and want to bring you home. Can you show me where you are?"

"I miss you too, Mama, but I like it here, it's fun. And I can't leave, I have to stay with Ashwyn."

"Is she ok? Is Ashlyn hurt?"

"She's really sad. I don't think she likes camp, that's why I need to stay. Aidan says he's gonna help her just like the others. I'm all right, Mama, I'm a big boy. I'll make Ada proud, I promise."

"Baby, we are very proud of you..."

"Sorry, Mama, I hafta go. I wuv you."

"No, Jackson, wait!" I shouted, but there was no reply.

"He's gone, Mama," Olivia said. "Ada looks mad."

"Why do you say that?" I said as I opened my eyes, but still kept the connection to my daughter. I looked behind me and saw Cameron standing across the room with his back to us. Victor stood next to him with his arm around Cameron's shoulders and talking closely in his ear. "He's not mad, baby girl. He just wants Jackson to come home, like we all do. Can you help us? Can you help us bring him home?"

"How, Mama?"

"Just keep drawing your pictures, draw everything Jack-Jack shows you. Tell me or Ada everything that he tells you, even the tiniest little thing could help us. Can you do that for us?"

"I like drawing," she replied.

I removed my hand from her back and petted her soft hair. "I know you do."

Olivia looked up from her drawing. "Can I have ice cream now?"

"Honey, you just had breakfast..."

"But Grandfather said that if I spoke to Jack-Jack I could have all the ice cream I wanted!" she wailed.

I looked across the room to Victor who gave me an apologetic shrug. "A means to an end, child, a means to an end. Come, little one, let us see what Christine has stocked in the freezer."

Olivia quickly slid off the antique desk chair and bounced over to Victor, her red rain boots squeaking as she traveled across the floor and then jumped in his arms. The two of them looked very peculiar together, she in a tiara and purple petticoat, he dressed for battle in ancient Rome.

"She dressed herself, I take it?" I asked, trying to lighten the mood in the room. Devin hadn't moved from the other side of the desk and Cameron still stood with his back to us. He didn't even flinch at my joke. Slowly I walked over to him, threading my fingers through his.

"It was harder to hear his voice than I had anticipated," he said in a strained tone. I kissed his hand and then pressed it into my cheek. "What is our son's infatuation with Aidan? He speaks about him like…"

But he couldn't finish once the many emotions overtook him.

"At least we know they haven't hurt him," I said.

"But we still do not know where he is," Cam replied as he put his hand through his hair.

"There is someone who might know," Devin said behind us causing Cam and I to whip around and see him holding Olivia's drawing. "I believe she's in the library with the team."

I ran to Devin, took the picture from his hand, and was out the door in a matter of seconds. The hallway and corridors were a blur as I ran to the library, and although I felt bad about doing it, I did Push a couple of Warriors out of my way.

The door to the library was open and on the far side of the room was the one person who might recognize where Jackson was being held.

"Nikki!" I shouted as I placed Olivia's drawing down on the table she was sitting at. "Do you know this place? Where is this?"

Nikki's eyes were wide with fear as she looked from me to the drawing and then to the others around the room. "That's a child's drawing, Brianna, I don't understand…"

"Did Aidan ever take you here?" I said impatiently. "Jackson called it a camp, did you ever go here?"

"N-no," she replied as her eyes fluttered.

Cameron stepped up next to me. "Nikki, please think back. Did Aidan ever mention a place like this? A retreat in the woods, a large plot of land, anything?"

Nikki shook her head vigorously. "No, never."

I slammed my palm down on the desk. "This is our son, Nikki! He's just a little boy. So take a moment and think, please!"

Nikki's cheeks reddened with anger as she stood from her chair. "I'm sorry, Brianna, I was probably too busy being tortured by Elaina's goons.

Does anyone ever remember that? It wasn't like I was always with Aidan and skipping through fields of daisies or something. I rarely got to leave that warehouse you found me in, and Aidan certainly didn't take me to some camp for fake father-daughter weekends."

Cameron held up his hand as he said, "Nikki, all we are asking is for you to think back…"

"No matter what I do, none of you will ever let me live my past down," Nikki interrupted as she began walking to the library door, but stopped just before she exited. "Thanks for the support, Jer. You're the best boyfriend a girl could have."

And with that Nikki slammed the library door. I looked over at Jared who was standing in front of the enormous monitor with Connor.

"Shouldn't you go after your girlfriend?" I asked.

Jared shrugged and pointed to the monitor behind him. "Er…well, we're kinda busy. Plus she'll just bitch at me, so might as well let her cool off for a bit. But…uh…good to see ya, Bibi. You're always good for an eventual entrance."

Cameron placed his hand on my back as he said, "We have just heard from Jackson, little brother. Olivia has drawn a picture of the images he is showing her. It is not much but it is all we have to go on so far."

"So what is it we know?" Connor asked.

"Only that their base is in a heavily wooded area."

"That only narrows it down to about seventy percent of the country," Jared responded sarcastically. "Anything else to go on?"

"Cabins," I replied. "Jack said something about having his own cabin. He said it was like camp. So could you stop being a condescending dick wad and at least pretend we're giving you some helpful information."

Jared smiled. "It's good to have you back, Beebs."

Chapter Thirty-nine

Jonah

Things had gotten weird. Brianna drank my blood and I was her first live donor. The weird thing – Cameron hadn't killed me. After sleeping for almost a day and a half I woke to find out that they had heard from Jackson. The weird thing – he had spoken to Livy telepathically. Jack and Ashlyn had been taken to some kind of rustic encampment. The weird thing – Jack wasn't scared, not in the slightest. I guess that's more worrisome than weird. Because of Jack's lack of fear, he was reticent about giving details on his location. At least I knew that Ashlyn was ok, though none of us knew how long that would last. The fact that Aidan said he would "help" her, made me close to throwing up more than once. And no matter how many pictures Livy drew, it didn't make me feel any better, even when she said drawing Ashlyn's multi-colored patchwork bag was her favorite part.

Ashlyn had only been gone for eight days, but it felt more like a month had gone by. There was an overall feeling of despair that weighed on my soul. I knew I was being totally dramatic considering I've only lost a girlfriend versus a child. Frankly, I was just in a bad mood. So it was good that tonight was a night away from the manor.

A family dinner at Ollie and Maddy's new place meant I had to take a real shower and actually put some time in my appearance. I shrugged in the mirror at my semi-spiked hair. I hadn't spent near enough time on it, but I was going to be late. I buttoned up my green plaid shirt over my t-shirt, slapped a little cologne on my neck, and headed out the door. Thankfully Tosh's room was only a few doors down from mine. When I knocked she called for me to come in, but when I entered she was nowhere in sight.

"Tosh?"

She opened the bathroom door and poked her head around its edge, keeping her body hidden behind the door. "So sorry, I'm running late. I just need a few more minutes," she said and then disappeared into the bathroom, but left the door cracked open a few inches.

I plopped down on the bed and noticed there was an addition to her room. "When did they make your room a double?" I asked, looking at the new twin bed tucked into the far corner.

"Today," she groaned. "Nikki must have pissed someone off. Big surprise, right? I guess now that we both live here she doesn't get her own room when she has her period. So now *I* get to suffer through her crazier than normal hormones."

"Maybe you pissed someone off instead," I laughed and heard her laugh with me. "So why are you running late?"

She groaned again as she stood at her sink. I glanced away, realizing that she was only wearing jeans and a bra. It was hard not to look over again since I also caught a glimpse of the infamous scars crawling up her back.

"Devin came in about the time we were wrapping up so training went late, and then that meant my session with Connor went late."

"Session? Is that what the kids are calling it these days?" I teased as I pushed further across the bed and propped my back up against the wall. "You spend every afternoon with that guy. When are you going to admit…"

"He is *not* my boyfriend, Jonah," she growled.

"That's what I used to say about Ashlyn."

The door to the bathroom flew open, a little shower steam wafting out from inside as Tosh stepped out, now fully dressed. "Connor offered to help me with extra training sessions to help me keep up with the guys. That's all, and I'm sick of everyone thinking it's more than that, because that's just not possible."

"Er…why isn't it possible?"

"Errr…scars," she replied and pointed to her abdomen.

"What does that have to do with it?"

"Uh, asshole, everything. Are you ready?" she said and grabbed her keys.

I nodded and scooted off the bed, leading the way out the door and into the hallway. "Thanks for driving. It's totally weird being without a car."

Tosh shrugged and smiled. "Anytime. I know I certainly didn't want to go through all the convoy hoopla. With all the detours they're taking, we may even beat them there."

I laughed lightly to myself having been present when all the preparations were being made for what should only be a fifteen minute trip, but would take the three cars almost an hour. No one was taking any chances this time.

As we headed down the expansive spiraling staircase, Tosh nudged me and said, "So how's the research going? Did you find anymore missing hybrids?"

"I sort of gave up on that," I sighed.

"Why?"

I shrugged. "It's not making a bit of difference, really. It was mostly something to keep me busy. We didn't find that many anyway and then I started thinking that maybe the reason for that is they're taking hybrids that don't have anyone, like Ashlyn. Seriously, if someone had taken Ash before she came across that Gatherer, no one would ever have reported her missing. They could have been taking people under the radar for months or years. Honestly, if that guy hadn't come for Lyla we never would have known there was still a real danger. But I guess they just couldn't pass up on a Firestarter."

Tosh shivered at the thought of a Firestarter, and I suddenly felt stupid for mentioning it. But she continued with the idle chatter as we walked across the main foyer and then exited the manor. "So if you're not searching for missing hybrids, then what have you been doing?"

"Mostly helping Alex and your sister with their research on the dual projection," I said as I followed Tosh through two rows of cars parked in the gravel parking area.

"Better you than me," she joked as she pulled her keys out of her pocket and stopped next to a brilliant black Mercedes coupe. "Hop in, it's open."

I didn't move, simply looked at her dumbstruck. "You're not serious."

Tosh shrugged coyly and sank into the driver's seat. A moment later the car hummed to life and I couldn't help but miss my silver lady. I shook the sad thoughts out of my head and walked around to the passenger side door, still hesitating when I closed myself in, thinking someone would come out and grab us for trying to steal this elegant sports car.

Slowly she drove us through the tall black gate, and then sped down the main drive. I gripped the door handle and sucked in a breath as the trees blurred past.

"Oh don't be such a baby," Tosh teased. "I know these streets like the back of my hand."

"Sorry, not used to someone else driving," I said relaxing my grip, but then squeezed the door handle once again when she came upon a curve and didn't slow down in the slightest. "So seriously, this is your car?"

"No, I just stole it from the parking lot."

"Oh my god!" I shouted and splayed all four limbs across the car.

"Jesus, Jonah, I'm kidding," she yelled back at me. "Of course it's mine. Why wouldn't it be?"

"Uh…because it's a really expensive car and you're barely twenty-one."

"You have a nice car," she rebutted.

"Yeah, because Brianna gave it to me. So what's your excuse?"

Tosh glanced at me through the side of her eye, and by her delay I knew that whatever she was going to say would be a lie. "My…uh…dad left me some money when he died."

When she glanced over again to see if I had bought her lie, I gave her a skeptical eye and she quickly looked back through the windshield. Knowing I wasn't going to get any further, I changed the subject.

"Do you know where we're going?"

Tosh rolled her eyes. "No, Jonah. I just thought I'd get in the car and drive around San Francisco hoping that someone would wave a sign saying 'Oliver's new house here' with a great big arrow pointing to it."

"Wow, have I done something to offend you today?"

"No," she replied annoyed. "You're just asking stupid questions. Of course I know where I'm going. I told you, I know these streets like the back of my hand. Trolling around in my car is kind of what I do."

Amen to that. I could more than relate, and yet again my stomach sank at the thought of my car.

"So a little birdie told me that today was weapons selection."

Tosh immediately blushed. "Yeah. It was."

When she didn't answer further, I pushed. "And?"

"And what?"

"Did you pick a weapon today or not?"

Tosh's blush continued as the engine revved up the curving ridge. "I did."

"Ok," I prompted, but again she didn't answer. "So…any reason you don't want to tell me?"

"Whips, ok? I chose whips," she blurted out.

"Seriously?"

Tosh rolled her eyes again. "Why would I lie about that?"

I shrugged. "I don't know. You lied about how you got the car, so…"

"How do you know…" she began and then caught herself.

"Tosh, you lie about as bad as my sister does. Why so shy about whips?"

She pursed her lips and sighed. "It's just that…the guys kept making comments about how I must be into S&M or something."

"Well, a woman with whips is pretty sexy," I teased, and got a hit in the chest for it.

"I'm being serious, Jonah."

"So am I, Natasha," I replied and received another hit to the chest. "Ow! I'm a human, you're not supposed to hurt me."

"That's Vamps, Jonah. I'm a hybrid, I can do whatever I want to you," she laughed, and then a moment later her worries weighed back down on her shoulders.

"Listen, Tosh, forget about those guys, they're just being douchebags and they're probably jealous that they're not going to be as good or look as cool as you will."

Tosh glanced over at me once again, this time a half smile stretched across her face. "Thanks, Jonah."

"Just telling it like it is, that's all."

"But really, thank you. The only other girl trainee dropped out yesterday, so now I'm suddenly the little sister that everybody picks on."

"Well, can't help you there. But if I were to channel Devin or Alex, I'd say just kick their asses left and right. They'll back off once they realize you're not to be messed with. Plus, all the Warriors like you. So don't let it get to you, Tosh. You're better than that."

Tosh tried to covertly wipe a tear with her left hand as she turned the steering wheel with her right and pulled into the driveway of an L-shaped, ranch-style home with red siding. Ollie's new digs. It was quaint and one level, similar to the house in North Carolina, and perfect for an elderly couple.

Tosh put the car in park and I reached to unbuckle my seatbelt when she placed her hand on top of mine. "I got a settlement."

"Huh?"

"When I got burned, I got a settlement from…Ty's family. That's how I paid for the car. Maddy went ape shit when she found out what I did. It's the only thing I've ever splurged on, and the rest has gone toward college or is in savings. There are only two other people who know about the settlement, so…don't tell anyone. I really don't like people to know."

I nodded and unbuckled my seatbelt. "If you don't want anyone to know, I'd stop driving around in a car like this. It leads to fewer questions."

I jerked back and laughed as Tosh's fist came close to hitting me again. The two of us continued to laugh as we exited the car and started making our way down the driveway where three large SUVs sat. As we approached I noticed Cameron and Bri standing between two of the trucks. Bri was nervously rocking back and forth with her arms crossed while Cameron rested his hands on her shoulders trying to comfort her. I gave them an awkward nod as we passed. Only Cameron looked up at me, and thankfully he nodded back. I knew Bri was nervous about today because it was the first time seeing Sera since the blow up in North Carolina.

When Tosh and I reached the front door she asked, "Is she ok?"

"She'll be fine once she gets over her guilt."

Tosh widened her eyes with a worried expression, and I knew how she felt. Brianna held more guilt than any other person I knew. Tonight would be hard for her, no doubt.

I opened the front door and was immediately hit with the sound of screaming kids.

"Jonah! Toshy!" Livy screamed as she ran to us, Will only a few steps behind her, both of them holding pieces of construction paper in their hands. "Look, we made signs!"

"Yeah, wook at our signs," Will said proudly as he held his sign up next to Livy's. Whereas Livy's said 'welcome home Daddy O', Will's was mainly scribbles and then his name. And just as quickly as they ran to us they fled to torture someone else.

The living area was a perfect square with the living room, dining room, and kitchen all open to one another. The kitchen was straight ahead and to the back with Maddy fluttering around making dinner while Kyla hovered behind her trying to help and Renee poured herself a big glass of wine. Business as usual, really. Tosh ignored her sister as she walked into the kitchen, though Nikki didn't really seem to care all that much. She seemed way too occupied with sulking on the couch and watching Jared play with the kids.

"Well don't just stand there, Jonah," Oliver said to my right and gestured toward the living room, "come on in and have a seat."

"Thanks, Ollie. Nice place."

Ollie smiled. "Well I certainly had nothin' to do with it. Can I getcha somethin' to drink?"

"Uh...maybe in a bit," I replied and looked around the room. "Where's Seraphina?"

"She got hit with a spell and Eris took her outside for a bit," he said pointing to the sliding glass doors at the opposite end of the room.

I gave him a curt nod of thanks and walked the width of the house to the sliding glass doors where I could see Sera and Eris sitting out on the large patio outside. They both looked up in my direction as I opened the door, though Eris stood and shook my hand.

"How was the trip, sir?"

Eris forced a smile. "Fine, fine. Though I believe Vlad is sick of the constant back and forth lately. Would you mind staying with Sera-phin-na while I locate my ungrateful daughter?"

"Eri, please," Sera begged, but her plea fell on deaf ears as Eris turned quickly and went back into the house. Sera gave me a smile and gestured to the lounge chair in front of her. "Would you like to sit with me?"

"Of course," I replied and sat down across from her. "Are you feeling all right?"

Sera nodded and began fanning herself with her hand. "Just a hot flash, c'est la vie. Zhough zhey always seem to come when you are near." I could feel my cheeks become flush, but when she laughed I laughed along with her. "How are you holding up, my dear?"

My hand rubbed my mouth nervously before I answered, "It depends on the hour, I guess. I'll be mopey and depressed then later on I'll be laughing and joking around, then I feel guilty about that so I become mopey and depressed again."

"Zhat seems pretty normal under zhese circumstances," she said, still fanning herself as her neck and face turned beet red.

"What about you? How are you holding up?"

Sera took in a deep breath and let it out slowly. "It is times like zhese zhat it is difficult being an Empath. But it is even harder when zhe woman you love as a daughter zhinks you have betrayed her."

"Sera, trust me, Brianna's much better now. She didn't mean those things she said. You two will get through this."

"Such a good boy," she said as she patted my hand. "How are zhings with your mozer?" But before I could answer she patted my hand again. "Do not worry, zhat will work itself out as well, I know zhis."

I couldn't help but smirk, but then a thought hit me. "Have you...by any chance...uh...had any visions about Ashlyn?"

Sera's chest fell slightly as the lines in her face creased into a sympathetic expression. "I am sorry, no. My vizions have almost always been about Brianna or zhe bébés. Zhat is until zhe night she died. Since zhen it has only been of how zhe Vampires look in zhe future. Sometimes zhey are zhe same as today, and ozher times it is chaos. Even when Aidan..." she paused for a moment as she held back tears, "Even when he took mon petit Jacques-Jacques, nozhing changed. Nozhing has tipped zhe future one way or zhe ozher. I just wish ma petite chute would believe me."

"Ah, who?" I asked.

"That's me," Brianna said from behind me. When I turned around she was standing at the corner of the yard, her arms clasped behind her nervously. "I'm the cabbage. One small, smelly cabbage."

"Petite?" Sera said as she held her arms out in front of her.

In the blink of an eye Brianna was sitting next to Sera and resting her head against her stepmother's chest. Sera wrapped her arms around Bri and the two of them began sobbing between expressions of apology and forgiveness. It was my cue to leave, and neither noticed me slip back inside the house.

My mouth instantly began to salivate at the savory smells of Maddy's cooking. Oliver and John were already sitting at the dining room table, both with plates overflowing with what looked like pulled pork, cornbread, and vegetables. Maddy wrapped her fingers around my arm and pulled me toward the kitchen where serving dishes lined the counter.

"Mr. Thorne, I want to see you eat a good-sized meal tonight. I've heard you haven't been eating lately," she said waving her index finger at me.

"That is true, Maddy," I replied. "But the manor chef can't cook like you."

Maddy narrowed her eyes, but curled the left side of her mouth into a smile. "You, my boy, are quite a charmer. Now get something to eat before Ollie gets to it all."

Ollie laughed from the table and after I filled my plate I sat between him and John. Just as I plunged my fork into the pile of pulled pork, someone placed an ice cold beer next to me. I looked up to my right and saw Cameron standing over me.

"Thanks, man," I said nervously.

Cameron gave me a one-sided smile, patted my shoulder, and walked outside to join Bri and Seraphina. Hopefully this meant he and I could go on like before. Cameron was a good friend, certainly not one I wanted to lose because I was tired and stupid. Twice.

"So John, how was your first week at Facility West?" I asked as I took a big swig of my beer.

"He didn't kill anybody," Renee answered for him from the kitchen.

"And neither did you, honey," John replied, toasting his wife and causing us all to erupt in laughter.

Over the next couple of hours everyone came together, including Bri and Sera, and got their minds off the stress of the week. Also during that time Oliver and I began testing who could eat more. Sadly, I lost. Ollie Morgan could eat his weight in pork. Bri warned me it was a pointless attempt, but I usually had to find out these things myself.

"Ollie, I give," I said as I pushed my chair away from the table so that its edge wouldn't press into my stomach.

"Lesser men have failed," he laughed before scooping up his last spoonful of pulled pork.

The sight almost made me want to barf, and I guess it showed on my face since John brought over a garbage can and placed it in front of me. At the same time Olivia came running over to the table with several pieces of construction paper in her hand.

"Hey Da-e-o, I made you more drawings for your new house!" she said happily, waving the papers above her head. "Wanna see?"

"Well a course I do, chillun," Oliver replied and pulled Olivia up onto his lap. After sliding his empty plate out of the way, Livy placed her drawings down on the table. "Now tell me 'bout these masterpieces that are gonna make your great-grandfather a wealthy man."

Olivia giggled and then began going through each picture. There was a picture of a horse with Livy dancing next to it. A second picture of a snowman with Livy dancing next to it. A third with a field full of butterflies with, you guessed it, Livy dancing next to them. But it was the last one that got everyone's attention.

"What's this one, chillun?" Oliver asked.

"Oh, that's camp," Livy replied in a very bored tone. Everyone else in the room went silent and suddenly all eyes were on Olivia.

Oliver sensed the sudden change and proceeded lightly. "Camp, heh? I used to love camp when I was little. Is that where uh…your brother…is?"

Livy nodded her head. "And that's Jack-Jack right there," she said as she pointed to a small figure on the paper with black hair. "And that's Ashwyn. Jonah, see?"

I forced a smile as Livy pointed to the blonde girl on the page with a multi-colored bag slung across her chest. She was holding hands with Jack-Jack and thankfully this time Livy hadn't drawn big blue tears falling from her face.

Oliver pointed to a small grouping of people Livy had drawn next to Ashlyn. "And who are they?"

"Those are Aidan's friends," she replied, then pointed to another grouping on the far right side of the page. "And those are some of the mommies."

"Wh-what was that?" I asked, my stomach leaping into my throat.

Livy's eyes fluttered, surprised at my question. "The mommies. There are the Vampys, the hybies, and the mommies."

My head started shaking, my mouth not working as fast as my brain. "Wh-wh-what does that mean? The mommies?"

"Baby, are you sure?" Brianna said as she knelt down in front of Livy, but also glanced down at the new drawing. "You've never drawn them before. Are you sure they're not just hybies…uh, hybrids?"

Livy's face scrunched up tightly. "No! They're mommies!" she replied angrily. "Jack-Jack said they were mommies cuz of the babies in their tummies. That's what he said."

"When, baby?" Brianna pushed.

"To-day!"

"Olivia Sera, you will watch your tone," Cameron warned from the kitchen, and Livy immediately calmed herself. "When did Jackson tell you about these mothers?"

"This afternoon," she replied quietly. "But I forgot until just now."

"C-can we go back for a sec," I said as my heart started to pound in my chest. "Can we talk about these...these mommies?"

"Bro," Jared said from the living room, "it's just like last time, remember?"

"What last time?"

"There was that kid, the one that wanted pudding. The pudding kid, uh...er...Mickey?"

"Mikey!" John corrected. "You're right, Jer. He called them the mommies. My God, do you think Aidan's picking up where Elaina left off?"

"It's plan B," Brianna said gave Cameron a worried look.

"Ok, can someone bring me in the loop here!" I shouted as I stood from my chair, accidently kicking the garbage can over and causing it to spill its contents onto the floor.

"Jonah, we do not know for sure..." Cameron began but I wasn't buying it.

"Livy seems pretty sure," I said, pointing to her and she nodded vehemently. "And Bri is talking about some plan B, so what the fff...ff-freak is plan B?"

"Mama," Livy began and pointed at me, "he almost said..."

"Yes, baby girl, but not now," Brianna said to her daughter, and then turned back to me and squeezed my arm. "Jonah, we don't know enough to get upset about anything. Just because Jack-Jack says there are mothers there doesn't mean..."

"What is plan B?" I asked plainly.

Brianna sighed and looked nervously at the others around the room before she said, "Livy, why don't you and Wills go into the back bedroom and play."

"I don't want to," Livy replied matter-of-factly.

Maddy came into the dining room and pulled Livy into her arms. "I'll take them back. Ollie?"

Ollie looked up at Maddy with a confused expression. "I'd rather stay here."

Maddy raised only one eyebrow and Oliver was out of his seat and taking Will by the hand. Once the back bedroom door closed, Brianna moved over to the small kitchen island and propped her back against it.

"The night Elaina took me…"

"The night you voluntarily *went* with her," Renee corrected and Brianna squinted her eyes at her.

"Fine. The night I went with Elaina she told me that she had almost given up on ever finding me so she came up with her plan B. Basically if she couldn't have my Vampire children, then she would make her own."

I looked past Brianna and up to Cameron. "And she succeeded?"

Cameron shook his head. "No. She only succeeded in producing normal hybrids."

"But they were still pregnant! So you're saying that they what…" I lowered my voice and whispered, "are…raping…women? You all knew this and didn't tell me?!"

"Jonah, we didn't know," Brianna pleaded.

"My girl is out there! It was bad enough when I thought they were torturing her, but now she could be…oh Jesus," I said, suddenly feeling lightheaded.

Brianna squeezed my arm gently. "Joey, Ashlyn is ok, we know that. She's not one of the mothers, otherwise Jack would have told us. We're going to find her, honey, I promise we're going to find her."

"I need some air," I said and walked to the sliding glass door. The cool air hit me immediately, though I barely needed a jacket. The San Francisco winter felt like spring to my New England blood. I almost longed for the biting cold and snow.

Just then the sliding glass door opened and closed, and a second later Tosh rested her hand on the small of my back.

"Did you know?" I asked before she could say anything. "About before, I mean, about those other women."

"I…did," she began, but paused again. "When they found that last place I was still recovering from my burns, and only heard about it. It's one of those things they kind of swept under the rug, I guess."

"Just like everything else that happens in the Vampire world."

"Do you want a beer or something?"

"No," I replied, taking a step away from her. "I really just want to go back to the manor. Would you mind?"

She shook her head and pulled the keys out of her pocket. "I'll even let you drive."

Chapter Forty

Jonah

I didn't take Tosh up on her offer to drive her beautiful car, although I'd probably hit myself tomorrow. I kept transitioning from fits of anger and frustration to unbelievable sadness over what could be happening to my girl. The last place I needed to be was behind the wheel of a car. Tosh drove us around the city, staying silent while I spewed my thoughts or had bouts of silence of my own. It took us over an hour to get back to the manor, and I found that the secure stone structure was not a comforting sight. With everything that had been thrown at me tonight I was definitely too sober.

"We should have run to the package store," I groaned.

"The what?" Tosh replied as she turned off the car.

"The package store, you know, for alcohol."

"Do you mean a liquor store?" she said with sarcastic distain.

"Yeah, fine, a liquor store. They call them package stores by me."

"Why?"

"I...I don't know, Tosh," I whined. "Can we just go in then?"

Tosh didn't answer, but merely opened her door and I followed. We walked silently across the gravel driveway and through the manor's massive front door. Just as I turned toward the spiral staircase Tosh took my hand and gave me a sly smile.

"I have an idea," she whispered as she pulled me down the main corridor. Oddly there weren't many people around, I guess everyone was enjoying the start of the weekend. The main dining room was pitch black and as we approached the kitchen I could tell it had been closed up for the night which made me curious as to why Tosh was pulling me inside it.

"Just watch the door," she whispered before disappearing around the corner.

"And do what?"

"Shhh," she replied as she rummaged through a cabinet. "Just tell me if you hear anyone."

"This is a house full of Vampires, Tosh, they can probably hear me hearing them, or some shit like that.

"Just…just do it!" she hissed.

"What are you looking for?" I asked as I peeked out into the empty hallway and then stepped back inside the dark kitchen. "Tosh? Tosh!"

"God you're impatient," Tosh said as she came back from around the corner. Once again she grabbed my hand and began pulling me through the kitchen.

"Where are we going?"

"Just wait for it. I promise it's worth it," she replied as we came to the back wall of the kitchen. Tosh released my hand and began feeling the wall. A second later she pushed open a portion of the wall revealing a dark, narrow passageway. The doorway on the other side was cracked open allowing a sliver of light to illuminate our path.

"Seriously, Tosh, where are we? Usually this is the point in a movie where the walls start closing in, or big spikes come up out of the floor."

Tosh groaned and pushed the other door open all the way to reveal an enormous and lavishly decorated room.

"Jonah, no joke, you need to think about medication," she said as she walked to the center of the room. "This is the grand ballroom of the Warrior manor, and that is the server's passageway that connects to the kitchen. So I'm sorry to say there are no spikes or moving walls."

I stepped out of the passageway and began admiring my surroundings. Moonlight was streaming in through the tall glass doors to my left, illuminating and catching the crystals hanging from the multiple chandeliers. This obviously wasn't Tosh's first time in this room, but from the expression on her face she was still in awe of it.

"How did you know about this place?" I asked

Tosh giggled. "I'm a Warrior groupie, I guess. Plus, Jared's been nice enough to show me the cool stuff like that passageway and even some of the vaults. I'm fascinated by how much history is here. Five hybrids have had their Claiming ceremonies here, including Brianna. Only sixteen Warriors have been inducted into the coven in this room, hopefully someday I'll up that number to seventeen."

"Is that why you brought me here? For a history lesson?"

"No," she replied softly. "I come into this room when I'm really upset. It's just so beautiful and grand that it makes me feel like I'm in a different place for a little while. And then I start to imagine what my induction ceremony would be like, who would be there, all the sights and sounds, and it just makes me…happy. So that's why I brought you here."

I tried to smile. "Thanks, Tosh, but I don't think…"

"And I also brought this," she said and revealed a bottle in her hand. "Hope you like tequila because that's all that was left."

I took the bottle from her hand and didn't recognize the brand of alcohol, but also didn't care. "I thought trainees and donors can't have alcohol."

Tosh took the bottle back and removed the cap. "Victor doesn't want his Warriors drinking tainted blood and Devin doesn't want the trainees hungover. But everyone needs a drink every now and then, that's why there's a secret stash. So I just can't get caught."

"Ok, who are you and where's Natasha Cushlin?"

"Hey, I can break a rule every now and then. Besides, I have two days off from training and I'm the only surviving girl in the group. I think I deserve a little celebration." Tosh gave me a wink before tilting the bottle up and drinking what must have been a double shot. But afterwards her face was priceless. "Blehck! God that's awful," she laughed as she handed me the bottle.

Not wanting to be shown up by a girl, I swallowed as much tequila I thought she had. And she was right, it was awful. "This is why we need limes and salt."

"Pussy," she replied as she took the bottle from me and grabbed my hand. "Come on, there's more to see."

Tosh pulled me across the floor and through one of the glass doors out onto a terrace that extended on both sides. We stepped down and proceeded to a wide concrete railing that looked out onto the manor's sculpted grounds.

Tosh took another swig of the tequila and then handed me the bottle. "Isn't it beautiful out here?"

"Yeah," I replied and then took another drink.

"That's all you can say? Yeah?"

I shrugged as I walked back to the wide steps and sat down. I took another drink before saying, "I'm sorry, Tosh. It is the most beautiful sight that my eyes have ever seen."

"You're an asshole."

"Yes I am," I replied and handed her the bottle. As she leaned back against the railing I realized that this truly was her happy place. "So you're really going to become a Vampire."

Tosh gave me a smirk. "Why does everyone keep asking me that?"

"Because you're so young."

"It's because I'm a girl," she grumbled. "I'm older than Jared when he was Turned."

"Yeah, but he can…" I began, but then got uncomfortable. So much so that I got up from the steps, took the tequila from her and took another drink.

"What? He can what? Still have kids? That's what you were going to say, wasn't it?"

"Sorry, I think it sucks, but it's a fact that once a woman is Turned she can't have a baby. You're still young, Tosh, and you're going to give that up. That's all I'm saying."

"Newsflash, Jonah, not all women want kids. But it doesn't matter anyway because I can't have them. So what's the difference if I stay human or become a Vamp?"

I extended the tequila out to Tosh like an olive branch and she drank it quickly.

"Tosh, I didn't know. Is it because of the…the scars?" I asked and sat back down on the concrete step.

"When a Firestarter explodes while he's in you, things get destroyed," she replied and then took a long drink. After she shuttered from the alcohol, she continued, "And even if I could have kids, I'd still need a guy to help me with that, and there are certainly none jumping at the chance to be with me." I opened my mouth to contradict her and she leaned forward with her finger pointed at me. "And if you say Connor's name I swear I'll break this bottle over your head."

I laughed and she went back to her stance against the railing.

"Tosh, all I'm saying is, just because there isn't a guy now, doesn't mean that years from now…"

"No, Jonah!" she shouted. "There won't be. There will never be a guy who can get past my scars."

"You don't know that."

She laughed and took another drink. "Yes, Jonah, I do. I didn't give up on men right away. There were several that helped me make that decision."

"They weren't men, Tosh, they were douchebags. There's a difference."

"Men want perfect and little and beautiful and smooth. They don't want…this," Tosh said as she angrily rubbed her abdomen.

"A good man, a truly good man sees past that, Tosh. He'll see what a great person you are inside and out."

Tosh laughed again, and it was insulting to say the least. "Jonah, that's what perfect people like you say to make people like me feel better."

"Oh don't give me that crap," I groaned. "Everybody has problems, Tosh, no one is perfect. And frankly I don't like that you're putting my entire gender into one senseless category."

"I'm just telling you what I know. No guy has ever been able to look at them."

"Try me," I challenged.

"Wh-what?"

"Let me see them." She didn't reply, just stood frozen up against the railing. "If I freak out like all the other guys, I won't say another word about your decision to become a Vamp."

"And if you don't?"

"And *when* I don't, you promise me not to give up on love."

The muscles in Tosh's face twitched as she worked through my challenge in her head. When she finally took another long swig I knew the choice she had made. She handed me the bottle of tequila and stood in front of me.

"Fine," she began, her hands shaking at her sides. "But promise me, no matter what, that you'll keep your opinions to yourself. I can't handle being made fun of, especially by a friend."

I squeezed one of her shaking hands. "Tosh, I promise you can trust me."

I held onto her left hand as she gripped the edge of her shirt and lifted it six inches up her stomach. Although I had seen small glimpses here and there, seeing the scars full on was intense. Red and pink skin melted and swirled together with no distinction of muscle underneath. I ran my fingers across a raised ridge of scar tissue, following it down to the edge of her pants. They were hard to look at, but not for the reasons Tosh assumed.

"And these go down your legs?" I asked as I continued to touch different ridges of her scars.

"To my thighs," she replied.

I pulled on her elbow, the alcohol visibly setting in as I steadied her down to her knees. Gently I pried her hand away from her face and looked her right in her eyes as I said, "Tosh, you have nothing to be embarrassed about."

"That's easy for you to say," she replied as she wiped the tears from her eyes. "You don't have to live with them every day."

"You're right, I don't, that's because what you went through would have killed me." Tosh blinked with surprise. "Don't you see? Anyone else would have died, but you were stronger than that. If I were you, I'd show those scars off every day, let people see what you survived. Every soldier has battle scars, these are yours. Show them off proudly, and if anyone ever makes a snide comment, you get right in their face and tell them that no way in hell could they have survived what you did."

"You...you really think so?" she asked tentatively.

"Hell ya!" I replied. "Show those suckers off. They're totally badass."

I saw Tosh coming at me, but the alcohol was already hitting me so I was slow on the uptake when she slammed her lips against me. Before I knew it, she pressed up from her knees and suddenly she was on lying on top of me. As she plunged her tongue into my mouth, my brain finally caught up with me and pressed into her shoulders to push her away from me. Her eyes were wide with confusion and she waited only a couple of seconds before she tried kissing me again.

I turned my head away, the back of my skull grinding into the stone underneath. "No, Tosh, I...I can't."

Tosh quickly rolled off of me, her breath becoming staggered as she started to cry. "I am...so...stupid."

"Tosh, I'm sorry," I said as I tried touching her arm, but she flinched and flung my hand away. "You are not stupid."

Tosh stood from the ground and began fixing herself, securing her shirt firmly below her waist and rebuilding the defensive wall around her. "I want to become a Vampire because I don't want to be a freak anymore."

"You are not a freak, Tosh."

"Yes I am, Jonah, and you more than proved my point."

"That's not why..." I started to say but someone else cleared their throat behind me. Tosh immediately froze. "Who is it?" I whispered, but she didn't answer so I slowly turned around to find a very short man with a very annoyed expression on his face.

"If you must have a lovers' quarrel, could you please refrain from having it outside of my office? Some of us do our work during these hours."

"Oh this isn't a...we're not..." I stuttered so eloquently, but the man put his hand up to silence me.

"You," he said and pointed at Tosh, "you are one of the trainees, aren't you? Yes, you are the other Cushlin girl. Of everything I have heard, I have to say I am surprised to find you like this."

"Victor...oh...my...god," Tosh cried, wrapping her arms around her before she fled back into the ballroom.

I turned back and looked at Victor. Surprisingly enough, after all these years of being connected with Brianna and Cameron, and having been in his home for a week, I had never met the leader of the Warriors. Brianna had told me he was short, but man he was short. But he only had to look at me with one eyebrow raised and I was ready to piss my pants. Intimidating couldn't even describe him.

"Was it something I said?" he asked, slightly amused and pointing in the direction of the ballroom. "She is the Cushlin girl, is she not?"

I nodded. "Yep, she is. I think that's why she ran," I said and then noticed the bottle of tequila at my feet. My eyes darted back to Victor who was also looking at the bottle. "This...this is all me, by the way. Tosh had nothing to do with this, she didn't have any of this, this was mine...my own bottle...that I...b-brought with me."

Victor raised his one eyebrow further. "Really? Because that looks like the bottle of tequila that has been in the secret cabinet for months."

My face fell. "You...know...about that?"

Victor laughed as he walked over and sat next to me. "I know everything that goes on here. For the protection of my Warriors and humans that live under my roof I have to know everything. For instance, if Jonah Thorne had a criminal record, I would need to know that."

"But I don't."

"Yes I know," he replied slyly. "The judge was very lenient on you and dismissed your DUI due to the extenuating circumstances. It was around the time of your father's death, was it not?"

"H-how did you know that? Brianna doesn't even know that."

"Ah, but you see again, it is my job to know. Even though we have never met, I know just about everything about you, Jonah Thorne."

"Yep, that's me, Jonah Thorne, non-criminal Jonah, truly. It was a stupid thing at a bad time..."

"Jonah," Victor said as he held up his hand, "You do not need to explain yourself to me. Because of your close connection to my family, and with all the praise you have received over the years from Facility East, I have actually been following you quite closely. Merely as an interested party, that's all."

"For Cameron and Bri's protection," I said as I nodded skeptically.

Victor gave a sly smile. "I take an eager interest in all my children's affairs whether they like it or not."

"So...uh...you're ok with the alcohol thing?"

"My Warriors must have clean blood from our donors, that is a must," he began firmly, but then lightened his tone. "But I understand that every now and then there are occasions where a human needs a bit of alcohol, which is why I look the other way when it comes to the secret cabinet."

"Well, you don't really look away," I corrected. "You look directly inside, it seems."

Victor's face was blank at my joke, and I thought for sure he was going to kill me. But a second later he erupted with laughter and patted me on the back, though a little too hard. "You have got me there, young one. I do look in the cabinet, only to see how quickly the supply disappears. Tonight it seems many of the trainees are celebrating surviving their first week of training. Which I cannot blame them, it is quite a feat. I do not blame any of the humans as long as it is not a regular occurrence and that they do not donate their blood if they have partaken. The rules are pretty simple, although there are always those that cannot abide by them."

"Like Charlotte?" I asked and received a curious glance. "Charlotte Shaw? She was one of your blood donors a while..."

"Yes, Jonah, I know who she is."

"Charlotte is Ashlyn's...er...my girlfriend's mother. Cameron told us about why she was kicked out."

"Ah, Charlotte," he sighed. "Such a beautiful person on the outside, and so terribly troubled on the inside. She was one of my favorites. I was the first to discover her tainted blood and I tried helping her, but she convinced me that she had everything under control. It wasn't until several Warriors came to me with complaints. I realized that I needed to protect my children more than a troubled human, even if I did have feelings for her.

"It was sad to see her fall so low. I even gave her money several times to help her back on her feet, but an addict is an addict. Or at least so I've read. But all my feelings of guilt were shed the minute she accused me of fathering her child. Such a betrayal could not be forgiven."

"Yeah, but you still had Cameron go out there and make sure. You must have thought there was some possibility."

Victor looked at me with another blank expression, and I thought that this time he would kill me for sure. "Jonah, there are many hard and fast rules that I have lived by my entire existence. One of which is that I do not sleep with humans, specifically because they can reproduce. This world does not need a little Victor or Victoria running around. My Warriors are the closest thing I will ever have to children, and I am resolved to that. Charlotte knew very well she was wrongly accusing me, and for what? Money? By sending Cameron, I sent a message to anyone who might try to threaten me. I do not back down, Jonah, not under any circumstance. It is that perseverance and drive that will get my grandson back, and your girlfriend for that matter. Although after what I saw tonight, do you still want her back?"

"Of course I do," I replied and then looked back at the ballroom where Tosh had disappeared. "Oh, that was just a misunderstanding." Victor tightened his lips as he nodded slowly. "Really, sir, I love Ashlyn, I wouldn't be here if I didn't. Tosh just got the wrong idea, and between the alcohol and the picture at Oliver's, I just wasn't seeing the signs."

"What about a picture at Oliver's?"

"Livy drew a picture tonight, there was this group of women she was calling the mommies. Looks like Aidan is making hybrids of his own."

"I suppose Cameron will be informing me of this upon his return. This is not quite the news we wanted."

"You and me both," I replied as my hands went through my scalp and scratched it harshly. "Like Bri said, we don't know if it's true and it doesn't look like Ash has been hurt yet."

"It doesn't make you feel any better though, does it?"

"Not a fucking bit," I replied and Victor gave a little snicker.

"I can see why everyone is so fond of you, Jonah," he said as he stood from the stone steps. "When this nonsense is all said and done, are you planning on returning to Connecticut?"   .

"I believe so."

Victor nodded with a surprised expression. "Well, if you change your mind, let me know. I can always put in a good word for you at Facility West."

"But they don't use drivers."

"You can't be a driver forever, Jonah. You are meant for bigger and better things. Just promise we'll talk before you leave."

"Why me?" I replied honestly. "You don't even know me."

Victor laughed as he started walking back to his office. "I would hardly say that."

Slowly I pushed myself up from the steps, groaning at the way my back and butt hurt. Knowing there was one last thing I needed to do.

After making my way back through the maze to the human wing, I knocked on Tosh's door, but no one answered. I knocked again. "Tosh? Tosh? I know you're there, please open up. I look like an asshole standing out here."

"Go away," she cried from inside.

"Tosh, please. Just talk to me."

"I said go…"

"It wasn't the scars, Tosh."

Suddenly the door flew open. Tosh's face was red and blotchy, her eyes swollen from the tears that were still flowing down her cheeks.

"Tosh, I'm sorry if I led you on. It wasn't my intention."

Tosh's fingers curled around the edge of the door, trying desperately to pull it from my grip. "Stop, Jonah, please."

"I love Ashlyn. That's why I pushed you away, not because of the scars. I just can't do that to either of you."

Tosh gave up trying to get the door back and hit it with the palm of her hand. "I know you love Ashlyn, that's why I'm so stupid. I'm just like my sister."

I opened the door fully and took a step inside. "You are nothing like your sister, and if you ever say something like that again I'll…well I don't know, but I'll do something." Tosh laughed slightly and had to wipe the tears from her cheeks. "Listen, I meant everything I said about your scars.

You should wear them proudly, show people what you've survived, and I promise you will find the right person who accepts all of you. You shouldn't settle for anything less, Tosh."

Tosh crossed her arm in front of her chest, every brick of her wall back in place as she said, "Says the boy with the perfect skin, the perfect girlfriend, and the perfect family living the perfect fairytale life. I know what I am, Jonah, and I don't need people in my life trying to convince me otherwise."

I took a step back into the frame of the door, and wrapped my hand around the doorknob. "If you consider what I'm going through now a fairytale life, then you really do have your foot up your ass. No one's perfect, Tosh. When you grow up you'll realize that."

I closed the door before she could throw anything at me, or even just punch me in the face. But once I got out into the hallway the guilt hit me. She was Katie Bell's age, dealing with the same uncertainties, fearful of both the path she was taking and the one she wasn't. I took another breath and opened the door back up again. Tosh was standing in exactly the same place, her hands covering her face while she sobbed. She looked up as I stepped back inside her room, a questioning look on her face.

"It wasn't the scars," I said firmly. That was all I needed her to know, and with a slight nod of her head I had a sliver of hope that she believed me.

Chapter Forty-one

Brianna

"They look so precious, I hate to disturb them," I said to Cameron who was standing next to me, the two of us looking down at Daddy O sleeping in his recliner with Livy tucked tightly into his chest.

Cameron smiled as he leaned down and lifted Livy into his arms, her body flopping over his shoulder like a ragdoll. Daddy O flinched awake, panicked at first and then relaxing with realization. He began the slow process of trying to get out of his chair, sliding and pumping his way forward.

"Daddy O, you don't need to get up," I said as I extended my arm to him, but he pushed it away.

"I ain't dead yet, 'Lil Bri. I can say g'bye to ya's," he grunted as he got to the edge of his chair and pushed himself up. He gave me a quick kiss on the cheek and then stepped past me to get to Cameron. He petted Livy's curly hair and kissed her temple, then patted Cam's arm. "Take care a my girls, son."

"Yes, Da," Cameron replied with a sad, crooked smile. "I always try, though not always successfully."

Daddy O squinted his left eye.

"Now don't go getting' all mopey on me," Daddy O warned. "I think 'Lil Bri calls it your moody broody act."

"Daddy O!"

Cameron let out a little laugh as Daddy O shrugged.

"Just tellin' the truth, sugar. Just like I'm gonna tell you, son. I know yur workin' hard over there. You all will get it done."

Cameron gave a slight nod. "I am going to put Olivia in the car," he said and turned toward the door.

I watched him walk out the front door, the revelations of the night sinking into his shoulders. No one was the same after Jonah left. We all knew the stakes were higher now. The pressure was intense before, now it would start crushing people. Daddy O's warm hand squeezed mine, bringing my attention to him. I found his blue eyes looking at me with a mixture of concern and love.

I gave him a little smile as I patted his hand. "I'm happy you're here. We haven't lived this close to one another since I was little."

"You and Cameron seem to be doin' better," he said, getting right to the point he'd probably wanted to make all night but couldn't.

"Yeah, we're much better," I smiled. "Just give us our son back and things will be just peachy."

Daddy O sighed with an understanding nod. "I'm glad ya made things right with Miss Sera. I kept tellin' everybody ya would, you just had to do it in yur own time. Always been that way, ain't about to change now."

"At least I'm consistent."

"Well, ya get that from me. It would drive yur Mama Jo up a wall. I'm tryin' to do better with Madelyn, but you know I'm just an old dog sometimes."

"But you're my old dog."

Daddy O smiled, pulled my forehead to his lips and then patted my cheek. "I'm glad yur better, sugar. Ya had me worried there for a bit."

"I'm sorry. I just couldn't get outta my head."

"Unfortunately you know who ya got that from."

Great. He was comparing me to my mother. Sadly, he was right. Although when Shelby went crazy they committed her to a mental institution.

"Now ya'll take care goin' home," he said once he realized I had no comeback. "And don't think that just 'cuz me and Maddy are so close you have to always come around. Ya'll gotchur own lives and enough to worry about now, don't think ya gotta take care of us old folks. Don't need ya'll comin' here all hours of the day and night."

"I get it, Daddy O," I said rolling my eyes. "You and Maddy wanna run around naked, and you don't need your granddaughter comin' in and cramping your style."

Daddy O squinted his eyes warningly. "Language, little girl."

"I didn't say one bad word," I laughed, and then hugged him tightly. Just the feeling of my grandfather's arms, his smell, the feel of his wrinkled cheek against mine always brought me back home. It grounded me, made me feel safe and secure. It was why I always ran to him when I was losing myself. Daddy O was my shelter, and now he was closer than he had ever been before. I loved that, and I would need him. He knew that.

And that was proven when he nuzzled his nose to my ear and whispered, "You're strong, sugar, you're strong like yur Mama Jo. Don't give into those dark thoughts, you got too many people countin' on ya. An Cameron can't get through this withoutcha either. That boy's got the weight of the world on his shoulders."

"I know," I replied, hugging Daddy O tighter, trying not to let the tears fall from my eyes. "I need to do better."

"Yes you do," he said sternly as he released me and gave me another warning look. "Neither of ya's gonna get through this without the other. Ya'll owe it to those chiluns."

"I know."

"I know ya know. I won't lecture ya anymore. You know it's only cuz I love ya, sugar."

I smiled and gave him a goodbye kiss on the cheek and then said goodbye to Maddy and my parents. I left the adorable ranch and crunched across the gravel driveway to the SUV convoy. Cameron had successfully fastened a still sleeping Livy into her car seat and through the opened backseat door I could see Dr. John locking Wills into his seat, although he was very much awake. Cameron turned when he heard me coming across the driveway and gave me the cutest little wink as he closed the backseat door.

You really are the sexiest thing alive, I Pushed lightly into his head.

His head flinched slightly and then he gave me my favorite crooked smile as he touched his fingertips to his heart.

"Oh stop making googly eyes at each other," Renee groaned as she crooked her arm through mine. The wine had hit her hard. I could smell it on her breath. I missed wine, especially at times like these.

"I have to say I'm a little jealous of you right now."

"This hair, these boobs, I'd be jealous every day if I were you," she laughed, but then hugged her cheek against my arm. "Sorry. Tonight kinda got awkward so I kinda got drunk."

"I would have been right there with you if I could have," I sighed.

Just then Alex came around to our SUV, his defenses up as he continued to survey the surroundings. His deep voice was very firm as he said, "Bri, we need you to do a perimeter check."

"Is everyone settled in?" I said noticing Kyla in the front seat of the SUV behind ours.

He nodded. "Jer, Dev, and Fabi are in the first truck, Cam in the second, Ky and I in the third, and your father is in the house. Let us know if you see any others."

I took in a deep breath and exhaled in order to clear my head, but before I could survey my surroundings, Renee flinched on my arm. "Do I need a metal jacket or something? Is this like an X-ray? I don't want to get cancer from your Vampire-mind-trick-radiation beam."

Slowly I looked down on Renee, doing a quick scan of the area as I performed the slowest and most dramatic eye roll of all time.

"I guess we'll find out," I said and then looked at Alex. "We're good. John, take your wife before I smack her."

"Can't do that, twin," Renee said as John took her away from me. "I'm a protected person. Vampire laws say so."

Cameron shook his head from the driver's seat and suddenly three SUVs roared to life. Knowing there was no way John would be able to fit in the third row, I took the job of sitting with Renee in the back. She didn't seem too worried about getting cancer from me anymore since she practically collapsed across my lap.

Once everyone was settled we bobbled down the gravel driveway and began our winding trip home. They had called it a heat run. Some kind of tactical term for dodging anyone who might be following you. Darting down back streets, taking a very circuitous route instead of a direct one. With the number of turns, hills, and the speeds they were driving, I wasn't sure if Renee was going to make it. Her face was turning green and I could see the muscles in her throat contracting and relaxing as if she were trying to hold it in.

Five minutes later she was squeezing my hand tightly, her free hand covering her mouth, and a panicked look on her face.

"Cam, we gotta pull over. And don't argue, I know it's bad, but I'd rather not have the children covered in vomit."

Cameron glanced at me in the rearview mirror, a tiny bit of fear in his eyes over stopping now. Dr. John threw his arms up in frustration, cursing his wife from the front seat. Renee muttered an apology through her hand, and held on tight as Cameron pulled over and slammed to a stop. The truck was barely in park before I had the backseat door open and Renee out in the open to heave her guts out.

Kyla came out of her SUV and stood next to me while the boys yelled at one another about the dangers of stopping in the middle of a heat run. Dr. John stepped down out of the front seat and went to shut the door to shield his son from seeing his mother in such an embarrassing state. Just before the door snapped shut, there was a coo from inside.

"Aw-awbie," Wills said tentatively, "I fink Wivy is havin' anudder bad dweam."

John quickly pulled the door back open and stepped aside as I quickly transferred Renee into Kyla's arms. Livy's little hand was flexed and stretched out in front of her while the muscles in her face winced. I stepped up into the truck and squeezed into the space between Livy and the driver's seat.

Just as I was about to take Livy's hand, the other passenger door flew open and Cameron stood staring at me with an intense and worried expression. His hand stretched toward me, ready to take the ride into Livy's dream with me.

"I'll last longer if it's just me," I said as I squeezed his hand and lowered it down. "I'll send you as much as I can, just stay where you are."

Cameron nodded and circled his finger in the air causing his brothers and Kyla to surround the SUV while Fabi and Nikki took control of Renee. I closed my eyes, pressed my fingers into Livy's outstretched hand, and melted into her.

The night was pitch black, the moon barely peeking through the canopy of trees overhead. Only a few feet ahead I could see myself standing at the edge of a high ridge, Jackson curled tightly around my left leg while Livy hung from my back. My left arm was stretched out behind me, my hand cupped and tense. The rest of the scene looked almost frozen as members of our direct family hovered low to the ground clawing at the rich earth beneath them while their faces contorted with pain.

I stepped closer to the ridge and looked down to see a large gathering of what I assumed were Vamps. I knew they'd be there, I'd seen this scene before, and every time I saw them their numbers seemed greater. From my gut I Pushed the image out to where I imagined Cameron to be. He would be worried at the enemy's numbers, as well he should be. They looked like an army filling the small valley below us. In front, as usual, were Aidan and Gorum standing there poised and ready to pounce.

"Baby, please!" my other self screamed, but Olivia shook her head.

"Just do it, Wivy!" Jack-Jack yelled up to his sister.

"Baby..." Bri number two grunted for reasons I didn't understand, "...I...n-need...you."

With a shaking hand, I watched as Olivia placed her small hand flat against my doppelganger's neck, bowed her head slightly, and closed her eyes as I stretched out my right hand. A second later a bright crimson light shot out from my outstretched hand like a laser beam. It was Livy's gift, her power of controlling hybrids like Jack and I controlled Vampires, flowing out of me and shooting toward the enemy. I followed the bright red beams and saw a sea of cloudy crimson lights. Why had we never seen this before? There were never lights of any kind, Vampire or hybrid, in all the other versions of this dream. Why now?

Before I could ponder on it any further, a big wave of energy jetted from my doppelganger and I watched as she fell to the ground. Everyone in sight, our side and theirs hit the ground, all had been hit. The twins were crying underneath me, Cameron was stumbling toward me, finally pulling Jack-Jack up into one arm and the other Brianna into his side. Livy, still sobbing, clung to my doppelganger's chest while Cameron ran us all through the battlefield.

And that's exactly what it became, a total battlefield. Vampires from our side flew over us toward the enemy, the enemy flying overhead towards the Warriors. I ran along the sidelines of the battle, keeping pace with my dream family, crashing through anything and anyone in my path like a ghost. Brianna and Cameron, each with a child tightly wrapped around them, dove and dodged and leapt out of the way of both friend and foe as they covered hundreds of yards of forest, and I took note of everything around us and continued projecting to where I thought the real Cameron stood outside.

Finally, dream Cameron and Bri came to a stop on the topside of *another ridge, and again the dream took a nasty turn. Aidan stood in front of them, his arms outstretched towards Jack who immediately fled to his side. Olivia's arms were tightly clasped around dream Bri's neck. Aidan grabbed Livy around her waist and tried pulling her to him, but Livy cried and clawed at dream Bri's neck.*

"Baby girl, you have to go," my doppelganger yelled as she pried Livy's hands from her neck. "Let go, baby, you have to go!"

"No, Mama!" Livy screamed and stiffened her body. "Mama, pwease!"

My feet kept inching toward them, wanting to step in and stop the madness. I had done it before, but I knew I had to keep watching and taking note of everything. My nails were digging into my palms as Livy continued to scream and wail, begging her mother not to give her away.

Aidan leaned in closer and was able to wrap one arm around Livy's chest and pull her away. Livy screamed and cried at me to help her. She could see me in her dream, watching as Aidan ran away with her, away from her parents who were supposed to protect her, but were now simply letting her go.

Unable to take anymore, I broke up the dream and snapped back into my body.

Before I even opened my eyes I could hear my daughter's cries. Olivia sat crying in her car seat, pulling and pushing at the seatbelts to unfasten them. I fumbled with the buttons and after a few seconds they snapped free. Livy untangled herself from the straps and pushed forward out of the seat. I thrust my arms forward to catch her, but instead she leapt into her father's arms. Shaking and sobbing into his chest, her tiny hands clinching handfuls of his sweater for dear life. Cameron looked at me in shock over her shoulder while he tried consoling her. I placed my hand on her back and she climbed further up her father's chest to get out of my reach.

"Don't let her, Ada, don't let her give me away," she wailed, sending daggers into my heart.

Cameron placed his hand on the back of her head and nuzzled his mouth to her ear. "No one is giving you away, lovey. No one will ever..."

"I saw her, Ada!" Livy cried as she pushed up from Cam's chest and then pointed accusingly in my direction. "Mama gave me to Aidan again!"

Cameron quietly shushed her and pulled her back into his chest. My mind was racing, emotions spanning from hopelessness to anger and I didn't have the slightest idea what to do. My son had run away, and now my daughter was afraid of me. A parent's worst nightmare. Someone should just take me out back and shoot me.

I looked over to my darling nephew, little Wills, still sitting in his car seat, his eyes large with uncertainty. My fingers trailed down the side of his left cheek, the corners of his mouth creasing into a smile. Carefully I unsnapped his harness and freed him from the car seat straps. I pulled him from his seat and whispered in his ear, "Can you make Livy feel better?"

"Sure I can, Awbie," he replied while he vigorously nodded his head. Quickly he climbed over me onto the floor of the car near the door and pulled on Livy's shirt to get her attention.

Seeing that I would merely be in the way, I slid from one passenger side to the other and exited the SUV. Kyla stood right at the door's edge, but her expression and concern was not what I wanted to see. I needed Southern avoidance right now. I didn't want to talk about why my daughter was terrified of me.

Renee was leaning into Fabi's side, still slumped and moaning while Nikki held out a tissue for Renee to wipe her mouth. Alex came to stand next to Kyla while Devin and Jared stayed with Cameron and John on the other side of the truck.

"Well?" Alex asked. "What did you see?"

I leaned my butt up against the side of the truck, my knees bent with my hands resting on them for support. My head was achy, my body suddenly feeling tired from the Dreamwalking. I titled my head up to see him and replied, "Same battle as last time. Very large wooded area. I'm sure Cam can draw a picture later."

Alex shifted his weight back and forth between his legs, impatient and unhappy with my response.

"Any other details?" he pressed. "Position of the moon? Landmarks? Type of trees, even."

I sighed and closed my eyes, trying to picture the scene again. "It was night, the moon was coming through the trees. There were lots of trees, very tall trees, pines maybe. Very hilly, lots of steep ridges. That's all I got, Alex."

"Come on, Bri, think," he kept pushing, but Kyla squeezed his arm to stop. He gave her a deep sigh in reply and then lowered his eyes. After a second or two of silence he shook his head and said, "What about...was there anything different?"

"Just more of them," I groaned as I pushed myself off the truck. "Everything was the same. Us on one side, them on another, me on the edge of the ridge standing there like a fool."

Nikki snorted, and then realized it. Her head shot up in my direction and looked at all of us with worried eyes. She cringed and tried to distract herself by helping Renee. And then it hit me.

"Wait!" I said to Alex and grabbed his arm. "There was something different. I could see Livy's Push." Alex knitted his brows together. "I was standing on the ridge, Jack's on my leg, Livy's on my back. I was begging her to help me, even Jack was egging her on. She put her hand on my neck and a second later red mist came out of my hand. That's her Push, it's red because she sees hybrids. It shot out of my hand toward Aidan's army. Most of their lights were red, but cloudy. They must be drinking a lot of hybrid blood."

"And you didn't see it any other time?"

I shook my head. "No, and I only saw Livy's. If Jack was helping me too, why couldn't I see his Push, or my own?"

"Because it wasn't your dream," Nikki answered, causing everyone's head to flinch in her direction, and even startling Nikki into silence.

"Go on, Nikki," Alex pressed.

She swallowed nervously and then responded, "Brianna was in Livy's dream. Livy can only control hybrids, she can only see her power. She can't see Jack's, right?" I shook my head. "So it makes sense that you wouldn't see Jack's because you were only seeing her dream."

"But every other time I saw nothing," I challenged.

Alex turned toward me. "Yes, but the twins were together those times, weren't they?" I nodded. "Jack can't see Livy's power, and Livy can't see Jack's. So maybe when they're together it's neutral. This is great news, Bri."

"How's that?"

Alex gave a sly grin. "Let's say Aidan has his people drinking hybrid blood, he's doing it to protect them against you and Jack. He doesn't know what Livy can do, he might even think she's just like Jack. If the dream is accurate, we have a huge advantage."

"If the dream is accurate, Alex, I hand my daughter off to Aidan."

"Your dreams weren't always one-hundred percent accurate."

"Ok then," I replied snidely. "Which part do we bet on? Which piece of that dream do you want to take the chance on?"

Alex sighed and tightened his lips into a thin line, but Kyla stepped forward just behind his shoulder with an eyebrow raised at me.

"The first part, of course," she answered. "We all know there's no way in hell you'd ever voluntarily give Livy over to Aidan."

I scoffed. "Doesn't mean I don't do it un-voluntarily."

Our group went silent just as Cameron came around the front of the SUV.

"Olivia has calmed down," he said. "We should get moving."

Everyone hopped to attention and filed back into their assigned trucks. I climbed into the backseat, kissing Wills on the forehead and thanking him for helping with Livy. My daughter sat in her car seat next to him, her cheeks flush and wet while she continued to sniffle. She was still visibly upset and frightened and there was nothing she wanted from me. I thought I at least had until she was a teenager before she began to hate me.

Before I could sulk any further, Dr. John pushed Renee up into the backseat and I guided her the rest of the way to the third row. She smelled like vomit and sour wine, and strands of her red hair were sticking to her face. She plopped down next to me and sighed her foul breath into my face.

"What did I miss?"

Chapter Forty-two

Brianna

Renee wanted to buy a house, a place to raise Wills in comfort and where he could easily run and play with any future siblings. But we weren't standing in a house, we were standing in a mansion that swallowed the one I had in Connecticut. She and Dr. John had been saving, he made a hell of a lot of money at Facility West, and she wanted to show it. The kitchen was almost the size of the first floor of her Boston apartment.

"Re," I started, "why do you need a kitchen this big? You don't cook."

Renee popped her hip and placed her hands on the enormous kitchen island.

"I don't, but you do," she replied. "And I know for a fact you're gonna get itchy to cook being in the manor, and this will provide that opportunity."

Kyla and Fabi laughed under their breath as they also congregated around the island. The realtor was keeping an eye on Wills and Livy who were playing in the empty living room.

"So you're just thinking about my needs if you buy this house," I said.

Renee quirked her lips and scrunched her eyebrows together. "Well, not so much of an if."

"You bought the house already, haven't you."

"We haven't 'bought' it," she replied with a sly smile. "But we 'might' have put in an offer this morning."

Fabi and I rolled our eyes while Kyla popped her hip and raised her eyebrow in Renee's direction.

"So the whole I-can't-do-this-without-you-guys-I-need-you thing was a scam?" Kyla asked without even a smidge of humor, and Renee immediately noticed.

"Ky," Renee began with puppy dog eyes, "none of you have left the manor since we had dinner at Daddy O's, and that was almost two weeks ago."

"I have," Fabi corrected.

Renee gave him an evil eye. "That's only because Devin won't let you stay at the manor."

Fabi made a hissing noise, and clawed the air in front of him. "Well I see motherhood hasn't taken out the b-i-t-c-h out of you."

I titled my ear toward the living room, waiting to hear if Livy would tattle on her aunt, but nothing came. Honestly, there was very little noise at all which worried me because that usually meant trouble.

Kyla relaxed her stance and leaned over the island. "Re, it's dangerous to have Livy outside of the manor. We shouldn't have done this, it's too risky."

Renee sighed. "There are three trucks out there filled with Warr..." Kyla squeezed her arm and Renee rolled her eyes. "The house is surrounded and my realtor is probably thinking we're part of the mob. Thanks for that, by the way." She looked across the island at me with sad eyes. "I just wanted to get you out for a couple of hours, Bri. My niece still needs to be a kid." Renee lowered her voice and looked at each one of us. "And I really wanted you all to see this place. This...this could be my home. My 'home', John's 'home', the place where my grandchildren will run around some day. And...I just wanted you all here before I take another terrifying leap into being a grownup."

I walked around the island and squeezed her shoulder into my chest. The other half of the twins gang came to her other side to complete the moment. Renee sighed deeply and patted our hands.

"Ok, ok, kumbaya moment over. I'm officially a human-vampy sandwich," she said with a little relief as we all took a step away. "So, have you changed your minds about Christmas shopping?"

"No," Kyla replied before I could. "It's too risky. Livy's pictures are getting worse. We need to stay close to the manor where we're safe."

"And where you don't have to keep looking ahead," I pointed out sympathetically.

Kyla just about had a panic attack when we left the manor, watching every second ahead in case something was to happen. She looked ragged, which in Kyla's case meant her long orange hair was frizzy with several strands dangling in front of her face rather than perfectly coiffed. Everyone was on edge, especially since time continued to pass without results. Cameron and I were just numb. It was our only defense against the blows that kept coming at us.

To make matters worse, shortly after our night at Daddy O's, Livy began asking how she and Jack were made. At first we gave her the explanation that when mommies and daddies love each other, a mommy can grow a baby in her belly. Livy rebutted with, 'then why are all of Aidan's mommies so sad?' We couldn't explain that, but it didn't really matter since she corrected us in her meaning and was asking why she and her brother had fangs and other kids didn't. Our 'because you're special' answer only satisfied her until the third time she asked. When I finally asked her where this was coming from she stated Jack kept asking her. Apparently Aidan wasn't too happy with our answer either. Aidan was getting desperate, and desperate people did dangerous things.

"Bri?"

I flinched my head in Renee's direction. "Hmm?"

"Yes or no?"

"Um, yes," I replied trying to cover myself.

Renee squinted her right eye at me. "Oh good. So I'll go bleach my hair as soon as we're done here."

"Wait, w-what?"

Renee pursed her lips and shook her head, I had been caught.

"I knew you weren't listening," she scolded. "Stop thinking for a couple of hours, will ya?"

"Give her a break, Re," Fabi scolded right back.

"If I give her any more breaks there won't be a single bone left in her body," Renee replied, though I could see through her tone to her sarcasm.

I straightened up from the island and looked around. "I hate your kitchen, and the paint in this house is hideous."

"We're so dysfunctional it's not even funny," she said with a smile as she, too, saw through me. It was the benefit of being friends for so long.

"Fabi, what time do I need to take you to the airport?"

I looked at Fabi. "I thought you weren't going to Boston for another couple of days?"

Fabi fluttered his lips in frustration. "Ormond is being a pill and demanding that I come back. The coven is drowning in debt because no new business is coming in."

"But what about standing clients?" Kyla asked. "Dante's coven was always tremendously successful."

"They're being poached," Fabi replied. "It's as if someone stole the client list and they're being swept up left and right. So Ormond is calling an emergency session and basically told me that if I don't come I'll be excommunicated."

"That's awful," I said. "Do you know who they're all going to?"

He nodded. "It's a new firm, Fiba Consulting."

"Fiba?" Kyla said, squinting her eyes at Fabi. "As in F-I-B-A? As in flip the two vowels around and it spells Fabi?"

"Damn you're good," he said. "It's been almost a year now, and Ormond still hasn't figured it out."

"But Fabi," Renee began, "if you hate the coven so much, why don't you just leave?"

Fabi's face fell as he sighed. "I've thought about it, but I...I just...can't. I'm sabotaging my own coven, and yet I can't bring myself to just pick up and leave."

"Er...why not? Kyla did."

"I didn't leave, Re," Kyla replied. "Vivienne isn't my maker, I just joined them because I was tired of being a solitary. I can't imagine what it would feel like if..."

"It's like your ripping yourself in two," I interrupted, causing all heads to turn toward me. "I was so messed up I even gave Victor my pin. It was like I was giving him an appendage. Of course he didn't take it seriously because he knew I was just..."

"Effing crazy," Renee answered.

"*Anyway*," I continued, "Fabi, you know we're all here for you. We're your family, too."

Fabi gave a skeptical look. "That is until Devin decides he's done with me."

"That's not true," all three women answered at once.

"Let's be honest, ladies. Devin holds all the cards. I alienated the

Negotiators the minute I started sleeping with a Warrior, yet Devin won't even entertain telling Victor we're together. He could turn around tomorrow and say we're done, and I'd have nothing. Hell, he won't even let me stay in the manor during this whole ordeal. Do you honestly think he'd let me drop by the manor and visit you all if we weren't together?"

I shrugged. "Fabi, we're not going anywhere. We're family. But if Devin ever stupidly breaks up with you, we can all hang out in Renee's obnoxiously big house."

Everyone around the island laughed, and kept laughing since it felt so good. I could suddenly picture us gathered around this very kitchen island for years to come, laughing and gossiping just as we were now. I couldn't help but want this house for Renee as much as she did.

Just then little Wills padded into the kitchen and pulled on the edge of my sweater. I knelt down to his level as his face scrunched up with a very concerned expression.

"Awbie, somefing's wong wiff Wivy," he said.

"Really? What's wrong?" I replied.

Wills shrugged. "I dunno. She says she doesn't feel good."

I stood from the floor and directed Wills over towards Renee before taking a step out of the kitchen. Kyla was next to me in a flash, which wasn't a good thing since Renee's realtor was in the living room. Thankfully she had her back to us, but turned as soon as she heard our heels clicking across the hardwood entryway.

"Could she be getting a cold or something?" Kyla asked.

I gave her a worried look as I whispered, "That child hasn't been sick a day in her life."

Olivia walked somberly across the large empty living room, her usual sprightliness gone. Her cheeks were slack, her bottom lip and jaw hanging in a pitiful pout. Anyone else would think exactly like Kyla, she looked like a child with a cold. But I knew it had to be more than that.

"Baby girl, what's the matter?"

She didn't answer at first. Instead, she held her arms up and waited for me to pick her up. Once I did, she nuzzled her head onto my shoulder, her fluffy black curls tickling my chin and ear.

"Mama, can we go home now?"

I turned to Kyla who immediately nodded. "I'll get the trucks ready," she said, and left through the front door.

"Is she feeling all right?" the realtor asked.

"I'm sure she's fine. She just might be coming down with something," I lied. "'Tis the season and all. Thank you so much for letting us in to see the house, it really is beautiful."

The realtor smiled and stepped over to Renee as I walked Olivia outside. Her little body was glued to my chest and she didn't move a muscle as we approached the convoy of SUVs. Alex was calling out orders to the other Warriors while Kyla held open a door to our truck. When I tried lifting Livy into the truck, her grip on my sweater tightened so I stopped and gave her a quick kiss on the temple. When I tried lifting her again, her legs cinched around my waist and her arms were like a vice around my neck.

"Is everything ok?" Alex asked as he came around the SUV.

I placed my hands on my hips and Livy clung to me like the monkey her father nicknamed her after.

"Do you have a crowbar?" I asked flatly, not sure why my daughter was acting like this, or what I was going to be able to do about it.

By this time Renee and Fabi had exited the house, and I laughed a little to myself thinking that the massive two-story colonial suited her. She had definitely moved up from the one-bedroom condo in Connecticut. It seemed like such a distant memory. Just me and her - partners in crime singing in the church choir, sneaking a lunch here and there to talk about what we would do if we'd been dealt another hand. Funny enough, this was that magic hand, and it could all be taken away at any moment.

"Earth to Bri," Renee said, waving her hand in front of my face. "You space-out way too often, you know that, right?"

"And you're buying way too much house, you know that, right?" I replied and received a loving smile.

I smiled and kissed Renee on the cheek before she pulled Wills up into her arms. Livy didn't even lift her head as I leaned over and kissed Wills on the head.

"Mommy," Wills began, "can I go to the manor with Awbie? I want to stay wif Wivy."

"Sorry, little man, we need to go see Daddy at work and then take Uncle Fabi to the airport," Renee replied and Wills gave her a very sad pout.

"But Mommy, Wivy needs me."

"Wills, your mommy needs you to help her right now. You'll see Livy later tonight," I said, trying to distract him.

"Wivy, I'll come back soon," he said as he reached over and touched Livy's shoulder.

Livy shuddered in my arms and didn't answer. I gave Renee an apologetic look, and she shook her head in a silence response telling me not to worry. I stepped up into the SUV with Livy still clinging to my chest as I sat down in the backseat.

"Baby girl, you need to get into your seat," I begged softly in her ear. "Uncle Alex can't drive the car until you do."

Olivia pushed herself up from my chest and looked behind her to where Alex sat in the driver's seat.

"Uncle Alex, is that twue?"

"Sorry, Livybean," Alex replied in his deep voice, "that's absolutely true. Everyone's waiting on you because you're the most precious cargo we have."

Livy thought about it for another second and then resigned to climbing over into her car seat. After I buckled her in she snaked her little arms around mine and pulled it to her chest. I gave Alex the go-ahead to start moving, but leaned into my daughter to comfort her. Jack was the snuggler. Jack was the needy one. This was so unlike Livy.

"Baby girl, what's the matter? Can you tell Mama?" I asked, nuzzling into the side of her face.

In a very soft and pitiful voice she replied, "I dunno know, Mama. I just feel funny." Livy lowered her voice even further when she said, "I fink it's Jack."

I tried not to react to Olivia's statement, but then had to try harder not to react to Kyla's gasp from the front seat. After counting calmly to five I finally said, "Has he said anything to you? Is something happening?"

"I dunno," she sighed as she snuggled back into my arm and officially stopped the conversation. She certainly was my daughter, bad habits and all.

The rest of the ride was quiet. With so many turns and backtracks I was surprised when the manor actually came upon us. As the guards waved us through the gates it saddened me how our new home had become more like Fort Knox. Yet another reason I wanted this nonsense to be over with.

Livy unbuckled herself from her seat even before Alex had pulled up to the front of the manor and climbed into my lap, draping herself over my chest. As we pulled up to the front door I noticed Cameron stepping out onto the landing. Once the SUV was in park, Kyla kindly opened my car door and I awkwardly stepped down from the truck with Livy clinging to me like a tumor. Cameron gave me a peculiar look as I walked up the stone steps to meet him.

"How was the house?" he asked as his hand gently caressed Livy's head.

"Beautiful and insanely big, but it's Renee so what do you expect," I replied and then bounced Livy a little to see if she would loosen her grip. "But this little one says she isn't feeling well."

Cameron knitted his eyebrows together in confusion, and then a second later his expression changed to worry.

I nuzzled my face into Livy's hair as I said, "Do you want to go to Ada?"

Slowly Livy lifted her head from my chest, a very pitiful pout etched into her face as she looked at her father and nodded her head. Cameron extended his arms and pulled Livy from my chest. Livy gave a little smile when Cameron kissed her cheek a dozen times very quickly, releasing even a tiny laugh. But her happiness was short lived and the sadness settled in once again causing her to rest up against Cameron's shoulder. I shrugged and shook my head. I didn't know what to do. I felt helpless as usual. Cameron pulled me into his other side and walked his girls into the manor.

"Any news this morning," I asked as we stepped inside.

"It is too soon to know. Connor and Jared are still fielding calls," Cameron replied as he steered us toward the kitchen. It was the tail end of lunch so we were swimming upstream against the current of humans returning to their activities. Among them were the Warrior trainees heading back to the training area, although Jonah seemed to have tagged along with them today instead of looming around in the library.

"Did you go and see the house?" he asked.

"Yeah, it's gorgeous. You should have come with us."

"Nah," he replied, "I decided to watch Tosh and the others train today. Plus, that was totally girl time. I didn't want to get in the middle of that."

Cameron laughed in agreement and opened his mouth to comment, but in the same moment Livy snapped upright. Her eyes were wide with fear as she looked to her left and right and then stared blankly in front of her.

"Monkey?" Cameron asked softly as he placed his index finger under her chin and tried turning her face toward him, but she resisted. "Olivia is it Jackson? Are you…"

"No, no, no, no!" she screamed, causing everyone in the busy corridor to freeze and stare.

"Livy, what's the matter," I said as I tried taking her hand to see if Jack was in her head, but she slapped my hand away.

"No, no! Go away, go away!" she yelled as she pushed away from Cameron and launched herself into the air and then landed on her feet like a cat. Cam and I knelt to the ground, trying to get close to her, but she slowly started backing away. Her face was full of fear, her little chest heaving up and down while she stretched her arms out in front of her defensively. "I want Mama," she cried.

"I'm right here, baby," I replied, edging closer and trying to take her hand again, but she screamed and backed away another few steps.

"I want Mama," Livy cried again, this time with tears streaking down her cheeks. "I wanna go home."

"But you are home, Olivia," Cameron said in a calming tone as he crawled closer.

I touched his shoulder and pointed at Livy's face. Her eyes were looking past us, slightly unfocused even. "I don't think it's her, Cam. I think she's channeling Jack."

Cameron whipped his head back in Livy's direction, terror on his face over what might be happening to our son. He rose from the floor quickly, his arms extended about to forcibly take Livy away when she let out a scream so loud and high-pitched that I thought my head was going to split in two. My hands instantly covered my ears and when I looked around I noticed that every hybrid that was standing in the corridor collapsed to the floor. Their screams echoed off the stone walls as they covered their heads with their hands and convulsed in pain.

Knowing it was Olivia who was attacking the hybrids, I lifted her into my arms in order to run her out of the corridor. The second I touched her, an image of Jack flashed before me. He was being held down on a table by someone I didn't recognize, but at his feet was Aidan standing in front of a machine. Jack screamed as Aidan began turning a knob on the machine and suddenly a wave of electricity went shooting through my body. I fell backwards onto the stone floor, Livy's hand still touching my neck and sending me the shocks of electricity her brother was feeling. Streams of white light shot out from my forehead and fingers. No Vampire in the corridor was spared from my attack, and no hybrid from Livy. There was no controlling either of our powers, not even to stop it.

Suddenly Olivia was lifted off of my chest. I opened my eyes and saw Jonah running away with her.

"This way," I heard someone say in the distance.

Slowly and painfully, I rolled to my side. I could see Jonah's sneakers flicking up and down as he ran away from us. I tried pushing myself upright when someone pulled me into their side and began leading me in the direction Jonah had gone. I looked to my left and saw nothing but people strewn across the floor, some moaning, some crying, but all recovering from shocking pain. My feet still weren't under me, more like dragging behind me as I tried to regain my focus. My head fell back heavily and I was able to see that it was Julian who was helping me down the corridor. I had to admit that I wouldn't have guessed that in a million years.

"Liv...where is..." I said breathlessly.

"Father's quarters. That's where I'm taking you," Julian answered.

"Cam?"

"Behind us," he said as he looked over his shoulder. "One of the blood donors is helping him. Looks like they were the only ones that weren't affected."

"They're human, that's why," I moaned. "Lucky bastards."

Livy's cries echoed from Victor's suite. My motherly instincts made me press into the floor and pull away from Julian. By the time I reached the door Cameron was next to me squeezing my hand tightly and pulling me inside.

Livy was standing in the middle of the room, Jonah and Victor kneeling down in front of her while she wept uncontrollably. Immediately we ran to her, causing her to take a few cautious steps back. Her cheeks were wet and bright red, strands of her black hair sticking to her face. Carefully I pulled Jonah out of the way and took his place down in front of her. Livy's breathing began to slow and I was hoping it meant that the worst was over. Gently I pulled one of the strands of hair away from her cheek, and thankfully she did not pull away.

"Baby," I began softly, "can you tell us what's happening?"

She sniffled and jerked as she said, "They were hurting Jack-Jack, Mama. It weally, weally, hurt."

From the corner of my eye I could see Cam's hand clamp down on his mouth. I pulled another strand of Livy's hair away from her cheek in order to appear calm, although my insides were flipping around.

"Are they still hurting him?" I said, trying not to let my voice crack with emotion like it wanted to.

Livy shook her head and then her eyes unfocused and looked to the right, a sign that she was connected to her brother.

"No, they're yelling," she said and then paused, almost looking like she was eavesdropping. Then in a deep voice she said, "Tell us, Jack. Tell us, and we'll stop."

I bit my lip as I realized Livy was relaying the scene as it was unfolding. In the next moment she raised her voice back to her own timbre, sounding like Jack as he said, "I told you, Aidan, I told you. I dunno! Mama says we were born this way, we were just born."

Livy lowered her voice once again. "Your mother is a liar! Now tell us the truth, or I'll turn that dial again."

Cameron crushed my shoulder with his hand. We both knew what Aidan was after, and he had become desperate. Our son was being tortured because of Cameron's mistake, and now we were all feeling the effects.

"I dunno!" Livy cried. "Pwease, Aidan, pwease, I dunno!" Livy began to pull away once again, her brother's fear and actions becoming her own. "Mama, I want Mama. I wanna go home, no, no, no, not again!"

Livy let out another ear-splitting scream, her body shuddering violently as her brother shared his torture.

"Ada! Ada help me!" she screamed, tears flowing from her eyes. "Ada, Mama, pwease!"

"Brianna, do something!" Cameron yelled at me, his hands pulling at the ends of his hair.

"What do you want me to do!" I yelled back. "If I touch her…"

"Cut the connection, Bri!"

"NO! We can't leave Jack…"

"Our daughter is suffering," he yelled even louder, trying to drown out Livy's screaming pleas.

Victor grabbed my arm and pulled me off my feet and down into the floor. "Brianna, you are the only one who can break the connection between the twins. There is no sense in making Olivia suffer." I opened my mouth to protest, but Victor put his hand up. "You are not abandoning Jackson, you are helping Olivia. You must do this and do it now, look at your daughter!"

Olivia's screams were worsening, her shirt collar soaked with tears and snot. I felt my own tears start dripping down my cheeks. Cameron helped me back up to my knees, squeezing my shoulders tightly. I took a deep cleansing breath, clearing my head and blocking out the sounds of my daughter's screams. Carefully I took Livy into my arms and immediately I was taken into her mind where her screams were now replaced with Jack's. My baby boy was begging for his mother and father to help him. I gritted my teeth as the electrical current that was flowing through him was burning through me as well. It took all my strength to stay in control through the pain and keep from attacking Cameron and Victor.

With another deep breath I placed Olivia into a deep sleep and raised a shield between the twins, effectively cutting their connection like a knife. Livy went limp in my arms making me squeeze her tightly against my chest as I wept. Cameron fell to his knees, his hands covering his face as he folded to the floor.

Victor patted my arm. "You did the right thing, child."

"Screw you."

Chapter Forty-three

Cameron

My worst fears had come true. Aidan had resorted to violence against Jackson, an action that took down my daughter, my lover, ten hybrids, and five Vampires. I wanted him dead more than ever.

Brianna sat in the far corner of Victor's quarters, surrounded by her parents, Oliver and Maddy, Kyla and Renee, and even Fabiani who skipped his flight back East when he heard what had happened. Bri was devastated over having to break the connection between the twins. In her mind she had forsaken her son for her daughter. Although she was still quite hysterical about it, Victor practically had to put me back together piece by piece.

Olivia, surprisingly enough, was in good spirits considering all that she had endured. She slept for almost ninety minutes, and when she woke there was no word from Jackson. The lack of communication sent Brianna over the edge, and I could not blame her. The only thing keeping me from being an angry mess was the fact that Olivia seemed fine. Even now she lay on the floor coloring with William, refusing to allow John to examine her. He begged, he bartered, even tried tickling her. Each time she either shook her head or wriggled away from him. Alexander, Devin, and I simply stood back and watched, getting a bit of a laugh over John's struggle. Even Jonah tried to help, but gave up and came to stand with us.

"Well, if she's putting up that much of a fight, she can't be doing too badly," he said, trying to be optimistic.

I extended my right hand out to him and placed my left on his shoulder. "Jonah, I did not thank you earlier for rushing to help Olivia."

He shrugged humbly. "Honestly, it all happened so fast. Everyone was down on the ground screaming, and instinct just told me to grab her. Thankfully Victor started yelling at me to follow him."

"You did good, kid," Alexander said proudly, nearly knocking Jonah over when he slapped him on the back. "Sometimes it's good to be human."

Jonah rubbed his back. "Yeah, and sometimes it's not."

From over Jonah's shoulder I saw Olivia run a wide circle away from John. Finally, William stood from the floor.

"Wivy, wook, it doesn't hurt," he said as he walked over to his father. "You can do it to me first, Daddy."

"Thanks, little man," John replied relieved, placing his stethoscope up to William's heart. "You see, Livy, there's nothing to it. You won't feel it at all, I promise."

Olivia quirked her lips back and forth as she knitted her eyebrows together. After a few seconds she sighed, pouted, and then shuffled slowly over to John. She stood next to William who held her hand while John lifted the stethoscope to her chest.

Someone cleared their throat behind me, and when I turned around I saw Nikki standing tentatively in the doorway. I waved her inside and she stepped over to us with something behind her back.

"How is she doing?" Nikki asked as she peered around us.

"Better than we expected," I replied and Nikki sighed with a sense of relief.

"I...I wasn't sure if you'd mind, but I brought her this," she said as she pulled her right arm from behind her back, revealing a large chocolate bar in her hand. "There was a doctor at the warehouse that would always sneak them to us. I found chocolate made me feel a little better after they would...do...that to me."

If anyone in the manor knew the pain that my children had just endured, it was Nikki. Even with all the devious things she had done, she still suffered through Elaina's and Aidan's experiments.

"If she can't have chocolate..."

"Oh no," I interrupted. "I know she will love it." I looked over to Olivia whose eyes were large and hopeful at the sight of the chocolate bar in Nikki's hand. "And she can have it once her uncle is done examining her."

Olivia's face fell into a pout, her brow furrowed deeply over her eyes. She maintained that look through the rest of John's examination, proving how much she was like her mother. Nikki handed me the chocolate bar and then excused herself, leaving just as quickly as she had appeared.

I watched as John tried conducting a few more tests, trying to get Olivia to follow his finger, squeeze and pull his hands, all checking for neurological damage.

"Cam?" Alexander said, nudging me to attention and then gesturing behind him. "Julian is asking for you."

I turned around again and this time Julian was standing in the doorway. Suddenly it seemed like a revolving door of visitors. Julian looked oddly nervous as I approached him, but I extended my hand out to him gratefully.

"Julian, thank you for helping Brianna earlier."

He nodded his head, though his eyes stayed on the floor. "Thankfully my meeting with Father was delayed today. Otherwise we may not have heard all the commotion."

The two of us stood awkwardly silent for several moments. I was waiting for him to state his business, but when my patience ran thin I asked, "Was there something else you needed?"

"Ah…yes," he replied nervously. "I don't pretend to know what a little girl likes, but after seeing what Miss Olivia went through today I thought she deserved something." Julian held a shopping bag at his waist and pulled out a small doll with long, curly black hair and dark eyes. The doll looked similar to Olivia, which I assumed was the reason he selected it for her. "It's nothing much, she doesn't have to keep it. I just wanted her to know someone was thinking about her."

I smiled at his remarkably kind gesture and patted his shoulder.

"Julian, she will love it. However, I believe you should present it to her yourself."

He shook his head. "I do not want to intrude. Just let her know…"

"But Julian, you are her friend," I interrupted. "And she would love to see you."

Julian fidgeted nervously, finally dropping the shopping bag on the floor and allowing me to escort him into the room. Olivia's eye lit up at the sight of him, causing a wide smile to stretch across Julian's face. His nerves melted away and he no longer needed me to guide him as he went to Olivia's side.

My brothers and Jonah gave me shocked and confused looks as I returned to them, making me laugh just a little. With the presentation of yet another gift, John's attempt at a full examination was hopeless. Knowing he had gotten all that he could, he rose from the floor and walked over to our little group.

"How is she?" I asked.

"We definitely know whose daughter she is," he grunted. "Frankly I'm starting to get a complex when it comes to the women in this family. But in all honesty, she's fine. Heartbeat is strong, no neurological damage that I can detect. There's nothing I can see off hand. Thankfully kids are resilient. She seems fine, which is more than I can say for her mother."

John looked back to the far corner where Brianna was now being consoled by Sera, most likely helping to remove some of the acute emotions for a short time.

"Brianna is resilient as well, Brother," Devin said as he squeezed my shoulder.

"Everyone has a limit, Brother," I replied.

"Ada, look," Olivia squealed as she peered around Julian and showed off her new doll.

"She is beautiful, monkey. Did you thank Julian?"

I smiled as Olivia hugged Julian and thanked him for the doll, but my smile was short lived as I heard a commotion coming down the hall.

"Bro! Bro!" Jared shouted as he came running into the room. He was about to share his news when the sight of Julian on the floor caught his attention. "What the fuck is going on?"

"Jared!" I growled.

"Ada, Uncle Jer said…"

"Yes, Olivia, we all heard him," I interrupted and then directed my attention back to my inappropriate little brother. "What did you need, Jared?"

"Yeah…uh…" he stuttered, still unable to take his eyes off of Julian.

"Focus, Jared," Devin said, hitting our youngest brother in the chest.

"Crap, bro, that hurt."

"It was meant to. Do you have something or not!"

Jared smiled. "I think we might," he replied in a soft voice. "A Tracker hasn't checked in."

The room became eerily quiet, even Brianna stopped crying and stood from her chair.

"Jared, are you sure?" I asked, turning Jared to face me directly. "Or is he just late in checking in?"

"Connor's been trying to contact him all day since he missed the morning check-in. I tried triangulating his cell phone signal and I got nothing. This might just be the break we've been looking for."

I looked across the room over to Bri, silently looking for approval to leave and she nodded her head immediately.

I patted Jared on the shoulder. "Good work, little brother. Pull everything you and Connor have, we will look at it together shortly."

"Will do," Jared nodded and turned to leave, but froze when Julian approached our group.

"Gentleman," Julian began, "I know that when it comes to battles I generally leave that up to siblings like you. However, in this particular case I would like to actively be involved."

My three brothers and I blinked several times, shocked into silence over Julian's statement. Julian rarely left the manor, let alone fought alongside us. He had always made his position within the Warriors very clear.

"Why?" Devin asked, saying what we were all thinking.

"I am doing it for Miss Olivia," he replied plainly. "You may all think I am heartless, but no child should have to endure what she and her brother did today."

Devin held his hand up. "Julian, it is very nice of you to offer, but I..."

"I am also an expert on imprisonments," Julian interrupted. "I can spot a weak point in their encampment so we can get in."

Devin glared at me when he saw that I was actually considering it. He still saw the old Julian, but I saw a side to him I had never allowed myself to see.

"Of course, Julian," I responded. "We would love your help. As soon as we have something we will let you know."

Julian gave me a curt nod and bid my brothers good day before he disappeared through the door.

Jared squeezed my arm, pulling my attention to him, a very serious expression on his face as he said, "Seriously, is someone going to tell me what the fuck just happened?"

"Language, Jared," I moaned, but knowing it was no use.

Chapter Forty-four

Jonah

We shouldn't have been happy that a Tracker was missing, he could be dead. But it was hard not to be excited at the prospect of our first real lead. The library was finally buzzing with activity, at least for the first couple of hours. Then it hit a lull. Although the Tracker went missing, there was still a several hundred-mile radius he could have disappeared in. The only information we had was the last cell tower the Tracker's phone pinged against the day before. The problem was the tower was in the middle of nowhere where cell towers were scarce. Now there was the debate of whether it was worth sending one of the other Trackers there, or since the cell tower was roughly a day's drive away should a Warrior team be sent instead. Either way, we needed more information.

So now, we waited. Jared was hiding behind several laptops, feverishly typing and cursing. Who knew how many laws he was breaking. Alex, Cameron, and Devin were looking at the map now with a big black X marking the Tracker's last signal. The rest of the family was scattered around the room – some reading, others chitchatting, or in the case of Livy and Will, coloring. Me? Using Alex's computer to surf the internet but then something caught my eye.

"Hey, Alex, what's this?" I asked as I pointed to a file on his desktop screen titled Lineage – All Types.

Alex stood over my shoulder and let out a grumbled laugh when he saw what I was referring to.

"That is a project I don't think I'll ever finish."

"Is it a family tree?"

"Even bigger," he replied as he clicked open the file. "We have hundreds of historical documents that detail coven members, makers and sires, that sort of thing. Forever ago I started pulling all the documents together and put them into this database."

"It's not a database," Jared corrected, an air of annoyance in his voice. "It's only a spreadsheet. I told you I could create a real database…"

"You charge too much," Alex interrupted, making several people in the room laugh, including Jared. Alex turned his attention back to me. "So I started putting this information into this *spreadsheet*, basically giving a listing of Vampires along with their maker, coven, if applicable, and any subsequent sires. Then when the Gatherers were established, I started working with Lanashell to cross-reference hybrids with our Vampire information."

I started scrolling through the spreadsheet, only seeing a couple of names pop out that I recognized. "So I could search for any known hybrid, see who her father is, and then see all his information?"

"In theory," he shrugged. "It's not near complete, and I realized quickly it never will be. Keeping that document up-to-date is almost a full-time job. But hey, search away, it can be pretty interesting."

Jared groaned. "Yeah, if you have absolutely nothing else to do."

Alex gave him a dirty look, and Jared pretended he didn't see, though he was smiling behind his laptops. But like Alex suggested, I started searching and found Brianna right away, and I could see things were a little outdated. Brianna Morgan: hybrid. Father: Eris. Coven: none. Siblings: none. Aliases: Brianna Lewis. It was weird seeing Bri's ex-married name. I looked around the room and found my next search.

"Seraphina, your dad's name is Jean-Luke?" I asked as I looked at the screen.

"Oui," she replied shortly, and didn't look up from her book.

"Did you ever meet him?"

"Oui," she answered as she turned a page. "Once was enough."

Ok, moving on. Next search, Cushlin. Natasha Cushlin: hybrid, father: Charles Cushlin, siblings: sister not found. Not found? Really? She's sitting on a couch in front of me.

"Hey Nikki, how come you're not in here?"

Nikki turned her head curiously, shrugging as she put her magazine down in her lap.

Alex, however, cleared his throat uncomfortably. "Er…I think it might be under Williams," he said as he pushed my hands from the keyboard and did a search under Nikki Williams, and just like that her record came up.

"Really, bro," Jared sighed. "It's been four years."

Alex shrugged in embarrassment. "I said I hadn't…let's just update that now," he said as he quickly updated the records.

"So…ah…" I began, "what's with being under a different name?"

"Move on, Thorne," Jared commanded, and so I did.

I started searching and following the hyperlinks from one Vampire to the next. Alex was right, it was interesting to see how people connected to one another.

"Alex, what are these numbers in the notes?"

Alex came back over my shoulder and took a quick look. "Ah, those are document numbers. A lot of this information came from old documents we have locked up in the vault."

"You have a vault?" I asked curiously. "Can…can I see it?"

Alex shrugged and waved me toward a wall of books. Hidden on the side of one of the shelves was a small keypad that Alex typed in a short code. A second later the wall of books opened, just like in the movies, revealing a secrete passageway. I followed the big man down several feet to a wide steel door. Alex typed in a code on another keypad and the thick pneumatic locks released causing the vault door to open slowly. A motion light clicked on as I stepped inside and I was amazed at the sight of so many historical documents rolled up and neatly stacked. Alex filed in after me, though there was little room to move around once he did. He went straight to the far wall, and began moving his fingers across the different reference numbers that were labeled on the shelf. A second later he pulled out a long piece of rolled parchment and turned back around.

"I always found this one interesting," he said as he handed the parchment to me. "It's one of the first attempts at documenting the covens and many of the solitaires."

"Can I bring it back into the library?" I asked tentatively as I held the document at its ends.

"Jonah, this document is centuries old. You can't just…" he began, but then began laughing at me. "I'm kidding. Of course you can."

I laughed, but didn't mean it, and then followed him back into the library. I stepped over to the small desk I had claimed as my own, moved Alex's laptop so I had more room, and carefully unrolled the document. The parchment crinkled softly, releasing a musky smell as it revealed columns of tightly scrolled script.

"What are you up to?" Brianna asked as she stood at the front of my desk, glancing down at the parchment.

"It's like a Vamp family tree," I said as I pointed to the column of names listed under the title of Warrior Coven. I saw several names I knew – Victor, Devin, Cameron, Julian. But it was obvious that the document was too old to display Alex and Jared due to their age. What was curious were the nine names at the top of the list, all with the initials DWA next to them.

"Alex, what does DWA mean?"

Alex thought a moment and then said, "There should be a key at the bottom of the page."

I looked at the bottom of the document, and there it was in small script. "Death by Warrior Assassin," I said aloud, and then looked up to where Devin was standing at the front of the room.

Brianna skimmed her fingers across the names. "These are Victor's first sires, aren't they?"

"You killed your own brothers?" I asked, completely shocked.

Devin finally turned around, his arms crossed and his expression less than amused. "When they betrayed our Father, they were no longer my brothers. I'm sure those three letters show up many times on that document."

Fabi huffed from the other side of the room, but Devin didn't acknowledge it and simply turned back around. I looked down the column titled Negotiator Coven and did notice Fabiani's name listed.

"Wow, Fabi, you're on here. How old are you?"

"A man never reveals his age," he replied dramatically.

"I believe that's a woman," Bri corrected.

"And I don't believe anyone asked you, Miss Smarty-pants," he retorted and moved to where Kyla was sitting in the window seat.

Brianna smiled and looked back down at the piece of parchment, tracing her fingers down the columns of names listed under the other covens. Whereas she followed the lines down, I noticed that all the coven leaders came from a small group of Vampires at the top of the page. The first thing that struck me was that the origin of Vampires were simply two boxes with the words "Brother 1" and "Brother 2". No names, just two oddly labeled boxes with family lines drawn down. Something else I found odd was that Eris seemed to be floating all by himself with no family lines connecting in or out. Bri flinched as I pointed to her father's name.

"Dad?" she asked as she took a pen from the cup that sat on the desk. "What was your father's name?"

Eris stared at us with a very stern look on his face. Sera patted him lightly on the leg, and then caressed his cheek with the back of her hand.

Finally, through his clinched jaw, he answered, "Hanif. Why?"

"No reason," Bri replied as she wrote the name Hanif on the parchment.

"Bri! You can't do that!" I said as I lifted her hand away. "This is a sacred document."

Bri raised her left eyebrow and then looked over her shoulder as she said, "Alex, can I write on this sacred document in order to make it more historically accurate?"

"I...guess...so?" Alex replied with a shrug.

Bri shook my hand away, stuck her tongue out at me, and then drew a line down from Hanif's name to Eris's. Next, she wrote the name Gorum and drew a line down to Hanif. Gorum was a name I knew.

I leaned into her ear and asked softly, "Eris's father Turned him?" She nodded. "And Gorum had Turned him?"

She nodded again, this time showing me sad eyes. "My powers come from Gorum. We're exactly the same, except that he's much stronger than I am."

"I would not say that, mia figlia," Eris chimed in. "You have overcome him twice."

"A lot of good it did," she replied flatly, and went back to looking at the document.

I knew Brianna well enough to know that the previous topic of conversation was finished and instead she decided to take an interest in those listed at the top of the document, a thick line drawn separating them from those listed below. According to this document there were only seven still living, three having a small "d" etched next to their name, which according to the key meant death, and not by anyone in particular.

"Bri, why are these guys separate from the others?"

She tilted her head slightly, the corner of her lips squeezed tightly before she answered, "I think these are the Ancients. Alex?"

"Yep," he replied.

"And all Vampires come from the Ancients?" I asked.

"The story we've always been told, was that there were two brothers," he said as he pointed to the two boxes at the very top of the document, "who were given the gift of immortality, but at a price – they would have to feed on the life force of others in order to remain alive themselves. After spending a century together, they grew tired of only having each other and they finally discovered how to create sires. The two of them created Alastor, Magnus, and Cassius, the first children of our race. Magnus sired Anu and then Isidor, whose line is associated with the Cleaners. Cassius sired Heron, who eventually sired Dante who formed the Negotiators. And lastly there's Alastor, who is the eldest Ancient, but created Victor very late compared to the others. Father is technically third generation, but because of his age is not considered an Ancient.

"Now for a very long time it was thought there were only six Ancients, all stemming from the two brothers. It wasn't until Eris, pardon me sir," he said as he looked over my shoulder at Eris, "started making trouble, did they realize there was another family line. Only now do we know it starts with Gorum, who is probably older than the two brothers. He's probably the only one who knows the true origin of Vampires."

"The two brothers never documented anything?"

Alex shook his head. "Not before they were killed. We don't even know their names, and the Ancients have never told us."

"Because then they would have to acknowledge what they did," Eris said behind me.

The room became quiet, only Brianna dared to asked, "Care to share something, Dad?"

Eris grinned and didn't answer, simply put his arm around Sera and began reading her book. Brianna kept her eyebrows up as she shook her head at me. It was probably best we didn't know all that Eris did. And with that, Bri and I went back to scouring the document, following the trails of the different sires, covens started and then disbanded, and then counting the number of Vamps killed by Devin. When we were done with the first page we carefully peeled it back to reveal a second page that had twice as many names with dozens of branches fanning down to the bottom.

"These must be the solitaries," Brianna said as she started skimming down the page, but from across the room Olivia gasped and jumped up from the ground. Instantly the room went quiet, all eyes on Livy while she titled her head slightly as though she was listening intently to something.

Finally her eyes found Bri as she said, "Jack-Jack's ok."

The room was suddenly filled with a mix of cheers and sighs of relief. Bri quickly left my side and went to her daughter, although Cameron had already picked her up from the floor and held her tightly in his arms. It felt like an intrusion to keep staring at them while they all held back tears as Livy relayed what her brother was saying.

I looked away and began scanning the document again, this time going a little slower to look at each name. The page looked like small grapevines – some solitaries only on their own strand while others branched off into small bunches. Only a few minutes went by before a name leapt out at me. Why at first, I didn't know, but something kept telling me to look at it. Andrew Williams – DWA, Death by Warrior Assassin. At first he looked like the dozen plus others, but he had a son, a son with a human woman, something that had a star next to it. It wouldn't have caught my eye if the son's name wasn't Aidan. I must have looked at the grouping for almost five minutes. It wasn't until I glanced over at Nikki did I ask, "Nikki, where did Williams come from?"

She flinched her head up, already on the defensive. "Why do we keep going back to this!"

"Nikki, please, just humor me," I begged. "You're listed as Nikki Williams in Alex's database. Why?"

Nikki threw her magazine down at her feet. "I told everyone my name was Nikki Williams, ok? I was just doing what Aidan and Elaina told me to do."

"Did you pick the last name Williams?" I pressed. "Or was it given to you?

Nikki thought for a moment and then answered, "Aidan told me to use it. Why?"

Suddenly I realized the room had gone quiet again.

"Where are you going with this, Jonah?" Brianna asked as she and Cameron stood slowly from the floor, leaving Livy to stand in between them.

I looked down at the document again, right where my index finger still lingered. "One of our biggest questions has always been Aidan's motive. Well, I...I think Devin killed his father."

No one in the room moved except Devin who shook his head and said, "That is not possible. I have never killed a Pierce."

"But you have killed a Williams," I replied. "Andrew Williams, to be exact. According to this, Andrew Williams had a son named Aidan with a woman named Anna Pierce. Anna was human, therefore their son was a hybrid, the first documented hybrid according to this. It's not listed like the other sires, it's bracketed like a real family tree."

I felt Alex's huge hand completely cover my right shoulder. "Slow down, Jonah. Let's take this one step at a time."

"Ok, so there's a guy named Aidan Pierce, and according to Jared he's practically a ghost. No credit, no property, and no known history. Am I right?"

Jared nodded from behind his screen, his fingers feverishly typing on his computer. Brianna came to stand next to me and I circled the grouping in question as I continued.

"Now here is a guy named Aidan, whose mother's maiden name is Pierce. So there is coincidence number one. Next, this guy's given name is Aidan Williams, *Williams*, the same last name that Nikki was told to use. There's coincidence number two. Lastly, his father, Andrew Williams, was killed by the Warrior Assassin, a.k.a. Devin, a.k.a. secret vendetta against the Warriors."

"Jonah, that is a big leap," Cameron said from across the room.

"No, he mentioned something," Brianna began, but paused as she searched her memories. "His mother died when he was young. I didn't remember that until just now. He said his dad raised him, and eventually Turned him, but was killed shortly afterwards. Aidan wouldn't tell me why, though."

All heads turned to Devin who simply stared back. "What?"

Bri groaned in frustration. "Why did you kill Andrew Williams?"

"I don't remember," he replied flatly with a shrug.

"Try, Brother," Cameron said firmly.

Devin grumbled something under his breath before he disappeared into a cloud of black smoke.

Fabi, who was still sitting in the window seat with Kyla threw his arms up dramatically. "Does it bother anyone else that he's either killed so many people that he can't remember why he had to, or that maybe he didn't even care to ask?"

Before anyone could answer, Devin Projected back into the library holding a black leather journal. We all watched as he began flipping through the soft pages and I realized then that Devin wasn't holding just any old journal, it was his kill log. Everyone in the room was tense with curiosity while he casually flipped through his book.

"For f's sake, Devin," Renee yelled, "this isn't book club!"

Devin looked up from his journal, paused a moment, and then began flipping through the book once again. I thought for sure Renee was going to leap across the room. Finally he stopped, flipped back a page, and said, "Ah, Andrew Williams, kill date twenty-seventh of November, 1769. Interesting, Jackson was also taken on the twenty-seventh of November."

There were several gasps in the room.

"Kill reason," Devin continued, "killing of adult humans, killing of human children, blood experimentation…on children, and unlawful Turning…"

Devin's voice trailed off as he looked slowly to Cameron who answered, "Of a child. Andrew Williams Turned a child, and Father ordered his death."

Devin nodded sadly as he closed his journal and tucked it in his back pocket. Brianna's face was frozen in shock, her mouth gapping open as she looked down at Olivia.

"Is anyone gonna explain this to the humans in the room?" Renee chimed in.

Alex turned in Renee's direction. "Turning a child is punishable by death. One of the most sacred laws that the Warriors must uphold. There are references to Vampire children in hundreds of books throughout the ages. It was one of the plagues of the apocalypse in the Bible until we had it remove. Horror movies…"

"We get it, Alex!" Renee complained. "You can't Turn children, got it."

"Seriously, the Bible?" I asked Alex softly, truly curious, and he nodded stiffly.

"Focus, Thorne!" Renee yelled. "We're getting to a good part. But someone besides Alex has to explain what's going on, he's too wordy."

"Renee," John groaned loudly as he buried his head in his hands.

"So what we're thinking," Kyla began, trying to take the heat off Renee, "is that Aidan's done all of this to get back at the Warriors for killing his father?"

"It may have started out that way," Cameron replied. "Aidan and I were acquaintances for many years, I am sure in order to get in close to find our weaknesses. However, I think it is more than that now. One of the reasons why Aidan's father was killed was because he Turned a child. At some point Aidan became aligned with Elaina, hears about a prophecy that two Vampire children will be born, through Jazlyn he sees the connection to the Warriors, and then simply lies in wait until it happens."

"The twins are not Vampires, Brother," Devin corrected.

"But to outside eyes they surely look like it," Cameron replied. "I am sure this fueled his anger, thinking the Warriors created the same thing his father was killed for. How could you not remember the similarities, Brother? This would have saved us years of speculation."

Devin waved his journal in the air. "Do you know how many kills are in here?"

"Devy, honey," Fabi said calmly behind me, "you're not helping yourself."

"This is not my fault!" Devin yelled.

"No one is saying it is," Brianna fired back. "And I don't think we should be talking about this in front of the kids."

"I'm ok, Mama," Livy replied.

"Me, too, Awbie," Will chimed in as well.

"Son-of-a-bitch!" Jared cheered as he jumped up from his chair, and then realized everyone was looking at him. "Sorry, but totally called for." Jared ran to the big monitor that displayed the map. "The black X is the last cell phone tower the missing Tracker was near. We gave him a five-hundred-mile radius where he could have gone missing. So while you all were talking about nonsense crap, I've been doing a search under different name combinations thanks to Jonah's awesome find. And what came out?"

"See, Jared has more flare and is more to the point," Renee announced.

"Thanks, red," Jared winked.

"Back atcha, jailbait."

"Jared, for god's sake…" Cameron shouted

"One property listing," Jared began smoothly, "under an Anna Andrews, right within our radius." Jared feverishly circled an area north of the big black X. "It's part of a huge nature preserve, a.k.a., wooded area, lots of land for Aidan to hide, and not many people to have to bribe or Glamour." The room was stunned, everyone staring at the map. "Yeah, this is where you applaud."

Jared didn't get his wish.

"Alex, find Connor and tell him to suit up," Cameron said. "It will take roughly eight hours to get that far up into Oregon."

"Eh…six, maybe five the way Connor drives and this late at night," Alex replied.

"Fine," Cameron nodded, "I want wheels up within the hour. Devin, get Julian, he will go with Connor to help with the recon."

"Connor won't be happy about that," Jared muttered.

"As you would say, little brother, I do not give a shit. What additional equipment will they need?"

Jared thought for a moment and then replied, "I'll get them infrared cameras, laser sensors, high range binoculars, and then some mini-cams so we can get a live feed of what they find. How many others on the team?"

"Just the two of them," Cameron replied.

Devin pulled on Cameron's elbow. "Brother, shouldn't we send a whole team?"

Cameron shook his head. "Our Tracker was only one man, and they found him. We need to get as close as possible without getting caught. Any more than two could put this whole thing at risk. We need to get a lay of the land before we go charging in there. There are too many human lives at stake if we do not plan our attack to the tee."

"Now that we're able to speak to Jack again," John chimed in, "maybe he can give us an idea of how many humans we're talking about? If there are pregnant women and others with newborns, you're going to need medical staff. We just need to know on what scale."

Cameron nodded. "Agreed. We should get counts on their numbers overall. Bri, could you…Brianna?"

Bri ignored Cameron as she stood staring at Olivia's latest picture. When she finally looked up from the drawing her eyes met mine. "Jonah, I'm so sorry."

Chapter Forty-five

Jonah

"I just need to be alone," I shouted at Brianna as she called after me, begging me to stay. But I couldn't stand there for another moment while everyone gave me sympathetic looks. I just wanted to make it to my room without losing it, and by losing it that could mean a spectrum of things. I wasn't really sure what would come out.

My pace quickened as the tall spiral staircase came into view and I ran up the stairs two at a time. My room door was a welcomed sight and I ducked inside quickly, slamming it loudly behind me. What came out of me could only be described as an animalistic wail. Next I swept the top of the chest of drawers clean, causing everything to crash loudly on the floor. The door was my next victim as I kicked and pounded it with my fist, calling the innocent plank of wood things I wouldn't call my worst enemy. I decided the door had had enough when the skin around my knuckles broke open. When I stepped away from the door I slid on the debris on the floor and fell right on my ass.

"Son of a bitch," I growled to myself as I pushed my back up against the side of the bed and pulled my knees up near my chest. My eyes closed as my head fell back on the edge of the mattress. The door creaked open, but I didn't move. "Go away, Bri."

"It should trouble me that you automatically think of my fiancée when

454 ~ C.R. QUINN

someone comes into your room," Cameron said as he clicked the door closed.

"She's the only one who would keep bothering me," I replied and held my hand up in the air. "I'm bleeding, so don't bite me or anything. I'm having a tough time as it is." Cameron didn't reply and simply sat down next to me. "You have much more important things to do than sit here with me."

"I am right where I should be," he replied. "Jonah, we do not know anything for sure. It is just a drawing."

I lifted my head and finally opened my eyes. "We've been looking at Livy's drawings for weeks. Why would this one be wrong?"

"Perhaps it is Jackson who is wrong. You must remember he is not even four years old."

"He knew who the mommies were, he knows what that means. And now he's saying my girlfriend is one of them," I said as my head fell to the top of my knees. "They touched her, man. They fucking hurt her and now she's...fucking...pregnant." My eyes burned as tears formed in the corners and I didn't care that I was breaking down in front of Cameron. "And what's with the 'she's having an Eris baby' horseshit? What the hell does that mean?"

Cameron shook his head. "Yet another reason to believe Jackson does not have all the facts. I think we can say with confidence that Eris has not had intercourse with Ashlyn, although Seraphina had some choice words for him in her native tongue."

"But Livy kept saying it over and over again. Ashlyn's having an Eris baby, Jack says it's a baby Eris. Why would Jack say that unless someone said those words to him? It's not like he said it was a baby Kevin or Chris. There is only one Eris."

"Jonah, it only goes to show that we should not jump to any conclusions."

"But what if she's really pregnant? What am I supposed to do?" I asked. "Ashlyn and I still barely know each other. We were just starting to talk about moving in together, and now what? I'm supposed to raise a rapist's child? Who...who can do that? If I decide it's too much, then I'm a douchebag. But every time I'd look at the kid I'd see the rapist asshole who did that to Ashlyn." My lungs burned from talking too fast and not bothering to breathe.

"Jonah, we have failed you and we have certainly failed Ashlyn. I cannot begin to tell you how sorry I am. I know how you feel…"

"No," I interrupted, jerking my head up. "No, you don't. I don't think anyone could know how I'm feeling right now."

"Actually, Jonah, I can," he replied and then paused, looking extremely conflicted. Finally, "Brianna has told you about her ex-husband, has she not?"

I nodded. "He was a real bastard, wasn't he?"

"Samuel Lewis was an evil, evil man. One of my greatest achievements was the day I took Brianna away from him, but even twelve-hundred miles away he could still hurt her."

"How?"

He paused for a moment. "Brianna insisted that I take her to Oliver's so that she could sort everything out, so I did. What was supposed to be a few days turned into a couple of weeks. We were still just getting to know one another when she discovered she was pregnant and it certainly was not my child. Bri was devastated and completely inconsolable.

"Now this does not leave this room, Jonah, but when I say I understand what you are feeling, I truly mean that. Being with Sam was never Brianna's choice and being pregnant with his child was a constant reminder of that."

Shit. Cameron really could relate, and that made my heart sink for Bri as well. I knew Sam was a bastard, but I didn't know he was *that* kind of a bastard.

"What did you do?" I asked. "How did you handle it?"

He sighed. "To be honest, it was not easy. But I kept reminding myself that she had no control of what happened to her. I loved Brianna, so I would love her baby. It was not the baby's fault Sam was an evil bastard. So whatever Brianna wanted to do, I would support her. But Jonah, that was my decision, my situation. You have to do what is right for you and no one can judge you on that."

"Now, not to pry too much, but Jack and Livy obviously don't have an older brother or sister running around."

Cameron nodded sadly. "Brianna miscarried a short time after we left Oliver's. I made the choice to support Brianna and her baby, but I was never truly tested, so I cannot honestly say I was successful in raising someone else's child. I say again, you have to do what is right for you. And know that we will help you and Ashlyn in any way we can. Never doubt what lengths Brianna will go to for you."

"I tell her not to."

Cameron laughed. "You can never tell Brianna to do anything, she will simply run the other way."

I smiled at Cameron's very truthful statement, but then a curtain of depression engulfed me. My brain started rushing through every possible scenario, and there wasn't one where I didn't get screwed. Christ, I was only twenty-four, hadn't I already been through enough? In what world was this worth it?

"You should probably be getting back," I said flatly, and I could see that Cameron noticed the sudden change in my demeanor. He didn't pry, simply patted my back and moved to the door.

"We are all here for you, Jonah, whatever it is you decide to do."

After Cameron shut the door the silence was deafening. I wanted to be alone, but then again, I didn't. Without any kind of noise to distract me, thoughts of Ashlyn began to creep into my head. Had they held her down? Did she scream for me to help her? Had it happened more than once? Holy shit, this was my life. Cameron was my friend, and I appreciated him coming to me, but I needed someone else, someone even closer. I looked around on the floor and found my cell phone among the debris. The other line only rang twice before it was picked up.

"Hel-hello?"

The sound of her voice made my nose tingle. "Mom?"

"Jo…" she began, but then yawned loudly. "Oh…sorry, Joey."

"Shit, Mom, I'm sorry," I said as I looked down at my watch and realized the time difference. "It's after midnight there, I'm so sorry, I'm such an idiot. I didn't mean to wake you, Mom, I'm so sorry."

"Joey, honey, it's fine," she said over me. "It's fine, really. I was actually falling asleep behind the wheel. I would have run off the road if you hadn't called."

"Off the road? Why are you out so late?"

"I'm just driving home from the hospital."

"The hospital? Why? Are you ok? Is it Katie?"

"Joey, honey, calm down," she pleaded. "I've been picking up some extra shifts. It's just been so long since I've worked this many hours. Your mother is old now, honey."

"No she's not," I corrected. "But why are you working the late shift?"

She waited another few seconds before she replied, "The overtime is helping me pay for Katie Bell's tuition, and then it's Christmas…"

"Where's Paul? Why isn't he helping you versus you having to work so many hours? I'll send you some money tomorrow."

"Joey!" she yelled over me. "Honey, I need to do this myself. I'm not taking your money, Joey."

"But Mom..."

"But nothing, Joey, I'm a grown woman and I need to take care of my expenses. Thankfully there are shifts available, you don't need to worry about us." I sighed loudly, guilt weighing heavy on my already overloaded shoulders. "Honey, I'm...I'm really glad you called. I've been so worried about you out there. How's Ashlyn? Is she...safe now? I'm not sure of all that happened..." my mom stopped talking when she heard me breakdown. Just the sound of my mom saying Ashlyn's name hit a nerve and brought on emotions from hidden parts inside of me, places only a mother was allowed to see or hear. "Joey, honey, I'm pulling over. Can you hear me? I'm pulling over so we can talk. Stay with me, baby, are you there?"

"Yeah, I'm here," I finally replied once I could inhale a solid breath. "I'm sorry, Mom, not sure where that came from."

"Honey, I'm your mother," she said and the road noise subsided. "You don't need to apologize, it's part of my job description. I only wish I was there with you. I can't take it when one of my babies is upset. Now tell me what's going on. Is it Ashlyn? Did something happen? The last thing you told me was that she was in trouble, that the people she was with wouldn't let her go."

"Yeah, sort of. I can't give you any real details, but...they still have her. Her and a bunch of other girls. And today they...we think...hell I don't even know how to explain it. We got some info a few weeks ago that some of the girls were..." I sighed and realized there was no good way to say it. "We think Ashlyn's pregnant. That's the news I got a little while ago."

There was silence on the other line for several seconds as my mother processed this bizarre revelation.

"Are you sure?" she finally said.

"Relatively sure. There are other girls, too."

"But how do you know?"

My hand rubbed my face in frustration. "I...I can't tell you, Mom. It's just really complicated."

"So you think Ashlyn is pregnant."

"Yes."

"And…not by choice."

"Yeah, that's….that's what they're saying."

"That is…just…" she said through soft sniffles, trying to hide it, but unable to fully hold it inside. "Joey, I…I cannot imagine what she's going through right now. When are they going to get their act together and go after her?"

"Soon," I replied. "I just don't know how to handle this. I…I'm beginning to think you were right, Mom. We've only known each other for a couple of months, and she's been gone for almost half of that. Now this? How much am I supposed to endure here? It's not like it's been easy since day one. So like you said, maybe this isn't worth it."

"Honey, when it comes to love, don't listen to me. In fact, please forget everything I ever said. Your father, god rest his soul, would be ashamed of me. The things I said…"

"Mom, you don't have…"

"Joey, please, I need to say this," she interrupted, and then sighed deeply into the phone. "Your father was everything to me, and when he passed, I didn't know how to live without him. I've been so lost and angry these last few years that I decided I wouldn't allow myself to ever feel that kind of love again because I never wanted to go through that much pain.

"When I saw you and Ashlyn together, I saw how you were with her and you reminded me so much of your father. I didn't want you to have to go through what I did if you ever lost her. I was scared for you, that's why I said those things. And Joey, I was wrong, I was so wrong and you were right. If something ever happened to me, your father would have fought tooth and nail to get to me. You're doing all of this because you love Ashlyn, and the reason you're hurting so much now is simply *because* you love her that much."

"But it's only been a couple of months."

She laughed. "Honey, your father asked me to marry him after our third date. I said yes a week after that only because I didn't want him to think I was too desperate. We would have gone down to the justice of peace right away if your grandmother hadn't threatened to disown us if we didn't get married in a church."

"I never knew that," I replied with a smile.

"Parents don't like to admit they were once stupid kids, too," she replied lightly and then we hit another quiet lull in our conversation.

Finally I said, "Why the change of heart?"

"A couple of reasons," she replied. "The biggest one being that…" she cleared her throat and took a second before she continued with, "I'm leaving Paul."

"What!" I said as I sat up away from the bed. "Why?"

"You need to ask?"

"I know why I'd leave him, but you've defended him the whole time."

She groaned. "Thanksgiving was an absolute nightmare. Katie and Paul did nothing but fight, then Paul kept arguing with me about Katie, then Katie kept arguing with me about Paul, and then my son was so mad at me that he didn't even tell me he went to the other side of the country."

"Mom…"

"I kept thinking about our last conversation and I'm disgusted at what I've become."

"Mom, don't say that."

"Joey, it's true. I let fear run my life and I ended up putting a man before my kids. I just hope you and Katie can forgive me. I know I have a lot to make up for, especially with you. Honey, I'm so sorry."

"Are you ok?"

"Yeah," she said happily, "I'm doing ok. At first I was worried about having to do everything on my own, but I'm getting it done and I'm actually finding it uplifting that I can do this without help. I still need to sell the house, but I've figured it out that if I get a good enough offer I can move into an apartment closer to the hospital. By saving on gas and keeping up the overtime, Katie Bell might not need to move home after all."

As I listened to my mother I realized I was speaking to a completely different person than I had a few weeks ago. My mom was back, and with a vengeance.

"That's great, Mom, really great," I said, feeling a little sad that I wasn't there with her.

"Thank you, honey, but I wouldn't have been able to do it without you."

"That's not true."

"Joey, we would have been out on the street if it weren't for you. When I was at my lowest, you picked our family up. Now you need to do the same thing for Ashlyn."

"But Mom, it's a baby."

"Yes, Joey, it's a baby, but you're not the one having it," she replied firmly. "Being pregnant is scary enough without having to deal with...my god I can't imagine."

"So what am I supposed to do? Marry her and raise the child of a rapist?"

"No," she said in a very motherly tone, "I think you need to wait and find out what Ashlyn wants to do. She may want marriage, she may want to hide, you just won't know until you get her back. You are all that she has, Joey, don't give up on her because of something she couldn't control."

"I...I'm not," I whined, hating that she was right. "It's just hard, Mom."

"Of course it is, honey, it's life," she replied at the same time someone knocked on my door.

"Mom, I'm sorry, I need to go. Someone's at my door."

"Honey, I'm really happy that you called, and keep calling if you need me, no matter what time it is."

"I will," I replied as I pushed myself up from the floor. "I love you, Mom, thanks...I really needed this."

"I love you, too, honey."

And with the sound of two kisses through the phone, my mother hung up. When another knock came through the door, I trudged through the debris on the floor and opened it.

"Tosh," I said surprised. "What are you doing here?"

"Nikki came and found me," she replied, sympathy filling her eyes. "Wanna talk about it?"

I shook my head. "I've been talking about it for almost an hour. I don't want to think about it anymore, honestly."

"Good," she said as she pulled a six-pack of beer from behind her back. "You can have a few beers, and whatever comes out, comes out, and I promise there will be no kissing of any kind. What do you say?"

I took the beer from her hands. "Sounds perfect."

Chapter Forty-six

Cameron

I knocked on the door of Victor's office and waited several seconds before he called for me to come in. When I entered he was sitting behind the elaborate desk in his tall chair with the phone held up to his ear. He waved his fingers for me to come further inside, it appeared I would need to wait. Honestly, it was the last thing I wanted to do. Everything was coming to a head. We were so close I could taste it which made me want to jump out of my skin.

Connor and Julian had arrived in the nature preserve early this morning, but needed the cover of night to do any real surveying. Thankfully the sun set early in the winter months. They confirmed they had found Aidan's base of operations and now we were only moments away from seeing it via a live feed. Unfortunately, I had to wait for Victor to get off of the goddamn phone!

"Yes, Ormond, I will take your concerns into consideration," Victor sighed and shook his head, "but the timeframe is the timeframe. You have three more months, that is all. Now I must go, I have urgent business I must attend to. We will talk soon."

As he hung up the phone I could hear Ormond screaming on the other end. It seemed as though the pressure was setting in for the Negotiators with only three months to go.

"Father, we are ready for you," I said, but Victor just sat there, his hands crossed in his lap while he looked quizzically into space. "Father?"

Finally, he lowered himself from his chair as he said, "Ormond has accused us of preventing Fabiani from returning to Boston."

"Fabiani stays to support Brianna. He was planning to leave for Boston when the episode with Olivia occurred."

Victor nodded. "That is what I said as well, and do you know he believes we are keeping Fabiani in order to prevent the Negotiators from being successful? As if he is the only Negotiator that can make them money."

"In some ways that is true, Father," I replied knowing about Fabiani's side venture. "The live feed should be starting any moment."

"Yes, yes, child, I know you are anxious to get there," he said as he walked past me and opened the door. "You know I have to say I am happy that Fabiani's loyalty seems to lie more with us. I truly hate that Ormond is technically a peer of mine simply by his title. Every time I have to talk to him I miss my dear friend Dante."

"Dante was a great loss for everyone."

"Child, I have been meaning to thank you for what you did for Julian," he said as we turned down the main corridor.

"He volunteered, Father."

"Yes, but you allowed him to go."

"It was nothing."

"Child, do not sell yourself short. I know how you dislike him. What you did took a great deal of strength."

"I had a moment of weakness when he brought Olivia the doll."

He laughed lightly. "Deep down he is a good man, a little needy maybe, but a good man. Like Fabiani. He has been such a good friend to Brianna. He also seems to handle Devin quite well, don't you think?"

"I cannot say I have noticed," I replied, knowing Victor was fishing. Thank goodness Renee was not with us. I could hear her voice in my head saying some remark about just how well Fabiani handled Devin.

Thankfully the library was in sight. I did not have a tremendous amount of confidence that I would be able to withstand more questions regarding Fabiani. The door to the library was left slightly open and I could hear the sound of raised voices coming from inside. When Victor and I entered the room, Jared was holding his laptop over his head while he shouted at Devin who was putting the large monitor back on its stand.

"For fuck sake, Devin, the bull in this china shop should be Alex. You could have destroyed my computer and then we'd be shit up a creek. It's not like this hasn't been connected for the last hour!" Jared shouted as he began plugging the cords from his laptop into the monitor. Victor cleared his throat and Jared's head shot up. "Oh hey, Dad. Your assassin is a fucking klutz."

Victor raised an eyebrow. "I would prefer that you use more appropriate language, child."

"Er...that's really a lot to ask of me," Jared laughed as the monitor clicked to life.

While others began to take seats around the room, Devin walked swiftly to stand in front of us.

"Father, Brother, I am sorry. The delay is completely my fault," he said quickly and then gave me a very worried look.

I glanced to my right and noticed Fabiani shaking his head. Seeing the exasperated look on his face I realized that Devin must have heard Victor in the hallway and that caused the accident.

"There is nothing to worry about, Brother," I said calmly and with dual meanings.

Devin nodded and turned to face the monitor which now displayed a night-vision view of a wooded area.

"No Brianna?" Victor asked, looking up at me curiously.

I shook my head. "She and Renee are putting the children to bed."

But everyone else in the family was here, including Jonah who did not look as green as he did the other day. The night-vision camera shook as Connor turned it on himself, Julian sitting just over his shoulder.

"Can you see me?" he said in a low voice, and Jared acknowledged that we could. "Well, we found it, obviously. We were able to get pretty close without tipping anyone off, and we took some infrared video which I've sent over. Jer, if you want to open the first one?" Jared obliged and the screen flashed to a video where many purple and orange and yellow figures moved back and forth through the frame. "The orange and yellow figures are the hybrids and humans, the hybrids showing a little cooler than the humans. From what we were able to see, we're estimating roughly twenty hybrids..."

"Twenty isn't bad," John said from the far corner of the room.

"With another ten that appear to be pregnant. There could be more, we were just going off the size of their stomachs," Connor continued.

A shiver went through Jonah, prompting Kyla to sit next to him and hold his hand supportively.

"Thirty is still not bad," John muttered.

But yet again Connor continued, "As you can see from the footage there are a few humans walking around, but we also found a large cluster of them in one of the larger cabins. We believe these are blood donors."

"How many?" Victor asked.

"Fifty plus," he sighed, as did everyone else in the room. John chose not to comment this time. "They seem to be restricted to this cabin, but Vampires are going in and out. Jer, if you open the second video you'll see what I'm talking about."

The screen refreshed as Jared opened the second file and on the screen was a long rectangular building with rows and rows of orange figures lying next to each other. They appeared very stationary, lethargic even, and I could see John's mind analyzing each and every one of them.

"Jer, can you open the third video? This one's for Brianna and Cameron."

Once again the screen flashed and another video began to display. At first it looked similar to the others until the camera panned to the right and focused in on a small yellow and green figure skipping around a cabin. I had to clamp my jaw down tightly as I saw my son for the first time in nearly a month. All eyes were on me, Devin's hand squeezing my shoulder, all of which made it difficult to keep my emotions in check. Needless to say I was happy when Connor began speaking again.

"We followed Jack as much as we could. As you can see there are four Vampires surrounding the cabin, but they also follow him wherever he goes."

"Go on, John," Jared said from the front of the room, "you know you want to say it."

John smirked and then said, "Four doesn't seem so bad."

"What about the Vampire numbers?" Victor pressed once the muffled laughter died down.

Connor sighed deeply. "In looking at the main encampment we saw roughly thirty Vamps monitoring the area, but then we found a second camp. Jer, pull up the last video."

When the screen flashed again the picture was almost solid purple from the sea of Vampires. Victor stood stoic while Devin's jaw became slack.

"How did Aidan recruit so many right under our nose?" I asked.

"Child, there are many out there that would rather not have to live under the rules we enforce."

"There are so many," I sighed as I looked to my father. "There are not nearly enough Warriors to conquer all of them, and do not forget all the humans we will need to help as well."

"Cameron, we can handle them," Alex said, trying to be positive, but I could hear the uncertainty in his voice.

"Even with our full ranks it would be nearly five to one. Now take away Warriors for security of Facilities, getting the humans and hybrids out of danger, and protecting our own basecamp, then we are looking at ten to one. Alex, that is difficult even for you."

"What do you propose, Father?" Devin asked.

Victor rubbed his chin with his index finger while he walked slowly in a circle around himself. Finally, "We should go to the other covens and seek their help. What we need are numbers. At our core we are all Vampires, the fiercest creatures in existence. You do not need to be a Warrior in order to fight this war. We are fighting for a common cause here and everyone needs to understand that. Devin and Cameron, you and I will begin calling the coven heads. Kyla, Alex, Fabiani, start contacting all the solitaries you know. Bring in Lanashell as well, there are always solitaries passing through Facility West. Start with those furthest away, we will need to allow for travel time. I want everyone convened here the day after tomorrow."

"Well, I best be off then," Eris announced as he stood from a couch several feet in front of us.

"But Eris, we need you," I replied quickly. "Brianna needs your help protecting Olivia."

"Mia figlia needs my chits more," he said as he extended his hand to Seraphina to help her from the couch. "I am going to cash in every one. Victor, I will make sure Vlad has me back the day after tomorrow. I hope that Seraphin-na may continue to stay under your protection?"

Victor assured Eris that Seraphina would be safe with us, and from the carefree look she had upon her face everything was still as it should be. My brain was screaming at me to stop Eris from leaving, but I knew it was no use. The only person stubborner than Bri was her father.

"What do you want us to do, Father?" Connor asked into the camera.

"Find a way in," Victor replied. "That is what we need most of all. There has to be a weak spot somewhere. Stay safe and check in with Jared every hour, more if you feel you need to. We also need to start devising battle plans. Work with each other, work with the whole coven, it is your choice, but I want to see drafts by tomorrow. And Jared, I do not care if the FBI, CIA, or Homeland Security come knocking on our door, I want satellite images now, not tomorrow, is that understood?"

"Yeah, Dad, I understand," Jared mumbled like a punished child.

Once the camera feed was turned off, everyone in the room went to work. Jonah began taking notes while John rattled off the supplies he would need while Alex and Kyla began searching for any and all solitaries. As Victor began discussing who would speak to which coven heads, Fabiani interrupted our circle.

"Victor, excuse me," he began, "I can contact Ormond on your behalf if you would like. Considering how things are between our covens right now, he might be more accepting of my call."

"I believe you may be right, Fabi," Victor replied with a rare smile. "Consider him yours. Hopefully we can at least confirm the covens within the next couple of hours."

"Yes, Father, but what do we say?" Devin complained. "On the rare occasions we've asked for any kind of support it is like pulling teeth. What am I supposed to say to convince them to help us?"

"We will tell them the truth, child. Aidan is not just an enemy to us, he is an enemy of our entire race. For years he and his followers have been trying to create a new breed of Vampires in order to gain power. Because we know his endeavors are fruitless, all he is succeeding in doing is torturing poor humans and hybrids, and we need to bring it to an end. From the number of followers he has acquired, Aidan is obviously preparing for a battle and we need to shut him down."

"But Father, Jack's kidnapping spread like wildfire. No matter what we say, they are going to think this is all for him."

Victor patted Devin's shoulder as he said, "Let them think what they want, we know the truth. Aidan's obsession with creating a living Vampire is what has caused this."

"Yeah, bro," Jared scoffed, "it's not like we had anything to do with how Jack and Livy are. They were just born that way."

Suddenly there was a burning in the pit of my stomach. If I had simply kept my blood to myself none of this would have happened.

"Jared, is the feed dead?"

"Yeah, bro, why?"

I turned to check that the door was closed and when I turned back around Victor squeezed my arm tightly.

"Child, before you say anything, think about the repercussions."

"And I deserve them, Father," I replied, prying his hand off of me. It was time to confess my sins. "Jared, unfortunately you are incorrect. Jackson and Olivia are more Vampire than human because of me."

"Brother, it is more likely because of Eris's blood…"

"I activated the twins," I interrupted and Devin froze. "I am sure that John can attest that the children were born perfectly normal and it was not until I had a moment of weakness did they become living Vampires. All of this rests squarely on my shoulders."

"What is wrong with you!" John yelled from across the room. "They were only infants and you gave them Vampire blood!"

"Doc, calm down," Jared said in my defense.

"No, I will not calm down! It was bad enough he Turned Brianna against her will, but the twins too? Where do you draw the line? I thought there were laws against Turning children."

"John is right, Father," Devin said sadly. "I killed Aidan's father for doing the same thing, no wonder he has a vendetta against us. To him we are hypocrites hiding behind our own laws. If we are to uphold order I should technically kill Cameron, kill my brother…"

"Child, you will not be asked to kill Cameron for he didn't break our law. He activated the twins, he did not Turn them. It is a thin line but there is a definite difference."

"Have you known all along, Father?"

Victor looked nervously at the others in the room. When he finally answered he rested his eyes on me. "It was more of a suspicion. When Eris and I discovered that the children had fangs, it was Seraphina who hinted that Cameron might be responsible. Because the children were very much alive I didn't pursue it any further."

"You chose to look away so you wouldn't have to punish him," John said angrily.

"Dr. Ryan," Victor began warningly, "you are a friend of this coven and relatively new to our ways so I will excuse your accusation this time."

"I may be new, but apparently I'm the only one with the balls to say something," John continued as he eyed Alexander and Kyla. "I am the only one thinking of my god children. All I am saying is that if it was anyone else he would have been killed or tortured."

"John, I assure you I have been tortured every day since I realized the effects of my blood on the children." John huffed and rolled his eyes, finally turning his back to me. "My guilt has been unbearable since Jackson was taken."

"Does Brianna know?" Fabiani asked tentatively.

"Yes, but only for a few weeks."

"Unbelievable," John muttered in the corner.

"John, I absolutely deserve your anger, and if you feel you cannot participate in this mission…"

"Don't you put that on me, man," John shouted as he turned violently around, "don't you even dare. I'm doing this for Jack and Livy and all those other women, but I am certainly not doing it for you. I honestly can't believe Brianna forgave you for this."

"If it makes you feel any better, I am just as surprised."

Victor wrapped his hand around my arm and pulled me toward the door.

"Child, we can handle things from here. Perhaps your time would be better spent with Brianna."

"But Father…"

"It wasn't a request. Allow everyone a little time to process this without you in the room."

I took Victor's cue and exited the library, leaving my family to deal with the bomb I had dropped. I walked slowly down the corridor, my feet feeling as though they were trudging through thick swamp mud. By the time I reached the top of the stairs my legs were shaking with fatigue. Everything had finally caught up to me and the weight was unbearable. Thankfully Olivia's room was only a few feet away, however, when I opened the door and found her bed empty I went into a panic.

We're in here, babe, Brianna's voice rang in my head.

I stepped across the hall and when I opened the door I sighed with relief at the sight of my daughter asleep and draped on top of her mother.

"I didn't mean to scare you," she whispered. "Sera found me and said that Dad had to leave all of a sudden so he wouldn't be able to watch over Livy tonight. Our bed is more comfortable than hers."

"Did Seraphina tell you why he left?" I asked as I closed the bedroom door behind me.

"No, just that he went off with Vlad. Cam, are you ok? You don't look so good. I'm afraid to ask how the call with Connor went."

I walked around to the other side of the bed and crawled up next to my girls. My hand instantly cupped the back of Olivia's head, her soft hair soothing me as I twined it around my fingers. I looked up to find Brianna staring worriedly down at me. Unable to handle her gaze I rested my head upon her shoulder.

"Aidan has an army."

"Well, we knew that," she replied, her hand combing through my hair.

"His army is bigger than ours, much bigger."

"But…nothing we can't handle, right?"

"Father is seeking help from the other covens, but I doubt we will obtain any real numbers. All I want is to bring our son home, not worry about all the other…pardon me…the other bullshit."

"You're such a potty mouth, Mr. Burke," she laughed softly, but then she sighed and became very serious. "I need you to say we can handle it, Cam."

"I cannot lie to you, angel, it does not look good."

Brianna remained quiet for several minutes, a million thoughts running through her head I assumed. Her hand, however, did not stop combing through my hair and I was very thankful for that. I was practically asleep when she said, "We're going to be fine. We'll get the help we need. We'll convince them, Cam."

I tilted my head back so I could look Brianna in the eye as I said, "I told the family what I did to the twins."

Brianna blinked several times before she answered, "And? Death by Devin? Board and chains?"

"Surprisingly, no. Father is actually defending me. It is John who may never talk to me again."

"John? Really? Honestly, I would have guessed Kyla before John. Crap, this means I'm going to have to deal with Renee tomorrow."

"Brianna, please try to be serious about this."

"I am, Cam," she replied. "My best friend is a complete psychopath and I take handling her very seriously. I also understand how serious of a situation this has become. Babe, in the four years we've been together our life has been nothing but serious. Right now we have more to worry about than John having a fit. He'll get over it. I know I have."

"Have you?"

"Yes…well…mostly."

"Mostly?"

She sighed. "There are moments when I start cursing you inside my head for what you did, but then I realize you're punishing yourself for it just as much. Every time you see the children you'll be reminded of what you did. I believe that's enough."

"You know me well, my love."

"Now not to say that when the twins get older there won't be times I'll throw it in your face," she said firmly. "I believe I'm owed that much."

I smiled and nuzzled back into the crook of her shoulder, realizing that our roles had been reversed. Usually Brianna was the one curling into my side while I comforted her.

"I have to say, love, I am surprised at your reaction to John."

"It's probably misplaced."

"How so?"

"Wills got into the primary school," she sighed. "Renee told me today."

"But that is wonderful news."

"Yes, but it's not our kids," she snapped. "Our babies are twice as smart as Wills…"

"Brianna…"

"I know, I know. It's not their fault that we have a maniac hunting down our family."

"No, it is mine," I replied truthfully and then rolled away from her to sit on the edge of the mattress. "I should really get back downstairs."

"Do you really need to?" she asked as she tugged on the back of my shirt. "Couldn't you stay here with us instead? Take one night off, Cam. You can watch Livy dream about her butterflies. She was giving them another recital."

"Monkey and her butterflies," I laughed and then curled back into Brianna's side. "Tell me again that everything will be ok."

"It has to be."

Chapter Forty-seven

Jonah

What did one wear to an emergency gathering of covens? Hopefully it was a pair of jeans and a button-up shirt because that's all I had. I picked the nicest one at least, not that there was much choice. I decided to forgo the spikey hair and go with a more mature hairstyle. Not sure why I was focusing on it, no one was going to be paying attention to me. Today was the battle before the war, I guess you could say. Everyone was on edge and the tension only grew as Vampires from all over started trickling into the manor, although we were all hoping for a flood.

After today everything would be full steam ahead. There would be battle plans and bloodshed, and surprisingly I wanted to be a part of it. However, Devin and Alex made it pretty clear last night that no humans or hybrids would be allowed to go except for John and a couple of his nurses. Even that made people uncomfortable. I had tried fighting my case, but Brianna laid into me, just like a big sister would have. It still didn't change my mind. I needed to go so I could find Ashlyn, but to also help my friends. I hadn't given up, though. There was still a full day left to wear them down.

Just as I wiped the last bits of shaving cream off my face there was a knock at the door. From the sound of a little girl's laughter a second later I knew my escort to the coven gathering had arrived.

"So, do I look good enough to eat?" I joked as I stepped into my bedroom.

Brianna rolled her eyes and shook her head while Livy climbed up onto the bed and began bouncing on the mattress.

"You know, Jonah," Bri warned as she reached back around my neck and fixed my shirt collar, "on a day like today, someone might take you seriously." Once she had finished straightening my shirt she looked up at me curiously. "No spikes today?"

Nervously I patted my hair down. "I was going for the sleek, mature look."

"I like the spikes," Livy squealed as she fell flat on the mattress.

"Hey, Livybean, bounce some more on the bed," Brianna said, causing me to give her an odd look. Once Livy was jumping on the bed again and squealing with joy, Bri took me by the arm and pulled me over to the far corner. "How are you doing? With all the chaos we never did get to talk about Ashlyn."

My stomach sank and my heart started to beat faster. "Cameron and I talked about it and then I spoke with my mom."

"You spoke to your mom? Jonah, that's wonderful."

"Yeah well, I've been thinking about it and..."

"Look, I know it's overwhelming, but don't make any decisions right now. Just wait until we know the truth and you talk to Ashlyn face to face."

"Bri, I..."

"Jack-Jack could have it wrong, we just don't know. And what's with that whole Eris is somehow the father."

"Bri..."

"Jonah," she interrupted again and lowered her voice even further and couldn't look me in the eye, "I...I know what she's going through. Shortly after I met Cam..."

"I know, Bri," I interrupted. She looked at me curiously, a thin red tear gathering at the corner of her eye. "Cameron told me."

"W-what?"

"Not details, just that you were in a...similar...situation."

She nodded and quickly wiped away the tear that was about to fall. "And he still stayed with me."

"Because he's a good man."

"So are you, Jonah."

I narrowed my eyes at her. "Bri, I'm not giving up on Ashlyn."

Brianna sighed with relief and patted my arm. "Ok, we should go then, we don't want to be late. Come on, baby girl."

"Mama, can Jonah give me a ride?"

Without another word I leaned down and Livy quickly leapt onto my back. She was so light I barely noticed her hanging from my shoulders. Before we were out the door Brianna grabbed my hand and held it tightly all the way down to the first floor. The main corridor was full of people coming in from outside, milling around and catching up, or like us just trying to get through to the Council Hall. Curious eyes started to stare as we pushed through the crowd which made Brianna so nervous that she pulled Livy from my back and held her tightly against her chest until we reached the courtyard.

Brianna pulled on the sleeve of my shirt and brought me to a stop near one of the several stone archways. Her voice was low and nervous as she said, "Jonah, it's important that you stay close to me. There are way too many Vampires around and not all of them have the control you're used to seeing from the Warriors."

I nodded as I cautiously looked at those around us. "Not a problem."

"The same goes for you, baby girl," she continued and adjusted one of Livy's curls. "You need to stay with me at all times. Do you understand?"

Livy blew her cheeks out and sighed loudly. "Yes, Mama, I know. You told me already."

"Yes well, I'm hoping you'll actually listen and do what I ask," Brianna muttered just as someone squeezed my arm from behind.

I turned to find Tosh with her hair tied back tightly, her face beaming with pride and sporting a black jumpsuit. I looked past her shoulder and noticed several others in the same outfit.

"Is this your uniform?" I asked.

She nodded with a wide smile. "Yeah, we all decided to wear them and go in together. And look," she said and pulled on her collar with a small circular pin, "it's almost like the pins the Warriors get when they're inducted, but it's stainless steel instead of gold. But I'll get there, right Brianna?"

"Of course you will, sweetie."

"Oh, there's Lana! I'm going to say hi to her before we go in. I'll see you guys in there," Tosh said and stepped over to a well-dressed blonde woman.

"Is that Lana as in Lanashell?" I asked, jutting my chin in the blonde woman's direction. "Like the head of Facility West?"

"Yep, that's her," Brianna grumbled.

"Not a fan?" Brianna didn't answer. "Well, you better become one, she's a..."

But before I could finish, the blonde woman known as Lanashell was standing next to us.

"There's no need for you to warn Brianna," she said with a smile which made me oddly uncomfortable. "I am very well aware how she feels about me, and she certainly has her reasons. You must be Jonah Thorne."

"Er...a...yeah," I replied and fumbled to give her my hand. "I forget about Vampire hearing sometimes, I didn't mean to offend..."

"Oh nonsense," she replied. "You can't run Facility West and not have a thick skin. I've heard a lot about you, Mr. Thorne."

"Really? That can't be good."

"On the contrary. Victor tells me you have been an asset to his family during this ordeal."

"Well, uh...I wouldn't say that," I replied and pushed my hands awkwardly into my pockets.

"Then you'd be lying, Jonah," Brianna corrected.

"And modest, too," Lana said, crossing her arms and suddenly becoming very serious. "You know, I am always looking for good people to work for me. The Facility can't run just with Vampires, I need good humans that the hybrids can count on and feel comfortable with."

"But you don't use drivers to transport the hybrids."

Lanashell shook her head. "Mr. Thorne, you misunderstand me. No, I'm thinking you definitely need to be in administration, be part of my direct staff."

I blinked slowly and looked over to Brianna whose eyes looked as big as mine felt.

"W-why?"

Lanashell laughed and then leaned her body in closer as she whispered, "Because I want the guy that Facility East can't seem to run without."

"I'm sure that's not true," I replied, although Brianna gave me a look.

"Mr. Thorne, the writing is on the wall. Facility East is crumbling and Diana is the cause. Everyone sees it. It's only a matter of time before she's walked out the door. Ah, and speaking of the train wreck, here she comes now."

I whipped my head around so fast my neck cracked. Lanashell was right, coming down the short set of stairs from the corridor was Diana, similarly dressed to Lanashell in a tight fitting suit. Diana flinched nervously as she caught all of us staring at her.

"Thanks for waiting for me, Lana," she said as she stood next to us. "Brianna, Olivia, nice to see you again. I wish it was under better circumstances, of course."

Brianna nodded awkwardly. "Nice to see you as well, Diana."

"And Jonah, I was hoping I would get to see you today."

"You were?"

"Yes, I'm hoping that after the session is over we could find some time to talk."

I must have stared at Diana for nearly a minute before I finally answered, "Uh…sure."

With a nod and a slight smile, Diana turned and walked away with Lanashell falling in line next to her.

"That was weird," I muttered softly and Brianna nodded.

"We should get in there," Brianna said, switching Livy to her other hip and stepping into the flow of people.

"We're not waiting for Cameron?"

She shook her head. "He comes in with Victor and Devin."

"Will Ada sit wiff us?" Livy asked and Brianna shook her head again.

"No, baby, Ada has to sit with Grandfather, remember?" she said as we entered the Council Hall.

I had heard descriptions, but nothing could have prepared me for the tall ceilings, the wide stone steps that cut into the hall's oval shape, or even how the sun came through the glass in the windows near the ceiling giving it a heavenly glow. The Council Hall's stone seating was cut into two sections, divided down the middle by its wide entranceway. The right side, where we were making our way up to Alex, Kyla, and Jared, was definitely the Warrior's side. Almost everyone was either in black combat attire, or sitting next to someone who was. I waved up to Tosh who sat with the other trainees on the top row, all of them looking nervous and proud at the same time. The other side of the room was filling up with members of the other covens, and sadly it was just over half occupied. Brianna sat on the edge of our row with Livy on her lap, staring intently at the other side.

"Have you heard from Eris?" I asked.

"Hmm?" she replied startled. "Um...no, not yet. Sera said he would be back today, she just didn't know when. Let's just hope he's bringing a freakin' army with him."

I squeezed her hand supportively just as Victor paraded through the wide double doors with Cameron and Devin only a few steps behind him. The Warrior side of the hall rose to their feet, as did many of the Vampires on the other side, although there were those who dug their way firmly into their seat. When Victor had reached his throne, Cameron and Devin stepped past him to theirs and the three of them turned around together.

Victor waved his hands down, gesturing for everyone to sit so he could call the meeting to order. Apparently Livy decided it was her time to make a break for it and leapt out of Brianna's arms. Brianna's hands were grabbing at her as she flipped through the air, landing gracefully on her feet and running towards the front of the hall. Cameron lunged forward to catch her, but Victor placed his hand up and allowed Livy to hug his leg. Brianna was mortified, her head shaking in her hand while mummers and soft laughter echoed throughout the crowd.

"Brianna, calm yourself," Victor said while he turned Livy around, "everyone here should see who we are fighting for. I am not merely talking about my granddaughter, but the safety of all our children and the future of our race. Our enemy has tortured and killed for too long and we finally have the opportunity to stop it once and for all. However, we Warriors cannot do it alone.

"Aidan's numbers are too great and there are humans in delicate situations that must be rescued. There are simply not enough Warriors to fight this war. That is why we have had a call to arms. We are bringing the covens together to fight for a common and important cause. With that, the floor is now open to each of the coven leaders. Let us start with Vivienne."

While Victor took his seat and pulled Olivia on his lap, Brianna looked across me over at Kyla who shrugged and returned a worried expression. I patted Brianna's arm for an explanation.

"Kyla's old coven," she whispered in my ear.

"Victor," the woman named Vivienne said as she stepped into the center of the room, "my coven and I are grateful for the protection the Warriors have always provided us. And although you have used your granddaughter to pull at our heartstrings, I think I speak for many of us when I say that protecting our race is your coven's only function."

Victor was stone-faced while Vivienne continued, "My Vampires are artists and actors, not soldiers. That is why the Warrior coven was created, to protect and fight for the weaker members of our race. I could not with good conscience ask my sires to go off to war. It would be leading the lambs to slaughter."

"And you believe that Aidan's army is filled with soldiers? I assure you they are not. We have all seen what your actors can do in their films," Victor said as he pointed to several gentlemen behind Vivienne, and yes they looked oddly familiar. "We are not asking anyone to be as skilled as us, but you are still Vampires. I assume even you, Vivienne, could scratch a man's eyes out."

Vivienne straightened her posture and quirked her lips at Victor's dig.

"Needless to say, Victor, I will not force my coven to participate."

Suddenly Kyla stood from her seat. "Victor, you know you have my full support, and if I have to be the only representative from my coven then so be it."

Victor smiled and nodded in Kyla's direction while Vivienne glared at her.

"Honestly, Kyla," she said in a nasty tone, "I don't think anyone here is surprised by your declaration. You're practically a Warrior yourself. You certainly don't share my blood."

Alex squeezed Kyla's hand tightly for support, and from the tears that were welling up in the corners of her eyes she needed it.

But then with a quick shake of her head she retorted, "Thank goodness for that. I certainly wouldn't want a coward's blood running through my veins."

The entire room gasped. Vivienne just put her nose in the air and sat back down next to the three gentlemen from her coven who all concentrated guiltily on the floor.

Victor sighed and tapped his fingers on the arm of his chair before finally saying, "Let us move on to the Cleaners. Santino, the floor is yours."

A slender, meek-looking man stepped down from the second stone landing. He was dressed in white from head to toe, and the dozen or so that were sitting in the same row were similarly dressed. At least he had brought more people than Vivienne.

Once Santino stood in the center of the room he bowed slightly to Victor and in return Victor tapped his heart with his fist.

"Victor, your Warriors keep my coven busier than any other," Santino began in a light-hearted tone, receiving soft laughter in response. "But I have to agree with Vivienne in the fact that my coven is not equipped to battle like yours."

Another round of groans echoed from our side of the room. Brianna folded over her knees. I could see Cameron digging his nails into the wooden handles of his chair. The only person who seemed unaffected was Livy. She was sitting on Victor's lap, swinging her legs freely and happily.

"However," Santino continued through the murmurs, "my coven has seen enough humans and hybrids tortured, mutilated, and killed at the hands of Elaina and Aidan. By not volunteering to help the Warriors, we are sending a message that we Vampires are more important than our fragile children of flesh and blood.

"Victor, my Cleaners may not be equipped for battle, but we can provide the additional security needed at the Facilities so that those security teams and your Warriors can be where they should be."

Brianna's head shot up while others sighed with relief.

"Santino, thank you," Victor said calmly.

He nodded and gestured toward the others from his coven who stood up proudly as Santino said, "Thirteen of my Cleaners have also volunteered to go with you to help with the rescue and transport of the humans that are being held captive. And afterwards they will aid in cleaning up what mess remains."

Victor shifted Livy off of his lap and stood from his throne with Cameron and Devin following suit. All three of them put their fists against their hearts as Victor said, "Santino, I am truly grateful for your coven's service. Their bravery will not go unrewarded."

As Victor bowed, others around us beat their chests with their fists, including Alex next to me. Feeling a little out of place, my right hand went up to my chest, but Brianna lowered my arm and shook her head slightly.

Once Santino and his coven members were seated, Victor called another one of the coven leaders down, and whatever relief Brianna had felt previously was suddenly gone. I nudged her, silently asking her why.

"Ormond isn't going to help us," she replied quietly.

"Ormond? Isn't that Fabi's coven?" I whispered and she nodded.

"Victor, there is no point in beating around bush," Ormond said with a smirk. "I think it is preposterous that the Warriors are seeking help from any of the covens. It is your job as our protectors to do just that. If you are unable to do that, then perhaps we need to find protection elsewhere."

I hated this guy and his stupid smirk. Victor, however, seemed to find it amusing.

"Ormond, considering we are having a hard enough time finding any help for this battle, I'm not sure where you think you're going to find others to protect you. I believe you are unable to see past your personal vendetta against us."

"Of course this is personal, Victor," Ormond shouted. "Not two days ago you were calling for our disbandment, and now you are begging for our help. It is a bit hypocritical in my opinion."

"So you are refusing to help, is that what you are saying?"

"Yes, that is what I am saying," he replied. "If your coven fails, let the cards fall where they may. Our race will adjust and survive. I have informed the members of my coven that they are prohibited from volunteering for this suicide mission. If they disobey this order, then there will be consequences."

"Then bring 'em on," someone said in the crowd. When I looked to the other side I saw Fabi standing alone, others around him with shocked expressions as they looked up at him.

"Fabiani," Ormond growled, "think before turning your back on your coven because we will do the same to you."

Fabi's lips tightened while he remained silent for several seconds. Devin was sitting calmly in his tall chair, but I knew he must have been going crazy on the inside. Finally, Fabi turned his body toward Victor and said, "Victor, I may not be a soldier, but like you said before, I can scratch out someone's eyes like nobody's business. Consider your numbers up by one."

"We all know why you're doing this," Ormond said over the gasps.

The family members around me froze, all eyes on Devin as his hand tightened over the arm of his chair.

But Fabi remained calm as he responded, "I am doing this for Dante."

"Dante?" Ormond laughed. "Please. You're doing this because…"

"Because I'm ashamed of my coven," Fabi interrupted. "Our maker and mentor was killed by Aidan's men. We should have been the first ones in line wanting to get our revenge, but no, you are forcing us to cower in the corner. Dante would be ashamed."

"Dante believed in peace, not war."

"And he also knew that there were some battles that no amount of mediation could resolve. This is one of those battles. If Dante were here he would be working on convincing everyone in this room to help these young women and children. Anyone who doesn't help, should be ashamed of themselves. And frankly, if I can grow a set, anyone can."

Ormond didn't seem to appreciate the soft laughter and some congratulatory claps. "Well, Fabiani, I hope you'll be happy without a coven. At least now you can stick your newly grown set into whatever Warrior you want without any guilt."

Devin flinched, but it was Cameron who stood from his chair.

"Ormond, you have gone too far."

"Cameron, it's fine," Fabi said calmly as he stepped down from where his other coven members sat. "I've never felt guilty a day in my life, Ormond. I'm proud of everything and everyone I've ever done. Now, Victor, do you mind if I sit on your side?"

"By all means," Victor answered and gestured to our side. "Very well, who is next?"

I probably wasn't the only one who thought that Fabi's defection would cause others to do the same, but that hope was lost when the remaining coven leaders sided with Ormond and Vivienne. Only a handful of the solitaries ended up volunteering when all was said and done. The disappointment was not lost on Victor as he addressed the room.

"Thank you to those who are willing to fight with us, but we still do not have enough to secure a victory against this enemy. If we are defeated, our way of life will cease to exist. Our children will continue to be hunted, as will those that stand against Aidan's new ways. If that day comes, I hope you look back and remember you chose to do nothing."

"Then let us help," a female's voice said behind us.

Everyone turned around to see who had spoken, and honestly I shouldn't have been that shocked to see it was the bravest girl I knew.

"Natasha Cushlin," Victor said proudly, "as always your loyalty moves me. It also makes me very proud to see a hybrid be braver than many of the Vampires in this room, but it is simply too dangerous."

"Victor, you are training us to be one of you. This is what we've signed up for. Let us help you. We are well aware of the risks."

"Yes, Natasha, I'm sure you are, but you are the only one that would be able to heal. Your fellow trainees would not be as lucky."

"But..."

"I'm sorry, Natasha, that is my final word."

"But it should be her choice," I said a second before I could clamp my mouth shut. Brianna slowly turned her head, her eyes burning into the left side of my face.

"Mr. Thorne?" Victor said curiously. "Do you have something to say?"

"Y-yes?" I replied tentatively, but Brianna clamped down on my arm.

"No he doesn't," she said firmly, glaring at me.

"Brianna, let him speak," Victor said, flicking his fingers up for me to stand.

Carefully I pulled Brianna's hand free from my arm and stood up slowly.

"I'm sorry, Victor...uh...sir," I stuttered and bowed slightly thinking that was what I was supposed to do. "I was just saying that it should be Tosh's...er...Natasha's choice. She knows the danger, she knows what they did to her sister, and I'm sure the other trainees have either suffered themselves or know someone who has at Aidan's or Elaina's hands."

Victor nodded slightly. "Yes, but the point of this battle is to save hybrids, not cause more fatalities."

"I understand that, truly I do," I tried to say as respectfully as possible. "But I think most hybrids are tired of being hunted. They're sick of having to look over their shoulder even if they're the lucky few that get released from a Facility. And we all know it's not going to stop. I was nearly killed by one of Aidan's goons because I was transporting a hybrid Firestarter. The girl had been in hiding her entire life and the first time she literally leaves the farm, she's almost taken. I'm just a lowly human in your world, but I for one think they deserve a better life than this. What boggles my mind is that so few of you over there do.

"I grew up with the horror movies and myths and books about Vampires, and honestly the first time I saw a Vampire up close I almost pissed myself. If the world could see you all now, they'd laugh. Squabbling over vendettas and whining about not being soldiers. You all could plow through those woods and all of this would be over. But you're scared. Victor, if you'll let me, I'll be there on the battlefield."

Cameron cleared his throat and gave me warning eyes.

"Ok, maybe help Doc Ryan," I said with a laugh. "But let me help, let the trainees volunteer if they want, look to Facility West, you never know who else might want to help end this. Let's stop another hybrid from being hunted, another child being experimented on, another woman being..." I had to stop and clear my throat of the lump that had formed, "...let's stop another woman from being raped. If what Aidan is doing doesn't disgust you, then you are no better than he is. By not stopping this you're supporting it, it's as easy as that."

You could have heard a pin drop in that Council Hall. I realized I was laying it on pretty thick, but I had to do something. Victor strummed his fingers on the arm of his chair again, letting the painful silence continue for nearly a minute before finally saying, "Jonah Thorne, your bravery outweighs your insolence. On a day like today that makes you a very lucky young man."

I sighed with relief and suddenly needed to go to the bathroom.

"With that said," Victor continued, "I will allow you to help us."

"You also have the ten of us," Tosh announced and nine other hybrids stood around her.

"And me," Nikki said to my right, hidden the whole time on the other side of Jared. To say we were shocked was an understatement, but Nikki stood nervously, exchanging a quick glance with her sister before saying, "I'm a Healer, I can help Dr. Ryan as well."

From there it wasn't like the movies where one guy stood starting the "slow clap" causing everyone else in the room to rise and volunteer to stand together as one against the enemy. Instead, only an additional twelve Vampires volunteered to help, mostly solitaries, but including the gentlemen from Vivienne's coven. It was more than we had before at least.

Victor stood from his throne and placed little Livy to stand in front of him. Just as he opened his mouth to speak, the wide double doors flew open and Eris walked down the center aisle with six other men following behind.

"My God," Alex muttered next to me.

"What?" I whispered and both Brianna and I whipped our heads in his direction.

"Those are the Ancients," he replied quietly, although the hall was quickly becoming loud with the sound of gasps. "Eris has all six Ancients with him. It's…it's historic."

"I guess he really did cash in his chits," Bri said stunned.

"Father," Victor said breathlessly as he stepped down from his throne and knelt down in front of a very rigid dark-haired man. Sadly, the respect and longing seen on Victor's face was not reciprocated.

"It has been many years, child," he said in a very disinterested tone.

"Grandfather, who's that?" Livy asked as she climbed up Victor's back and hung on his shoulder.

"Olivia, this is my father, Alastor. Father…"

"Is this the other one Eris spoke of," Alastor interrupted and pointed in Livy's direction.

"The other one?" Brianna growled softly through very tight lips causing Cameron to look up at her nervously.

"Yes, Father," Victor replied quickly. "Olivia's twin brother is the one that was taken."

Alastor scrunched his brows and scanned Livy up and down before saying, "I guess I don't see the allure. She doesn't seem special to me."

Brianna flinched forward, but Alex and I grabbed her arm and pulled her back. Livy, however, wasn't fazed by Alastor's insult.

"But I am special. I have fangs, see," she said as she opened her mouth wide and her small fangs extended down.

All six Ancients flinched backwards, as did others on both sides of the room. Once the initial shock wore off, one of the other Ancients inched forward and knelt to the ground.

"May I have a closer look at her?"

"Of course, Cassius," Eris replied and Victor lowered Livy down to the floor.

Cameron closed in on the group, but Eris held his hand up in Cameron's direction. The Ancient named Cassius had a much kinder face than his brother Alastor.

"You are a very pretty little thing, aren't you?" he asked.

"Ada says I am," Livy affirmed. "Have you come to help Jack-Jack?"

"Yes, I do hope we can," Cassius replied in a kind voice.

"Only because Eris is holding his leverage above our heads," Alastor grumbled, causing those around me to look at each other curiously.

"Which will be paid in full once your service to us is complete," Eris replied, making Alastor and a couple of the other Ancients sneer and roll their eyes. "Now, Alastor, how about giving everyone a demonstration of your unique gift."

Victor looked at Alastor curiously. "What gift, Father?"

"Victor, I am happy to say I have solved one of our little mysteries," Eris said proudly. "Alastor, why not demonstrate with your only child."

Alastor glared at Eris before exhaling dramatically and taking Victor's hand. A second later both men disappeared into a cloud of black smoke. The entire hall was suddenly in an uproar, except me and Brianna. We had seen it done before. Now no one could say we were lying or crazy.

A few seconds later Alastor returned to his original spot, although Victor wasn't with him. Victor Projected back inside the Council Hall a second later, a look of hurt and embarrassment on his face. Alastor was an asshole.

"So you see, Warrior," Eris said in Cameron's direction, "it is not just Gorum who has this extraordinary Projection ability. Since Alastor is the eldest, it might very well have to do with age versus blood."

"Especially since we know you certainly don't share a bloodline with us," Alastor said nastily.

"Alastor, please," Cassius said calmly while still kneeling in front of Livy, "we have come here to pay our debt, not drudge up old feuds."

Alastor scrunched up his face angrily and shook his head. "I will honor my agreement and that is all, not a minuscule amount more."

"Thank you, Father," Victor said. "Your help is greatly appreciated."

"Yes, well you certainly aren't going to be risking your life for anyone. That is why you have a coven, isn't it? You always were the one staying behind while the others did the real fighting."

Before Victor could reply, Devin launched himself from his chair at the front of the hall. Cameron dove in front of him and tackled him to the ground. In the middle of the chaos, Cassius lifted Livy into his arms, I assumed to protect her. However, when he took a step back it must have been one step too many for Brianna's comfort because Cassius was suddenly flattened out on the floor, writhing in pain from an invisible force, although from the way Brianna held out her hand I knew it was her. Livy landed on her feet gracefully while the other Ancients looked on with horror.

"Mia figlia," Eris said lightly, "I assure you Cassius meant no harm. Perhaps you could refrain from torturing him."

Brianna lowered her hand and as her body relaxed so did Cassius's screaming.

"She certainly is your daughter, Eris," Alastor said in a snarky tone, but Eris just smiled.

"You haven't seen anything yet," he replied proudly. "Now shall we release the cowardly ones so that the real Vampires can get to work?"

Chapter Forty-eight

Jonah

How did you tell your mother that you might never come home? I'd been trying to figure that out for the last two hours. I would go to dial her number and I'd glance down at my father's watch and hang up. When I spoke up in the gathering I was standing up for what was right. I was volunteering to help my friends and the woman I loved. I was thinking only of them at the time, not the fact that my mother and sister might have to suffer through another loss. I was selfish and honorable at the same time. Either way, I still needed to talk to my mom, even if it was for the last time. Holy shit this was real now.

After a deep exhale I finally dialed my home number, thinking I would need to try her cell when she didn't answer after three rings. But just as I was about to hang up, a surprising voice came on the line.

"Wow, so you are still alive."

"Hey, Katie Bell," I replied, startled a little by the irony. "What are you doing home?"

"Duh, school's out."

"Oh, yeah, sorry. How do you think you did on your exams?"

"Great on some, shitty on others, same old same old."

"And how's Chemistry boy?"

"Who?"

I sighed. "The kid in your Chemistry class, the one you had the hots for."

"Oh please, Joey, that's like three guys ago."

"And I thought he was the reason you wanted to stay on campus."

"Yeah well, I didn't think he'd be such a mama's boy. Anyway, I've accepted the whole having to commute to class. It won't be so bad, I guess."

I was shocked at her complete one-eighty.

"What...a...changed your mind?"

She was silent for a few seconds and then her voice was very soft as she said, "Mom broke up with Paul. I came home and all his stuff was gone."

"She mentioned she was thinking about it."

"And then today," she continued, "we went and looked for apartments."

"Apartments?"

"Mm-hmm. She got an offer on the house."

My head fell into my free hand. "That's...uh...great."

"Liar," she laughed. "So seriously, since you and Mom are talking again, when are you coming home? More importantly, when do I get to meet Ashlyn?"

"Uh...well...a visit is gonna be a little hard."

"What do you mean?" she said, raising her voice. "Tomorrow's Christmas Eve, Joey! We always go..."

"It's Christmas Eve?" I asked, truly shocked.

"Joey, what is up with you? Are you stoned?"

"No! I just...lost track of time."

"So you're coming then?"

"Hey, is Mom there?" I asked, hoping to change the subject.

"Ok, so that's a no," she said before calling out to our mother.

"Katie Bell, I'm sorry. I'll be home as soon as I can."

"And buy me extra presents to make up for my pain and suffering."

"Fine," I laughed. "Hey, I...uh...love ya, Katie Bell. You're the best little sister a guy could have."

"Um...ok," she replied slowly. "Love you, too. Here's Mom."

I could hear the phone being passed, and then my mom came on the line.

"Joey?"

"Hey, Mom," I replied, pinching the inner corners of my eyes to hold in the tears that were suddenly forming. "You got an offer on the house?"

"I'm calling it my little Christmas miracle," she laughed lightly. "It came in yesterday."

"And you took it already?"

"They offered the asking price and they're paying in cash. Of course I took it. Katie Bell and I started looking at some apartments today."

"Yeah, she said," I answered sadly.

"Hopefully you'll be able to come home soon?" she asked in a prodding tone.

"That's actually why I was calling. We're going to try and get Ashlyn back tomorrow."

"Hold on," she whispered, "I'm going into another room." After another few seconds I heard the sound of a door close and then she said, "Did you just say *we're* going to get Ashlyn?"

"I'm going with them, Mom." She sighed loudly into the phone. "Mom, I'm sorry, I have to go."

"But you don't have those kind of skills," she said, her voice shaking with emotion. "How can they expect…"

"Mom, I'm just going to help any way I can. After everything Ashlyn's been through I need to be there for her. Can you understand that?"

"I can," she sniffled. "Sometimes I wish you were more of a punk kid who didn't care about anyone. Instead, your heart is big enough for everyone, but you've always been that way. It's what makes me so proud of you."

I bit the inside of my cheek and looked up at the ceiling, trying to keep my emotions at bay.

"So, Mom, if anything should happen…"

"No," she interrupted, "you will not finish that sentence. As your mother I demand that you keep yourself safe. I know you've been sucked into this top secret kind of world and I can't know all the details, but I'm telling you right now that you better come home to me. And if anything should happen to you, I will hunt Brianna Morgan down like a dog. I don't care how good she's been to us, I will see to it…"

"Mom, Mom, calm down," I said, actually laughing at her a little. "It's good to see the fight back in you."

She laughed back. "It's amazing what comes back when you don't have a parasite sucking the life out of you."

"Katie said she noticed that Paul's stuff was gone."

"He didn't take it very well," she sighed. "But at least he was out of here before she came home. I didn't realize how uncomfortable he made her feel. As soon as I told her she just let loose about how she'd catch him leering at her and that she'd purposely wear loose-fitting clothes if he was here. I...I just wish I'd known."

"He's gone, Mom, that's what's important. I wish I was able to be there."

"Nonsense, honey. You're where you should be, and don't let your sister make you feel guilty about it."

I could hear her getting emotional again, and it struck a chord inside me making it almost impossible not to cry with her.

"I love you, Mom. I'll be safe, I promise."

She sniffled loudly. "Just come home to me, Joey. I'll be praying for another Christmas miracle."

"I'll be calling you very soon."

"And be gentle with Ashlyn," she said softly. "She's been through a trauma, honey, she'll need some time to adjust."

"I know, Mom, I will. I love you."

"I love you too, honey. I will...talk...to you...later," she cried, and then hung up the phone.

But before I could wallow for too long there was a knock at the door. Quickly I wiped my eyes and pushed myself up from the floor.

"It's open, Tosh. Come on in," I said, remembering she was coming by to take me over to Cameron's poker game. You'd think I'd know where his room was by now.

But when I turned to face the door I didn't find Tosh, and my body language must have conveyed my disappointment.

"Yes I know I'm not Tosh," Diana said tentatively, "but you did say it was open."

"What are you doing here, Diana?"

"I wanted to talk to you, remember?" she asked and closed the door behind her.

I rolled my eyes with a sigh and sat down on the edge of my bed, purposely not inviting her to sit down. "Fine. What's up."

"Jonah, I know we got off on the wrong foot."

"Ha!" I shouted. "Diana, you found out I was human and decided I was beneath you. I saved a hybrid, almost got myself killed, and you fired me. You wouldn't have given me a goddamn thing if Cameron hadn't fought for me. So yeah, you could say we got off on the wrong foot."

"I know, I know, and I really am here to apologize."

"For what?" I asked skeptically.

"For not trusting you," she replied. "More so, for putting my trust in people I shouldn't have."

"Cole didn't work out so well, huh?"

Diana gave an embarrassed smirk as she straightened the skirt of her suit.

"Cole has left Facility East," she said. "And me, for that matter."

"I can't say I'm surprised," I replied and then felt like I needed to correct myself. "About leaving the Facility, not...uh...you. So if you're here and he's gone, who's looking after things?"

"Warren," she answered. "He says hello, by the way. I'm sure he'll be thrilled to hear about what you did today."

"Be sure to say hello for me. Now if that's all...

She shook her head and clinched my forearm when I rose from the bed.

"Jonah, I need you."

I paused. "Sorry, what?"

"Jonah, I need you back at Facility East. Come back and work for me."

"I don't think that's a good idea, Diana," I replied and removed her cold hand from my arm.

"I know Lana offered you a job," she said nervously.

"She didn't offer me anything specific, so don't get worked up about it. Besides I think it's mainly to get back at you for something."

"That woman hates me with a passion. I don't know why."

"Well maybe it's your charming personality," I said and thankfully she laughed.

"This is what I need, Jonah. I need someone to stand up to me, tell me when I'm being a jerk and help me with relating to the hybrids. All the warmth and camaraderie is fading away from Facility East and that's what made it so special. I know one of the reasons is because I'm there and another is because you're not. Jonah, I want you to come back and be my right hand guy."

"Diana, you have a lot of balls coming here and asking that of me. You were happy to see me leave. You didn't even care when Ashlyn was taken. She's technically one of your hybrids, did you give her even a second's thought?"

"Yes, I did!" she replied defensively.

"Bullshit. You didn't even call when it happened."

"I know you didn't want to talk to me in the first place and I'd been bothering you. So when everything happened I stopped calling. I had Warren use his contacts in order to get daily updates about her. And when I heard she might be…" she paused and looked at me compassionately, "…a…victim, my heart went out to her and to you. I just knew you wouldn't want to hear anything I had to say. But please believe me, I do care about what happens to both of you. I want you both to come back to Facility East when this is all over with. I'll do whatever it takes to bring you back, Jonah, anything."

"Go home, Diana."

Diana opened her mouth to say something, but at the same time Tosh pushed open the door.

"Oh, sorry, Jonah," Tosh said as she straightened up in the doorway. "I didn't mean to interrupt. I can come back."

"No need, Tosh. Diana was just leaving."

Diana adjusted her jacket and skirt before extending her hand to me. Hearing my father's voice in my head, I reluctantly shook it.

"Whether you believe it or not, you and Ashlyn will be in my thoughts tomorrow. If after the dust settles you change your mind, let me know. I'm sure we can work something out."

I didn't respond, simply gave her a curt nod and watched her squeeze past Tosh to exit through the doorway.

"So…um, should we go?" Tosh asked, gesturing toward the hallway. "Or did you want to hit something first?"

I laughed and walked over to her, holding the door open so she could duck out.

"Dare I ask why Diana was in your room?"

"I'd rather forget about it, actually," I replied as we began to make our way down the hallway toward the big spiraling staircase. "Maybe you could explain why this poker game is such a big deal."

"Because it's *the* poker game," she replied like an excited teenager.

"You know that doesn't actually tell me anything."

Tosh groaned at me, making me feel really stupid.

"Before every battle, Cameron and his brothers play poker. It's strictly family only, so the fact that they invited you is pretty cool."

"But why play before every battle?" I asked as we started our assent up the staircase.

"Because it might be the last," Tosh responded. "But if you think about it, they're all still alive so maybe it's a good luck thing now."

"I shouldn't be surprised that you know all this. Was it in the Warrior training handbook?"

She punched me in the arm in response.

"I'm human, you're supposed to protect me, not hurt me."

"I keep telling you, that's a rule for Vamps, not hybrids. I could kick the crap out of you if I wanted to."

"Have you forgotten already that it was me who stood up in front of that big ass crowd of Vampires and got Victor to change his mind about you? Yeah, that was me, by the way."

As we reached the top of the landing she nudged me with her hip and said, "I'll never forget that, Jonah. You were a good friend today."

"Eh, I'm not so sure. A good friend wouldn't have asked Victor to put his friend in danger."

"You didn't ask him to do it, you asked him to give us the choice. That's the major difference. And hey, you even got Nikki off her ass to help, too. You should become a motivational speaker."

I glared at her from the side of my eye. "Smartass. So what are your plans tonight before that restriction thing sets in?"

"I'm hanging out with Nikki, actually," she replied as we turned down the hallway for Cameron's rooms.

"That's really great, Tosh."

She shrugged. "Yeah, we'll see how long it lasts. I know she's nervous about tomorrow."

"About something happening to you?"

"That, and I think she's nervous about being where Aidan is. She technically still has a bounty on her head, so I know she's worried about being around Vamps she doesn't know, and about what Aidan might do to her if he gets his hands on her. So yeah, I'm doing the sisterly thing tonight. Hopefully we won't kill each other."

"You'll be fine," I laughed and she gestured to an open door on my right. When I peered inside I saw Nikki talking to Ollie and Maddy while Alex, Jared, and Devin sat around a circular table.

"Maddy!" Tosh said next to me before stepping inside the room and hugging Maddy. "I didn't know you were going to be here tonight."

I extended my hand out to Ollie who gave me a warm smile and hugged me instead.

"Are you guys just visiting?" I asked him once he released me.

"Nah," he replied. "'Lil Bri didn't want us staying at the house unprotected so we're staying here for a couple of days. Anything to ease her mind. She's got enough to worry about."

"How are you doing with all of this? You've been keeping it together pretty well from what I've seen."

"Only 'cuz I'm old, son," he smiled. "Maddy gets the worse of it. Ain't no point in me makin' a scene in front of the family. But, I know Cameron and them'll do just fine tomorrow."

"Just keep saying that to everyone, Ollie. I think we all need it," I said, patting him on the back and stepping over to the circular table where Devin and Alex were divvying up different colored poker chips. "Where's Cameron?"

Alex jutted his chin towards another door a couple of feet away. "You're lucky if you can't hear them yelling at each other."

I tilted my head toward the door and could hear the faint sounds of voices coming from the other side.

"What are they yelling about?"

"What aren't they yelling about," Jared laughed and Devin glared at him, causing his tone to change and speak in a whisper. "They're arguing about what's happening tomorrow."

Jared didn't have to say anymore, and I knew he wouldn't with Ollie in the room. Basically, the plan was to get Jackson out before any fighting broke out. The only way to locate and speak with him was through Olivia, and the only one who could hear her was Brianna. Cameron fought pretty hard against it, for obvious reasons, but even Bri shut him down. I couldn't blame Cameron for being upset. If I were in his situation, I'd probably be screaming too.

"Where's Livy?" I asked to no one in particular, but Alex chose to respond again.

"Coming down the hall from the sounds of it."

Not ten seconds later Livy came bursting into the room with Wills clutching her hand, barely able to keep up with her. Unfortunately, he almost took a face plant when Livy saw Ollie and leapt half the distance across the room to get to him. Thankfully Kyla caught Wills before he hit the floor. Once she placed him back down on the ground he scurried over to Ollie just as Renee and John came through the door. I was happy that John came, although he didn't seem all that thrilled. Honestly, he looked exhausted and a little perturbed. Renee, on the other hand...

"Don't tell me they're still in there arguing," she said as she crossed the room.

"Afraid so," Jared replied.

"Renee, leave them…" John started to say, but then sighed as she went through the inner door and shut it behind her. "I'm not sure why I try. It's not like it's going to stop her or anything."

"I'm glad you came, man," I said, patting him on the shoulder.

"Only because Renee's been yelling at me for almost three days. Seems like I'm the only one with issues about…you know," he said, realizing he couldn't say what he wanted in current company. "So I'm here. But I heard you grew some brass ones today. Standing up to Victor?"

"I didn't stand up to him," I replied, shaking my head. "I was just the idiot that made a comment under his breath and got caught. And because of that, you now have another assistant."

He laughed. "Yes, I heard that. Do you have any experience in first-aid?"

"Took a class in high school," I answered with my most charming smile.

"So no obstetrics training?"

"Sorry, man, maybe that was covered in the college classes I didn't get to."

John laughed again, although it was more of a worried laugh than anything else. In the same moment, Tosh came up behind me and placed her hand on my shoulder.

"We're taking off," she said. "I'll see you in the morning, right?"

I nodded. "Yep. I think we're in the same convoy."

"Cool. Are you sure you can get back to your room on your own? Or are you going to need a GPS?"

Without waiting for a response, she gave me a quick peck on the cheek, and headed out of the room with Nikki close behind her. I knew the kiss was innocent enough, however, the questioning look I received from John made me a little uncomfortable. Thankfully at the same time the inner door opened and Renee came walking in with Cameron and Brianna.

I broke away from John's side when Bri stepped in my direction. She and Cameron looked like they had both been through the ringer. So it surprised me when she asked, "Are you ok? Your eyes are red."

"Really?" I answered and blinked quickly several times. "Just a long day, I guess."

"Did you call your mom?" I nodded. "Does she want to kill me?" I nodded again. "Did you tell her I tried to stop you from going?"

"Eh...I might not have gotten that far." She glared at me, so I turned it around. "How are you?"

"I'd rather not say with Daddy O right behind you. He'll yell at me for swearing."

"But playing cards always makes you feel a little better."

Jared snickered behind me causing Bri to roll her eyes.

"Actually, I'm not allowed to play anymore, but it's fine. The ladies and I are doing bath time with the kids. Daddy O, you're welcome to join us or stay here with the guys, but know they don't play pennies."

Ollie smiled and stepped toward the table. "I could play a hand or two. Whadaya got to put down?"

"It's a five-hundred-dollar buy-in," Devin replied and Ollie's jaw dropped.

"Da, I will buy you in," Cameron said with a smile.

"Nah," Ollie replied. "I ain't worth that. I'll go on with the girls."

"Yeah!" Livy squealed and pulled him toward the inner door causing Bri to call after her, begging her to take it easy on her great-grandfather.

Once the ladies had filtered out of the room and the inner door was shut, I patted the back of the chair in front of me and said embarrassingly, "Look guys, I didn't know the buy-in was so high. I don't have that kind of cash. I'll just hang and turn in early."

"You've already been bought in, Jonah," Alex said as he gestured to a pile of chips next to him.

I looked over at Cameron and said, "Thanks, man, but I can't let you do that."

"He didn't," Devin responded. "I did."

"Why?" I asked stupidly. "I mean, thank you. But seriously, why?"

Devin shrugged as he began to deal out the first hand. "Because of what you did today. You showed great courage and said what none of us could. Now instead of challenging my decisions, can we start the first game?"

I nodded and quickly sat down, suddenly realizing I was sitting between Cameron and John. Jared caught the awkwardness I was feeling and smirked before looking at his cards.

"So why isn't Brianna allowed to play?" I asked while studying my own cards.

"She cheats," everyone except Cameron replied simultaneously.

"You do know how to play poker, don't you?" John asked.

"Yeah," I replied and then laughed, "Bri taught me."

Cameron laughed a little to himself while the others groaned around me. But they didn't have anything to worry about, at least for this hand because I had crap. It would, however, give me a chance to see if Brianna was right about everyone's tell. I may not be able to count cards like she did, but I could at least see if they were bluffing. I noticed Jared rubbing the top edges of his cards. If Bri was right, that meant he had nothing.

"Ok, confession time. Who's going first this time?" Jared said and then folded. Jared's tell, check.

"Confession?" I asked.

"Yeah, it's kind of a tradition," he replied. "We all tell a big secret we've been keeping."

"It is not a tradition, little brother. It just happened one time when we were playing," Cameron said, and then began picking at the cuff of his shirt. According to Bri that meant he had the start of something.

"Well maybe it should be a tradition," Jared continued. "It did us all a lot of good. If we hadn't, we'd still think Devin was a celibate straight man."

I would have laughed, but the man just put up five hundred dollars for me. The others around the table didn't have the same consideration, but Devin didn't react. In fact, after putting in his bet he kept his eyes firmly on his cards and became very quiet. That meant he had something good, really good.

"All right then, since no one else wants to go, I say John gets to go first."

"Why me?" John whined.

"Because you've barely said a word since you got here."

John sighed loudly and shifted uncomfortably in his seat while he exchanged two of his cards.

"I'm not sure what you want me to say. Um…we…uh got that house," he said as he looked across me and gave Cameron a terse smile. "I think Bri calls it the monstrosity."

Cameron nodded with a soft laugh while others around the table congratulated John on the new house.

"It's not much of a secret if you ask me," Jared muttered.

"Um, ok," John sighed. "I'm still mad at Cameron."

"Yeah, that's totally not a secret," Jared laughed. "What you don't know is that we're all a little mad at Cameron for what he did."

"You certainly don't show it."

"There's not much we can do about it now. The twins are what they are. We, as their uncles, just need to do everything we can to help them get through life. It is going to be hard for them, so they need to know how loved they are. There is no one else who knows what they're going through so that makes our roles in their lives even more important. That means all of us together as a united front."

Everyone at the table was dumbfounded at Jared's declaration. No one even reacted to Devin's winning hand.

"Did you hear that in a movie recently, little brother?" Cameron smirked as he threw his cards over to Devin.

"Don't make fun, bro. All I'm saying is that it sucks what you did, but it's done and we all need to help the twins get through it. But when BiBi used to have those dreams about battles and shit, they came true. Now the twins are having them. If their dreams are accurate, we're going to need those powers of theirs."

"Can we please stop talking about this?" Cameron asked. "I have argued enough this evening about the children's involvement tomorrow."

Devin gathered everyone's cards and began to shuffle them quickly. I had to admit they played pretty fast, and I probably needed another hand in order to get the rest of their tells. I had completely forgotten to look at John or Alex. Bri would have had them down in five seconds flat. While Devin began to deal the next hand, Jared leaned back in his seat and started staring me down.

"I think Jonah should go next," he said as he picked up his cards from the table.

"You're going to keep bugging me until I say something, aren't you?" I said as I examined my own cards. Not a bad hand, a pair of nines and the start of a straight, so I put in a couple of chips.

"Yes I am," he replied. "You might as well give it up, Thorne."

"Er...let me think," I began, wondering what in the world I could say. I took my time, even trading two of my cards before finally saying, "Well, in case anyone is wondering, I've decided not to make any rash decisions when it comes to Ashlyn. I love her. So I'm going to wait and see what she wants to do. If she wants to keep...the...baby, then I'll be there with her...if she wants me."

"Seriously, Dev, stop dealing me this shit," Jared cut in and threw his cards down on the table. "And Jonah, please, we all knew that's what you'd do."

"Wha-how did you know?"

"Because you're Mr-All-American-Boy, who always does the right thing for everyone else. So yeah, we all knew you'd never throw Ashlyn away like that. That said, it doesn't count, you need to tell another secret."

"I don't have anymore," I replied, trying to keep my eyes on those still in the game.

"Like hell you do," Jared said with a raised eyebrow.

"Well then, why don't you tell me what you want to hear."

Jared leaned forward to put his chair back down on the floor and said, "I want to know if you slept with Tosh."

The table suddenly became really quiet, and all eyes were on me. I tossed in my final bet and said, "Of course not."

"Aw come on," Jared whined, "she's been hanging on you for weeks."

"So?" I laughed. "We're just friends, Jared. She's affectionate."

"Yeah, to your pants," Jared grumbled and threw a twenty dollar bill across to Alex who took it with great pleasure.

"Wh-what's going on? Did you guys have a bet on whether Tosh and I were sleeping together?"

Cameron patted me gently on the back. "Unfortunately, Jared and Alex will bet on nearly anything."

"But I bet on your good moral code," Alex said defensively. "And I call. Show your cards, boys."

So far Bri was right on the money. Even with my measly two pair I had won the pot. Alex narrowed his eyes at me, and I'll admit I thought about throwing the next hand just so I wouldn't be on Alex's bad side.

"Come on, Jonah," Jared droned on while Devin dealt, "you did nothing? Not even a little over the shirt action?"

"NO! Nothing happened. Besides I don't think she can do anything with those scars that she has."

"Whoa, wait, what do you mean? How do you know that? You did do something, you dawg! I caught you!"

I rolled my eyes and shook my head as I looked at my third hand.

"Little brother, let it go," Cameron said firmly.

"Bro, how would he know she couldn't have sex unless he saw where the scars were?"

"She showed me the ones on her stomach, Jer," I said. "She told me they went down to her legs. Considering what's in between there I just assumed she couldn't."

"Not entirely true," John said next to me, although he was concentrating on his cards. When he realized we had gone quiet and were all staring at him he finally looked up and said, "I shouldn't have said that."

"But you did," Jared said excitedly. "So..."

John grimaced and sighed uncomfortably before giving in and saying, "All I mean is that she technically can have sex, that's all. It'll probably be uncomfortable, maybe even painful, and she'll most likely receive absolutely no pleasure from it."

Jared gave a loud harrumph. "What's the point then."

"Come on, Jer," Alex began, "Nikki still sleeps with you, and I doubt she gets that much pleasure from it either."

The table exploded in laughter.

"Alex, just because the entire manor can't hear us having sex doesn't mean I'm bad at it."

"Doesn't mean you're good at it either," Alex laughed.

"Eh, it won't matter for long," Jared said dismissively as he put in a bet. "Once all this nonsense is over with I'm going to cut her loose."

Alex folded and threw his cards on the table. "Let me get this straight, Jer. You started dating Nikki after everything she did to Cam and Bri. You've stayed with her for the last four years when she's basically been sitting on her ass doing nothing. And now, when she's finally starting to do things to support the family, you're kicking her out."

"She's miserable all the time."

"You're just realizing that now?" John grumbled before putting in his bet.

"I thought you guys would be thrilled. You've hated her since the beginning. Are you saying I should stay with her?"

"Let's not be rash," Alex answered, causing the table to laugh once again, except Devin.

He was the one to beat this hand apparently so I took my chances and raised the bet. Devin's eyes rose from his cards for the first time this round and raised the bet again. Everyone else folded, but I called Devin's bet and showed my full house.

Devin folded and gave me a nasty look. "It appears Brianna's tutelage has been very successful."

Slowly I took my winnings from the middle of the table, afraid the initials DWA – Death by Warrior Assassin, would be etched on my gravestone. Thankfully he gave a smirk and dealt out our new hand.

"Ok, I think it's Devin's turn," Jared said.

"For what?" he asked as he threw in his bet.

"Duh, your secret," Jared said, rolling his eyes as he put in his bet.

"Let Cameron go first."

"Uh, Cameron's already laid down enough secrets lately. I think we can give him a break."

"Thank you, little brother," Cameron responded.

"Eh, don't thank me. I just can't handle John throwing another fit. I have a very delicate constitution, you know."

"Well you better go get a tissue," John answered and laid down his cards. "Read 'em and weep boys."

John had a straight flush and based on everyone's reaction they had nothing. At least John had taken the heat off of me, even if it was just for one hand. Once John had his winnings situated, Devin dealt out the next hand.

"Fine, Jared," Devin groaned after Jared's relentless whining. "I guess my secret would be that if we win the battle…"

"When we win," Cameron corrected sternly.

Devin looked up from his cards apologetically. "Yes, Brother, after we win the battle, I think I am going to tell Father about Fabi."

"Always playin' the gay card," Jared said in a disappointed tone and shaking his head. "How are we supposed to compete with that?"

"Brother," Cameron said, flatly ignoring Jared, "I believe that is a wonderful idea, especially after what Fabiani did for us today. Father likes him very much. I think it will go over much better than you think."

"And here he is now," Jared announced just as Fabi opened the outside door to the room. Devin nearly dropped the chips he was counting, causing most of us to stifle a laugh.

After shutting the door securely, Fabi glided into the room dramatically and said, "Oh I'm so glad you were gossiping about me. Was it about my choice of shoes today? Or my incredibly brave act of mutiny?"

"I think you mean defection," Devin muttered as he put his chips in the pot. "And please don't make a speech…again."

"But I had another one prepared," Fabi whined and pouted. "You always ruin my fun, Devy."

"Yes, yes, I always do. Where have you been?"

"I was meeting with Cassius and Heron," Fabi began as he walked to the other side of the room and sat in one of the chairs in front of the fireplace.

"Why?" I asked as I placed my bet and traded my cards.

"Because I belong to their bloodline, they're trying to mediate the whole defection thing. They're actually afraid I'll start a chain reaction since Ormond basically made our coven look like assholes today. I'm not sure why they care now, it's not like they've cared about us since Dante was killed."

"Are you going to go back?" I asked, trying to stay cool when I didn't get the card I needed to make my hand. I'd have to bank on others having nothing.

"Hell no, I'm not going back," Fabi shouted. "Cassius even suggested putting me in as coven leader."

"What did you say?" Devin asked.

"Don't worry, Devy, I said no," Fabi replied and Devin relaxed. "If anything, I'll go and make a ton of money with all my new clients and build my own coven. The Fabi Fabulous coven. I think it has a ring to it. Come join the Fabi Fabulous coven, where everyone is fabulous, just not as much as me."

Everyone at the table laughed except Devin, who just shook his head and raised his bet. He wasn't eyeing his cards, so I hoped that he was bluffing.

"Oh, but then," Fabi said excitedly as he stood from his chair, "Victor came in to speak with Cassius. I guess he's going with us tomorrow. He asked Cassius to stay behind and protect the manor in his place."

"What!" Devin shouted while the others whipped their heads in Fabi's direction.

John and I just looked at each other. Apparently this was a big deal and I was hoping someone would explain, but just then the inside door opened with Livy and Will spilling out into the sitting room.

"Ada! Ada!" Livy squealed as she jumped into Cameron's arms with a head of wet curly hair. "I'm all clean! Mama used the special shampoo. Don't I smell good?"

"Yes, monkey, you smell wonderful. But you interrupted…"

"Did you lose all our money yet, John?" Renee asked loudly as she and the rest of the adults came in.

"No, not yet, but Fabi was just saying…" John began but was interrupted by Eris and Sera coming through the outside door.

"Buono sera, la mia famiglia," Eris said loudly and dramatically as he entered the room, causing both children to squeal and cheer.

"Enough! Quiet, all of you!" Devin yelled as he stood from his chair. The entire room instantly went silent, even Livy and Will froze in place. "Fabi, repeat what you just said."

Fabi's eyes were wide as he answered, "Victor asked Cassius to stay behind and protect the manor."

"And why?" Devin growled.

"Beee…cause he's coming with us tomorrow. Why is that so bad?"

"Father doesn't come with us on missions, never has. He stays to oversee everything, he ensures we still have leadership if the mission fails. It's that son of a b…Alastor," Devin shouted as he slammed his fist on the table causing chips to jump in the air. "You heard what he said to Father. You shouldn't have stopped me, Brother. You should have let me tear him apart!"

"Brother, calm down…"

"I will not calm down! How dare that man, his own maker, make him feel inadequate. Father is a legend in his own right, damn that Alastor!"

Devin released another growl and slammed his fist down on the table once again, this time causing chips to fly everywhere. Livy ran to her uncle's side, Brianna chasing after her and pulling Livy back by her arm to stay out of Devin's trajectory. But as usual, there was only so much Bri could ever do since Livy definitely had a mind of her own.

"Devy? Do you need a hug?" she asked sweetly.

Devin's breath slowed as he looked at his niece, her big, black eyes melting his almost impenetrable heart. Bri leaned down to take Livy away when Devin answered, "Yes, monkey. I think I do."

Without a second's hesitation, Olivia leapt into her uncle's arms, hugged him tightly around the neck, and gave him a kiss on the cheek. Will followed after her, of course, and hugged Devin around the leg.

"Ok, well this game's a bust," Jared announced and threw his cards down. "I guess we'll have to divvy this out since Devin threw a tantrum on the table."

Cameron grabbed Jared's hand as he placed it near the pot.

"Little brother, you had exactly twenty dollars left. You're lucky that Devin stopped your hemorrhaging. You should really take some lessons from Brianna. We are all tired of taking your money."

"I'm not," Alex replied.

"And he doesn't listen to anything I tell him," Brianna chimed in. "Unlike Jonah, who took to it like a pro."

I returned her wink and started pulling my chips back over to my side.

"So Jonah," Alex began, "she taught you how to cheat, didn't she?"

"Absolutely," I replied and got whapped in the arm by Bri. "So are we going to keep playing? Or are you all too afraid?"

While I ducked incoming chips coming from Jared, Fabi climbed up on one of the end tables and clapped his hands to bring our attention to him.

"Oh crap," John muttered quietly into my shoulder, "he's going to make another speech."

And that he did.

"Friends, Romans, countrymen…"

"Fabi, that's Julius Caesar," Devin interrupted.

Fabi stuck his tongue out at Devin, and then started again with, "For he today that sheds his blood with me shall be my brother…"

"Can we please refrain from Shakespeare altogether?" Devin groaned again.

"I am trying to bring some culture to you brutes," Fabi answered flustered and then raised his arms again. "All the world's a stage…"

Chapter Forty-nine

Brianna

Out of everything I'd been through the last few months, tonight seemed the hardest of all. Cam and I had argued for nearly two hours straight. Daddy O broke down in front of me for the first time in my life. Renee screamed at me and threw a fit. And to top it off, I would be fighting to save my son in less than eighteen hours. I was crawling out of my skin. I had every intention of laying out my clothes for tomorrow and then packing a bag for the twins, but instead I found myself sitting on the couch in front of the fireplace and flipping through Cameron's photo book of our family. I was even being a good girl and drinking a bottle of freshly warmed blood.

I slugged down a large gulp of blood and was about to close the book and start it again when a piece of paper slipped out from in between two of the blanks pages. Carefully I slid the paper out, noticing the crinkles from being crushed and then flattened. When I unfolded it I found what I thought at first was a penciled sketch of Jackson, but there were slight differences in hair and eyes, a crooked smile like Cameron's that my baby boy never had. I realized then I must be looking at Christian Burke, a little boy not much older than mine when his life was taken. I wondered when Cameron had drawn this, and why he had tried to throw it away.

But I guess I could ask him since he just opened the door behind me, the rumblings of others saying their goodbyes in the sitting room before the door latched shut.

"I'm keeping a bottle warm for you," I said as I ironed out the sketch of Christian and secured it in one of the blank photo pages.

"Thank you, love. I take it Olivia is asleep?"

"Yes. She decided to sleep with Daddy O and Maddy. Poor things, she'll probably kick them all night. Who won?"

"Who do you think?" he grumbled, now only inches behind me. "Jonah may very well have played himself out of games for life, like you have."

I closed the photo book and let it rest on my lap as I responded, "Maybe the real problem is that you are all really bad at poker."

Cameron laughed lightly and snaked his arms around my neck from behind. He kissed my temple and began to say something when he noticed the photo book on my lap and pulled away.

"Where did you find that?" he asked defensively as he walked around the couch.

"Well, the first time I found it was in your overnight bag. But tonight I found it when I was snooping in your nightstand."

"Why were you snooping in my nightstand?"

"I was looking for the photo book," I replied, patting it gently and seeking forgiveness. "Why have you been hiding it from me?"

He shrugged awkwardly as he sat down on the couch and pulled his bottle of blood from the warmer.

"I was not hiding it," he said and then took a drink from his bottle. After he wiped his bottom lip he continued, "It was just a way for me to get through all the traveling and time away from all of you. No man wants to admit when he feels weak, especially to his...lover."

"You really wanted to say wife, didn't you?"

"What I really want is not to start another argument," he replied and drank a large amount of blood.

While he drank, I opened the book to the page where I had stuck the drawing of Christian. The picture immediately caught his attention, although he didn't stop drinking.

"Why was this crumpled up and put in the back?"

Cameron swallowed and placed the bottle of blood back into the warmer. "Why is that important?"

"Because we only have a few more hours together and I think we should have everything out on the table."

"You will not like my answer."

I paused before finally saying, "Christian looks a lot like Jack-Jack."

"Yes, Jacky does look a lot like his brother," he replied while his hand raked through his dark curls. "I became uncomfortable with the déjà vous and tried to throw the drawing away, but then I hated myself for doing it."

I didn't answer, instead I finished my bottle of blood.

"I warned you."

I put my empty bottle down on the table and wiped my lips clean. "Jackson's not dead, Cam."

"I know, love."

"So it's not déjà vous."

"Yes, love."

"I'm just stating fact, Cam. I'm not trying to start an argument."

"Could have fooled me."

I smiled and transferred the photo book from my lap to his.

"I think you should redo the picture. Maybe we could even have it sent out and have a professional paint a real portrait."

"We do not need a portrait of my dead son, Brianna. I sketch all of you when I need to occupy myself. It is just a...a mindless doodle."

"Cam, a stick figure is a mindless doodle. We should do...something for him."

Cameron closed the book and placed it on the table as he said, "Let us get through tomorrow first. Then we can discuss it further."

In Cameron-speak that meant he didn't want to discuss it all, even after tomorrow.

"Is everything all set for Jonah?" I asked, pulling my legs up underneath me on the couch and gently combing my fingers through Cameron's hair.

"Yes, everything is with the lawyers now. There is nothing else we need to do. So in the case of our deaths, everything will still go through."

"Thank you for taking care of that."

He shrugged before finishing off his bottle and placing it on the table.

"It is your money, angel. You can do with it what you choose."

"I don't know what it is, I have to take care of that boy."

"Did you handle things with Oliver and Renee?"

I nodded and pointed to the manila folder on the table. "Daddy O and Renee are now the twin's legal guardians if something happens to us."

"How did they take it?"

"Well…" I sighed, "Renee said 'don't effing die.' Daddy O just cried, but then later said that even though he signed the paper, he's already been a father to his granddaughter, he didn't need to be one to his great-grandchildren. I would have rather he told me not to effing die."

"I would rather no one said anything about you dying, Brianna." Cameron took my hand from behind his neck and kissed the tops of my fingers. "I lost you once, I have lost a wife and son, there will not be enough of my heart left if I fail you and the children again."

"Cam, you won't…"

"Brianna, my anger from earlier has nothing to do with my faith in you, but my confidence in myself and those around us. I am angry that after tomorrow that photo book may be the only memories my children have of me. I am angry that I am not a better Warrior. And I am most angry that I have only had these few short years with you. If only your father had reached out to Victor sooner…"

"Do you remember that day in the bookstore?" I interrupted and he nodded. "You scared the crap out of me and I dropped all those books on the floor. And then I took one look at you and fell into your chest like I'd known you for years. You were a perfect stranger and yet it was the first time I'd ever felt safe. And it didn't hurt that you smelled so damn good."

"Was that what you were doing? Smelling me?" he smiled. "What do I smell like?"

I climbed into his lap and snaked my arm around his neck. "You smell like autumn leaves and rain. It's always been one of my favorite smells and then here you come smelling just like it. I guess that's the way it's supposed to be with your soulmate."

"Soulmate?"

"I never knew what it was like to be loved," I replied and put his hand on my stomach. "I couldn't carry a child until I met you."

Cameron pulled his hand away. "And because of me our son is being tortured and our daughter can feel the effects of it."

"We'll get him back."

"At what cost?" he said and then sighed. "Are we really putting everything on the table?"

"I think we need to," I replied and exhaled nervously.

Cameron squeezed my hand before finally saying, "I have let Aidan get away too many times. Tomorrow I cannot stop until he is dead, even if that means that…I do not come home."

I cupped his cheek with my hand. "I know, Cam. I just hope you know it's the same for me." Cameron lowered his head, but I tilted it back up so I could look in his eyes. "And you are a good Warrior, Cam."

"As are you, love. Right now I wish it was less so." I knitted my brows together. "That way you would have to stay here where it is safer."

"Well, you and Dad insisted that I learn to defend myself, so you only have yourselves to thank," I said lightly, but then sighed. "As long as my brain doesn't get in the way, everything will be fine."

Cameron smiled. "Love, you have found your way out of that place."

"Thank goodness," I replied. "I'm sorry I've been such a hormonal bitch for the last three years."

Cameron flinched in surprise and then smirked. "I am sorry that I activated our children."

"I'm sorry that I was so mad that you Turned me."

"I am sorry for having to leave you alone so often."

"I'm sorry I've been such a hormonal bitch."

"You said that one already," Cameron laughed.

"Well, I'm really, really sorry about it," I whined. "Why couldn't I get my shit together sooner? Then you'd have better memories of me."

Cameron shook his head. "Angel, you are being too hard on yourself. I treasure every day we have been together. Like I said, I just wish we had more of it."

"Maybe we will."

Cameron smiled. "You are right, love, let us hope for that."

"And if we do, I'll be the best mother and the...the best wife...you could ever ask for." A dead silence hit the room as Cameron froze with his eyes wide. "If we survive this thing, I...I will marry you."

"Brianna, do not tease me."

"I'm serious, Cam. I'll change my name, exchange rings, vows, all that stuff."

Cameron crushed his lips against mine. Good thing I didn't need oxygen anymore. His kiss was so hard and wanting I would have suffocated if I was still human.

When he released my lips, his kisses traveled down my neck as he said, "Please let me make love to you."

I pulled away from him, and he instantly knew why.

"Let me make up for last time," he said. "If tomorrow goes badly I cannot have that literally be our last time together."

I looked at the clock on the nightstand in the distance.

"It's close to midnight."

Cameron kissed me softly, staring at me with pleading eyes before saying, "Can you be quiet?"

"Probably not," I replied and he laughed against my lips. "Do you want me to be quiet?"

"Only if you want me to last longer," he said with his crooked smile. "I beg you, angel, let me make love to you."

I rose up from his lap and pulled him from the couch.

"Drop your pants, Burke," I said and stepped back.

Cameron raised an eyebrow, waiting to see if I was serious. After another second he undid his belt, and when he unbuttoned and unzipped his pants I mirrored his actions. His eyes grew with desire as we both slid our pants down our legs. When he reached for the edge of his shirt, I mimicked him again and pulled my T-shirt up and over my head. His chest began to heave when I pulled the straps of my bra down my shoulders and then unclasped it from behind, letting it fall to the ground. Cameron tugged at the elastic of his boxer briefs and waited with a raised eyebrow until I did the same.

Seeing him full on like this still took my breath away. His arms and chest were perfectly muscular and broad, but not overly developed. His sleek abdomen cut down the middle and separated into six soft sections that gave way to his slim pelvis. I'd said it before, he was a god – carved in pale marble for all eternity.

And then there was me, plain old Bri. But from the way he was looking at me he saw something desirable. Despite all my tantrums and depression, he always made me feel like I was the most beautiful woman in the room. His fingers combed through my hair until they were tangled and wrapped around the back of my neck. His kiss was tentative, his eyes open as his other hand traveled down to the curve of my lower back and pressed me into him. My arms curled around his neck and I easily pulled my legs up around his waist. His hands fell to the back of my thighs as he carried me over to the couch and laid me down gently.

There was little foreplay. He wanted inside of me and I needed him to be there. Our rhythm was slow and sensual, nothing that would cause our eyes to part from one another. And even though our bodies were silent and cold, a staggering heat generated between us, fueling the need to somehow be closer, deeper, further into each other's skin. Cameron's dark curls fell in his face and I raked them back with my fingers, digging my nails into his scalp which caused him to moan and reluctantly close his eyes.

When he was close to finishing he anchored one of his arms around my pelvis, locking me into him as close as possible before his body tensed and then released with pleasure. He rested his forehead against my cheek for a moment while he gained his composure, but when he lifted his head again there was a thin red tear gathering at the corner of his eye. I reached up and cupped his cheek with my hand, wiping away the tear with my thumb. Cam's face melted into my hand before completely falling into my chest.

We stayed there silently for a while, merely touching and petting while still entangled in one another. The silence was only broken when he began making circles around my breast with his index finger and I giggled from the sensation.

"That tickles," I said, but that didn't stop him from continuing to do it.

"You really have the most amazing breasts."

"All boobs are amazing to men."

Cameron lifted his head. "I have to disagree, love. I have seen breasts for almost three hundred years…" he said but stopped and laughed when I hit him in the arm. He laid his head back down on my chest as he said, "But I stand with my first statement, they are amazing. Perfect in size and shape, proportional and playful…"

"They're just breasts, Cam."

He laughed softly as he nuzzled in closer, but then another silence fell between us. This one a little more awkward and heavy than the last.

"How long until you leave?"

"Only a couple of hours," he replied. "Devin wants us to speak to Father before we go."

"Why?"

"He wants to convince Father to stay here and not go to battle simply to prove something to Alastor," he said and then propped his head up on his fist. "It is pointless, of course. Once Victor has made a decision he is not going to change it, like someone else I know," he smiled and I tried to look coy. "But it is important to Devin, so I promised I would try and help."

"Alastor is an ass."

"That he is," Cam replied. "And tomorrow you get to work with him personally."

I sighed. "I have to say I'm not particularly excited about that part."

"You could always back out," he said hopefully.

"Cam, no one is touching our babies but me...and Kyla...or Jer...oh you know what I mean. I let Jack-Jack get away, it's my job to bring him home."

"And you will," he said softly and gave me a quick kiss.

"How long will it take you to get ready?"

He shrugged. "Ten, maybe fifteen minutes. Why?"

"Where do you want me?"

Cameron blinked once before realizing what I was offering. Quickly he lifted me from the couch and carried me over to the decorative table that sat next to the fireplace. He cleared the table of all its contents, letting everything crash loudly on the floor before placing me on the tabletop. He spread my legs open and entered me once again, crushing his lips against mine as he squeezed my breast tightly.

With only a couple of hours left together we made the most of it. There wasn't a sexual position or location in the room we didn't use. Even the wall wasn't free from attack. We made love intensely and passionately, and then would slow down in order to take each other in. I tried to stay quiet, but when the moment would take me, I didn't care who came barging in, no one would stop me from enjoying my time with Cam.

We waited up until the absolute latest possible second before we finally stopped and gave in. Cameron retreated into the changing area while I picked up our discarded clothes from the floor. When I stepped into the closet myself, Cam was already donning his black combat pants and tucking in his black T-shirt. I threw our dirty clothes in the corner and then began dressing while I thought back to the first time I had seen him in his combat gear. It seemed so long ago, but even now the sight of him gave me butterflies.

When I was done putting on a pair of pajama shorts and one of his shirts, I stepped out of the closet to give him some time to himself. I knew this wasn't easy for him. The risks couldn't be greater, or our numbers smaller. He needed some time alone in order to disconnect from his feelings, like clicking a button that would instantly put him into Warrior mode.

A few minutes later he stepped through the archway of the changing area with a small bag slung over his shoulder. He was very stiff and quiet, his Warrior mode had set in. When he kissed me I had to bite the inside of my cheek in order to keep tears from forming. I couldn't let my emotions affect him, there would be plenty of time to cry once he left.

When he finally took a step back I realized that we had gotten through the moment without a meltdown. But as was usual in my life, the other shoe had to drop from somewhere. Just as Cameron backed away, the door to our room flew open and in came running our daughter in pink footie pajamas, her curls wild and bouncing around her face.

"Ada!" she squealed and wrapped herself around Cameron's leg.

Cameron's face began to twitch with emotion, his jaw taught and tense, and he was unable to look down at his daughter. His Warrior wall was beginning to crumble. This wasn't what he needed. I leaned down and pried Livy off his leg.

"Baby girl, what are you doing up? You're supposed to be with Daddy O and Maddy."

"I had to say goodbye to Ada," she said and launched herself around her father. Cameron petted her head of wild black curls while he took in a deep breath of her scent.

"You should be in bed, monkey," he cooed as she lifted her head from his shoulder.

"But I had to say goodbye," she said with a pout. "Can't I just come wiff you now?"

"No, lovey, you have to wait and go with your mother."

"Oh all right," she grumbled and then kissed him on the cheek. "I wuv you, Ada."

Cameron held Livy tightly to his chest with his left arm and extended his right out to me. I stepped into his side and wrapped my arm around him and Livy. We all hugged each other tightly, although Livy complained. Cameron was able to give her one last kiss on the forehead before she wiggled free. She wasn't trying to get away, more so that Devin had come into the room. Livy ran to him and he easily picked her up in his arms.

While Livy was distracted by Devin, Cameron gave me a long kiss goodbye. When Devin cleared his throat we knew our time together was over. Cameron pulled away from me, and I could see he was struggling with having to step away. I knew at any second my tears would start and it would be unbearable for him. So I took the step away and called for Livy to come to me. Devin waved goodbye and pulled Cameron to the door.

I love you, Cam, I said in his head.

He paused before closing the bedroom door and turned slowly back around, bowed his head, and placed his hand over his heart. He didn't need to say anything, his gesture was enough. To us it meant everything. When he finally closed the door I was ready to breakdown, but Livy snapped me to attention.

"Mama, why is all that stuff on the floor," she said as she pointed to the mess her father had made.

"Um...the...table broke," I replied and lifted her in my arms.

"The table isn't bwoke."

Damn she was too smart for her own good.

"We need to get you back to bed, baby girl."

"Can I sleep in here wiff you?"

Her big, round, pleading eyes were too much for me to say no to her at the moment so I acquiesced and pulled down the comforter of my bed. Livy leapt from my arms and dove into the mountain of pillows.

"Under the covers please," I nagged and pulled the sheet back, loving the way her little legs in footie pajamas kicked the air and finally snuggled underneath the blankets.

When I went to slide in next to her she said, "Mama, can you brush my hair again? I can't sleep wiffout my hair brushed."

I retreated to the bathroom and then returned to the bed with hairbrush in hand. Livy sat up expectantly and allowed me to place her between my legs while I tried to get through the mess of curls.

"Mama, why was Ada sad?"

Really? Couldn't one thing get past her?

"He's just nervous about getting Jack-Jack back."

"Why?"

"Because something bad could happen."

"But...I don't want anything bad to happen."

I sighed. "Neither do I, Livybean."

Chapter Fifty

Brianna

"Mama!" Jack-Jack squealed as he ran to my doppelganger who had Livy on her back.

It took all my strength to keep my feet on the ground. I wanted Jack to run to me, I wanted to hold him and hug him and kiss him, but this wasn't my dream. I watched while the other Brianna scooped Jack up into her arms while Livy hung tightly around her shoulders. Just as she stepped toward the woods to run away, a stick snapped in the distance, causing her to freeze.

"Going so fast?" Aidan said as he and Gorum stepped out from the woods.

I took a step forward just as the other Brianna was slammed into the ground. Both children were thrown in the air, but still landed on their feet, scrambling to help their mother. Shivers went up my spine as I watched the other Brianna scream and writhe on the ground.

"Gorum, stop, pwease!" Jackson cried.

"Mama!" Livy screamed while tears streamed down her face.

Gorum must have let go of his control over my doppelganger since she stopped screaming, although she lay limp on the ground.

"Mama, you ok?" Livy asked weakly.

"It's just starting, Miss Olivia," Aidan said. "Gorum, again."

The other Brianna started screaming again, her head grinding into the ground causing Livy to wail loudly.

"Olivia, do you love your mother?" Aidan said calmly over the screams.

"Yes!" she cried.

"Do you want her pain to stop?"

"Yes," she cried again.

"Then come with us."

"No, Wivy!" Jack yelled. "Don't do it, Aidan isn't nice anymore."

"Awe, Jacky boy, that hurts me," Aidan said smugly and then quickly picked him up by the scruff of the neck and put him under his arm. Jack kicked and flailed his little arms and legs from Aidan's side. "Now, Olivia, your brother has made his choice, are you ready to make yours?"

"Baby...don't," the other Brianna groaned through her teeth, but then she was dragged forward by an invisible force.

"Mama!" Olivia screamed and ran to her mother's side. "Stop hurting my mama, pwease!"

"Olivia, your mother can't take much more of this," Aidan said very matter-of-factly. "Do you want to see her in pain?"

"Wivy, don't listen to him!" Jack-Jack yelled from under Aidan's arm.

"Olivia! Your mother is going to die if you don't come with us," Aidan shouted, causing Livy to sob louder.

The screams from the other Brianna grew even louder and I could see that Olivia had already made up her mind. When she took a step in Aidan's direction I immediately broke the connection...

My eyes were open first, Livy still lying limply on my chest. But the peace was quickly interrupted when she jerked awake.

"Mama!" she cried and wrapped herself around my neck, her hot wet cheek sticking to mine.

"It's ok, baby," I cooed. "It was just a bad dream."

Livy lifted her head to look at me directly, her dark eyes still leaking tears.

"Mama," she said with a pout, "are you all right?"

"Yes, baby, I'm fine."

"But...I saw you, they were hurting you."

"It was just a dream, honey," I said and petted her hair.

"Why didn't you stop them? You can always stop them."

"I don't know, baby," I lied. "But remember it was just a dream."

"But what if it comes true?"

I sighed and brought her cheek to my lips and kissed her several times before saying, "Olivia, no matter what happens to me, you cannot go with…"

"Petite!" Sera yelled from down the hall. I squeezed Olivia to my chest and rose from the bed just as Sera burst into the room with my father. "Petite, petite…"

And then everything else she said was in French and so fast I couldn't even begin to pick out words I might know.

"Dad?" I said to Eris over Sera's speedy French, but he shrugged.

"She woke up in this panic, but I cannot get her to calm down."

"It changed," Livy said as she pushed up from my chest.

"What?"

Livy pointed to her hysterical grandmother. "That's what Mémé is saying, something changed."

"Oui, oui!" Sera cried. "Qui passé? Vite! Vite! Qui passé?"

"What changed, Mama?"

"Ch-changed? Nothing…that I know of," I replied. "Cam left a few hours ago, and I've been here with Olivia."

Sera leaned down in front of Livy and asked her a question in French. Livy sucked her bottom lip in as she listened to her grandmother and then looked up at me with scared eyes. When Sera tugged on her arm she turned her attention back and replied, "They hurt Mama. She couldn't get up, she was hurting. Aidan said they would stop if I went wiff them."

My stomach dropped at how similar we were. Livy sniffled and buried her head in the crook of my neck.

"Nothing's going to happen to me, baby girl, nothing," I cooed to her and looked over at Sera whose eyes glazed over meaning she was suddenly having a vision. "Right?"

So this morning was not quite how I wanted to start this whole ordeal. A surprise to us all was it appeared that our future rested with my baby girl. Somehow her choices and actions would determine our success. It was too much for one little girl. It was too much for me as her mother knowing it would come down to her, and even harder that I couldn't tell anyone else. Sera had made that very clear. Olivia was on a precipice and we now knew what could tip her over to either side. If anyone else knew, more things would change making many more possible outcomes, and too many for Sera to sort through.

"Mama? I'm ready," Livy said from the bedroom. "Are you ready yet?"

I looked at myself in the long mirror and almost had to laugh. For the first time since becoming a Warrior I was wearing a female's formfitting battle jumpsuit. In some ways it reminded me of Jazlyn and her skintight outfits. It was odd that in this moment I wished she was here. She lost her life because of Aidan, yet another reason he needed to be brought down.

"Mama?" Livy called again.

"Coming, baby," I replied as I smoothed the sides of my ponytail and gave myself one last look before grabbing my daggers and heading out into the bedroom.

I'll admit I gasped a little at the sight of my daughter standing on top of my bed suited up in battle gear herself. She was a miniature version of me, except that Kyla was putting the finishing touches to a tight little bun. Every motherly instinct was telling me that this was wrong. How could a mother willingly put her child in danger?

"Bri," Kyla said as she squeezed my arm and brought my attention to her, "don't freak out."

"Where did she get that outfit?"

"I had it made," she shrugged guiltily. "What did you want her to wear? One of her frilly dresses?"

"Mama," Livy interrupted before I could respond, "I look like you and Auntie Ky!"

"Yes, baby, you do," I replied and pulled her down off the bed. "Now be sure to give Daddy O and Maddy big hugs and kisses, ok?"

I patted her back and prodded her toward where my grandfather and Maddy sat on the couch in front of the fireplace. Sera was standing in the opposite corner speaking softly with my father, her hands clasped tightly in his.

I looked at Kyla. "Are we sure…"

"Yes," she replied and squeezed my arms again.

"You know, Ky, sometimes I actually like getting out my entire question before you answer it."

"My way saves time," she answered.

"Your way pisses me off," I said with a glare and pulled at the high collar of my jumpsuit. "I hate this freakin' uniform. It's strangling me. How come the men get to be comfortable and we have to wear crap like this?"

"Because men run the coven," she laughed and pulled at her own jumpsuit. "Pack up the rest of your stuff, it's almost our call time."

I nodded to her and turned to the bag I started to pack which had clothes for Jack-Jack, extra clothes for Livy, snacks, juice boxes, and now my harness and daggers. My mother alarms were going off again. Bad mommy! Bad mommy!

But I couldn't torture myself for very long since from down the hall I could hear the wails of my nephew. I zipped up my bag and took a step toward the door just as Wills came running inside.

"Awww-beee," he cried and ran to me, hugging my leg tightly. I looked up to see Renee running into the room and stabilizing herself breathlessly in the doorway.

I unclasped his hands from around my leg and knelt down in front of him, wiping his very wet cheeks. "Wills, honey, what is the matter?"

With a trembling lip and ragged breath, he replied, "I…I'm supposed to come wiff you. I a Warrior, too, Awbie. Mommy says I can't, but I hafto to come wiff you."

I looked over Will's shoulder to Renee who merely shook her head and threw her arms in my direction meaning he was all mine. Kyla handed me a tissue and while I cleaned his drippy nose I said, "Honey, I'm sorry, but your mommy is right. You can't come with us."

"But Wivy gets to go," he cried. "I hafta help bwing Jack-Jack home."

He didn't know how much he was breaking my heart, and obviously torturing his mother.

"Wills, baby, you have to stay here," I began, but his immediate high-pitched wail stung in my ears.

Livy gently took Will's hand and pulled him away from me.

"Wills, you can't go," she said very directly.

"But why?" he whined.

Livy leaned into him and although she whispered I heard her say,

"Because you have a mission, too. You have to stay here and protect Mémé and Aunt Re and Da-e-O and Maddy."

Will's tears instantly stopped and he nodded to Livy in understanding. "Ok, Wivy, I'll stay."

Renee's head jerked back in shock, not knowing what Livy had said. When her son retreated back into her arms, her exhaustion and frustration was heard by all. But before I could say anything, Alex stepped into the room.

"Bri, it's time," he said in a low, serious voice. "Our convoy is waiting."

I nodded and looked around at the worried faces of my loved ones, and as I had done so many times I plastered a fake, confident smile on my face. While Olivia gave her final hugs, I pulled my bag up on my shoulder and took one last look around my bedroom.

When I turned back around, Olivia's hand was wrapped around Eris's finger while he led her out of the room with Alex and Kyla right behind them. Maddy was the first to meet me at the door, giving me a silent hug and then a kiss and pat on the cheek. Her eyes bore into mine and gave me the message of love and worry her mouth couldn't because of the tears that were stuck in the creases. When she finally took a step away from me, she extended her hand out to Will who wiggled out of Renee's arms and escorted her out of the room.

"Sugar," Daddy O said softly as he came around me from behind, and then struggled to look up at me, "I...I just don't know what to say in a moment like this."

My jaw was tense as I replied, "I'll see you in a couple of days."

He nodded and cleared his throat. "Yep, 'dat's right. I'll see ya in a couple days and then I can rip those papers in half."

"It's just a precaution, Daddy O."

"I'm too old fur them twins, so you come back safe and sound with Cameron next to ya, and that's an order, 'lil girl," he said with his stern face and index finger pointed at me. But a second later it faded and his arms were squeezing me tightly for only a moment before he left the room without even the slightest glance.

When I looked over to Renee her cheeks were already wet with tears, her hand covering her mouth to muffle the sound of her sobs. I took a step toward her but she put her hand up in front of her and shook her head.

"I can't," she cried and ran to the door. "I can't effing do this again."

I quickly wiped the tear away that escaped from my eye, not wanting the stain on my face for all to see. I couldn't blame her for leaving, she wasn't just crying for me.

The only person left in the room was Sera, and she had an uncharacteristic worried expression on her face. She glided over to me and wrapped her arms around my neck and waist, cradling my head against her shoulder. Even though we weren't blood related, despite that I was now an immortal creature, she was for all intents and purposes my mother. I wanted and needed more time with her, more time to have that relationship I had always been missing from my life. But just as I thought I wouldn't be able to let go, Sera released me and patted my cheek.

"Chute, ma petite chute," she began and kissed my cheek.

"Please tell me everything will be ok."

She sighed. "Olivia is zhe key. Our future lives or dies with her choice, and her choice is over helping you."

"But how do I…"

"Show her, petite, show her how strong you are. Everyzhing was ok until she saw you being hurt. She makes zhe choice to go with Aidan because she believes zhere is no ozher option. Show her zhere is. Prove to her zhat her mozer is zhe strongest Warrior, zhe strongest Vampire, just like her grandfazer. Zhis is key, petite."

"Oui, Maman," I replied and made her smile.

"Now go, go. Everybody is waiting."

I nodded and stepped into the corridor with a nervous sigh. The manor was unusually quiet, even with many of the humans gathering in the corridor to wish the Warriors off. When I finally stepped through the front doors there was a row of SUVs and vans with groups of people waiting to board them. Alex waved me over to a grey SUV a few feet away, but Livy wasn't with him. I quickly looked to my left and zeroed in another few feet ahead to my baby girl giggling and dancing in front of Cassius. In less than two seconds I was scooping Olivia into my arms and resting her on my hip.

"Livy, don't bother Cassius. I'm sure he's much too busy today."

"Not a bother at all," Cassius replied and extended his arms which prompted Olivia to launch herself into them. He was definitely different than the other Ancients, seemingly the only one with a heart as he tickled Livy underneath her chin.

"I'm sorry about yesterday," I began. "I didn't mean to hurt you."

Cassius gave me a smile. "Yes, you did indeed inflict quite a bit of pain, however, it was purely my fault. I was simply too curious about this enchanting little creature," he replied as he tickled Livy once again. "May I see those little fangs of yours again?"

Livy complied and opened her mouth wide to show her little incisors growing to lethal points. Cassius giggled almost as high-pitched as Livy while he touched the tips of her fangs.

"Figlia!" Eris yelled behind me. "We must get going!"

"Bye, Cassius," Livy squealed as she jumped out of his arms and ran toward our SUV. "I hope we get to play again soon."

"She is truly remarkable," he said quietly as he watched her over my shoulder. "As is, I assume, her brother."

"That he is. They make quite a pair."

He nodded and his glance came back on me. "But it is best that there are only two of them in our world."

His sudden change in tone took me aback, and it took all of my strength not to say some snarky comeback. So instead, "What does my father have over you and the others?" Cassius raised his eyebrow at me, so I raised mine as well. "There's a possibility I won't be coming home after all of this, so if that's the case I'd really like to know what my old man holds over all of your heads."

Cassius narrowed his eyes at me and then finally sighed and said, "He killed our fathers."

"Your fathers? As in the original two brothers?"

He nodded. "We knew Eris didn't know who they were, and he thought by doing this for us it would allow him entry into our circle. Little did we know he would hold it over us for all eternity."

"But why?"

"Why does any son kill the father? To be set free."

"I thought it was to be with the mother," I replied snidely, but thankfully he laughed.

"Yes, but in our case it was so we could build our race, flourish throughout time with sires of our own. If we were to live forever, we wanted a different kind of world to live in. So we contracted Eris to do what he did best."

"You treat him like the bratty stepchild."

"And he behaves like the bratty stepchild," he laughed lightly, although he stopped when I didn't join in. "I apologize, Brianna. We took Eris for granted thinking he would fade away, but he has surpassed most of us with his skill and fame. We certainly underestimated him."

"Something I'm sure you won't make the mistake of doing again."

He laughed. "There is no doubt. Today of all days we cannot afford to underestimate him or you. Good luck today, my dear. I'm afraid you will need it."

I nodded nervously, but tried to keep a confident smile. "Take care of the manor, ok? It kinda holds a special place in my heart."

"I will do everything in my power, Ms. Morgan," Cassius replied and bowed his head.

Even with Alex and Eris calling me to get into the SUV, I had to take one last look at the manor. It was my home, no matter how often I cursed about leaving Boston. I always ended up back here. It was where I became Brianna Morgan, daughter of Eris, lover of Cameron, mother of twins.

"Hey Bri," Jonah said behind me, "we're the ones that actually have to go. The manor is staying here."

"Thank you, smartass," I said, realizing my final dramatic moments in front of the manor were over and started toward the SUV. "Are you sure I can't talk you into staying?"

He laughed and fell in line with me. "Not after what I said in front of everyone yesterday."

I shook my head. "Stupidest thing you could have ever done. Your mother must hate me."

"She's not a fan, I'll tell you that."

"I'm not much of a fan of myself, either," I laughed as we stepped up to the SUV. Kyla was fastening Olivia into her car seat while Eris took position in the front. "Sorry, Jonah, I think you're in the back."

"But my legs are longer than yours," he whined.

"Well when your son gets kidnapped and tortured I will let you sit where there is more legroom when we go to rescue him."

"You always cheat."

"Yeah she does," Alex groaned, and I couldn't help but laugh.

While Jonah begrudgingly climbed into the far backseat I noticed that Vlad had suddenly climbed into the driver's seat. I leaned into Alex. "I thought you were driving us."

He laughed. "Thankfully you missed that lovely confrontation. Your father feels more comfortable having his own man drive on such an occasion." I jerked to respond, but he put his very large hands up in front of me. "It's fine, Bri. I'll be in the car ahead of you. If anything comes at us, it'll come through me first and Vlad can divert you."

"But…"

"And Kyla will be with you to see anything."

"But…"

"It'll be fine, Bri, I promise."

I nodded nervously, and then noticed Nikki standing alone waiting to board one of the many waiting vehicles. When I called her name she snapped her head around to face me, but when I waved for her to come over, she stayed put. I waved her over again, and this time she shook her head.

"Alex, give me one more minute," I said and ignored his heavy sigh as I walked away from our SUV and took the few steps over to where Nikki was standing. "Nikki, what are you doing in this line? You should be with us."

Nikki shook her head again. "They said that was the family car."

"Yes," I nodded. "Which is why you should be with us." Nikki's head flinched and her eyes became glassy when I extended my hand to her. "Come on, Alex is getting impatient."

She smiled and allowed me to direct her to our SUV. I had every reason not to like her, but on a day like today all of that seemed so minuscule compared to what we were headed into. Kyla gave me a less-than-thrilled look when Nikki climbed into the backseat with Jonah, but I merely shrugged her off and positioned myself next to Livy.

"Everybody in?" Alex asked.

"I'm ready, Uncle Alex," Livy said excitedly.

"Ok then, we'll see you there," he replied and shut the SUV's door.

"Now, figlia, I know you wanted Alex to drive…" Eris began.

"It's fine, Dad. Thank you, Vlad, for being here."

Vlad looked at me through the rearview mirror and replied, "There is no other place I would be today than with you all."

"You know, figlia, if we weren't going to war, this would almost feel like a family vacation."

"What kind of family vacations have you been on?" Jonah asked from the backseat, causing even Eris to crack a smile.

Chapter Fifty-one

Brianna

It was nightfall by the time we pulled into the Warrior camp deep within the woods just over the Oregon border. Vehicles from earlier convoys had been abandoned miles behind us, but ours was one of the few allowed to drive right in. Knowing how many people were actually here, you could hear barely a murmur and there was only a faint glow of light coming from several tents a few feet away. As we bumped slowly along the wooded path we were greeted by someone dressed like a swamp creature that waved us forward until giving the signal to cut the engine. It wasn't until the swamp creature opened my door did I realize it was Jared. He was dressed in a set of fatigues with bushy netting and fake leaves draped around his body, his face completely painted with dark green and black camouflage grease.

While the others opened their doors and began to exit, I immediately turned to Livy and said very quietly, "Ok, baby girl, you need to listen to me very carefully." She nodded while I wiped away the peanut butter cracker crumbs from her mouth. "This is not playtime, you have to be quiet, you cannot run around, and you must stay with me and do what I say at all times. Do you understand?"

"Yes, Mama," she whispered. "I'll be good, I promise."

"I know you will," I replied and unlatched her car seat harness.

"Can I bring my crackers?"

I had to smile. "No, baby. No more crackers," I replied and pulled her out of her car seat. Jared came to my side, glancing behind me briefly to see Nikki climbing out from the backseat and then looking back at me questioningly.

I shrugged and said softly, "It's the family car."

Jared shook his head and pointed to a large tents few feet away. "Beebs, everyone is waiting for you in there. Nik, Jonah, the medical tents are up behind me. There are people along the way to help you since the sun is down."

Jonah hesitated for a moment, but Nikki pulled him up into the woods, only giving Jared a quick look knowing she would get nothing in return while he was in full Warrior mode. They were barely three steps up into the woods when Jared nudged me toward the dimly lit tent. Squeezing Livy into my chest I followed behind him and Kyla while other Warriors gathered in small groups preparing their weapons for battle. When we came to the main tent Jared held the flap open for us to enter. Once we stepped inside a few other Warriors dispersed out the other side revealing Cam and Devin standing in front of a large map with various colored circles and arrows drawn all over. Cam was all business, his serious expression barely cracked when he saw us. Devin waved us over just as Julian, Connor, and unfortunately Alastor stepped in from the opposite side. Livy's head popped up from my shoulder before she pressed her hand against my neck.

Mama, can I say hi to Juwian and Connor?

I nodded and placed her on the long table that was next to me, allowing her to run to the other side where she curtsied to Julian before leaping into his arms. I was thankful she was quiet, especially when she transferred to Connor who snuck her a piece of gum that I knew he'd put in his pocket especially for her. She instantly put the gum in her mouth before Cam or I could object.

But at Devin's insistence, mostly due to Alastor's impatient groan, the debrief began. Connor placed Livy back on the table as I stepped to Cam's side. I noticed Cameron making side glances in her direction. He seemed as uncomfortable with her looking like a miniature Warrior as I was.

"Brianna," Devin began in a low voice, "you, Olivia, Kyla, and Alastor will go into the encampment together and locate Jackson. Once you have him, get to as many of the women as possible, leaving the most critical for

Alastor to dual Project back here. My suggestion is that once you have Jackson, have Alastor Project the twins as well."

"Not happening," I replied.

"Bri…"

"Dev, I'm not allowing anyone to Project my children anywhere. That's how we got in this mess in the first place."

"The fewer children I have to Project the better," Alastor muttered.

"And I'd rather not have your…"

"Bri," Cameron warned, and I promptly shut my mouth. "Connor, I believe you can take it from here."

Connor nodded with a smirk and pointed to a large green area on the map that was circled in red. "This area here is the encampment itself, and it's a good hike in from the laser border closest to us. Julian and I have a way to take it out at least long enough for all of you to get in. We'll do everything we can to keep the grid down so that as many humans can cross over into our camp before Aidan's tipped off and they attack. Our forces will stand at the ready until then. The longer we can prevent any fighting, the better. It'll be dangerous as it is trying to get some of these women over to our side."

"And how are we getting them here safely?" I asked. "You said it was a hike."

Connor nodded with understanding. "The most direct and covered path is by the stream," he replied as he moved his finger along a thin blue line that cut through the edges of Aidan's property. "Jared will provide cover up in the trees. We have a few other volunteers willing to post themselves along the way to keep the women moving."

"Where are they keeping Jack?"

"Julian and I have been keeping ties on him, and they seem to keep his schedule pretty consistent. Usually around this time he is in his cabin, located here," Connor continued and pointed to a small circle. "His cabin is on the side of the stream, second row, second one in. He does have four guards at all times. Take them out, and you'll be golden. Now, if for some reason he's not in his cabin…"

"He is," Livy interrupted, causing us all to whip our heads in her direction. "I told him we were coming."

Devin shoulders tensed and his jaw was tight as he said, "Olivia, you might have just jeopardized the operation by telling him we were here. He might let it slip…"

"He already knew, Devy," she replied. "He saw Ada first and just waited for everyone else to come. He says hi to you too, Mama."

I bit the inside of my cheek. The last thing I wanted to do was show weakness in front of Alastor. Cameron couldn't seem to take it anymore and took Olivia into his arms, carrying her away from the group in order to have a moment with her on his own. Livy carried on as if today was like any other and she was getting her daddy's attention, however, Cameron was taking in every inch of her as if he wouldn't see her again.

"Beebs?"

I shook to attention and looked at Jared, still uneasy about his painted face and camouflage. "What?"

"Connor asked if you had any questions. You ready to do this?"

"Yeah," I sighed. "I just need to strap on my daggers."

Jared grinned slyly and released a low laugh. "Strap on."

"It's good to see you can still crack jokes when you're dressed like that."

"Underneath, I'm still me," he replied with a wide smile, but then it quickly disappeared as he said, "Now get your shit strapped on, we've got work to do."

"Inspirational as always, Jer," Connor muttered.

"Let's give the family a few minutes alone," Julian announced and directed everyone. But before he ducked out himself, he waved goodbye to Olivia who responded by leaping out of Cameron's arms and curtsying. The gesture made Julian smile, which seemed to create a glow around him before he bowed deeply in response and then disappeared outside.

While Cameron lifted Olivia back into his arms, I unpacked my daggers and harness from my bag. As I pulled the harness up onto my right shoulder, Devin came up behind me and pulled my arm through the other side.

"Are you ready for this?" he asked.

"Is anyone every ready for something like this?"

"I believe I am always ready."

"That's because you're a freak," I replied and he narrowed his eyes at me. "Take care of Cam for me."

He nodded in reply but then something caught his attention over my shoulder. I turned around to see Fabi Projecting into the back corner of the tent. Unfortunately Devin's defenses immediately went up.

"Fabi, what are you doing in here?" he whispered nervously.

Fabi rolled his eyes. "To give you an update, Devin. If you wore underwear I'd tell you not to get them in a wad, but since you don't..."

"Fabi," Devin growled.

"All the medical tents are staffed and prepared," Fabi interrupted as he unzipped the high collar of his uniform and revealed a bright red ascot.

"What the hell is that?!" Devin said, pointing at Fabi's neck. "You weren't wearing that before. Where...wha...you can't wear that."

"On the contrary," Fabi replied and stretched out the ascot to be even wider than before. "I am not part of your coven, in fact I'm covenless. I find your uniform drab and depressing, and since I am a volunteer I don't think you can prevent me from having a splash of color, one of Dante's favorite colors in fact. I'm wearing this in honor of him, so if you ask me to take it off you'll look like a real ass. Now do you want to continue this pointless argument, or say thank you for the update and get this show on the road?"

I raised an eyebrow in Devin's direction and tightened my harness around my waist.

"Thank you, Fabiani," Cam replied instead. "I believe we are ready."

A lump formed in my throat, but instead of panicking I pulled my new gloves on and looked up at Devin as I pushed, *You should tell him you love him. You might not get another chance.*

Devin's jaw tensed, his breath sounding like a bull ready to charge.

"Come on, Olivia, it's time to go," I said and opened the slim wooden box with my daggers inside. My fingers grazed over the swirling pearl faces, feeling for the first time in years a connection with them. When I clicked the first one in place over my shoulder, a surge of energy went through me as though the daggers were waking up Eris's half of my DNA. Once the second dagger was secured at my lower back, Olivia jumped on me and wrapped her arms around my neck. When I turned around, Cameron was only inches away, his face strained from having to keep himself together.

"I wuv you, Ada," Olivia cooed over my shoulder.

Cam didn't answer, merely kissed her on the cheek and then pressed his forehead against mine. Nothing was said, it had all been said last night. Win or lose tonight, no matter how hard I tested our love it was unbreakable. Win or lose, the lives of our children were more important than our own. Win or lose, we were thankful for the time we had together, no matter how short.

With a sudden jolt, Cameron turned his back and left the tent. Fabi looked at me sympathetically, but I knew he was in pain too.

"Think about what I said, Devin," I said and turned around to the opposite side of the tent. "Regret is a bitch."

From the corner of my eye I could see Devin stepping over to Fabi, and I hoped he would tell Fabi those important three little words. As I stepped through the tent's flaps, I was unfortunately reminded that I had a three-year-old on my back.

Mama, she said as she pressed her little hand to my neck, *you said a bad word.*

I know, baby. You might hear a lot of that today. Just don't tell Ada.

I knew she'd probably rat me out, but I couldn't worry about it now. Once I stepped outside I found my team standing together, except for Alastor who stood off to the side and seemed annoyed. Livy only took a couple of seconds before she leapt from my shoulders over to where Julian and Connor stood. There was no point in yelling at her, at least she wasn't going to Aidan like she had in her dream.

"Can't you keep a leash on that thing?" Alastor growled lowly.

"By that 'thing', do you mean my daughter?"

"Perhaps if you kept a closer eye, we would not be in this particular situation."

"You're just mad you have to help us."

"And what is there to stop me from leaving whenever I choose?"

The dagger was in my right hand before I knew it and I was pressing it against Alastor's abdomen. "I swear if you screw us over I will tell everyone the Ancient's dirty little secret."

The left side of Alastor's lips curled up into a sinister smile. "You know nothing."

"I know what my father did for you."

"And if Eris truly told you, then he broke our agreement…"

"Eris didn't tell me."

He sighed and narrowed his eyes at me. "I say it again, you know nothing."

Casually I put my dagger back into its holder as I said in his head, *I know you all wanted your fathers dead, and got the needy, blood-thirsty stepchild to do it.*

Alastor's face flinched at my Push and then contorted in anger as he growled, "Cassius and his endless guilt. He told you, didn't he?"

"Does it matter? Do what you're here to do and no one else will know the truth about their precious Ancients."

"Like I care what anyone thinks," he growled again and looked back ahead into the darkness. "But I will honor this agreement. Dual Project the mothers most in need and not a single thing more."

"Well let me get your medal ready," I groaned and stepped over to Jared and Kyla. "Can we get going?"

"Sure, if we can get Connor and Julian to stop playing with Livy," Jared said. "And yes, that's the weirdest thing I've ever said."

"I doubt that," Connor responded as he stepped over to us. "We're ready when you are, Brianna."

I nodded and brushed past him to where Julian stood allowing Olivia to use his arms like a set of uneven bars. She noticed me just as she completed her second flip around, climbed up to Julian's chest, kissed him on the cheek, and then leapt over onto my shoulder.

"Now remember, baby," I whispered in her ear, "you have to stay with me no matter what."

"No matter what, Mama," she replied and tightened her arms around my neck. "I'm telling Jack-Jack we're coming."

I patted her hand in a silent thank you, and turned to tell Connor we were ready when suddenly...

Mama?

The sound of Jackson's voice filled my head causing me to barrel over my knees from the sudden emotions that took over. I covered my mouth with both hands in order to soften the sounds of the heaving sobs my stomach and lungs were making. Kyla grabbed me around the waist to hold me while Julian removed Olivia from my shoulders. Jared turned to run for help when I shook my head and held my hand.

"It's...Jack," I stuttered, trying to whisper and not let my sobs overpower me.

Mama? Are you there?

I waved Olivia back over and she lifted her hand up to my cheek so that I could respond to Jack. *Yes, baby, I'm here. We're all here to come get you.*

Wivy told me. I'm in my cabin, I wanna come home now.

We're coming, baby, just stay where you are. We're coming.

I pulled Olivia's hand away from my cheek and apologized softly to those concerned around me. "Jack's in his cabin. He knows we're coming."

"Good," Connor replied and pulled me up to a standing position. "Let's go get him, then. Everyone ready?"

We all nodded except Alastor, who simply rolled his eyes. Livy climbed up on my shoulders again and a moment later we were following Connor and Julian down a recently made path through the woods alongside the stream. The run only took us a few minutes, and several times I had to quiet Livy down. She was enjoying the ride a little too much.

Several minutes later we came upon a clearing where a metal stand stood shooting a grid of green lasers to several other receivers to create the edge of Aidan's secured border. Connor pointed and directed us to climb up into the trees. After warning Livy to be silent, I climbed up the tree nearest me until we were both hidden by the canopy of braches and leaves. Kyla and Jared were in the tree next to me, Alastor choosing one further away while Connor and Julian ducked into the brush a few feet behind us.

A minute later they returned carrying a live deer they must have trapped earlier in the day. I prayed they wouldn't kill the deer right in front of my daughter, but I was pleasantly surprised to see that they seemed to be aiming the deer directly at the metal stand. Once the deer was in place, Connor waved Julian away and he immediately Projected onto a set of branches that hung dangerously close to the laser grid with his weight.

You could see Connor's body flinch with each interval he counted down – 3, 2, 1...then he released the deer and jumped up into the tree above him. The deer ran directly into the metal stand, causing it to crash over and bring the entire laser grid down. Both Julian and Connor held their hands up, instructing us to wait, which we did for almost two agonizing minutes until it became clear why. From out of the darkness came two men, one carrying a large rifle, the other a crossbow, both held at the ready and looking for targets.

Livy placed her hand against my neck and in an instant I could see the red halos glowing around their heads. The lights were cloudy, murky, meaning they weren't real hybrids, but Vamps drinking hybrid blood. I had a feeling we'd see a lot of them tonight. I took Livy's hand away from my neck and kissed it gently. She needed to save her strength as much as I did. Just then their radios began to crackle from their hips.

"Perimeter, report," someone said through the radio.

The man with the crossbow ripped the radio from his belt. "There's no one here. Looks like another damn animal took the grid out."

"Smells like deer," the other man replied as he slipped the rifle's strap off his arm and smelled the blood and hair the deer had left behind on the metal stand. "That's the third one in two days. They really need another way to protect us out here, this is ridiculous."

Crossbow-boy shook his head and pressed the button to talk again. "Base, this is perimeter, we've got to fix the grid stand again. We'll need about twenty minutes to get it up and running."

"More like forty," the other man replied. "It's completely smashed. We'll have to take parts from the destroyed ones to piece this together."

The radio crackled again. "Perimeter, this is base, Aidan wants that grid back up in ten."

"Then he should come out here and do it himself," the gunman grumbled and threw the stand back down on the ground.

"We'll get it up as soon as we can. Over," crossbow-boy replied and replaced the radio back on his belt. "Tell me the parts you need and I'll run back to base and get them."

Just as the man placed his crossbow on the ground, Connor gave a signal to Julian and the two of them jumped gracefully from their hiding places, each taking a man down. I tucked Livy's head down into my shoulder so that she wouldn't see the men being killed. A moment later their lifeless bodies were dragged into the bushes, and what little blood there was, was buried over with dirt and leaves. Julian and Connor took the weapons and radios and then waved us down from the trees.

"Stick to the stream," Connor said softly and pointed in its direction. "Second row of cabins, second one in, four guards. We'll keep the grid down as long as possible, but you might only have ten minutes before they start getting curious. Jer, one klick in should be a good perch."

Jared nodded and patted the heavy artillery bag that was on his back. I'm glad he knew what Connor was talking about, I certainly didn't. But there wasn't a second to question it since we were off and running behind him, all the while keeping the winding stream to our right. Livy tightened her grip, and I could feel her little heart racing against my back. I patted her arms and legs as we darted around trees and leapt over brush, trying to alleviate the fear that was suddenly coming over her.

After a few minutes Jared motioned us ahead of him before darting up a tree to provide us cover from above. It was only me, Kyla, and Alastor left running toward the cabins whose dims lights were finally coming into view. As we got closer, our pace slowed, making sure that our approach was as silent as possible. Kyla put her hand up a couple of times to warn us to stop, but each time the threat passed and we continued forward. Only another minute went by before the rows of cabins were only a few feet ahead.

Suddenly a woman's cry broke through the night. Kyla whipped her head back around to me, a questioning look on her face, but I shook my head. Our mission was for Jackson first and then the hybrids, we had to stick to that. Kyla nodded her head in understanding, worry still etched into her face. Alastor just sighed impatiently behind me, so I waved us forward to the first row of cabins.

Thankfully the wall of the first cabin had no windows so we all pressed our backs firmly against it, hiding in its shadows as best we could. Gently I kissed Livy's hand before pressing it against my neck, and she instantly pushed her power into me. I could see clearly that there were four red halos surrounding Jackson's cabin, two in front and two in back.

Just then, another scream broke the silence of the night and at the same time two muffled shots rang out, hitting the guards in front of the cabin in an instant. When the other two guards ran forward to investigate, I pulled my daggers from their holsters ready to strike when Alastor suddenly Projected behind the one on the left and disappeared with him, returning a second later and Projecting away with the other. When he returned the third time he stood in front of Jackson's cabin waving us over. What happened to helping the hybrids and nothing else? He was an ass, but I wasn't going to complain at this moment.

Kyla and I quickly ran across the aisle, Livy ducking her head into the nape of my neck. I stepped up to the door, hesitating for a second with my hand on the door handle, but when Kyla nudged me I quickly opened the door and the three of us piled in. There were no lights on in the room, but even through the darkness I could see my baby boy sitting atop his bed, his little legs dangling and kicking over the edge.

"Mama!" he cheered softly and ran from the bed to my waiting arms. As soon as he was secured in my chest I rose from the ground and sobbed into my baby's hair while I gave him endless kisses. His hands and arms were grabbing at my neck and shoulders trying to find a way to get closer, all the while crying into my chest that he would never leave again.

Kyla tapped me on the shoulder lightly. "Bri, we need to go."

I nodded and kissed Jackson one last time on his fluffy curly head, reluctantly pulling him away from my chest and wiping his tears from his cheeks. "Ok, baby, where are the hybrids that need help?"

"I'll show you, Mama. Sybil is having her baby tonight."

Well that explained the screams we heard before. Having a baby in the woods probably meant no pain killers. I didn't envy her in the slightest. Jack-Jack took my hand and pulled me to the door, Kyla and Alastor following after us as we stepped outside and darted between cabins. After crossing one aisle over, Jackson burst into a cabin just as a woman released a deafening scream.

"Ashwyn!" Jack-Jack squealed too loudly. The front of the cabin was empty except for a curtain that hung from the rafters, cutting the room in half. Kyla shut the door quickly just as Ashlyn came from around the curtain wiping her hands with a towel while the cries and moans of the woman in labor echoed throughout the room.

"Jack, I told you that you can't..." she began, but then was startled by the sight of us. The towel fell out of her hands as she broke down in front of us. "You're here...I prayed you'd....you'd come."

I pulled Olivia down from my shoulders and stepped over to Ashlyn who sobbed heavily into my chest. "We're here to take you all away, everything's going to be ok," I said, hoping it was true. "Jonah is here too."

Her head shot up. "He-he is?" she stuttered and put a hand on her stomach. "I-I'm..."

"We can talk about it later, honey, but right now we need to get you and the others out of here. This is Alastor, he is going to Project the most critical. I take it the woman back there is…"

"Yes, that's Sybil. She's started to push but the baby isn't crowning yet."

Without waiting for any further invitation, Alastor stepped behind the curtain causing several of the other women to scream. He pulled the curtain back slightly and said, "Where am I to go next?"

I looked to Ashlyn who replied, "Next door and then down the row. Each cabin works its way up to this one, this is the birthing cabin."

"What about the babies?"

"They're with the mothers so they're spread out all over. But there's a bleeding house too…"

"We know about that," I interrupted. "We're trying to get the mother's out first since they're mobile. Alastor, start with the woman back there and then continue on down the line."

Alastor nodded and within seconds the woman's moans completely stopped. Three other women came from around the curtain, confused and scared expressions on their faces.

"We're Warriors," I said softly. "We're here to help you. This is Kyla, she'll help you to the path."

"But, Bri!" she protested, but I held my hand up.

"*Kyla* will help you to the path," I stressed again, which caused her eyes to flare and her posture to straighten, but in the end she extended her arm and waved the three hybrids over to her.

Once they had left I looked to Ashlyn. "Show me to the others, we'll get them ready."

She nodded and Livy climbed back up on my shoulders while Jackson jumped in my arms. Ashlyn poked her head out first and then waved us all to follow her. We darted to the next cabin where there were three women looking as though they would go into labor at any moment. We had to hold one woman down she was so emotional and desperate to escape. Thankfully Alastor came in a moment later and was able to disappear with her first. The other two promised they would wait for him to return since they were in no condition to run through the woods.

The next two cabins contained over a dozen women, some that were left for Alastor to Project, while others were grouped together and escorted to the path, all under the watchful eye of Jared.

When the last group had left with Kyla, Olivia pulled on my sleeve and said, "Mama, can we go home now? I don't feel good, I wanna go home."

Her sick feeling tended to mean trouble, almost like a sixth sense. I picked her up in my arms, cradling her to my chest. "Come on, Ashlyn. We'll all go to the Warrior camp together."

"But what about the other cabins?"

"We'll send in more help, I promise, but I need to get the twins out of here and you with them."

She nodded reluctantly and followed us to the door. Livy chose to stay in my chest, meaning Jackson had to take the catbird seat on my shoulders. Taking Ashlyn's hand, I pulled her outside and we headed toward the path. Suddenly my head was struck with blinding pain and I was forced to the ground, pinning Livy underneath me. Ashlyn screamed and tried to grab Jackson, but in the same moment I was dragged backwards, bringing him along with me while Livy was pushed deeper through the dirt.

"Gorum, stop, pwease!" Jackson screamed.

Through the pain I could hear a raspy cackle behind me before I was elevated from the ground and turned around to see Gorum and Aidan staring up at me. My entire body was shaking from the pain in my head. Livy looked up at me from the ground, big wet tears cutting tracks through the dirt on her face. This was it, this was her dream coming true and her actions could change the course of our future.

"Olivia, my darling girl, I'm so glad you've come to join us," Aidan said lightly.

"S-st-tay a-way," I stuttered, trying to push through the pain. Gorum clamped down on me even harder and slammed me hard into the ground.

"Mama!" Livy screamed.

"Aidan please!" Ashlyn cried as she ran in front of me and pulled at Aidan's arm. Surprisingly Aidan cupped her cheek with his hand, but then in the next second slapped her so hard in the face she fell to the ground.

"Having Eris's baby has afforded you some leeway, but this little stunt will cost you," Aidan growled and reared his leg back to kick her.

"No," I screamed and leapt forward a few inches, breaking Gorum's connection for only a second.

"Keep a grip on her, Gorum, for fuck sake," Aidan shouted and received a deathly glare from Gorum.

"I do not want to kill her, Aidan," Gorum said and then looked back to me, "at least not until her grandfather's debt is settled."

"Fuck your debt," Aidan snapped as he stepped over Ashlyn and pulled my chin up to his face. "You could have made it simple, Morgan. All you had to do was stay with me and have those babies. But you had to go and run away, didn't you? That's why you died and your life turned to shit."

"Nn-nn-o..."

"N-no?" he teased. "Is that what you're trying to say? Well, it really doesn't matter much anyway. I was going to kill you eventually, so whether it was then or now, I'm easy."

"NO!" Olivia cried.

Aidan dropped my chin and immediately shifted his attention to Livy. Jackson ran at Aidan, but he merely grabbed my son by his collar and lifted him off the ground. "Jacky boy, you really have hurt my feelings. I thought we were friends."

"I'm not your fwiend! Don't touch my sister!"

"How cute," Aidan laughed and looked over his shoulder. "Squeeze her harder, Gorum. These kids need to learn a lesson."

Everything around me went white as Gorum's Push cut through my head. I could hear Jack and Livy crying and begging for it to stop. Hearing Sera's words in my head, I Pushed at the thin veil of white light, even seeing a tiny opening tearing near my fingers. But in an instant Gorum applied more pressure, causing me to convulse in the dirt.

"Wivy, help Mama, you can Push them!" Jackson yelled but Livy was frozen with fear.

"Yes, Olivia, you can help your mother," Aidan cooed.

"No, Wivy, don't listen."

"Oh yes, Olivia, you do need to listen to me. Do you see your mother? Do you see how much pain she is in? You can stop all of that, you can stop her pain. Don't you want that?"

"Yes," she whimpered.

"Wivy don't," Jackson yelled and kicked at Aidan's legs. Aidan responded by throwing Jackson a few feet behind me.

I dug my nails into the ground and painfully pulled myself forward. Gorum grinded his teeth and pushed down into another gear. Wails came from deep in my throat, but I kept inching forward against the stream of white light that was pushing against me, all in an effort to get closer to Livy who was being sucked in by Aidan's lies.

"Olivia," he cooed sweetly, "come with us and all your mother's pain will go away. Don't you want that? You don't want to see her like this, do you? And what about your dad? Your Ada?"

Livy's head shot up, her eyes like saucers spilling over with tears. "You promise? You won't hurt Mama or Ada if I come wiff you?"

"Wivy don't!" Jack yelled again, running up behind her and trying to pull her away.

I could see that Aidan was getting impatient and that his pleading would only last for another minute before he forcibly snatched my children away from me again. Livy struggled against her brother, finally pushing him away and taking another step toward Aidan. The nightmare was coming true. Our future was slipping away and I couldn't get out of Gorum's grip. Livy paused and took one last look at me, fear written all over her tiny face.

"Olivia you must choose," Aidan shouted, startling Livy and causing him to adjust his tone. "Come with us now, Olivia, or Gorum is going to kill your mother right in front of you. Is that what you want?"

Livy shook her head and took another step, but I was able to stretch my hand out just enough to grab her ankle. Instantly I could see the murky red lights of Aidan and Gorum and with one Push I launched them back into the depths of their camp, unable to even see where they had landed. Gorum's connection on me was immediately cut and I finally felt like I could breathe, oddly feeling as though my lungs needed the air. Jackson jumped on my chest, but Livy was frozen. I pulled on her arm slightly, and with a sudden wail she collapsed into my side.

"It's ok, baby girl," I whispered and panted. "Mama's ok."

"I sorry, Mama, I sorry."

"Don't be sorry, baby," I replied and awkwardly rose from the ground trying not to drop either of my children.

Just then Kyla came running from the woods.

"Bri! What happened? What happened to Ashlyn?" she shouted.

"Shit, I forgot," I replied, handing Olivia and Jack to her and running over to Ashlyn. Her face was swollen from Aidan's hand, his three fingers even taking shape on her cheek. When I rolled her over she groggily opened her eyes and sat up.

"Wha-what happened," she said as she came to. "Where's Aidan?"

"He's gone for the moment, but we've got to go," I replied over the sudden shrill sound of an alarm. Quickly I helped her to her feet. "You've got to run, Ashlyn, go with Kyla now. Go find Jonah."

She struggled to walk the first few steps, squeezing my arm and looking at me in a panic. "But I need to tell you…what you heard Aidan say about me being pregnant…"

"We know, Ashlyn, it's ok."

"You…you do? But how?"

"Long story."

"But what Aidan said about being Eris's…"

"We'll talk about it later," I replied as we all ran to the end of the dirt aisle to where the stream cut through the woods. Ashlyn tripped and stumbled over the roots rising from the ground causing Kyla to pick her up altogether, it was faster anyway. Shots rang out in the distance, the shouts and battle cries echoing through the woods. The battle had begun and we were running along the outskirts. Ahead of us I could see a cloud of white light coming in our direction, and behind us a cloud of murky red. Just ahead, a ridge rose to our right and it was eerily familiar.

"Mama! We have to go up there," Jackson shouted.

"No, Jack-Jack, I wanna go home," Livy cried, but Jack was right. We had made it through one dream, now we had a second to contend with. Although the tide had turned with Livy, there was still a chance this all fell apart.

"I'm sorry, baby girl, we have to," I said, leaping off the path and running up the ridge.

"Bri what are you doing?!" Kyla screamed.

"What I have to!"

I ignored the rest of her screams and tried to soothe my whimpering daughter.

"Livy, baby, I can't do this without you."

"But Ada said I can't use my powers on hybies," she cried.

"But they're not hybrids, Livy," I yelled impatiently as we neared the center of the ridge, the two sides converging on the three of us.

Four Warriors broke from the pack and leapt off the edge of the ridge with weapons drawn. But in the same moment a bright white stream of light hit all four of them and they instantly disappeared. I followed the white stream of light to see Gorum standing in the middle of the rebel group of Vamps, hundreds of red lights filling in behind him.

Before I could even warn the rest of the Warriors heading our way, an array of white light came right at us. Jackson jumped out of my arms and wrapped himself around my leg, allowing me to thrust my left arm behind me trying to keep the Warriors from disappearing. My hand was shaking from the amount of power I needed to keep so many Warriors from being forcibly Projected away.

Just then I heard my name and slowly looked to my left to see Cameron and Devin digging their hands into the ground while pieces of their essence flew away like white dust. To my right I could see Connor and Alex suffering in the same manner and I wasn't sure how much longer I could hold everyone around me.

"I'll help you, Mama," Jack-Jack shouted as he placed his hand on my calf. Suddenly I was filled with a surge of power, the Warriors around us lurching forward while Gorum stumbled back.

Aidan pushed his way through the crowd, his eyes wild as he screamed, "This is your last chance, Morgan! I will tear you limb from limb and eat your fucking throat. You hear me? We will kill every last one of you!"

My head was burning and my left hand shaking almost as much as Livy who was sobbing in my chest. Even with seeing those that I loved suffering, I couldn't give in. I had to show my children that their mother would fight for them and never give up.

"Go...to...hell," I growled through clinched teeth and lifted Livy to curl around my shoulders. "Baby, I can't do this without you."

"You're going down, Morgan," Aidan shouted and waved his troops to move forward.

The Warriors behind me were screaming in agony while Gorum and I fought over their essences. Even with Jack's help, I could feel my grip lessening. I was out of time and Aidan's Vamps were coming right for us.

"Livy, please! You have to help me!" I begged.

"But Ada said..."

"We're going to die if you don't help me."

"But Mama, I'm scared," she cried.

"Livy, if you don't use your powers," I began, my skin crawling because of the horrible, but necessary thing I was about to say, "I'll put you in time out for rest of your life!"

Livy's tears didn't stop, but she did place her little hand on my neck, allowing her power to run through me. With my right arm now free, I thrust it out in front of me, red sprays of light coming out of my fingertips and Pushing Aidan's troops back.

There is no winning, daughter of Eris. You will die like the rest of them unless you release your power, Gorum's voice rang in my head.

My entire was body shaking with exhaustion. I could only hold onto everyone for a few more moments. I looked down at my son and then over my shoulder at my daughter, the two people I had sacrificed my mortality for and I was ready to give up my immortality for.

"Always...remember," I struggled to say, "Mama loves you."

With all the energy I had left, I pulled my powers back inside and compressed them tightly into the depths of my soul. With one last Push, a wave of white and red light exploded out of me, leveling anyone it came in contact with. I fell to the ground, taking one last glance to my left to see Cameron sprawled out and rolling onto his side. His eyes met mine, and I was complete.

Jackson climbed up my side and draped himself around me. "Mama, are you ok?"

My fingers were weak as they petted his sweet head. Livy ran around to my back and before I could stop her, pulled a dagger out of its sheath and then scurried back in front of me.

"Olivia, put that back," I said weakly.

"But I need a sword, Mama."

I struggled to form a smile. "You are your mother's daughter."

"Don't worry, Mama, I'll protect you."

"I know you will, baby girl."

Chapter Fifty-two

Cameron

We gathered and stood at the ready on the front line once Alastor Projected the first hybrid into the hospital tent. Devin stood on my left which was normal, but having Victor on my right was odd. No one had ever fought with Victor at their side, but we all knew why he was here – to prove to Alastor he was not a failure. Unfortunately, I could relate.

"Anything, Brother?" Devin whispered and I shook my head, careful not to make any sudden moves. With the adrenaline and anticipation building, our line was on a hair trigger.

"The longer it is quiet, the better," Victor said. And although I agreed with him, I wish we had heard something by now. Did Brianna have our son? Was he hurt? Were they on their way back? When could I hold him in my arms again?

A stick broke in the distance causing most of the line to crouch in preparation to pounce, but a moment later three young women came running through the darkness.

"It's working," Alex whispered as volunteers took the women up to the medical tents.

"We should go in," I said impatiently.

"Give them a few more minutes, Brother," Devin replied, squeezing my forearm to keep me in place.

Barely a minute went by before I was struck by an uneasy feeling in the pit of my stomach. Even though it was quiet, something was wrong. I feared my loved ones were in trouble. I took a step from the line and Devin was instantly pulling on my arm.

"Brother, what are you doing!"

"Something is wrong, we need to go in."

Victor stepped forward, shaking his head. "There is no indication that there is a problem, child. You need to stay calm."

"No, there is…" but my statement was cut short when my son's voice was suddenly yelling in my head.

Ada help!

"Child," Victor cried out as he caught me before I hit the ground.

"They are in trouble," I said, pushing out of Victor's arms and running forward.

The line broke as soon as Devin and Alex came after me.

"Brother, stop!" Devin called behind me. "There are no signs of trouble."

Just then a screeching alarm echoed through the woods around us.

"Is that a big enough sign for you, Brother?" I shouted. Devin barked orders over his shoulder and within seconds a black cloud of Warriors dissented into the depths of the woods. Suddenly mid-stride, my head was snapped back with the image of Brianna lying face down in the ground while Olivia stood in front of Aidan and Gorum. The image must have come from Jackson and he sent it so hard that I fell backwards. Thankfully Alexander picked me up and held me upright for a few paces until I could run on my own.

"Was it Bri?" he asked, keeping a steadying arm at the ready.

"No, Jackson. Bri's in trouble and Olivia…she might be more like her mother than I feared."

He did not quite understand my meaning, but he knew enough to shout at those around us to get the lead out. Would my daughter go to our enemy in order to save her mother? Aidan sure knew how to manipulate my girls. I had to get to my family, yet my legs would not move as fast as I wanted them to. If only I was able to speak with my son and Bri the way they were able to speak with me. I could tell them we were all coming as fast as we could. I just needed them to hold on for a few more moments. I could not fail, not again, not after all the times Aidan had slipped through my fingers.

Several Warriors were ahead of us and I could see a clearing stretching out in the distance. As the tree line thinned I could see Brianna darting up the clearing's edge with the twins on her hip and suddenly my surroundings seemed scarily familiar.

Right at that moment the Warriors ahead of us leapt up in the air to jump the distance to the area below, but within seconds their bodies disintegrate into a fiery black smoke.

"Stop! Everyone st..." I shouted, but was cut short when an intense pain hit me in the head and chest, pushing me back several inches before I fell forward and dug my fingers into the ground.

I strained to look next to me and saw that my brothers were experiencing the same phenomena. Even Alexander with all his girth was struggling to stand and I could see his skin shimmering away behind him. In fact, everyone was beginning to shimmer away. The feeling was almost as if someone was Projecting me away. My fingers were digging into the dirt to try and keep me grounded, and just when it seemed as though I would be pushed away, another invisible force pulled me forward. My body was raked with pain as it was pushed and pulled, two forces fighting over me. One trying to send me away while the other fought to keep me here.

Looking forward I saw Brianna still standing at the edge of the ridge, her left arm stretched out behind her while Jackson clung to her leg and Olivia hung on her shoulders. It was the dream the children had had so many times. I realized now that although I could not see it, Brianna and Jackson were the ones trying to keep all of us from being Projected away. My skin started to burn as deeper layers started to flake away. I screamed as I was suddenly pushed back several feet, my fingers leaving ten distinct trails in the earth.

Come on, Bri, I growled in my head, since speaking was not an option. Finish them, finish them all, I kept thinking and clawed my way toward her. As if she heard my thoughts, she pulled both of her hands in as if she was harnessing all her energy and I knew what was coming next, and it was not going to be pleasant.

Just as I had expected, a sudden wave of energy exploded from around her, taking out everything in its path, including me. No amount of clawing into the ground would have kept me from flying back. My head and chest were pounding as I hit the ground, and it was difficult to concentrate through the ringing in my ears. I lifted my head and saw that all the

Warriors were down, strewn about and moaning while they pulled themselves together. Brianna was curled up on the ground with Livy standing protectively in front of her with a dagger in her hand.

"Get up you dogs!" Victor shouted as he pulled himself up from the ground.

Alexander looked over at me, punched his fist in the air and yelled, "I'm going to puke!"

"Hell yes we are!" I shouted back and fell in line behind him, pushing through our own men in order to get to Brianna and the twins.

"Ada!" Jackson shouted and leapt into my arms as I fell to my knees at Brianna's side.

"Jacky, oh my sweet boy," I said into his hair, suddenly having to clamp down on my emotions while my son wept into my shoulder.

Alexander was circling protectively around us and looked down over the ridge. "They're coming, Cam. We need to hurry."

I nodded and brushed Brianna's cheek. "Are you able to run?"

Slowly she pushed herself up to her knees. "Not without a little help, Cam, I'm so sorry."

"Do not be, but we need to be quick," I replied and lifted up my sleeve. Brianna's fangs were already extended and she quickly sank them into my wrist.

"Thirty seconds," Alexander warned.

Brianna sucked in another mouthful of blood before removing her fangs and licking the wounds clean. Quickly I wrapped my arm around her waist and pulled her up to a standing position.

"Fifteen seconds, Cam!" Alexander yelled over his shoulder.

"Jackson, hang on to me. Olivia, you will need to hold onto your mother," I instructed, releasing my hold on Brianna and helping Olivia climb up to her mother's chest.

"They're coming, Cam!" Alexander shouted again and began pushing us all forward.

"Dagger, please," Brianna commanded and took the silver dagger from Olivia before starting a slow gait.

With Jackson clinging to my chest, I kept one arm around him and the other held out protectively at Brianna's back. While we ran I could hear Olivia's soft whimpering through the wind whipping past. It tore at my heart, as it did Bri who has cooing her as best she could while trying to dodge the Warriors coming at us and the enemy nipping at our heels.

We were only fifty feet ahead when Alexander had to stay behind with the others to hold off the oncoming Vampires. I shouted at Brianna that we needed to go faster and I could tell she was already digging deep. Only another twenty feet and the ridge ahead marked we were halfway to base.

"Hold on, Jacky," I said in his ear, causing him to tighten his grip around my neck as I leapt forward toward the ridge, grabbed the edge with my hands and launched the two of us up onto higher ground. Immediately I extended my hand down to Brianna who was now making the jump and pulled her effortlessly up to the top of the ridge.

As we turned to continue running to base, we were jostled back around, the ground shaking underneath our feet as an explosion sounded in the distance.

"Bombs?" Brianna asked fearfully.

"Or landmines," I replied.

"Oh that's much better, Cam. Are we running in a minefield?!"

"How would I know?" I shouted. "Nothing triggered when we were running down. Maybe they are being set off…"

But I could not finish my statement since at that moment a flood of Vampires, Warriors and enemy alike, came running in our direction.

"Go! Go!" I shouted and pushed Brianna forward, however, we were once more stopped in our tracks when the ground shuttered again with an explosion, this time sending Vampires and dirt and shrapnel scattering every which way. Olivia screamed and covered her ears while Jackson watched those below shout and cry for help.

"It is a silver bomb," I said, taking her hand and pulling her away.

"You mean the shrapnel is…is…"

"Is silver, or coated with silver. Head toward the path, perhaps that is safer."

Brianna nodded and we began crossing the open terrain while Devin was yelling below to hold our lines. The enemy could not crest that ridge, it was imperative. Halfway to our camp was too close. They were pushing through us too easily.

As the path grew closer Brianna pointed to Kyla and Julian coming toward us.

"Give them to us," Kyla shouted over the chaos behind us. "We'll get them out of here."

"They have bombs, Kyla."

"I know," she replied, extending her arms out and reaching for Jackson.

"I'll be able to see them before they hit. Julian and I will protect them. Devin needs you two down there."

Reluctantly I nodded and shifted Jackson away from my chest, kissed him on his forehead, and wiped the small tear from his cheek. "Go with your aunt and Julian, son. Help them with your gift, use all the power your mother gave you. Do you understand? Use everything you have, Jacky."

"I will, Ada, I will," he replied tearfully and allowed Kyla to pull him from my arms. There was no way I was able to do it myself, and at first it looked as though Brianna was having a hard time giving Olivia to Julian. But then I realized it was Olivia that was not letting go of her mother.

"But you love Julian, baby, you need to go," Brianna said, trying to pry Olivia's hands from around her neck.

"No, Mama, pwease no, Mama," Olivia cried and tightened her arms around her mother's neck while Julian tried pulling her away. Suddenly the sight of them struggling with Olivia triggered the memory of the twins' other dream, however, instead of Julian pulling Olivia it had been Aidan. Whether it was Brianna or the twins, their dreams weren't always exact, but they were always warnings. This had to be a sign.

"Julian, let her go!" I yelled.

"I was just trying to…" he began as he released Olivia, causing her to wrap her little legs around her mother's waist.

"It's not you, Julian. Bri, this is the last dream," I said to her and suddenly the recognition flashed in her eyes.

"But what does it…"

"Get down!" Kyla screamed and launched herself forward with Jackson tucked into her chest.

I immediately turned to Brianna and pushed us all forward just as the ground around us erupted, spewing dirt and projectiles into the air. I covered Brianna as best I could while Olivia was tucked underneath. While dirt rained down upon us my back was suddenly struck with a sharp pain. I lurched forward, crushing Brianna and causing Olivia to squeal. The pain was piercing and burning through layers of my skin and muscles.

"Cam?" Brianna said weakly as she tried moving from underneath me.

"Shrapnel," was all I could say as I crawled to the side of her. Once she took hold of Olivia she stood from the ground and screamed. "That bad?"

"Julian!" she screamed. "What do we do!"

Julian knelt down in front of me, but looked over my head to speak to Bri. "Brianna, you'll have to take it out."

"Me! Why me?" she replied in a panic.

"Because you're the only one with gloves on," Julian shouted. "I'll hold him, you take it out." Julian braced his hand around my neck tightly. "Hold onto me, Cameron."

"Wh-here's...Jackson."

"He is unharmed. Kyla has him," he replied softly and guided my arm over his shoulder. "Now hold on, brother, this is going to hurt."

"You will enjoy this then," I tried saying with a laugh, but the object in my back sent ripples down my spine.

"I only enjoy it when you deserve it," he replied and then titled his head up to see Brianna behind me. "Now, Brianna, grab hold and pull straight up in three, two..."

I screamed and held onto Julian for dear life while the shrapnel was pulled out of my body. It must have sunk in several inches by how long it took to take out, but with a big exhalation of breath my body was finally free. Julian released me and I collapsed to the ground while my body started to heal.

Brianna draped herself over me, crying into my ear that she was sorry for having caused so much pain.

"Love, you had to," I replied and patted her hand. "You need to go, Bri. Go with Kyla and Julian. Get the children out of here."

"I'm not going without you," she said firmly and pulled me up to a standing position.

I groaned from the pain in my back stretching and stitching itself together. On the ground was a long, wide piece of metal coated in blood. This wasn't just small pieces of shrapnel. This was major hardware. No wonder so many had gone down in the blast.

Olivia tugged on my pant leg, her face covered in dirt except for the two small tracks down her cheeks where her tears had cut through. "Ada, are you ok now?"

"Yes, monkey, thanks to your mother," I replied.

"Ok. I can go with Juwian now," she said happily and leapt into the air.

Julian was so surprised that he almost did not catch her, and looked to me for an explanation, which of course I had none. Kyla lifted Jackson into her chest, and Brianna gave him a tearful kiss on the forehead and hugged Kyla tightly.

"Julian," I began, "keep them safe."

"With my life, brother," he replied firmly.

It was such an odd feeling that in that moment he was indeed my brother. "Thank you, brother. Now go!"

Brianna shook with emotion as we watched our children disappear into the darkness. When we could no longer see their figures, Brianna squeezed my hand and oddly it was wet and sticky. I held it up and saw a thin, sharp piece of silver cutting into the skin of her forearm.

"Brianna, you are injured," I said in a panic and pulled her arm into my abdomen to stabilize it. I dug my fingers into her skin trying to get ahold of the silver, but causing it to slip further up her arm and burn my fingertips in the process.

"Just leave it," she growled and tried pulling my hand away.

"Hold still!" I shouted.

Just as I removed the silver shrapnel, Brianna screamed and was suddenly thrown backwards across the clearing and in her place stood Aidan Pierce.

"Shall we dance?" he said with a smirk.

"Only if you let me lead," I replied, shoving the silver splinter into his abdomen, wrapping my arms around him, and launching us down into the midst of the fighting below.

Aidan bit into the side of my neck as we flew through the air, ripping out a chunk of skin and muscle when we finally hit the ground. The pain was dazing and allowed the quick second he needed to throw me off of him. He stood above me, grunting while he tried pulling the silver shrapnel out of his stomach. Quickly I kicked his legs out from underneath him and leapt on top of him, pummeling his face with my fists. But with each hit he gave me a daring smile, almost as if he was enjoying the pain.

I pulled the small knife from my vest and thrust it towards his heart, but Aidan held my arm above him with both hands keeping the knife's tip only inches away.

"Does Brianna...still taste as...good as she used to?" he grunted, but I ignored him and shifted all my weight into pressing my knife into him. "What about your daughter?"

His baiting worked and I punched him in the face with my left fist, losing my leverage and rolling forward off of him. Instantly he sat on my back, grabbed the back of my head, and slammed it into the ground once, twice, each time burying my face deeper and deeper into the rich earth. When he reared my head back a third time he flipped me head over heels and into a dead tree a few feet away.

Slowly I pushed myself up to a standing position, as did he, both of us panting like bulls and preparing to strike. In three steps we were clashing into one another, grabbing and pushing at each other's shoulders when another loud blast came from my left. Suddenly I was thrown several feet back, shards of silver flying in my direction. My ears rang painfully while dirt cascading down on top of me. A large shard of silver sank into the outside of my forearm, sending shooting pains through to the bone. The only thing worse was the radiating pain coming from my stomach. I looked down to see a piece of rebar coated in silver disappearing into my abdomen. My palm sizzled as I grasped the rebar, trying to pull it free from my body.

"Let's leave that in, shall we?" Aidan growled and planted his foot on top of my hand, pushing the rebar deeper inside my body.

The pain and continued ringing in my ears made it almost impossible to focus, even causing my vision to double. Aidan lifted his foot and grabbed me by the throat, holding me nose to nose with him.

"There's nowhere your kids can hide that I won't find them," he said while tightening his grip on my throat. "I will find them again, groom them, torture them…"

"Not…about…them," I struggled to say.

"Say again?" he laughed. "Is that silver going to your brain, ol'buddy? Look around you, all of this is about them. Elaina started this, and I'm finishing it."

I pulled at his wrist with my right hand as his grip became tighter and tighter. "It's…for…your father."

Instantly Aidan threw me to the ground and kicked the rebar in my stomach through to the other side.

"You know NOTHING about my father," he shouted and kicked me again in the stomach.

"I know…Devin killed him," I said and coughed up dark red blood as I rolled over onto my side.

Aidan knelt down beside me and pulled my head back. "My father was a pioneer."

"He was a murderer and a forgetful kill."

Aidan's eyes flashed with fury as he wrenched my head back further. "I will tear your son apart until I can recreate him in my own image. I will breed your daughter until I have an army of my own."

With each word Aidan opened himself up further and further, letting his anger fuel his tirade. He did not see me tense my left arm before I swung it around, slicing his throat with the shard of silver that was still stuck within it. He stumbled back and fell to his knees with shock, blood leaking out of his wound and dripping down on his shirt. Painfully I crawled over to him, grabbing the back of his head to hold him firmly while I pushed my left forearm into his wound, allowing the silver shard to continue to burn through his throat.

"It was me, Aidan," I whispered, enjoying the pain in his eyes. "Decades of experiments, hundreds of kidnappings, all to create something I did the day they were born. It was me, not Brianna, that made them the way they are. They fed from me, Aidan, that is all. Something so simple yet the only thing you never thought of."

Aidan's eyes grew wide while his body shook with pain and pending death. I wanted this to last longer. I wanted him to suffer what Brianna and I had. But then I realized there were others that had to pay.

"Enjoy seeing your father in hell," I growled and ripped through Aidan's throat with the crude weapon sticking out of my arm. His body fell heavily to the ground when his head finally came off clean, blood dripping from the underside.

I yelled and screamed all the anger inside of me and threw Aidan's head into the battle. While the battlefield started to thin and change direction toward the enemy camp, I painfully pulled the rebar from my stomach, burning my hands in the process. I was debating whether I could take the piece out of my arm when Devin came in from the surrounding woods with panic stretched across his face. A sight I never saw in battle.

"Brother!" he yelled and waved me in the direction of the woods. "Brother, it's Father! Hurry!"

Without a second's hesitation I followed my brother. He gave no explanation while we sped to the wood's edge, but after only a few seconds I saw why he was in such a panic. There lying on the ground was the mighty Victor, sprawled out and growling in pain from a long, thin piece of metal coated in silver that was practically cutting him in half lengthwise. Natasha hovered over him, a long open gash bleeding across her forehead while her left arm hung at an awkward and painful-looking angle. My knees sank into the ground next to my maker, my hands shaking as they traced the entry point of the metal from the side of Victor's abdomen up to the left side of his chest.

"Is it...is it touching your...heart?" I stuttered.

Victor grunted slightly and found my hand as he answered, "I believe...so. I can feel it burning...through."

"I think it's also slowing the bleeding," Devin said over my shoulder. "We need to do something, Brother. Do something!"

I looked up at my eldest brother and saw his absolute worst fear coming true right before his eyes.

"I'm so sorry, Victor," Natasha cried and then looked over to me. "I'm so sorry, Cameron. I was helping some of the mothers. There were Vamps coming up on the path. I was trying to fight them when Victor came to help and then a bomb...it just...they just kept going off and then Victor went down trying to..."

"I think I am responsible for child's broken arm," Victor said, squeezing my hand.

"I'll heal, Victor, I'm sorry..."

"Brother, what do we do?" Devin shouted at me again.

"Everyone just be quiet for a moment and let me think!" I yelled and then had to take a breath to think through all the options. "Brother, what if we both carried him to base."

"With this terrain we'll cause the shard to push through even faster. Look at him, how would we even keep him together!"

"Thank you, child," Victor grimaced. "That option also sounds very painful."

"Ok then," I continued, "we take the shard out and then you Project yourself to base."

Victor shook his head painfully. "I doubt there is enough blood or energy in me to do so."

"Besides, Brother, you take that shard out and it opens the wound to his heart and it drains in seconds."

"Then you come up with something!" I shouted.

"Child," Victor said softly, "a wound to the heart cannot heal on its own. We all know what needs to be done here."

"NO!" Devin yelled.

"Child..."

"We stitch the heart, Father," I interrupted. "We stitch it to stop the bleeding and give you blood directly to heal it."

"Impossible," he replied and then squeezed my hand again while his face tightened with pain.

"Not impossible. We have John here, he can do this, Father."

"And I can give him blood," Natasha said as the cut above her head began to slow it's bleeding.

"Even if that could work, how do we get him there, Brother," Devin said as he paced next to me.

My mind was racing, thinking of all the different ways we could get Victor to the base without injuring him even further or causing his instant death. Damn, damn, damn. Think, Cameron, think. If only he could Project somewhere, we could have John ready and waiting. But Victor was right, especially with the damage to his heart there was no way he could do it on his own. And then it hit me.

"Where's Alastor!"

Just at the sound of Alastor's name Devin knew what I was thinking and stood up in the direction of the wooded path. "Jared, come in!" he said into his comm unit.

"Jared, here."

"Do you have a location on Alastor?"

The was an agonizing silence for nearly five seconds before Jared replied, "Copy that. He's headed north."

"On the path?"

"Er...no. Just walking through the clearing towards base."

"Devin, stay with Father," I commanded. "And get Jared here. We are going to need him."

Devin nodded and took my place at Victor's side. I ran quickly into the clearing where bodies and debris were scattered everywhere. Just when I looked to my right I saw Alastor's head pop up in the distance. Jared was right, he was just walking through the clearing as if he was taking a stroll in the woods. I ran to him and strangely he smiled.

"Good, I am glad I found you," he began. "I was afraid you might be among the dead."

"Victor needs you, Alastor. He is injured very badly and we need you to dual Project him to..."

Alastor put his hand up in front of me. "Our agreement was that I would Project the most critical women to your medical tent, and I have done just that. No more, no less. That was the agreement."

I was stunned. "But...he could die."

"The spoils of war," he replied callously and stepped past me. "His injuries are not my concern."

"But he is your only sire!"

"I don't see why that has any bearing."

"He is dying!"

"You said that," he replied. "He should have been faster or fought harder, as the rest of you did. I gave my blood to him once, that never meant I was bound to him for all eternity. Now, if you will excuse me, I have fulfilled my contract. Whatever happens to your kind now is all up to you."

"Our kind?" I responded. "You are an Ancient! You are turning your back on your people, even your child."

"Victor is my sire, not my child, and he serves no purpose for me. Now, I will return to my peace."

My vision went red when he turned away from me again and began walking away. "I will defile your name at every instance. I will tell our world the likes of who you really are, what a vile and greedy and disgusting Vampire you are."

Alastor jumped up onto the ridge a few feet ahead and looked down at me as he replied, "As if I care what your kind thinks of me."

Before I could say another word he Projected into black mist, taking with him the power needed to save my father. But lying there at the ridge's edge was Aidan's head, his dead eyes eerily staring at me and reminding me that there was one other with extremely powerful blood.

"Brother!" Devin shouted from the wood's edge as I bolted to where the battle was still in action.

"I have to find Gorum!"

Chapter Fifty-three

Brianna

Just as Cameron dug out the silver from my arm I was suddenly pulled backwards through the air. The battle was in full swing below me, and when I finally collided with a tree I landed right in the thick of it. Immediately I got back up on my feet, unsheathed my daggers, and was ready to fight my way back up to Cameron. It was only a second before two enemy Vamps were in front of me. Block up, swipe down, swing around, dagger to the throat, head off. One down. The second Vamp looked scared and took a step back to run. I swung my daggers around in front of me causing him to step back again, but then in the next second a white light lassoed him around the head and he was flung into the battle, and I was suddenly pushed into the ground face first.

The pain in my head was excruciating as I was forcibly pulled up to my knees to come face to face with Gorum.

"If only you were a son of Eris rather than a daughter, then we could easily fulfill your family's contract and be done with all of this."

"Wha...what do...you want," I growled through the pain.

"I want you to scream," he replied with a sinister grin.

Suddenly the stream of white light that connected us grew thick and pierced the inside of my head with such pain that I couldn't help but give him what he wanted. My screams were deafening and Gorum dropped me back down on the ground. Like a dog on a leash, he pulled me through the clearing, moving battling Vamps when they got in his way. When I would try and muffle my screams he would tighten the vice-like grip in my head. I tried focusing my power in order to break through the connection, but it was impossible to think through the pain.

"Figlia!" I heard my father shout in the distance, but before I could warn him not to come to me, Gorum stepped on the side of my face, pushing me into a mound of wet dirt and leaves.

A moment later Eris was standing in front of us with both his swords drawn.

"I knew a father couldn't resist the sound of his daughter's screams."

"Let her go," Eris growled and took a step forward.

Gorum responded by sending waves of pain into my head and down through my body.

"Stop, stop! What is it you want?" he begged.

"My contract with your father was for one daughter and one son. I was given your sister, and you never came. For thousands of years I have waited to collect."

"A son and daughter?" Eris asked flabbergasted. "For what?"

Gorum took his foot off my face and stepped toward my father, the white stream that connected us stretching out behind him. "I was promised a family. A son and daughter for all eternity, to spread my blood and create an even greater coven."

"But you killed Anoi, you drained my sister."

"Only because your father broke our contract. But now you can rectify that."

Eris began lowering his swords. "How?"

"By coming with me and answering only to me."

"And you will release my daughter?"

"Of course not, she is the other half of the contract, Eris. One son, one daughter."

"No!" I screamed and was flung through the muddy brush and then brought back to lay helpless at Gorum's feet.

"I haven't spent all these years with Aidan and Elaina to come away with nothing. I knew that my patience would win out in the end and receive my family."

Eris threw his swords down. "You can have me, but not my Bri-an-na. You can Turn any other woman and I will surrender to you as I have surrendered my swords, but only if you let her go."

When it seemed that Gorum had finally conceded to Eris's request, another white stream grew from his hand and stretched to touch my father. Eris knelt to the ground in pain, his head forcibly lowered into submission.

"Get used to that position, Eris," Gorum said with a sinister grin.

"Let...her...go," my father struggled to say under Gorum's control.

Gorum turned his gaze on me and slowly shook his head. "I have a feeling Brianna will not just let me take her precious father away. She will hunt me, send her Warriors for me, all to get daddy back. Won't you, dearie?"

I couldn't answer. The white mist thickened as it drilled through to the back of my head. He was going to kill me and take my father away from Sera. I was willing to sacrifice myself for my children, and I would suffer any amount of pain for my stepmother.

"Let...her go!" Eris shrieked.

"Say goodbye to your precious figlia, Eris," Gorum replied and strengthened his Push.

Everything around me was white. White mist, white light, white hot pain that radiated through my nerves. Suddenly I could feel every particle of Gorum's power circulating within me, somehow becoming one with my own. Painfully I looked up at Gorum and placed my hand up through the stream of white mist, catching the light in the center of my palm and slicing it free from my forehead. Gorum stepped back in shock as I literally held his power in my hand.

"You're wrong about one thing, Gorum," I said and stood from the ground. "If you dared to take my dad away from me I wouldn't send Warriors after you because I would want the glory of hunting and killing you all to myself. But in this moment, I will give him the pleasure."

Gorum lunged toward me and I thrust his power back at him causing him to flip over backwards and fall face down in the mud. Before he could get to his feet, Eris picked him up by his throat.

"For my family," he growled and plunged his sword into Gorum's chest until it came out his back.

Gorum was frozen on his knees, shock on his face while his heart emptied down his stomach. Eris released a feral howl as he pulled his sword from Gorum's body and threw him to the ground. Then he began thrusting his sword back in over and over again, thrust after thrust, causing blood to drain and soak into the ground underneath. Thousands of years' worth of anger went into each cut, guilt and grief over the murder of his sister Anoi and the eventual draining of his other sister Eliah. With the last cut taking Gorum's head clean off, Eris threw his sword to the ground and fell to his knees.

"Brianna!" Cameron shouted in the distance.

I turned around to see Cameron running through the clearing.

"Over here," I shouted back and in the blink of an eye he was in front of me.

"Where's Gorum!" he said in a panic and I pointed at the mutilated body lying on the ground.

Immediately Cameron fell to the ground and shoved my father out of the way. Eris recovered quickly and grabbed Cameron by the throat.

"I need...his blood," Cameron grunted and ripped my father's hand away.

"Gorum is mine, Warrior," Eris growled and pushed Cameron back.

"And I will not take him away from you. I just need his blood, Eris. Please!"

When Eris didn't respond, Cameron knelt down to the ground and buried his face into the underside of Gorum's exposed neck.

Gross.

When he finally lifted his head, blood was smeared across his mouth and chin like a child who ate red ice cream.

"Cameron, what the hell?"

He grabbed my wrist and dragged me into a run. "Eris, he is all yours now."

"Cam, wipe your face and then tell me what the hell is going on."

He wiped his chin clean of blood before responding, "I needed Gorum's blood to help Father."

"Why, what's wrong?"

"You will see soon enough," he replied in a fearful tone as we raced across the clearing, skipping over the bodies of fallen Vampires. At the edge of the clearing I could see Devin and Tosh kneeling next to someone on the ground. As we approached, my stomach sank at the sight of Victor lying on the ground with a piece of metal cutting him vertically in half.

"Oh my god."

Victor gave me an effortless smile although he must have been in so much pain. "I can always count on you to give me a truthful reaction, my dear."

"I'm sorry, Victor," I replied as Cameron pulled me closer. "Cam, what's the plan here?"

Cameron edged Devin away from Victor's side and pulled me down beside him. "Bri, you will need to pull the metal from Father's body…"

"How did that become my job today!"

"Brianna!" he yelled at me and I saw the absolute fear in his eyes. "The timing has to be precise. You will need to pull the metal from his body and I will stop his heart from bleeding. Then I will dual Project us to the…"

"Wait, what?! No," I yelled and stood up from the ground. "No, you don't know how to…no…I'm sorry, no."

Cameron took my wrist gently and pulled me back down to the ground. "It is the only way, Bri. That is why I took Gorum's blood. If Aidan's goons can do it, it cannot be that difficult. Please, love, you have to help us."

"Brianna," Victor said with effort, "please know that I did try and talk them out of this."

"Father, be still," Cameron demanded. "Brianna, the longer we wait the more blood he loses."

"Cam, what if you don't…"

"I will find my way back, I know I will. I am the strongest Projection skills in the coven. Please, love, we are running out of time."

"Jesus, Cam! You can't just drop this on me and…oh my god, what's that in your arm?"

Cameron lifted his forearm and saw the thick piece of metal he had somehow forgotten about. "Please, love?"

"Seriously, how did this become my job today!" I shouted and yanked the silver out of Cameron's arm.

"Jared," Devin began over Cameron's groans, "take Tosh to camp and ensure that everything is clear for Cameron and Father's appearance." Jared nodded and gently pulled Natasha into his arms before disappearing down the trail in the woods.

When Cameron's arm had mostly healed, he positioned himself at Victor's chest. "Father, are you ready?"

"I don't think anyone can prepare themselves for something like this. So come now, Brianna, give it a yank."

"Before I do this, just know I totally disagree with this whole plan."

"Brianna," Devin growled.

"Ok on one, two, three," I said and then pulled the long piece of metal from Victor's body and at the same time Cameron placed is hands inside the cavity.

Gross. Everything about this was gross.

"Brother, are you sure you have plugged the leak in the heart?"

"I believe so," Cameron replied as Victor groaned in discomfort.

If I were still human I would have puked on the battlefield again.

"Ok, Brother, it's now or never."

Cameron nodded and I stepped around in order to see him face to face. "I love you."

"Always, my love," he replied with worry behind his eyes making me take his face between my hands.

"Come back to me," I said sternly.

"I will see you at camp," he replied nervously before looking back down at Victor. "Are you ready, Father?"

"Last chance to just cut off my head and put an end to this," Victor replied, but with no takers. "Alright then, I guess I am ready."

Cameron took in a deep breath and exhaled. His lips flexed as he counted to himself – one, two, three, and then both he and Victor disappeared into black smoke.

Devin looked over at me and said, "Meet you th…"

But I didn't bother letting him finish and began Projecting myself to camp. If Cam survived the battle only to be ripped apart trying to save Victor, I was going to be pissed. Pissed! He'd said before that he would never forgive me if I died, well back at you, Mr. Burke.

Chapter Fifty-four

Jonah

"John, are you sure I can come in there?" I asked at the curtain divider while a woman screamed in labor on the other side.

"Jonah, get your ass in here now! I need those blankets, this baby is coming now," John shouted back at me.

Gritting my teeth, I opened the curtain and stepped inside the makeshift birthing room where a nurse from the Facility and two other women from Aidan's camp held the hands and legs of the screeching woman giving birth while John sat with a front row seat between her legs.

"Is that a head!" I accidently said out loud.

"Blanket, Jonah," John said with an outstretched arm. I placed the stack of blankets in my arms on top of an empty table and then handed him one from the top. "Now get out unless you really want to help."

"Nope, I'm good," I replied quickly and ran out of the room.

"You ok?" Nikki said looking up at me while she cleaned the head wound of a girl who couldn't have been older than Katie and was pregnant.

"Yeah, just…ah…don't go in there. It's…it's terrifying."

She laughed, which was weird since she rarely even broke a smile. But the moment was broken when the ground suddenly shook beneath our feet and the sound of an explosion came in the distance.

"Was that a bomb?" I said as women began running into the tent.

"Well don't just stand there, get to work," Nikki growled.

Quickly I began directing women to different areas based on their injuries and in most cases the size of their stomachs. Only a minute later did the ground shake again. This time the sound of frightened screams and the wailing of a newborn baby filled the area around us.

John stepped out from behind the curtain wiping his hands with a towel. "Were those bombs?"

"I think so," I replied nervously as I helped a woman into a chair, her knees and ankles scratched and bleeding.

"Find the extra bandages and tape. If those were bombs, there could be shrapnel. Just what we need, right?"

John really was destined to be an emergency room doctor. Even with everything going on around him, he was perfectly calm and going from patient to patient checking who needed his attention most. Thankfully only one woman had actually delivered her baby, although others looked as though they would go at any moment. As each wave of women came inside our tent I hoped one of them would be Ashlyn. Now there were bombs. Bombs! I can't say I was prepared for that. What if she was injured and...

"Dammit, Jonah! Don't just stand there, help that girl!" Nikki shouted at me from across the tent. "Useless! Absolutely useless!"

I snapped back to attention and knelt down in front of the young woman in front of me.

"Sorry about that," I said, "I'm just a little distracted. My girl's out there somewhere." The young woman smiled and then gasped as I began cleaning the cuts on her shins with disinfectant. "Sorry, I know it stings."

"That's ok," she replied with a loud exhale. "I'm the one who tripped. I couldn't see anything out there."

I looked up to see her place a hand on her stomach. "You're a...one of the...a..."

"Yes, I'm pregnant," she replied with an awkward laugh. "Only six months, though. Man that hurts."

"Sorry," I replied and started cleaning her other knee. "At least you didn't have to have your baby in the woods without painkillers."

"Poor Sybil, she couldn't hold out one more day," she laughed softly. "So, you said your girlfriend is out there? Is she one of the fighters?"

I shook my head. "No...uh...she's in the camp. Her name is Ashlyn."

Her eyebrows went up. "So you're Eris?"

"Uh…what?"

She bit at her bottom lip. "Um…she got to keep her baby because the father was someone named Eris. I just assumed…"

"No, I'm uh…Jonah."

"Oh, I'm so sorry. Just forget what I said, I must have heard wrong."

"I doubt that. I know who Eris is. It's just…uh…confusing."

But before the moment could get any more awkward the ground shook again with the sound of a bomb blast in the distance.

"Here they come!" Nikki shouted as a dozen injured women entered the tent. Heads and arms were seeping blood, ankles were turned, and shrapnel was cutting into skin.

John was a machine and didn't miss a beat. He just delivered a baby in the woods. I'd be running around the tent demanding high fives, but John just….

"Jonah!"

I looked over my shoulder to see Fabi waving at me from the front of the medical tent.

When I took a step toward him Nikki shouted, "We need him, Fabi."

"She needs him more," Fabi replied and waved at me again.

"Who? Who needs me?" I shouted over the noise as I walked to the front of the tent.

Fabi grabbed my shoulder and pulled me outside. "Who else…dammit where did she go?"

"Who, Fabi!"

"Jo-Jonah?"

She was hard to hear over all the activity around us, but I knew that voice, I had longed to hear it for weeks. I turned to my right to see a pale, exhausted-looking Ashlyn with her blonde hair frizzy and tangled around her face. Tears were cutting tracks through the dirt on her cheeks.

"I told you she needed you more," Fabi said next to me, but then was off.

Nervously I took a step toward Ashlyn which caused her to sprint the fifty feet that separated us. As she ran into my chest I found that I had forgotten how little she was. I had to bend down in order to get my head to rest on her shoulder. She smelled of dirt and sweat and days without a real shower and I didn't care. I pulled her face up to mine and kissed her until I had to wipe the dirt out of my mouth. Ashlyn was crying so hard that mud was forming on her cheeks. I pulled my sleeve down around the palm of my hand and wiped her face, but she gasped and pulled away.

"Ow, that hurts," she said and cupped her hand over her cheek.

Gently I pulled her hand away and could see now that her cheek was swollen. "Did someone hit you? Who! I want a name, and then I'm going to give that name to Devin so he can hunt him down..."

"Jonah, Joey!" Ashlyn said and placed her hands on either side of my face. "It doesn't matter. It just hurts, I'll be fine."

I didn't respond and kissed her gently on her cheek, and then her eyes, and then her forehead, only stopping when the taste of dirt in my mouth was too much.

While I wiped the dirt from my lips, Ashlyn took the opportunity to say, "Jonah, I-I know this isn't really the place, but I need to tell you..."

"That you're pregnant?"

Ashlyn's jaw dropped, a new tear leaking from her eye. "H-how did..."

"Long, weird story. Just please tell me that it isn't Eris's."

Ashlyn froze. "How did you hear about..."

"Please, Ash, just tell me the truth."

"Of course it isn't Eris's."

"Then why is everyone telling me you're having his baby."

Gently Ashlyn cupped my check and the anxiety that had built up in me dissolved. "Jonah, just trust me for a minute. Shortly after I got here I started getting sick every morning. I was forced to take a pregnancy test and it was positive. They took me to Aidan and Gorum and I was afraid they were either going to kill me or get rid of my baby. I knew any connection to Brianna was important to them. So I lied, Jonah, I told them it was Eris's and I felt their feelings change instantly. I just kept the whole thing going because I couldn't lose this baby. Your baby."

"Oh thank god," I shouted and lifted Ashlyn off the ground as I tightened my arms around her. Then a second later reality hit and I placed her back down on the ground at same time the blood ran from my head. "It's mine. Holy shit, it's mine. Mine? You're really sure?" She nodded. "Yeah, ok. That's good then. Can you hold on a second, I just need to..."

I didn't finish my statement, I just sat down on a tree stump and rubbed my eyes. There was always this possibility, frankly it was the better one, but still. Holy shit, there was a baby in her stomach and it was mine and we weren't married, hell I didn't even have a job, my mom sold the house so I have no place to live, no place to raise my child. Holy shit, holy shit, what was I going to do. What the hell, what the hell...

"Jonah! Get off your ass!" Nikki yelled from the medical tent.

"Go to hell, Nikki, I'm dealin' with something..."

"Tosh is hurt, asshole! And Jared needs your help. Wanna get up now?"

I looked up to Ashlyn, mortified at the choice I had to make. "Ash, I'm sorry..."

"Later," she replied and lifted me up from the tree stump. "They need you."

"But..." I said and placed my hand on her stomach, "I love you."

She smiled with a tiny laugh and kissed me quickly. "I love you too, now come on."

"You should be going on the transports, especially in your condition."

"I survived this long, Jonah," she said and pushed me toward the medical tent.

Nikki threw up her arms as we approached. "About f-ing time."

"Where's Tosh and Jared?" I asked as I looked around.

"They should be here any second," she replied just as Jared came around the trees with Tosh hanging from his arms.

"Nik, take Tosh. She's fine, just taking a little longer to heal than usual. Give her a boost and bring the doc to the main tent," he began as he put Tosh down on the ground and into her sister's side. "Jonah, come with me, I need your help with...oh hey Ashlyn. Sorry I gotta take him away from you for a bit, but I promise..."

"It's fine, Jared, I'll help Nikki with Tosh," she replied, squeezing my hand and kissing me one time on the lips before helping Nikki take Tosh inside the medical tent.

"Great, you found her, so happy for you, now come on," Jared said and pulled me down toward the tent in the center of our camp.

"What happened to Tosh?"

"What do you think? Bombs are going off, shrapnel's flying everywhere, she got caught in the middle. But it's not her we have to worry about."

"Wh-who then?" I asked nervously as we approached the tent.

Jared held open the flap and allowed me to enter. "You'll see soon enough. Clear everything off those tables," he said and began moving the maps to the far sides of the tent's walls.

"Jer, tell me what's going on!"

"Just clear the damn tables, Jonah!" he shouted and then caught himself. "Sorry. It's Dad. He's in really bad shape and Cameron's trying..."

"Did he make it?!" Brianna shouted as she came running through the entrance with Devin. "Where is he? He Projected before we did!"

"Who!?" I shouted.

"Cam," Brianna whimpered and then held her hand up to her mouth.

"Cameron is dual Projecting with Father," Devin answered. "Only...if he's not here then..."

Suddenly a loud snap broke through the tent and in the same instant Cameron appeared on top of the table covering someone else with his body. His eyes were wide while he heaved like he desperately needed air. Brianna yelped and immediately went to catch him when he began to slide from the table, not only exposing that his hand was inside Victor's chest but also that Victor was practically in two pieces. I covered my mouth to keep the vomit inside.

"I told you it was bad," Jared said next to me.

"Child, are you all right?" Victor asked Cameron softly.

With Brianna's help, Cameron put his feet on the ground and answered, "Yes, Father. Just a little shaken."

"Where's John?" Devin asked as he moved to Victor's side.

"Right here...good lord," John said as he entered the tent.

"Everybody else out," Devin commanded. "Now!"

I jumped, practically landing in Jared's arms. Devin didn't have to tell me twice. The less time I had to see Victor cut in half the better. Just before I stepped through the flap, Brianna pulled on my elbow. Her eyes were stenciled in red from the tears she was struggling to keep inside.

"Did Ashlyn find you?" I nodded and she squeezed my hand. "Wonderful. Now get her and get on one of the transports."

I leaned away from her. "No, I'll stay here until..."

"You've both been through enough, and in her condition...please just go. The least I can do is deliver you to your mother unharmed. And if you go now, you can catch Julian and Kyla taking the twins."

I nodded. "I'll tell them you and Cameron are ok."

"Just don't say anything about..." she began and looked over her shoulder at Victor.

"I won't," I replied and hugged her before Jared pulled at my shoulders and brought me outside. Warriors were starting to gather around the tent, somehow the news of Victor's condition was spreading.

"Beebs is right, Jonah. You and Ashlyn should get out of here," Jared said, patting me on the shoulder. "I'll tell Julian to wait until you get there. See you back home, brother."

I didn't waste another second and ran back up the hill to the medical tent. As if she knew I was coming, Ashlyn stepped out from within.

"Ash!" I said and grabbed her hand, not stopping for a second and pulling her along with me to where the transport vehicles were being loaded.

"Jonah, where are we going?"

"We're getting out of here," I said and then turned around to face her. "We're getting our...our baby out of here."

She smiled and threw her arms around my neck. "I know it's scary, but we'll figure it out."

"I'm usually the one saying that to you."

"Who do you think I learned it from," she said as she lowered herself and wiped a tear from her eye.

I squeezed her hand and pulled her into my side. "I'll never let you go again. Either of you."

"You'll never have the chance."

Chapter Fifty-five

Cameron

"I'm not sure what exactly I can do here," John said while looking down at Victor's body.

My fingers were still plugging up the hole in his heart, although it was not completely effective. Blood was still seeping from the wound and if he bled out, he would be finished.

"Just sew him up," Devin snapped.

"A needle won't penetrate a Vampire's muscle," John replied.

"Then spray it with silver first."

"Why isn't he healing?"

"Because he has punctured his heart," I answered, looking sadly into Victor's eyes. "If you can suture the wound, the rest of him might heal with some help."

"Or you could just let me bleed out like I asked you to," Victor said painfully.

"Shut up, Father," Devin growled and everyone's eyes shot in his direction. "We will not stop trying."

John waited a beat before he finally looked over to Brianna and said, "Go up to the medical tent. Ask one of the nurses for a surgical kit, all the suture wire we have, and we'll need a can of the silver spray. I guess it's worth a try."

Brianna nodded and gave me one last look before disappearing outside. I knew my dual Projection scared her to death, and frankly it did me as well. My body was still aching from the pain. I wondered if it was always that painful, or if it was just because I was forcing the activity through a small amount of Gorum's blood.

"Jared, I said to stay…" Devin yelled, but Jared held his hand up.

"I know, bro, but Tosh insisted," Jared said and held the opening to the tent so that Natasha could limp inside with help from Nikki.

"Natasha, you should not be here," I scolded, worried that her wounds were still healing slowly and her coloring was very pale.

"I know, but I can help," she replied slightly out of breath.

"And how is that," Devin said angrily.

"My blood. My Healer blood could help his heart heal faster, maybe it'll even soften his skin so that Dr. John can sew him together easier."

John looked over his shoulder at Devin, and then to me and Victor. "It could work."

I shook my head. "Natasha, you are too weak."

"I'll do it," Nikki said and stepped in front of her sister. "I'm fine and I have the same blood as she does."

"Nikki, you don't…" Natasha began, but Nikki pushed her sister into Jared's arms.

"I'm doing this, Nat. Jared, get her out of here."

The tent became awkwardly quiet as Nikki sat down near the table. When Brianna came back inside with John's medical supplies, she instantly felt the change.

"Did I miss something?" she asked as she placed the supplies on the table and gave a confused glance in Nikki's direction.

"Nikki is going to provide some of her Healer blood to help Father," I replied.

"You're kidding," she said. "Shit, did I say that out loud?"

I nodded.

"Sorry, Nikki. It's been a long day. Thank you for helping."

Nikki rolled her eyes in response.

"Ok, we should get started," John said, thankfully breaking the tension. "This could take me a while, and I'd really rather not have an audience if that's ok."

Devin made eye contact with me, and I could see he was about to refuse, but Victor lifted his fingers up in the air.

"I would like to say goodbye to my children first, if you don't mind."

John nodded. "Of course. Nikki, let's get a bloodline going," he said and began pulling out the tubing and needles needed to draw Nikki's blood. Brianna stepped toward the tent's opening when Victor called to her.

"Brianna, wait," he said softly and she immediately came to his side, carefully taking his hand in hers. "Thank you, child."

"For what?" she sniffled as red tears leaked from her eyes.

"For giving me two of the most beautiful grandchildren ever made."

She gave a tearful laugh. "I think Cameron had more to do with that."

"Brianna," he continued in a more serious tone and wiped away Brianna's tear with his index finger, "you gave your life for them, do not minimize your sacrifice. And do not forget how strong you really are. Others would have crumbled where you have risen again and again. Never lose that, my dear."

"I won't," she cried. "Thank you for bringing me Cameron," she replied and kissed Victor's hand before rising from the ground. With her hands covering her mouth she left Victor's side and stepped out of the tent.

"Cameron," Victor said and moved his gaze to me. He cupped my cheek and I instantly felt the bloody tears welling up in my eyes. He so rarely called me by my name that it affected more than I expected. "My one mistake, they said, and now look at you. I cannot be more proud of what you have become. Always be true to who you really are, not a stubborn soldier like me. Be that loving father I always wanted to be."

The tears finally broke over my lids. "You are a loving father."

He smiled. "Not like you, child. You will always amaze me in how much you can love."

"But there is still so much I need to learn from you, Father. You need to stay with us because I am not ready."

"Child, you will learn as you go and you will have your brother," he said and removed his hand from my cheek, reaching out for Devin who eagerly took his hand. My brother's tears were already streaming down his face. "The two of you must work together to keep our coven going."

"Father, no. I don't want it like this," Devin said with a break in his voice.

"Devin, listen to your brother. Learn from him in the ways you lack, and work as one to continue our mission to protect our race and our ways."

"I will, Father," Devin replied as he buried his face in Victor's arm.

"And Cameron," Victor continued, "listen to your brother. He is older and more experienced in battle. Learn from him in the ways you lack, and work as one to bring our coven into the future."

"Of course I will, Father."

"We should get started," John said quietly behind me.

"Yes, doctor, of course. I just need to say one last thing," Victor said and pulled Devin's face up to see him directly. "Devin, you are my oldest child. You have always done as I asked and I have never questioned your loyalty."

"Because you are my father, a true father. I acknowledge no life before you."

"Thank you, child, but you must promise to do one thing for me, whether I survive or not."

"Anything, Father."

Victor cupped Devin's cheek and held it firmly as he said, "Do not hide who you are."

"Father?"

Victor paused for only a moment, gathering his own emotions before saying, "Do not keep Fabiani in the shadows. He is a good man. A good man who left his coven for you and what you stand for."

Devin looked up at me in shock, but I shook my head.

"How...how did you know, Father," Devin stuttered, his face contorted with conflict over his darkest secret being known.

"Child, I've always known."

"Why didn't you say anything?"

"Because you obviously didn't want to tell me. If I do not survive this, I cannot die having you think who you are was ever shameful to me."

"But loving a man isn't very...Warrior-like," Devin said softly.

"Who says," Victor replied flatly. "And if anyone tells you differently, you show them the Warrior Assassin that you are. I just want you happy, child."

"He makes me very happy, Father," Devin said and wiped his face clean. "I would like you to live so you can get to know him better."

"Thanks for not adding any pressure, Dev," John said behind us. "We really need to start, especially with the amount of blood he's lost just here on the table."

"Yes, yes, doctor, I am done with all my speeches," Victor said and released Devin's face. "Now in the presence of my two children, Dr. Ryan, if it appears that I cannot be saved, rather than continue fruitless options I ask that you end my life as quickly as possible."

"Victor, I'm not sure I can do that," John replied nervously and looked at me and Devin.

Victor sighed. "Then I ask that you call in Eris. I'm sure he would jump at the opportunity. Now kick my children out."

John looked up at the two of us with sympathetic eyes. "I'm sorry, guys, you heard the man."

"You don't need any help?" Devin asked reluctantly.

"Nikki's here. She wants to be a nurse someday, so this'll be great practice. Plus, I really don't need the two of you watching over me. I'll do everything I can."

"Listen to him, children, please leave him to do his work," Victor commanded.

I sighed and moved my body so that Nikki could replace my fingers with hers. I counted to three and reluctantly moved my fingers from within my father's heart.

"We love you, Father," I said and stepped away from the table, wiping my bloody hands on my shirt.

"Then I have done something right," Victor replied with a smile.

I wrapped my arm around Devin's shoulders and pulled him away from the table. Once we were outside we were taken aback by all of those gathered in front of the tent. Warriors and others who had joined us in battle, all standing and waiting with tension pulsing through their extremities.

Alexander stepped forward, but was unable to form words, so he merely knelt to the ground. The crowd followed in mass, all kneeling and Warriors placing their fists over their hearts. It was a sight I wished our father could see.

Alexander lifted his head, a sense of fear in his eyes that I had never seen. "Brothers, what can we do?"

Devin looked at me and I replied, "Pray."

Chapter Fifty-six

Cameron

"Cam, your tie is fine," Brianna moaned impatiently since I had re-tied it at least ten times.

"No it is not," I snapped back and undid the damn thing one more time, looped it around itself unevenly and then just ripped it from my neck and threw it down on the floor.

"Feel better," she said with a lifted brow.

"Much. But it means my outfit is no longer historically accurate," I replied as I straightened my long black Victorian-era jacket over the matching waistcoat.

"And why is that important?"

I sighed. "Father said that you should always be a symbol of your era, show others where you came from. That is why he always wore his robes."

"But this isn't your era," she replied.

"I am aware, love, but I would look ridiculous if I marched into my induction in a frilly shirt, knee-high pants and tights." She raised her brow at me again. "And I like this era's style better."

"There he is! There's the clothes snob I love," she said victoriously, but then saw my nervousness. "Cam, everything will go perfectly. You and Devin being inducted is a really big deal. You should be happy."

I pulled at my collar and unbuttoned the top button. "I am, and I am very happy for my brother. His dream is finally coming true."

"Mama," Jackson said as he came to stand between us, pulling roughly at the bowtie around his neck, "do I hafta wear this thing? It itches and chokes me and…" but the rest was lost while my son struggled to undo the knot.

"He becomes his father more and more every day," Brianna smirked as she bent down and removed the bowtie completely. "Now let's unbutton the first button of your shirt, then you'll really look like your Ada."

"Really?" he said with big hopeful eyes. With his dark curls and well-tailored miniature tuxedo he really did look just like me.

"We will make a new family rule," I began and picked Jackson up into my arms. "The Burke men shall no longer where bowties. Sound good?" He nodded. "Now how about your mother, how beautiful does she look?"

Brianna pursed her lips and shook her head with a little embarrassment, but no one could deny how exceptionally beautiful she looked in her bright red satin dress with plunging neckline and slit up the front that caused the fabric to billow effortlessly as she walked.

"Mama looks so pretty," Jackson replied. "She looks like a Christmas present."

Brianna smiled and kissed our son on his cherub cheek. "Thank you, baby. See, Cam, I can dress myself without your help."

"What about me, Ada," Olivia cooed from behind me.

I placed Jackson down on the ground and turned to my daughter in her red and green plaid dress that was stiff with tulle in her skirt. I knelt down in front of her and whispered in her ear, "Monkey, I am afraid of making your mother jealous at how lovely you look tonight."

Olivia smiled widely while her mother laughed behind us.

"Incoming," Brianna said a moment before the library doors were open and young William burst into the room.

"Did we miss it?" he said breathlessly.

"No, Wills," Olivia replied and ran to him. "Devy isn't even here yet."

"Devin's not here?" Renee asked as she and John walked into the library. "I thought for sure we'd catch you as you were walking in. Totally my fault, shoe emergency."

"There is no such thing," John said with a big sigh.

"Yes there is, I was just in one."

"Having a limb cut off is an emergency. A gunshot wound is an emergency. Putting shoes on your feet, not an emergency situation."

"Twin? A ruling?" Renee said impatiently just as Kyla came storming into the library.

"Of course there's such a thing as a shoe emergency," Kyla said and looked down at Renee's sparkling silver shoes. "You chose well. Ok kids, time to get this show on the road. Everyone is seated and anxiously waiting for the ceremony to begin. So chop chop, Renee and family first…"

"Ky," Brianna interrupted, "we're still waiting for Devin."

"Waiting…what? He's not here? Where the hell…people are waiting."

"And they'll have to keep waiting," Fabiani said flustered from the doorway. "That man…he finally comes out and now he's going to…I'm mortified, absolutely mortified."

"Fabi, what's the matter," Bri began but then the sound of metal pieces grinding and hitting the ground echoed from the corridor.

"Mama," Jackson shouted from the doorway, "Uncle Devy looks like the tinman!"

"What?!" Renee squealed and ran to take a look.

Brianna turned slowly toward me, both brows up and creating thick creases in her forehead. "Is he wearing a suit of armor?"

My jaw dropped, unable to speak, but knowing the answer would be coming into view any second.

"He couldn't do this before he announces to the world we are together?" Fabiani shouted and then walked in the direction of the Council Hall.

"Ok, ok, everyone else, let's go," Kyla directed as she shooed everyone out of the library.

"But I wanna see the tinman," Olivia whined.

"Come on, Wivy," Wills said excitedly, grabbed Olivia's hand and ran with her out into the corridor.

"No, no, no," Kyla cried and gave us all dirty looks. "We're running late as it is, take control of your children and get into the Council Hall!"

"So hurricane Kyla did hit the coast today," Renee groaned before kissing her friend on the cheek and following John to capture the children.

"I guess that's my cue," Brianna said as she squeezed my arm.

I took her face between my hands and kissed her lightly on the lips, not enough to smudge her makeup, but enough to convey how much I loved her for the sacrifice our family would be making after tonight.

"I can still say no," I said softly as I rose from her lips.

"If you did, Kyla would have your head," she replied with a smile.

"You really do look beautiful."

"I know," she replied with the sassiness I loved. "And don't worry, you'll be fine. This is what Victor wanted, nothing can go wrong."

"Nothing can go at all if we don't start this thing," Kyla said angrily just as the clanging noise became almost deafening. "Good lord in heaven."

Brianna stepped away from me as we turned to see Devin coming through the library doorway. The suit of armor he was donning was polished to a high shine, although every hinge creaked and every piece of metal scraped against itself.

"Well that's a choice," Brianna said as she tried to kiss Devin on the check through the opening in his metal helmet. The only thing she accomplished was causing the visor to fall down and clang Devin's helmet shut. Kyla groaned but Brianna simply bit the inside of her lip. "Good…luck. Come on, Jack-Jack."

"You all have five minutes before that fanfare starts to play. You better be there, I'm not going to make those people wait any longer," Kyla said as Brianna ducked around her and the library doors were closed.

"Well, Brother, the time has finally come," I said as I stepped over to him.

"Brianna was laughing at me," he said flatly through his closed visor.

"She was not," I lied and he lifted the visor to show me that he knew I was. "Brother, in all the years we have been together, I have never known you to actually put on one of your suits of armor. I thought they were merely decoration."

Devin took his helmet off altogether and held it in the crook of his arm. "But Father always said that a leader should represent their era. This is my history, my legacy."

"Brother, you were too poor and too low in class to ever have a knight's armor," I said delicately.

"And your outfit is about a hundred years forward from when you were Turned," he rebutted in a challenging tone.

"We are both nervous, Brother, and want to make Father proud."

Devin sighed. "Tonight has to be perfect. It's our first impression as leaders of this coven. Everyone will be looking for the slightest error in order to challenge us."

"And we will put them in the ground if they try," I replied.

"Yes we will, Brother," he laughed.

"You will what?" a voice said as the faux bookshelf door to the vaults opened and revealed Victor coming toward us. "Child, whatever are you wearing?"

Devin touched his chest. "But Father, you always said we needed to represent…"

"You must forget everything I've said," Victor replied kindly. "Well, not absolutely everything. But you and your brother must make your own rules about how to handle yourselves."

"But you still wear your robes," Devin said and pointed to the white Roman robes that Victor was wearing.

"Yes, my robes are part of the time I came from, but they are also…comfortable," Victor answered with a guilty smile. "Now, child, if that is what you want to wear…"

"Hell no," Devin said quickly and ripped the armor loudly from his body. Thankfully he was wearing black combat pants and matching shirt. "This feels much better. There wasn't one piece of that fucking armor that worked correctly."

"What about shoes, Brother," I asked and pointed to his bare feet.

He shrugged. "I don't need shoes to kick someone's ass."

"And there's your signature," Victor said and directed us toward the door. "I believe the fanfare is going to start any second. I fear Kyla's wrath if we are not in our place."

"You'd think she was running this coven," Devin groaned as we exited the library.

"Oh child, you will soon come to find that the women close to you run more of your life than you realize."

I smiled and laughed to myself because I knew it was the truth.

Just as we approached the Council Hall's doors, Victor turned to me and Devin one last time, placing a hand on each of our shoulders.

"Always know that in this moment I have never been prouder of the two of you. My dream of passing the coven to both of you has finally come true. Now just be sure to say yes to whatever I say in there."

The three of us laughed together before the wide oak doors were open at the call of the trumpets. As Victor led us into the Council Hall, five hundred guests stood proudly. When we passed my family, Jackson shouted "that's my Ada!" and my chest swelled with pride. I was the first to admit that I never wanted to lead my brothers and sisters, and even when Victor began grooming me I was only doing it to satisfy him. But that day on the battlefield, my hand keeping his heart together, hearing his last words to me and Devin, I could not stop myself from wanting to take care of my siblings. I was proud of myself, proud of my brother, and weighing the task ahead of us made me smile nervously over at Devin. He responded with a smile of his own, but I knew it was from the pure joy of having his longest dream come true. I had never been so happy for my eldest brother, he deserved this honor much more than I did. I was humbled by his gratitude of sharing the throne with me. Most brothers would kill the other to gain absolute power, but not my brother Devin, the deadliest and most honorable Vampire alive.

When we reached the front of the Council Hall, Victor stepped up to the landing where now only two thrones sat. Once the fanfare was finished, Victor directed everyone to sit except for Julian who came forward with a display of two medals. Devin's chest began to rise and fall, but we all knew it was not in anger. It was excitement at what those medals meant.

"Warriors, friends and colleagues, this is a very joyous day, but it is also an emotional one for me. This will be the first time in more than five hundred years that I will not be sitting at the head of this coven. Now I know for many of you this transition could be difficult, and yes even a Warrior can be scared, especially when it comes to change. But know that I am entrusting the safety of humans and Vampires everywhere to two of the greatest Warriors and all-around good men that I have ever come across in my long life.

"Now to my Warriors, my precious children, just as you were loyal and loving to me, you must also be to your brothers here. A coven, as we have seen, will fall without solidarity amongst its members. And as your father and maker, I expect all of you here to raise your brothers up with all your gifts, and help them bring in a new era of our great coven."

The Council Hall echoed with the sound of my siblings pounding their chests while others applauded. Victor turned and took one of the gold circular medals, a larger recreation of our sacred seal dangling from a red velvet ribbon.

"Cameron, son of Thomas, sire of Victor, I hereby bestow the leadership of our great Warrior coven in conjunction with your elder brother, Devin. May this seal remind you of our history, inspire you for our future, and demonstrate our never-ending commitment to the protection of our kind and established way of life. Do you accept this commission?"

"I do, Father, and all the responsibilities that come with this obligation," I replied and puffed my chest as Victor placed the metal over my head. He extended his hand to me, and when I took it he pulled me down into his chest and patted my back lovingly.

Next he took the remaining medal, similar to mine except that the ribbon was adorned with thin gold rods. Victor lifted the medal from Julian's tray as he said, "Devin, eldest sire of Victor, you have honored us with centuries as our Warrior Assassin. These gold rods represent each kill you have made in our name. And yes, there are two more ribbons full of gold rods if you want to be completely accurate with your numbers."

Devin smirked and lowered his head. "Thank you, Father."

"And thank you, child, for the sacrifices you have made for our coven and our race. I would like to show my gratitude by bestowing the leadership of our great Warrior coven in conjunction with your brother, Cameron. May this seal bind you together as one, made stronger by how you complement one another in almost every way. Do you accept this commission?"

"Of course, Father, it is my greatest honor," Devin replied, beaming as Victor placed the medal and golden adorned ribbon around his neck. When he lifted his head, Victor embraced him and kissed his forehead.

Together he placed a hand on each of our shoulders and turned us to face the large crowd that was already on their feet. You could not even hear Victor pronounce us as the new coven leaders through the deafening applause. Brianna was beaming while the children cheered and jumped wildly around. I was a failure no more. Somehow after three hundred years, a new life was just beginning.

Chapter Fifty-seven

Brianna

"Do you have the envelope?" I asked Cam softly, seeing that Jonah was at the food table alone.

Cameron reached into his jacket's pocket and pulled out the legal papers I'd asked him to hold for me.

"Are you sure you want to do this now?"

"He leaves in the morning, and I don't know when he's going to…you know," I whispered, looking around nervously.

"Fine, love, it is your present to give."

"Now don't go getting all cocky just because you're one of the grand poohbahs," I said and took the envelope from his hand.

"Grand poohbah, really?" he said as he followed me over to Jonah who had just stuffed a large scallop wrapped in bacon in his mouth. Oh how I missed those.

"Heywuyswuh," he said with a full mouth.

"Nothing's up, but do you have second?" I said, hiding the envelope behind my back.

Jonah swallowed hard before finally being able to say, "Sorry, you caught that?"

I nodded. "I often spoke with my mouth full."

"Boy did she," Cameron said, pinching my side.

"So…" I began, prodding Jonah with my eyes, "…do you have the…you know."

Jonah sighed and patted his suit jacket's pocket. "Got the ring right here. I keep checking every few minutes, I'm terrified I've lost it. Mom is thrilled. I finally got through to her today. She's been so busy packing and getting the new condo ready. I'm not sure what she's more excited about, me proposing or her being a grandmother."

"Being a grandmother, definitely," I replied. "Well, before you go back home, I wanted to give you something…"

"No, Bri, no. No more gifts, no more help. Both of you have given me way too much already. Hell, the new job is more than enough."

"Job, what job?" I asked, and then looked back at Cameron who had a devious smirk on his face. "What do you know that I don't?"

Cameron put his hands up in front of him. "It is Jonah's news. And Jonah, I assure you, you got the job based on your merit. Diana realized her mistake the minute you left."

I turned back to Jonah. "Spill it."

Jonah shrugged and put his hands in his pockets. "Diana reached out to me about maybe coming back to Facility East. So I gave her a call and she offered me the janitor position."

My head flinched. "Wait, what? How dare she bring you back and demote you…"

"Bri, I'm kidding," Jonah laughed.

I hit him lightly in the arm. "Jerk."

"Sorry, I couldn't help myself. No, I'm her new Director of Operations. We're going to run Facility East together, and she's going to pay me a boatload of money to do it."

"Ohmygod!" I shouted and threw my arms around him. "That's incredible! I'm…I'm so…proud of you."

I released Jonah's neck and held my hand out for Cameron's handkerchief that was quickly put in my hand to catch the red tears leaking from my eyes.

"Thanks, Bri. I thought for sure you had pulled some strings."

I shook my head and Cameron answered, "Like I said, Jonah, you got the job based on your own merit."

"So with a new job, you certainly need this," I said and handed the envelope to Jonah.

He eyed me and then Cameron before taking the envelope from my hand. When he opened it he scrunched his brows together. "It's a deed."

"Keep going," I prodded, hoping he would read a little faster.

He unfolded the paperwork all the way and his eyes bulged when he saw the piece that was the most important. "My house? This is a deed to my house?"

I clasped my hands together and nodded in excitement, but he quickly folded the paperwork and put it back into the envelope.

"I can't accept this, Bri, this is…way too much. I…I can't. I haven't done anything to deserve this."

"Yes you have," I snapped. "Jonah, you've supported our family, supported me in my absolute darkest moment. Because you were with us, the mother of your child was taken and held for weeks in that awful place in the woods. The two of you deserve this. Your baby deserves this. And your mom and Katie can move back in if you want. I just wanted you to have that house. It's where you grew up with your dad, now you can raise your child there. Just take it, damn it."

"So you're the reason it sold so fast. Mom said she had a buyer right away who offered the asking price. Of course that was you."

"Look, you and Ashlyn and that baby need a little head start and I can give you that. It's the least I can do."

"The least you can do! I can never pay this back…"

"Jonah," Cameron said, stepping between us and putting his hand on Jonah's chest, "take the house. It is futile to keep arguing with her. And Bri, no more gifts or favors, you are making Jonah anxious. Does that make everyone happy?"

Jonah sighed but nodded. When I didn't respond, Cameron raised his eyebrows at me. "Fine, but that doesn't count for the baby."

Cameron sighed. "Of course, love. Now, Jonah, I think you have some news to tell Ashlyn."

"I guess I do," Jonah replied and shook Cameron's hand. "I better do it now, you never know what might happen next."

Jonah gave me a curious look before he hugged me.

"What's that look for?"

"Nothing," he replied as he buried his face into my shoulder. "Thank you, Bri. My family owes you so much…"

"My family owes you too," I said as I released him and cupped his cheek. "I need you to have this happy ending, Joey. It's all I've ever wanted for you."

He smiled and looked up at the ceiling to hide the emotion in his eyes. "You too," he said weakly and stepped away from us.

"We'll see you off tomorrow," I said to his back and he gave a little wave as he kept walking toward Ashlyn who was having trouble getting Kyla to stop talking to her stomach.

Before I could start to cry, Cameron pulled me back out onto the dance floor and easily slid me into his arms. While he rocked me back and forth I played with the gold medal that hung down his chest.

"Where are we going to put this thing?" I asked.

The left side of Cameron's mouth lifted into his famous crooked smile. "I was thinking you could wear it," he began and I tilted my head in confusion, "with nothing else, of course."

"I was thinking where could we put it where our devilish twins won't find it to play with."

"I think my idea is a solution to that as well."

I squinted one eye at him, but how could I resist that handsome face. "Just once," I replied. "I guess I'm glad you don't have all those gold rods on yours like Devin does. That would just be…uncomfortable."

Cameron laughed and twirled me around, allowing my satin red dress to billow around me.

"Remember when we danced at your Claiming?" he asked and I smiled up at him. "Your arm was injured, you were terrified Jared would attack you…"

"My feet were killing me all night," I interrupted. "At least that's one thing I'll never have to worry about again."

Suddenly Cameron's smile dropped and he became surprisingly serious. "Are you happy?"

We stopped dancing and I looked directly into his eyes as I replied, "Yes, Cam, I'm happy."

"Still love me?"

"Always," I replied and held up my left hand. "Besides, I really don't want to give up the ring."

"Remember you said that," he laughed and kissed me on the cheek.

"Brother, we need you," Devin said from behind me.

I gave Cameron a pout which only got me another kiss on the cheek. "I will see you shortly, my love, I promise."

Reluctantly I let him go, watching him walk across the dance floor until he disappeared through the grand double doors. I caught a whiff of

Renee's heavily applied perfume before she crooked her arm around mine and placed her chin on my shoulder.

"The job's taking him away already?" she asked.

"I can't complain," I sighed, "I told him he should do this."

"So what are they calling you? The First Lady?"

"He's not the president, Re."

She lifted her chin from my shoulder and stepped in front of me. "If he's the coven leader then you're the…the…Mistress of the Manor."

"That makes me sound like a whore, Re."

"Well then you think of something," she said and then laughed, as did I but then I looked around with a sudden worry.

"Where are the kids?"

Renee waved her hand dismissively. "They ran out with Jared. I think he promised them ice cream or something. I'll be peeling Wills off the walls for days after all of this excitement. Did you finally hear from the school?"

I nodded. "They're allowing us to interview next week."

"That's great! I don't think the kids could get through school without each other. More so, I don't think I could deal with Wills if he didn't have his Livy and Jack-Jack."

"I know the twins feel the same way. Can you imagine if we ever went to school together?"

"Um…yeah. I wouldn't have let you speak to Sam. Boy would your life have been easier."

"Thank you so much for throwing Sam in my face yet again."

"You're welcome, now come on," she said and pulled me off of the dance floor.

"Where are we going?"

"I…uh…just want to talk to you out in the hallway."

"Why?"

"Shut up."

"You know I am stronger than you and could stop you at any time."

"Shut up some more, please."

When we got out into the hallway I saw my father and grandfather standing together.

"What's going on?" I asked, but neither of them answered and it was actually Renee who squeezed my hand and brought my attention to her.

"Do you remember my wedding day? Before the ceremony we were in the bridal suite and I was basically having a 'mental' breakdown?"

"Yes," I replied slowly.

"Do you remember what you said to me?"

"I think I said bam a lot and you yelled at me."

"I didn't yell," she said, squinting her eye at me. "You told me that when I got into the aisle, I just needed to find John and let the love I saw in his eyes bring me to him."

"Why are you telling me this?" I asked skeptically as she walked me over to my father and Daddy O.

"Honey, in life we all do things that scare the crap out of us. And now it's your turn to find Cameron, look at him, and let the love you see in his eyes bring you the rest of the way."

"Wh-what's happening?"

"Mia figlia," Eris began and extended his elbow to me, "allow me and your grandfather to have this great honor in escorting you inside."

"What's going on inside?"

Daddy O's worn, wrinkled hand patted mine as he said, "Sugar, give me this one thing."

"You're playin' dirty, old man."

He smiled. "I gotta do what I gotta do."

I felt a knot forming in the pit of my stomach as Renee opened the door to Victor's office and my fathers led me inside. I was shocked to see Jonah and Ashlyn huddled together with Tosh, Nikki, and Jared up against the far wall. Kyla and Fabi were practically jumping up and down when I entered, while Victor, Maddy, and Sera simply beamed.

Cam was standing at the far end of the room in front of the fireplace with Devin standing just to his right and Alex on his left. I froze when I truly realized what was happening, but it wasn't made vocal until the twins and Will jumped up and down screaming, "Happy wedding, happy wedding!"

The thin lines on Cameron's face were creased with worry, but I did as Renee had instructed and looked for the love in his eyes. It was easy to find, it had always been there, it was only missing when I didn't want to see it. I loved him with all my heart, even now that it was silent. Our children were miracles of our kind, survivors like me and Warriors like their father. It was finally time to show them that even their mother could face her worst fear.

When I resumed walking, Cameron's chest heaved with relief and his smiled reached his ears. My feet no longer felt like lead, and instead my body was almost floating toward him.

When we reached the front of the room Daddy O kissed my cheek with loving tears in his eyes. When he finally stepped away, I turned to my father who hugged me and whispered something in Italian in my ear before kissing my hand and placing it in Cameron's.

"What did my father say," I whispered to Cam as I stood opposite him.

Cameron shrugged. "Something about killing me if I do not keep you happy."

"Ah, your Italian is improving, Warrior," Eris said with a laugh, although we all knew he wasn't kidding.

"I can't believe you didn't tell me about this."

Cameron gave me his crooked smile. "It is a little easier to ask for forgiveness than permission."

"Wow, you really do know me well," I laughed and Alex leaned forward over Cameron's shoulder.

"Apparently better than we do, Bri."

"Lost money, huh?"

He nodded and the room bubbled in laughter.

"Ok, let's begin before our guests miss us too much," Devin began very authoritatively.

"Wait a minute, you're marrying us?"

Devin smiled proudly. "As coven leader, I have that authority, and I am honored I get to officiate a marriage for two people I most treasure."

"Ah, Devy," Fabi cooed, but rather than be embarrassed like usual, Devin gave Fabi an adorable wink.

"Eternity isn't just a figure of speech among our kind," Devin began. "Immortality can be a curse for some, but when you have someone to share the endless journey with, it can be a most precious gift. Now will each of you extend your fangs and bite the inside of your left hand."

I looked up at Cameron who gave me a comforting smile as he released my hand, putting his own up to his mouth and sinking his fangs into his palm. Nervously I did the same, truly not knowing why the heck we were doing it. Cameron took my left hand in his and Devin placed his Warrior medal on top of our hands and wrapped the gold rod embellished ribbon around our wrists.

"Brianna, do you take Cameron as your husband? Committing yourself as his one true partner, not as two, but as one soul bound together by love and blood. Do you promise to love and support and lift him up to succeed?"

"I do," I replied easily and squeezed Cameron's hand.

"And do you, Cameron, take Brianna as your wife? Committing yourself as her one true partner, not as two, but as one soul bound together by love and blood. Do you promise to protect and honor her in every way, never forsaking her needs for your own or our coven's?"

"I do," he answered and stopped a tear at the corner of his right eye.

"As co-coven leader of the great Warriors, I hereby pronounce you husband and wife, partners and lovers for eternity. You may kiss your bride!"

The cheers rang out as Cameron pulled me into his chest and kissed me. He lifted his head for a brief moment and smiled as he said, "Hello, Mrs. Burke."

I couldn't help but smile. "Now Jared's nickname isn't so stupid."

"Hey! Bibi was never a stupid nickname. I knew this would happen," Jared said proudly despite the laughs around him.

Brianna Burke, that was me. A new name for the new life ahead. No more Sam, no more Elaina or Aidan, just my happy little family that included humans and hybrids and Vampires. Nothing conventional or traditional besides the love we felt for one another.

After one last kiss, Cameron released me and Devin removed his medal that bound our hands. The puncture wounds in my palm had healed, but what was left was a small smear of blood, a mixture of mine and Cam's, a bond in blood as Devin called it. As I licked it away I looked up to Devin and said, "Ok Dev, your turn."

Devin's eyes shot open as he jerked his head up. "Wait...what?"

"I do!" Fabi shouted.

STAY TUNED FOR BOOK FOUR IN THE

Blood-Borne Series

VISIT **WWW.CR-QUINN.COM** FOR THE MOST UP TO DATE
INFORMATION ON THE BLOOD-BORNE SERIES AND
OTHER PROJECTS FROM C.R. QUINN

Acknowledgments

The first person I have to thank is of course my husband, John. For over five years you've shared your evenings with a woman whose face is buried in a computer screen, and all the while being my biggest supporter and pushing me to continue. Although I'm sure you didn't mind rolling around on the ground and helping me block some of the scenes. The battle scenes of course!

About the Author

C.R. Quinn is a budding author whose prior accomplishments include a bachelor's degree in Biology, surviving the corporate world for over fifteen years, and a singer/dancer/actor/director in community theatre. She lives in Connecticut with her husband, and is lucky to be the stepmother to two wonderful children. Even though a trilogy would have been a great stopping point, this great cast of characters is keeping her writing juices flowing.

43239062R00350

Made in the USA
Middletown, DE
22 April 2019